The Eastern War

Book 4
of
The Master of Fate

William Price Jr

Other Books by William Price Jr:

The Master of Fate series:
Into The Northlands
The Northern Keep
The Western Empire
The Eastern War

The Fallen Angel series:
Fallen Love
Fallen Justice

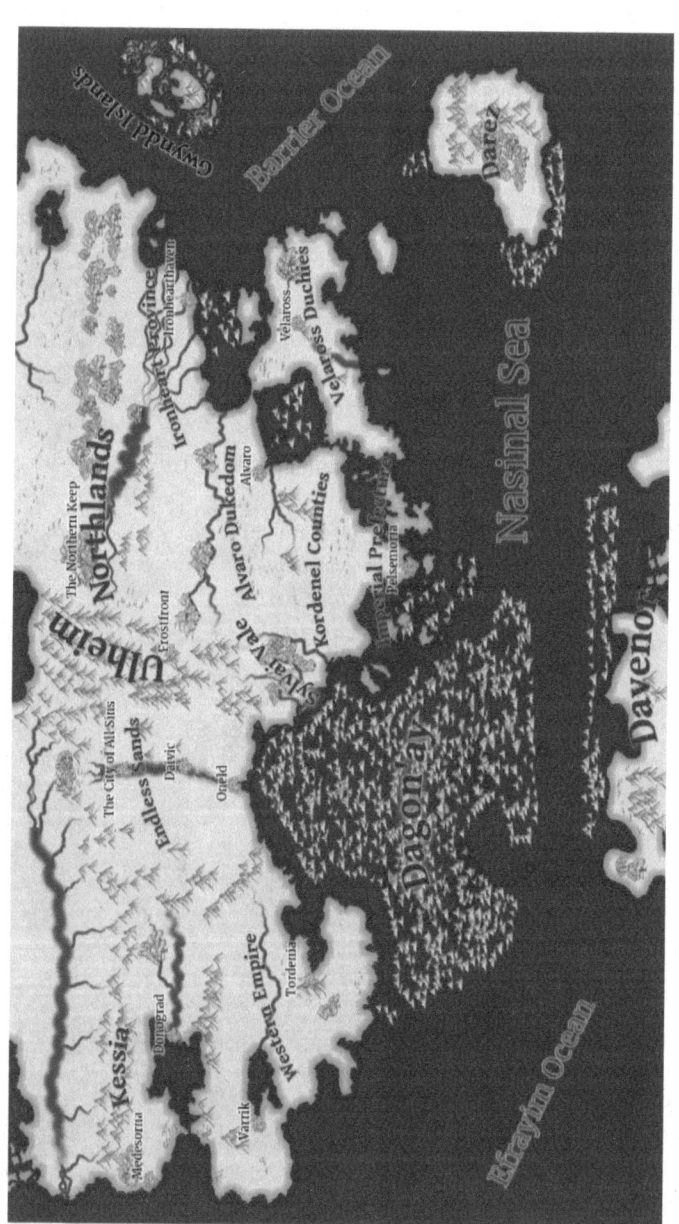

The Heroes Abroad

I

Dagon'ay

Chapter 1

The enemy galley approached rapidly, the sound of its drums clearly audible. Somewhere in the back of Tomas' mind, in that quiet part that could remain still even during the terrifying moments before battle, facts seem to drift forward of the approaching warship. The squire could not recall from where he had learned these facts, probably some journal or diary of a past war. Even after the destruction of his home and the end of his formal schooling, still he had continued in his exploration of the past through whatever books and scrolls he could save from the predations of time, the elements, and the uncaring cruelty of men.

The ship was a quadrireme; that much was obvious. Four banks of oars clawed through the water, dragging the monstrous enemy towards them. A single, angular sail jabbed sharply towards their smaller ship, indicative of the Western Empire's incorporation of newer sailing technologies within their fleet. The galley had no towers either fore or aft, Tomas noticed. The protective designs favored by the east for their maritime archers had never been popular in the west; rather, the lords of Tordenia preferred large contingents of marines, nautical soldiers that Tomas could even now see lining the decks of the approaching warship. If the armored prow jutting ahead of the encroaching beast failed to ram and mortally wound their delicate ship, the eager soldiers swarming aboard that monster far outnumbered the *Blue Lady*'s crew.

Tomas hated the waiting that preceded a battle. The fighting itself was little comparison to the tension before one. Even the horror afterwards did not compare to the terror of anticipation. Rogan had tried to teach his squire calming techniques, methods of emptying the mind and simply awaiting what was to come. That quiet part of Tomas' mind also tried to still his beating heart, to whisper soothing words of faith and surrender to Fate. Despite this, the young man could not help but let his imagination run wild before a battle. Would someone be injured, he wondered? How much suffering would there be? What would be the White Lady's claim? Worst of all, would he make a mistake that cost someone their life? Tomas was willing to risk his own life; but to cause the suffering or death of another? To be able to save someone, but fail?

His young eyes drifted back, from the oncoming warship to the receding coastline of Tordenia. The screams of that dying city had faded within hours of their departure the previous dawn. The strange buildings in their mesh of eastern and western designs had dropped beneath the horizon. Tomas could no longer see the horrid darkness of the Shadowed Mage's umbral curse consuming the homes, shops, and places of worship. He could no longer smell the carnal wind that blew out from the dying city, nor could he taste the rotting evil he, himself had mistakenly unleashed. Despite this, despite the distance the *Blue Lady* continued to add between him and his unforgivable sin of carelessness, still the squire felt the terrible burden of ten thousand damned souls. His victims.

The large galley made contact. Rather than ramming them, as many had feared, the enemy ship had turned upon its final approach and wrapped its oars on the near side. There was a horrible grinding sound as the bodies of the two ships made contact. Sliding along the hull of the *Blue Lady*, the crew of the quadrireme made ready to board, throwing across grappling hooks and brandishing weapons. With a loud groan, a massive wooden ramp, lashed to the enemy's single mast with a stout rope and clawed with a giant metal spike at its tip, came crashing down onto the *Blue Lady*'s deck. A *khorvus*, the thought came. Tomas looked at it and, somehow, recognized the design. A boarding ramp the Uldra had devised centuries ago for their own ships, when they still built them. A strategy they had created during the War of the Black Sea, when their slower hulks would board the sleek cutters of their hated enemy, the Sylvai. Adopted by the Western Empire, the boarding ramp was a means of bringing infantry warfare to the sea.

Almost before the *khorvus* had finished coming down, the enemy came spilling across it. The marines, though, were not prepared for what awaited them. Through the thousand-year reign of the Republic, the quadrireme had dominated the coastal seas of Lanasia. Their massive crews overwhelmed all opponents with ease, ramming and sinking smaller vessels, or boarding and claiming them. The handful of these massive warships that had survived Lanasia's worsening civil war had all sworn allegiance to the Western Empire, patrolling and defending House Balshazzar's coastline in return for the right to claim whatever slaves and other booty they won. They were the terror of the waters around western Lanasia.

In all the years since the fall of the Republic, however, the quadriremes had never engaged the forces of House Calonar.

Had they only been facing the crew of the *Blue Lady*, perhaps the piratical marines would have had more success, although that also was doubtful. The navy of the Western Empire was accustomed to fighting the ships of other, less organized nations and raiding merchant ships. Their sailors were often pressed into service from captured ships and coastal towns. These unwilling crewmen suffered under brutal discipline and harsh conditions, earning release only through loyal service or the touch of the White Lady. In the navy of good King Cylan, every sailor was a volunteer, paid a fair wage, and trained well. The crew of the *Blue Lady* served together eagerly, and each man and woman was prepared to fight and, if necessary, die in the service of their ship, their King, and House Calonar.

Unfortunately for the marines of the Western Empire, they not only faced this difficult and determined group, but also the combined might of Rogan's team and the Archaeknights.

Rogan and Tomas leapt forward, each easily countering the clumsy swings of their opponents and cutting a bloody swath through the boarders. The leather vests the marines wore offered no real protection against Talon and Steelheart. The two swords, both Uldra-forged and battle-tested against the strongest of opponents, cut through the weak armor of the marines as easily as they cut through the weak metal of their upraised weapons. Even in the hands of an unskilled warrior, either of the master-forged blades could defeat most opponents; combined with the martial skill of knight and squire, the swords became the fingers of Death Herself. Rogan and Tomas danced among the marines, spinning and slashing their blades to the accompanying song of dying men. Their form was flawless and their timing precise; only their coordination showed signs of imperfection.

A marine jumped forward, stabbing towards Tomas. The squire moved to block the strike but was surprised when Rogan deflected the attack and countered, sending the dead man spinning away. "What?" the squire demanded.

"Look out!" the knight barked and swung Talon over Tomas' head giving his apprentice only a hair's breadth of space and a moment's reaction to move. The young man glanced back and noticed another dead marine falling away. The squire looked back to his knight in time for Rogan to shake his head slightly. "Pay attention..." he began to say.

Tomas roughly elbowed his mentor aside and stabbed an approaching enemy in the chest. He then pulled Steelheart free and kicked the dying man away before turning to watch Rogan pick himself up off the deck. "You were saying?" the young man asked.

Rogan casually disarmed and dispatched another attacker. "I was saying there's plenty more work to do," he replied. "So stop standing around and get to it."

Knight and squire separated then, finding their own places in the spreading fight.

Tomas forced his way towards the ramp, across which the boarders were still coming. The squire hoped to stem the tide of the enemy, not really knowing how, fearing their overwhelming numbers. While individually the marines posed little threat, the constant tide of them could make the difference. Tomas swung Steelheart twice, killing one enemy and sending another stumbling back. The squire advanced, intending to finish his opponent, but his foot caught on some coiled rope and he fell, losing his grip on Steelheart. The retreating marine, seeing his chance, leapt forward and raised his shortsword to strike. Tomas raised his hands to try to ward off the attack but was shocked when the marine, rather than delivering a deathblow, suddenly jerked and stumbled past the startled young man. Tomas looked up and shook his head, more than a little annoyed at needing to be saved again. "I didn't ask for help," he grumbled.

"You're welcome," Sarah replied. The flame-haired archaeknight offered the squire her hand, which he accepted with a grimace. She also handed him his sword with more than a little dry amusement showing in her emerald eyes.

"Shut up."

Sarah just shrugged and gestured back to the fight.

"Yeah, yeah."

Tomas and Sarah moved towards the ramp, engaging the knot of marines surrounding it. The squire swung his sword in a wide arc, trying to scatter them and forcing each of the enemy back a step. Exploiting this opening, the newest archaeknight darted in with her weapons held low. She carried a pair of simple straight shortblades, each emerging from long wooden handles. These danced in a blur of reflected sunlight, Sarah bringing to bear her mystically-enhanced speed and agility with strikes faster than a serpent's tongue. Wrists were slashed, thighs sliced, throats opened, all in a whirl. The marines faltered against the dance, Sarah becoming almost a flame-haired avatar of the White Lady, unable to defend themselves.

When Sarah couched low, under the high swing of a mace, Tomas stabbed with Steelheart. Although not as nimble as the arcane warrior, the squire did make a fulcrum upon which she could turn. He became an immovable object around which she danced, keeping the marines occupied while the archaeknight lashed and countered. The enemy simply could not defend against Tomas and Sarah. The seasoned warriors of House Calonar moved among the marines, swinging their blades in tight circles, covering each other's backs, exploiting openings the other provided and generally unleashing a horrific level of carnage.

The crack of whips and snarling voices, growling commands in Varresi, the common tongue of the Western Empire, caused another surge of marines across the *khorvus*. Tomas and Sarah tensed to counter the rising enemy tide, but were joined by Rogan and Ward, commander of the Archaeknights. Ward, bronze skinned and raven-haired, picked up two struggling marines and threw them into the sea. He caught the high swing of a sword against the strange black bracer he wore, the seemingly-stone material easily negating the attack. Rogan stabbed under Ward's upraised arm and, in pulling Talon free of the dead man's chest, used the motion to slash across another's throat. "We have to end this!" the knight insisted.

Ward pointed out to the open water on the left side of the ship. "We have bigger problems," the large Human said.

Rogan and Tomas looked in the direction Ward had pointed and grimaced. Two more galleys had appeared and were obviously approaching. "Damn," the squire muttered. He parried an attack and kicked the attacker, Sarah then slashing at the man's torso until he fell in a bloody, screaming streak tumbling into the waves. "Ideas?" he asked no one in particular.

Rogan turned towards the quarterdeck and raised his voice. "Ahmed!" he called to the ship's master.

The Shamashi captain finished off the lone marine who had dared to profane his *Lady*'s high deck and looked to where Rogan and Ward were pointing. "How long until they get here?" Rogan shouted.

"Ten minutes at battle speed!" Ahmed estimated. "Fifteen at most!" The captain then turned to engage another intruder.

"Are we sure they're with Balshazzar?" Tomas asked. "We're due for a little luck."

Ward glanced up at the mast. "Deriel!" he shouted to the young Sylvu. The leader of the Archaeknights jabbed has finger out towards the approaching galleys. "Recon!"

Deriel, newest among the Archaeknights but for Sarah, understood his instructions and grinned, anxious for an opportunity to prove himself in the eyes of his comrades. The boyish Sylvu sheathed his short sylvai blades and ran his long-fingered hands though the short, tangled mane of light brown hair atop his head. Gathering himself, he leapt free of the mast. Stretching his long arms out, the small warrior thrilled at once again being free of the limitations of gravity as the mystical power of King Cylan coursed through his soul. He took flight away from the *Blue Lady* as free as any bird.

"He'll remember to come back, right?" Rogan asked.

The continued wave of boarders was beginning to push against the combined might of the warriors of House Calonar. Though Rogan and Ward held their ground, Tomas and Sarah were being forced back as the attackers relentlessly continued their advance across the *khorvus*. "This can't last," Tomas pointed out as he swung Steelheart over Sarah's head, separating an enemy's head from his shoulders before the man could complete his own attack on the archaeknight.

The red-haired warrioress, who had ducked her partner's strike, tumbled in front of him, stabbing out with one of her own blades at another enemy who had hoped to kill the distracted squire. "Agreed," she replied. Sarah had never been one for unnecessary words, even in calm situations.

"We're too outnumbered," Rogan declared, slicing his longsword under Ward's upraised arms.

"We need some way to even things out," the archaeknight leader added, snapping the neck of the marine he held and throwing the body at his fellows, knocking a few into the sea.

Tomas put his back to Sarah and parried several attacks, countering when he could.

"Thoughts?" she asked, matching his movements and meting out death from her long-handled blades.

One of the Western Empire marines made a desperate lunge, which Tomas intercepted with his left hand. The squire twisted the man and, in the same motion drilled into him by his mentor, spun his hips, sending the enemy to the ground. Once there, the marine was sent to the White Lady at the point of Sarah's blade.

Free the slaves. "Free the slaves?" Tomas asked, unsure of from where the idea came.

"'Might work," Sarah replied, slashing another opponent across the eyes before a reversed second slash opened his throat. "If they're carrying any."

Tomas stabbed an attacker in the chest and kicked him off Steelheart. Knowledge came flooding into his mind, ideas and facts and estimations like a flood of unremembered lore from some forgotten book. Tordenian galleys spent most of their time attacking foreign merchant ships. Cargo was stolen and crews were either killed or captured, to be sold later to Xeshlin slavers. "There's a prisoner's hold below decks," Tomas said as he continued to fight. "It'll have people from their latest patrol."

"You sure, kid?" Rogan asked as a pair of marines charged him. They bodily pushed at the knight, forcing him back. Ward grabbed one by the arm and leg, lifting the screaming man and tossing him into the water. His sword arm free, Rogan swung Talon low, severing the other man's leg.

"Yes," he lied. Tomas was not sure of what he said. He could not remember where he had learned so much about Tordenian galleys.

"How do we get over there?" his knight demanded.

Sarah spun, kicking out one of her legs in a broad arc that forced away her attackers, giving a moment's respite. She brought her hand up to her small mouth and blew an ear-splitting whistle, getting the attention of her teammates. Once several sets of eyes, each bearing the Calonar-sigil tattoo, were upon her, Sarah gestured to Tomas and herself, and then pointed to the enemy ship.

From high above the melee in the crow's nest, Ilaywin the archer took aim at the *khorvus*, focusing a moment and said, "*Ven'aya.*" The Human archaeknight then let fly with one of his enchanted arrows. As the missile flew, a blue aura formed around it, building in intensity until the mystical weapon struck the center of the boarding ramp. There was a flash of brilliant arcane energy and all the men charging across the *khorvus* were violently thrown in all directions. Before the stunned attackers gathered at the base of the ramp could react, Gendo and Rei, the husband and wife from Tramaya who always fought at each other's side, leapt amongst the stunned enemy. The oriental pair slashed at their enemies, he with a strange lance tipped with a curved blade and she with a pair of metal warfans, in a dance that scattered their opponents. When the marines tried to regroup, Genma raised his lance and brought the butt down, striking the deck of the *Blue Lady* and sending a shockwave that brought a groan of objection from the ship; her rigging lashed out in all directions, sending many marines into the sea. Of those among the enemy who survived Genma's assault, most retreated. Any foolish enough to try and continue their attack on the pair was greeted by the horrors of Rei's illusions, dredged up from each of her target's worst nightmares. Within moments, the combined attack of the Archaeknights cleared the *khorvus* of all enemies, if only for a few seconds.

Sarah grabbed her open-mouthed partner. "Move!" she snapped.

Tomas shook off his surprise and followed, as quickly as he could, the flame-haired archaeknight as she effortlessly flipped onto the ramp. Even sheathing Steelheart and using both hands in the effort, the squire had little success in pulling his armored body onto the ramp. "Uh," he grumbled, "little help."

Sarah glanced back and rolled her emerald eyes, grabbing the shoulder of Tomas' armor and hauling the squire up onto the *Khorvus*. "Have you considered wearing less?" she asked.

The young man glanced meaningfully up and down his companion's frame. As usual, despite knowing the likelihood of battle that day, Sarah had worn only a loose-fitting tunic of some thin fabric belted at her waist. It was sleeveless and only reached mid-thigh. Based on Tomas' conservative upbringing, such an outfit left far too little to the imagination. "Have you considered wearing more?" he replied pointedly, though with little confidence. Sarah never wore armor, trusting instead to the speed and agility granted to her by King Cylan. Despite this, her pale flesh was without a single mark, unlike Tomas' own body, even with his chainmail.

Sarah reached a hand into her tunic and flipped her wrist, sending a small blade flying across the *Khorvus* into the throat of an approaching marine. "Speed wins fights," she insisted.

Another enemy leapt onto the ramp and, screaming in fury, charged them. Tomas met the charge and redirected his opponent's energy, again with a move painstakingly taught to him by his knight, and hurled the attacker into the sea. The squire glanced back at his friend with a victorious grin. "But power wins battles," he pointed out.

Sarah shrugged and flipped over her partner's head, somersaulting across the ramp and striking at the gathering enemy on the other side. Tomas rolled his eyes and drew Steelheart, unwilling to be upstaged.

Charging onto the enemy ship, the squire looked around, knowing they had only moments before the crew recovered from the opening the Archaeknights had provided. "There," Sarah pointed at a staircase at the rear of the galley that led down, into the lower decks of the ship.

"Watch my back," Tomas instructed and charged forward, slashing Steelheart at anyone who approached.

The two sprinted for the stairs, the squire nearly diving down, into the dim opening once he reached it. When confronted with a marine, Tomas kicked the man solidly in the chest and followed him further down, leaping onto his unfortunate enemy almost before the man landed and thrusting his sword all in the same motion.

The squire knew that speed was their only ally, despite his argument with Sarah, and mercy was a luxury that would only lead to their deaths.

Sarah shot past her partner before he could even begin to pull Steelheart free, spinning in tight circles that cut down the few soldiers left. The low ceiling was a minor encumbrance to the squire and archaeknight, both being nearly the same height, forcing them to stoop a bit. A handful of the crew, rowers, Tomas realized without knowing how he knew, remained in the large, open bay. Anyone foolish enough to come within arm's reach was separated from their limbs by Sarah's unending dance, the long, tight braid of her fiery hair almost a weapon in itself. Most of the remaining crewmen retreated.

Tomas blinked to try to speed the adjustment his sight struggled to make in the dim chamber. Rows of openings lined both sides of the bay, each housing a long oar. These had been pulled in and were now at rest, forming two opposing rows that ran the length of the great bay. The dim light only managed to come through a series of grates that lined the center. The smell of unwashed bodies was pungent, slithering down the backs of their throats. A pair of guards, drawn to the screams and pleads for mercy that Sarah's entrance into this place had brought, climbed up from the stairs on the opposite side of the large bay. The squire reversed his grip on Steelheart and, ducking low, charged forward, growling fiercely to hold their attention. As he shot ahead, Sarah, still in the midst of her own carnage, darted to the side and ran, stepping from oar to oar. As the two overseers, though how Tomas knew what they were was uncertain, confronted the squire, his Archaeknight partner shot past and behind them. The squire swept his sword in a wide arc, brushing both of his opponent's short blades aside. Sarah accompanied this attack with a shallow slash against their backs. He then shoved his shoulder into one of the men, using his momentum to continue the spin and cut the throat of one guard. Without pause, she swung her blades low and cut the tendons behind the knees of the second doomed man before opening his throat.

"Is that all of them?" the squire asked.

Sarah listened and pointed to the ladder they had used to enter. Heavy bootsteps from above betrayed the approach of more trouble. Tomas jerked his head towards the stairs leading down. "We'd better free those slaves fast," he suggested.

Sarah nodded.

The squire led the way down to the next deck, again moving quickly. Fortunately, the pair found no more guards to kill. Sarah moved forward. The oar stations on this level had been cleared as well, with the slave hold in compartments beneath the floor. Metal grates covered the only visible openings, with heavy chains and locks keeping the grates secured. The flame-haired archaeknight took one of the heavy, iron locks in her calloused hand and looked meaningfully at her partner.

"There has to be a way," he insisted.

She glanced down at the slaves, many of whom looked up at her with the empty stares of defeated men. "Do any of you know my words?" she asked in broken Velish. "Do any understand?"

Fingers appeared from among the holes of another grate. "I," a weak voice speaking with a heavy accent drifted up. "I speak."

Sarah moved over to that grate while Tomas maintained his post at the stairs, ready for the inevitable trouble. The archaeknight knelt down and clasped the upraised fingers as best she could. "We want free you," she said carefully, her knowledge of Velish being limited. "But not know how. How open cages?"

"Key," the slave replied. "One key for all."

"Where key?"

"Drums. Whips. Beat we."

Sarah glanced at Tomas. "Did you kill a drummer?" she asked, switching to Gunnic.

The squire thought for a moment. "I don't think so," he replied. "But I can't swear to it."

The archaeknight grimaced. "Without the key, we may have to break the chains."

"Great." Tomas grunted, glancing about at the large network of thick chains securing the many cages. He thought about it. "There's got to be another way." *Use magic*, the thought came. He glanced about, almost in desperation, but saw nothing. "Get back," he sighed. "Keep watch, I'm going to try something that will…" he shrugged.

Sarah moved to the stairs leading up, though she kept one emerald eye on him.

Tomas went to the cage possessing the slave with which they could communicate. "Have everyone get as far away from me as they can," he advised in Velish.

The slave nodded and spoke to the others in Varresi. The other slaves pushed back.

Tomas took several deep breaths, trying to clear his mind. Since he and his teammates had left the Northern Keep, a strange power had been growing in the young man. Several incidents had occurred centered around Tomas that could only be explained by his development of magical talent. A few times, his friends had been hurt by the manifestations of Tomas' abilities, so Rogan had ordered his squire to avoid any deliberate use or experimentation, an order the young man had only been too eager to obey. Tomas feared this unknown, unknowable, perhaps unholy power. It seemed a thing of great danger, great uncertainty. Despite this, Fate conspired, time and again, to force him to tap into this power. The necessity of their mission had demanded that Tomas bring these growing skills to bear on occasions, often with limited and unpredictable results.

Like all educated Lanasians, the squire had a basic understanding of magic. Before the fall of Pelsemoria, Tomas had even taken a class on magical theory in school.

Therefore, he felt that he understood the basic concept. An adept simply had to clear his mind, focus his thoughts on whatever it was that he was trying to accomplish, draw into his body sufficient energy from the appropriate Wind of Magic, and release that energy in a focused manner. All the chanting, ingredients and so on was simply a matter of helping the adept to maintain focus. Surely, Tomas could do something as simple as break the locks.

The squire breathed and relaxed his mind. Rogan's lessons on focus, on finding calm amidst chaos, returned. "You never know when you need to find your center," his knight had shouted as he banged to cooking pans together, circling his increasingly-irritated apprentice. They had spent that entire morning while traveling through Wildelves Wood on meditation. "The world'll never stop when you need a moment," his knight continued, still yelling and banging, much to Aebreanna and Beraht's amusement. "But you'll still need to find that point of calm, that focus."

Now, Tomas breathed, not forcing away the world, but letting it slide through and past him. He reached out with his mind, sensing the currents in which all things flowed. They were always present. It felt like standing in the ocean. Magic flowed through everything, with everything having some sort of effect, some ripple, amidst the currents. Tomas was aware of the battle raging above them, the ships approaching from the north, the individual slaves beneath his feet, and even the small insect that had just landed on his hand. But, he let all these things drift past him. Everything that lived radiated magic and caused ripples in its currents, even the White Lady Herself and those she claimed. Tomas let himself blend into the soothing current of the world and its magic.

He began concentrating on the locks. They were cold, metal things at his feet. Tomas concentrated on pure, explosive energy and began drawing in that aspect of magic within himself. The Wind of Fire responded. Instead of passing through and around Tomas, it flowed into him. When the squire thought he had enough power, the hopeful-sorcerer pointed Steelheart at the first lock and willed it to explode.

Nothing happened. The Wind of Fire flowed into his hand, but then stopped.

"Dammit!" Tomas released the magic, letting it rejoin the surrounding currents. "What am I doing wrong!?!" But then, another thought arrived: *Steelheart is hardened against magic.*

"Oh, yeah," the squire grumbled. He shook his head, feeling foolish for forgetting a key fact about his own blade. Master-forged using a process once thought lost, Remm Stonebearer had created Steelheart for his friend and lord Cylan Calonar long ago as a weapon against magic. Obviously, no spell cast while holding the blade would work. Tomas glanced back towards Sarah, hoping she was not aware of his mystical fumbling.

The squire's thoughts were cut off when his eyes made contact with the archaeknight. As with so many things at that time, Tomas had let another fact slip from his mind. When he opened himself up to those strange currents, he did not perceive the material word, but rather the mystical one, the one composed of the Winds of Magic. When he looked at Sarah, he did not see his friend, but the shining truth of her radiant soul.

"Ow! Ah! Ok!" Tomas jammed his eyelids shut and turned away, the image of an immaculate warrior-goddess, wreathed in flame and crowned in glory, forever burned into his mind. "Ouch! No, not good! Not fair! Not funny!"

Sarah looked at her partner with an even gaze. "Are you alright?" she asked calmly.

"Yes. No. Flames. Brain. Soul. Saw you. Stupid, very stupid."

The archaeknight pursed her lips at the young man's obvious discomfort and then glanced up the stairs, where the sounds of trouble were drawing ever closer. "So," she said, "how are those locks coming?"

"Right," the squire blinked. "Locks." Tomas turned back to the damned locks in the damned galley to free the damned slaves so he could continue with the damned mission.

This time he carefully, but deliberately, sheathed Steelheart. Fortunately, Tomas had anger and pain to draw upon, which made for wonderful catalysts when trying to destroy something with the Wind of Fire. The currents responded quickly to his call, swirling into the squire's outstretched hand. To Sarah and the slaves, it appeared that a ball of green and violet energy swirled to life. Tomas grabbed the ball, reached back, and hurled it at the offending lock, shattering it into a thousand pieces. Seeing the destruction made him feel a little better.

In short order, all the locks were destroyed and the chains removed. With the help of Tomas and Sarah, the slaves were freed. A small cluster of Tordenian marines came charging down the steps, but were intercepted. The freed prisoners, spared the horror of enslavement to the Xeshlin, swarmed their captors. Bones were broken, flesh torn, and screams descended into wet gargles until there was nothing left. The once-slaves grabbed at anything that could become a weapon and surged upward, roaring their fury like a vengeful wave.

"Most of them are going to die," Sarah pointed out.

"It's still a chance at life," Tomas insisted. "A chance at living free." He turned to his partner. "Would you rather die fighting or live in chains?"

The archaeknight shrugged. "Some value their lives over all else."

"Well, either way, we need to get back to the ship."

The two warriors returned to the weather deck, unmolested further by the enemy crew. Every man loyal to the Western Empire was occupied by the scores of slaves who were not trying to take over the ship, but to unleash bloody wrath upon their captors. Tomas and Sarah looked about in confusion once they exited the darkness of the lower decks, taken aback by the violence that superseded even the boarding of the *Blue Lady*. In their bid for freedom, the slaves were vicious, clawing at their former masters and tormentors, mutilating bodies, and delighting in the terror they unleashed. Their desperation and prior hopelessness now made them fearless, and that fearlessness made them merciless.

"Quite standing around you two!" Rogan bellowed from the deck of the *Blue Lady*. "Get back over here!"

A small burst of blue energy directly in front of them gave the pair a start. When the flash passed, Drystan held out his hands to them. Tomas shook his head, having had to endure magical translocation before, and never enjoying the process. No matter how short the distance, nor the experience of the Archaeknight's jumper, magical teleportation was one of the worst experiences Tomas could think of. He gritted his teeth, closed his eyes, and grabbed Drystan's hand.

The squire recalled, a few hours earlier, the native of the Gwyndd Islands saying that he actually enjoyed what he called jumping. He claimed that it kept him healthy, that the more he translocated, the less chance there was that some disease could catch up with him. While Tomas did not know the archaeknight very well, given the wiry man's predilection for off-color jokes, the squire was not inclined to believe the statement.

Blue energy surrounded them that Tomas could see even with his eyes closed tight. *Here we go,* he thought grimly. Then, a thousand times a thousand flaming ants leapt onto the squire's body and began biting, tearing his flesh into the smallest pieces they could manage. Just when the pain could not get any worse, the vicious ants stopped biting him, instead pouring freezing seawater into the voids where his body had once been, sealing the breaches. Tomas opened his eyes and realized he was standing on the deck of the *Blue Lady*.

And then his breakfast caught up with him and tried to leap from his body.

"Wipe it off, kid!" Rogan barked from the quarterdeck. "We've still got problems!"

The squire spit out the last of his meal and moved up to join Rogan.

The knight turned to Ward. "He's sure?"

The leader of the Archaeknights nodded. "Both galleys are flying red and gold."

"What do we do?" Rogan asked Ahmed.

The ship captain pulled his cap off and wiped the sweat away. "I've got an idea but I need to be free to maneuver."

"We'll handle that." Ward moved down to the main deck, his gigantic stride covering the distance in moments. "Archaeknights!" he roared, jabbing his finger at the *khorvus*. "Clear the deck!"

Fikri, the Archaeknight's chronicler, briefly put his hands to his belt and then flicked his arms outward, sending a number of small metal stars shooting out towards the rigging that had held the boarding ramp secure. The rope snapped and seemed to fling itself away, causing the mast of the Tordenian galley to groan and rear away itself.

One of the remaining marines approached the archaeknight, attempting to take advantage of his distraction, and raised his sword.

"Look out!" Beraht called.

Fikri turned his shaved head and smiled. The marine stuck and the archaeknight's body exploded into water, showering his surprised attacker. The flood pooled at the marine's feet and quickly reformed, building into a humanoid form. In only a few heartbeats, the water once again took on the form of the Archaeknight's chronicler, who drew a dagger and dispatched his would-be dispatcher.

By then Ward had reached the *khorvus* and, firmly grasping it, began to lift the enormous ramp. Wood groaned under the strain of the archaeknight's enchanted strength. A few of the remaining enemy crew, no doubt desperate to escape the wrath of their prisoners, had been in the process of crossing and now held to its ropes as it was raised up. Higher and higher Ward raised it, even shaking it back and forth to try to clear the few men that stood upon the thing. "Now!" he barked, once he had reached to maximum his impressive height allowed.

Khwezi, the dark-skinned archaeknight from the continent of Davenor, jumped to the *Blue Lady's* rail. He held his hands together for a moment, concentrating and spoke a single word, then slowly pulled them apart. Between the tribesman's hands, as he slowly pulled them apart, grew a ball of blue flame. Once he had it to sufficient size, Khwezi leaned back and threw the fire at the far end of the *khorvus,* where the ramp was secured to the enemy ship. The ball impacted and exploded. Khwezi directed the motion of the flames with his hands and his mind, quickly burning through the vulnerable wood and rope.

Ward twisted the ramp, using the advantage of Khwezi's fire. The *khorvus* groaned, its wood snapping under the combined archaeknight assault. Finally, with a victorious roar, Ward hurled the burning ramp into the sea between the two ships.

"Now what?" Rogan asked.

"Now we need wind," Ahmed replied. "A lot of it."

"Asaya!" the prince called out. "We need wind!"

The Halvan woman sheathed her twin rapiers and nodded. Of all the female Archaeknights, Asaya was the only one who did not braid her hair, instead letting her long, black locks fly freely in the breeze. Even the clothes she wore matched the unencumbered nature of this Archaeknight; with loose-fitting skirts and sleeves of many bright colors, and simple boots to match. She despised restrictions of any kind.

Asaya moved to behind the mainsail, nearly dancing as she did so. Taking a deep breath, the Archaeknight put both of her hands over her heart and smiled. With pursed lips, she began to lightly whistle. Asaya whistled, and the wind responded.

"Holy-!" Tomas stumbled back and desperately grabbed for the railing on the quarterdeck as the *Blue Lady*, suddenly assisted by the extreme winds Asaya had summoned, leapt forward.

"Still working on those sea legs?" Ahmed joked.

"Funny," the squire grumbled. "Now what?"

"They were going to try for a ram," the captain explained. "One comes straight at us; the other harasses us with arrows. We're going to sweep one."

"Sweep?"

"Just watch."

By then, the two approaching galleys had closed much of the distance. One of the warships had broken off and begun a wide arc to the front of the *Blue Lady*. The second ship continued its advance, the oars on either side frantically clawing at the sea. Ahmed watched this and grinned, turning the ship slighting towards the approaching enemy. "Prepare to sweep!" he shouted to his crew.

In response to the command, the sailors of the *Blue Lady* scrambled about. To Tomas it seemed a mass confusion as ropes moved, rigging was reset, sailors ran about, and nothing in particular seemed to happen. "Should we be doing something right now?" he asked the captain.

"Stay out of the way," Ahmed replied. "You also might want to get over to the starboard side."

"Uh..." Tomas moved forward but paused looking left and then right.

Rogan shouted to the typically land-bound warriors to move over to the right side of the ship, grabbing his squire and directing him to grab the railing along that side of the quarter deck.

The *Blue Lady* continued its advance, as did the approaching galleys. Ahmed continued holding his course until some point he had been waiting for and then, as the approaching enemy warship seemed to be close enough to touch, swung hard to the left. With the extreme speed the *Blue Lady* had built up and the uncomfortable proximity of the other ship, Tomas winced in preparation for a collision, but was surprised when none came, instead there was only the snapping sound of wood as dozens of oars on the enemy ship were destroyed by the *Blue Lady* as she slid past.

"So that's a sweep, huh?" Tomas noted.

"She's crippled now," Ahmed confirmed. "It'll be hours before they can maneuver."

"What about the other one?" Rogan asked with a look behind them.

The captain glanced behind at the other warship, still trying to adjust its course to compensate for the *Blue Lady's* maneuver. "Forget about her. Galleys may be maneuverable, but once a ship like my *Lady* gets a head start, we've got more speed on open waters with a good wind behind us."

"Then let's move," the knight said. "We've lost enough time as it is."

Chapter 2

When the sun had begun to dip behind the retreating Western Empire, the last of their pursuers had finally given up. The open waters of the Aebreka Sea beckoned ahead, and with Asaya's constant winds driving the *Blue Lady*, the galleys of the Western Empire were hopelessly outpaced. Although danger laid both ahead and behind, the sea around them was calm, and the ship's crew and the warriors of House Calonar breathed a collective sigh of relief. Even with the ominous mystery of Dagon'ay before them, they had at least this small time to gather themselves.

The next morning, Tomas rose before his knight, as had become his practice. He pulled on his undershirt and pants but carried his boots out to avoid disturbing Rogan. The weather was fair and warm with this, the first day of summer, so the young man did not bother with a tunic or cap. Instead, he pulled on his boots and rolled up the sleeves of his shirt as he made his way forward, yearning for the feel of the free air on his skin.

Tomas spoke briefly with the ship's cook, arranging for a meal to be prepared and sent not only to Rogan, but to Aebreanna and Beraht in their own shared cabin. Although he had yet to see her that morning, the squire knew the change of the season would be affecting his Sylva companion. He had already seen the impact of Aebreann's Wyrdmark during their trip into the Western Empire. On the first day of each season, the mystical sign of her profound and unwanted magical heritage caused a profound shift in her appearance. When winter had become spring, her great, flowing mane of white had resurrected into a flow of golden life, glowing with the rising sun. When the mystical Sylva had awakened with the rising sun that morning, the azure glow of her opalescent eye instead looked out with verdant magic. For these outward changes, and whatever inward ones about which Aebreanna never spoke, the Wyrdmark drew a price. Tomas knew she would wake with a fierce, almost ravenous hunger.

As for Beraht… the squire was wall-acquainted with his Uldra friend's own insatiable appetite.

Taking a small piece of salt pork and a ship's biscuit for himself, Tomas made his way into the hold. Urge grunted at the squire's arrival, making a passing attempt to bite his rider, but more out of habit than any true animosity. Tomas moved into the very tight stall in which his chestnut warhorse was slung, squeezing past the beast's bulk to the wall behind. There, he worked the strange pulley that lowered Urge a few inches, letting the warhorse step onto the new conveyor system the Uldra had installed at the *Blue Lady*'s last stop in Clayton. Tomas made his way forward again and stood, staring expectantly at his mount. "Do we have to do this every time?" he demanded.

Urge started unwavering, unyielding stone at his rider.

"C'mon," the squire negotiated, as he was forced to do each time. "You know how this works. Get your exercise and I'll feed you."

Urge snorted his contempt at the indignity of his situation. Although none of their horses were especially happy with being confined in the hold like this for so many weeks, Urge, in particular, had become increasingly sullen. Each morning aboard ship, Tomas came down to offer what exercise was available, and each morning Urge resisted.

"I'm not going anywhere," the squire insisted. "And you're not eating until you do a little walking, at least."

Urge reached out and snapped his teeth at Tomas. Restrained by the sling, though, he could not make contact. The squire had been careful to note how far his irascible chestnut warhorse could reach on the very first day. "How will you feel when Stick finishes his exercise and is eating while you're still just standing there?"

Urge huffed and looked away, greatly offended at his imprisonment.

"Suit yourself," Tomas shrugged and made to turn away.

Stick, slung in the next stall, tossed his head and offered a low squeal at his progeny. Urge threw a hard look at his sire but then lowered his head and sighed. The warhorse began walking. The Uldra-built conveyor slid beneath his hooves, overing at least some small approximation of true exercise.

"You can do better than that," Tomas insisted.

Urge snapped his teeth at the squire again.

"Too bad," the young man sighed. He reached into the large sack he had brought with him and pulled out a carrot. "I guess I'll just have to give this to Stick."

Urge perked his ears. In their months together on this difficult journey, Tomas had learned that his warhorse had a special weakness for carrots. Though Stick preferred apples, his progeny had a special passion for the vegetable. The chestnut stallion broke into a trot, licking his lips and thrashing his tail.

Tomas shook his head with a soft smile and continued his work. Tomas reached over and flipped the sand-timer, then lowered the other horses for their own exercise. Stick was first, the black warhorse walking almost before he was in place. Then Beraht's Sus came down, the wench groaning against the shire horse's massive body. Finally, and with minimal effort, Tomas lowered Aebreanna's tiny Mayva. The Sylvai pony eagerly pranced, almost frolicking, along her own conveyor. Each seemed relieved to move along the strange machines at the bottom of their narrow stalls, showing none of the stubbornness of Urge. With all the horses exercising, Tomas pulled the grooming and care tools from a low cabinet at the back of the hold.

"It's hard on them." Rogan's voice came from the opposite end of the hold.

"On all of us, I think," Tomas nodded.

The knight moved to Stick's stall, offering an apple to his black warhorse. "He's never liked sea travel."

"What about you?" the squire asked.

Rogan shrugged. "Give me the open sky and the open road," he sighed. "Leave the sea to the fish."

Tomas went back to Urge, who sniffed around his rider. "It's back there," he noted, jerking a thumb back at the cabinet where the carrot rested. Urge snorted his irritation, but kept trotting. "They need real exercise," the squire then said. "These things may be better than nothing, but they can't replace a good run in the open air."

Rogan nodded. "There's an island ahead. Ahmed says we'll reach it tomorrow. He'll stop there for fresh water and other provisions. There's supposed to be fruit trees and even some game. We'll take them off-ship for a few hours so they can run around."

Tomas glanced up. The complex pulley the crew had used to lift Urge and the other horses off the deck at Oneld and lower them down into the hold had been broken down. It's major components were tightly strapped to the ceiling, ready for reassembly. "Can we afford the time?" Tomas pointed out.

"The ship has to stop anyway," Rogan pointed out. "There's no telling if we'll be able to resupply in Dagon'ay, so we have to do it before we make the run."

"Dagon'ay," Tomas whispers. The young man shook his head and then laughed ruefully.

"What?" his knight asked.

The sand-timer ended and Tomas signaled for Urge to stop. His chestnut warhorse did so and began nudging at his rider. "Alright, alright," the squire sighed. He retrieved the carrot and offered it, making sure to snatch his hand away as the vegetable disappeared. He then lowered each of the other horses.

Rogan followed. "What is it?" he asked again.

Tomas glanced at his knight. "It's…" He picked up the feedbags and filled them with oats and barley. "The ruins of Uldron," the young man said. "Lost capital of the Uldra." He strapped a bag onto each of the horses. "Frostfront, the Free City of the Arcane Guild. The Endless Sands and Daivic, home of the Shamashi. Oneld and the Khepri. The Hoppi River." He finished with Urge's feedbag and stopped. His head lowered and his hand lingered, resting against the chestnut stallion's head. Urge paused in his eating and nudged at his rider.

Rogan crossed his arms over his chest and leaned against one of the stall posts. "Tell me."

Tomas unstrapped a shovel from beneath the cabinet. "All my life," the young man said, moving to the back of Urge's stall. "The whole time in Pelsemoria, after the

Madness. The only thing that kept me going were the stories." He started cleaning out the manure. "Histories, journals, diaries, geographies. Anything that talked about distant lands. I dreamed of visiting those great places, those historic peoples."

"And now you are," Rogan pointed out.

Tomas lifted the filling bag he was filling and moved to the next stall. "Yeah. I'm seeing a lot." He glanced at Rogan. "And look what I've seen... what I've... done." He continued shoveling. "We almost die in Uldron. Aebreanna gets scarred." The squire continued to angrily shovel the manure into the bag, forcing away the water that was threatening to fill his eyes and had nothing to do with the smell. "We find slaughtered women and children in that oasis in the Endless Sands. House Parano made a deal with Balshazzar and got slaughtered. Every damned one of them." He punctuated his words with hard movements of the shovel. The squire glanced at his knight. "Oh, and I certainly saw the Hoppi River, as well as its river monsters." He moved to the next stall. "Oneld is crumbling and the Khepri are a beaten people. And Tordenia..." The young man stopped, looking away from his knight.

Rogan nodded. He moved to the cabinet and retrieved a brush. The knight did not look at his squire or forcefully expose the young man's shame. Instead, he moved to Stick and began brushing down his black warhorse. "After Pelsemoria," he said softly. "After the Madness. People spent weeks trying to tell me and Kyla that it wasn't our fault. It was the Greysoul's magic; it was Balshazzar's scheming; it was Fate." Rogan shook his head. "With everything that was happening, there really wasn't time to take it all in. We had to get back to the Keep. Then we were attacked by the Greysoul. Then Aebreanna was kidnapped, so me and Beraht had to go rescue her." He sighed. "Only after things calmed down did it really start to sink in." The knight looked at his squire. "Do you remember me telling you about that mission Kyla came along on? The one when we first found out about Senen?"

Tomas glanced back. "Yeah. That's when you were investigating the child disappearances, when you found out about what he'd been doing." The squire sniffed and continued mucking out the stalls. "You said she had some kind of breakdown after."

Rogan nodded. "The reason she was with me on that mission was because we needed to get away for a while. We were both hurting after Pelsemoria, but never had time to deal with it. We went on what was supposed to be a simple, straightforward mission. Help some kids. Easy hero stuff."

"But it wasn't?"

"Never is," the knight shook his head. "It's always pain and suffering. Ours or theirs or both. The bad guys make their plans and hatch their evil plots. We try to help. People always suffer. Sometimes, all we can do is minimize the damage."

Rogan put away the brush and walked up to his squire. Tomas was still keeping his back to his knight. Rogan put a hand on Tomas' shoulder, pausing him in his work. "Tordenia was your fault, kid. People will tell you it wasn't; they'll forgive you, make excuses for you. But, in the end, it was your actions, your choices, your mistakes. You can either let it destroy you or motivate you."

"Motivate me to do what?"

Rogan straightened. "To make damn sure it never happens again. To make sure that the next tyrant or warlord or spell-slinger gets the kicking he deserves." The knight walked to the end of the hold but paused at the door and glanced back. "Take whatever time you need, kid. Remember, though, that you're not alone. You have Beraht and Aebreanna and me. We've all been through the same things. We've all seen what you have. If there's anyone to share this with…" The knight shrugged and left.

"Ow!" Well before reaching the door leading into the aft cabins, Tomas could easily hear Beraht's shouted objections. The bark of outrage came from the large cabin that was a shared space used by the ship's officers for dining. "Damn your race!"

Tomas stood in front of the small hatch that led to the tiny cabin he shared with Rogan. The thought of sleep was a wonderful one, and as tempting as the most forbidden sin. Since Tordenia had been destroyed by his carelessness, the squire had been greatly tempted to remain forever in bed. Despite this temptation, though, Tomas glanced towards the common room ahead. Its door was open and morning light spilled from within. The voices of his friends, his companions in this terrible journey, drifted out, like the sweetest song of home.

Rogan, who had been cleaning his sword with an oiled rag, noted the arrival of his apprentice to the common room with a nod. "Horses all taken care of?" he asked. When Tomas nodded, the knight continued wiping down Talon with great care, pausing only occasionally to take sips from a cup at his elbow. Tomas' mentor did not indicate, with either word or glance, their earlier conversation, nor of his squire's suffering. "Did you clean your weapon yet?" he asked instead.

"No," Tomas replied. "I…"

The knight pushed a small box with oil and a rag across the central table towards his squire.

The apprentice sighed. He retrieved Steelheart from their shared cabin and sat down opposite his mentor. He drew the flawless, legendary blade of House Calonar, noting that the sword did, indeed, need to be cleaned. Tomas took up the oil and cloth and began his work. "What happened to you?" the squire asked Beraht.

The Uldra grumbled a curse in his native Uldric language. Even sitting on a low stool and bending low, Beraht towered over them all. A sullen expression soured his already-ugly face from behind the beard of unkempt, coal-black hair. During their battle in Tordenia, the Uldra's beard had been burned off by Inquisitorial magic. When Beraht had been healed by the Seal of Life, his facial hair had been restored, but since then, the massive warrior had refused to replace the heavy braids that had once kept his long beard in place. In one of the rare instances Tomas could recall, the Uldra warrior was not wearing his helmet, having instead laid it on the table before him. His long, braided hair, black as the night sky, was still held in place by his purple headband, but what drew Tomas' first attention was the large gash on the top of his barbarian friend's head.

"Is that from the fight yesterday?"

The warrior grunted.

"Why are you only getting it looked at now?"

"Because the courageous Sir Beraht is even more stubborn and foolish than typical in your obtuse gender," Aebreanna replied coldly.

"Ow!" Beraht objected again when his treatment became unnecessarily rough.

"If you stopped squirming," Aebreanna heartlessly replied, "you would stop hurting." The tiny baroness stood over her brooding Uldra friend with a clean cloth, needing a stool to reach Beraht's head, even with the mountainous warrior bending low. The Sylva had the sleeves of her linen undershirt rolled up, and was ministering to her friend as she often did whenever one of the boys, as she called them, were injured. Tomas noted that the seasonal change brought on by her Wyrdmark had, indeed, occurred. The spy's great mane, held only partially by a leather thong at the base of her graceful neck, now carried a cedar glow, and spilled over the right side of her face. This had become her custom since their disastrous trip to the ruins of Uldron, in which Aebreanna had been horribly scarred and lost her eye. The remaining one, now glowing with hazel opalescence, stared at the bloody gash at the top of Beraht's head. She rarely spoke of the Wyrdmark, and almost never of her mystical heritage. In the few times Aebreanna had talked to Tomas of such things, she had intimated that her seasonal change was a time of renewal for her, when both her spirit and her body are reborn. When winter had shifted to spring, Aebreanna had hoped the Wyrdmark would heal her injuries; with spring was now summer, and Tomas saw even the subtle power of her bloodline had once again failed to restore the Sylva's once-unmatched beauty.

"Damn it!" The Uldra flinched once more away from the cloth his Sylva friend held. He looked at Aebreanna with hate-filled eyes. Their respective races had despised each other for uncounted millennia, with cruelty shared upon both sides. Even the great fire of the Uldra Uprising could not consume the fuel of their peoples' shared animosity. Tomas had noticed over the past months that, although Aebreanna and Beraht went out of their way to express the traditional feud, their words were only performative.

The Sylva calmly returned the look, putting her delicate-seeming hands on her curvaceous hips. "The wound must be cleaned," she explained. "As hard as your head is, that cudgel was harder. Now summon your courage, O mighty son of Uldron, and stop moving."

"What did you do to the guy with the cudgel?" Tomas asked, thinking to distract Beraht.

"I broke him," the Uldra replied, sullenly allowing Aebreanna to finish. "Damned Humans kept knocking my helmet off and some lucky bastard caught me when I wasn't looking."

"At least they did not strike you someplace vital," Aebreanna mused as she finished her treatment of the massive Uldra. Stepping down from the stool, the Sylva gathered her various healing implements and moved over to Tomas. "Strip," she commanded the squire.

"Wha-" Tomas was about to object but, instantly realizing the futility of arguing, obeyed.

Despite his obedience, Aebreanna still gave voice to her matriarchal authority. "We have all suffered a great many minor injuries lately," she said. "You foolish boys have the idiot habit of shrugging off wounds that, properly treated, would heal adequately. I'll not have one of you forcing me into the unpleasant conversation of having to explain to your wives why I let some simple scratch or bump turn foul."

Beraht grunted, reaching for the platter of food in front of him. From what Tomas could tell, each of his friends had brought their breakfast into this common room, sharing the meal together.

As Tomas removed his tunic and shirt, Aebreanna stared daggers over at her uncouth companion, who casually tore at his ship biscuits. "You know," she sneered, "if you boys demonstrated a little more finesse in your actions, you would, perhaps, require less assistance after said actions were complete." She turned and began examining Tomas, administering a salve in whatever places she deemed necessary.

"Huh?"

"We're sloppy," Rogan translated.

The Uldra, now realizing the nature of the insult, turned back to Aebreanna. "Oh, oh! And who was it that slipped on the deck and landed on her big butt!?!" he demanded.

"That was you, actually," the Sylva replied primly. "I, in attempting to assist you, was tripped by those ungainly limbs you call legs."

"And I still managed to kill two Humans while on the floor! When you got grabbed and pinned, I had to save you... AGAIN."

Aebreanna finished with Tomas, who had managed to escape serious injury, and moved over to Rogan. The knight removed his hose at her gesture, having long-since learned not to object. "As I recall," the Sylva was saying over Rogan's grumbling, "I was only surprised because I had to keep one of those sea-men from stabbing you while you were lying on the deck."

Beraht hurled the biscuit to the table and stood, banging his head against the low ceiling. Fury shone on his face, but no more than was normal. "No Sylvai saves a son of Uldron!" he roared.

"*Sylva*," Aebreanna snapped. She snapped her fingers with each syllable. "*Syl-va*. The word cannot be hard to remember." The spy ran her hands along every inch of her sensuous curves, looking at the ignorant Uldra through her glowing eye. "In what world could a creature such as I be mistaken for anything but female?" she demanded.

"Bah!" Beraht spat on the floor. "Where's your strength? Where's the braids? Where's your meat!?! THAT'S what makes a real woman! You? Nothing but skin and bones!"

Beraht and Aebreanna sneered at each other but returned to their respective tasks, the Uldra to his eating, the Sylva to her healing.

Aebreanna knelt and examined Rogan's groin, the source of the knight's obvious discomfort. Only a brief glance revealed the injury. She glanced up with an empty expression. "That must be quite uncomfortable," she noted.

"You have no idea," the knight grimaced.

"Being female, I fear you are correct." The Sylva reached for a mixture of materials and spread them around Rogan's injury.

Tomas glanced at his knight.

"Shut up," Rogan commanded, seeing the look on his squire's face.

Aebreanna finished and stood, cleaning the viscous material from her hands.

"So," Tomas said after a few attempts at keeping his voice level. "Any contact?"

"No," Rogan answered. During the battle in Tordenia, King Cylan had reached out through his Archaeknights. In addition to the magical abilities granted to each of the warriors, the last of the Heroes of Fate had also formed a mystical connection to his bodyguards. King Cylan had spoken to Rogan, informed him of much that had been happening at the Keep. The legendary warrior had also been clear in recalling them home. Since then, though, the Archaeknights had reported that the connection seemed to fade, almost to nothing.

The knight carefully returned Talon to its scabbard. "We know the King is getting weaker," he said. "That poison will make it harder for him to use his magic, so he'll only risk it if there's something important. We all know what's happening and what we're doing. Fak'Har is heading to the Keep, where Vagris has taken command of a mercenary army." This, the knights said through gritted teeth, his voice almost a growl. "We'll cut through Dagon'ay to get home in time to stop the attack."

"And finish the fight Fak'Har started," Beraht added.

"Indeed," Aebreanna added. "Just try to avoid being knocked down again."

Again Beraht leapt to his feet, and also again banging his head on the ceiling. "No Sylvai-"

"*Syl-va.*"

"No FEMALE knows better than a son of Uldron how to fight!"

"Nor how to drink excessively or demonstrate poor hygiene, apparently."

"EXACTLY!"

"Ugh," Aebreanna rolled her opalescent eye. "You must be the most obvious example of your entire, misbegotten race!"

"What? Sorry, I don't speak uptight female!"

As their arguing continued, Rogan glanced over at his squire. "Why're you smiling?" he asked.

Tomas blinked. "I am?"

Chapter 3

Three days later, Tomas stepped onto the main deck after finishing his care of the horses. They had spent the day before at Ahmed's small island. A rocky outlet had also held a rough wood pier. This strange outcropping ran a great length from a wide, secluded lagoon, allowing the crew and passengers of the *Blue Lady* to avoid the need for longboats.

"Who built this?" Tomas had asked as the ship carefully made its dock.

"Pirates," Ahmed had shrugged from the whipstaff, easing the *Blue Lady* towards their sanctuary.

"What!?!"

"Anyone who sails this part of the world but refuses to kneel to House Balshazzar is called a pirate," the aging sailor explained. He was following the shouted commands of the men he had posted ahead, making subtle corrections to left and right as directed. "Tordenian taxes are oppressive, and this island makes for a good layover for some honest smuggling."

"Why would pirates all agree to build this?" Tomas had demanded.

Rogan chuckled. Like his squire, the knight had also come up on deck to watch the docking. "Common purpose can unite people," he had said. "But it helps when a wealthy, anonymous benefactor chips in."

Tomas had blinked before understanding. "House Calonar is helping pirates?"

The knight had shrugged. "We're helping people who are fighting House Balshazzar."

The crew had disembarked the horses, allowing Rogan and his squire to give them proper exercise and to graze on the tall grass resting back from the soft white sand of the wide beach. Aebreanna had lost herself among the many trees, moving dreamily towards a towering waterfall. Beraht and Teka Ironhands helped the crew with restocking their supplies, while the Archaeknights went hunting. The island had an abundance of fruit and nut trees as well as some game. That night, they enjoyed a great feast. Music was played and Aebreanna, refreshed from her time alone, led several of the Archaeknight women in dancing to the delight of the men. Asaya seemed especially adept at the graceful movements of body, arm, and leg, flowing about their great bonfire as freely as did the gentle breeze that seemed to forever envelop her. Tomas had been a bit surprised with Sarah joined this, the seemingly-reserved Archaeknight bringing to bear her mystical agility to spin and stretch and flow like a flame-tipped wind. Laughter, music, and merrymaking filled the air well into the night, fortifying them all against the hard days ahead.

The wind had become something of a mixed blessing. Asaya had delivered on her promise. Using the power granted to her by King Cylan, she had maintained a constant wind that drove the *Blue Lady* east at speeds that, once the passengers and crew had grown accustomed, most found exhilarating. The cost of such speed, however, was the constant labor of the crew to keep the *Blue Lady*'s sails and rigging secure. This unending series of tasks left little patience for the inexperienced passengers who rarely had sense enough to stay out of the sailors' way. More than a few harsh words had been barked in exasperation to prevent catastrophe, finally convincing most of the *Blue Lady's* passengers to remain out from underfoot.

Another disadvantage of the powerful winds Asaya had summoned was the rough seas that accompanied such winds. Beraht and Teka Ironhands, the Uldra of Rogan's team and the Archaeknights respectively, both complained bitterly at the unnecessarily-strong winds, the constant swaying of the ship, and the crippling tightness of their quarters. The races of Lanasia knew the Uldra were a land-bound people and did not take well to traveling by water. Even during the War of the Black Sea, that time when their Uprising had spilled into the waters around Pelsemoria, the Uldra had built only hulks with minimal seafaring ability. The mountainous warriors hugged the coast and used their vessels for little more than the transport of their soldiers. As both Beraht and Teka had pointed out, the Uldra were made for the mountains, not the waves.

Tomas had assumed Beraht would take kindly to having another of his race aboard. The morning of their boarding the *Blue Lady*, however, proved the matter more complicated.

Tomas and Rogan had left Ahmed to the running of his ship and gone below decks. There, they had found Teka Ironhands in the common room the passengers shared for meals and socialization. Aebreanna had been sitting with her back to the narrow door, for once, her flowing main pushed back, away from the horrid scars marring the right side of her once-flawless face. Teka was kneeling in front of the Sylva, her hand outstretched and moving slowly down Aebreanna's disfigured side. A soft blue and gold light floated out from the Archaeknight's hand, like an impossibly-fine mist composed of the bright heavens. This light drifted from among Teka's fingers, languidly crossing the brief distance, bouncing against Aebreanna's flesh and failing to find purchase.

Beyond the two females, Beraht had crouched on one of the Human-sized seats, near, but not too near, the Sylva. The brutish Uldra's ugly face had shown no sign of concern; in fact, he had even tried to force a look of apathy or even annoyance at the procedure. Still, his coal-black eyes had shown with worry for his oldest friend. He had glanced at Rogan and Tomas, jerking his hand to demand silence and stillness. The two Humans had obeyed, remaining in the far corner of the small cabin.

After several minutes, Teka had lowered her arm and her head, breathing heavily. "I'm sorry," she had whispered. "The wound is Fated. No lesser magic can restore your flesh. Only Fate Magic can restore it, or something of equivalent power."

Aebreanna had said nothing, only nodding and moving her mane to obscure the right side of her face once again.

Teka had stood then, ducking her head to keep from banging it on the ceiling. She turned to Beraht. "Your beard is restored," she had noted, "but unkempt."

The warrior's face had remained superficially-blank. "My mother is with the Allfather," he had replied.

"You are grown," the Archaeknight had said then, in a tone that had sounded to Tomas as though she were reciting some ritual phrase. "You no longer sit at your mother's table. Let me take her place, and offer care for your body." Her hands had started to reach up, towards Beraht's unkempt beard.

The Uldra had leaned away, only an inch, but in that gesture putting miles between him and her. "She who holds my heart, cares for my body," he had said, again in that tone that seemed to Tomas as though he were reciting some ritual, some mystical incantation. "She, alone, decides the care of my beard."

Teka had nodded and backed away. The Archaeknight gathered her few things, including the thick cudgel she always had at hand. Reaching the door, she had paused a moment and glanced back. "If ever you are in need of another, consider me."

Beraht had nodded solemnly, and Teka left, closing the door behind her.

Tomas had taken a breath then glanced at Rogan. "Can I ask?"

"Uldra courtship," his knight had replied.

"That was courtship?"

"Teka was only expressing her willingness to proceed with a courting," Aebreanna had explained, standing. The spy had retrieved the food provided to them upon their boarding of the *Blue Lady* and placed it in the center table. "The Uldra are so inherently violent, so quick to destruction, that they must place great restrictions on every element of their lives."

"There was no dishonor in her actions," Beraht had insisted, taking some of the food and, not bothering with the Human-sized chairs, simply sat on the floor. Even then, the Uldra had still sat above Aebreanna's eye level. "She was interested, but misunderstood the situation."

"So that was letting her down easy?" Tomas had asked, also retrieving food.

Beraht had nodded.

"What was all that about your beard?"

"Adolescent Uldra are braided by their mothers," Aebreanna had explained, taking small, delicate bites from her plate. "Female children have their first braids put in when they begin the transition to adulthood. The mother teaches them, over time, the proper care of themselves and marks special occasions or achievements with particular braiding styles and decoration. When a young Uldra male begins the transition, as marked with the appearance of his beard, his mother assumes the responsibility for the maintenance of that growth until the Uldra marries, at which time the wife takes over."

Tomas had looked at Beraht. "So, you can't comb your own beard?"

The son of Uldron had shaken his head. "Taboo. A warrior shouldn't send the wrong message."

"What message?"

Rogan had chuckled. "That he doesn't need a woman in his life."

They had been quiet then. As had often become the case during the long, hard miles of their journey together, Tomas assumed responsibility for breaking a difficult topic. "What does it mean that the wound is Fated?" he had asked.

Aebreanna had stopped eating and taken a deep breath. "You understand the Winds of Magic, that they flow in different aspects?"

Tomas had nodded. "Sure. Earth, Air, Fire, Water, Life, Death, Time, and Fate."

"The ordering is significant. Earth: creation and construction, is fundamental. Nothing else may appear without it. But, Earth can be undone by Air: adaptation and perception. These may be destroyed by Fire: evocation and assertion, which, in turn, can be undone by Water, intuitive thought and inspiration. So the order continues…"

"And ends with Fate," Tomas had finished, starting to understand.

"Indeed," Aebreanna had agreed. "Fate, destiny, the purposeful organization of all reality. A form of magic so fundamental, and so fundamentally powerful, that after Stalline the Wise, no other could master it through all the long centuries. Until…"

"Cyras Darkholm," Tomas once again had finished. "And his brother."

The Sylva had shaken her head. "No. Fak'Har can no longer wield Fate Magic or any of the Corporeal Winds. With the loss of his body, he lost his connection to those Winds. Over the centuries, he has mastered the Ethereal Winds: Dream, Thought, and Shadow."

They had said nothing for a time, sitting and eating their meal and considering the implications. Finally, again, Tomas had broken their awkward silence. "So, if the wound is Fated…?"

"It was inflicted not only by the brutality of the Druug, but also by the manipulation of Fate itself. Only another manipulation can undo what has been done."

Tomas had leaned back then, his eyes going to the locked cabinet at the back of their shared cabin. "What about…?"

Aebreanna had firmly shaken her head. "No," she had stared a hard look from her remaining eye at Tomas. "A Seal of Stalline is the most powerful, most fundamental manifestation of each Wind of Magic. But, it is neither infinite, nor all-powerful. Consider *Bjorgatkin*, the healing spring beneath Uldron. Even with its great magic, it could not fully restore… It still had limitations. And its healing of all our grievous wounds depleted the spring's natural magic. In time, that power will be restored. This is also true of the Seal of Life. We employed the Healing Sphere to save Beraht. His wounds were fatal, and his life nearly spent. The Seal brought him back; this required nearly all of its power. In time, that power will return."

"How long?" Rogan had grunted.

Aebreanna had shrugged. "As long as is needed. As such, we must conserve the Sphere's power. We must protect it and conserve its power for the King."

"What about you?" Tomas had asked softly.

"I am not dying. My needs are second to the King's."

Some of the passengers had a less vocal, but no less violent, means of objecting to the constant tossing about of the *Blue Lady*. As Tomas reached the main deck after their departure from the pirate cove, a blur of movement shot past him. The squire briefly caught sight of long, blonde braids in the breeze before they, like the head they were attached to, were thrown over the side of the ship to the violent accompaniment of vomiting. Tomas grimaced in sympathy for the poor woman as she continued to retch, her whole body spasming in objection to the ship's motion. She had been doing that ever since boarding the *Blue Lady*, her only respite coming during the battle against Tordenia's galleys.

"Again?" Sarah asked, moving up beside Tomas.

"Again," he confirmed. "Has she always been like this?"

Sarah shook her head slightly. "Kara never had problems with sea voyages that I'm aware." The flame-haired Archaeknight looked around, the sunlight shining off of the Calonar-sigil on her left eye. "But then, I can't recall a voyage this…"

"Exciting?" Tomas suggested.

Sarah shrugged.

Kara, once relieved of her stomach's contents, moved unsteadily towards them. Sarah reached out to help but let her hand drop when her blonde teammate's bright blue, pearlescent eyes widened before spinning and bending over the rail once more.

"Maybe we should get Teka?" Tomas suggested.

Sarah looked towards the forward area of the ship, from where an unending torrent of Uldric obscenity pinpointed the location of Beraht and Teka Ironhands, the Archeknight healer. "I rather doubt she is in the mood to tend to a bought of sea-sickness," Sarah mused.

"Maybe I can get Aebreanna?" Tomas offered.

"Would the baroness be willing to tend to a Halvan?"

The squire shrugged. "I don't think Aebreanna has a problem with Halvans. Besides, she's a member of House Calonar. How could she hold onto an old prejudice against her own king?"

"She's still a Sylva." Sarah looked at the sagging Kara. "Although," she mused, "it couldn't hurt to ask."

Ilaywin the archer walked up behind them. "Don't bother the baroness," he advised. "Kara just needs to rest." The Gwyndd native walked up to his fellow Archaeknight and said something softly to her. Kara, in response, gave the archer a weak smile. Ilaywin, with great care and tenderness, took his teammate in one arm and guided her uncertain steps towards the cabins below. As the two passed, Kara sent a glance and a grin to Sarah that belied the overly-weak steps she took with Ilaywin's support.

"Is that allowed?" Tomas asked.

The flame-haired Archaeknight shrugged. "Our first loyalty is to the King. We all understand that. But we're not monks." She nodded towards Rei, the Tramayan illusionist, and her husband Gendo. "Two of us are even married. The King doesn't want us to live loveless lives."

Sarah began walking along the deck, carefully grabbing the railing and rigging as needed in the strong wind but taking great care to stay out of the way of the working sailors.

Tomas followed, mirroring the movements of his nimble friend as best he could. Looking ahead towards the pair of Uldra, a thought entered his mind. "Does Teka ever fight?" Tomas asked. "I don't think I've seen her shed blood."

Sarah shook her head slightly. The two paused while a small group of sailors worked to secure several ropes that had torn free. "Teka took a vow called *Batront Efshar Hada* when she was younger. I think it means 'non-violence.'"

"Not exactly," Tomas supplied. "I studied Uldric in school. That oath was for the daughters of a village's Keeper of the Well. It means that she's a healer and teacher, free from any responsibility of tribe or family until she gets married. She can't fight or even defend herself if attacked. She can only defend those under her care."

"And she only carries that cudgel," Sarah added, nodding significantly towards the Uldra healer who stood with Beraht. Despite what Tomas had thought would be awkwardness between the two after Teka's failed proposal of a courtship, she and Beraht had nonetheless spent a great deal of time together aboard ship. They spoke together in the Uldric tongue and shared a great many friendly insults and challenges.

The Humans moved on past the cantankerous Uldra once the crew signaled it was safe.

Tomas looked up and smiled. With the force of Asaya's wind propelling the *Blue Lady*, it was very nearly worth a man's life to attempt to climb up to the crow's nest. The rigging the sailors customarily used as ladders was whipping about much too dangerously.

"How long has Drystan been up there?" he asked.

Sarah glanced up at the small perch from which her teammate was hanging onto. "Less than an hour," she replied. "He has another one to go."

"Two-hour watches in this?" the squire asked in surprise.

"For most of us, it's not that bad. Drystan can translocate, after all. If anything happens, he just jumps down."

Tomas shuddered at the memory of what Drystan called jumping. Seeing her friend's discomfort, Sarah patted him on the shoulder. "He swears that eventually you get used to it."

"He can get as used to it as he likes," Tomas replied, walking away from the mast. "I'll stick to horses and ships."

The pair reached the bow, looking out at the clouded horizon that stretched before them. Ahmed was already there with a strange device held to his eye. It looked somewhat like a small cross-staff, but much smaller and with strange, curved devices attached. The captain seemed to be looking through one end of the device, making notes on a map he had secured at a small table near his hip.

"Problem, Admiral?" Sarah asked.

"Not at all," he smiled, looking away from his arcane device. "Quite the opposite, in fact. I've been taking measurements throughout the night and now most of the morning. Thanks to your teammate, we're making much better time than I thought possible."

"I thought we were supposed to call you 'Captain?'" Tomas pointed out. The squire had made the mistake not long after boarding and been corrected.

Ahmed shrugged. "You asked, so I told you. The master of a ship is the captain. As his Majesty has also made me the commander of his fleet, I'm also an admiral. This makes me senior to the other ship captains. As they're not around, I don't use the title much."

"Sounds confusing," Tomas admitted.

"Not really. Prince Rogan is also Sir Rogan, is he not?"

"I guess."

"He has both titles, but one supersedes the other. It doesn't change the fact that he's still a knight. He just happens to be the knight that outranks all the other knights."

"So which do you prefer to be called?"

"Since you're not a member of my crew, I really don't care."

Tomas nodded slightly. "What is that?" he asked, gesturing towards the strange device Ahmed carried.

"A new Uldra design," the sailor grinned, holding up the invention. "They call it a back-staff. It's for determining our position."

"Land ho!" Drystan called out from above.

Ahmed set down his back-staff and pulled a traditional spyglass from beneath the small table, looking towards the horizon.

Tomas grinned again up to the crow's nest. "He's really getting into this," he noted.

Ahmed shrugged as he tried to see through the gathering clouds. "Let him enjoy it while he can," he replied. "That duty gets very old, very fast."

Tomas and Sarah looked out into the clouds and mist that had collected to obscure the east. Despite the pleasant warmth of the spring winds Asaya had called upon, a strange chill seemed to push back as the three gazed eastward. Over the shouts of the crew and the thousand other sounds that accompanied the *Blue Lady*'s dance across the waves, there was a new, ominous one in the distance. The booming of surf against hard cliff and the shattering of water against reefs. Among the light clouds and gentle mists that hugged the eastern horizon, several dark claws were slowly dragging themselves up from the cold sea ahead.

"Is that Dagon'ay?" the squire asked softly.

"Yes," Ahmed replied. "The one place in all the world every sailor knows to never enter. The place where the sea grows angry and swallows a ship faster than her crew can scream a prayer. The place where even great Kayalkiel, goddess of the angry sea, fears to enter. The place where the great Vaeyen make their lairs. The place where dragons be."

"And we're going in there," Sarah added.

The admiral shrugged. "Did you have something better to do?"

"Has anyone ever tried this before?" Tomas asked.

Ahmed laughed ruefully. "Oh, God yes. Why, just last year we were chasing a Xeshlin slaver that had been raiding the southern coast, near Pelsemoria. Her captain somehow managed to convince his crew to try and lose us in those islands."

"Did he make it?"

"No. She tore her bottom out within ten minutes of entering the straits."

"Has anyone ever made it?" Sarah asked.

"Well, there is an old tale about a captain from long ago, before the Heroes of Fate. This captain was fearless and ruthless. He attracted the eye of Kayalkiel, who blessed him with a vision of Her unclothed self. He reached for Her, but she laughed at him and slipped away like seawater through the fingers. The captain sailed every sea across the world in search of Kayalkiel, but She forever remained just out of reach.

Finally, he thought to trap Her, to lure the goddess to the one place from which none may escape."

"Dagon'ay?"

Ahmed nodded.

Tomas felt a slight lurch forward, as though the *Blue Lady* were increasing in speed without an increase in the wind. The squire put his hands on the rail for support. "What happened?" he asked, noting that the sound of crashing surf was growing, along with the chill in the air.

"Well," Ahmed mused, putting a hand to the rail himself, "the legends say that his ship made it through. After weeks of fighting off dragons and other monsters, of battling the sea itself, he and his crew found a safe passage, forged by Kayalkiel Herself."

"That's good news," Sarah insisted. The nimble Archaeknight had not yet needed to grab onto additional support with the additional speed, but she did have to adjust her stance. The wind, which had once come consistently from behind them, now battered the ship from several directions.

Ahmed continued his tale. "Not entirely," he warned. "The captain was killed on the last day of their journey home. Just as he caught sight of Kayalkiel, as the Lady of the Misty Waves emerged with open arms, he fell into the violent sea."

"Well," Tomas said, shivering a bit, "at least the ship made it."

"Actually, she ship was sunk by Xeshlin raiders a week later."

"So the path is lost," Sarah noted.

"One man made it out." Ahmed secured his map. The admiral handed it to a waiting crewman and turned back to the horizon, where the dark shapes that stabbed towards the sky were growing without end and multiplying like an army of Umbra. "That sailor had the chart his captain had drawn," he continued, staring at their destination. "On the chart was marked the route they had taken, but the sailor himself had lost the power of speech. He could only write down on the chart a few ravings about what had happened."

"If the route survived, why isn't it better known," Tomas demanded. The squire gathered his cloak tighter around his shoulders.

Ahmed shrugged. "Most sea dogs know it, but every ship that's tried to follow the route has been lost. Most men say it was cursed by the spirits of the crew that died in its discovery."

"Then what use is it?" the squire snorted.

"It may be deadly, but it's still the safest route, the only known way through."

"Safest?" Sarah snorted.

"Alright then, how about the least deadly?"

The flame-haired Archaeknight narrowed her emerald eyes at the approaching peaks. "That's the route we're taking," she surmised.

"That's right."

"That was the reason for your calculations through the night and morning. You had to approach Dagon'ay from the proper position."

"Are you nuts?" Tomas demanded. "You're taking us on a cursed route?"

"If you know another path," the old sailor laughed, "now would be a wonderful time to let me know. Otherwise, I'm taking us through the only route I know."

Before the squire could reply, the *Blue Lady* rocked violently to the right. Everyone was caught completely by surprise and made desperate grabs for anything stable. Tomas grabbed Sarah and spun, taking the blow of the right-side railing onto his back.

"You alright?" he asked with a grimace of pain.

"I was until you grabbed me," she replied, though making no effort to free herself from Tomas' arms. "Magical reflexes, remember?"

"Sorry."

Ahmed was already back on his feet, moving as much by way of the rigging as he was by his legs. "Report!" he roared to anyone that had information.

"Captain!" one of the crew called from the rear of the ship. "Whirlpool to port!"

"Batten down!" the admiral roared over the wind and tides. He grabbed a rope and slung himself up onto the railing, looking out the left side of the ship. In the distance, barely discernible over the building mist, was a gaping maw that threatened to drag the *Blue Lady* down to her destruction.

Tomas and Sarah joined Ahmed as he leapt back to the deck. "Damn!" he muttered darkly. "We're not even in Dagon'ay yet!" The admiral raised his voice to the quarterdeck. "Twelve points port! Secure stations!"

"Shouldn't we turn away from it?" Tomas asked.

"Too late," Ahmed replied as he stormed up towards the whipstaff. "She's got us. Kayalkiel must be hungry today! Damned stupid, putting inexperienced eyes on the watch." Seeing Ward and Rogan emerge from below, the admiral again issuing orders. "Get your boy down!" he barked to the leader of the Archaeknights. To Rogan he said, "Have everyone below get down and hold! This is going to get rough!"

Both warriors nodded and complied. Rogan disappeared below decks and Ward called Drystan down. Tomas and Sarah looked to Ahmed. "What can we do?" the squire asked.

"Shut up and hang on!" he barked. "Sarah, get Asaya!"

The nimble Archaeknight nodded and shot to the main deck to retrieve her teammate. The dark-haired Halvan woman often fell into a near-trance when she summoned the wind. For most of the day, Asaya seemed to prefer standing near the main sail, whistling a joy of freedom and flight as the long folds of her brightly-colored skirts danced about her lean body. She seemed nearly-oblivious to the world, even to growing danger, instead swaying with the winds she called.

Tomas grabbed one of the lines a sailor had secured to the quarterdeck and tied it around his waist.

"You'd probably be happier below!" Ahmed called out over the howling wind.

Tomas shook his head violently. "If I'm going to a watery grave, I want to see it coming!"

Ahmed nodded in understanding. "Lock one end of that rope to those posts," he said, pointing to a row of posts in front of the whipstaff. "Wind them around the rail to use up the slack, and then tie another end good and tight around me too! Get one around those women when they get here!"

The squire nodded and had just finished tying off Ahmed when Sarah and Asaya arrived. Without a word, Tomas tied lines around the two Archaeknights.

"Wind, Asaya," Ahmed commanded. "As much as you can give from behind! We need speed!"

The Archaeknight nodded and turned, facing the sails. Even over the howling wind, Tomas heard the high-pitched whistle she emitted. Moments later, a force like the fist of God stuck the *Blue Lady* from behind, nearly lifting the entire ship out of the water and carrying it forward amidst a wall of air. The ship groaned in objection, but only a moment before slamming her bow back into the water and leaping ahead, no longer dancing, but charging through the increasingly-angry waves.

The whirlpool yawned before them like the mouth of a massive beast. The *Blue Lady* approached it from the right side, giving Tomas an uncomfortably-excellent view. Water spiraled into that portal to oblivion, along with some random debris and particles of ocean matter, all caught in the vortex's grip. Nothing could escape such absolute hunger.

"We're going to skip it," Ahmed barked. "Let Kayalkiel think she's got my *Lady*, get in real close, and let her give us all that speed, and then break off at the last second." The aging sailor laughed in a surprising burst of joy. "The Mistress of the Open Sea likes to be teased, to be danced with! Let's give Her what She wants!" He turned to Asaya. "This only works if you keep that wind on us!"

The Halvan continued her whistle but glanced back at Ahmed and winked.

Faster and faster the *Blue Lady* approached the terrible monster before her. The ship groaned under all the pressures working against her hull, but she determinedly held together. The crew worked tirelessly at their stations, adjusting the rigging and preparing for what was to come. The tension was terrible as all those on the deck knew their fates rested on the captain. Should Ahmed turn away too late or too soon, all was lost.

Tomas could now see over the edge, down into the darkness of forever. The ship began to lean, ever so slightly, towards that eternity. A spiral that led into nothingness, with cold mist that chilled the soul and an awful grumbling howl like a hungry beast waiting at the bottom. The squire looked into that pit and felt as though his soul was sliding down into the darkness.

"NOW!!!"

The *Blue Lady* pulled hard to the right. The crew moved as one, moving ropes and sails. It seemed as though, through sheer force of collective will, the sailors urged their ship away from the awful beast that wanted to devour them all. Ahmed pushed at the whipstaff, turning them away from Death and towards another chance at life. Asaya increased her whistle, calling even more wind from behind. All these things happened together and the *Blue Lady* responded.

The ship shot away from the whirlpool. The great beast at the bottom of that pit howled its fury but could not hold on to the *Blue Lady*. The flagship of House Calonar's fleet danced across the jagged waves as it tore a new path through the sea away from the danger behind and towards the danger ahead.

"Get a watch up!" Ahmed called out. "Rufino!" he called out after spotting a particular face. "Get your sorry carcass up to that lookout!"

A weather-beaten sailor looked up at the wildly swaying mast and threw his captain a look of pure hatred. "What makes you think I'm goin' up there?" he demanded.

"Because if you don't I'm telling the cook to serve you nothing but seaweed until we get back to port, after which I'll have you hanged for mutiny! Now get your tail up there before I have Beef throw you up!"

The weather-beaten sailor put a hand up in surrender. "Alright, alright. Just askin'." Despite his hesitation, Rufino climbed up the treacherous rigging with ease and only slipped to his death once.

"Well," Ahmed grinned, "now that the preliminaries are over, I suppose it's time for the main event."

Chapter 4

The storm was worsening. Both sea and sky growled warnings like angry guard dogs snarling at intruders drawing too near their home. A curtain of dark clouds pushed down, as though to smother the *Blue Lady* and her crew. The ocean became an unending, frothy cascade of wave after wave. The separation of the two could no longer be seen, with white-capped waves blending into the lightning-streaked mist. They had yet to enter Dagon'ay proper, with the first of the reefs and islands still laying ahead, and yet the world thrashed against their intrusion into that most forbidden of places.

"Are we sure about this?" Tomas shouted to his knight over the crash of surf and the boom of thunder.

"No choice!" Rogan called back. The two were with Ahmed near the whipstaff. Although most of the passages had heeded their hosts' advice and remained below decks, knight and squire spent much of their time on the quarterdeck.

Tomas moped at his face with one hand while maintaining a firm grip on one of the guidelines. Sheets of rain had come with the dawn. Hair and clothing was plastered to the body, and an omnipresent chill made mockery of the summer sun, which had long since retreated. "Can you even see where we're going?" the squire asked.

Ahmed shrugged. "The sea will tell you when to turn," he offered. "You can feel when something draws close." He adjusted the whipstaff and, a few moments later, Tomas spotted a reef, barely visible beneath the thrashing sea, slide to the *Blue Lady*'s left side.

"You're steering by feel?" the squire asked.

"By everything," the aging sailor replied. "You've got to use all your senses, all your instincts. The sea'll warn you when danger comes close. The warning'll be subtle, but it'll always be there."

Everything went still. The wind became less than a whisper. The waves vanished, with the sea calming into a featureless mirror, reflecting the ship. The growing thunder quieted, and the ship's groaning stopped. There was not even motion of current beneath them. All that remained was the grey mist, the impenetrable curtain surrounding the *Blue Lady* that obfuscated the world around them. "Or," Ahmed whispered, "sometimes it's not so subtle."

Rogan's hand went to Talon, his longsword as always belted to his waist. "Kid," the knight said in a voice as flat as the surrounding water. "Get everybody up here."

The squire was moving even before his knight had finished the command. "Armor?" he asked as he climbed the steep steps down.

"No time. Weapons."

Tomas roused their team and the Archaeknights. All the warriors of House Calonar responded to the summons, grabbing for blade and bow and hurrying to the main deck. Voices were hushed. Eyes rolled to the horizon, now only just out of reach because of the heavy mist enveloping them. Every step, every creak of rope, every breath seemed an impossible crash. The crew, suddenly without crisis, stood about, looking at each other in wide, terrified eyes.

Tomas rejoined Rogan and Ahmed on the quarterdeck, his own hand staying near Steelheart's hilt. Like his knight, though, the squire did not yet draw the fabled blade of House Calonar. "Is this natural?" he asked.

Ahmed made a half shrug. "It can happen," he whispered. "The sea can grow calm, the wind can still. But this…"

Aebreanna and Beraht climbed up, with Ward and Sarah close behind. Rogan glanced to the Sylva and his squire. "Can either of you sense anything?" he asked.

Aebreanna briefly closed her eyes and seemed about to take a deep breath, but jerked as though having been slapped. She gasped in surprise and held a hand to the side of her face. Beraht caught her before the Sylva could do more than stumble half a step, easily supporting her tiny frame.

"Wait!" Rogan snapped to Tomas, even as the squire was about to also try tapping into his mystical senses.

Ward turned to the main deck. "Perimeter!" he snapped. "Secure and hold!" In response, the Archaeknights spread across the *Blue Lady*, weapons drawn. Asaya flowed to the base of the mainmast, her rapier held ready and a commanding whistle at her lips. Gendo and Rei, their strange Tramanese weapons also in hand, moved to the bow. Kara, for the first time in days not stumbling in stomach-turning illness, moved to protect Teka Ironhands, as the archaeknight healer put her back to a wall. Deriel drew his Sylvai blades and flew up to the crow's nest, trying to force his Sylvu sight to penetrate the oppressive mist. Ilaywin held his bow ready and stood beside Asaya at the mast. Khwezi, Drystan, and Fikri, an odd collection of Humans from far-flung corners of the world, stood back-to-back at the center of the *Blue Lady*'s main deck, ready for an instant response to anything.

The wait was not a long one.

"There," Tomas said grimly, pointing to the right.

Something approached. The mist parted for it. The grey curtain was not blown aside as it might be for some great bird, but instead the heavy cloud seemed to pull itself back, though from fear or respect was unclear. The now-still water also gave way, retreating, dipping low as though the sea was made to bow in the presence of this new arrival. Rogan's team and the crew of the *Blue Lady* stared as though mesmerized by whatever approached. Only the Archaeknights, bound by duty and skill, maintained their vigil in all directions. Though even these, the most elite of House Calonar's warriors, could not help but have one eye on the strange arrival.

As the thing approached, Tomas could begin to make out a form. It drew closer to the *Blue Lady*, but did not do so in any great hurry. It drifted on a non-existent breeze as a leaf would float lazily upon a gentle wind. It had a body, the squire discerned. A head, torso, and limbs became solid and seen. Backed by the venerating grey mist, the thing had no color. Instead, light seemed to slip around the shape, unable to fix it with any permeance. The approaching thing passed over their heads, turning and floating along the length of the ship. It's nature become clearer to Tomas as it did this, though not, the squire realized, because of its proximity. The shape was changing, altering itself as it flew. The head became more pronounced and waves of hair spilled out. The limbs lengthened and became defined, ending with fingers and toes. The torso adjusted, swelling with breast and hip. Still, though, there was no perceptible face.

The strange, female-thing passed around the bow of the *Blue Lady* and turned, again floating down its length to the very rear, hovering over the quarterdeck. Ahmed wrapped a thick rope around the whipstaff, locking the steering lever in place, and retrieved a shortsword. The aging sailor said nothing, but only retreated, eyes wide and mouth agape, as the warriors of House Calonar moved forward.

The female-thing descended. Rogan and Tomas moved to the center, facing her. Aebreanna and Beraht, weapons ready, stood to their right. Ward and Sarah, equally-weary, moved to the left. Behind, the Archaeknights moved into supporting positions. "Enough of the show," Rogan said, not in a threatening voice, but neither in a welcoming one.

The female-thing glanced towards him, eyes forming. They were almond-shaped, and the color of an angry sky filled them. Nose and ears similarly appeared, and with them, a mouth twisted into a sneer of contempt. The face should have been a beautiful one, reserved for statues of goddesses or ancient empresses, without flaw or feeling, and frozen forever in breath-taking beauty. This, however, was a face of cold indifference, of supreme arrogance in the face of lesser beings. It was the face of someone forever looking down and seeing nothing of worth.

Most frightening of all, though, remained the eyes. Tomas recalled the eyes of the Triumvirate, the leaders of the Arcane Guild at Frostfront. All the starry heavens seemed to have rested behind the eyes of those three, supremely-powerful archmagi. But with that appearance also came the distance, the indifference of the night sky. There had been no humanity in the Triumvirate's eyes, no curiosity or joy or anything but cold calculation. This creature, however, had eyes of angry power.

She stared at them, her sneer perpetual. Brief flashes of power, like the lightning of a devastating storm, danced behind her eyes. The faintest blue of a clear sky rested behind whirling grey like clouds ready to shower an unsuspecting village with death and destruction. These were the eyes of power, raw and cruel.

Those storm-wracked eyes moved from one face to the next, barely pausing with Ward or Ahmed. They scanned briefly Beraht and Sarah and Tomas. They fixed for an unending moment on Aebreanna, and Tomas thought he saw the faintest hint of something alter the sneer bending her lips. She was not happy, for happiness was alien to this creature. No, the squire decided, it was amusement and perhaps anticipation that danced ever so briefly along that hard face. Finally, the female-thing rested her stormy gaze on Rogan.

"I am Ravana," she said, her sneer replaced with an amused grin.

Gasps and oaths and strangled prayers for God's mercy choked the air. All, seasoned warriors, enchanted protectors, champions, sailors, took an involuntary step back. Weapons, once held ready were raised in shaking hands. Faces paled and breath came in gasps.

Ravana ran her hands through her long hair, thrilling in the waves of fear she sensed, as though empowered by them, rejuvenated by them. "I bear a message from the Vaeyen," she said.

"How?" Rogan demanded through clenched teeth. He held Talon at the ready, though his hands trembled. "You were banished."

"I am restored. I sit once again with my family."

"What madness!?!" Aebreanna's voice was choked. Tomas glanced over and saw that she had, without thinking, taken a step behind Beraht, as though seeking shelter as a child would.

Ravana glanced at the Sylva, once again betraying that strange look of gleeful anticipation. "You should not judge, Daughter of Fate," the Mad Vaeyen chastened. "Your own restoration draws close."

Beraht growled, the sound coming like the low rumble of the avalanche before it buries a hated, insignificant thing. His mighty Uldra waraxe, without command, began crackling with holy rage.

"Ha!" Ravana laughed, her cruel sneer becoming only more insidious. "You are not Fated to die here!" She glanced again at Aebreanna. "And not by my hand." The Mad Vaeyen stood a moment, arm half-raised, but soon she waved away Beraht's looming threat. "Enough of this, I grow bored." Ravana looked at Rogan. "And your master has certainly warned you of the danger in boring me."

"What do you want?" Rogan said, his voice still not showing the terror his body betrayed.

Ravana leered with mad, murderous lust at Rogan and all his friends and comrades. More flashes of power sparked from her stormy eyes and the tip of a serpentine tongue drew along her lips. "If you only knew what I really want," she hissed, her mouth growing row upon row of dagger-like fangs. Her face then returned to its sneering-indifference. "Alas, duty compels otherwise. The Vaeyen command you to leave our home."

"We're just passing through," Rogan replied. "No stops this time."

Ravana laughed then. It was a horrid sound, without joy or even mirth, lacking in anything but the delight in others' suffering. "Yes, my family told me about that. How delightful. To hoard the Seal of Fire for centuries, only to have it stolen by," she waved at them all as though a child might dismiss the lives of tiny insects. "Marvelous." The Mad Vaeyen then leveled a gaze at Beraht. "But drawing our blood, wounding a child of the Radiant?" She shook her head. "That demands…" her eyes narrowed, "retribution."

Beraht set himself, as implacable and undeniable as a mountain. He raised his mighty waraxe.

"Oh, not yet," Ravana laughed again, raising a finger that became distended and clawed. She leered at him, and then at Aebreanna, her hand returning to deceptive simplicity, "But soon."

"Speak your business," Rogan demanded.

"As I said, the Vaeyen demand you leave. You are Fated to return to that little city of yours, but nothing dictates how long your trip takes." She turned her stormy gaze out and ahead. "You have chosen to violate our home, not doubt, in some foolish hope of a shortcut. This will not be. If you turn around now, the Vaeyen will not further hamper you with storm and sea. If you continue, your little boat becomes my plaything."

"We can negotiate," Tomas suddenly said, though why he spoke and from where his words came, he did not know. Even his tone was strange. The squire was nearly mindless in his fear of the Mad Vaeyen, of the legends of her brutality. And yet, a serenity appeared within that swirling terror, an eye of peace and clarity. His voice, speaking without his knowledge or instruction, became calm, gentle, and wise.

Ravana threw her head back, her mocking laughter booming out into the unmoving sea. "What could such a tiny thing as you offer a child of the Radiant?" she said though chokes of derision.

"You said yourself," the squire's voice pointed out, though Tomas himself was still unsure of what was prompting the words. "We are Fated to return home. This ship is Fated to make safe port. Nothing you can do will change that."

The Mad Vaeyen's smile fell to nothing. Her stormy eyes flashed in irritation and she took a half-step forward.

"The Vaeyen don't want us in Dagon'ay, but we need to get home as quickly as possible. We can minimize our intrusion." He stepped forward and looked up at the much-taller female. "Give us a safe path, a quick route to the far side of Dagon'ay."

"Or what?" Ravana sneered, her fingers extending once again into talons.

"Or nothing," Tomas calmly replied. "Show us a quick way through and you will have fulfilled your obligation to the other Vaeyen." The squire sheathed Steelheart and put his hands together. A pristine light appeared between his fingers, then. He flung his arms out to either side, and the mystical light spread out like a white mist that saturated the *Blue Lady*, her decks, her rigging, her sails, and her passengers and crew. When the golden light threatened to touch Ravana, the Mad Vaeyen hissed and pushed into the air. She screamed her fury and lunged at Tomas, but was repelled by a flash of the white light.

"The White Lady's gaze has been drawn to this ship," the squire told her. "Any creature, even one normally beyond the sight of Death, is now vulnerable to Her when in contact with it. You cannot touch the ship or anyone upon her, either through your body, or your magic."

Ravana floated for a moment, seething. Finally, "So be it!" she hissed. The Mad Vaeyen drew herself up. "I cannot touch you; you are Fated to make the passage. But I can make you suffer in the crossing!" She pointed to the sky and shot like an arrow of hate into the grey mist, her mortal form sliding off like rain. All was still and silent for a few heartbeats, and then the sea and sky crashed upon the *Blue Lady*.

They were all quiet, staring at Tomas. After Ravana's retreat and the return of the storm, the crew had returned to their work in navigating the angry sea. The Archaeknights joined in the effort, lending their mystical abilities to the struggle. Rogan's team went below, needing no order to gather in the small common cabin at the rear of the ship.

"You want to tell me what in Underworld you were thinking?" Rogan muttered, pouring himself a cup of rum. "And what was that light?" The knight was struggling a bit with the unpredictable turning of the cabin, but finally managed to half-fill the wooden cup.

"Death Magic," Aebreanna supplied, sitting on one of the chairs and bracing herself with her legs.

"I thought Death Magic was forbidden," Rogan said. "The Guild said they'd blocked that Wind." He took a seat and, matching Aebreanna, used his legs to brace against the constant back and forth rocking.

"Apparently not." Beraht simply sat on the floor, wedging himself into a corner.

"Indeed," Aebreanna agreed. "After the destruction unleashed by Karnat, the Arcane Guild promised that their Triumvirate had locked away that particular Wind of Magic. Nonetheless, Anninihus did still become a Deathmage.

Tomas stood apart from them, as much as the small cabin would allow, and held to a pair of cabinets for stability. "I…" words failed. He was trying to recall how he knew to say what he did, or how he was able to access the magic he had employed. Now, however, his mind was blank. "I don't know." He closed his eyes and breathed deep. "For a while now, it's felt like there's this part of my mind, this place in the back that I don't really have access to. There's information there. It just lets me know when I need to know something. It's like a voice, but not a voice."

"Does it tell you to kill people?" Beraht asked. "Because, I guess that would be alright."

"Must you?" Aebreanna demanded wearily.

"What?" the Uldra replied innocently. "The kid's possessed. So what? We've all be possessed. Do you remember that time you got possessed by that-"

"I remember perfectly well, thank you very much," the Sylva snapped.

"You built that nest up in Darkholm's tower!"

"Thank you, Beraht."

"It took us a week to get you down!"

"I said I remember."

"By the Allfather, you stank."

"I SAID I REMEMBER!"

"Um," Tomas raised his hand. "I'm still panicking a little."

"Take a breath, kid," Rogan advised. "Can you deliberately access this voice, this information?"

The squire shook his head. "I'm not sure. It's always been in some emergency. It's like whenever I try to use magic. I just... do it."

"Breathe deeply," Aebreanna instructed. "Close your eyes and let your mind wander where it will."

He did so.

"Remember how to find your calm," Rogan advised. "Let the world flow in, through, and out of you. Don't fight, just abide."

"Indeed," Aebreanna agreed. "Do not try to force knowledge. Do not try to pick at certain ideas or impulses. Simply let your mind supply what it will. Breathe and just exist within the moment."

Tomas felt a lassitude, a still, peaceful calm fill his soul. He opened his eyes and looked at Aebreanna. "Your mother's name was Aevasaleth, daughter of Aeanveniel, daughter of Salethesal, matriarch of House Tressalon." Whence this information came, Tomas did not know. He did not seek it out. Somehow, though, when he looked at Aebreanna, knowledge seemed to flow in from some other place, separate and yet within the young man. "All bore the Wyrdmark. You inherited it not from your father, but your mothers."

Aebreanna gasped, her opalescent eye going wide.

Tomas' serene gaze floated to Beraht. "*Beraht benhel Frodr.* Before you left home, your father told you the secret of your family, that you weren't cursed by the

Nameless, but burdened with a Fated responsibility. Everything you do, just as everything your father and his all did, has been in service to that destiny, to prepare the way for the One Who Comes."

Beraht narrowed his eyes but said nothing.

The squire looked at his knight. "Rogan Eigenhard, cousin of Dwyer, Baron of Grania. Your first love-"

Rogan held up a hand, silencing Tomas. "We get it," he snapped. He turned to the others. "What's it mean?"

"One person in all the world knew what he just spoke," Aebreanna said.

"Alexia," Beraht nodded. "She's the only one I told about what my father said." The Uldra paused then, his brow furrowing. "She knew, but my father knew, and his father."

"But how?" Rogan demanded. He glanced at his squire.

Tomas thought, his brow furrowing.

"Not like that," Aebreanna reminded him. "Just breathe. Let the knowledge come without force."

The squire nodded and breathed. "I was dying," his mouth said, his voice becoming lighter, empowered with a mother's love. His eyes, now opalescent, turned to Aebreanna. "I knew it was not your father, despite the Shadow's deception. That was why I hid you. Even after he violated me, after he tortured me, I would not give you up. You are the last hope of our House, born of two great legacies. I wanted to comfort you, to wipe away your tears, but I could only watch and see the hope drain from you. I am so glad you found your way to our cousins in House Calonar."

Aebreanna said nothing, but tears fell from her opalescent eye and her breathing was rapid, even as her lips quivered in long-suppressed grief.

Tomas' now-granite eyes went to Beraht. A voice spoke in Uldric, telling his son of the night Fak'Har came to their village and slaughtered their family. He spoke of battling the Shadowed Mage, and of falling to his magic. He reminded Beraht of their family's legacy, one of service and loyalty, and the urgency of preparing the way for the One Who Comes.

Beraht said nothing, made no move or response. The Uldra only bowed his head slightly at the sound of his father's voice, unheard in decades.

Tomas turned emerald eyes to Rogan. "I was dying," a woman's voice said in Gwenish. "Anninihus had poisoned me and escaped. You could have caught him, killed him, but you stayed with me. I whispered to you one last request, and you've done it. You are still a good man."

Rogan tried to remain as stoic, as unflinching as Beraht, but his shaking body belied the act.

"I was dying," Tomas' voice said then in Gunnic. His now opalescent eyes, shining with hazel love, were not looking at any one thing, any one person. His voice became matriarchal: gentle, loving, and wise. "I knew Tomas would survive. He was Fated: the Final Host. Somehow, he would live through the attack and reach Cylan's Keep. I used the last of my gifts. He became Fatetouched: he can change things that are Fated."

"Is that possible?" Rogan asked, clearing an old grief from his throat.

"Apparently so," Aebreanna replied, shrugging away her own old wounds.

"While I was dying, I used the Truthsight, what little remained to me after passing it to Nora all those years ago. I saw what Tomas needed to do…" He stopped, then, his eyes losing Alexia's opalescence and his voice losing the harmony of her loving wisdom.

"What is it?" Aebreanna asked.

"Something's missing," the squire noted in his own voice. "It's… like a part of has been cut out, like I'm not seeing all of it."

"What else?" Rogan asked.

"I… she… Alexia saw something, something to do with Cyras, or maybe Fak'Har. She wanted to disrupt what one or both of them was… will do. I woke up, and she decided…" The squire's eyes snapped wide. He collapsed to his knees, cradling his head in his hands. Aebreanna was there, beside him, holding him. "She knew she was going to die, there, then," the young man said in a trembling voice. "She somehow tapped into my… her ability to cheat Fate. She put something in my mind, awoke a power that's only existed sporadically in my family…" The squire tilted his head, filtering through memories that were not his, echoing from beyond the White Lady's Veil. "In my mother's family. She had it; my mother reached out to Father Konrad, who taught her how to suppresses it. Alexia had been tracking my family for generations. I think… I think she was waiting for me." He could not stop the tears.

Rogan was quiet, thinking. Then, "Alexia couldn't use Fate Magic," he glanced at Beraht, "I think."

The Uldra shrugged.

Aebreanna snapped her finger at Rogan, who handed over the cup of rum. She offered sips to Tomas. "Like all matriarchs of House Calonar," the Sylva reminded them, "Alexia had the Truthsight passed to her, and she, in turn, passed it to Queen Nora. This ability is a natural manifestation of Fate Magic, even as Tomas' abilities are a natural manifestation of the Wind of Death. Tomas is using her wisdom and her skill to tap into his own natural abilities."

"Is that what he did to Ravana?"

The Sylva nodded. "Apparently, this ship is Fated to endure."

"We're Fated to make it to port," Tomas confirmed. He continued to deeply and, with Aebreanna's help, sat at their small table. "Alexia saw this journey, years ago, when she looked at Ahmed. She knew he would sail to Tordenia with all of us, and then return home. No matter what, this ship is Fated to get through Dagon'ay. We will get back to the Keep. What I did… it wasn't part of that."

"What did you do, then?" Rogan asked.

"Not me," the squire objected. "Or… not just me. Alexia's insight, her knowledge, and…" Tomas' eyes widened in awe. "And my grandmother. She received training as a death mage… from… someone." The squire breathed deeply. "Ravana is Vaeyen. She's normally immortal, beyond the touch of the White Lady. I could… sense her absence from the Wind of Death. I couldn't touch her, but I could touch the ship. I wove the Wind into the ship, all around it."

"This is a ship of death, now?" Beraht demanded incredulously.

"Not the way you mean," the squire countered. "It's more like, now the White Lady can see, can touch anyone who makes contact with the *Blue Lady*. They become mortal, even if for only a minute. It's not that they will die or they must die. They just…"

"Can die," Rogan finished.

"So," Aebreanna sighed. "We are protected from her explicit, overt attack. Even in her madness, I doubt Ravana will risk herself attacking us, no matter her hatred for House Calonar. Despite this, I fear she will not relent in her vendetta."

Tomas stood, with some help from Aebreanna, and braced himself again. "What vendetta?" he asked. "I could feel how much she hates you, hates everyone in House Calonar."

"The Siege of Velaross, kid," Rogan answered.

"When Cylan Calonar almost died?"

"He did die," Beraht countered. "He was brought back."

"Only the Heroes of Fate knew the true story, and now, with them all gone, only the King knows. During the Siege of Velaross, when the Golden Army sought to defeat the Nenic Twins and their unliving army, Ravana appeared and attacked, killing the King. The other Heroes brought him back, and they defeated the Mad Vaeyen, driving her off."

"The vendetta goes further than that," Aebreanna added. "The Queen once revealed to me that King Cylan accidentally caused the death of Ravana's child. This is what triggered her madness. This is why she inflicted torturous death upon Kyle Calonar."

"And now she's targeting us," Tomas shuddered.

"But she can't stop us," Beraht insisted.

"No," Rogan sighed titling his head at the latest crash of thunder. "But she can make the trip… interesting.

Chapter 5

Waves crashed over the deck of the *Blue Lady*. One after another, walls of seawater surged, towering above the mast. Although the ship rolled away from the danger each time, trying desperately to protect her vulnerable crew and passengers, those pounding blue fists still came with pitiless, relentless fury. There was no respite from the endless tidal barrage; even as one wave finished its assault, the crew of the *Blue Lady* would look up to see its brother looming above them from another direction. The sea hurled herself at them relentlessly.

Ravana's magic was fully upon them. The sun had fled behind an angry burial shroud of inky clouds. The sky had become as dark as fresh grave dirt, with only the frequent claws of lightning, slashing across the clouds and plunging into the unquiet waters to illuminate the growing terror on the crew's faces. The wind howled from every direction, heedless of Asaya's command. Anything not secured to the deck was cast about, becoming a deadly hail of rage and vengeance. Any breath taken frozen the lungs and burned the throat. The loudest yells of command, instruction, or supplication were swallowed by the Mad Vaeyen's wrath.

The moon and sun were lost, nearly forgotten in the unending assault. Despite this, flashes of lighting were nearly-continuous, creating an unearthly glow that swallowed hope. When those sailing aboard the *Blue Lady* risked a look skyward, they saw the shadow of the Mad Vaeyen. She was following them, floating within the maelstrom, directing it. Ravana used her unimaginable power to lash at them, while remaining safe from the touch of the White Lady.

Each island the *Blue Lady* desperately tried to sail around was nothing more than a jagged stone claw, grasping for the delicate ship. Little vegetation grew on the small outcroppings of rock or the ominous peaks towering over the intruders. Coral reefs lurked amidst the foaming surf of each narrow channel, with uneven currents, whirlpools, and unpredictable shallows as their nefarious companions. The mountains of Dagon'ay, once a great range of majestic peaks swallowed and deformed by the Disaster of Nassinalia, drew around them like the fanged maw of some ancient, chthonic beast. Yet still, the brave crew and passengers of the *Blue Lady* sailed on.

Tomas gripped the railing near the whipstaff on the quarterdeck with all his strength, constantly checking the rope that secured him to the deck. He occasionally tried to wipe some of the water from his eyes, despite the futility of such an action. He leaned against the wind and looked in the direction in which he knew Ahmed stood, seeing only a dim shadow as the veteran sailor struggled to hold their course against the savage combination of storm and tide and the Mad Vaeyen's rage. "How many sails to you have?" the squire shouted in between howls of thunder.

Ahmed shook his head, clearing it of at least some of the accumulated rainwater. He opened his mouth and spat away the storm before answering. "We were lucky to have the spare!" he roared back.

Their original sail had torn not long after Ravana's departure, the first victim of Dagon'ay, but not its last. The process of raising the replacement had cost the lives of two sailors as the Mad Vaeyen's power had thrashed, again and again, upon them in an effort to halt their work. So vicious had been the watery attack, so rapid the waves, that the two men who fell to their deaths in the cold water had not even had the chance to scream.

"Two points starboard!" the relayed command came from below Tomas' feet.

The squire turned and repeated the words to Ahmed, and the captain responded by pulling at the whipstaff. With their loss of visibility and the constant wind, Ahmed had ordered a relay system into effect. Four lookouts were posted at the *Blue Lady's* bow who knew the sea best. These sailors would shout course corrections to a series of people who were evenly spaced along the deck. Since the storm's arrival, their system had worked, if only barely.

"If there's no replacements," Tomas continued, again struggling to be heard over the storm, "is it wise to risk this?"

Ahmed wiped his face and looked up at the battered mizzen sail, swinging wildly in its desperate bid to keep the *Blue Lady* balanced against the sea's unrelenting assault. He could not maintain his raised eyes for long, though, before the rain forced his gaze down. "You're right," the captain shouted. "Even if another sail doesn't go, we're damaging the masts!" He was again forced to clear his face of the buildup of water. "Call down; get a team to secure the sails! Have Ward's team ready!"

Tomas nodded and turned. The young man tried his best to keep his shoulders into the wind, with his head down as the wind and rain continued to assault his senses. He hailed the next sailor in the chain and relayed Ahmed's orders.

Within seconds, a group of sailors emerged from below. They carefully tied ropes around each other and to the deck before spreading out to each of the *Blue Lady's* three masts. With the work detail came several Archaeknights, none of them bothering with a securing-line. Tomas thought he spotted Sarah among them, but could not be sure with the storm surging all around.

Each team of sailors split into two smaller groups, with one climbing up the left side rigging, and the other the right. The Archaeknights stood ready below, waiting for whatever must inevitably come.

"Five points port!" came the shouted correction.

Ahmed jerked the whipstaff and the *Blue Lady* turned sharply. At the same moment, another of the hidden currents aided the ship's correction, sending her spinning much further than intended. Everyone standing was sent tumbling to the right. Tomas struggled to maintain his grip on the rail even as Ahmed desperately clung to the steering lever, scrambling to his feet, cursing, and trying to correct their course.

Too late. Four of the sailors who had been climbing the rigging, at that point a little more than half-way up, were thrown. The crew on the left had been pinned against the ropes and able to curl amongst them. The men on the right had no such advantage as the ship was torn from their hands and feet and the dark, thrashing sea beneath them growled hungrily in anticipation of its meal.

"Archeknights!" Ward barked. No other command was needed.

Two of the elite warriors leapt forward. Kara, the blonde woman, slid through the deep water on the deck and thrust out her arm. The Calonar-sigil covering her left eye blazed to life and, in response to her gestures, one of the falling sailors stopped in midair. Kara then jerked her arm back and the terrified man flew towards her. The woman caught him and they both fell into the ready arms of the crew.

Sarah moved even faster than her teammate, her own sigil blazing to life as the Archaeknight leapt into harm's way. She grabbed one of the securing lines and dove off the deck, throwing the rope back in the same motion without a backwards glance. Ward caught the line and braced himself. Once the rope went taught, he heaved; Sarah and the sailor flew up onto the deck, drenched but alive.

The sailors continued to work at lowering the sail, despite the danger, under the protection of the Archaeknights. Tomas observed this and finally shook his head. The squire turned to Ahmed. "How long can we keep this up?" he demanded.

"As long as we have too!" the captain shouted. "We'll be through in a few weeks!"

"A FEW WEEKS!?!"

Another wave crashed over the deck.

"Don't worry," Ahmed laughed. "This storm is good!"

"HOW!?!"

"I'll dance with Kayalkiel any day!" he laughed in spite of the roaring sea. "No matter how temperamental She may become!"

More waves tossed the ship. Ahmed briefly lost control of the whipstaff but, with Tomas' help, straightened the *Blue Lady*'s course.

"Are you mad!?!" Tomas panted. The rain ripped away any air he tried to draw in.

The aging sailor shook his head, wiping away some of the rain. "We'll be fine if all the Mad Vaeyen throws at us is storm and surf. The weather keeps away any…"

As dark as the sky already was, somehow it grew darker. A massive shadow passed over their heads, drawing all eyes upwards. A blast of light, not from any bolt of lightning spawned by nature, arced ahead of the shadow.

All at once, a dozen cries came from all over the ship. "DRAGON!!!"

A blast of lightning shot down the length of the ship, missing it by only a hand's breadth. Sailors threw themselves down, begging any god that might listen for mercy. Even the Archaeknights, greatest of House Calonar's warriors, were stunned by the arrival of so great a terror. The sky roared an accompaniment to the fury of the massive beast. The *Blue Lady* rocked against not just the surging ocean, but also the buffeting air that was further stirred by each flap of those enormous wings.

Rogan came running back from the bow. "On your feet!" he roared. The prince's fury was so great that he no longer had any trouble being heard over the storm. He grabbed a sailor at random and pulled the trembling man to his feet. "Yes, it's a dragon! Yes, it'll attack! Nothing will change that! If you lay down, you die! So stand! Stand and fight! Fight for your lives! Fight for your crewmates! Fight for your ship!"

By then, Tomas had arrived from his trip below. The squire held both his blade and his knight's. He tossed Talon to Rogan, who caught it effortlessly and drew the Northlands blade, its flawless steel catching the light of the dragon's next blast.

"Fight because no lizard is going to make cowards of you! For House Calonar!"

The crew of the *Blue Lady* leapt to their feet and roared in fury. Fists were clenched and raised high. Curses and challenges were spat at the circling dragon. Weapons were retrieved from below and handed out. The warriors, under the leadership of their prince, made ready to humble a dragon.

Something exploded from the sea. Something small and long launched itself up from the dark water and wrapped itself around a screaming sailor, pulling him into the depths below. From the other side of the *Blue Lady*, another surge of water and another scream as something of claws and fangs dragged a sailor to his death. They were under attack from above and below.

"What in Underworld?" Rogan roared.

Beraht came forward from the stairs leading belowdecks. The great warrior squared his shoulders, somehow remaining planted despite the rolling deck. The son of Uldron slowly cracked his neck and raised high his waraxe. In a blur of speed that belied his race, Beraht shot to the right, knocking a sailor aside with merciless force and swung his weapon in a wide, overhead strike. A serpentine head with two long tendrils trailing from its snout exploded from the Uldra's blow. A long, sinuous body made of blue-green scales collapsed, writhing to the deck. It's serpentine form was covered in small spines that sparked with tiny bolts of lightning. Beraht swung his waraxe again, sending pieces of the creature back into the sea.

"Hatchlings!" Aebreanna called out to Rogan. She stood behind the towering Beraht, sheltering herself from the stinging rain against his great torso. The Sylva pointed up to the circling shadow. "Their mother seeks to trap us! This is their first feeding!"

"And their last!" Beraht announced.

Another hatchling launched itself from the sea. This one was caught in mid-flight by Ward. The Archaeknight leader, ignoring the arcs of lightning the creature delivered, broke the creature's spine before returning it to the water. "Spread out!" he roared. "Cover the ship!"

No longer content with their individual attacks, the hatchlings launched themselves all at once. Dozens of the monsters hurled themselves onto the deck from every direction. The air filled with the screams of the dead and dying to accompany the howling of the wind.

Tomas ducked under one of the creatures as it came flying towards him. The squire turned and swung Steelheart, lopping off the hatchling's head before it could reorient. Seeing Rogan hacking at two of the beasts, Tomas decided to help, but was surprised as a leathery tail wrapped itself around his legs. He fell to the deck with an oath and tried to turn but jerked as pain spasmed through his body.

Then Rogan was there. The knight cut off the hatchling's head and uncoiled its body from his squire. "You alright, kid?" he asked, offering a hand up.

"That really hurt!" he panted, taking the hand.

Rogan wiped some rainwater off his face. "We've got to get the initiative here!" he bellowed over the wind.

Tomas spun around his knight and sliced a huge chunk of flesh off an approaching hatchling. "What do you usually do in cases like this?" he asked.

Rogan caught a small spark of electricity with Talon and kicked the attacking hatchling back. The knight then reversed his blade and buried it into the beast's head. "Cases like this?" he demanded. Looking up, the prince cursed and grabbed Tomas' arm, pinning them both against mast.

A massive wave crashed onto the deck, flooding it with water. The *Blue Lady*'s defenders were knocked off their feet by the force of the tidal wall, many being sent screaming over the side. The entire ship leaned dangerously before correcting itself. The hatchlings did not relent in their attack.

"In cases like this," Rogan gasped, "I have no idea. What've you got?"

"Nothing," Tomas groaned, trying to clear his head, to find the calm center that would allow him to access Alexia's wisdom. "Maybe Aebreanna."

Both warriors looked over, but their friends were faring little better. The wave had sent Beraht tumbling towards the railing, and he now dangled precariously over the side. Only Aebreanna kept him from going into the sea, somehow holding his massive weight with both hands as she strained to pull her Uldra friend back onto the relative safety of the ship. Again and again, the hatchlings leapt from the waters as Beraht swung helplessly in the air. The warrior knocked each of the beasts away the moment they came within range of his waraxe, cursing them and demanding they give him a proper fight.

"Would you please desist in your damned swinging!?!" Aebreanna demanded. Veins bulged in the Sylva's neck as she struggled to pull her companion up.

"Oh, I'm sorry!" the Uldra shouted back. He batted another hatchling away. "I'll just hang here and LET THEM CHEW ON ME!"

"I should just let you drop!" she growled through clenched teeth. "You could use the bath!"

"Y'know what!?! Drop me! Just DROP ME, DAMN YOU!"

"*Fal'elesh'a* Uldra!"

"*Bjhud* Sylvai!"

"*SYLVA!!!*"

Four hatchlings approached Aebreanna from behind. She spotted them but could do nothing. The Sylva maintained her grip on Beraht, desperately trying to pull him to safety, clenching her teeth in defiance of her approaching death. The monsters hissed and crouched low, preparing to strike.

Rogan and Tomas leapt between them. The warriors swung their swords, doing their best to ignore the pain the hatchlings inflicted with each shock. Within moments, the beasts were dead. Knight and squire then turned and ran to the railing, grabbing Beraht and heaving, pulling the massive warrior up.

"I'm not that damned heavy," he growled.

His three friends, gasping for air against the rain and wind, all looked from Beraht's face to his stomach, and then at each other.

"We need to end this," Rogan shouted to Aebreanna.

"The mother," she replied heaving breath. "Kill her and the young may flee."

The knight jerked his head to the quarterdeck and his team followed. Ahmed was doing his best to maintain control of the ship while fending off several of the hatchlings. Seeing this, Rogan led his friends in a short, vicious assault that made quick work of the monsters.

"Do you have any ranged weapons onboard?" Rogan asked.

Ahmed shook his head, clearing his eyes of the rain. "What did you have in mind?"

The knight pointed Talon up towards the circling dragon.

"Are you kidding?" the captain started to say before another wave began pulling the ship upwards. Everyone grabbed the whipstaff and held onto it for dear life as the watery fist came pounding down.

Ahmed eventually shook himself. "This is a carrack!" he shouted to Rogan. "It's meant for exploring, raiding, assaulting! Not fighting a damned dragon!"

"Well," Tomas shouted, pulling himself to his feet, "it's fighting one now! There has to be something we can do!"

Ahmed waved his hands towards the Archaeknights, busy fending off the hatchlings. "Ask them!" he insisted. "They're the ones with the magic!"

Rogan turned and, with the impact of another wave, nearly flipped over the rail. With Beraht's help, though, the knight managed to hold fast. Rogan called out to Ward. The leader of the Archaeknights threw the hatchling he had been fighting back into the sea and approached his prince. A sudden change in the tides caused the massive warrior to lose his footing, however, and caused him to tumble into Rogan, Beraht, and Tomas. Aebreanna had the good fortune to dance out of the way.

"Well," Tomas noted grimly, "this is fun."

Rogan picked himself up and grabbed a nearby railing. "Can your people attack the dragon!" he shouted at Ward. "Can they drive it off?"

Ward called out to his archer. "Ilaywin, can you hit it?" he roared.

"No!" The Gwyndd archer shook his head, not bothering to look away as he ducked beneath an attacking hatchling, drawing an arrow from the quiver upon his back and firing it into the hatchling's hissing mouth. There was a moment's pause, then the beast's head popped. "The wind is too strong and it's too high! Right now I couldn't hit anything more than a span away!"

"Rei!" Ward called out to the Tamanese woman, "illusions!"

The small Tramanese woman shook her head. A hatchling leapt at her from behind but she spun and unfolded one of her steel warfans, slicing its head off with one perfectly placed attack. "I have been trying!" she called back. "It seems immune!"

"Gendo?"

The lance-wielding Archaeknight shook his head. Never far from his wife, Gendo kicked another hatchling that had tried to attack as she recovered from her last battle. He then thrust his large-bladed weapon into its body and twisted.

Tomas looked around the deck. "What happens if we finish off these hatchlings?"

Aebreanna also looked around and suddenly looked very worried. "The mother will call them before that happens," she shouted back. "She will then attack us herself."

Ward made a face and turned. "Asaya! Kara!" he called out. "When that thing comes down, you two keep it's lightning off of us as much as you can!"

Both women nodded.

"Illaywin, Khwezi, when it gets closer, you two throw what you can at it!"

The warriors jerked their heads and moved into position.

Ward turned back to Rogan. "It's not much of a plan," he warned.

The knight grimaced. "Better than nothing."

The battle continued. Waves crashed over the deck, bringing with them more hatchlings. The crew rallied under Rogan's leadership and the Archaeknights' example. Clubs and short blades sent the monsters hissing back into the angry sea. Thunder roared in the sky and bolts cut through the air and from the attacking beasts.

Fewer of the hatchlings came to replace those that were sent bleeding into the water. The crew of the *Blue Lady* roared their fury at the attackers and forced them off their ship. A hissing, screaming, bleeding eternity passed as the warriors of House Calonar raged against the newest wrath of the Mad Vaeyen.

Without warning, a thunderous roar shattered the clouds above. In response, the hatchlings broke off their attack and leapt back into the sea. All eyes turned upwards, heedless of the stinging rain.

"Get ready," Rogan barked. He and Tomas moved towards the mast, uncertain of where else to be.

To the right of the ship, far in the distance, a dark shape dropped out of the clouds. Its wings reached from one island to another. Its endless body, one long, continuous tail from snout to the barbed tip of its tail, seemed much too large for flight and yet still it defied gravity. The creature's eight legs clawed at the sea as it flew, as though it could gain more speed by running along the water. Dark blue, almost black, in color, the dragon matched the storm and sea perfectly in both hue and rage. It oriented on the *Blue Lady* and charged.

Again, there came the monster's roar and again the sailors began screaming in panic. The giant monster opened its cavernous mouth, revealing row after unending row of serrated teeth, each longer and more deadly than any sword. Large barbs, all along the dragon's scaly hide, bristled as it moved through the air. Lightning arced across its body, building in intensity as it moved and channeling up to its mouth.

"Archaeknights!" Ward bellowed. "NOW!"

A burst of lightning erupted from the dragon's mouth. Asaya and Kara called out to their individual magics at the same instant. A burst of wind hit the monster's snout at the same moment as Kara's power, turning it aside just enough. The lightning flew over the *Blue Lady*, searing the top of the mainmast.

A mystical arrow and a ball of flame both lanced out, striking the dragon in one of its massive eyes. The creature flinched and lifted upwards, soaring over the ship.

"You did it!" Tomas cried.

"She will return," Aebreanna warned. "She has been wounded, and will now want vengeance."

Beraht spat on the deck. "Enough of this!" he thundered. "I'll be damned if I end up as lunch for an iguana!" The Uldra grabbed Drystan by the collar and pointed with his waraxe towards the dragon. "Get me up there!" he ordered.

"Beraht, no!" Rogan yelled.

A roar split the air around them and all heads craned up at the shadow as the dragon passed over them again.

Beraht pointed straight up. "Let's go!" he growled.

Drystan looked at Ward for orders. Seeing his leader nod, the young man crouched slightly and both Uldra and Archaeknight vanished in a flash of blue light.

The Archaeknight reappeared a moment later on the deck of the *Blue Lady*. In answer to several obvious questions, he could only point to the dragon, which was already lining up for another attack.

Tomas forced his thoughts to stillness. He swallowed his fear and his rage, the pain of his many small cuts and the ache of his muscles. He called upon all the techniques Rogan had taught him these many months. He slowed his heart and the drew in peaceful breaths. He reached out to the Winds of Magic and opened his eyes. Before, he had done this by accident, and was nearly blinded by the sight of Sarah's mystical radiance. This time, he deliberately looked through the aid of the Winds.

Beraht was climbing up the dragon's neck. He shone within the Winds of Magic like a pillar of holy fire. His faith, his absolute certainty in the glory of his Allfather, beat back the storm. Tomas saw the resolution, the unwavering, undeniable purpose compelling the son of Uldron forward. All Beraht cared about was the righteous fury building in his heart, guiding him forwards, towards his enemy's head. He made no prayer to the Allfather; as a true son of Uldron, he would prove his worthiness for his God's favor, or he would die. His belief was that simple, that pure.

As huge as the dragon was, as brutal as the storm pounding them both, the beast could not feel Beraht's advance along its back. It continued its own advance towards the *Blue Lady*, heedless of the monster inching its way up towards its head.

Even as the dragon lowered its head and beat its wings in anticipation of crushing the ship, Beraht acted. He used nothing more than the strength of his hands and back, blessed to him by the Allfather. The Uldra dug his hands under the scales of the dragon's neck, finding the soft, vulnerable flesh beneath. He dug until he could grip the scales from underneath, and then he heaved. Beraht pulled and pulled, ripping up several massive scales. Once done, the *Uldra* rammed his steel-toed boots into these crevasses and stood.

This, the dragon felt.

With soft skin suddenly exposed to the storm all around them and worse, the fury of Beraht's attack, the monster roared in pain. The dragon reared up, once again deflected from the *Blue Lady*, and raising up back into the clouds. Lightning shot all around as the two monsters, dragon and Uldra, soared upwards. The wind howled and the dragon roared. It twisted its neck around, trying to reach the source of this new pain, but could not.

Beraht laughed in defiance of the dragon and the storm. He reached to his belt and freed his waraxe. As incandescent as Beraht's faith had been, in raising the symbol and spirit of the children of Uldron, that blaze became an inferno of divine power. Here, in the clouds, with so worthy an enemy, Beraht became a conduit for the unwavering fury of the Allfather.

Tomas had to look away. His mortal eyes could not bear the sight of true divinity manifesting within the world.

"What's happening?" Rogan demanded.

The squire could only shake his head, trying to clear his fallible eyes, and point.

From the deck of the *Blue Lady*, everyone aboard gasped. The storm itself, a manifestation of the Mad Vaeyen's power, was stilled. Ravana herself emerged from the clouds, stunned nearly to sanity at Beraht's feat of strength and faith. Dozens of lightning bolts, each thicker than the trunk of the oldest tree, hit the dragon from all directions. Again and again bolts of divine wrath hit the creature, illuminating the entire sky and shattering Ravana's power. Then, with an earth-shattering cry, the dragon died. The men and women aboard the *Blue Lady* watched, stunned to silence, as the giant creature fell, its huge body hitting the water and creating a massive wave.

"All hands!" Ahmed called out. "BRACE!!!" He yanked on the whipstaff, turning the *Blue Lady* into the towering wall of water.

Rogan and Tomas threw themselves against the railing and rapped their arms around it as tightly as they could. The mighty wave reached their ship and pulled it up. The *Blue Lady* leaned over, far over, until they all looked to the side and saw beside them what should have been below them.

"We're going over!" Ahmed roared. "Make for land!"

Tomas' heart froze. He blinked and looked around, seeing the terrified faces of his friends. Knowledge entered the squire's mind. In one moment, he did not know something, and in the next, he did. The squire stood and let go of the railing.

Before Rogan could object, Tomas fully opened himself to the Wind of Death. All the thoughts and dreams and hopes of a thousand, thousand generations of adepts filled his mind. He was not carried away, though. Beside him, somehow apart and yet, fully connected to his soul, were two others. He glanced to the side and saw opalescent eyes and a gentle, loving smile. Beside his dear friend, her arm reaching across the Veil itself, was another like her, but dark-haired, grim, and armed. With the fallen Walker were others still. Generations of champions and heroes. And there was another group, another line unbroken. This began with his mother, and her mother, and hers besides. The entire lineage of Tomas' mothers, all sensitive to the Wind of Death and all sharing their knowledge. Together, Tomas and Alexia and all the heroes of House Calonar and all the adepts of his family turned and faced the broken sea.

They reached out with their shared power. They guided the tender White Lady, merging Her with all the Winds of Magic. The colossal wave stilled and spilt, gently guiding the fragile *Blue Lady* down. Not satisfied, Tomas and Alexia, with all the help their comrades could give, soothed the angry storm. They calmed the waves and the tides. They unclenched the rain and bid the clouds continue on their way. They even reached out towards the mind of the Mad Vaeyen. Ancient adepts from the very dawn of history joined in the effort, employing the Lost Winds of Dream and Thought. The mind of Ravana was, for the first moment in centuries, made serene.

The Mad Vaeyen, mad no longer, floated in the peace created by Tomas and his chorus of magic. Her formless body once more assumed mortal shape, looking down at the *Blue Lady* with all the centuries of her wrath melting away. In their place, her stormy eyes revealed horror, not at what had befallen her, but at what she had done. Tomas sensed this through the Wind of Thought, briefly grifted to him by Khepric adepts from the distant past. Ravana looked at them, at the young man and the spirits helping him, and she fled.

All eyes on board looked in shock at Tomas.

"Ah, kid?" Rogan said.

"Yes?" he replied through a chorus of voices.

"You're glowing."

Tomas looked down and realized that he was, in fact, glowing. A radiant white aura surrounded the young man and he was floating above the deck, a manifestation of the power shared from Alexia and his mothers and all the others. "Sorry," the squire mumbled, "I got a little distracted." He released the magic, letting it flow back into the Winds. He wistfully, though without grief, smiled at Alexia and waved farewell, as she, Raven, his mother, and all the others returned to their proper side of the Veil. This done, he collapsed to the deck, breathless and drained of nearly everything.

Rogan caught his squire before he could finish falling.

Aebreanna's opalescent eye darted out, into the now-peaceful seas. "Beraht!" she cried.

Without need of command, Deriel launched himself away from the *Blue Lady*. The young Sylvu shot like an arrow, straight across the small waves which were still trying to settle themselves, and circled the sinking carcass of the beast itself. All abord watched as the Archaeknight spotted something in the water and dove, coming out again and flying as quickly as he could back to the ship. The Sylvu hit the deck with a hard crash, carrying the unmoving Beraht.

"Teka!" Rogan barked. The Archaeknight healer ran to them. She knelt beside the unmoving son of Uldron and spread her hands across his massive chest. A golden light intensified, growing in brilliance until it was blinding and everyone had to turn away. When the light dimmed, Teka gasped and Beraht was healed.

The Uldra sat upright with a gasp and a curse. The entire crew cheered.

Aebreanna pounded on her friend's shoulder. "You are quite simply the dumbest, most insane Uldra to ever curse this world!" she declared, tears flowing from the opalescent eye.

Chapter 6

With the death of the dragon and Ravana's retreat, the storm that had been assaulting the *Blue Lady* dissipated. The wind became little more than a steady breeze at their backs. The reborn sun warmed their faces and their hearts. Merry waves only playfully butted against the ship's hull, almost rocking the heroes of House Calonar into a false sense of serenity.

Despite this seeming tranquility, already the natural threat of Dagon'ay rumbled its replenishing vigor. The jagged peaks of that harsh land, mortally wounded by the Disaster at Nassinalia, loomed over the *Blue Lady* like a predator's hungry claws. These mountainous islands could neither hold back, nor conceal the encircling wall of dark clouds. Distant thunder growled a counter harmony to the restful surf upon the many nearby points of rock. Brief flickers of menacing lighting peaked from behind the mountains. Even the helpful breeze held within it the chilly hint of danger regathering its strength.

The crew and passengers of the *Blue Lady* had decided to take advantage of their respite. A small cove, sheltered from the unpredictable tides, offered temporary anchorage for the weary ship. Rotations were quickly arranged for sleep. Those awake worked feverishly to make repairs. The watch scanned constantly for threats not only from the sky, but from beneath the waves. Everyone knew that the longer they remained in one place, the greater the chance increased that Death, the tireless White Lady who was every mortal's companion, would find them again.

With the crew hard at work, and being made increasingly aware of how useless, even obstructive, they were to those efforts, Rogan's team and the Archaeknights retired to the aft cabins.

"I was just trying to help," Tomas insisted wearily as he and Sarah entered the common room.

"How many masts have you reinforced?" the junior Archaeknight asked.

"Oh, come on!" the squire replied, trying to stifle a yawn. In truth, the young man was keeping his eyes open through sheer force of will. Since his spectacular summoning of the fallen, Tomas felt as though all the strength had been sapped from his body. He was tired to his very soul, and only his fierce sense of duty kept the squire on his feet, Tomas unbuckled his sword and placed it in the small cabin he shared with Rogan Then, taking the small cup of water Sarah offered in a trembling hand, he joined his friend at the table of their common room. "It's just nailing wood to the mast. I can follow instructions as well as the next man."

"And yet," she argued, "you were asked to leave." The Archaeknight grinned. "As a matter of fact, I noticed a couple of men tearing up your help as we left."

"Well that's gratitude."

"It raises a point, though," Ward added from where he stood with Rogan. "We're only really useful to this ship when it's under attack."

The knight nodded. "And we'll only stay useful if we're rested."

"I've already ordered my people to sleep," this the Archaeknight leader said with a meaningful look at Sarah. In response, the newest of their order sighed and went to the cabin she shared with Asaya.

Rogan looked at his squire. "We should bed down as well. There's no telling when we'll get another chance." The knight did not point out his apprentice's obvious weariness, nor had he pushed Tomas for any explanation of the fantastic conclusion of their most recent battle.

Aebreanna entered with Beraht. Like Tomas, the Uldra seemed very near dead on his massive feet. Even after being healed by Teka's magic, the lumbering warrior's head and eyes drooped and he leaned heavily on the tiny Sylva supporting him. Despite the tremendous disparity in their sizes, still Aebreanna supported her titanic friend, showing no discomfort as he leaned upon her tiny frame. "There is a matter of some urgency we wish to discuss while this time of rest is afforded," she said.

"Yeah," Beraht agreed. The odd pair moved to a corner and the Uldra sank to the floor. His eyes blinked heavily and slowly, though he obviously fought to remain awake.

"Why don't you get some sleep?" Rogan suggested.

"After we talk."

The knight glanced at Aebreanna. "He will recover," she said in answer to the unspoken question. "As always, despite all logical insistence of the White Lady's claim upon his malformed soul, the lumbering oaf will recover." She glided over to Tomas and examined the young man, looking intently into his eyes, and feeling the pulse at his neck. "Much like your squire, I should think."

"Any idea what he did? How he did it?"

"HE's sitting right here," Tomas insisted.

"Hush," Aebreanna instructed, listening to his breathing. "Although I cannot be sure, I believe our young friend has finally manifested his mystical alignment."

"Right," Beraht agreed, clearly not listening.

"Translation?" Rogan requested.

Aebreanna loosened the squire's shirt and dipped her hand under, probing with small, delicate fingers along his neck and shoulders. "All adepts spend some time fumbling about with the various Winds of Magic, but inevitably settle into one specific orientation. As his power is apparently gifted from the Matriarch, his matching of her specialization seems logical." She looked meaningfully at Rogan. "You will recall which of the Winds Alexia most frequently employed."

"Death Magic," Tomas said, the knowledge drifting up unbidden. He blinked at started at Aebreanna and Rogan. "I'm a death mage?" he demanded. "Like Anninihus!?!"

The Sylva sighed wearily and sat down opposite the squire. "Not in the way I believe you mean." She glanced about and Rogan offered her a cup of water. "Since the time of Karnat, the term has become increasingly derogatory. Anninihus' actions no doubt contribute to this." The Sylva drank. "But yes, in answer to your question. Your orientation within the Winds of Magic is toward that discipline. Your actions today reflect what a death mage is supposed to be, not the perversion Anninihus became."

"I don't understand," Tomas admitted.

"Death magic is supposed to be about communion with those beyond the Veil, not dominion over them. Appealing for their wisdom and aid, rather than exerting mastery over the deceased. A true death mage, a master of that Wind, can not only summon the dead, but from them be granted knowledge and even a measure of the skill."

"So, it wasn't him?" Rogan guessed. "It was Alexia and Raven and all the others?"

"Entire generations of our predecessors working through him," Aebreanna clarified. "He reached through the Veil and called upon them for help. They responded."

Tomas shook his head. "I've read legends about death mages from the ancient past," he countered warily. "I've never heard of anything like what happened today."

Aebreanna took his hand. "All magic, no matter the type, requires communion. The adept opens herself to the Winds, becoming a vessel, a conduit into our world. But there always remains the will of the person. Our own sense of self limits to what degree the Winds can manifest through us, since we are unable, or unwilling, to sacrifice our own identity to the powers brought to bear."

She glanced at Beraht, who had his head back against the wall. His eyes were barely open and his breathing was becoming deep. "I believe both you and Sir Beraht performed what was essentially the same act: you fully relinquished yourself to your mystical power. He gave himself utterly to his god, and you gave yourself to our fallen kin. In both cases, such a selfless sacrifice, allowed for a... rather spectacular manifestation of magic."

"Why am I so tired?" the young man asked.

"You had a hundred dead people running through your brain," Rogan said with a chuckle. "That'll take it out of anybody."

"Indeed," Aebreanna sighed, weary herself. "Rest. Your strength will return." She looked at Rogan. "Our greater problem is more dire, however."

"What now?" the knight sighed. sighed.

"The time has come to reevaluate our strategy."

"Again?" Tomas asked blandly.

"Shut up, kid," Rogan snapped. He then shook his head. "Sorry."

Aebreanna grimaced. "A certain frustration is to be expected. Very little of this mission has proceeded according to any plan or expectation. We have been forced to change course many times."

"And you think this is another of those times?" Tomas guessed.

"We do."

Rogan shook his head. "We're already in Dagon'ay," he insisted. "We're committed. We have to get home and the enemy's got a huge advantage in time and speed. Vagris has begun to attack the villages in Wildlelves Wood. A siege can't be far off, and Fak'Har is heading towards the Keep right now. We've got to catch up somehow."

"I will not dispute that our disadvantages are many," Aebreanna replied. "Our basic strategy of taking some type of shortcut was a good one." She held up one small finger. "However, I believe that we made two serious errors in judgment. We underestimated the dangers of Dagon'ay, to include the lingering resentment of the Vaeyen due to our last visit. Secondly, we overestimated our abilities to meet those dangers."

"Either will get a warrior killed," Beraht added softly, clearly paying attention even through his weariness.

"So where does that leave us?" Tomas asked. "If we keep going forward the danger will only get worse. Ahmed said we've got weeks left in these islands at least. And that's assuming we don't get lost. Do we try to back out and go around Dagon'ay?"

Rogan shook his head. "Too much time," he insisted. "It'll take months to sail around to the south and with the Shamashi starting a war in the Endless Sands, it would take even longer to get through by land to the north. Speed is everything."

"I disagree," Aebreanna whispered. "Life is everything." She looked directly at Rogan. "We fight to defend life. We risk our lives to defend the lives of those we love. But what good would our deaths accomplish? How would our deaths defend the lives of our families? We must reach home quickly, true. However, we must do so alive."

"How?" the knight demanded.

"There is a path that we have not considered," she said. "A route that offers even greater speed than Dagon'ay, with far less direct danger."

Rogan leaned back in his chair, suddenly aware of what it was his friend was suggesting. Tomas leaned forward and asked, "What route are you talking about?"

"Otherworld," she replied. "We can travel through Otherworld."

"What!?!" the squire snapped. He shot a glance of disbelief first to Rogan but, seeing that his knight was considering such a suicidal move, looked next to Beraht. "You have to see what a stupid move that would be!"

"Hear her out," the Uldra said.

The squire crossed his arms and looked to the Sylva.

Aebreanna sighed. "Your brief experience in Otherworld notwithstanding, Tomas, that realm does offer some benefits. We, ourselves, once journeyed into that mystic realm in search of the Seal of Earth. You only saw one tiny part of a greater world. We may even find, once more, the Fael, who could be called upon for aid."

Tomas huffed.

"Further," she continued, "Time moves differently there. A trip of weeks or months in Otherworld should only see the passage of days here. Distance is also different there. Our journey across the breath of Lanasia could seem little more than a few leagues."

"I'm hearing a lot of 'could,' and 'should' coming off this idea," Tomas pointed out.

Beraht sighed again and raised his head. "Otherworld doesn't work like the real world," he rumbled. "Our world has rules. We've got laws like up and down. In Otherworld, magic is the only law."

"A crude, but not inaccurate assessment," Aebreanna conceded. "Magic emanates from Otherworld. The Winds are given form there. In Otherworld, the strong mind can shape reality to suit it."

"And there are monsters," Tomas added.

"There are native creatures," she agreed. "Like our own world, some are malicious, but most are indifferent. Your own experience was unfortunate, and unusual. Typically, the denizens of Otherworld do not specifically target mortals."

"What about the Zafael that said it was hunting your family?"

Aebreanna lowered her head, her flowing hair that so strategically covered the right side of her face spilling lower to cover nearly all her features.

Beraht leaned forward. "Back off, runt," he growled.

"No," the Sylva said softly. "Our young friend is correct." She raised her head slightly, allowing the left side of her face to show. "House Tressalon is hunted by the Terror that Feeds. Where once my family was second only to the Imperial House in size and eminence among the Sy'lva'n, because of that Zafael, I am now all that remains." She looked at Tomas. "My aunts, cousins, everyone who has ever held the name Tressalon has fallen victim to the Terror that Feeds. I am all that remains. Should we enter Otherworld, I will be saving it the effort of hunting for me through my nightmares. You fear repeating your own brief experience. You asked me once, Tomas, if I sleep, if the Sylvai as a whole, engage in sleep. I explained that what we do is not, exactly sleep, but that was an evasion." She stood, looking up at the squire in unshakable resolution. "Sylvai must dream, as do all intelligent creatures, even Uldra. And every time, in every instance that my mind is opened to the wonders of Otherworld, to the Wind of Dreams, the Terror that Feeds is there, as he has been for all my mothers. It has spent my entire life twisting my dreams into wretched, painful nightmares, false memories and horrid visions. The Zafael does this because, under normal circumstances, it cannot reach my body. Instead, it delights in tormenting my mind. Should we enter Otherworld, the Terror that Feeds will sense my arrival, and it will come in search of my flesh. I believe I have much more to fear than you, and yet, I am willing to risk the horror of my bloodline for the sake of all those who we hold dear."

Shamed by Aebreanna's words, Tomas looked away.

Rogan came to his squire's defense. "It's a moot point anyway," he argued. "I'm sure Dagon'ay has plenty of portals, but how to we find one? How do we get it open?"

Aebreanna reached into the folds of her cloak and pulled out a small silver branch. It was the same mystical device she had used, months ago, to rescue Tomas from Otherworld.

The knight shook his head. "You told me that thing can only open a small breach for one or two people."

"True," she replied, staring down at the branch. "This item lacks sufficient power to open a portal large enough for our needs. You forget, however, the nature of all devices created by the Trickster Mage."

"I don't get it," Rogan admitted.

"He was never a creature of moderation. Anything he creates will always have the potential of channeling vast amounts of energy."

"So all you have to do is… what? Focus more magic through it and create a bigger portal?"

"Not I." Instead, she glanced at Tomas.

"Whoa, whoa, whoa," the squire objected. "I don't know anything about opening portals." Despite his objections, the knowledge for how to accomplish Aebreanna's idea floated into his mind. He took a deep breath. "Damn," he muttered.

"More wisdom from beyond?" Rogan guessed.

The young man looked at his knight and grimaced. "It's actually not hard. I only need to gather the Winds and focus them into the branch. But I need to focus a lot of them." Tomas shook his head. "I don't think I can do it right now," he added, rubbing his eyes.

Aebreanna stood and placed a gentle hand on the squire's shoulder. "Rest. Sleep as long as you can and gather your strength. In the morning, we shall do what must be done." She looked at Rogan. "You must keep watch on the horizon. Ravana will renew her assault."

"No," Tomas objected, "she won't."

They looked at him.

The squire and nascent death mage shrugged. "Something happened, when I was… merged with those spirits. Adepts from long ago, ones of Thought and Dream, they did something to her."

"What?" Rogan asked.

Tomas shrugged. "I can't be sure, but I think they cured her madness. Through them, I could feel her mind, and it was… well, not peaceful. She was rational, but something was still tormenting her."

They said nothing. Aebreanna pursed her lips in thought. "Still," she finally said, "while this affects our predicament, it does not alleviate all danger. Ravana said she was acting on behalf, or at least with sanction from, the other Vaeyen. They will not relent." She looked at Rogan. "Wait for as long as you dare, then wake us before the storms return."

Tomas felt as though he had only just put his head down when Rogan shook him awake. "It's time, kid," his knight said grimly.

The squire wearily rose and belted Steelheart around his waist. Rubbing the sleep from his eyes, far less than he had hoped for, Tomas climbed the ladder to emerge onto the main deck.

The *Blue Lady* had moved out of the cove in which she had sheltered and back into the connecting channel. Storm clouds had gathered overhead, growling at the ship and flashing in anger at their attempt to escape. The sea was once again thrashing against their ship's hull, the rocking increasing even in the brief time since Tomas' return to the waking world. The wind thrust against them, chaotically pushing first this way, then that, gathering its strength for a renewed assault.

Feeling a pulsing within the Winds of Magic, Tomas looked up, behind the ship, to the island that had given them an all-too-brief shelter. There, atop the highest peak he saw Ravana. The Mad Vaeyen had once again assumed a Human-like appearance, a women of middle-age wearing a flowing dress of white and with long, flowing hair to match. She did nothing but watch them.

The crew of the *Blue Lady* all looked as Tomas did, staring at Ravana, the deadly enemy of their King. The men and women, still mourning for their lost crewmates, did not flinch, either from the evil behind them, or the uncertainty ahead. They silently parted way as Tomas made his way to the bow, turning their backs on the Mad Vaeyen.

The squire joined Aebreanna at the place furthest forward on the *Blue Lady*. Occasional droplets fell from the sky, silently urging them to hurry. The wind was picking up speed, pulling at the rigging. Tomas glanced back at where Rogan stood with the Archaeknights. The Northlands prince grimly nodded.

Aebreanna wordlessly handed over her silver branch. Tomas took the arcane device and glanced down at her. The winds, both mundane and those of Magic, pulled at her hair, tossing it about, removing her ability to conceal the deformation that brought her such shame. Feeling Tomas' eyes on the angry, jagged crevasse that deformed the right side of her once-beautiful face, the spy looked down and grimaced. But there was more, the young man realized. Aebreanna was not only ashamed of her grievous wound, the distortion of her once-proud smile and the destruction of her glorious eye. The Sylva' entire body shook, not with cold, but with terror. She held herself, stiff and proud, all while her breath escaped with choking sobs.

Tomas said nothing. Words could not ease the Sylva's obvious suffering in being forced to confront the generational nightmare of her family. No empty cliché, no matter how soothing in its attempt, could undo the wound to Aebreanna's soul. The squire took the silver branch, but also took his friend in his arms. Tomas said nothing, but only shared the warmth of his body and his heart to succor his suffering friend however it could.

"It'll have to get through me, first," the squire swore.

Aebreanna, for only the briefest moment, flinched back. But then, she pressed into the squire. Her shame was hidden within the dancing folds of his cloak and smothered in his love for her. As though defeated, however briefly, by the display of selfless compassion, the gathering storm relented. The wind faded and the thunder muted. The frothing seas stilled and the bizarre pulsation Ravana generated within the Winds of Magic stilled. Tomas held Aebreanna, trying to offer comfort to the member of their team who so frequently had to comfort them, and demanded the world give them a moment.

At last, Aebreanna sighed. She closed her small hand over Tomas' so that they both held the silver branch. Together, they grimly raised the mystical device and called out to the Winds of Magic. All those gathered took an involuntary step back. A brilliant, multi-colored light gathered around Tomas and Aebreanna, as though a great rainbow had shattered into starlight and was then were drawn towards the pair of adepts. The light grew in intensity and slowly began to turn, thickening into a mist. The pair concentrated and drew even more upon the Winds. The swirling mist grew and expanded. The *Blue Lady* continued to sail forward, passing through the turning ring of rainbow-mist and into what lay beyond.

The sky overhead was filled with various shades of red. This crimson coloring was shared by the surrounding mountains. The ocean channels of Dagon'ay were, in this place, mere rivers, slowly flowing with prismatic water. An unnatural haze clouded the eyes, obscuring everything more than a few hundred paces away. The surrounding land was filled with trees covered with strange pink and white leaves caught in a non-existent breeze and fell to the dark ground. Eerie silence pressed in all around.

Tomas glanced back. Ravana still stood atop that high peak. The wind still pulled at her dress and her hair. She still said nothing, did nothing, as the *Blue Lady* slipped away from Dagon'ay. Once the ship passed through, the mystical portal began to close, the connection between two worlds repairing itself. The last Tomas saw of Ravana, the once-Mad Vaeyen raised a hand to them, not in threat or anger, but as though to communicate something else.

A disturbance drew all eyes to the shore on the left side of the ship. A brilliant white stag burst from the treeline, chased by a pack of wolves covered in equally white fur. The predators ran their prey down and pulled it to the ground, ripping bloody chunks from its flesh. One of the wolves, the largest of the pack, clamped its powerful jaws down upon the stag's throat and shook his head. Without warning, all the creatures, predators and prey alike, halted their gory dance and stared with eyes the color of blood at the new arrivals. In total silence, the undying stag and the wolves devouring it watched as the *Blue Lady* passed by.

"Great," Tomas noted. "Otherworld."

The Heroes Abroad

II

Otherworld

Chapter 7

Sleep was impossible. All the elements for a peaceful slumber were in place, but still they lay awake. The river on which the *Blue Lady* drifted was placid, a welcome, gentle swaying compared to the vicious tumult of the seas around Dagon'ay. The current gently guided them onward, and Ahmed found within the first hour of their arrival in Otherworld that he did not need to steer his beloved ship. Repairs were completed within a day, and the mainsail was patched and reset. No obvious threats presented themselves, so the leaders of their expedition ordered a return to rotating shifts. Those relieved of duty made their weary way below decks, to bunks and hammocks and the hope of rest. Despite all the possible comforts, however, sleep was impossible.

Tomas was exhausted to his core. He was already soul-weary by his horrid destruction of Tordenia, the battle to escape the Western Empire, and then the struggle to survive Dagon'ay. Any one of these would have been enough to drain the strength of any mortal. Together, they should have sent Tomas into the deepest clumber. Moreover, Tomas had twice opened himself to the Winds of Magic: once in saving the *Blue Lady* from destruction by the dragon's death, and again in opening an escape from Dagon'ay's wrath. His shoulders drooped as low as his eyes, but he did not sleep. For uncounted hours, he lay in the narrow bunk, not moving, not thinking, only resigning himself to the non-existence of wakeful exhaustion.

"Is it everyone?" the squire overheard his knight ask.

Tomas rosed himself, moving as though through mud. He stood and half-stumbled into the central cabin, finding Rogan and Aebreanna in weary discussion with Ward and Ahmed.

The captain of the *Blue Lady*, a veil of gray on his bronze face, was nodding. "The whole crew," he said. "I checked again at the last bell. Those off-duty are just lying in their hammocks. No one sleeps."

"It's the same with my people," Ward confirmed. The large man was leaning against a cabinet, rubbing his eyes. "Asaya and Deriel are holding up, but the rest of us..."

"Halvan and Sylvu," Aebreanna noted. She was sitting upright, her opalescent eye alert. "We do not need sleep as do Humans and Uldra. Rather, we can go longer without."

Rogan sighed, cradling his head in his hands. "No one's sleeping," he grumbled.

"In fact," Aebreanna corrected, "you are sleeping, but only lightly, for a few minutes at a time. Little more than a doze, really."

"Is it because of Otherworld?" Tomas asked, stepping in and taking the seat beside Aebreanna. "Is it something about this place?"

The Sylva shook her head. "Sleep is possible within Otherworld. Easier, in fact. The Wind of Dreams is as powerful here as any of the others, perhaps even more so. Dreams come more quickly in this realm, more vividly." She looked squarely at Rogan. "This is an attack."

"Of course it is." The knight shook his head and glanced to the ceiling. "Just once on this trip, we deserve something easy." He took a deep breath, squaring his shoulders and looking back at Aebreanna. "How bad will this get?"

"Terminal," she replied. "You are feeling the symptoms now. Fatigue, difficulty with thought, impaired movement. As our situation worsens, speech will become impaired, confusion and hallucination, loss of bodily control. If we are denied sleep for too long, the mind will eventually fail and, soon after, the body.

"Humans are most vulnerable. You spend a third of your brief lives amidst the Wind of Dreams. You suffer its absence more profoundly, more quickly than the children of the Radiant. The Uldra," this she said with a glance at Beraht, who's bowed head spoke to his weariness, "will be next. Their minds are resistant to attack, to manipulation of either the Winds of Thought or Dream. Their slower functions offer some protection, some resistance. Still, Teka Ironhands and Sir Beraht will succumb. The Halvans will fall next; they share some blood of the Radiant, though not as much as pure Sylvai, so they are only partially susceptible. Even we, full-blood children of the Radiant, will eventually fall victim to this assault."

They were quiet for a time. "What do we do?" Tomas asked.

"Our options seem few," Aebreanna conceded. "As with any attack, defeating the attacker would be the most obvious, most direct solution."

"Any chance of finding out who's doing this?" Ward asked.

The Sylva shook her head. "Otherworld is the source of the Winds of Magic. Here, they are potent, and nearly uncontrollable for mortal beings. I attempted a mystical detection some time ago, and I still suffer the ill-effects." She glanced at Tomas. "Should one already weakened, unschooled in withstanding the Winds make the attempt…"

The squire nodded, needing little prompting to avoid tapping into his own arcane power.

"What does that leave us?" Ahmed sighed.

"I am uncertain," the Sylva replied. "We cannot neutralize or even detect our attacker. We have no trained adept aboard to shield us or otherwise counter the attack. Tomas and I lack the strength to open another portal without rest."

They were quiet again. "How long?" Tomas said softly.

"Humans? Days, perhaps a week. Uldra can normally spend two weeks without sleep, but Teka was already as weary as the rest of us, and Beraht..." Aebreanna blinked slowly and sighed. "The Halvans can last a few weeks, I believe, though there is no certain knowledge. We Sylvai do not sleep as you do, but still require our dreams. In perhaps a month, we will deteriorate."

Rogan had been looking down and rubbing a finger along his lip. The other hand had been at his chest, stroking the small pouch in which he kept his wedding ring tied around his neck. "There might be a way," he mused.

"What?" Ward asked.

"Something," the knight mumbled. He looked at Aebreanna. "I need to be asleep," he declared.

"As do we all," she reminded him. "The question remains as to how."

"You don't get it. I need to dream. We might have help, but I need to contact her."

"Her?" Tomas asked.

"Kyla."

Aebreanna shook her head. "Even with her heritage as a daughter of Calonar," she objected, "Kyla lacks the power to penetrate Otherworld."

Rogan held up a hand. "I don't really understand myself. She's got a... She can contact me. Through dreams."

"You're sure?" Ahmed muttered. "It's not just... you missing her?"

"I'm sure. It happened the night we stopped at the pirate cove. At first, I thought it was just me missing her, like you said. But night after night, she kept appearing, talking to me." The knight glanced at his squire. "Among other things," he said with a weary grin.

"Those were some pretty... extreme dreams."

"My wife's enthusiastic," Rogan shrugged. "The point is, she can reach me through dreams. She might be able to do something about this. At the least, she can talk to her father, to Esha. But I have to dream." He stared hard at Aebreanna. "Is there a way?"

She seemed about to refuse, to reject the strange idea, but then paused. The Sylva put her hand to her temple and breathed deep, forcing her thoughts into focus. "Perhaps not true dreams, but something similar enough," she mused. "I can render you unconscious easily enough, but that is not true sleep." She glanced at Ward. "Can Rei employ her abilities?"

The Archaeknight leader shrugged. "Not with any real control. We can all access our gifts, but-"

"That is sufficient," Aebreanna interrupted. "We need only for her to trigger a hallucination on Rogan while he is unconscious." She looked at the knight. "This is, at best, a wild leap bearing little resemblance to logic. It may work exactly as we hope but, more likely, you will suffer horrors."

"Are there any better ideas?" he asked.

The sun was shining upon a restored Pelsemoria. Tomas and his friends, having finally left behind the horrors of the past months, had arrived in his childhood home to find it resurrected. The Forum Biblithecea, the capital's great library, once again stood tall and proud, filled to overflowing with the knowledge of a great civilization. Restored homes once again housed the elite of Lanasia. A mighty wall once more enfolded his old home protecting his loved ones from the evils of a hard age. The Nassinal Sea no longer beat upon the broken and pitiable skeleton of mercantile docks; instead, the commerce of the entire world again flowed through the great harbor of Pelsemoria. The Inn of Lost Hope was repaired beyond its past life, now filled with marble and wood fixtures, rich tapestries, and the gladful cheers of a community reborn. A joy more powerful than any other filled Tomas' heart as he led his friends through the familiar streets.

They somehow found themselves at the old Imperial Palace, no longer a crumbling relic of past glories. The mighty building, built long ago by the Sylvai to house their own rulers, reflected all the ages of Lanasia. Great columns adorned the front and sides of the central building. Open plazas and gardens adorned the residence of the Imperial Family. Pointed arches and stained glass prevailed in the newer construction, meant to house the growing needs of a modern government. And there was even the newest designs, those just beginning to flourish before the civil war, emphasizing symmetry, proportion and the geometry of regularity. Praetorians, the sun gleaming upon their gold-trimmed breastplates, once again stood watch over the heart of Lanasia.

Within the chamber reserved for the Council of Elector Lords, Tomas saw the leaders of all the Houses, great and lesser, debating the welfare of the people. Cylan Calonar of the Northlands led the Plebeian Party, intent upon the protection of the common people. Theodorico Balshazzar of the Western Empire stood amidst the Senatorial Party, preserving the traditions and authority of the nobility. These two leaders looked upon one another with respect, arguing their perspectives and finding compromises that benefited all. There was no rancor in this august chamber, this sacred place of diplomacy and governance. Only the responsibility of leadership prevailed here.

And there, no longer a blasted scar upon history, sat the Redwood Throne. Upon the raised platform that once housed the now-lost Crystal Dais, symbol of the fallen Sylvai Empire, was the seat of Human power in Lanasia. More than a simple chair, the Redwood Throne was an icon. A flawless wooden sculpture, the back flowed up in the image of a living forest, the branches fanning out like the wings of the Radiant. Within these branches were carved the heraldry of the founding Houses of the Republic, many lost to history, but some few still alive today. The arms stretched out from the wide seat in benediction upon the world, and the legs were shaped as a complex root system, somehow merging into the marble floor. This was once again the center of power and hope for an entire continent.

Within this great chamber were all the people Tomas had ever loved. Father Konrad debated theology with Alexia. Elpidius and Kineus, his oldest friends, laughed together with El's younger sister, Cecilia. Luigino Mariano stood amidst his fellow Praetorians, the elite warriors restored to their honor positions. And in the center of them all was Alessandros Fidelis and his loyal wife. Tomas' mother smiled at him, a glow of warm pride in all her son had accomplished, and she gestured that he come forward, to stand once more with his father.

The milling crowd retreated. Even the sun seemed to fade a bit in veneration of this reunion. Tomas stepped forward, calling to his father, who had his back turned. At last, with his son only a few paces away, Alessandros turned. Tomas started, choking back a scream. A darkness, like liquid obsidian, was spreading from his father's chest. The burning cold clawed at Alessandros' torso; the man tried to scream, but was choked to silene by the slithering mass of shadow and vile hatred.

"What's happening to him?" Luigino Mariano asked from somewhere distant.

"He's having a nightmare," Fiametta replied. The innkeeper's daughter from Nunzio had arrived at some point and was now standing behind Tomas.

"Why did you give him a nightmare?" Luigino demanded.

"I didn't. He's doing this himself."

The insidious darkness consumed Tomas' father and reached the floor. Tendrils of smoke and shadow probed out, away from the mass that had been Alessandros Fidelis. Terrified screams filled the air as the vile magic grasped at the Council of Elector Lords. It wrapped around ankles, pulling the noblemen to the floor and consuming them. The hateful curse reached the Redwood Throne and, with vines of dripping evil, crushed it. Tomas looked about for any help and spotted Cylan Calonar. The ancient hero was grey and pitiful, a frail excuse for a ruler. He stood, doing nothing, only sighing away his life as the darkness enveloped him.

"This is getting out of hand," Father Konrad insisted. "You've got to stop it."

"I'm trying!" Alexia insisted.

Tomas fled from the chamber. He and Rogan, with Aebreanna and Beraht just ahead, sped through a maze of twisting tunnels. His Sylva and Uldra friends stopped at each of the endless intersections, lost for which path to choose. Panic showed on both their faces as they looked, again and again, to Tomas for an answer the squire did not have. He tried leading them out of the labyrinth, but at every turn the seeping darkness had cut off any path of escape. At last, after an eternity of running amidst walls of stone, of dark forests and wintery mountains and desert cities, Tomas spotted the ladder leading up and away from the spreading curse.

The squire turned back in time to see his friends die. The hissing, baleful darkness had caught them, wrapping itself around them and pulling them back, screaming, into the night. Tomas reached out, he tried to grasp at their desperate, trembling hands, but they were consumed like all the others.

"Can't we just wake him up?" his father asked.

"He's too exhausted," his mother noted sadly. "Too dream-deprived. This has to end on its own."

Tomas turned and exited the dungeon, and somehow exited the world entirely. A blurring force swept around, pushing in and through and beyond the squire. Everything around seemed to grow brighter, and yet somehow also darker, warmer and colder, more clear and more opaque. Tomas felt as though he were slipping out of a river's current, and into the restless waves of the sea.

He emerged into the streets of the Northern Keep. The spreading darkness was there, as well. The great walls protecting the city had a great, gaping hole in them, and wrathful extensions of the dark curse were pouring through. The Walkers stood amongst a dead forest surrounding the city, trying to battle the invading evil, but were consumed. The people within the broken walls screamed and fled in all directions, but a few stood and fought. Velaera stood before her shop, the seamstress swinging a sword but falling beneath the waves of hate. Higal stood with his family at their restaurant, the Sylvu making a desperate stand but being consumed like all the others.

The squire tried to turn away, but was confronted with more of the horror he had unleashed. The Temple of the Harvest Mother echoed with the agony of children being devoured by the evil shadows, Ilse and the other clerics helpless against the dark tide. Cardinal Tain stood with the other priests, helpless as the Adamic Church as destroyed. Medaka and the Sisters of the Lady of Light tried to employ their loving magic to protect their temple, but were carried off as their sanctuary collapsed. Tomas reached Castle Calonar, desperate to help anyone, any possible survivors, flee the spread of the slithering death. He was too late, though, as a mountain of darkness had risen from the heart of the Northern Keep and forced its way through the castle's defenses. Tomas spotted the body of Roland the butler, already being devoured. The squire could not find Princess Karen or Aebreanna's twins. The King and Queen were similarly missing. The only remaining inhabitants for this proud House seemed to be the mutilated bodies of its Guard, still with bloodied weapons in hand.

"There's got to be something that can snap him out of this!" King Cylan barked.

"This isn't a dream!" Queen Nora replied.

"What is it!?!"

"I... I don't know! It's still the Wind of Dreams, but there's something else here, something more powerful!"

"Tomas!" a voice called out. "Help me!"

The young man turned and tried to scream. He tried to roar, to bellow, to make any sound at all. He was mute, though. Struck dumb and frozen in place. Mary stood at the center of the castle's main doors. Her beautiful face was twisted in horror. Her gentle body spasmed in pain. Her large eyes were wider-still in agony. His fiancée, the truest love of his life, was caught by the darkness. It lifted her up and cast her shattered body from the balcony.

At last, Tomas found his voice. "NO!!!"

"NO!!!" Tomas flung aside his blanket and shot to his feet, Steelheart in hand and his soul aching for vengeance.

"It's ok!" Rogan said. The knight stood at the door to their cramped cabin. His hands were widespread and he was careful to speak gently. "It's ok, kid. It was just a nightmare."

The squire looked about, his breath heavy and his body soaked in sweat. He was standing in the cabin, he forced himself to realize. He was aboard the *Blue Lady*. They were still on their way home. None of it had been real, no matter its vivid horror.

"Well?" Rogan asked.

Tomas straightened. He took a deep, purifying breath, and nodded.

"How about putting that away?" his knight suggested with a nod towards Steelheart.

The squire glanced down, having nearly forgotten his naked blade. He retrieved the scabbard and sheathed the legendary sword of House Calonar, belting his weapon around his waist. "Wow," he grunted. "Dreams really are more... everything here in Otherworld."

Rogan nodded, relaxing just a bit to match his squire. "Yeah. Everybody reported some pretty powerful dreams. Nothing like this, though." He jerked his head out, towards the common room. Tomas nodded and followed his knight out.

Aebreanna and Beraht, looking very nearly their normal selves, were seated in that cabin. They looked to Rogan and Tomas as the two Humans arrived. "Finally awake?" the Uldra noted.

Tomas nodded, rubbing his temples. "Am I the last one up?"

"You seemed in most need," Aebreanna replied, handing him a cup of water. "The rest of us have been awake from some short while, but we thought it best to allow you the extra time. That is, until your obvious distress."

"Yeah," the squire grumbled, sipping at the water. "That was just about the worst nightmare I've ever had."

"An effect of Otherworld," the Sylvai informed him. "All things of the mind and soul are intensified in this realm."

Tomas shook off the remnants of his violent dream. "Did Kyla do that?" he asked Rogan.

The knight shook his head. "Once I contacted her, and told her what we needed, she put us all under, into our own dreams. She didn't create anything we dreamed, and apparently couldn't stop them, either." He punched his squire in the shoulder. "She feels pretty bad about this, kid. Expect one serious round of apologies when we get home."

The young man shrugged. "You said she's still new to this whole dream magic thing," he pointed out. "There were bound to be mistakes. No permanent harm, I guess."

"Still," Aebreanna added, "Kyla is a woman of deep passions. She will carry a great deal of guilt for what she will believe is her hurting of you. No doubt, you will have to make an extraordinary effort to ease her pain."

Tomas leveled a look at the Sylva. "So, I have the nightmare, but I have to make her feel better?"

"Welcome to life with women, kid," Rogan laughed.

Aebreanna leveled her own look at the knight. "And what, exactly, do you mean by that particular statement?" she asked in a voice that could shatter stone.

"What, Ahmed?" Rogan called up the hallway. "You need us on deck?" He turned and made his escape. When Aebreanna glanced at Tomas, the squire, too, employed the better part of valor.

As the two men made their way to the main deck, they were intercepted by Ward. "Rogan," the Archaeknight leader called down. "We've got a problem."

"Of course we do," the prince growled. He grabbed Talon, belting his longsword to his waist and climbed up to the main deck. "Just one damned thing after another."

Chapter 8

The *Blue Lady* was at a dead stop. The iridescent river on which she coasted had also halted its gentle current. The glowing flowed both forward and back, from one side to the other, as though the river was unsure of its path. The sails were limp and the rigging as silent as the sailors. All hands on the main deck were assembled forward, staring ahead. They made a path with the approach of Rogan, Tomas, and Ward. The knight stopped at the bow, standing beside Ahmed. He glared ahead and swore.

A wall of fallen trees, loose stones, and dug-up earth stretched across the river.

"It's recent," Ward noted. He pointed to fresh leaves still clinging to the branches of newly-fallen trees. "Somebody's blocking us."

Rogan scanned the banks on either side of the ship. "Can your people clear it?" he asked Ahmed.

The aging sailor shook his head. "Even with all hands, without heavy equipment, that's a job of weeks."

The knight looked to Ward. The Archaeknight leader narrowed his eyes at the blockade and nodded. "We can do it. It'll take a couple of hours, but we can get it done." He looked back at Rogan. "But we'll be vulnerable."

A chorus of monstrous screams then tore at their souls. The crimson sky darkened as an evil wind began pushing at them from all directions. Tomas looked up and gasped, for its seemed as though a horrid curtain was being pulled from horizon to horizon. This darkness then exploded into a shower of flying creatures. They were female, though only in a vague sense of their shape. They wore flowing, mist-like gowns of a sickly green that hugged curves of hip and arm. They had no breasts, but instead muscular torsos that rippled with inhuman rage. Long hair of midnight black flowed from too-small heads, from which blazed eyes of amber insanity. Overly-large mouths stretched from one pointed ear to the other, and within these near-caverns was a serpentine tongue slithering amidst horrid fangs. Their torsos extended impossibly down, gradually replacing flesh with scales, what should have been two legs instead blending into a single serpentine tail. In their hands, the creatures held cruel rapiers with barbed points and serrated edges. On their backs was the source of the monstrous screaming, insect-like wings like those of some nightmarish dragonfly that vibrated against the air and kept the horrors aloft. Tomas shook his head and pulled Steelheart free of its scabbard. He looked to his knight and the two nodded at one another.

"Spread out!" Rogan barked. "Pairs and threes! Cover each other!"

The flying not-women dove upon them. They attacked in mass, seemingly wanting to overwhelm through the strength of their great host. Swooping down, the monsters swung their cruel weapons, trying to scatter clutches of sailors. When a person was isolated, two or three of the screaming flyers would pick up their victim and drag him into the sky, with chunks of the struggling body raining down. With each kill, with each wailing sailor dragged into the sky and mutilated, the evil, joyous scream of the attackers' wings grew louder.

The flying creatures revealed a preference in their attacks. The few women aboard the *Blue Lady* went unmolested, perhaps even unnoticed, even when they swung attacks at the monstrous things. Sarah and Kara, the two archaeknight women having arrived on deck, immediately leapt to the attack. When Sarah employed her mystical agility to leap upon one of the monster's back, the nightmarish not-woman ignored her completely, even when the Archaeknight buried her short blade into the creature's heart. Kara, similarly, was ignored when she took to the air; the serpentine horrors only dodged away from her, but made no other acknowledgement, not even of her heavy daggers as they sliced and slashed. Only the men aboard the *Blue Lady* held the monsters' murderous attention.

Tomas and Rogan stood back-to-back. When a creature dove at them, the warriors did not flinch away. Instead, the knight deflected the strikes from the cruel rapier while his squire spun and sliced with Steelheart, cutting the monster's legs free of its body. One of its sisters screeched and dove upon them, its serpentine tongue drooling a vengeful hunger, Tomas intercepted the wide sweep of its rapier even as Rogan stabbed upward with Talon. The monstrous female wailed in pain and despair as the knight's longsword cleaved its heart. More of the alien beasts came swooping to the attack, but they all met the unflinching pair of knight and squire.

One of the not-women dove at Ward, thinking the Archaeknight leader alone and vulnerable. A moment before she was within reach with her vicious rapier, a high whistle disrupted the scream of her wings. There was then a blast of purifying wind that forced the monstrous female down onto the deck. Ward dove forward and grabbed the creature with both large hands. A single twist of his mystical strength and the monster was broken. The Archaeknight leader glanced at Asaya and nodded. The Halvan woman nodded back and whistled again, sending another blast of wind at the attacking creatures.

The remaining Archaeknights were surging onto the main deck, followed closely by Aebreanna and Beraht. The massive Uldra looked about and roared, "What in Underworld!?!"

His Sylva companion flipped onto his shoulders and, with a spinning kick of her graceful leg, sent an attacking serpentine not-woman to the deck. "Zafael!" she announced. "The Doom of Men! *Lam'i'ai!*"

Ilaywin the archer ducked one of the swooping monsters as it reached to capture him, rolling along the deck and coming back to his knee with an arrow knocked. Sighting, letting the missile lose, and rolling again from another attack, the experienced man began striking the creatures from the sky with his explosive arrows. With fire and water, Khwezi and Fikri protected each other by forcing away the not-women, driving them back into the sky where Ilaywin's missiles could pick them off. Kara joined in the archer's deadly counterattack, the woman gesturing at sections of the heavy rigging which whipped out under her mystical command. The ropes and pullies thrashed at the sky, forcing the flyers to the deck where the crew was waiting with blade and club to vanquish this newest threat.

At the rear of the ship, Beraht and Aebreanna were an unmatchable force. The sky filled with the gleam of flawless Sylvai blades, each intercepting one of the non-women in eye or throat even as their single-minded wrath for any male drew them to the largest on the ship. Any of the insect-winged monsters foolish or fortunate enough to survive Aebreanna's bladed protection of her towering friend were dismembered and destroyed by the edge of an Uldra waraxe. Whether the creatures drew close or stayed away, they were brought low by these unlikely friends.

At some unknown signal, the entire swarm of monstrous females surged to the rear of the ship. They disregarded the attacks of the Archaeknights and crew, leaving for dead those of their number who fell. Instead, perhaps consumed only with their hatred for all males, they focused upon Beraht. The Uldra swung his great weapon again and again, severing limbs and insect wings in a shower of gore, but was overwhelmed. As mighty, as unstoppable, as Beraht was, even he could not defeat such an unrelenting wave of evil. He was forced back and away from Aebreanna.

The Sylva was nearly as deadly as her Uldra friend. She slashed and stabbed with her iridescent blades. She killed one monster after another. But a strategy had appeared in the seemingly-mindless attack. Beraht and Aebreanna were separated in combat, for perhaps the first time Tomas could recall. The Uldra was distracted in forcing away the swarm of screaming, thrashing not-women, and so lost sight of his Sylva friend. A small clutch of the Lamiai broke from the others and slithered through the air, wrapping themselves around Aebreanna. Even when they lifted her from the deck, still the Sylva continued dispatching the not-women. She did not scream or give any indication of fear, instead grimly fighting on as they pulled her into the crimson sky, away from the *Blue Lady*.

There was a great roar of maddened outrage. Beraht, through the implacable force of his unwavering loyalty, drove away dozens of the monstrous serpentine women. He spotted the capture of his friend and cleaved a great swipe with his waraxe.

Another score of the insect-winged monsters fell and the son of Uldron leapt in pursuit of Aebreanna.

"Beraht!" Rogan roared from the bow as the Uldra reached the shore in one mighty leap, only to continue bounding through the alien landscape. The son of Uldron did not waver, did not alter his course. Any obstacle was destroyed or forced aside: monsters, trees, or hills. Rogan looked to Ward and thundered, "Protect the ship!" The knight then jerked his head at his squire and charged towards the side rail.

"Drystan!" the Archaeknight leader barked. "Get them to shore! Sarah, go with them!"

The teleporter appeared beside Rogan and Tomas just as Sarah landed beside the two men. The squire gritted his teeth as the world once again dissolved against the sting of a thousand thousand vicious wasps, only to reform through the haze of blazing lava. This time, though, the squire's stomach remained stable and his vision clear. He, Rogan, and Sarah took only the briefest moment to orient themselves and charged after Beraht.

The son of Uldron's trail was not a difficult one to follow. The prismatic light of the river was quickly swallowed by the bizarrely-spiraling trees, but the warriors needed no light. Beraht had obliterated anything in his path. Thick clumps of uprooted moss lay scattered and the white branches formed a straight line away from the *Blue Lady*. Far ahead, they could hear the thunderous crash of the Uldra's charge, and the Humans had only to follow it, their path made free of any possible obstruction. Even the great white stones and sodden hills had been uprooted by Beraht's rage.

They ran through the alien landscape of Otherworld. Tomas and Rogan, even unencumbered by armor, could not match Sarah's speed. The youngest, newest of the Archaeknights obviously restrained herself, but her breath remained light and steady, even as that of the two men became labored. The terrain was rough, even without trees or stones. The pink and white foliage, now obliterated, was replaced with soil in shades of blue. The red sky, absent any sun or moon, still cast its crimson light down, blending with the ground to cast the three warriors in a bizarre violet glow. There were no sounds, beyond breath and heartbeat, as all the creatures of Otherworld seemed to have fled Beraht's wrath. There were not stars or clouds, no distinguishing terrain features. Nothing about this place seemed capable of remaining in the memory, except for the upheaval of Beraht's passage.

The attack came without warning or preamble. In one instant, Tomas was running beside Rogan and Sarah and, in the next, he was screaming on the ground. Angry, boiling slashes seared across his back. Part of the squire's mind noted that the suddenness of the insect-monsters' attack had not given Tomas and Rogan the chance to put on their armor. The young man's back, then, had been fully exposed and his undershirt, its only protection, fell away in bloody shreds.

Rogan and Sarah skidded to a stop in the same moment the squire had fallen. The knight turned but also screamed and fell to his knees as his own back suffered bloody slashes. The champion of House Calonar was back on his feet without pause, though, and he swung Talon in a wide circle. Tomas similarly forced himself to his feet, Steelheart raised and ready. Sarah grunted as she dove forward, twisting and turning through air and ground. Her great dexterity, though, had not spared her the attack, but only minimized it: thin red streaks were slashed into her back, and her tunic hung against her shoulders.

"Back-to-back!" Rogan barked and they did so, circling together and eyes probing the unbroken twilight for this newest threat.

Tomas heard his knight scream again and turned to see Rogan stumbled back, three great gashes carved into his face and blood flooding down onto his chest. Sarah leapt over his shoulder and slashed her short blade at nothing. The squire raised his sword and swung a great circle over his friends' heads, hoping to luck for a hit, but slicing nothing but air. Rogan regained his feet somehow, desperately trying to clear the blood from his eyes even while holding Talon at the ready. "Ears and air!" he growled.

The two younger warriors obeyed. Tomas half-closed his eyes against the uselessly-dim light. He shifted his attention away from sight and to his other senses. Sounds came to his ears and scents to his nose. The hairs on his arms and the back of his neck pricked up, scanning their surroundings and reporting all. The stench of old blood and deadly speed came from Tomas' left. The three heroes moved in the same moment. Sarah took once more to the air, flipping above them slashing horizontally, not trying to hit their unseen opponent, but only trying to drive it. The men, moving a heartbeat slower than Sarah, turned in that direction with deadly intent, instinctively taking advantage of the opening she was trying to provide. Rogan swung high and his apprentice low, both warriors sweeping in opposite directions so that their blades passed by in a near-perfect scissoring. But they struck nothing.

A hideous laughter came slithering from the trees to their right. Knight and squire and Archaeknight reoriented and stood ready. "Close," the darkness congratulated them. "So very close, but not close enough." The smell of blood and gore came from behind, and the men dove to the ground and rolled, coming back to their feet as some impossibly-fast attacker lanced overhead. Sarah leapt once again, her emerald eyes intent upon her prey.

Too late, Tomas realized the trap. "Look out!" he called.

The newest Archaeknight intercepted the murderous blur, but struck at nothing. Instead, she then twisted in mid-air, screaming in pain as gashes were cut across her entire body. Her light tunic was shredded, only wet tatters left in the furious assault. Her short, long-handled blade fell uselessly to the ground, without having landed a single attack. Sarah herself fell also, crumpling to the ground and mewling in her agony. Tomas and Rogan sprinted to her side and gasped. They could not tell where individual wounds were, so great was the damage. Her strong body trembled weakly, her flesh desecrated and coated in its own blood.

"How delightful," the darkness surrounding them rejoiced. "Maiden blood mixed with an ancient power! Delicious!"

"I know that voice," Rogan growled, his rage ignoring the fresh blood coating his face and clogging his eyes.

"The thing from the forest," Tomas agreed in a harmonizing growl.

"I feared Time would deny me vengeance against you short-lived cattle," the darkness hissed. "But then, I was promised my chance." Another wave of blood, gore, and deadly speed short towards them, this time from the front. Knight and squire spun away in opposite directions, turning in unison to slash at the space between them.

This time, they were rewarded with a scream of outrage and pain. A stream of ichorous blood painted the ground, spilling across Sarah's nearly-still body before the Zafael could again retreat into the oppressive darkness.

"He's physical here," Tomas spat, forcing away the pain and the dread. "He's solid." The squire could only offer the briefest glance to Sarah. He saw that she was breathing, if only barely. He stood over his friend, stilling his heart and focusing his mind. There was only one way to help her, the squire told himself: the Zafael first had to be defeated.

"Solid and eternal," the darkness countered. "I am beyond Death, beyond Time. You cannot kill me, you cannot banish me." A blur of murder shot from the darkness, this time without warning of smell or sound. A horrid gash running the length of Rogan's right arm opened and Talon fell to the ground. Tomas swung Steelheart but hit nothing. His knight stumbled but kept his feet, retrieving his longsword with his left hand and holding it in a trembling, weakening grip.

"Then why hide?" Tomas demanded. "If we can't kill you, why are you afraid?"

More laughter set the young man's skin crawling. It was an unnatural sound, filled with nothing but the perverse joy of inflicting suffering and stripping hope from helpless prey. "This is not hiding," the darkness said with vile mirth. "This is savoring!"

Months of training flowed through Tomas. His mind quieted. "The worst is going to come," Rogan had advised him as they had walked through the great tunnel beneath Ulheim. "Moments when you think it's over. That's when panic will kill you. Stay cool, find your peace. What will happen, will happen. Just let it come."

Something the Zafael had just said. *I am beyond Death.* The nascent adept half-closed his eyes. He opened himself, not to all the Winds of Magic, but to the one to which he was most attuned. Even here, in Otherworld, the White Lady was present. Most natives of this realm did not die of age or disease, but they could be killed, they still felt the touch of Death. The Zafael were one of the few exceptions. Tomas felt the Wind moving through everything subject to the White Lady, sensed them through Her. And there, just at the line of still-standing trees, was a void in the Wind of Death.

Before even his senses could give an alert, the Wind of Death cried out, and the squire reacted. He spun Steelheart, the legendary sword of House Calonar, even as he pivoted. There was another scream and another jet of ichorus blood. This time, though, Tomas did not pause. Some distant memory recalled the workshop of Remm Stonebearer, and the mighty Uldra smith leading him into the squire's own fighting style. In their mock battle, Tomas had accessed the skills of a dozen teachers across his lifetime and blended them together. Tomas spun with Mary, he deflected with Beraht, he countered with Rogan. He even moved with Aebreanna and Luigino Mariano, the Paretorian who was first to give him guidance. There had even been Alessandros Fidelis, his noble father, adding to Tomas' unique style. Tomas tapped into all of this once again, all his friends and loved ones together, to battle the Zafael. But more came with his loved ones. Through the Wind of Death, he felt the skill of Raven, the Walker-companion of Alexia. With her came warriors of legend, offering their own skill and experience. These blended together, guiding Tomas' movements as he brought the White Lady to the Terror that Feeds.

The bestial shadow tried to dodge away, but Tomas was there. It slipped down and around, but Tomas was there. It tried to strike, to block, to retreat, to advance. But, in each of its shadowy movements, Tomas was there. The assembly of warriors, moving within the squire's body, slashed and stabbed and blocked and parried with Steelheart. The legendary blade of House Calonar became a glowing blur of light-on-steel. The assembly of legends moved with perfect grace, unmatched fluidity, unrivaled skill, but could find no purchase. They were stalemated, neither opponent able to best the other.

There was then a swooshing in the air. Beraht's mighty waraxe came spinning from the darkness, crackling with righteous, holy rage. The great blade of the divine weapon impacted the shadowy mass engaged with Tomas, knocking it to the ground. The Nameless' weapon then jerked away, spinning back whence it came. Tomas looked and there was Beraht, standing atop the shattered trunk of a great tree and covered in the bloody remains of those who would harm his friends. His waraxe returned to his outstretched right hand, still shining with its great power. The squire could see, through the holy light, that Aebreanna, bloody and weak, was cradled in Beraht's left arm, sheltered against his massive frame. "You talk too much," the son of Uldron declared.

Another outcropping of insipid laughter clawed at the young man's soul, forcing him and the assembly of heroes to look at the dark thing Beraht's attack had forced to the ground. The oily shadows were melting together, framed by the light of the waraxe. The Zafael was every bit the horror Tomas remembered: as tall as Beraht but twice as broad and covered in dark hair matted against its hide by the gore of a thousand victims. Its long, trunk-like arms scratched at the ground with six-fingered hands ending in jagged claws. Eyes of pure black evil stared around a huge nose at Aebreanna, and yellowed fangs dripped with noxious, hungry drool. "Daughter of Tressalon," the Zafael leered. "My feast was interrupted. Shall we begin again?"

In their last encounter, Aebreanna had suffered from a generational terror. Those many months ago in the wintery forest surrounding the Northern Keep, the Sylva could not bear what her mothers had named the Terror that Feeds, the nightmarish monster that had haunted all the dreams of her family for an uncounted age. This time, though, she stared at the monster that had hunted her family to near-extinction without fear, without flinching. "Your feast ends this night," she declared in a weak, but unwavering voice.

The Zafael laughed again, delighted at Aebreanna's defiance. "I am beyond Death, beyond Time!" it once again declared. "You can never end my feast!"

"Not I," the Sylva said with a cold smile. "You are beyond the White Lady's notice, true, unless Death is made aware of you."

Tomas understood. The young man dropped Steelheart and raised both hand towards the Terror that Feeds. He calmed his mind and opened himself once more to the Wind of Death. He released the assembly of heroes and instead called out to the White Lady Herself. A purifying white light misted into existence around Tomas, coalescing around his hands. He sent the Wind forward, not as an attack, but as an invitation. The gentle light suffused the Zafael, bonding with it and setting it alight as a beacon to the White Lady.

The Zafael looked at its own body, eyes widening in terror at the realization of what had been done. The Terror that Feeds stood and tensed, ready to leap once more into the sky, but stiffened, its impossibly-long arms outstretched in agony, and its muzzle raised to the crimson sky in its own terror. A blade had erupted from its chest, forced through from the back. Emblazoned upon the blade was the cross-diamond sigil of House Calonar. Sarah, bloodied, nearly spent, but undefeated, leaned over the monster's shoulder and hissed her vengeance.

"It is mortal," Aebreanna declared.

The warriors responded to her command as an undeniable condemnation. Sarah ripped her weapon from the Terror that Feeds and threw herself back, away from the onrushing men. Rogan leapt forward in defiance of his near-blindness, trusting to his other senses and his instincts. Talon slashed downwards, severing the Zafael's hand. The Terror that Feeds screamed and tumbled away. Beraht charged, cradling Aebreanna to his left side and swinging his great waraxe. The weapon did not make contact with the bladed end, but with the blunt, crushing into the monster and knocking him towards Tomas and Steelheart. The squire, having retrieved the legendary sword of House Calonar, stabbed forward. His blade lanced into the Zafael's chest in an explosion of black gore.

The Terror that Feeds gasped and stiffened. Its eternal life cut short, the eyes that had seen uncounted generations tormented to madness flickered with the agony of mortality, of its great feast finally forced to end. Strangely, the monster grinned through the flood of ichorous blood flowing from its fanged mouth. "It is done," it said in a gargling whisper. "As I was commanded."

The Zafael collapsed to the ground. Tomas stood, uncertain, for a moment. He then looked down, and saw the hilt of a small dagger protruding from his chest. The squire looked up to his friends, seeing the horror of realization on their faces. He then sighed and fell.

Chapter 9

Consciousness only gradually returned to Tomas. Rogan and Aebreanna were standing over him, shouting, then all was dark again. Sarah, her body still gowned only in the tatters of her tunic and the mixing gore of her blood and that of the Zafael, was cradling his head in her lap, then all was dark again. A commotion stirred him back as gentle, twinkling lights suffused the sky, accompanied by a chorus of gentle bells, then all was dark again. Tomas was being carried, rocked gently as the crimson sky passed overhead, then all was dark again. At last, reluctantly against the pain of wakefulness, the squire opened his eyes.

Tomas was lying on a cot of woven clouds and starlight. He lie on the mist-soft material for an unmeasured age, his conscious mind refusing to accept the information his senses were relaying. Bandages of sapphire light were wrapped around his chest, holding in check the spread of black veins from a still-bleeding wound. Tomas could breathe, though not without discomfort, and his life seemed as though suspended, for his heat did not beat. This possibility most of all the young man's thoughts rejected as impossible. And yet, the reality doggedly persisted.

Tomas sat up, feeling discomfort but not pain. He pressed a hand to his chest and the mystical bandages, but could not gain purchase. Some unseen force guided his probing fingers away, like the surface of an impenetrable bubble. He could not touch the sapphire light wrapped around his chest, nor penetrate it to reach the moving black tendrils struggling against that light. He looked about for something, any believable reality that could anchor his delicate sanity.

He was in a large room. The walls seemed to be made of marble, though upon closer view, revealed faint veins of iridescent blue. A pleasant warmth radiated from this impossible material, and it yielded just slightly to the touch. Small, steady lights glowed form each meeting of two walls, a wall and ceiling, and a wall and the floor. These pinpoints looked as though distant stars had been captured and locked within the material comprising the strange building, free to float within their prison, but nonetheless contained. There were no decorations, no murals or tapestry, nothing to break up the unrelieved white of the building's interior except two oval-shaped openings.

One of these portals, the closer of the two, was nearly as wide as a man's outstretched arms. Tomas went to this opening and looked out on a mythical dream. His strange room was a part of a larger building, one of many, within a great city. All construction within this place was of the same unreal material, and contained the same imprisoned starlights. Each of the buildings had similar wide, oval-shaped windows and doors, and broad balconies wrapped around most levels. Some time passed before the young man noticed what his eyes were seeing, that the bizarre city was a ruin. Most of the buildings had great scars and cracks in their walls. Many of the blue-tiled roofs were missing. Some buildings were little more than a few fragments of wall. The destruction seemed ancient and random.

The room from which Tomas now looked out was very high in an impossibly-tall building. Those of its fellows still standing and relatively undamaged were equally tall, with a great many equal levels. Surrounding the dream-like city were a series of prismatic waterfalls, spread evenly as far as the young man could see. These poured into a central series of canals that crisscrossed the entire city. In fact, there were no roads in this impossible place, but instead a connected system of waterways separating the various tall buildings. Looking down, Tomas spotted the *Blue Lady* at anchorage, docked alongside the very building from which the young man looked out. Even from his tall vantage, he could see the crew moving about their ship, and interspersed with them were several Archaeknights, identifiable by their unique weaponry and clothing. But these familiar people were not the only inhabitants of this strange place.

Tomas did not realize how long he stood at that glassless window. He looked out for an eternity, open-mouthed and uncomprehending. Flying amidst the many buildings, standing upon the broad balconies, and serenely rowing the tiny boats that navigated the prismatic waterways, were a species the young man could not accept as real. They were tall, he realized, nearly as tall as an Uldra. But they were thin, as lithe as a Sylva. They wore only the most minimal shifts made of some ethereal green material that seemed little more than vague afterthoughts of cloth. Sparkling lights of gold and silver followed their every movement, their slightest adjustment, as a trailing afterimage. Most alien of all, though: each of the figures had flowing from their backs bright butterfly wings.

"Hey kid," Rogan's voice hailed softly from the other portal, which the squire now realized must be a door. The knight's face bore three angry red scars, and the tatters of his undershirt were stained with still-drying blood.

Tomas stood, open-mouthed, at the glassless window. He glanced at his knight, then back out upon the impossible city. "What?" he tried to asked. "Where?"

Rogan moved up beside his apprentice and also looked out on the mythical city. "Welcome to Ayabalia, Lost City of the Fael."

"The Fael," Tomas repeated, his eyes trying to follow the mystical denizens of Otherworld as they sailed, floated, or flew amidst the ruined buildings of their city.

His knight nodded. "They sensed the Zafael's attack," he said. "They fought off the flyers, saved the *Blue Lady*, then came after us. They showed up just after you were stabbed."

The squire looked down and again reached for the pulsing black wound on his chest, but his fingers again slid off the sapphire light bandaging him. "The Fael did that," Rogan explained. "They stopped the curse."

"It's still in there," Tomas whispered. "I can still feel it."

Again, Rogan nodded. He put a hand on his squire's shoulder, leading him towards the door. "There's someone you need to meet."

They walked through the wide oval-shaped door into another room. This one was even larger than that in which Tomas had awoken. The walls, ceiling, and floor were all the same marble-like material. The same points of light slid along the room's joints. Furniture of the same woven clouds as the squire's cot adorned this place, wide couches, singular chairs, and tables. They all floated above the floor, and seemed as though they might drift away with the slightest breeze. More oval-shaped windows looked out on the ruined city of the Fael, and a large door opened onto a broad balcony wrapping around the building. Beraht stood in the farthest corner, still wearing his gore-streaked scalemail and helmet, and with his great waraxe hanging from his thick belt. Aebreanna sat on one of the couches, still wearing the tunic she had on when the flying Zafael had attacked the *Blue Lady*. Her bare legs were drawn up and tucked under herself and her long cedar-colored mane had been smoothed to once again cover the right side of her face. She turned on Tomas' and Rogan's entrance, her opalescent eye glowing with barely-contained hazel power. "Your words were true," she commented, looking at Tomas' injury.

"Yes." Standing behind and to the side of Aebreanna was a Fael. As Tomas had guessed from his vantage in the other room, she was as tall as Beraht but as lithe as Aebreanna. Her proportions were perfect, without blemish or other flaw. Her coppery hair cascaded down, nearly to the floor upon which she stood with unshod feet. Her green shift was little more than a forest mist, concealing none of her nakedness and tied at her throat, waist, wrists, and ankles with what seemed pink ribbon. Upon her back, constantly swaying backwards and forwards, were a pair of butterfly-like wings that glowed with a sapphire light and, with their motion, let fly a gentle shower of gold and silver lights. "The curse has been contained, for now." Her voice was a chorus of tiny bells, the sound perfectly harmonizing with itself, and somehow forming words within Tomas' mind.

"Kid," Rogan said. "This is Genaea. She's the one who…" he gestured at the sapphire bandages wrapped around his squire's chest.

The Fael's wings fluttered as she curtsied with exquisite grace. "The honor was mine, to give comfort to the one who finally defeated the Terror that Feeds."

Bemused, lost in the chaotic scene in which he found himself, Tomas could only stare. He blinked then, and asked, "Sarah?"

"Aboard the ship," Rogan answered. "Alive, and resting. Teka healed her."

Tomas nodded, relieved. "My heart isn't beating," he said then, as though commenting on the weather.

"Your life has been suspended between one beat and the next," the perfect Fael explained. "As I was explaining to your belovéds," she gestured to his friends, "our power could only delay, but not deny, the curse leveled upon you by our curséd kin."

"How long will this hold?" the squire asked.

"For twelve more heartbeats," Genaea replied, her words flowing in odd symmetry, emphasizing unusual syllables. "Your suspension has paused that countdown, but the spell can only endure a little while longer."

"Why?" Tomas asked.

"The curse upon you," the Fael explained. "comes from Fate Magic, but twisted by the touch of the Demon-God. This is stronger, more enduring, more relentless than the Wind of Time, which we employed to preserve your life. We can delay, but we cannot stop a Fated event." She looked to Aebreanna. "Only the employment of true Fate Magic can remove the curse."

"I was Fated to get stabbed?" the squire asked, looking at the grievous wound. "This is how I…?"

Aebreanna lifted his eyes to hers. "This is not how you end," she insisted.

"This curse is not the result of destiny," Genaea agreed. "It is a corruption of the Keys."

"Keys?"

The Fael looked to Rogan, who nodded. She then turned back to Tomas. "In recent months, you have encountered some of the Seals of Stalline. You even have the Seal of Life in your possession."

"The Healing Sphere!" Aebreanna gasped, turning to Rogan.

The knight shook his head. "I already though of that," he replied. "I asked Genaea. She said the Seal can't remove it."

"What is it?" Tomas asked, his hand going to the wound. "I still feel it in there."

"It is the Nightshard," Genaea explained, her bell-song voice adopting a minor key. "It is a piece of the Narasin Medallion, prison of the Demon-God. Before Stalline the Wise hid the Medallion, the followers of the Demon-God attacked, seeking to capture it and engineer an escape for their master. In the battle, the Narasin Medallion was damaged, a single piece breaking off. The followers, whom we have cursed the Zafael, retreated back here, to Otherworld, and have kept it hidden."

"Then why use it…?" the squire again gestured to his wounded chest.

"We do not know. For uncounted ages, even as measured within the folded Time of Otherworld, the Zafael have dedicated themselves to hiding the Nightshard. That the Terror that Feeds would use it now suggests something greater at work, some design."

"It said something," Tomas mused, trying to remember. "Right after it stabbed me, it said something about being commanded."

Aebreanna shook her head. "Nothing has either the power, or the authority, to command a Zafael," she insisted. "Let alone the Terror that Feeds."

"Nothing except the Demon-God," Genaea countered. "Or his agents."

"The attack was organized," Beraht grumbled. He was looking out from one of the large open windows into ruins beyond. "They were deliberate in their tactics," the Uldra declared. "The dam to block us. The swarm to engage us. Kidnapping the Sylva to draw us away, to split us up. Then, wounding the kid." The mountainous warrior shook his head.

"Look," Rogan snapped, slamming his glass back down on its tray. "All this is beside the point." He looked at Aebreanna. "I'm sorry, but they've already told us how to get it out."

The Sylva turned a hateful glare at the knight. Tomas realized what the point of dissent was. He calmed his mind and let Alexia's wisdom come forward. "Fate Magic," he whispered, taking Aebreanna's shoulder in his hand. "They want you to use your power to get it out."

The spy did not face him, instead turning so that her cedar mane covered even more of her shame. The squire looked at Rogan. "Can you give us a minute?" he asked.

The knight nodded and, with a jerk of his head, Genaea and Beraht left with him. The trio went out onto the broad balcony, offering privacy to Tomas and his Sylva friend.

Aebreanna had not moved as the others left. Nor had she turned to face Tomas. For his part, the young man had kept his hand on her shoulder, waiting for Rogan and the others to leave before enveloping the Sylva in a tight embrace. "I know," he whispered.

She tensed in his arms but said nothing.

"Alexia was a matriarch of House Calonar," the squire explained. "She had Truthsight. She visited Pelsemoria when you were a child. One look at you, and she knew. Before passing the Truthsight to Nora, she made arrangements so that you would eventually join House Calonar.

"You let the others think, you encouraged them to think, that your hatred for your magic is connected to your hatred for your father. You let them believe you hate that your power makes you feel connected to Cyras Darkholm. But that's not it."

"No," Aebreanna whispered. "I do not hate my mothers' power."

"You fear it."

The Sylva pulled away, crossing to the same window Beraht had been staring out at the ruined city of the Fael. She crossed her arms over her chest, hugging herself against the awful thoughts and emotions coursing through her soul. "All the generations of my family have been attuned. Just as you are naturally drawn to the Wind of Death, so too are the Tressalons attuned…"

"To the Wind of Fate," Tomas finished.

"We are not Truthseers, like the matriarchs of House Calonar. We cannot control the Wind of Fate, but are merely sensitive to it. That sensitivity is what first drew the eye of Darkholm and his brother," she sneered. "They have been manipulating my family since before the *Im'peri'a*. Breeding us like horses, like cattle. Encouraging us in the expansion of our magic, our greed for more. The last matriarch of House Tressalon founded the Disciples of Time," Aebreanna confessed. "She wanted mastery of Fate, but could not. So, in her arrogance and spite, she turned to another of the greatest Winds. She spent her entire life exploring the Wind of Time, attempting to gain dominance over it. Her arrogance, her unrestricted greed, caused the Disaster at Nassinalia."

She breathed deep and continued to look out on the Lost City of the Fael with her remaining eye. "Do you know why Ayabalia is in ruin?" the Sylva asked.

Tomas shook his head.

"The war against *Ethroi'sa'kai* did not just shatter our world, but Otherworld as well. Just as the *Sy'lva'i*, the Uldra, and the other children of the Radiant had their traitors, so too did the Fael. This was the last great city of the *Sa'kai*, their last attempt to create a paradise. When *Ethro'sa'kai* started its war and corrupted the Zafael, the resultant war destroyed this glorious city. The Radiant ascended to Overworld, and took with them the secret of building this place. The Fael do not know how to mend the wounds of their home, so they can only live in its corpse."

Aebreanna turned to face Tomas, the misery and guilt of a hundred generations playing out on her once-flawless face. "This is the curse of *Ar'ay'el*," she declared. "We suffer the same mistakes, time and again. The powerful want only to accumulate more power, and they unleash horrid suffering upon all others in their quest."

She sat back down on the long couch, pulling her legs up and hugging them close to her chest. Tomas joined Aebreanna at the seat, but remained a small distance. "Every time I access my mothers' power," the Sylva said, "I feel it. I sense their lust, their unquenchable thirst for more." She put a hand to her temple. "I know the unrestrained ambition of my family, that they would burn the world if it meant sating their hunger. I see, like true memories, myself sitting upon a throne of blood, surrounded by slave-warriors, laying waste to the world. I see a coven of hateful adepts, a sisterhood of forbidden magic, bound to my command. I see a horde of men, enthralled to my will." This last she said with tears flowing from her remaining eye.

Tomas reached out, but Aebreanna flinched away. "You would never…" he tried to say.

"I ALREADY HAVE!!!" she screamed, turning away to bury her half-ruined face. "I already have," she whispered. The Sylva crumpled into the far corner of the couch, her small body shaking with self-disgust.

Tomas stood and then knelt before her. He did not put a hand on her, but only crouched close, available to her. "Rashid," he said. "Alexia knew you would enthrall him."

Aebreanna looked at him in shock. The squire nodded sadly. "She knew you'd be taken by the Greysoul, and that Rogan and Beraht would come after you. She let it happen, knowing it would bind the three of you, especially you and Beraht. She also knew that you'd enthrall Rashid and have the twins. She knew about the Seal of Fate."

"I tell myself it was an accident," Aebreanna whispered. "The Greysoul's abduction of me triggered *shel'iel'enim'or*, the Change of Maturity. I could not control…"

"Alexia knew. She thought it needed to happen, so that the Seal of Fate would be ready when Rogan needed it. She tried to help you, to ease the pain."

The Sylva nodded. "She explained to me what was happening. My own mother had died before she could warn me of the power within *Sy'lva* tears. Alexia warned me about the danger of the Change, my violent emotions, my… desires. She warned me of the power of my tears at that time."

"She also warned Rashid," Tomas pointed out. "She saw his desire for you, and tried to warn him."

"We were little more than children, playing at seduction." Aebreanna held a hand to her remaining eye and lifted free a tear from her cheek. "Even know, without a fertility cycle, my tears could enthrall you, if I desired. My mothers' magic, our power within the Wind of Fate, means I could change your destiny, bind you to my will, even outside of a normal mating cycle. Within one…" She clenched her fist around the dangerous tear and closed firm her eye. "And Goddess protect me, I want to do it."

Tomas was quiet for a moment. Then, "Alexia saw the temptation you felt, every time you were forced to use your Fate Magic."

Aebreanna sniffed loudly, cleaning the dangerous tears from her face with a cloth. "Odd," the Sylva commented. "Since she frequently encouraged me to learn more of my mothers' magic, to explore it."

"But safely," Tomas countered. "She didn't want you to be afraid of it." He again put his hand on her shoulder and turned her to meet his gaze. "You've been telling me how dangerous Death Magic can be, but also how useful, how beneficial to our loved ones. You've encouraged me to learn more about it, so that I can better control it."

The spy laughed softly. "Your logic is as obvious as it is… inescapable."

"Neither of us asked for this," he said. "I don't know if my magic comes from something Alexia passed to me, or if it comes from me. You don't really know from where your magic comes, either. Is it your mothers or your father? We can both live in fear of our power, or we can live with it, accept it and try to learn its safe use."

Aebreanna breathed deeply, closing her eye and nodding. "I hear the echo of our beloved matriarch in your words." She looked at him. "I begin to see her great faith in you, in why she wanted you to help us." The Sylva stood, then, raising Tomas to his feet. "I can do no less," she declared. "Let us see to your latest injury."

Chapter 10

"So how do we do this?" Tomas asked.

Aebreanna stepped up to him, her opalescent gaze fixed on the Darkshard's rippling black tentacles. The horrid veins of the umbral curse flinched as though sensing the Sylva's approach and seemed to try burrowing deeper into Tomas' chest, held back only by Genaea's sapphire magic. "In my experience," Aebranna said, her voice breathy and low, "Fate Magic understand the will, not the word." She glanced up at her young friend. "The other Winds are willful and errant. They require managing, shaping, a strong and demanding mind to force them into a particular shape." She looked back to the Darkshard, her remaining eye spilling its hazel glow in the Sylva's growing intensity. "Fate, alternatively, knows what I want; it needs no prompting. Destiny desires only to be freed."

Tomas took her chin and raised it so that their eyes could lock. "You're still with me," he said firmly.

"You cannot imagine the feeling of letting go," she said in a voice that was some darkening blend of growl and purr. A terrible hunger seemed just barely restrained behind her opalescent eye, an aching need so terribly close to being, at last, fulfilled. "Of finally being free." A soft tongue, dexterous and aching, slipped from between the spy's supple lips. It flickered out, teasing, testing.

"You are Aebreanna Tessalon," Tomas said, his voice and his resolve unbending. "You are a daughter of House Calonar, and a Sister of the Lady of Light. You are a wife, a mother, and a friend. You have faced, and defeated, the worst horrors of Arayel. You control this, it does not control you."

He could see the battle within his friend, the impossible struggle she waged to maintain herself against the pull of all the generations of her family. A thousand emotions played across her beautiful, flawed face, from anger and desire to fear and loathing. Beyond this, though, there was Aebreanna's implacable, undeniable control, her unyielding will. "Yes," she whispered. "I am here. I am in control."

The mystical Sylva, the power of all her mothers radiating from her very skin, reached a hand up. She gently held Tomas' cheek for a moment and then cradled the back of his neck. "There will be pain," she warned in a voice of loving silk. "You will suffer as I extract the Darkshard."

The squire braced himself and nodded.

Still holding the back of his head, Aebreanna slowly moved her right hand up to hover just over the thrashing tendrils of the Darkshard. Maintaining her opalescent hold on his eyes, she asked, "Once I penetrate the spell protecting you, we will have twelve heartbeats only. I must be fast, harsh, perhaps cruel. Are you sure you wish me to do this?"

The squire nodded.

Aebreanna took a deep breath. Tomas could feel the moment she accessed the power, the terrible heritage of House Tressalon. There was light, for no magic seemed possible without some display of shining color. There was a sound, as well. Ancient, forgotten words of power flowed as though unbidden between her lips, echoing like the chorus of a thousand ravenous female predators. There was even the sense of the Winds of Magic, flowing about them as they stood close. Their clothing struggled against the mystic breeze even as Aebreanna's glowing cedar mane rose in joyful abandon as the last Daughter of House Tressalon made use of her bloodline.

More than anything, though, Tomas was aware of the warmth. Not heat, but rather a comforting, loving, cradling warmth radiated from Aebreanna's flesh. From her very soul flowed the power of the candle, the hearthfire, the very sun. That gentle heat reached out and took hold of the young man, claiming him and reassuring him, asserting itself such as a great bonfire would subsume a pitiable stick.

The squire was aware, though only vaguely, of Aebreanna reaching a hand up. She pressed in, penetrating the spell that was maintaining his life. Genaea's gentle sapphire magic retreated, fading as nothing before the raw power of the Sylva. She reached out with firm but gentle fingers, probing, grasping, taking hold. In response, the pulsing tendrils of the Darkshard tried, for a single heartbeat only, to assert themselves, to lay claim to Tomas. This could not endure, though, against the raw power Aebreanna wielded. She took hold of the hateful veins, the umbral curse trying with all its might to devour her young friend, and she pulled.

Tomas screamed. The world became a white-hot blaze without end. He would have fallen, but a single, small, loving hand held him up, supported him and gave him the strength to endure. The flesh, organs, and bones of his entire body seemed to be ripping free, torn asunder. The young man screamed and would have pleaded for mercy could he but form the words. Somewhere, though, deep in his heart, he felt his friend's love and support. He endured only because she was there with him.

And then it was over.

Tomas was held for a moment. He could breathe and once again feel the steady beating of his heart. The young man blinked his eyes, forcing the world back into focus. Aebreanna was still standing before him, but her opalescent gaze was no longer fixed with his. Instead, its hazel glow thrumming with power, her remaining eye was locked on the thrashing claws of the Nightshard. It writhed and throbbed in her upraised hand, seeming as though trying to escape her implacable grip. "Wh-" was all Tomas could say before she dropped him.

With a grunt, Tomas fell to the floor. He made as though to rise, but Aebreanna put a small foot to his chest and forced him back down. No matter the grace and athleticism of her body, the Sylva should not have had the raw power to hold him, to keep him pinned, and yet the young man was unable to move. He could only stare open-mouthed up that impossibly-long leg, up along her perfectly-feminine body, up to the exquisite joy of her power, at last unleashed.

Aebreanna was on the verge of losing herself. The mystic breeze was now a gale, her glorious mane a cedar halo of power. Her opalescent eye blazed with hazel power as it beheld the Darkshard. Her grip, as unflinching, as undeniable as was the foot she held pressed against Tomas' chest, maintained its grip upon the weakening evil in her hand. Her lips, one end forever curled into the hideous mockery of a grin, were turned on the opposing side into a smile of imperious will. The last Daughter of Tressalon then hissed at the Darkshard, commanding without words for it to obey.

Once more, Tomas tried to rise, but Aebreanna forced him back down with only a minor push of one hip. She did not spare him the slightest glance, holding him as an afterthought. The Darkshard seemed to surrender to that implacable will. Its insidious tendrils collapsed upon themselves. It withdrew its writhing mass of evil, hardening even as it was weakening. The impossible darkness coalesced into a dagger. It was a vicious mockery of Aebreanna's sylvai blades. It was in the waving pattern of her people's metalworking, and had the same watery sheen, but its edges held the promise of suffering, of torment unending. Rather than the polished, iridescent metal, the flowing grace of sylvai steel, the dagger was of obsidian, or some other hard, polished stone of unyielding black. Aebreanna held the weapon close, her face nearly lost to her power and authority.

"You-" Tomas tried to say, but she pushed her small foot forward so that it cut his breath short. The young man struggled, grasping at her unmovable leg. "You... are... Aebreanna... Tressalon." Each word needed a titanic effort.

She looked down at him, far down along the length of her leg as though she was looking at the smallest insect from atop a throne.

"You... are... a... daughter... of... Calonar."

She hissed at him, at the naming of that House.

"You... are... my... friend."

There was an unending moment. No conflict passed over Aebreanna's face, no tortured struggle. She merely paused. Then, the mystic breeze seemed to fade. Her cedar mane calmed its dance, folding back down, along her back. The hazel blaze of her opalescent eye quieted. The Sylva blinked and looked about, confused. She looked down again, seeing where she still held her young friend beneath an imperious foot, and jumped back. She looked down at her hand, seeming to see the Darkshard dagger for the first time. She yelped and threw it away, the hateful weapon clattering to the floor. Aebreanna's hands went to her temples and tears flowed from her eye. She tried to shake away the thoughts, the horrid temptations that had filled her mind. Unable, she collapsed to the floor, retreating to a far corner and curling into a ball.

When she sensed Tomas leaning down beside her, Aebreanna made to shrink further away and object, but her voice died on her lips. The squire was holding the small cloth she had used before to wipe away her dangerous tears. She looked up at him, and the young man just shrugged with a half-grin splitting his honest face. Unable to stop herself, Aebreanna laughed.

"We wish you well upon your journey," Genaea was saying. Hundreds of butterfly-winged Fael had come to see them off. The words, though they came from the Fael before them, seemed to echo amongst her kindred, rising into a great symphony. "We perceive that you are meant to stand against the rise of the Demon-God. For this, if for nothing else, we wish upon you all possible blessings."

"Your help is appreciated," Rogan said, bowing deeply not only to Genaea, but more generally to the assembled Fael. "And your friendship means much to us. Signs seem to keep pointing to some great battle in the near future. If you could help us with that…"

Genaea held up her hand. "Otherworld is our home," her voice range with finality. "We can only cross to yours for moments at a time, and even then, we do so greatly reduced and vulnerable. We have aided House Calonar before, and we shall do so again, I suspect." She turned then to Aebreanna, who stood behind and to the side of Rogan. "You do not need to bear the Nightshard's burden."

The Sylva put a hand to the hilt of the insidious dagger now sheathed at her hip. "My hand pulled it free," she told Genaea. "The only way to free my friend was to force the Nightshard to bond with me instead. Until we return to the Northern Keep, and there are able to properly imprison it, I must bear its burden. I will not inflict this upon another."

As one, the Fael bowed, their butterfly-wings fluttering. "We do not agree with your decision," Genaea said. "But we accede to your wishes."

"If we left the Nightshard here," Rogan stepped in, "would the Zafael try to recapture it?"

"Without a doubt," Genaea confirmed.

"And they are as limited as you on our world?"

Again, the Fael nodded.

"Then better it comes with us. You and your people won't be in danger of a Zafael attack, and they can't easily take it from us. Plus, our King and the adepts who serve him have experience in containing…" the knight glanced at the obsidian dagger now sheathed at Aebreanna's hip. "Let's call them, great evils."

Genaea nodded once again and gestured to the horizon, between two of the great, iridescent waterfalls. "We have opened a path for you. The portal ahead will lead you safely out of our realm, and into the seas beyond Dagon'ay. May your journey home be free of further hardship."

"Be nice for a change," Tomas grumbled.

The Heroes Abroad

III

Pelsemoria

Chapter 11

Pelsemoria had changed. It was not a city restored, for the ruins were still there, still in the midst of their decomposition. The spiraling towers of the various guilds were still gone, crumbling fingers clutching for a glorious past forever gone. The magnificent palaces of the wealthy were still hollowed-out crypts, vainglorious monuments to the folly of the powerful. The great arena and amphitheater were both still crumbling, desperately trying to hold on to the echoes of lost celebrations. Even the mightiest of monuments to Humanity's rule, the Forum Biblitheca and its cache of knowledge, the Holy Basilica and its sacred relics, and even the Imperial Palace, all stood empty and rotting. No, Pelsemoria was not restored, it was reborn.

Tomas stood at the bow of the *Blue Lady*, staring in wonder at where his home should rest. The dockyards and merchant wharfs were still broken skeletons. Beside them, however, rested a new series of docks, small, yet functional, with a pair of Velarossi traders harbored. The walls, once an impenetrable bulwark against barbarians and monsters, was still a pock-marked blight, crawling across the seven hills of Pelsemoria. And yet, a new palisade stood, just to the east of the ruined city, manned by soldiers in service to the people. The buildings, homes, and shops still shrank from the summer sun, shedding stonework and tiles like skin from a dying animal. Within the new palisade, though, were new homes, new shops. Beyond were well-ordered fields with crops nearly ready for harvesting. These were not the decorative gardens or elite vineyards of the capital, but true food-producers. The ruin of the formal capital was empty but for scavenging animals and other parasites picking over the bones of the old metropolis. Within the new community of Pelsemoria, though, was life, bustling and vibrant. Tomas stared at this in shock.

What brought the squire even more surprise, though, was what greeted their ship. Lining the new docks, gaily dressed in bright cloths and cheering their joy, were the people, the survivors of Pelsemoria. But, Tomas thought, these could not be his friends and family. These people were not scarred with disease; these new inhabitants were healthy. Their clothing was not patched and threadbare, nor did those ragged tatters masquerading as clothes hung limply from emaciated bodies. These people wore new dresses and tunics, shirts and hose, and their bodies were full and strong. The women wore headdresses and the men full caps. Little girls had bright ribbons in their hair and the babies...

Babies.

Toms stood in open-mouthed shock as he stared out from the bow of the *Blue Lady*. There were babies in Pelsmoria. Women were holding children, less than a year old, and those tiny people were not squalling in sickness and hunger. The mothers did not stare with grim acceptance of their children's certain mortality. Parents laughed and cheered, children waved banners made merry. And in mothers arms, babies either slept peacefully or looked about in hopeful wonder.

"What?" Tomas asked. "How?"

Rogan, standing beside his squire, nudging the young man and nodded to a detachment of knights waiting back from the crowd that had gathered at the new dock. Tomas looked, and saw pristine white surcoats adorned with the sacred red flame. "The Knights of Mercy," he said reverently.

"Remember that we dispatched a message to them, asking for their help?" Rogan reminded.

Tomas nodded dumbly. "But," he breathed, "I never thought…"

"I guess they got the message," Rogan shrugged. He slapped his squire on the shoulder. "Come on, we should get changed." The knight turned his young friend away from the bow and started walking back to their cabins.

"Changed?"

"Aebreanna's been holding onto some clothes for us, something she picked up at Krykos when we docked there."

"She bought us clothes?" Tomas asked skeptically.

Rogan shrugged as he climbed down the short stairs leading to their shared cabin. "We knew we'd be passing by Pelsemoria, and she found out some of what's been going on here." The knight grinned at his squire. "I think she wants you looking your best when your people greet you." He entered the cabin.

Tomas paused. "My people?"

Colin, Pelsemoria's only remaining blacksmith, stepped forward. "On behalf of your people," he said in a great, booming voice, "Welcome home, my lord!"

The assembled crowd cheered and waved their ribbons and banners. Tomas had stared at those banners as he and Rogan disembarked from the *Blue Lady*. A silver lion was rampant on a crimson field. In one hand, it held a sword, in the other, a quill. The squire had quietly asked his knight whose heraldry that was, but Rogan had only grinned.

"My lord?" Tomas asked.

Colin raised a parchment scroll and unrolled it. He turned the document towards Tomas. On it were the seals of House Calonar and House Calexto, as well as more than a dozen baronies in Ironheartshaven and Velaross. Center of these was the seal of the Lords Cardinal themselves. "As declared on the last winter's solstice, and formally acknowledged by other noble lords, Tomas Fidelis is recognized as the hereditary Lord of Pelsemoria. His family is hereby named a Noble House, with sovereign rights over his lands and people." The blacksmith glanced back to the crowd and nodded. He then sank to one knee, as did all the people of Pelsemoria. "We swear fealty to House Fidelis and Tomas, our liege lord!" As one, the crowd lowered their heads.

Tomas gaped and moved his mouth, as though to form words, but nothing came from his lips but a puckering, stunned silence. Finally, Rogan nudged his squire in the ribs. "Stand," Tomas blurted out. "Please, don't bow." He moved forward and raised Colin to his feet. The young lord of Pelsemoria kept moving forward, motioning for his people to stand. "Please, get up."

One of the first to stand was a face as familiar to Tomas as his own. "Elpidius?" he gaped. "El!" the two young friends ran to each other and clasped their arms around each other's backs, laughing and slapping one another and joyous in their reunion.

Close behind Elpidius in standing was another familiar, grinning face. "Kineus!" Tomas pulled his other childhood friend into a rough bear hug.

"All hail the conquering hero!" Kineus laughed mockingly.

"Welcome home, Tomas!" Elpidius rejoiced, and the crowd cheered again.

"What is all this?" Tomas demanded.

"The Knights of Mercy came just before the winter arrived," Kineus explained, nodding towards the white-cloaked knights. "They brought food, medicine-"

"And news," Epidius finished. "We found out what's been happening since you left. The knights helped us rebuild, to start a new community outside the ruins. They've helped defend us from raiders and even sent word to the islands to restart trade."

"No more raids?" Tomas asked.

"Nothing we can't handle," another voice responded. The crowd parted to reveal a soldier wearing red and silver to match the banners flying overhead. At first, Tomas did not recognize the man, but in a few moments, the young man was able to connect the strong man before him with the wounded one from more than a year ago. "Mariano?" Tomas started. "Luigiano Mariano?"

"Thanks to you," the soldier grinned, "my wounds healed."

Tomas stepped forward and looked the man over. Nothing remained of the life-threatening wounds he had sustained. He stood tall in his chainmail and crimson cape, his gladius once more belted at his side and his crested helmet carried under the crook of his arm. "Why aren't you wearing your Praetorian uniform?" Tomas asked.

Mariano nodded. "The Praetorians did our job. We kept the people as safe as we could. We protected this community for years. But the Republic is dead. The Legions are disbanded. There were only a few of us left, anyway. When the Knights of Mercy arrived and brought hope with them, we decided the time had come to let go of the past."

"So, you're what now?" Tomas asked. "Just... soldiers?"

Mariano stood, if possible, even taller. He glanced back to the crimson-cloaked soldiers standing atop the new palisade and the detachment standing back with the white-cloaked knights. "We've all sworn loyalty to House Fidelis," he said. The soldier dropped to one knee and drew his gladius, presenting it to Tomas. "On behalf of my men, we swear fealty to you, Lord Tomas of House Fidelis. By your leave, we are, henceforth, your House Guard."

The detachment standing back with the white-cloaked knights drew their own blades and held them high. From the new palisade, horns blew and the soldiers there also drew their weapons. Tomas stared at them, and then at the warrior kneeling before him. He drew Steelheart, the legendary sword of House Calonar and saluted his new House Guard. "You honor me," he said in a voice he hoped would carry. "You honor my family, and you honor our community. The Legions may be gone, but in men like you, their spirit, their tradition, endures."

Mariano stood and sheathed his gladius. He took Tomas' hand with a grin. "Not that this changes much," he said conspiratorially.

"Wouldn't expect it to," Tomas replied. He then looked around. "How many are left?"

"I have twenty-four left," Mariano reported. When the Knights of Mercy arrived, they brought news that many didn't find very... acceptable."

Tomas glanced around. "Dunnalban?" he guessed.

"Our former Lord Commander has left, taking with him about a third of our people."

"Said he was going to Velaross," Elpidius snorted. "He said something about not protecting fools."

Tomas glanced back at where Rogan stood at the base of the *Blue Lady*'s ramp. Ahmed had been careful not to fly the colors of House Calonar, and of their overly-diverse team, only Rogan himself had come ashore. The Archaeknights, with their damning tattoos, to say nothing of Aebreanna, Beraht, and the other non-Humans abord, remained out of sight until Tomas could discern the type of welcome they might receive. "So, what have you been told about House Calonar and what's been happing in Lanasia?" he asked.

"I took the liberty," a voice weighed by age and hard years answered. The crowd parted, and Father Konrad stepped forward. He had aged somewhat in the past year, the thinning tufts of his hair carrying more grey, and the wrinkles across his weathered face growing deeper. Despite this, the clergyman walked with more surety and purpose than Tomas could recall seeing since the night of the Madness.

"Father!" Tomas called and went to his old priest. He took the holy man's hands and kissed them, then pulling the kind friar into a rough hug.

"Welcome home, Tomas," Father Konrad said gently. "I take it your trip was a productive one?"

Tomas smiled and stepped back, looking at all his assembled friends. "You could say that. I…" he stopped and stared as Father Konrad stepped away. "Mother!"

Tomas' mother was weeping openly, unashamedly. She ran to her son and threw her arms around him, pulling him to her and sobbing into his chest. To the squire's surprise, his mother was now significantly shorter than he. Despite this, she was fuller in body; her bones no longer stuck out from her skin and her long hair no longer hung limply about her withered shoulders. Instead, she was once more the vibrant, powerful woman of his memory. "You did it, Tomas!" she exalted, kissing his forehead, his cheeks, and his hands. She looked up at her son with more joy than should have been possible. "Your father and I are so proud!"

Tomas could say nothing, only hold his mother in joy. For months, he had said nothing, not even allowing himself to think of his mother. He had gone, leaving her behind to an almost-certain death. The people of Pelsemoria so frequently fell victim to raiders, slavers, starvation, illness, or injury. Barely a week could pass, let alone so many months, without another member of their community being lost. Tomas had, in the silence of his mind, accepted that he would never again lay eyes on his mother. But, in defiance of Fate and all the evils of a fallen world, she had survived.

"Father Konrad told us everything," his mother said, wiping away tears only for them to be quickly replaced. "He told us about House Calonar sending aid through him. About their Walkers trying to protect us from the Xeshlin and the bandits."

"And you believed him?" Tomas asked.

"Well," Kineus grinned. "The Knights of Mercy were supporting everything he said, so we sort of had to."

"What about all those reports Dunnalban kept bringing back from Velaross?"

Elpidius snorted. "Apparently, his Lordship was exaggerating. None of the Knights of Mercy had ever heard of him. The best anyone can figure out, when he told us he was going to Velaross, he really only ever went as far as Wignis. We sent some of our own people north, and found out he's been lying to them, as well. He's told them for years that we didn't want any help, nor any outsiders."

"Why in Underworld would he do that?" Tomas demanded.

"Power," Mariano growled. "He had a few loyalists among the Praetorians helping him. As long as they kept up the lies, they stayed in power here."

"Big fish," Elpidius snorted again. "Keeping his small pond."

"So, everything is cleared up now?" Tomas asked of Father Konrad, and the old friar nodded. "Well, then I can make some introductions." He turned and waved Rogan forward. "Everyone," the squire said whimsically, "meet the mercenary captain of House Calonar, servant and assassin for the Black Duke, and consort to the unholy priestess Kyla."

"Smartass," Rogan grumbled in Gunnic, stepping forward. He bowed slightly, keeping his hand far away from Talon's hilt. "Rogan Eigenhard, of the Northern Keep," this he said in accented Velish.

Tomas' friends and family stood wearily. The crowd had gone silent. Years of misinformation, of rumor and outright lies had buried themselves deep into the souls of the people of Pelsemoria. Tomas had, at first, suggested they sail around his home. As much as he wanted the very reunion he was now enjoying, the squire had admitted that chances were high they would not be welcomed. Having been the victim of a mob's justice once, Tomas was ill-at-ease in subjecting his friends to such horror.

There were few sounds coming from the people, but for whispers passed back and forth. Tomas' friends glanced at him and then back at Rogan. The air grew still and even the rough seas around Pelsemoria seemed to quiet their usual crash against the hard shoreline. No one seemed eager to take the first step, whatever that step might be.

At last, a young boy stepped forward. He had in his hands a tiny replica of the new crimson banner of House Fidelis. He walked up, ignoring his mother's hissed demand for him to return. The boy ignored his new lord, and instead walked up to Rogan. "Did you really kill the Emperor?" he asked.

Rogan slowly lowered to one knee so that he was more or less at eye level with the boy. "No," he said with a tone of surprising softness. "Tienel Uskera killed the Emperor, and most of the Elector Lords. I was there that day, along with a few of my friends, and the Praetorians, including Tomas' father."

"What happened to the Greysoul?" the body asked.

"He escaped. He ran away and kidnapped one of my friends."

Another child, a girl, stepped forward. "What happened then?" she asked.

"Me and more of my friends went after them. We hunted the Greysoul down to his tower and fought him. We rescued my friend and... we stopped the Greysoul."

"Actually," Tomas corrected, "Rogan threw a sword into the Greysoul's chest."

"Really?" the boy asked, his eyes wide.

Rogan threw his squire an irritated look. "It was his shoulder, actually," the knight grunted. "And I had a lot of help."

"From who?" the little girl asked.

Rogan glanced back over his shoulder and whistled. Beraht stood up and stepped off the *Blue Lady*, not bothering with the ramp. The great Uldra strode up the pier, stopping behind Rogan. Most of the crowd near Tomas gasped and took a step back. Even Mariano, trained and disciplined as he was, could not resist the instinct to put his hand to his sword when confronted with one of the most extreme examples of the great mountain race.

Beraht stopped and knelt, yet still towered over the children. "Hello," he said in a voice that seemed to echo up from the deepest, most impenetrable of mountain chasms.

"Did you help kill the Greysoul?" the little girl asked hesitantly.

"Yes I did," the Uldra replied, his Velish thick with the accent of the mountains.

"What did you do?"

Beraht leaned in and looked about, as though in fear of being overheard. "I hit him with a big rock." The Uldra punched himself in the side of the head with one boulder-sized fist. He then pantomimed becoming dizzy and falling over, bringing a great laughter from not only the two children nearby, but those still safely back with their parent. The laughter continued, growing, until the adults could not help but join in.

"You're really tall," the little girl observed to Beraht.

"You need to be, to see over the mountains," the Uldra replied. "Would you like to see over the mountains, too?" he asked.

The little girl excitedly nodded, and Beraht gently picked her up. He lifted the girl high and set her standing atop one of his massive shoulders. "You lied!" she accused. "I can't see any mountains!"

"You can't!?!" Beraht exclaimed. He made a great show of looking about. "Huh, I guess you're right. There aren't any mountains here!" The great Uldra then swung the little girl, spinning her in midair only to put her down on the pier with such gentleness, not a single one of the ribbons in her hair was disturbed. This quick motion and spinning brought a joyful squeal from the little girl, and a relieved sigh from several parents.

Rogan stood. "Much has been said of us over the years. Cylan Calonar has been called the Black Duke. Really, he's the last of the Heroes of Fate, still fighting to protect us all. His daughter has been called an unholy priestess, the head of an evil cult. Really, she's my wife, and I love her. We try to help, but we do make mistakes."

"The Madness?" someone from the crowd asked.

"There have been a lot of stories about that night," Tomas said. "But-"

Rogan put a hand on his squire's shoulder. "The Madness happened," the knight confessed. "There are plenty of excuses. Kyla had magical power she didn't understand and couldn't control. She didn't even know she had it. We had just survived battle with the Greysoul. All of these are excuses, but they don't excuse us. The truth is… the Madness was our fault. Much of what you all have suffered this past decade started because of us. We've tried helping you, sending food and medicine, sending our Walkers to fight off the Xeshlin. But none of that changes what we did. What I did."

Rogan breathed deep. "Someday, I'll ask for your forgiveness. Someday, I hope to earn your forgiveness. Until then, know that I, and all of House Calonar, will continue to try and help you, however you'll let us."

Mariano, like all the gathered crowd, said nothing at first. The soldier eventually stepped forward. He strode up and stood in front of Rogan, his fists on his hips. "A fine speech," he conceded. "Living in Pelsemoria, we heard a lot of fine speeches. Politicians, nobles, priests, adepts. All of them making speeches. Few of them ever really doing anything."

The soldier glanced back at Tomas. "Lord Tomas risked his life to quest, to bring back help for us. He did it. My loyalty, all our loyalties, are with him, and with House Fidelis. If our lord says we can trust you, then so be it." Mariano extended a hand to Rogan.

The knight took the offered hand, and the people once again cheered.

Tomas' mother put her arm through her son's. "Enough of all this melodrama," she insisted. "I started preparing a meal the moment our soldiers spotted your ship. Let's go home." She glanced to the side. "But first…" she motioned for the people to stand aside. The group parted, and Tomas felt his heart turn to lead.

Cecilia had clearly taken great care in preparing herself. Her dress, very nearly a gown, was of bright crimson, matching the new banners of House Fidelis. A silver lion had been embroidered over her heart, seeming to emerge from the intricate embroidery that flowed along the conservative neckline. A simple silver cap rested at the back of her head, holding back the elaborate coils of her long, dark hair. Her cosmetics were applied with deft skill, quiet probably with the aid of an older, more experienced woman. Her large, wide eyes stared at Tomas with joyful hope. Her already-rouged cheeks blushed even deeper. Her rose lips were slightly parted, her breathing heavy in anticipation of a question she, and all those around her, were certain must be asked. She was dressed and carried herself as a noblewoman, as the Lady of a new House, and the intended wife of a great champion.

Tomas sighed deeply. He had not been looking forward to this conversation. In the days since their departure from Krykos, he had tried practicing, tried examples of what he would say with Rogan. The knight had urged simple honesty and directness, but Tomas had dismissed his useless suggestions. On the last night he had seen her, the young man had taken her virginity and left nothing behind. He had abandoned Cecilia and gone north, where he found Mary. In the deepest silence of his heart, in that very moment as he looked at Cecilia in her new gown and earnest gaze, the squire realized that much of his suggestion in traveling around Pelsemoria had been a cowardly hope to avoid this very moment.

Tomas stepped forward, and the crowd parted for him and his supposed love. The squire, the newly-anointed Lord of Pelsemoria, reluctantly moved to face Cecilia. More than anything, he wanted to spare her this, to preserve for her the hopes she must have fostered since Tomas had been proclaimed a nobleman. There must be words to preserve everyone's happiness, he thought. There must be something to say that will spare her pain. There had to be some simple, elegant speech that would preserve Cecilia's dignity.

"I think we need to talk," was what he said.

Chapter 12

"I thought I'd find you here," Rogan noted, his words echoing across the great cathedral. Tomas glanced back from the front pew on which he sat. His knight was standing in the broken doorway.

"I was hoping for some privacy," the young man said with acid.

Rogan shrugged and walked down the center aisle. "Yeah, well... your mom sent me to look for you."

"I wasn't hungry," Tomas muttered, turning back to stare at the broken altar. As Rogan and the others had sat down for the morning meal, the young man had taken a quiet moment to slip away. The rest of the day had been filled with meetings and reunions, with plans and formalizing Tomas' authority over Pelsemoria. His mother had said little the rest of the day, serving food for her son and his guests, but her overly-neutral face promised a lengthy reprimand in the future. Tomas had tried, after her new house had quieted for the night, to talk to her. He had so many questions about her bloodline, about the mystical power he himself was now developing. She had refused, though, and sent him to bed.

His knight flopped down in the crumbling pew behind his squire. "So, praying or hiding?"

"Both, I guess."

"Yeah," Rogan nodded, noticing his squire fidgeting. "Still sore, huh?"

Tomas rubbed his still-burning face. "Yeah. I don't think that could have gone worse" he noted.

"Probably not."

The young man shifted, trying to take the pressure from his sore genitals. "Most of it... most of it I understand. Screaming at me, slapping me-"

"Repeatedly."

Tomas threw a hateful look at his knight. "Repeatedly," he confirmed. "Cursing me. Even punching me in the stomach-"

"Repeatedly."

"Fine! Yes! Repeatedly! Punching me in the stomach, REPEATEDLY! All of that, I understand." He shifted again. "But kicking me in crotch?"

"Re-"

"I KNOW!!! I WAS THERE!!!"

Rogan said nothing for a while. He looked around, letting his squire sulk at the poor result of his reunion with Cecilia. "You know," he finally said. "I always laugh when people talk about how unfair life is."

"What? Why?"

"Think about it," the knight said, leaning forward to clasp his hands against the back of Tomas' pew. "If life is unfair, then bad things happen randomly. They just happen, for no reason. On the other hand, if life is fair, then all the bad things that happen to us happen for a reason. They happen to us because, in some way, we deserve it."

Tomas stared at Rogan. "Are you saying I deserved all this?" he demanded.

Rogan just shrugged.

"You know, as I recall, you were the one who kept encouraging me to pursue Mary."

His knight held up a finger. "Actually, I was encouraging you to make up your mind. You were swinging back and forth. I told you to make a decision and stick with it." Rogan breathed in the dead air of the crumbling cathedral. "Life's all about consequences. You make a choice, you live with the consequences. I married Kyla, so now I serve her father. You fell in love with a Northlands girl, and confessed it to your last girlfriend, so now you've got a Pelsmorian girl putting curses on you."

Tomas rubbed at the side of his head, relieved that the bleeding had, at last, stopped. "Do you really think she's putting a curse on me?" he asked nervously.

"Who knows? Maybe she just wanted that clump of your hair for... I don't know... a keepsake."

The squire threw a flat look at his knight. "A keepsake?"

Again, Rogan could only shrug.

Tomas sighed again, squirming to try and find a comfortable position for his throbbing genitals. "Rogan, do you remember when you made the choice to leave home, to travel?"

"Oh, yeah. I was in my father's study. I'd run away from another art lesson. My father had a few books on the old adventures of the Heroes of Fate. I loved reading them. That night, I was reading the story about how the Heroes first met."

"Castle Rainer," Tomas noted, "near the town of Citta Muore."

"Yes. Something just hit me, as I was reading about the Heroes coming together, violating their orders and instead fighting Karnat. The freedom to do something that really matters. I liked that idea, so I left. My uncle gave me some help and, well, you know most of the rest."

"Some of it, anyway," Tomas countered.

"Why do you ask, kid?"

The squire looked around. Despite the building's decay, much of the Holy Basilica's beauty remained. The great murals were still overhead, cracks in the ceiling doing little to erase those depictions of some of the great stories from the Teachings. The marble pews and columns still have beautiful sculptures of saints and angels. The Alabaster Window, the great, stained-glass portal rising behind the shattered altar, was still intact. Still there was the holy flame rising above the waters of uncreation, casting its divine light across the world. "I started here," he whispered. "I was here, praying, when I had an epiphany. The idea just sprang into my head to find the Trickster Mage, to earn a wish and get our lives back. I made the decision to leave while sitting right here."

"Looking for more inspiration?"

"I don't know." The squire looked around. "Weirdly, I think I got exactly what I was going to wish for. My people are safe. My home is being... I guess rebuilt, rather than restored. My mother is alive and happy."

"Actually," Rogan corrected. "I think she's still stewing about the whole Cecilia thing."

"Long-term," Tomas grumbled. "My mother and my people are happy, long-term. But, right now, I feel the same way I did back at the Northern Keep. Do you remember that night we talked, after I realized that House Calonar wasn't the threat we all thought it was?"

His knight nodded. "You were pretty deflated, as I recall."

"That's putting it mildly," the squire snorted. "All that work, all that journeying, and for what? I found out it was all pointless."

"But it wasn't kid," Rogan corrected. "You went north and met Mary, if nothing else. You got experience and resources. You were able to get help for your people."

Tomas nodded, considering his knight's words.

"It's like traveling through a forest," Rogan explained. "You lose sight of the path because of all the trees, all the up-close things. When you're spending all your time looking down, behind, or directly ahead, you lose sight of the long-term."

"Huh. I never really thought of it that way."

"That's because your balls hurt," the knight pointed out. "A man should never try to make important decisions right after getting kicked by a woman."

They were quiet for a while. Tomas looked at the broken stain glass windows and the shattered altar. His mind drifted through all the memories he had collected since leaving this very spot, more than a year ago. As so often happened, when he let his mind wander, his thoughts inevitably turned back to Tordenia. "Rogan?" the squire asked softly.

"What is it, kid?" the knight replied.

"What was Vagris like, before he betrayed you?"

"That's an Underworld of a question," Rogan started. "What brought that on?"

Tomas glanced over at one of the more-intact windows, which depicted a famous scene from Adamic history. A great castle stood atop a mighty hill. It was surrounded by a forest in flames, and the wrath of God was sending monsters up from beneath the earth. Rogan followed his apprentice's eyes. "The Ruin of Castle Kordenel," he said, recognizing the art.

"You're familiar with it?"

The knight nodded. "Well, everybody's seen the play. The original painting at first from my art lessons. The window replicates one of the masterworks of the fourth century. I learned the actual history of the castle's fall later."

"One of the founding Noble Houses of the Republic," Tomas mused. "Feared and respected. Its members were leaders during the final days of the Uldra Uprising. But pride consumed them. They sought out the Umbra to increase their power and wealth, and even to take the Redwood Throne. They went from the heroes of one war to the villains of another."

"Kid," Rogan said, "you aren't the villain."

Tomas looked at his knight. "I destroyed a city. It doesn't get more villainous than that."

Rogan sighed and shook his head. He began to say something many times, but kept stopping. Finally, the knight jerked a thumb back to the main doors and the tympanum above them. "You know that story of course," he said.

Tomas looked and nodded. "The Siege of Velaross. When the Nenic Twins overwhelmed the Holy City with their army of unliving monsters."

"Yeah. The Heroes of Fate led a great victory in that battle. They saved the day, defeated the Twins, and stopped the Plague of the Walking Death."

The squire nodded. "One of the great victories over evil. So?"

Rogan leaned in. "Do you know how many people died in that battle?"

Tomas thought for a moment. "The histories only say that the city was nearly destroyed. That Velaross needed generations to be restored."

"Yeah. The city was all but destroyed. Thousands lived there. Tens of thousands, maybe. And most of them died. Most of the buildings were destroyed. The day was won, but at a high price.

"We beat the Greysoul, but Pelemoria was destroyed in the process. We beat Balshazzar, but Tordenia was destroyed. God only knows how many are going to die up north before we can stop Fak'Har. You asked me what Vagris was like? He was an arrogant nobleman. He never had a problem with sacrificing the low-born, or with inflicting whatever collateral damage was necessary for a mission. That's the difference between you and him. Tordenia was a terrible mistake, and you own it. Those deaths, that destruction, it haunts you, and it should. I saw Vagris burn a village to the ground once, just to locate a single target. And I'll tell you, he slept just fine that night. Me and you, kid, when we mess up, when we cause collateral damage, we live with it. We try to make it better, but it stays with us. I still have nightmares about the Madness, and I should. I doubt Vagris has ever lost a moment's sleep over the things he's done."

Rogan stood. "You're not the villain, kid. Some people will call you that. But as long as you hold onto that remorse over the mistakes. As long as you try your best to help and to minimize suffering…" the knight shrugged. "Let history make up its own mind. Now come on." He jerked his head toward the door. "We've got another mystery brewing."

Tomas stood, somewhat awkwardly. "What now?"

"Aebreanna and Beraht have found something in the old palace."

Rogan led his squire across the ruins of Pelemoria, up the Via Palatium. The great road that once marched through the heart of the city and led to the gates of the Imperial Palace had, for centuries been adorned with great marble statues. These were supposed to be eternal memorials to the greatest of generals, archmages, and guild masters, men who had dedicated their lives to the glory of the Republic. Like every citizen of Pelsemoria, Tomas had dreamed as a boy of one day earning a place amongst the great heroes of the past. He had walked with his father upon this very road and looked up whenever Alessandros Fidelis had paused to describe the history of one of those great statues. Tomas recalled looking from the marble icons to his father, believing he was one of them, a paragon of duty made flesh.

Little remained now of the statues or even the stone that had made up the great Via Palatium. "Building material," Rogan noted, as though reading his squire's thoughts.

"Yeah," Tomas mumbled. He paused at a lump of moss-covered marble, the remains of a pedestal that had once held the statue of Marius Kordenel, the great general of the Uldra Uprising, but whose family had fallen into shame.

"Stuck in the past again, kid?"

The young Lord of House Fidelis grimaced. "I understand the need for building materials," he said sadly. "And we don't have the resources, the people or the tools or the time, to quarry new stone. But…"

"The past is always sacrificed for the present," Rogan noted. "Old buildings are torn down to make room for new ones. Old memorials are forgotten. Old glories fade."

"Then what's the point?"

"Never reach for immortality, kid," his knight advised. "We just do what we can for friends and family. History'll always make its own decisions."

They continued on. "How'd your meeting go with… what was his name?"

"Roger," Rogan offered. "Sir Roger. The other Knights of Mercy call him 'Roger of the Old Mill.'" He shrugged. "Not sure why."

"Anything interesting, or just more diplomacy?"

"Actually," the prince of House Calonar replied, "he had quite a bit of intelligence." As they walked, Rogan pulled a small map from his tunic and handed it over to his squire. Tomas looked and noted several red marks along the southern coasts of Damaris and Mireio. "The Xeshlin have landed," Rogan said. "They've set up supply dumps in those areas, and the Knights of Mercy think they're also operating out of Remigis Island."

"Anything around Pelsemoria?"

"Nothing yet. It looks like the Xeshlin're concentrating on the Duchies of Velaross this time. I guess they don't think Pelsemoria is worth the trouble anymore." Rogan nodded at the map. "What's worse, the Gwyndd barons have also launched another campaign into the Duchies."

They reached the old gates to the Imperial Palace. The gold had long since been plundered, and the black iron showed recent harvesting, leaving only an uneven graveyard of rusting fingers breaking through a weed-choked garden. "The war's shifting," Tomas observed.

"What do you mean?"

"The fighting used to be here in the old Imperial Prefecture, and up around the Kordenel Counties. Now it's Velaross."

"Don't forget the Northlands, kid," Rogan advised as he led Tomas towards the palace itself. "We've still got that little problem at the Keep."

"And Frostfront's war in Jarek," Tomas added. "Seems like the whole of eastern Lanasia is going up in flames."

The Imperial Palace, so legend said, had been designed by the last Khepric architects and built by enslaved Uldra. The Sylvai had added their aesthetics to the great complex, adding beautiful sculpture, mosaics, fountained gardens, murals, and etchings. Every surface of the marble and gold palace had once been covered in beauty. For uncounted centuries, the empresses of the Sylvai, and then the Republic's emperors had lived and ruled from the great structure. The Imperial Palace had been the heart of Lanasia for more than ten thousand years.

Now it was a pock-marked cadaver. Any precious metals had been scavenged in the first year after Pelemoria's destruction. The sculptures were disfigured mockeries of art, twisted grotesques reflecting a decade of neglect and predation. Few doorways were intact, instead gaping out at an uncaring world like the moans of a forgotten martyr. Windows had long since lost their glass, now staring vacantly onto a world that had moved past its glorious past.

"I heard your people wanted to try and restore some of the old buildings," Rogan noted as the pair entered the great entrance hall. It's supporting marble columns were broken, gaping at them like the toothless grin of a mocking skeleton. The tiled roof was riddled with holes, the constant onslaught of Pelsemoria's hard weather taking a heavy toll.

"A few of them suggested it last night," Tomas replied, "but I said no. We need to focus on houses, shops, public works. We need to keep our community alive and focused on stability. There's no time for palaces." He tried to ignore the faded and broken murals along the walls and ceiling; the once-vibrant paintings had been depictions of glorious achievements in magic from the mythical past, now they were faded distortions of legend.

They passed out of the entrance hall and walked through the overgrown gardens. Trees and shrubbery, once immaculately-trimmed, now grew without constraint. The twin fountains on either side of the now-grassy path were still full, but now held mossy ponds, rather than crystal-clear reflecting pools. "You'll have time," Rogan noted. "Your people are safe again, they're rebuilding. Someday, you'll be able to restore all this."

"Should it be?" Tomas asked softly.

"What?"

The young lord of House Fidelis stopped, just in front of the yawning hole that had once been the gold-lined doors to the audience chamber. He looked around, at the north and south wings, at the distant baths and the Praetorian's barracks. All of its stood empty now. "My people are happy, Rogan," he admitted to his knight.

"That's good, right?"

"It's great. Honestly, it's more than I thought possible. In the past year, we've seen foolish kings, vengeful adepts, greedy politicians, and power-hungry tyrants. New kingdoms are forming, old religions are returning." Tomas raised his arms and gestured all around them. "And here we are. The Xeshlin are launching another invasion. God knows what's going to happen to the Western Empire. The Gwyndd are invading Velaross again. Fak'Har and Vagris are attacking the Keep. And here we are. My people are happy in their new village." The squire looked at his knight. "Should we reach for past glory? Can we... is it possible to just... be happy?"

Rogan closed his eyes and breathed deep. "In all honesty, kid, that question needs someone a lot wiser than me to answer. You've talked to the King, did he ever tell you his great wish?"

"To be free," Tomas nodded. "To take his family and just ride away."

"But he can't. He was one of the Heroes of Fate. He's the last of the Heroes. If there's a problem, if there's people in need of help, he'll help them. He can't not help. He'll never have a quiet life, because he cares."

"Like you?" the squire asked, half-jokingly.

"Like us," the knight corrected. "Like it or not, kid, you're one of us. You give a damn. You can't not give a damn. Your whole life, when you hear about people in need, you'll put your own life, your own wants and needs aside, to help." Rogan nodded out to the ruins of Pelsemoria. "You saw your people here, you knew how they were suffering, and you were the one to leave, to find help."

Tomas said nothing for a moment. "That's… kind of depressing," he admitted.

"Tell me about it." The knight took his squire's shoulder. "Come on, Aebreanna and Beraht're waiting"

Rogan led the way into the audience chamber. Therein, to Tomas' great relief, he did not turn left and head towards the Chamber of the Elector Lords. The young man had little interest in revisiting his father's deathplace. Instead, Rogan turned right and headed to the forbidden Imperial Vault.

"We always meant to come back," Rogan said, walking down the long corridor. Unlike all the other parts of the Imperial Palace, this passage was unadorned. There were never statues, frescos, or murals. This was not a place for visitors or grand ceremonies. In the time of the Republic, only the Praetorians and the Emperor himself were ever allowed to walk this corridor. "After we defeated the Greysoul, we meant to come and help your people."

"You'd have been killed on sight," Tomas pointed out.

"Exactly why we didn't come," his knight conceded. "Once the Greysoul was dealt with, the Republic was already well on its way out. The warlords were popping up, and we just didn't have the resources to fight our way here, let alone the warm welcome your people would've given us. But that left one big problem."

Rogan stopped in front of the great, round door. The entrance to the Imperial Vault. Designed by the Khepri, built by the Uldra, and sealed by the Sylvai, the door was three feet thick of cold-forged iron. Twenty men were needed to open and close it. An entire generation passed after the death of the last Sylvai empress before Chlodocar Majestos, greatest of the Human emperors learned the secret of opening the Imperial Vault. Only the Praetorians were told the secret, and then bound by the greatest of oaths. Perhaps even more than the lives of the Emperor and his family, the Praetorians were sworn to the defense of the Imperial Vault.

"Did Mariano open it for you?" Tomas asked.

The knight's expression was answer enough. "Oh, God," the squire gasped.

"Mariano swears that nobody's gone near the Vault," Rogan reported. "Not in years. Not only that, your father was the last person who knew how to open it. None of the other Praetorians knew the secret, except…"

"Except Dunnalban," Tomas finished. The squire grimaced at the open door and its implications. "What did he take?"

Rogan waved Tomas in and entered what was perhaps the most forbidden place in all Lanasia. The Imperial Vault was a single, great, open room. Eight unadorned pillars stood at identical intervals across the round chamber. There was no treasure within, for that was not the purpose of the Imperial Vault. Instead, each sitting upon its own pedestal of cold-forged iron, were various items, all deceptively common-looking. Upon one sat a hand mirror, covered in black silk and chained in silver. On another waited a small shepherd's flute, suspended in a bowl of viscous green liquid. A harlequin's mask grinned at them, the eyes glowing a soft, inviting red. Any one of these items, by itself, radiated impossible power, and infinite evil. Together, Tomas felt as though the air was pressing in upon him, somehow both hot and cold, pushing and pulling, and enticing as only the worst taboos can be.

At the far end of the Vault, at an empty pedestal that somehow stood alone amidst the great evil surrounding them, waited Aebreanna and Beraht. The great Uldra held his mighty waraxe close to his heart, muttering to himself in the language of his people. The Sylva was staring intently at the empty pedestal, and one hand rested on the Darkshard dagger belted at her waist.

"What was taken?" Tomas asked again, finding the words difficult to form against the alluring pressure within the Vault.

Aebreanna turned, glancing at Tomas with her opalescent eye. "The worst of them all," she replied with a helpless gesture to the empty pedestal. "*Sara'wabcusba'sarapum*, the Obsidian Tiara."

Tomas' body took a step back without his knowing. The young man gaped at Aebreanna, then looked to Beraht as though hoping for some denial. The Uldra could only nod. "The Crown of the Dark Empress," Tomas whispered, fearing even the name of that hateful artefact.

"You know of it then?" Aebreanna asked.

Tomas nodded mutely.

"Well, I still don't," Rogan interjected. "So, the kid's here. Will you explain now?"

"The Imperial Vault has, since the very founding of our *Im'peri'a*, been the repository, the prison, of the most vile evils to infect this world." Aebreanna looked again to the empty pedestal. "Creations of the worst, most irredeemable souls were stored here, in the hopes that they might be kept forever out of the reach of those who would let themselves be consumed by evil." She closed her opalescent eye and gently shook her head. "The worst of these was *Sara'wabcusba'sarapum*, the Obsidian Tiara."

"Created by Kelinva on the eve of the Uldra Uprising," Tomas continued. "Capable of enslaving men, of twisting their minds and stripping away their souls. The Dark Empress could use the Obsidian Tiara to enslave, to torture, to damn."

"The legends are, of course exaggerated," Aebreanna countered. "Nevertheless, the few surviving records from before the Uldra's Uprising are clear in the power Kelinva possessed, enhanced greatly once she crowned herself with *Sara'wabcusba'sarapum*."

"A thousand warriors died taking it," Beraht added through clenched teeth. "Worse than died. She ripped apart their souls."

"Why did the Uldra give the damned thing to the Republic?" Rogan asked.

"We didn't," Beraht grunted. "The Nameless would not allow that blasphemy within Ulheim. He gave it to the one Sylvai worthy of his trust."

"Naronor Calonar," Aebreanna said. "The King's grandfather. He, in turn, passed it to the Lady Alexia, who brought *Sara'wabcusba'sarapum* here."

"Why here?" Tomas asked.

"Alexia was Truthseer to Chlodocar Majestos," the Sylva answered. "She taught your Praetorians how to open the Imperial Vault so that *Sara'wabcusba'sarapum* could be secured herein."

"Why would Dunnalban take the Obsidian Tiara?" Tomas demanded.

"Dunnalban?" Aebreanna looked to the squire with an arched eyebrow.

"The former commander of the Praetorians," Rogan explained. "And a big part of the reason for the problems Pelsemoria was having."

"Interesting that a sworn Praetorian could steal from the Imperial Vault," the Sylva mused. "Their oaths should make such theft impossible."

"They're mystically bound," Tomas confirmed. "They CAN'T take anything from this room. Hell, it takes twenty of them just to open the door!"

"He had help," Beraht nearly growled. The Uldra glanced at Rogan and Tomas. "Where will he go?"

"Somewhere in the Velaross Duchies," the squire answered. He then squared his shoulders. "We have to get it back."

The others looked at him. "My father was a Praetorian," he explained, "sworn to keep this Vault safe. I will NOT allow that traitor to dishonor the oath my father took."

"Alright," the knight sighed. "There's not much we can do now. After we get home and deal with Fak'Har and Vagris, we'll figure out what to do about this."

"We should also revisit my husband's plan," Aebreanna added.

"Plan?" Tomas asked.

"There was a lot of discussion about moving all this stuff to the Keep," Rogan explained. "I don't know all the details, but there's a place under the city. A kind of vault, like this one. House Calonar has used it the same way the Sylvai used this."

"Then why did Alexia bring the Obsidian Tiara here?" Tomas asked.

Rogan could only shrug. "All of this is a problem for later," he declared. "Let's get back and have the Prae… I mean, let's have the Fidelis House Guard seal this place back up." The knight looked at his squire. "We'll talk with the King when we get home. Figure out what to do."

Tomas nodded.

Chapter 13

"I've packed some good clothes," Tomas' mother said, handing him a full canvas bag. "And some new undergarments."

"Mother," the young man objected, making as though to try and continue the conversation she clearly did not want to explore.

She held up a finger. "Don't start," his mother cautioned. She breathed deeply, clearly struggling with emotions. "There are…. there are things you need to know, things I should have told you." She glanced at Father Konrad, who noticed the look and smiled sadly. "Your father was a good man, a forgiving man. He was better than I deserved, really. My family…" She straightened. "When you get home, we'll talk. I promise.

"Besides," she said then, the maternal mask sliding once more into place and reestablishing itself as an impenetrable barrier against any child's questions. "The last time you left, I sent you out with little more than the shirt on your back. This time, I'll send you off properly."

Once again, most of the village had gathered at their new pier. The *Blue Lady* was restocked with everything Tomas' people could spare, more than enough to see them safely past the Velaross Duchies. When Tomas had objected, Colin the blacksmith and de facto village elder had insisted. "The Xeshlin patrols are everywhere," he had cautioned. "You won't be able to stop until you're well past."

"Don't worry about us!" Ahmed had called from the rail of the *Blue Lady*. "We're faster than anything on the sea! Even if they try to chase us, those damned Xeshlin will never catch us!"

More gifts were still being brought forward. New clothes and trinkets were offered, not only to Tomas, but to his companions as well. Little of what the people offered was of any real value, but it was all made with loving attention. The little boy and girl who had been first to welcome Beraht upon their arrival came forward again. The great Uldra knelt once more as they handed him their gift, a rough sketch of mountains. "Now you can always see them," the little girl declared.

Beraht marveled at the drawing and carefully rolled it, tucking the gift safely into his belt.

"Do you know how long you'll be gone this time?" Elpidius asked.

"The Northern Keep is under attack," he replied. "We have to go to Ironheartshaven to gather reinforcements, then march across the Northlands." The young lord of Pelsemoria looked to Mariano, who was standing in his new crimson uniform. "And then I need to track down Dunnalban."

The former Praetorian, and now commander of the Fidelis House Guard, nodded. Men had been posted at the Vault through the night. Although the secret of opening the vault had been lost with Dunnalban's betrayal, closing it was a simple process known to every Praetorian. Mariano had revealed to Tomas that the door could only be moved with the dawn. The lord of House Fidelis had stood and watched with the sun's rise as Mariano and nineteen of his men performed the simple ritual that allowed the Vault's door to be moved, then lend his own strength in closing it again. A feint blue light briefly pulsed as the great iron door was sealed.

Tomas took Kineus hand. "Keep doing what you have been," he instructed. "Homes and shops first. Use what you have to from the ruins, but…"

His friend nodded. "We'll keep clear of the cathedral and the library," he promised. "We've also started laying the groundwork for a new home for your books. Until then, we've got a few people sorting through what can be saved."

"Priorities," Tomas insisted. "Shelter, food, and safety. The rest is great, but it doesn't matter unless we survive." The squire then turned to Sir Roger. He took the knight's hand. "Thank you, Sir Knight," the lord of Pelsemoria said once more. "Thank you for all you and your men have done."

"It's our duty and our pleasure, my lord," the knight replied.

"How much longer can you stay?"

"We'll remain through the next winter. We cannot remain longer. Between the Xeshlin and the Gwyndd, Velaross itself might come under attack."

Rogan also took the knight's hand. "Like I said, once we safeguard the Keep, we'll hold to our oath. House Calonar will offer what aid it can."

The Knight of Mercy grimaced. "Doing so will likely put you in direct conflict with your own family," he warned.

Rogan shook his head. "House Eigenhard stopped being my family a long time ago. This idiotic war is just another reason." He turned, then, and boarded the *Blue Lady* with Beraht.

Tomas looked about his community. All his surviving friends and family had gathered. All the people who had been center to his life and his travels across Lanasia. All, but one. The young man looked to Elpidius. "Can you…?"

His friend nodded. "I talked with her a little last night. She's pretty upset, talking about leaving home."

Tomas sighed again. He reached into his tunic and pulled out a purse. "If she does decide to leave, at least have her wait and travel with the Knights of Mercy. He handed the money to his mother. "This won't make up for anything, but it can at least help her start a new life."

His mother accepted the purse and Elpidius nodded. Tomas then pulled the large traveling bag from his shoulder and handed it to Kineus. At his friend's inquiring look, the squire said, "I've been writing things down. Everything since I left. Meeting Cyras Darkholm and Rogan, then traveling to the Northern Keep. Meeting everyone there," he glanced at his mother, "especially Mary. Facing the Sorceress Vara, climbing Allfather's Throne. Our travels through the Endless Sands and into the Western Empire." The young man laughed gently. "Even our trip into Dagon'ay and Otherworld. I tried to put it all out as it really happened but," he glanced back at Rogan and shrugged.

"Sounds like quite a story," Kineus said.

"Maybe," Tomas agreed, "once it's finished. Take care of it until I can get back."

"I'll make a copy and send it off with the Knights of Mercy," his friend suggested. "Velaross is always interested in histories."

Tomas shrugged away any possible value in his writings, then stepped back and looked across the gathered crowd one last time. "Thank you all," he said. "All these months, not knowing if you were all alive or…" The squire shook away such dark thoughts. "You did it. We did it. We survived. We rebuilt our home. We faced Xeshlin and outlaws and weather. We've faced traitors and we've lost too many of our loved ones. But we faced all this together. We survived together. No matter what comes, no one can ever take that from us.

"I'm going back to the Northern Keep to help defeat the Shadowed Mage, once and for all. When that's done, I'll find Dunnalban and bring him back to face our justice. When I come home, we'll keep doing what you've already worked so hard at, rebuilding our homes and our lives."

Tomas' mother stepped forward and embraced her son. "And I assume you'll bring this girl you want to marry home with you?" she asked, somewhat archly.

"Yes, mother."

"Good. I look forward to meeting her."

Tomas had no idea how to take that, so he did what he thought a good son should do. "Yes, mother," he said again, and kissed her on the cheek.

The young lord of Pelsemoria turned and boarded the *Blue Lady*. The ramp was pulled away and workmen helped guide the ship out. Tomas stood at the rail and waved to his people, keeping his eyes on the cheering crowd even as the ship made its graceful way out. As they sailed away, Tomas moved to the aft, up to stand beside the tiller, marveling again at the change in his home. Pelsemoria was gone, but a new community had arisen in its place. The young lord of House Fidelis offered a silent prayer that he and his people might have the chance to build something worthy, something that could endure through the hard times to come.

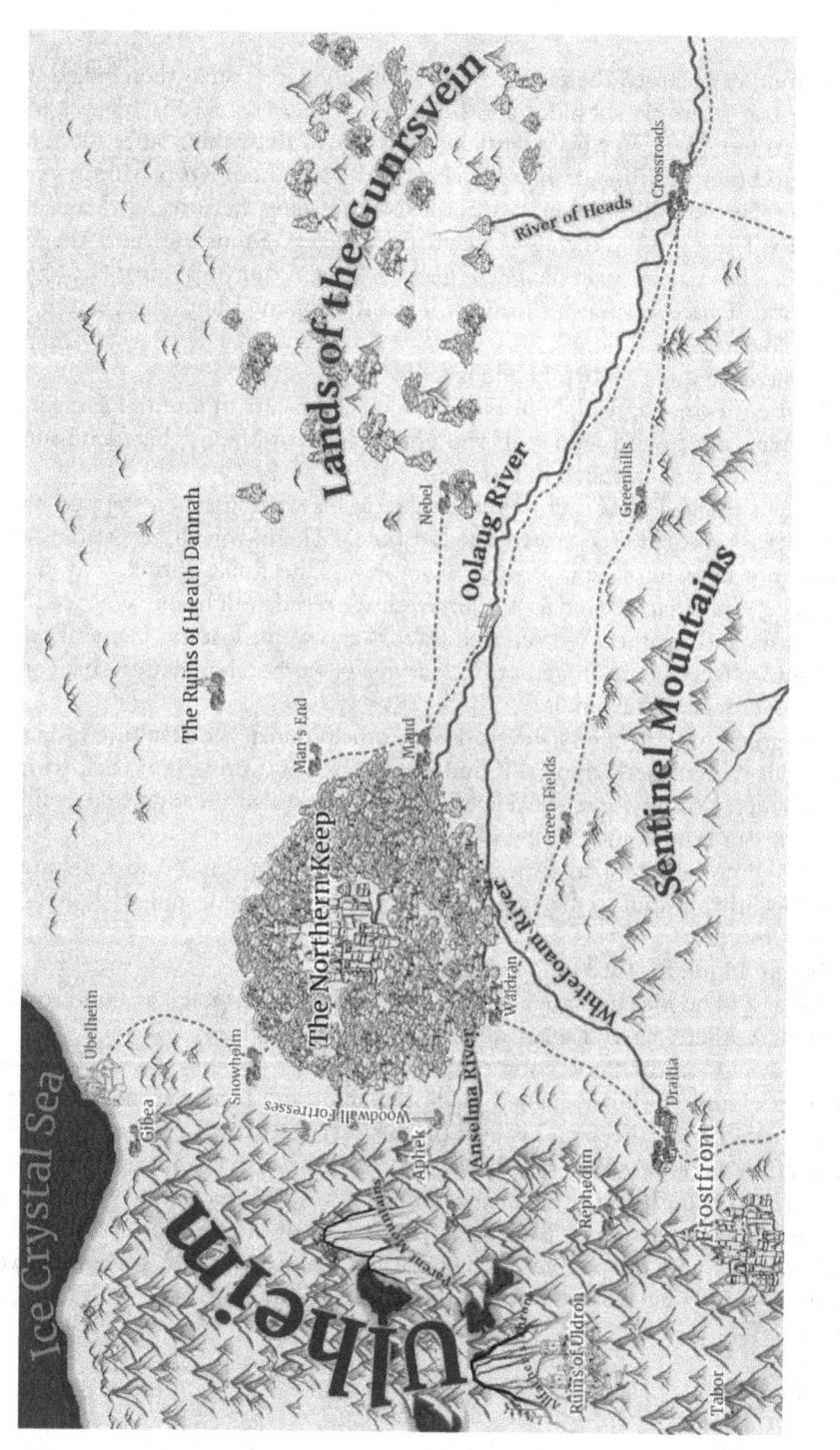

The Heroes at Home

I

Forest

Chapter 14

The *Sy'lva* maiden absently brushed back an errant lock of her honey blonde hair. She was a Daughter of the Wyld, reflecting the late spring season. Her opalescent eyes cast a verdant glow upon the crude huts in which her community had chosen to live. The cool ivory of her flesh absorbed the broken sunlight that penetrated through the forest's canopy. The flowers adorning every windowsill turned towards her as she walked by, responding to her inherent magic. The sodden world, still recovering from the recent storm, was made dry and blooming as this Daughter of the Wyld passed. She wore a lose dress of woodland green with a brown skirt that matched the various cottages, though her Wyrdmark made her noticeably stand out amidst the villagers.

She would soon be reborn, with the turning of spring to summer. Her coloring would reflect the progress of the seasons. The vitality that had replaced winter's chill must, inevitably, itself give way to the heat and trials of summer. As a Daughter of the Wyld, this maiden no doubt felt the shifting of the world beneath her feet. Perhaps she attributed this only to the seasons themselves. Perhaps she did not sense the approach of the White Lady. Xaemus hoped this was so; he hoped the *Sy'lva* had at least these final hours of blissful happiness.

Even without her mystical power, this one would not have blended into the background of her rural community. She walked through the rough but well-maintained village like a princess of one of the great Houses. Her chin was raised and her smile seemed just slightly forced. The maiden responded politely, though curtly, to the friendly hails of her neighbors. Though the cottage from which she had emerged with her water pail was no larger or finer than any other, still she looked at the rest of her village as though it were unworthy of her. She was regal in her step, purposeful and confident. Her country dress might as well have been the silks of an empress, and her tin bucket could have been a royal scepter. She was not dismissive of her fellow *Sy'lva'i*, but neither was she especially gracious.

A pair of House Calonar soldiers were walking on the same street, in the opposite direction as the Daughter of the Wyld. There were a dozen of the warriors stationed in this village. Added security, no doubt, in the face of the growing mercenary threat. They wore the blue and grey surcoats of their master, with chainmail beneath, but went about without helmets. They also were not carrying the traditional poleaxe of the Northlands, instead having shortswords belted to their waists. The men, Humans both, politely stood aside for all the villagers as they went about one of the periodic patrols in which their unit engaged. Upon approaching the maiden, though, they not only stepped far out of her way, but even bowed. Proof, perhaps, that even Humans could sense the nobility of a Daughter of the Wyld.

"Goodness in the morning," one of the soldiers attempted to say in broken *sy'lva'n*.

The maiden did not try to hide her smile, her amusement, at the Human's bumbling attempt at speech. She turned her nose further up at the soldiers sworn to defend her community with their lives and continued on her path, ignoring the men. The *Sy'lva* did, however, add an extra sway of her blossoming hips as she passed, glancing back once to ensure the males were watching her.

She was not far into the Change. As a Daughter of the Wyld, she would be expected to assume the position of Speaker, once a village was in need. That she had chosen to undergo the passage into maturity revealed that her training was nearly complete and the maiden would be ready for her destined role. Her mane was noticeably longer than the other adolescent females of her village, already becoming more lustrous. Her breasts, though not filled out, were swelling under her green blouse. Her body was adjusting in preparation for her first fertility cycle, which would begin with the completion of the Change. Any *Sy'lvu* she passed stopped and looked after her; the maiden's scent would already be carrying her power. She would have to choose a male soon or else risk the growing conflicts, the increasing violence, that was once the norm for *Sy'lva'n* communities. Even the Human soldiers responded to her scent, dull as their senses were.

The maiden reached the edge of the village and made her way down a well-worn path to the nearby creek. Though the trees blocked easy sight, the sound of a small waterfall echoed clearly. Summer was nearly upon the forest, and this one promised to be both hot and dry. The torrential storm last week had been the only of its kind, with little other rain all spring. The sky was absent of clouds, and the southern wind brought a strong heat up from the Wasteland of the Exiles. The leaves beneath her feet crunched dryly as she passed, and the small waterfall ahead was already lowering, as though the water seemed almost desperate to escape Wildelves Wood. The path upon which she walked, glided really, led to this stream. A Walker, an apprentice obviously, leapt from what he must have thought was a well-concealed perch, to land beside the maiden. "You should not tease them, Komalan," he reproached in *Sy'lva'n*.

"I do as I wish, Nesleph," she sniffed, continued without pause along the forest path. Her accent betrayed the nobility of her mothers. Even in this barbaric north, where the *Sy'lva'i* pretended at primitive lives, still the ancient bloodlines held true. Her words were flawless, and her tone and perfect enunciation reflected the great education of a future matriarch. In the time of the *Im'peri'a*, this would have been a princess of a great House. Yet even these dark times of Human supremacy could not thin her noble blood.

The youthful Walker fell in beside her. He was young, perhaps as young as the maiden. He had no beard, nor other sign of having been chosen and gifted the Tears. He was lean and lacking any muscle granted by the Change. His clothes, dyed to match the surrounding Wood, were without patch or repairing stitch or other blemish, likely fresh from his mother's thread and needle. Even his bow, carelessly draped over his thin shoulders, looked unused. "They are supposed to be protecting us," the youth was muttering, "not harassing our females."

"You speak from jealousy," the maiden called Komalan replied haughtily.

"I am not jealous!"

"You said nothing yesterday when one of the Calonar soldiers spoke with Vasalu."

The youthful Walker blushed. "Vasalu is training to be a Walker, the same as I," he declared weakly. "She can handle herself. Besides, she isn't undergoing the Change. I doubt those Humans even know she is female."

Komalan laughed. "Perhaps. That might explain why she so often volunteers to train with them."

"Vasalu's actions are none of my concern," the boy Nesleph declared.

"Nor are yours any of mine." The maiden glanced sideways at her companion. Despite her teasing, or perhaps with it, the maiden seemed interested in the male. If she chose him, he would be taken into the binding. Adolescent males were rarely allowed to be bound to a first fertility cycle. Such a sudden growth of muscle and size was painful enough for a mature *Sy'lvu*; for an adolescent, the process would be excruciating. Worse, even a mature male, with centuries of experience, had trouble enough controlling the protective instinct over his gravid mate. An inexperienced boy, suddenly forced into the body of a man, was often vicious in his defense of any perceived threat to the new mother.

Still, a *Sy'lva* undergoing the Change often lost sight of such practical matters. The first fertility cycle could be troublesome, with unpredictable desires and youthful passions overriding good sense. If the maiden's mother was aware of this flirtation, she would almost certainly end it. Komalan set down her bucket and stretched, incidentally putting a hand on her back and running the other along the front of her green dress. "This trip gets longer every time I walk it," she noted.

"Here," the boy Nesleph immediately and predictably replied. "Let me help you." He picked up the bucket, emphasizing how little its minor weight seemed against his strength. Komalan smiled and led the male further down the path.

The pair reached the small waterfall in minutes. The creek twisted its way amidst the low hills and many trees. It dropped some small height into a large pool before continuing its way. The forest had kept this area clear, though one could not see for any distance from the edge of the water. A collection of stones bordered the pool, though a platform had been smoothed out, likely by the local Speaker, beside the waterfall for easy collection. Despite the approach of summer, the water still looked very cold.

"The pool grows shallow," Nesleph observed.

"My mother is seeing to it," the maiden replied indifferently. "She and the other Speakers are more concerned with the mercenary intruders, though."

"The forest needs water," the youth insisted. "The spring has been very dry."

Komalan and her adolescent companion approached the water. She had the boy take the day's water while she went to the bank of the pool and removed her shoes. Seeing an opportunity for mischief, the maiden grinned and sent a small splash of cold water flying towards her bumbling suitor.

The boy Nesleph cursed and jumped back, startled and red-faced at being caught by surprise. He recovered quickly and grinned himself. "I should throw you in for that," he threatened.

Komalan raised her chin in imperious authority. "You would dare lay hands on the Speaker's daughter?" she demanded. "You would place an unearned touch upon the body of a female? You would dare violate the sanctity of my Change?"

The apprentice Walker took a step towards her, clearly feeling the pull of her scent, but caught himself and stopped. He dropped to a knee, looking up at her with sincerity. "Forgive me, Daughter of the Speaker," he said, realizing how close he had come to breaking the taboo. "I only… I am your servant."

"Careful, servant," the maiden said with rising heat. She put a hand to just under her eye. "Remember that I need only one drop from my eye, and you are mine forever." Even as the boy had that moment of weakness, feeling the pull of animalistic instinct, so too did the girl. The power of biology, of the reproductive drive, was great.

"We should stop," the boy Nesleph said without much conviction. He did not rise, nor make any other movement, trapped as he was within her verdant gaze.

Komalan held up a finger. "You are my servant, remember? I say when we stop." She reached out to touch his face, but the boy caught her hand in his, not breaking the taboo, but treading dangerously close to it.

"Komalan," he said in a weakening voice.

The snap of a twig drew their attention across the creek. Several Humans, carrying a variety of weapons and armor, approached. The mercenaries had been trying to move without sound, to take the young couple by surprise. For weeks, the murderers, thieves, and bandits masquerading as soldiers had made a habit of taking isolated *Sy'lva'n* by surprise, slaughtering the males and abusing the females. They were becoming quite proficient. The broken twig, echoing from high in the trees and far from the approaching marauders, had alerted Komalan and the boy.

A moment of shock passed between the group of Humans and the young pair. Discovery was startling, and inevitably caused a brief panic.

"Run," Nesleph whispered.

The youths broke for the village, but Komalan and the boy found their home in chaos. Several of the cottages were already ablaze, Humans seeming incapable of violence without arson. Several of the villagers had already been cut down, including the handful of Walkers, their weapons broken. The occasional scream indicated that a number of the mercenaries had disobeyed Vagris' standing orders and begun taking their pleasure with the village females despite the still-active battle. The maiden grabbed at her young friend and the pair ran along the outer perimeter of the village, perhaps in search of sanctuary, perhaps escape.

On the opposing side of the village, Vagris was arriving. The warlord was tall for a Human, sitting stiff-backed and proud on his horse. He was muscled as some trained warriors could become, wearing his half-plate without seeming discomfort. As was his custom, and that of his Brotherhood, he wore no heraldry or insignia, nothing that could identify him as anything other than a mercenary. A few light scars adorned his aristocratic face, though nothing disfiguring; they seemed more like adornments or badges of honor, proving his life on campaign. His iron-grey hair, by nature rather than age for he seemed barely at mid-life for a Human, was cut short in the old style of the Republic Legions, as was his matching beard.

The warlord rode with a small contingent of men, loyal bodyguards dispatched from his Brotherhood, no doubt. "What's the problem here?" he demanded in Velish only lightly accented of Frostfront, but carrying the steel of arrogant command.

The local captain, an experienced highwayman from near Alvaro, nodded his head at Vagris. "Calonar had a small group of soldiers stationed here, general," the officer explained. "We were taken by surprise."

Vagris grimaced. "Our scout didn't report their presence?"

The captain shook his head. "No sir. There's been no report or sign from him. We went ahead with our attack, since he only reports back problems." He nodded at the sounds of fighting ahead. "We managed to take most of them, even capturing one. But the last two are making a stand at that pagan shrine at the center of the village. They're giving us some trouble."

Vagris looked down at the captain. "If the problem is there," he pointed out, "what are you doing here?" Without waiting for a response from the stammering officer, the warlord pushed his horse ahead.

At the village's shrine, two soldiers wearing the blue and grey of House Calonar had indeed taken up a defensive position on slightly elevated ground. They had their backs to the stone altar, still covered with tatters of its purple drape. The spring offerings were scattered through the large, open area, fruits and nuts being of little interest to the pillaging invaders. The soldiers were seasoned professionals, standing close enough to aid one another, but at enough distance for mobility. Several mercenaries lay dead and dying near the soldiers.

"Back off!" Vagris barked and his men obeyed. The warlord approached but remained outside the soldiers' effective radius. He looked down at them and nodded in satisfaction when they did not back down. After weeks of growing attacks by the mercenary army, the Calonar House Guard would likely have been thoroughly briefed on what happened during one of Vagris' raids. They would know what Fate had for them, should they be taken alive.

"Your situation is hopeless," Vagris told the soldiers in flawless Gunnic. "You're outnumbered and surrounded. There's no hope of reinforcement. We only want the Sylvai and their village. We've taken one of your brethren." The warlord dismounted, handing his reigns to one of his bodyguards and gesturing them to move back. "You've done your duty, as well as any could expect." He gestured indifferently to his dead mercenaries. "I give you my word; put up your weapons, abandon the Sylvai, and you'll be allowed to leave with your comrade. If you resist, you die, and your companion goes to the Xeshlin."

The two soldiers glanced at each other. Their looks were identical, their faces locked in stony resolution. They both looked back at Vagris. One spat on the ground, the other gave a more verbal reply. "Duty, honor, humility," he growled, quoting the traditional motto of House Calonar.

"So be it," Vagris replied, drawing his weapon. He carried a blade of Tramanese design. It was straight, and longer than a Lanasian shortsword, with a hand-and-a-half hilt. The metal was engraved with the jade lettering of one of the Tramanese languages. The weapon was called Zhu Shasho, or so Vagris had declared once the men from his Brotherhood had presented it to him, claimed from an enemy, a betrayer of their order.

Vagris darted in and swung Zhu Shasho low, slashing the leg of the soldier on his right. The warlord then spun and caught the thrust of the second soldier, deflecting the attack and spun again, reversing his Tramanese sword and stabbing his opponent in the chest. Pulling his blade free, Vagris took a step and turned, bringing his weapon to a ready position. The first Calonar soldier had remained on his feet, despite the leg injury. The warlord raised Zhu Shasho in a brief salute and danced in, easily deflecting a hasty strike before delivering a single, killing blow. Even as the first Calonar soldier fell, the second attacked. Vagris stepped into this, ducking under the man's swing as though the breastplate were no encumbrance. The warlord dipped his Tramanese blade low and slashed his opponent's groin, then turned mid-strike and slashed again, across the small of the man's back. The second soldier fell beside the first, his life gushing out in seconds.

"Your form is impressive," Xaemus conceded.

Vagris tried showing no surprise at the Xeshlin's sudden presence. This, the monster of Davenor knew, was the betrayal. The Human worked so hard to maintain his seeming indifference that he might as well have screamed in surprise. Xaemus had made no sound, no stir of wind or leaf, but rather had emerged from the shadows and dropped down. Likely as not, the Humans would not have been able to follow the movement with their sluggish eyes, seeming to just appear beside their commander. The bodyguards swore and drew their weapons, but Vagris waved them back. "Where have you been?" he demanded.

Xaemus said nothing. The breeze drifting across the folds of his dark robe spoke louder. The subtle creak of his black-dyed leather armor was more communicative. Even behind the deep hood protecting his Xeshiln flesh from the burning sun and the heavy cloth covering the ruins of his face, Xaemus made no expression in response to this Human warlord. He was not in the habit of explaining himself to anyone. Only the Sorcerous Sisters who had birthed him, the Coven of Midnight Sun, could ever have commanded an explanation from the monster of Davenor, and he had long since disposed of them. Instead, the Xeshlin glanced around with his eyes of burning blood. "Your criminals are finished?" he asked in a voice that came as much from his deeply cowled hood as it did from any mouth.

"Answer me," the warlord demanded. He gestured with his blade at the dead soldiers. "You are meant to report any threat, especially if that involves the Calonar military."

Not for the first time, the monster of Davenor considered killing this Human. Xaemus' time in this place was growing oppressive. He had been promised an answer to his unending search in payment for his aid here. The months were dragging, however, and Xaemus was growing restless. "My service is not to you," he reminded Vagris. "You do not command me."

Vagris sheathed his Tramansese sword and drew himself taller. He already stood more than a head higher than the Xeshlin, and seemed eager to emphasize this at every opportunity. Still, he wisely remained several blade-lengths away. "Fak'Har is your employer," the warlord reminded.

"And yours."

"You are bound to assist me with this campaign. You are to be my eyes and ears in this damned forest. You are bound to report any and every threat as it manifests."

"Very well," Xaemus conceded. "There is a threat over your left shoulder."

A blast of mystical energy caught the warlord from behind, lifting him into the air and sending him tumbling into his collection of bodyguards. If it were possible, Xaemus would have smiled. Cowled and covered as he always was, the Xeshlin's near-amusement would not have been visible to anyone surrounding him. Still, the near-feeling of happiness in the moment was undeniable.

The gathered mercenaries turned and, as one, took a step back. A *Sy'lva* was walking purposefully from the far edge of the village. She was of only average height for one of their race, but carried herself with great purpose, with authority nearly lost since the collapse of the *Im'peri'a*. Her great honey-blonde mane was heavy with streaks of grey and flowed about her in a powerful manifestation of the Winds, held in check only by a crown of vibrant daffodil. The matron's green dress, spun from nearly-lost *Sy'lva'n* silk, flapped amidst her legs and matronly figure, bound to her waist by the golden cord marking her a Speaker. Her staff was raised high, its tip glowing with the same verdant power as her opalescent eyes.

"You dare harm my people!?!" the Speaker snarled in Velish, still marching forward. "You dare cut down those sworn to protect them!?!" The air grew colder. "You." The sky became dark and angry. "Will." Wind and rain emphasized her words. "Suffer."

Words of magic came forth and the Speaker swept her hand in a broad arc. The ground all about the village cracked and groaned. It erupted with the roots of the forest. Tangled vines, gnarled wood, and thorned bristles reached up and out, wrapping themselves around the invaders. Flesh was shredded, limbs torn, eyes and ears gashed, and screaming tongues eviscerated. The men of violence were, themselves, violently lifted up and stretched out, crucified with wood and leaf and flower. The air became a sea of agony and horror, of suffering and vengeance.

The ground in front of Xaemus also exploded, and the awakened forest reached for him. The Xeshlin spun his double-bladed weapon, shielding himself and severing the attacking roots. He danced aside, into an open area, still facing the Speaker. She turned her furious gaze at him and the thunder muttered, "The monster of Davenor."

"I have no quarrel with you, Speaker." The Xeshlin's dead, empty voice carried the faintest undercurrent of respect.

"You stand with them, child of Midnight Sun," the wind snarled and lashed at him.

Xaemus again spun his double-bladed weapon, trusting to its enchantment to nullify the attack. "I continue my search," he declared. "I serve their master, but do not join in their banditry."

The Speaker gestured to the side. The vines and roots lifted a pair of Xeshlin. Even through the cover of the forest canopy, the errant beams of midday sun burned their colorless flesh. Smoke was already rising and blisters forming on the exposed skin, but even beneath their *xcaupil* armor, their cursed flesh boiled; the overlapping layers of cotton offered little protection against the Mark of Kelinva. They were slavers, clearly, wearing the markings of the Coven of Puma's Leash; but they had no *heuatl* tunics, and their wooden, puma-carved *cuacalalati* helmets were unadorned; they were the lowest of the Coven's males. Xaemus regarded them with indifference in his eyes of burning blood, the match of theirs.

"Your countrymen enslave my people!" the earth rumbled.

"They are not my countrymen," Xaemus coolly replied. "I have no country."

The Speaker clenched her outstretched fist and barbed thorns erupted into the screaming Xeshlin, slowly tearing them asunder. "You die as do all the betrayers!"

"So be it." Xaemus leapt over the ground, dodging amidst stony obstacles even as they emerged. The Speaker pointed at her race's most hated enemy and spoke a single word of magic. The wind lashed out at the monster of Davenor. Rather than dodging or struggling, pitting his strength against the wind, even as the Humans had done, Xaemus joined with the wind, dancing within it. The Speaker snarled her frustration and clenched again her outstretched fist. The green canopy reached out at her command and slashed at the deadly Xeshlin. Again, Xaemus did not pit his body against the power of the forest. He did not slash or struggle, but avoided. He spun around each clawed branch, each thorny vine. He rolled along the jagged ground and continued his approach to the vengeful Speaker.

Xaemus reached her. His eyes of burning blood looked up at her… and paused. The monster of Davenor did not want to butcher yet another priestess of the old ways. He had slaughtered the Dark Coven of Midnight Sun. He had cut his bloody way through the vengeful Sorcerous Sisters who had hunted him after. He had traveled the world in search of his Dark Empress, of someone worthy of his devotion, and cut down all those in his path. He had performed acts of cruelty in the name of finding his true mistress, anything to achieve that goal. This was a mother defending her village, though. Murderers, rapists, thieves, and slavers had invaded her home, and she retaliated. There was nothing dishonorable, nothing wicked in her actions. Even her wrath at him was forgivable, as he was just as marked as all Xeshlin.

Vagris appeared behind the Speaker and slashed Zhu Shasho. He cut a vicious gash into the Speaker's out-stretched arm. She screamed and fell to her knees as the warlord raised his Tramanese blade for the killing blow.

Then the world was a blinding light.

Xaemus shook his head to clear his thoughts and his eyes of burning blood. He was lying on the ground, some distance from where he had been. Smoke was coming from his robes and his darkly-dyed leather armor. His sight and his hearing were only just recovering as he tried to force the world back into rational order.

Vagris was also on the ground, though on the opposite end of the central clearing. The stone altar was scorched black, having also been hit with what Xaemus realized was a bolt of lightning. The warlord was struggling to regain his feet, weapon still in hand. His mercenaries, those still alive, were also picking themselves up and reaching for blades.

Xaemus stood, but paused in whatever action he might have taken. A green light was surrounding the Speaker. She was floating mid-air, the light emanating from her growing more brilliant by the moment. The monster of Davenor sighed. He had seen such magic before, used only by the most desperate priestesses, only as a final defense against him. The Speaker was calling out to Otherworld.

Within the aura, with the Speaker, was something else. A second being was emerging, responding to the matron's call from Otherworld. The *Sy'lva*'s body was changing to accommodate this Fael protector. Her small nose extended, becoming a long snout. Her beautiful face twisted, with rows of sharp fangs punching their way into her mouth. Her graceful limbs distended, becoming long legs ending in clawed paws. A tail burst from within her dress, the priceless garment tearing free to be replaced with a great coat of grey and white fur. The Speaker tried to scream, tried to give voice to the destruction of her body, but the only sound that came forth was a howl of vicious intent. The green aura dimmed then, and eyes of furious amber looked out at Vagris, the surviving mercenaries, and Xaemus.

You will not harm her again. The thought entered their minds. Xaemus could tell the others heard this commandment as well, for they cursed and held their temples and swung their weapons as though they could fight off the terrible curse. Most fled; foolish, as the wolf would chase them down individually. Vagris stood his ground with weapon raised, but his eyes and his trembling hands betrayed his failing courage.

The great wolf, taller at the shoulder than even an Uldra, crouched and snarled. Xaemus did not run, nor did he cringe away. The monster of Davenor had faced creatures from Otherworld before. He opened his stance and held ready his double-bladed weapon. A soft green light, matching the still-fading aura the Speaker had summoned, flowed from Xaemus' sword.

The two, wolf and Xeshlin, circled each other across the uneven ground. The wolf leapt and Xaemus rolled, slashing with his weapon. There was a yelp of pain and a grunt of surprise as the two separated and turned, staring at each other. The monster of Davenor put a hand to his arm without taking his gaze from the mystical creature. There was a warm wetness coming from the folds of his robe. The wolf held its right foreleg off the ground, where drops of Otherworldly light, the closest one of its kind had for blood, fell to the ground. This was the imbalance in their confrontation: regeneration. The Fael wolf could at least partially restore its form in this world and, at the worst, retreat to Otherworld and be regenerated by the raw Winds of Magic. Xaemus, however, bore the Mark of Kelinva; his body could not heal without the assistance of magic. Even his bleeding would not stop or even slow if left on its own. In Davenor, the Sorcerous Sisters demanded obedience and supplication to their every whim in return for their mystical healing. As a renegade, Xaemus had no access to their supposed gifts.

They both leapt again. Xaemus slashed and the wolf bit. Both found their targets and both were rewarded with cries of pain. The stalemate continued. He had little time remaining. His injuries were worsening. The smallest cut, if left untended, could bleed a Xeshlin to death. The Fael wolf had open several great gashes in his arms and legs. He had only minutes to end this confrontation and locate one of Vagris' rogue adepts.

A plan formed within Xaemus' mind. The monster of Davenor continued to move, to back away, in a lose circle. The wolf followed. The Xeshlin put his back to an outcropping of stone spikes, their tips still decorated with the remains of some faintly-moaning mercenaries. He waited. The wolf pounced.

Xaemus rolled on the ground and kicked out with his legs, changing the wolf's trajectory onto the stone spikes. They startled the creature but did not harm it, as the Xeshlin knew would happen. They did, however, give him the half second he needed. Xaemus spun in the same instant that the wolf was briefly impaled on the spikes, and swung his darkly-enchanted weapon. The creature's head came away from its shoulders and there was a flash of green light. When the aura faded, the body of the wolf melted away like wax, streaming back into Otherworld. The Speaker was revealed within, her nude form exhausted and looking up at her race's hated enemy with the beauty of despair.

The monster of Davenor glanced back at the mercenaries. The Humans had found their courage, now that the threat was past. They would demand a terrible vengeance against the Speaker, despite the justice of her attack. Even should she survive such an ordeal, unlikely but possible, she would be handed to those whom she had called his countrymen. A Speaker sold to *Xesh'lin* slavers would be given to the Sorcerous Sisters; such a damnation Xeamus knew all too well, having seen it so many times across the Blighted Lands. The priestesses were merciless in the torments they unleashed, jealous of their cousins who still enjoyed a connection to the Winds of Magic. Of these, though, the Coven of the Puma's Leash were amongst the worst. They would not only torture a Speaker, they would force horrific atrocities upon her. He had seen, during his servitude to the Coven of Midnight Sun, the unending torments that fed horrid, Umbral rites, but the Coven of the Puma went further; they would ravage a Speaker's very soul.

Xaemus looked once more into the Speaker's eyes and raised his weapon.

Zhu Shasho was then at his throat. The monster of Davenor turned his eyes of burning blood to Vagris. The warlord was staring at him with undisguised malice. "She's mine," he declared.

For a moment, one brief, glorious moment, Xaemus was ready. The entire battle played out in his calculating mind. He saw each swing of a blade, each dodge, counter, retreat, and advance. He knew how to kill this offensive Human and, very likely, all his followers.

Vagris, his own mind equally tactical, smiled. He glanced down, at the gash cut into Xaemus' arm. Blood still flowed from the wound. The Xeshlin's strength was already fading, weakening with each beat of his cursed heart. His need for magical healing was dire, and worsening. After the exertions of his fight with the wolf, Xaemus was no match for Vagris, and they both knew it.

The monster of Davenor stepped back.

Vagris turned towards the Speaker, a leer of anticipation on his lips. But then another small bolt of green energy struck him. "What in Underworld?" he snapped, more surprised than harmed.

Both the warlord and Xaemus turned. The monster of Davenor found himself surprised at a sudden surge of feeling in his dead soul. The maiden, Komalan, had not escaped. Having been warned of the mercenaries' approach, she had been given ample opportunity for flight. Xaemus had last seen her apparently doing just that. But instead, the maiden had returned to pit her undeveloped magic against the attackers.

Komalan raised her hands and concentrated, chanting the words of magic. She summoned another ball of green light to her hands, this one even smaller than the last. The maiden threw her pitiable magic at Vagris, but the warlord easily ducked the attack. "Enough," he said flatly.

"You will not harm her, *leph'en!*" she said in a shaking voice. The maiden started pulling together another ball of green light.

Vagris huffed in irritation and threw a small blade into the girl's shoulder. "I said enough!" he snapped. The warlord stomped over to her as the near-child fell to her knees, holding onto the knife protruding from her still-developing body with a trembling hand. He reached down and grabbed the maiden's hair, pulling her had back and raising his sword.

"No," Xaemus declared. His hand was on the warlord's sword-arm. Vagris turned in rising anger, ready to play out their confrontation, but paused. He looked into the gaze of the monster of Davenor and felt, for a moment, the truth of that title. Vagris knew much of Xaemus' history, and that his moniker was well-earned. "She lives," the Xeshlin commanded in a voice no longer empty.

Vagris pulled his arm free. "Fine," he grunted. "She lives." He turned to a pair of mercenaries. "Put her in chains. Bind her and gag her." He stared for a long moment, taking in her developing body. The warlord glanced at Xaemus. "Be careful of her eyes," he warned. "Her tears can enthrall." He went back to the Speaker, watching for a moment as she clawed at the earth, clearly trying to reach the maiden being forced into restraints. The warlord glanced back. "Your daughter?" he deduced.

"Please," she begged. "Please."

Vagris stood tall and glanced at his mercenaries. "Secure prisoners," he commanded, returning his cold gaze to the Speaker. "Take anything of value, burn the rest." The warlord glanced at the moaning men, still crucified in branches and vines overhead. "Cut them down. Tend any still alive, leave the rest."

"Nesleph, no!" The maiden had called out, even as the Humans were trying to gag her, the men wearing thick gloves to avoid contact with her streaming tears. Xaemus had seen the juvenile Walker circling the ruined village center, but said nothing. He had watched as the boy had approached with commendable stealth, readying himself.

With Komalan's unintended warning, Vagris ripped his sword free and intercepted the attack. Nesleph did not pause, though, but immediately launched into a traditional, and predictable, sword sequence. Vagris easily parried each strike, waving his men back with his off-hand. "Nesleph, huh?" he asked casually, obviously amused at the boy's lack of experience. When the young Walker had completed the sequence and readied another, Vagris grabbed the boy's sword-arm and forcibly turned him, so that he faced Komalan. The warlord exerted his greater strength and forced Nesleph to his knees.

Komalan and Nesleph looked at each other with flowing tears. Vagris grinned evilly at the maiden. "He goes to the Xeshlin," the warlord declared. The young couple both looked at each other in horror, the great terror of their race realized. Human slaves had a great many uses for the cursed children of Kelinva; they could be laborers or athletes. Attractive ones could be kept in some female's home for as long as they maintained their aesthetic quality. Some were used as breeders, keeping the population of slaves constant. Most would live for years, once they were broken. Sylvai, however, had but one fate: the altar of Ramalech. But first, the Coven of the Puma's Leash would enjoy their new pets.

Nesleph's throat then opened. Blood flowed out and the boy died in moments, with a minimum of suffering. Vagris swore and threw the body to the ground. He turned and snarled at Xaemus, who calmly looked back. Another moment between them passed. "Treat his wounds," Vagris commanded. He glance then at the Speaker. "And bring up green wood."

So far as anyone knew, Xaemus was gone. One of the rogue adepts under Vagris' employ had mended the Xeshlin, and the monster of Davenor had seemed to leave. He lingered, however, to keep watch and ensure Vagris kept his word. There was a single moment when he considered intervening, but the warlord was surrounded by his bodyguard. Frequent grinning looks towards the trees suggesting Vagris was aware, or at least suspected, Xaemus' presence, as though daring the monster of Davenor to make some suicidal attempt.

The sun was setting by the time Vagris' men were finishing with their pillaging and murder. Vagris sat astride his horse, calmly supervising. The buildings were aflame, everything of value having been taken. Living prisoners were all in chains, already being led by their new *Xesh'lin* owners away for their gruesome end. The heads of the victims had been severed and put on poles in a ring surrounding the village's altar. The Coven of the Puma's Leash had wanted to erect one of their *olin*, the monoliths they used in as monuments of their perversions, and adorned with sacrifices to the Demon-God. Vagris, however, had sternly refused, unwilling to loiter for the many hours such a construction would take. He had informed the slavers that his forces would be leaving, and that the lesser male Xeshlin would either remain in his protection, or stand alone against possible Calonar reprisal.

Xaemus saw Vagris take another deep, satisfied breath. A younger officer, promoted following the causalities of the day, rode up and saluted to Vagirs. "Final casualty report sir."

The warlord nodded absently, still breathing deep his insipid victory.

"Only five of the men we cut down are still alive. Of those, I'd say only three have any chance of living out the week."

"Hold plunder for all five," Vagris commanded. "God knows they've earned it. If they die, divide the rest among the survivors."

"Yes, sir. Also, a messenger just arrived." The young man handed over a sealed scroll.

Vagris broke the seal and read. He humphed and casually tossed the message into the nearby pyre.

"Problem, sir? Or none of my business?"

The warlord shrugged. "Our employer is anxious to have another word with me. Trust a spell-slinger to use a lot of words to say something simple."

"Yes, sir."

Vagris glanced at the officer. "I don't suppose you want to take the meeting for me?"

The young mercenary shook his head. "No, thank you sir. That's why you get a bigger share than me."

"Well, one reason, anyway." He took another deep breath and sighed. "Well, I guess we're just about done here."

"Yes, sir. Shall I order the movement?"

"You might as well."

The officer saluted and rode off, shouting orders. Vagris remained for a moment longer, breathing deeply. "There really is nothing like the feeling of a day's work being finished," he noted.

With that, the warlord turned his horse and pushed it into a walk. Tied to the saddle, Komalan kept her gaze back on the large smoldering pyre they had just left. The maiden had run out of tears not long after her mother had stopped screaming. The monster who now owned her had forced her to watch as his men had built the stake   and   the   pyre   and   set   it   alight.

Chapter 15

The typical chaotic efficiency of Castle Calonar had been replaced with an even greater intensity. The normal staff continued about their work, preparing and serving meals, delivering and receiving dispatches, cleaning and maintaining the seat of power for House Calonar. The officials and functionaries continued in their unending service to the rulers of the Northlands. Unlike in normal times, if such a thing existed within the Northern Keep, the inhabitants of Castle Calonar moved with deliberate purpose, eager in their service to the good King Cylan and his loving Queen. On this final day of spring, however, very little was normal.

In addition to the serving staff and inhabitants of the castle, there were now a great many uniformed members of the Calonar House Guard. The blue and grey liveried defenders of the Northlands moved about with equal intensity. Traditionally, the Queen forbade the display of weapons within her home; now, however, the soldiers went about with swords and daggers belted and ready. Poleaxes, the traditional weapon of the Northlands, stood in row upon row, awaiting deployment. Though most of the warriors were not yet burdened with armor, many recent arrivals, or those preparing to depart, were fully equipped. The faces of these well-trained, hardened fighters were locked in grim determination. Their eyes remained nearly fixed upon their current duties, but often spared a glance beyond the high walls of the castle, beyond the city they were sworn to defend, and into the surrounding Wildelves Wood, for they all knew what was coming. War.

Amidst the efficient chaos of Castle Calonar, a single point of grim determination moved. Mary, wearing her favored green Northlands dress and white apron, descended into the loyal maelstrom. The handmaiden to Princess Kyla was as equally grim as were the men and women sworn to protect her, as devout in her duty. Her steps, though obedient to this most recent command, were burdened with reluctance. Not for the first time, the young woman cast a backwards glance, up into the recently-broken serenity of the higher floors and her princess' quarters.

Only a few days had passed since the jewel of House Calonar had been betrayed by her own bodyguard, and nearly killed. Mary had been there, and failed. The handmaiden's sworn duty had been to protect her princess and the heir growing in her womb, even at the cost of Mary's life. She shook her head once more, trying as she so often did to cast away the burdensome memories of her failure. She should be with the princess, not pulled away on some errand. She should be preparing Kyla's meals, keeping her chambers in good order, and helping the beloved elder daughter of the King content during the long absence of Prince Rogan. Instead, she was descending the grand staircase into the castle's main hall.

Queen Nora had sent a summons. The messenger, a downy-faced page wide-eyed at being pressed into service by the beloved mother of the Northlands, had been intent on the command. Kyla had insisted she would be fine, ministered by her other handmaiden, Ilse; still, Mary only reluctantly departed. In all the Northlands, in all the world, really, there was only one person who could have commanded Mary away from her penance at her princess' side. Even the King, had he somehow mustered the strength to walk again, appeared and tried ordering Mary away, still the handmaiden would have stayed. But, the Lady of House Calonar had given her summons. There could be no refusal.

Mary had reached the central hall of Castle Calonar to find her queen waiting. Nora was speaking to a small delegation. A half-dozen men wearing the regalia from minor houses across eastern Lanasia were making their apologies and final farewells. They would soon be leaving, as were so many foreigners, hoping to escape the imminent war. The queen bowed and the men left, leaving the mother of the Northlands standing with a sad look in her bright blue eyes as she beheld the death of her home. Beautiful carpets had once lined the floors, but were now rolled up and stacked in a far corner. The exquisite works of art, gifts from across Lanasia, had been taken down and moved to a secure vault for safekeeping. The once-cheery glow of the candelabras now illuminated the weapon racks, long tables bearing deployment orders and strategic maps, and the staging of supplies. This was no longer the great receiving area, where visitors from across the continent found warm welcome for, indeed, there were no more visitors; this had instead become the command center for war.

Mary paused at the top of the grand staircase. Everyone did, when passing by. She looked up at the portrait of House Calonar. The great painting still hung there, though now it seemed somehow diminished against the terrible buzz of war preparations. So much had changed, the handmaiden realized, in such a short time. King Cylan stood tall and strong, the grey of his short-cropped hair and beard mocked by those unbreakable shoulders. His face still shone with a gentle smile, warm and caring, yet firm and resolute. That image was not the frail shadow, the barely-living ghost, haunting the royal chambers. Despite the efforts at secrecy, word had escaped: the King was dying, poisoned by the enemies now marching on his city.

Princess Kyla stood at that past-king's side. Youthful and bright, the picture of noble beauty and joy. The princes, though with arms demurely folded and head meekly bowed, still shown with mischievous delight, the image of her teenaged-self somehow vibrating with hopeful positivity. That past-Kyla was to become Sister Superior of the Lady of Light. She had her marriage ahead, the great love affair with her noble Prince Rogan. The princess of the past was not weighed by the long absence of her noble husband, off to confront the men who poisoned her father. That Kyla was not bed-ridden, recovering from the assault of a traitorous assassin.

Even the Queen in that painting seemed so different from the one now standing in the great hall. Nothing physical had changed in Nora. The Lady of House Calonar was still the mature image of her eldest daughter. The grey streaks in her blonde hair and the faint wrinkles adorning her face were less marks of age, and more highlights of loving wisdom. The eyes were what had changed, Mary realized. The same blue as Kyla's and yet burdened. The noblewoman in that painting had not spent six long months emptying herself in a desperate attempt to keep her husband alive. The Queen Nora of the past was not draining every scrap of magic at her command, holding back a mystical poison in the hope that Prince Rogan returned with a cure.

"She's waiting, miss." Mary started at the words, but recovered when she saw Roland limping by. The aging butler, master and overlord of the castle's staff, carried himself as best he could against his many years and his nearly-broken body. Rumor had spread that the Queen had tried pensioning Roland, offering to have him escorted anywhere in the Northlands so that he might be spared this latest attack on House Calonar. The butler had firmly refused, of course.

Mary put a hand on the old man's arm as he limped past, smiling at him. Roland had been the one who first welcomed her to the castle, years ago. He had given her a purpose in this strange place. Most importantly, he had been the one who introduced Mary to her beloved Tomas. For that, she would hold the aging man eternally dear to her. The butler smiled at the former maid through the aches of his old body. There was no hesitation in his eyes, no possibility of yielding. Like all the others in service to House Calonar, who fought against the growing fear of the battles to come, there never seemed any doubt in Roland's eyes. He was the unshakable rock upon which the castle rested.

Mary hurried to her queen's side, curtsying deeply in defiance of Nora's standing orders. The noblewoman grimaced as she nodded acknowledgment of Mary's bow. "We must hurry," she insisted in a voice meant for a warm kitchen and gentle lullaby. As she led the handmaiden towards the double doors, the rushing tide of military men reverently parted. The hardened warriors, without exception, stood aside and bowed deeply, many even averting their eyes as their Queen passed. Voices once raised in barking command or heated debate became hushed in her presence. Objects in motion came to a sudden halt. Amidst the furious preparations for the battles to come, the mother of the Northlands had surrounding her a reverential serenity.

Only when she was within a half-dozen paces did Mary notice Princess Karen. As so often happened, the youngest child of House Calonar had disappeared into the background. The handmaiden cast a backwards glance at the family portrait, and realized that the younger daughter of the King and Queen was not in it, that Mary had not even noticed her absence. This had been the pattern for much of Karen's young life. Although the eldest daughter of Nora Calonar was vivacious and sociable in the extreme, her little sister was almost painfully introverted. Karen attended public events with enthusiasm and performed the duties required of her as a member of the Northlands' ruling family. But personal, individual interactions were nearly intolerable.

A page, the same one who had first brought Mary the Queen's summons, approached Karen. The young man, downy-cheeked and awkward, tried asking the princess if she needed anything. His words were an obvious ploy, a gambit to speak to a pretty girl. Karen, in response, only mumbled something nearly-inarticulate and seemed to wilt into her pink Northlands dress. Karen had reached that difficult time of transition, beginning her change into womanhood. She had always been a pretty girl, nearly matching the noble beauty of her sister and mother, and her developing body drew the eye of many boys. The princess, uncomfortable speaking to women, was painfully shy around the opposite sex. The pearlescent glow of her sapphire, adolescent eyes dimmed when directly confronted with an admirer. Princess Karen could not bear the direct attention of the page, turning down and away.

The page had seemed ready to give up on his ill-fated attempt to speak with the princess. The boy, however, clearly lacked the experience in how to gracefully and politely step away, and so had been continuing in the awkward, one-way conversation. He paled at the sight of his approaching Queen, though. The page bowed low, stammering an apology for any possible wrong or insult. Nora had that effect on many men, Mary had noticed. Faced with her scrutiny, males of every age, every race, every rank often began stammering apologies and looking guilty.

"It's alright," the queen gently said. "Thank you for entertaining Karen while she waited. I'm sure you have more important duties."

The page continued stammering, bowing and backing away and stumbling into a guardsman who had seen the exchange. The soldier's grin vanished in an instant, though, when Nora's gentle eyes regarded him. The younger women fell in behind the Lady of House Calonar as she turned to leave. Mary tried greeting Princess Karen, who mumbled a polite reply. The handmaiden recalled with a smile that only Tomas had seemed able to break through that awkward shell. Karen had joined his impromptu support team during the Harvest Festival's tournament, cheering him and aiding as best she could. The younger Calonar princess had seemed enthusiastic, nearly joyous, joining in the public events for the first time anyone could recall. With the departure of Tomas, however, Karen had returned to her introverted self.

"Are you ready?" the queen asked of her younger daughter. Nora's tone surprised Mary. The handmaiden glanced at the Lady of House Calonar, seeing a sorrowful veil over her warm face. Karen, too, heard the tone in her mother's voice and took Nora's hand. The princess nodded and tried to smile in confidence, though Mary guessed from the youngest Calonar's demeanor that she had as little notion of the day's outing as did the handmaiden.

A grand carriage waited in the courtyard. The gold-edged wood gleamed in the broken sunlight. The white horses were brushed to perfection and bore brilliant draperies of blue and grey. Attendants stood at attention in royal surcoats and an entire company of the House Guard were already mounted and awaiting their queen. "Oh, for Overworld's sake!" Nora snapped. Her normally tender blue eyes sought out the source of this latest display of loving devotion and locked upon poor Roderick. The stablehead looked abashed and seemed to wither into himself under the disapproval of the Lady of House Calonar.

Nora crooked a finger at Roderick, and the stablehead, a grown man in his prime, reluctantly approached like a schoolboy anticipating reprimand. "My Queen," he tried to rationalize.

The queen held up a hand, cutting off any explanations or justifications before they could be given voice. She said nothing, only pointed back at the stables. Roderick sighed and turned, whistling. A pair of boys came out leading three horses, saddled and ready. Nora remained silent as the mounts, the correct response to her wishes, were brought forward. She maintained a cool, unflinching gaze at Roderick, even as she moved to one of the horses and signaled for Mary to take the other. A young page sprinted forward with a stool, placing it before the queen's horse and holding out an arm to aid the mother of the Northlands in mounting. Nora sighed and accepted the unneeded help.

Mary patted Roderick on the shoulder as she too passed, and gratefully accepted another page's help in mounting. Karen did likewise, but blushed to the roots of her hair when the page holding her horse took her hand. Nora glanced back to ensure the others was set, then looked as though to move, but paused as the House Guard formed up around the three women. The Lady of House Calonar looked as though fed up with indulging over-protective men.

"Your Majesty," a voice called from the open gate. Captain Klug Rainer was riding in, having just returned from another inspection of the city walls. "We're in a state of war," he reminded his queen. "Standing procedure is extra protection for the entire royal family, especially the King and Queen." Dark circles marred the greying face of the career soldier. Rainer had a reputation throughout the Calonar House Guard for his whimsical, sarcastic behavior. Though professional to his core and exquisite in his manners, the veteran long had the habit of laughing at all things serious, and making light of tragedy. In recent days, though, the newly-promoted captain had turned serious.

"We're only going to the gardens, Klug," the queen insisted. "There's no need for all this, especially with your preparations-"

The captain cut her off with a raised hand. "Respectfully, ma'am," he said in a voice of hardest iron. "There was an assassination attempt against a member of the royal family. Your pregnant daughter nearly died." He broke the unspoken taboo of the Northern Keep and looked Queen Nora steadily in the eye. "There won't be another failure under my watch."

The mother of the Northlands sighed and nodded. She nudged her horse forward, beside Rainer's. She put a gentle hand on his arm, whispering something to him. The veteran said nothing in response, only bowing in his saddle. He then turned and barked a command to the assembled guardsmen to move out. Mary glanced at the captain as she passed under the heavy escort. He was as immovable, as professional as was the reputation of the Calonar House Guard. His eyes, though, betrayed his doubt. As much as Mary berated herself for failing to protect her princess, the acting commander of the House Guard felt his own failure even more keenly. They shared a brief look, one of mutual understanding. They would not fail again.

The city gardens were still a blasted wasteland. Once the beating heart of the Northern Keep, this island of peace had been shattered by the Deathmage's assault during the Harvest Festival. Gentle streams had once meandered through the small paradise, but were now angry veins filled with debris. The high-arched bridges that had once offered crossing to those walking the winding paths were nothing more than charred bones, broken and devastated. The great trees of fruit, nut, and flower were little more than blackened husks, skeletal arms reaching up in supplication from their disturbed graves to an uncaring sky. Shrubbery, topiary, flower patches and grassy hills were all bare, denied the rebirth of spring.

Even with the war preparations weighing upon the city, dozens of its citizens should have been in the gardens. Everyone took time to visit, to take in some of the natural serenity once offered by this place. Instead, the burnt and broken gardens were empty. No one came here anymore.

"The Speakers can't heal it?" Mary whispered as the women, with their many bodyguards, passed through the crumbling ruins of what had been the hedge wall bordering the gardens.

"The Speakers have their own battles," Princess Karen replied. "Our enemies assault them too, and they must defend the Wood." Mary was always a little startled when the youngest Calonar spoke, so rarely the sound was heard. The handmaiden was used to Kyla's voice and could not help but compare. At first glance, the two sisters sounded as alike as they could look, when Karen surrendered to Kyla's insistence on cosmetics and fancy clothes. But those who spent time with the royal daughters quickly recognized the fundamental differences. Kyla, no matter if her voice was commanding or pleading, seductive or serious, always carried firm tones. Hers was an undeniable voice to be heard, the roar of a predatory cat. Karen, though, only ever spoke in gentle harmony. Hers was a voice of whispering wind, of distant bells.

Mary looked at a nearby hill. Tomas had brought her there, an eternity ago, where they had shared a picnic and he had read to her terrible poetry. "Will it ever return?" she asked, only partly speaking of the desolate gardens.

Queen Nora glanced at Mary, something mournful in her soft eyes. "All things pass," she said gently. "The nature of a mortal life is its impermanence. We must enjoy what we have for the time we are allowed it. But new life, new love, new hope always comes."

They moved to the center of the gardens, to the Sylvai Shrine. The Queen called for a halt and summoned the detachment commander. "You must wait here," she said.

The sergeant was about to object, but Nora held up a hand. "Form a perimeter, keep everyone and everything out. Nothing must interfere with us until we come out. Do not let any man, any male of any kind, approach to within a hundred paces."

The guardsman clearly did not understand, and was not enthused about letting his queen go ahead alone, but bowed his obedience. Nora dismounted and signaled for Karen and Mary to follow as she approached the shrine.

Lying within the exact center of the gardens, the Sylvai Shrine had been there for as long as anyone knew. Stories of the Northern Keep always spoke of the Shrine's presence. Even those tales from before the city's foundation, when it was but a tiny village, lost amidst the forest, made clear that the Shrine predated even that community. Mary approached, as all Northlanders did, with reverence for the ancient, mysterious structure. The Sylvai never revealed the origin of this place, and some even admitted to not knowing. The domed structure was open to the Northlands' air, only a circle of eight marble columns blocking sight within. Despite this, the eye slid over the Shrine, unable to focus upon anything within, until entering. One could not make out those within, until joining them.

This place, alone, seemed untouched by the Deathmage's horrid magic. Of all the streams wandering through the gardens, only those wrapped around the Shrine ran pure, unpolluted of debris or death. Grass still grew around the building, though only an inch or two high. Not a single blemish marred the pure white of the unadorned marble, such that Mary could easily see the strange bluish veins within the stone. As she always did, the handmaiden drew and held a breath as she entered the Shrine, feeling as though she were entering some place profoundly holy.

The great oculus, that opening at the center of the dome overhead, still looked down on them. Sunlight, though broken in the Northlands' spring, nonetheless still shown down, illuminating the patch of flowers that seem to ever-bloom. In all the time the Shrine had stood in the heart of, not just the Northern Keep or its ancestors, but Wildeleves Wood itself; in all that time, there had only ever been one addition to the structure, and that in recent months. In the center of the flower patch stood a small sculpture, two birds, one white and the other black, rising together in a spiraling dance. Queen Nora went to this sculpture and knelt, putting a hand upon the white bird. She said nothing, only bowed her head a moment, then stood and straightened her shoulders.

The Lady of House Calonar turned and regarded the younger women before her with calm blue eyes that, despite the wrinkles speaking of her many years, still held much beauty. Legends throughout the Northlands spoke of Cylan Calonar and his beautiful wife sharing many adventures, many lifetimes through the centuries of their long lives. Stories were told of the great power of this couple, not only in magic, of which they had much, but in their loving devotion to one-another and the people under their protection. Mary did not know if she truly believed all the stories, there were so many, after all, but she did believe that her queen would give her life in service to the people. For as long as she had lived in the Northlands, House Calonar had sacrificed so much, even the life of Kyle, the Queen's first-born child. Mary, like so many others, had sworn loyalty not from necessity for survival or under threat of their great power, as was the case in so many lands, but out of a love she felt returned so many times over.

The Queen pushed back a lock of her graying blonde hair and cleared her throat. As she stared at Karen and Mary, the handmaiden felt again that strange sensation as all those did who fell under the Lady of House Calonar's gaze. When Queen Nora looked upon you, she saw into your very soul. All knew of her magic, of course. As the High Priestess of the Harvest Mother, she had power that, though subtle, was equal to any of the Lords Cardinal, perhaps even greater. "The time has come for you to learn secrets," the queen said softly. "Both of you."

Mary bowed. "As you wish, your Majesty."

Princess Karen said nothing, only nodded.

"What you both learn today, only a few in all the world know," she continued, stepping to her younger daughter and putting her hands on the princess' shoulders. "This is no gift I offer, but a terrible burden. I would spare you this, but someone must know and..." the noblewoman pause, again that mournful shadow passing over her face.

Karen pulled her mother into a tight embrace.

Queen Nora smiled, though sadly. "I wouldn't have even..." She sighed. "When you had your first bleeding; I should have brought you then. But... I wanted just a little more time. Childhood is short enough." She then turned and led Karen and Mary to stand in the flower patch. The Lady of House Calonar closed her eyes and raised her arms.

The Northlands was a place of wonder. Under Esha, Tower Mistress of the Northern Keep, local adepts were producing great and amazing devices and discoveries aiding in the comfort and protection of all people. Many believed that, in time, this city would eclipse even Pelsemoria, lost capital of the Republic, in its arcane wonders. Combined with the technological marvels delivered by the Uldra, the people of the Northlands had grown accustomed to startling miracles performed as though they were the most mundane of acts. Heatless light, plentiful clean water, abundant crops, ever-warm clothing, and easy transportation were but a few of the great works available to the people.

Despite this, Mary was taken aback at what she saw. Queen Nora reached her hands forward, whispered, "I am here, a seeker of wisdom," and slowly moved her outstretched hands apart. As though in response, the stone floor surrounding the flower bed spilled down into some unseen abyss as though it were water. The Lady of House Calonar turned in a circle, gesturing at the stone and it melted away. This done, Queen Nora clasped her hands before her waist and stood, facing Karen and Mary. Just as the handmaiden was going to ask a question, the world rose.

Mary did not move. She did not feel movement. The flowers on which she stood did not shudder or give any other indication of change. the world around them flowed up. The handmaiden's eyes told her they were descending, lowering into some darkness, but the rest of her body, her ears and her heart, all said she was remaining motionless as the world was lifted. Darkness arose around them, stretching up until the Shrine's oculus was only a small point of light.

"Come," the queen said then, and walked into the darkness. Her daughter followed without pause. Mary hesitated only a moment, but then followed as well. She tapped a toe onto where she had seen her queen walk and found the nothingness solid.

Once the women had stepped off the flowers, the queen paused and motioned for her companions to wait as well. "We must allow the guardians to recognize us, and to see we are no threat."

"Guardians?" Mary asked with a frightened look around. There was no light, no detail of any kind, nothing except the circle of flowers behind them and their small sculpture of two birds.

"Stand very still," the queen instructed. "Do not move unless I instruct, no matter what you see. Move only where I indicate. Do you understand?"

Karen nodded.

"No, your Majesty," the handmaiden admitted. "But I don't think I really need to, do I?"

Queen Nora smiled. The flower patch rose, then, lifting silently and without disturbing the still air around them. There was nothing beneath the patch, no pedestal or platform, nothing but more darkness. "We're being admitted."

Mary's heart beat faster. The flowers rose higher, back towards the light overhead, the only light left. In a moment, that too would be lost. However, in the moment the flowers were returned to the Shrine and all light was lost, a soft blue glow appeared. There was no source for the illumination. There were no torches, no globes of the heatless lamps Esha had designed. No gas-powered Uldra lanterns. In one instant, there was nothing. In the next, a gentle blue radiance surrounded them. Mary blinked, adjusting to the dim glow. She looked around and noted that this interior was far larger than she expected.

They stood in a great, rectangular room. The distant walls, only vague shadows, really, were far further than had been the marble columns of the Sylvai Shrine. After a moment, some still-rational part of Mary's mind realized that the corners of the chamber lined up with the cardinal directions. There were two doors on opposite ends of the strange room. "This place is older than you know," the queen was saying as she walked towards one of the doors. "It predates the Republic or the Sylvai Empire. Before there were even Humans walking upon this world, this place existed."

The Lady of House Calonar led Karen and Mary to an opening in the northwestern wall. There, Queen Nora paused and glanced back, but sighed and continued. Mary followed. The portal led to a tunnel, tall and triangular, with the point disappearing in the darkness overhead. The passage angled sharply down, with stone steps matching the blue-veined marble of the Sylvai Temple somewhere above them. As the noblewoman navigated this stairway, she continued. "The Sylvai no longer know of this place," she said. "Nor the Uldra or the Khepri. Its secrets were passed along the royal family of the Sylvai Empire, from mother to daughter. Only the empresses and one other knew of this place, let alone its function."

They reached a platform, a level area still encased in triangular stone. The path split to the left and right, each side descending into more stairs. Queen Nora turned right without pause and continued their descent. The steps were increasingly hard for the aging mother of the Northlands, so Mary offered help, letting the noblewoman lean on her as they negotiated the path. "You know about our family's lineage, yes?" the queen asked.

Karen nodded, walking beside her mother and lending her own arm whenever the aging queen needed extra support.

"Your great-grandfather, you remember his life?"

"General Naronor Calonar," the princess replied. "Commander of the Sylvai army during the Uldra Uprising."

"What is less-known is that, during the Uprising, the general had a priestess tending to his spiritual well-being. They became lovers and produced a daughter, Aunt Alexia. On the last night before the Battle of Lake Tragedy, Annakarala, the last Sylvai empress, summoned the priestess of House Calonar and her daughter, Alexia. There were no more heirs to the royal family, and Annakarala's Truthseer revealed that she and the Empress would fall in the coming battle. There were no other heirs, no one left in the Royal Family, so no one to inherit the Truthsight. Annakarala and her Truthseer revealed to the women of House Calonar the secret of this place and burdened them with Truthsight. Aunt Alexia and her mother assumed responsibility for the great secret. Alexia never had a daughter to whom could pass the Truthsight, so she entrusted it to me."

"And you pass it to your daughters?" Mary asked.

The queen stopped then. She sighed once more and shook her head. "No. The Truthsight only passes to one daughter. It reveals to the mother who should inherit the secret." Nora looked then to Karen. The younger Calonar daughter returned her mother's look. The princess nodded, understanding.

"Your Majesty," Mary said then. "If only the women, the mothers and daughters who inherit this great secret, can come here, then...?"

Nora paused again. She was breathing heavily, and so the handmaiden helped her sit on a step. Karen sat beside her mother, holding hands but saying nothing. "Truthseers are not the only ones who come here," the queen answered. "We are allowed companions, women we can trust." She looked steadily at her younger daughter. "This is not a burden we must bear alone, nor should we try."

Karen nodded.

"Why only women?" Mary asked.

Nora breathed deeply and glanced around the unadorned, perfectly-smooth marble. "There are many defenses, many layers of protection in this place. Truthseers are granted admission, and our chosen daughters. We may also bring a companion, someone to give us aid and comfort. Our Truthsight reveals to us who must inherit that power, and who can be trusted as a companion. For a reason known only to Fate, no male has ever been chosen."

After a short rest, Nora rose and they continued. At last, they reached the end of the stairs. The tunnel they followed turned to the left and quickly opened into a very large cavern. This place, like the tunnel, was triangular, the slopes of the distant walls sloping inwards and meeting in the darkness far overhead. The pervasive blue glow continued here, revealing two rows of low buildings. These had triangular openings, but no real doors or windows. The queen led them down the center avenue between these double-rows, towards a great domed structure at the far end of the cavern.

As they passed, Mary could not help herself but to look within the structures. She gasped and paused, a hand to her open mouth and her eyes as wide as could be. Karen joined her and, just as the handmaiden had been shocked, so too did the princess gasp. Tools of war rested within the first structure. Staffs, swords, armor, shields, and things unknown. Another room held rings and rods, crowns and wands. Yet another held whips and chains and devices for torture. A tension, an aura of mystic power filled these rooms, as though the objects within held a will of their own. The handmaiden took a step away, her body, her very soul, recoiling.

"Centuries of effort by the Heroes of Fate and their inheritors," Queen Nora explained. "The tools and trophies of evil." She spoke with a hard, unforgiving finality that carried ages of suffering, of effort spent in resistance to villainy. "First Aunt Alexia, then I," she looked at Karen, "and now you, will be responsible for this. We alone can bring these hateful things down, burying them here, where they can never again bring harm to the world."

The Lady of House Calonar took their arms and led them further on. "For generations, the women of our line have taken possession of all the evil our men have defeated, bringing it down here."

"Is that the purpose of this place?" Mary asked. "Is that why it was built?"

Nora stopped. "No," she sighed. "Or, not exactly. This place was built to contain great evil. Over the centuries, the generations of Truthseers have made use of it and its sentinels for other purposes. House Calonar has used it as a repository for the villainy you see." She looked ahead to the domed structure at the end. "And for one other use." She stopped then. Unlike the other buildings, this one had a closed door of iron. The door was unmarked by rust and covered by strange symbols that somehow resembled a fusion of all the oldest languages, of Sylvai and Uldric and more, and yet somehow even older. The Lady of House Calonar turned and put a hand on Mary's arm. "Much of this trip is for Karen, so that she might inherit her burden, her legacy. However, within this room, we come upon your burden."

Mary put her hand over the queen's and nodded.

"Once we are through this door," Nora continued, "you must not speak, nor take any action I do not command. You will never speak about what you witness inside, not even when alone... especially when alone."

"I... I don't understand."

"As you, yourself, said: you don't need to understand. In this case, your understanding would not help, and would likely harm." She turned to Karen. "There is great danger past this door," the mother warned. "Danger that you, and one day your daughter, alone, can face. Do as I instruct, and keep your mind focused, clear of distractions."

The princess nodded.

Nora turned back to Mary. "You must watch us very carefully. When we enter, you will follow behind. Only cross the threshold and wait. Keep part of your body in the doorway to prevent it from closing upon us. You will not understand much of what we say and do, but you will see us. If... if at any time, we seem to lose control, to become crazed, you must carry us out of that place, out of this vault, back to the room in which we entered. Call for the exit; the sentinels will respond. Ignore our words, or actions. Do not obey any command we give, nor threat, nor plea. Do not stop until you have dragged us into daylight."

Mary say the sincerity in her queen's eyes. She saw the fear within the noblewoman's determination. The handmaiden did not understand why this thing had to be done, but understanding was not important. She would not fail her House again. "As my Queen commands," was all she said.

The Lady of House Calonar turned then, facing the iron door. She held up her right hand, but remained silent. The alien symbols illuminated, glowing red against the omnipresent blue. They blurred, sliding across the iron door, swirling like oil sliding down a drain, forming the sigil of House Calonar, two crossed, four-sided diamonds. The iron door opened silently, revealing a green light within.

Nora looked at Karen, and the princess once again nodded. The two women of House Calonar joined hands and entered, followed closely by Mary. The handmaiden, once she had stepped within, felt more than heard or saw the iron door begin to slowly close. She backed up half a step, putting her body in the portal, and the door returned to its fully-opened place.

The chamber within was a nightmarish mirror of the Sylvai Shrine. The same blue-veined marble made up pillars supporting the dome, though the stone fully encased them. There was an oculus above, but this one was filled in with the darkest, red-flecked obsidian. At the center, rather than a serene patch of wildflowers, was a fissure producing the horrid green glow. The light seemed alive, pulsing and thrashing, undulating back and forth. Opposite the iron door was a giant throne of basalt stone. More of the alien symbols were carved upon that horrid seat. Surrounding them, spaced evenly between the columns, were statues. Each of these were made in the image of the Elder Races: Sylvai, Uldra, Khepri, and Xiana. They did not look as these groups did now, but as they appeared in the most ancient of myths. The Sylvai were lithe and graceful, masters of the arcane. The Uldra were tall and broad, immovable workers. The Khepri were winged and joyous, artisans and creators. The Xiana were water given form, beautiful and seductive. Each statue held in its hands a tool of war, and each, though facing the green pool, watched the empty throne.

A small hand touched Mary's face. The queen had reached out and turned her eyes away, focusing her gaze on the women of House Calonar. The handmaiden blinked and breathed deep, nodding.

Nora and Karen stepped forward. Mother restrained daughter when they approached the green pool, for the youngest Calonar seemed as though she might walk straight into it. As best Mary could tell, the queen did not look into the undulating fissure, but instead let her eyes drift anywhere else, from one statue to the next, and sliding past the empty basalt throne. "I have come-" she began to say.

"We know why you have come, Bride of Calonar." The words did not come from anywhere. Like the blue glow outside, the sound seemed to just be, to manifest at will from nowhere.

"My daughter has begun her journey into womanhood," Nora said. "My Truthsight revealed her as next in line."

"She is next." The words were a single voice, but also, somehow, a community of voices. Like different versions of the same person, joining together. "The Wind of Fate imbues her. The Great Queen will be a Truthseer of power not seen since our Founder, to aid or thwart the One Who Comes."

Karen said nothing, but moved closer to her mother. The adolescent princess stiffened suddenly, gasping, her pearlescent eyes wide as though a veil, forever present, was suddenly pulled away. Her mother turned and held her close, tears streaming from her eyes as she whispered, "I'm sorry."

The youngest Calonar relaxed after a moment. She stepped back from Nora's arms and slowly blinked. Karen looked at the queen, as though seeing her for the first time. The Lady of House Calonar nodded sadly. The princess then turned and looked at Mary, and the handmaiden sensed the same penetrating gaze as belonged to her mother. Karen looked as though she might say something, but then closed her mouth and sighed in the exact way as her mother so often did. She then looked around the chamber, pausing at each statue. "I see them," she whispered

Nora also looked at the statues. "They've always been here. They will never leave."

Karen tilted her head. "Yes, they will," she argued. "They must, when..."

The queen put an arm on her daughter's shoulder. They shared a look, one that spoke of knowledge and its terrible burden. "We should go," she said.

The princess shook her head. "We can't. We have to ask first."

"They won't answer."

"They'll answer me."

Nora nodded and took a half-step back. Karen raised her chin and spoke, for perhaps the first time in her short life, with authority. "A nexus is approaching," she declared. "The Death of Calonar is imminent. We need information to proceed along the correct path."

"You seek information to thwart the designs of the Dark Scion," the not-voice countered. "You wish to understand and defeat the Shadowed Mage."

"You have aided us in the past," Karen insisted. "Your sentinels have fought before. You can aid us now without violating the dictates of Fate."

"Only when the ziggurat is under threat can we act. We perceive no such threat."

"Fak'Har seeks the destruction of the Northern Keep," the princess insisted. "Your duty is to protect this place. House Calonar, though the Truthseers, have aided you in this. If the Shadowed Mage is victorious, you will lose that line of defense, and your most valuable ally."

"The Death of Calonar is Fated," the voice argued. "It cannot be thwarted."

"The Death of Calonar does not need to mean the death of the people or the city," Nora stepped in. "If Fak'Har succeeds-"

"The Dark Scion seeks the destruction of your family in furtherance of the Demon-God's return. He seeks the Dark Empress' newest incarnation. He has no interest in the ziggurat. Not yet."

"Please," Nora said softly. "Even if my family must... there will be survivors. There must be a way to save..."

The not-voice became almost gentle. "The Inversion is upon us," it said. "It begins in Dagon'ay, a sennight from now, with the Lost Mother. The Death of Calonar will signal the Inversion's completion. These are Fated. Your Truthsight fades even now, in favor of the Great Queen. You cannot prevent what must be."

"I can try," the queen said firmly.

All was quiet for a time. Then, "There is a price for navigating the Wind of Fate," the voice said. "Balance above all must be maintained. Our Founder set in motion a great design, and we must keep to that."

Karen put a hand on her mother's, stepping forward again. She tilted her head and narrowed her eyes. "There is a way," she mused. "A path forward that can maintain the balance."

"As we said, there is a price."

"I will pay your price," Nora insisted.

Again, there was a pause. "For our help now, for the few answers we can provide, you will sacrifice your place in the Inversion."

The queen blinked. She looked to her daughter, who nodded. "I'll still be there," the princess insisted. "I can help them."

Nora took a deep breath. "I swear it."

"Then ask."

Mother and daughter considered, whispering back and forth. Finally, Nora raised her voice. "What is the truth of Anninihus' attack?"

"The Shadowed Mage's disciple was never more than a pawn to be sacrificed. You suspected this already. His true mission was to lure the Heir and his companions away from the Northern Keep, to render it vulnerable."

Karen looked up. "Why did Vara bring her storm upon us?"

"Already the Great Queen sees further than her mother." The not-voice held an almost amused tone. "Vara does not possess the Truthsight, yet she can glean some of Fate. She perceived the threats to come and her ignorance of them. Her service to the Shadowed Mage gained her the Seal of Air, the Mind's Eye. With it, she can now chart a path of survival."

Karen considered a moment.

"Even now, the Great Queen emerges. Yes, in answer to your thought. Vara now holds the key to ending the Inversion. Her aid will not be easy to gain, but it can be purchased by the Heir."

"We can do it," Nora gasped to her daughter. "We can, if not prevent, minimize the Inversion! Your father-!"

"You are wrong, Bride of Calonar," the not-voice proclaimed. "And your interference has only worsened the Inversion."

"What?" the queen snapped.

"How?" the princess added.

"The Inversion would have only consumed the last of the Heroes of Fate. But, with your demand for knowledge, it will now take also a daughter of Calonar."

"What!?!" Nora exploded. "No!"

"Fate has already adapted. Both of your daughters are on the path of greater power, one through Fate, the other, Dream. One will stand against the Inversion, the other within it."

Karen paled and looked down, her eyes lost in this new pronouncement. Her mother turned and grabbed the princess by her shoulders. "No," she insisted. "We can fix this! We just need to know more!" The queen spun and took a step forward, staring into the thrashing green fissure. Karen grabbed her mother, pulling at her and screaming for her to stop.

"Let me go!" the Lady of House Calonar commanded. "I have to see! There has to be a way!"

Mary was there, grabbing bodily at the mother of the Northlands and, with Karen aiding her, hauling at the struggling older woman.

"You don't understand!" Nora screamed. "It's not what you think! I have to know more! I have to help him! It's coming! Let me go!"

Mary and Karen ignored the queen. They pulled, nearly lifting her from the floor as they dragged her out. The iron door, already moving shut behind them as they raced down the great cavern. The women retraced their steps, climbing up and out, ignoring their heaving lungs and burning legs as much as they ignored the blows, threats, and pleas from the Lady of House Calonar. They struggled back up the stairs, all the way to the dark chamber in which they entered that hateful place.

"Open!" Karen demanded as she and Mary pulled the limply-resisting Nora into the darkness. At the princess' command, the flower patch descended, resting only a moment before the three women fell breathless and exhausted within the light. "Up!" Karen   barked,   and   the   flower   bed   obeyed.

Chapter 16

Upon their return to the sunlight, Karen called for the sergeant of their escort. The young princess kept giving crisp, clear orders, but the guardsman stood agape at the sight before him. Queen Nora was curled into a ball, tears flowing and her voice whimpering. Karen's dress and hair were disheveled from the effort of dragging her mother out of that dark, terrible place. Mary herself, looking equally unkempt as the other women, was kneeling beside the mother of the Northlands, holding her tightly and trying to ease her sorrow. Perhaps most shocking to the loyal soldier, though, was the sight of Princess Karen asserting herself.

"Pay attention, man!" the youngest Calonar barked, snapping her fingers in front of the sergeant's wide eyes. Even with the recent burst of adolescent growth, Karen, like all the women of her family, would likely never stand very tall. She had to crane her neck in looking up at the stunned guardsman. Despite this, the normally wilted flower of House Calonar now stood as though she towered over the military man, meeting his gaze with unflinching, pearlescent ice. "Get your men formed up!" the princess commanded. "They are to escort my mother back to the Castle. Send a messenger to the Adamic church; Cardinal Tain needs to tend to the Queen."

The sergeant blinked again and shook his head, professionalism winning out over his shock. "Yes, your Highness," he said firmly with a bow. The veteran turned and barked orders to his men, getting them moving. "What about you, Princess?" he asked.

Karen paused, then glanced back at her mother and Mary. The princess, her new sight taking in things the handmaiden could not imagine, remained calm and unflinching, seeming as though Karen were looking through a catalogue, rather than at two women. "Keep a few guardsmen here. Mary and I'll remain for a little while."

The sergeant bowed again and obeyed. A messenger was sent galloping towards the distant church. When Nora seemed unresponsive and certainly unable to ride, the soldiers built and improvised litter and laid her on it. Within minutes, the queen was on her way back to the castle. With the departure, the remaining soldiers once again left the building Mary had, like all others, believed to be a Sylvai Shrine.

The handmaiden had watched all this, helping when she could but mostly staying out of the way of the efficient House Guard. Then, as the Queen was being carried away, Mary turned back to the sculpture resting at the center of the flower patch. She could not step upon those plants. Her entire soul recoiled from what she knew rested below. The young woman only stood there and stared at the memorial to two of the most respected women of House Calonar, the noble family that was supposed to be so much better than the others.

Karen said nothing for a long time. This was a familiar sensation, a familiar situation, to Mary. Even when the younger Calonar daughter visited Kyla, she said little to any but her older sister. The handmaiden was used to having the adolescent princess nearby while speaking little, if at all. In truth, her recent assertiveness had only added to Mary's increasing sense of unreality. Finally, after an age of silence, the handmaiden spoke. "We were going to get married here," she whispered.

"Tomas wanted that," Karen agreed.

"He wanted Lady Alexia to be present, in some form." Mary looked around the domed structure, her skin crawling at the sight of the blue-veined marble. She half expected there to be an empty throne of basalt stone on one end of the structure. "He didn't know what this place truly is."

"Do you?"

The handmaiden glanced back at the adolescent princess. She stood tall, shoulders firm, face unreadable. Her eyes, the pearlescent, Halvan eyes of House Calonar, regarded her. "Can't you tell what I know?" Mary demanded. "Don't you see...?"

"Yes," Karen replied. "I see you. I know what you believe."

"Then why ask?"

"Because you need to say it."

Mary turned away from the sculpture and walked to the edge of the columned building. She looked up to Castle Calonar, rising on its great stone escarpment, it's impenetrable outcropping. Even from so far away, the handmaiden could see the preparations. The castle's walls were being reinforced. Soldiers scurried along the battlements, emplacing weapons, ammunition, supplies. All the things they believed... all the things Mary had believed would help in surviving the coming battle. "We're all going to die," the young woman said in a surprisingly calm tone.

Karen said nothing.

"You won't even deny it?" Mary asked. "You won't continue the false hope your family is feeding us?" She turned again to the bird sculptures. "The false hope you women have always fed us."

The princess sighed softly and rubbed her newly-awakened eyes. "Truthseers can't see the future," she said. "We're not prophets or scrying adepts. I don't exactly understand myself, not yet." Karen again looked upon Mary. "When I look at you, I don't know everything that will ever happen to everyone around you. I don't know the future of this shrine or this city. That isn't what Truthsight is, how it functions."

"Then what?" Mary demanded.

"People," the princess replied. "Individuals. I see your past and your future, but just yours. I see you meeting Tomas." She pointed at the nearby stream. "I see you both removing your clothes and swimming there last summer." She turned towards the southwest. "I see you cheering Tomas at the tournament, and him pledging himself to you after winning the joust." She turned to the castle. "I see you after his battle against the Deathmage in the ruins of Heath Dannah, waiting in his bed."

Karen rubbed her temple, closing her eyes and grimacing. "It's all... together. Everything, all at once. It's hard to... to separate into then, now, and later. I'm having... it's hard to remember if I'm talking to you here, or if we're in the main hall, on the last night. Or... are we in Kyla's room, with the Fael?"

The princess was clearly having trouble, obviously suffering in some unreal way against what her new sight revealed. For the first time in her life, Mary felt no urge to comfort the adolescent girl. Before her was a member of House Calonar, the rulers of the Northlands, in need, and the handmaiden felt no compulsion to act. She simply stood and stared. "You'll get better, I suppose," Mary said. "After all, that was the bargain, wasn't it? The death of Calonar doesn't have to mean the death of its members, just the death of us."

"I go on," Karen admitted. "After the battle, I think I go on." The princess walked over to the nearby stream's bank and looked at herself in the water. "I can't see myself but, at least some of those soldiers survive as well, and they interact with me after the battle is done. I think that means I survive."

"Some of those soldiers," Mary repeated. "Not all. Not most. Some."

Karen turned back to face the handmaiden. "Yes, some. Do you want to know which ones will die in the battle?" she calmly asked. "Do you want to know which of them die screaming? Do you want to know which ones die only after seeing their family dead? Because I know."

Mary paused. "So," she whispered. "Everyone you look at...?"

"Yes, everyone. Every time I look at them. I see their birth. I see their death. I see every point of joy and sorrow between."

The handmaiden looked out, past the desecrated gardens, to the city beyond and its protective wall, even now being reinforced. "If you know how this all happens, that we fail and die, why bother?"

"Knowing the story and living the story are two different things, I think." Karen stepped beside Mary and joined in her view of the city. "Some events are Fated, fixed points that cannot be altered. Alexia knew this, I think. She knew Tomas would come here. She knew he would meet you and fall in love. She knew he would leave and..."

"And...?"

Karen shook her head. "Some things are fixed, but not all. Tomas would come here, but how he got here and when were variable. He could have walked all the way here from Pelsemoria. He could have spent weeks, months in Velaross or Alvaro or Ironheartshaven, only eventually making his way here. Instead he came with Rogan." She looked at Mary. "He was Fated to love you. But how much time you spent together was another variable. You could have had only days, or even just a single night. Instead, because of Alexia and my mother, you had months with each other."

Mary considered, saying nothing.

"My mother warned that you would learn unpleasant secrets," the princess reminded. "And you have. You know this city will fall. Fak'Har will penetrate our defenses. The mercenaries will kill many, but not all. We can work within the variables, within the space Fate allows, to save as many as we can." She gestured out at the city. "You can tell everyone what you've learned; warn them that Death is coming, that the White Lady will claim most of them. That won't change what's to come. They'll still die, but they'll die without hope, in misery for their final days. And you won't save those who otherwise might survive."

The princess began walking away. "Take the time you need to decide."

"Wait," the handmaiden called out. Karen paused and looked back. "You already know what I'm going to decide."

Karen smiled sadly. "There's a council meeting tomorrow at noon," she said sadly. The princess was about to turn when she paused. The adolescent girl glanced back at Mary. "By the way," she said softly. "You will see Tomas again. You will hold him, and love him."

Mary stared at the princess, wide-eyed and wanting to believe.

Karen shrugged. "As you said, the women of my family give hope. That's what we always   try   to   do."

Chapter 17

Mary stood at the top of Castle Calonar's western tower, grimacing. Princess Karen had been right, of course. A day spent wandering the city, and a night spent wandering the castle, had led her exactly here. Predestination was a frustrating thing, the handmaiden decided.

Captain Klug Rainer disturbed her gloomy thought as he came huffing up the curving stairs. His dress uniform, bright with medals, was rumpled as though hastily thrown on, and he looked as though he had run much of the distance from the Guard barracks on the southern edge of the city. The older veteran nodded at Mary as he arrived, working more to catch his breath than offer any of the bland courtesies neither he nor the handmaiden cared for. "You too?" he asked finally.

"Apparently," Mary shrugged. She reached out and helped smooth his rumpled tunic. "It seems neither of us has a lot of choice in our service."

Captain Rainer raised an eyebrow at her. "Odd thing to say."

"I'm... in an odd kind of mood, I guess."

"That can happen to you young people," the soldier advised. "You get torn between your urge to do what you want and the demands of what you need."

"What I want isn't..." Mary shook her head.

The captain said nothing for a moment. Then, "Did you eat this morning?"

"What does that-?"

"Did you eat yesterday?"

"Yes, why?"

"And the day before? You ate something then, yes?"

"Captain, I'm not seeing-"

"You decided to eat, but you also had to eat. You could have chosen not to eat, but then you'd starve. So, in one respect, you really had no choice but to eat. Except you did have a choice. Priests and the like twist themselves into knots trying to understand if there's such a thing as free will. I think that's the wrong question to ask, though."

"What's the right question?"

"It's not about free will or the Wind of Fate. It's about actions and consequences. I could, at this moment, take off this uniform and leave the Northlands. Maybe I die in the Wood, or maybe I live to old age. But either way, I have to suffer the consequence of knowing I might have done something, any small thing, to help here.

So, I can stay and very likely die in the weeks ahead. In that case, I suffer the consequences of... well not being alive anymore. It's all about choices, actions, and consequences."

The captain then walked forward. "What's that you brought?" he asked.

Mary glanced at the rolled parchment in her hands. "A map of Lanasia," she answered. "I'm not sure why."

"I'm sure the answers are coming." He stepped up to the large wooden doors ahead. Two guardsmen stood on either side, their uniforms crisp and their poleaxes polished to perfection. "Klug Rainer," the veteran announced to his subordinates. "Standing for General Killdare, representing the Calonar House Guard. As commanded by..." He interrupted the ceremony for admittance to the Council Chamber to check his notes. "As commanded by Princess Karen," he read, his voice trying, but failing, to hide his confusion, "I have come for the meeting of the House Advisory Council." The captain glanced back at Mary. "With me is Mary Fidelis, handmaiden to Princess Kyla."

Mary started at the use of Tomas' name. They had performed the betrothal ceremony before he left with Prince Rogan, months ago. Legally, this gave her right to his name and his property, but people so rarely used it that the handmaiden often forgot she was, technically, a part of his family now.

"I don't know," one of the guardsman said to his partner. "I've met Captain Rainer a few times, and this guy doesn't look like him."

The second guardsman nodded. "The real captain could at least dress himself properly." This, the soldier said with a glance at Rainer's still-disheveled uniform.

The captain rubbed his temples. "Would you two idiots just open the door please?"

"And whooom did you say this was again?" the first asked, glancing at Mary.

Rainer said nothing, only narrowed his eyes.

The second leaned towards Mary. "If this villain is holding you, blink twice. We've seen this kind of scum threaten pretty girls before."

"I swear to God," Rainer growled. "If you two morons make me late for this meeting, I'll transfer the both of you to the ruins of Heath Dannah."

"But Captain," the second objected, holding an offended hand to his burnished breastplate. "It's our sworn duty to question in detail any person of questionable character that try to gain access to this sacred place."

"And let's face it," the first added. "You do have a pretty questionable character."

Rainer stopped then and grinned. "Ok," he said in a far too-friendly voice. "Since you two professionals seem so eager in your duty, I guess I'll just keep you two on this detail." He leaned towards them, his face losing every hint of mercy. "For. Ever."

The guardsmen saluted. "Sir!" They each held a door wide for the officer and Mary to pass.

"What was that all about?" the handmaiden asked.

"I set the duty roster," Rainer explained as he led her into the Council Chamber. "Technically, that detail is a great honor, but it's also pretty boring. So, whenever I try to get in, whoever's on duty gives me a hard time."

They approached the great round table engraved with the double-diamond sigil of House Calonar. "Why not order them to stop? Mary asked.

The captain shrugged. "I did the same thing when I stood that post. It'd be pretty hypocritical for me to get too bent out of shape."

Rainer reached his assigned spot and nodded a greeting at his new aide. "Mary," the veteran said politely, "Have you met Lieutenant Aloisa? She's just back from Nebel."

The woman stood and extended a hand. She was much taller than Mary, and thickly-framed. Her blonde hair was tied back in a long braid, resting over the warrior's right shoulder. Her blue and grey tunic stretched a bit against her large chest, and the cloth hugged her powerful arms. When the handmaiden took her hand the slight squeeze offered silent testimony of restrained power. When Mary glanced down at that strong, callused hand, she blinked.

"You've seen the Mark of the Chooser?" Aloisa asked with a grin.

Mary mutely shook her head.

"In my tribe, a woman who defeats a man in combat and takes what's his, earns this mark." Her voice carried a strange, rolling pitch. She spoke Gunnic without flaw, and yet it was as though her use of the Northlands language was more primal, more authentically pure. The lieutenant rolled up the sleeve of her tunic, exposing the tattoo. A circle of strange runes surrounded the back of her hand. Within that an old compass-symbol indicating the eight directions. Trailing away was a tree, it's branches grasping towards the circle on Aloisa's hand, and its roots training along her arm. In the center of this, as though resting amidst the leaves, was a raven with wings unfurled.

"Your tribe?" Mary asked.

"Aloisa's of the Gunrsvein," Captain Rainer grunted as he took his seat.

The handmaiden gasped and took an involuntary step back.

In response, the warrior-woman's grin grew slightly savage, her eyes of northern ice narrowing and filling with a terrible hunger. "So," she said in a voice of chilling as the winter wind. "That means I lust for plunder. I'm just waiting for the right moment to sack the city." She took a step forward, pushing herself into Mary's trembling body. "It also means," she said in a growling purr and eyes that roamed across the handmaiden's shivering body, "that the only thing I love more than stealing your men is corrupting your women." She flicked a lightning-quick tongue across Mary's nose.

"Stop playing with the girl," Rainer said wearily with barely a glance behind him. "I'll feed you later."

"He always promises," Aloisa complained. She then grinned as evil a grin as Mary could ever remember seeing. "But he never delivers." She returned to her seat beside her commander.

Mary stood for a moment, unsure of what to do, but was spared with the arrival of Medaka. The Sister of the Lady of Light was, as always, dressed in brilliant purple, her skirt short and without sleeves in summer's heat. Her long hair was also styled as many Northlands women preferred, with a series of decorative braids, and yet hers seemed vaguely Uldric, decorated with rough gemstones bearing small Uldra runes. Amethyst was the dominant stone, though there were also small nuggets of silver, gold, and steel. Medaka saw Mary and smiled in greeting. She took the younger woman's hand and walked with her around the great table. "They finally forced you into this as well?" the Sister asked.

The handmaiden grimaced. "I've recently learned how little choice I have," she grumbled.

Medaka paused and looked at her. The Sister had been guiding Mary's investigations through the Temple archives. As such, they had spent many long hours together. In that time, Medaka had shown a quiet insight, a gentle, loving concern for all the younger Sisters. She had soon extended this to Mary herself. "That's a hard realization for one so young."

Mary shrugged. "I... There are secrets I'd rather not have," she confessed.

"True of us all." The Sister glanced towards the door. "There are, in every generation, those burdened with knowledge. To be awakened to the hardships of Fate, that's no easy thing. To know what lies beyond our own lives, our own small concerns, is a terrible kind of imprisonment."

"It's worse when you aren't given the choice to know or not."

Medaka stopped in front of her chair, placed beside Cardinal Tain's as representatives of the religions of the Northern Keep. "Would you choose not to know?" the Sister asked. She looked at Mary. "Would you inflict that knowledge upon another?"

Mary did not know the answer. She stared for a moment, the idea shocking her, as Medaka took her seat.

Cardinal Tain looked up at Mary's approach. "Good day, Mary," he said lightly.

"Your Eminence," the handmaiden replied, taking his outstretched hand.

"Now, none of that," he gently chided. "You know I leave such things to my esteemed brothers in their Velarossi palaces."

Mary smiled and placed a light kiss, not on the holy man's hand, as was traditional, but on his cheek. "Are you well?" she asked.

"As well as any old man can be in such times," Tain replied.

"Things do seem to be... turning."

The cardinal looked up at Mary. "Times always do," he said. "They always must. But remember, that turn does not stop. The bad comes, but good always follows close behind."

"I hope so, father."

Mary moved to her own reserved chair, the same one, she realized, that Tomas must have sat in himself, months ago. Prince Rogan customarily sat to the side of the royal place, and his squire would have been beside him. Mary traced a hand along the chair, as though she might feel Tomas' presence, the afterimage of his body. Sighing, she took the seat she did not want, and so deeply wished was filled instead by her husband-to-be.

Esha entered the chamber as the handmaiden sat, though only the tip of her head could be seen over the table. Mary was always a little startled when she saw the great archmage of the Northern Keep. In her mind's eye, Esha always grew whenever the tiny Sylva was not within sight. So great was her reputation, so awesome her faculty with magic, that Mary thought it was impossible for such power to be contained within so small, so deceptively frail a body. The mighty archmage's blue robes were, as usual, adorned with fresh burns. No doubt, some experiment of hers had once again detonated. Esha reached her assigned spot and stood on her tiptoes to put her books and parchments onto the table, straining at first to climb up her chair. That seat had been specially designed by Remm Stonebearer, and rebuilt after Esha had exploded at a council meeting last winter, to allow the great adept to sit level with the table.

Remm Stonebearer himself sat at Esha's side. The ancient Uldra metalsmith towered over the diminutive Sylva, but never to Mary's recollection, ever used his great size for intimidation. In fact, when he reached down and helped Esha into her seat, he did so with a light, friendly touch. Remm was a mystery to most residents of the Northlands. He was older, by far, than any Uldra, having been a part of the legends and histories of the Northern Keep for as long as it had existed. Despite this, he did not seem burdened by his age, standing as tall and powerful as any male in his prime. The greatest mystery, of course, was the source of his binary body. His left side was typical of his race, with coal-black hair and a full, if unkempt, beard. His right side, though, was anything but typical; the hair on that side was as white as mountain snow, and that eye was a piercing blue. Strangest of all were the dizzying tattoos that covered the right side of his body, markings that seemed to shift each time someone laid eyes upon them. Despite the centuries of racial hatred between them, neither Remm nor Esha carried any hint of that ancient vendetta. The two chatted as old comrades did, of unimportant matters.

Princess Karen entered then, and made her way around the large table. Each member of the Advisory Council stood and bowed to the princess, most showing surprise at her first appearance. Word had almost certainly spread of the Queen's infirmity after the mysterious incident in the ruined gardens yesterday. That, combined with Kyla's continued limitation to her bedchamber after the attempted assassination, logically left only one remaining member of the royal family to assume control of the Council. Despite this rationale, none likely considered the reclusive, self-effacing Princess Karen for any kind of leadership role.

Karen took the King's seat. This caused another round of surprised murmuring. There could be no question as to the princess' purpose, then. "Be seated," Karen said with heretofore unheard-of command in her soft, adolescent voice.

Each person slowly sat, never letting their eyes slip from the new mistress. Karen locked hard, pearlescent eyes on each of them in turn, letting the merciless urgency of the moment flow into them all. Finally, she said, "There is a traitor on this council."

No one moved. None spoke. For months, rumors had spread throughout the Council, the castle, and even into the city. Many feared what the princess had just confirmed. Within House Calonar's Advisory Council, the most powerful governing body left in Lanasia, there lurked a traitor.

"The suspicion has been here for months. Evidence has grown. Doubt and coincidence has piled atop one another. Now, I know." Her eyes were not those of her mother. Queen Nora looked at others with soft understanding, with gentle love. Her daughter, though, looked with unforgiving authority. "For weeks," the princess continued, "nothing was said and our actions were curtailed, all for fear of letting sensitive information slip into traitorous hands. House Calonar has tried to work in the shadows, to deceive, to cheat. In short, we have tried to operate as you, the traitor, operates. We have failed." As she spoke, the princess' eyes never stopped moving from one face to the next. Never once did she give any indication of one, specific person upon whom she would cast accusation. "Our failure has allowed great suffering.

"Each of you has failed my family. Some of you have done so deliberately. The rest of you have simply failed to fulfill your duty. The Harvest Festival was disrupted by an attack from the death mage Anninihus. My father has been poisoned and is dying. My mother expends every bit of her strength and magic to keep him alive. Our city has been attacked by the Sorceress Vara. Our magic, mobility, and communications have been disrupted for months. War has broken out in the south, drawing our army, and its leader, away. A horde of mercenaries is now raping, murdering, and burning at will through Wildelves Wood. Our allies, the Sylvai, suffer through our neglect. My sister has survived an assassination attempt by her own bodyguard only through the intervention of the next heir of House Calonar, an infant boy not yet even born."

She looked with unflinching, unforgiving accusation at the entire council. "A boy unborn has done more to protect House Calonar than any of you." She straightened. "For ten years, you have maintained peace and prosperity in the Northlands. A decade has passed since anyone challenged us. We have become powerful, influential. And you have become complacent. The time for that has passed."

The princess closed her eyes and breathed deeply. "I have undergone the ritual of my mothers," she said. "I now have the Truthsight." Karen opened her eyes, seeing the visible flinch of many people sitting at the table. "Additionally, my father has been in contact with Rogan through his connection to the Archaeknights."

Mary let out an involuntary gasp. Without looking away from the council, Karen put a hand on the handmaiden's. "My mother and I also consulted more esoteric sources of information."

"Was this the cause of her... incident, yesterday?" Captain Rainer asked gently, carefully, watching Karen.

The princess looked at the veteran soldier. "Yes," she replied. "The effort was more difficult than we expected. My mother is resting, and then will continue her ministrations of the King."

Esha straightened abruptly. The tiny Sylva, sitting in her newly-replaced chair, seemed like a child at table with her elders. Despite this, the great archmage, the Tower Mistress of the local Arcane Guild, spoke with the authority of her genius and years of loyal service. "Your Highness," she said in her tiny, musical voice. "If a mystical inquiry was to be made, I should have been included! We can't afford to risk two members of the House, especially now!"

"You are not a Truthseer, Esha," Karen replied evenly. "Your powers are formidable, but some things are still beyond you. The Wind of Fate is one."

"Your Highness," Baron Rashid Tressalon said calmly. Despite his easy words, the spymaster's face revealed his growing worry. His dark eyes were sunken, surrounded by even darker bags. His handsome face, olive skinned from his heritage of the Endless Sands, was growing pale in his unending work behind closed doors. "If your information is as sensitive as you say," the spymaster noted, "perhaps it would be better to dismiss all but the most critical personnel?"

Karen glanced at her spymaster. He and Chandra, his second, had been the first to arrive, as was their custom. Normally, the baron was every woman's dream, the epitome of sensuality with long, dark hair that often seemed to move with a life of its own, but now hung drab. His flawless skin had become blotched and unshaven. In the days since the nearly-successful assassination of Kyla, Rashid had slowly transformed, becoming less the unflinching master of secrets and more a broken man.

The princess shook her head. "You have tried for months to resolve the threat of the traitor your way Rashid," she pronounced. "The efforts have accomplished nothing useful. What your methods have only achieved is suspicion. House Calonar has operated blindly, not trusting our own people, nor using our own resources to full effect for fear that they may be turned against us. I will no longer allow us to operate in fear. Let the traitor learn fear. House Calonar is stronger than any one person. We are powerful together, in our unity."

Cardinal Tain, the ancient clergyman representing Velaross and the Adamic religion, raised his trembling hand. "If I may?" he asked. "What did your effort reveal?"

"Rogan's team and the Archaeknights have retrieved the Seal of Life. They are, even now, rushing home."

That information caused a great stir. Side conversations spilled over each other with new that the Healing Sphere, the most power engine of Life Magic in the world, was on its way to the Northern Keep. Princess Karen raised her voice to regain the council's attention. "We have a greater problem than my father's poisoning," she declared. "Although not unrelated. While in the Western Empire, Rogan's team discovered that the adept working with Emir Theodorico Balshazzar was Fak'Har himself. The Shadowed Mage is even now marching an army of his creations to reinforce the mercenaries. He will attack us."

Gasps escaped from everyone's lips. No matter their power or their experience, the Shadowed Mage was an object of terror. Mary saw, across the table, Lieutenant Aloisa begin trembling, the warrior-woman's eyes wide and her breathing short.

"Do we know when Fak'Har will arrive?" Chandra asked. Rashid's assistant rarely spoke during Council meetings, preferring her whispered consultations with the spymaster. As always, she was dressed as plainly as possible, letting her long hair cover much of her unadorned face. Instead of addressing the council, she usually only whispered into Rashid's ear.

Karen looked at the spy, saying nothing. The princess let a moment pass, one in which Chandra seemed increasingly uncomfortable. "I know exactly when the Shadowed Mage will arrive," the adolescent girl said. "I know what route he is taking, and what resources he is gathering. I know his strategy upon reaching the Wood. Now."

Captain Rainer cleared his throat carefully. "And… if we can ask?"

The princess nodded. "I reveal as much as I am able." She stood and nodded to Mary. The handmaiden took up the map she had brought and, without thinking, unrolled it across the table towards Captain Rainer. The veteran grabbed the map and finished flattening it, using weights that were on the table to hold the map in place. Only when she returned to her seat did Mary consider for a moment that no one had told her to bring a map. She had, for some unknown reason, chosen to do so.

Princess Karen took up a large, smoothed stick and used it to indicate specific locations on the map. "Even now, Fak'Har is traveling north, through the Endless Sands." She traced a path up the Hoppi River. "He will cross through northern Ulheim with the assistance of the clans there."

Remm Stonebearer leapt to his feet. The ugly barbarian, as disheveled as always, glared at Karen. The twisting tattoos on the right side of his face nearly clawed at the air, and his mismatched eyes burned in barely-controlled rage. "What!?!" he roared.

Karen looked at the monstrous Uldra calmly, examining more than his bifurcated body and hair. "The Shadowed Mage has spent the past several years corrupting the western Uldra. He has shown them secrets once lost to your people and guided their invention of new, terrible inventions. Any among those clans who would not be corrupted were sold into slavery in Tordenia. The Western Uldra are now loyal to Fak'Har and will join in the coming battle."

Remm half-turned. "I've got to warn the clans!" he barked.

"They already know," the princess replied. Somehow, her young voice froze the seething, belligerent barbarian. "There have already been skirmishes around Gibea. Word is already spreading to the eastern clans of what's happening. They are mobilizing, even now. The greater bulk of the corrupted Uldra are marching through Ulheim, intent on either spreading their corruption to the eastern clans, enslaving them, or simply wiping them out."

"God," Captain Rainer breathed. "Civil war among the Uldra."

"Has that ever even happened?" Lieutenant Aloisa asked. "Is it possible?"

"Before the Nameless," Remm growled. "Before our Uprising. Not since." He fell back into his own, specially-designed chair. Despite its reinforcement, the furniture groaned under the mass of Remm's thick body. "My people," he said in a voice of pain and horror.

"There will be war in eastern Ulheim," Karen said. "Just as there is war in all of eastern Lanasia. Frostfront will continue their campaign against Alvaro. The Xeshlin have landed forces in the southern Velaross Duchies, even as the Gwyndd launch another of their incursions north of the Holy City. Our own battle is only one theatre in much broader conflict."

Karen returned her attention to the map of the Northlands. "After crossing Ulheim," she continued, "Fak'Har will travel south, meet with Vagris and the mercenaries, and then march for the city." The princess looked at Cardinal Tain, again taking a moment to see further than any other was able. "The Shadowed Mage has learned the secrets of Soul, Thought, and Dream," she said. "He has used this power on the hundreds of Holy Knights and Inquisitor-Priests who defected to the Western Empire. These soulless creatures will form the core of his army when it attacks."

"The secrets of those Winds were lost forever," the ancient holy man noted.

"Yes," Karen murmured. "Fak'Har found someone to teach him."

"No defenses exist against Soul Magic," Tain sighed. "Nor Thought or Dream."

"And your Church has destroyed all the research into those Winds," Esha pointed out surely, her lower lip jutting out in accusation.

The Cardinal could only sigh and nod. "Yes. Once again, our Holy Mother has proven Her own worst enemy."

"Fak'Har will try to limit his use of those more corruptive Winds," Karen said then. "He has already used Soul to the extent of his ability in creating the unliving knights. He may, or may not, bring Thought and Dream to bear. The bigger, more immediate threat is Vagris' mercenaries."

"And General Killdare is trapped in the south," Rainer added grimly.

Rashid straightened in his chair, looked at the veteran. "What's the status of our forces here?" he asked, visibly forcing his mind back into its typical clarity and focus.

Captain Rainer glanced at Aloisa, who handed him a sheet of parchment. "I can assemble one full brigade from our remaining forces," he noted. "Plus another two battalions from nearby villages.

"I can add to that," Remm declared, retaking his seat. "When we're done here, I'm heading west. The main fight might be shaping up in the mountains, but if Fak'Har's bringing the traitors here, then we'll deal with them. I'll bring whatever clansmen can be spared."

"The Wood is crawling with mercenaries," Chandra pointed out. "It won't help us if you're killed trying to get through."

"We can send some security with you," Aloisa offered. "A little company for the road?"

"Perhaps magical support?" Medaka suggested gently. She glanced at Esha. "Perhaps one of your new archwizards? Jade is quite resourceful, and I understand Xathias is quite skilled at evasion."

The Tower Mistress shook her head. "Jade went south with General Killdare." The tiny Sylva glanced at Rainer and Aloisa. "Xathias…" Esha removed her thick reading-lenses and glanced at Karen. "He is… not available."

The young princess nodded.

Chandra glanced up, catching the look shared by Esha and Karen. "Um, is there something going on that the Council should be aware of?"

Karen glanced at the spy. "I have ordered Xathias on a sensitive task."

Rashid sat forward. "Princess," he said, clearly trying to summon some of his past dexterity with language and persuasion. "Normally, I am consulted on any covert operations."

"That is our job," Chandra added insistently. "Especially if you want to start operating more openly."

The princess stared at Rashid's second with unblinking pearlescence. "There are a few matters I will handle personally, just as my mother did in the past. The Truthsight has made clear to me certain unpleasant truths, certain actions that must come to pass. Xathias is seeing to one of these." Her tone was flat and hard as granite.

"I can move faster alone anyway," Remm stated, shaking his mangy head and ending any further debate. "They won't see me leave, and I'll have plenty of backup on the way home. With the clans, I'll swing by the Woodwall Forts and bring them along."

"No," Karen objected. "The Western Forts must remain secure. They'll be needed after."

An awkward paused followed. Esha broke this by saying, "All my students will aid in the defense, of course, as we are needed. But what about reserves? Are there any supplementary forces that can augment the regular ones?"

Rainer consulted more notes provided by Aloisa. "There are two hundred City Watch," he glanced at Remm. "Is that right?"

The venerable Uldra nodded. "Before I leave, I'll transfer their command to you."

Rainer nodded. "We'll use them as a fire brigade and reserve. I can arm as many of the commons as you like, forming them into an auxiliary. But for real fighting men, we're only going to have whatever Uldra Remm can bring back, plus a few hundred veterans. Maybe an additional thousand to add to the House Guard."

"You'll have more," Karen proclaimed. "Forces will retreat from the mercenaries. Survivors can be found in the Wood. They will be eager for vengeance."

"What about the Speakers?" Mary asked suddenly. The handmaiden bit her lip at the sudden outburst.

"Sora is out in the forest," Chandra pointed out.

Rashid nodded. "The Speakers are having a hard enough time coordinating their Walkers against the mercenaries. They won't answer any call for help. They won't be able to."

"They will come," Karen promised.

"What about General Killdare?" the spymaster added.

Captain Rainer stood and gestured towards the map. "We've lost most contact. Last we heard, he's somewhere near the Sentinel Mountains."

"He will arrive," Karen said. "His army is coming, but we cannot depend on his arrival for our defense."

"It seems time, in general, is not an asset," Rashid mused. He glanced at Karen. "Do we know when Fak'Har will arrive?"

"Anlanil 17th," the princess replied.

The spymaster leaned back in his chair. "About six weeks." He looked at Captain Rainer. "A couple of battalions. Maybe a thousand barely-trained reservists."

"And half our people, not to mention the Sylvai, our greatest fighting strength, are all scattered through the forest," the veteran agreed. "It's time for recovery."

"What does that mean?" Esha asked.

"Our best, most experienced, most capable will break into teams," Rainer announced. "While the rest stay here with the City Watch and begin preparations. The teams will spread into the forest, pulling everyone back to the city who can't escape the Wood."

Rashid nodded. "My people will go too, all of them. We'll scour the forest for anyone, everyone, and get them back here."

"Isn't that a big risk?" Chandra objected.

"Indeed," Esha agreed. "We already know our actions are being monitored and perhaps countered. If we dilute our already-meager forces, will than not risk weakening our defense, rather than strengthening it?"

Rainer shook his head. "At this point, it doesn't really matter. The mercenaries are already out there, already causing havoc. If we move in force, in large groups, there's less chance for any traitors to make mischief without exposing themselves."

"Then the path becomes clear," Princess Karen added. "Our efforts, for now, must center on the evacuation of as many people as possible. We consolidate our strength for a defense of the Northern Keep.

Rainer looked at Rashid. "It's not much of a plan," the veteran admitted. "But it's something. We still need to develop our siege defense, though."

Karen tapped the branch in her hands upon the table, calling for silence. "On that note, Klug Rainer, we arrive at an important decision. With General Killdare and Rogan both gone," she nodded at Remm, "and the departure of our Captain of the City Watch, command of our defenses must fall to you. A central commander is needed to organize the preparations and lead the defense when the battle comes.

Rainer stood, all color draining from his face. "With respect, your Highness," he objected. "There are several officers in the city who outrank me. I'm just sitting in on these meetings for the General, relaying his policies and instructions. There are even two retired Legion commanders here. One of them should take command."

"The choice is yours, Klug Rainer," the princess said. "You are a Northlander, born and raised. Your entire family is of the Northlands. Your children have served House Calonar, just as you. You have fought for decades in our House Guard. You know the soldiers, and they you. You understand the Northern Keep, its strengths, weaknesses, and its people. Do any others share your connection to this city and its people?"

The veteran looked to Aloisa. The lieutenant shrugged.

"The great strength of our community is how we welcome others," Karen relentlessly continued. "We empower ourselves by empowering one another. But you, alone, have the knowledge and experience so deeply rooted within this city. If not you, who else can lead its defense?" The princess resumed her seat. "But, the choice is yours."

Rainer opened and closed his mouth several times, as though trying to speak but unable to find the words. He was still then, for a while. Finally, the veteran bowed his acceptance, his choice to lead.

"You are right," Karen noted, "that several men outrank you. Hereby, you are granted the rank of colonel. Once General Killdare returns, he can decide whether or not your promotion be permanent." The faintest ghost of a smile passed over the princess' lips. "I supposed your success or failure of this campaign will be the determining factor."

Chapter 18

That evening, Chandra was sitting at the desk in her small office. Even in the days when she still held loyalty to House Calonar, the spy had little use for extravagance. The walls were bare of any of the dozens of citations and awards she had earned. There was no memorabilia of her innumerable missions. She had no art or other décor to brighten the otherwise drab room. Only a single cabinet held her personal clothes and a simple cot in the corner, were touches of habitation. In fact, there was little to distinguish the office of the Service's second-in-command from any other small room in the castle. Like Chandra herself, the room was plain and forgettable.

Second-in-command. The thought, the supposed title, never failed to make her inwardly seethe. Officially, if there were any records of House Calonar's intelligence service, they would have marked Rashid Tressalon as commander and Chandra as his second. In truth, she was, at best, a distant third. Though the other operatives all deferred to her and accepted her words as coming from Rashid himself, her authority had an undeniable limit.

As always, whenever Chandra sat at her desk, her hand moved of its own volition to the side drawer. Her hand pulled this open and reached inside, pressing the hidden release. The false bottom slid aside and her heartless, unfeeling hand reached inside. Chandra did not want to look at it; she never wanted to look at it. And yet, her eyes, the dull, unexceptional brown blobs, insisted on looking.

The tiny gold ring was such a simple thing. No jewels or inscriptions. No intricate design or mystical enchantment. Only a legacy. "This is the only thing I had when I left the Endless Sands," Rashid had told her. "Everything else is gone. There were so many times I almost sold it, traded it, lost it." He had looked at the tiny golden band with soft kindness, with loving memory he never revealed to anyone, even the Sylva witch.

They had just returned from Alvaro, from the mission that had proven the value of spies to then-Duke Cylan. Rashid, not yet spymaster, but only another refugee taken in by House Calonar, had learned of a kidnapping plot against Kyla. A minor noble had used the last of his squandered fortune, hoping to sell the mystical girl-child. Rashid and Chandra, herself just another orphan, discovered the plan and alerted their duke. The kidnappers had not even time to reach the city walls. The little girl was recovered and Rashid was named spymaster. They had saved each other's lives on that first mission; Chandra had even taken an arrow to the middle. She still carried the scar.

He had given her the ring as a gesture of gratitude. Not just for saving his life, they had done much of that. Rather, Chandra had been the first one who believed in him, trusted him, even more than that idiot brother of his. And, more importantly, he had been the first to see her. There had been others, of course, an orphan girl learns quickly the advantage of her body, but Rashid had been the first to really see her. To all others, Chandra had only ever been convenient, forgotten the moment she was out of sight. But Rashid, he had truly seen her. The day Duke Cylan had granted him the title of baron and named him to the Advisory Council, he had come to Chandra and given her the ring. "It's the only thing I have left of my old life. It belonged to my mother. I want you to have it."

As she recovered under the care of the Harvest Mother clergy, Rashid had spent much time with her. They made plans in those days. They schemed on what the intelligence service would look like. How to recruit, how to operate. Even as Rashid was the father of the Service, Chandra was its mother. They had been occasional lovers, not in terms of the emotion, for they both understood the absurdity of the word, but in the physical release. They had gone on a great many dangerous missions together in those early years and took frequent comfort with each other. They had defended House Calonar and neutralized so many threats before they could even manifest. They were the perfect team, the perfect partners. Chandra had even entertained occasional thoughts of their life together beyond the Service, and, when alone, considered the title of Baroness. But then she arrived.

Chandra's hand closed around the ring like a claw. The spy was one of only a handful of people in the world who knew the truth. Rashid had been her partner. They had sacrificed everything for one another. She had earned her place on the Council, in the Castle, in the Service. And then that whore, that heathen sorceress, stole what was hers. Rashid never trusted her, he did not even particularly like her. He seduced her, of course; over the years, he and Chandra both had used sexuality as the weapon it was. They harbored no delusions of intimate exclusivity, and what better way to monitor those newcomers than to twist the witch's heart? But then she was kidnapped.

Tressalon came back so terribly hurt. Chandra always huffed at the thought. How many times, the spy often thought, had she herself been captured, abused, abandoned? How many times had she lost fellow agents? How many horrid traumas had she endured, not with tears and wide, inhuman eyes, but with strength? Rashid always welcomed her home and treated her no differently. But when the witch came back, teary-eyed and weak from her time with the Greysoul, suddenly the spymaster was the one twisted.

Seemingly overnight, Rashid had gone from the solid, independent master of secrets to her plaything. He humiliated himself for her amusement, danced for her every tune. He was hers, and no one else's. Chandra had tried to snap him out of the spell, break him free of the witch's curse, to no avail. She lost him between Tressalon's thighs.

A knock at the door startled her. Chandra dropped the ring back into the drawer, even as the door opened. Rashid, unshaven, unwashed, and weaker than ever, stuck his head in. "A minute?" he asked.

Chandra nodded, sliding the drawer shut. Her supposed leader stepped in, forgetting to close the door behind him. The spy fought a grimace at how pathetic he was becoming. Each time Tressalon left to whore about Lanasia with Eigenhard, Rashid withered in her absence. The separations were of little note to most, with the spymaster putting on an effective show of strength and skill, maintaining his duties as spymaster. He never let the withering spell she had put upon him affect his service to House Calonar.

So, this time, Chandra had needed to exacerbate the issue.

"I've got the deployment orders," he said, handing a slip of parchment to her.

Chandra looked at it. "Some of these people aren't in the castle," she pointed out. "Some aren't even in the Northlands." His deterioration nearly broke her heart. This, the traitor could silently admit to herself. Rashid was a strong man, capable and loyal. His brilliant mind had attracted her even more than his sculpted body. But, if he was to be freed from Tressalon, this extreme measure was needed.

And her master had shown her how.

"Right," Rashid grimaced, rubbing his temple. "Just… switch out the names. Take care of it, would you?" He was getting worse every day, the spy noted. That idiot Lukas had failed in his assassination attempt on Kyla, and Chandra had been forced to kill him to prevent his questioning. The failure of House Calonar to defend its precious jewel was causing the real damage now. The spymaster had already become burdened with self-doubt, adding to the effects of Tressalon's absence. The Mindfog she had begun slipping to Rashid only added to his already fearful burdens. That had been the deal, after all. Chandra had insisted that the spymaster be freed and healthy after their plans reached culmination. Her master had approved, and shown her how to free Rashid.

Chandra grimaced. "So, what do you think of Karen showing up?"

Rashid sighed and fell into the chair opposite hers. "Hard to say," he grunted. "We knew she'd inherit the Queen's Truthsight at some point." The spymaster shook his head. "There's just no way of knowing what it's going to do to her. We don't know what Nora was like before the Truthsight, so we don't know how she was changed." Chandra's master had told her that the compound took time to build up, that it would hasten the deterioration inflicted by Tressalon. Only now, months after the traitor had begun slipping it to Rashid, was Chandra seeing the results.

"Can we really trust a little girl with these... visions?" the traitor asked, probing Rashid's mind. "Can we really listen to her commands?"

Rashid shrugged. "Not much choice. She's next in line of succession, until Rogan gets back. We'll just have to keep an eye on her."

Chandra stood and walked around her desk. She knelt beside Rashid and put a hand on his. "Is there anything I can do...?" She was not really sure why she made the offer. Neutralizing the spymaster was high on the list of objectives. He was simply too dangerous to leave active, too clever and too perceptive to be allowed to remain in play. Although she had not said as much to her master, Chandra's first priority, now that the attack was imminent, was to keep Rashid safe and inactive, in preparation for their escape.

Rashid sighed and patted her hand, then stood. "I just need a little rest. Take care of this new job, will you?"

"I always do," she replied with a smile.

The fading spymaster left, this time remembering to close the door. This would not last much longer, she predicted. A few months, at most. House Calonar would be destroyed and Rashid would be released from the witch's spell. Then, Chandra could wean him off the Mindfog and he would be restored to his brilliant, virile self. After that, freed of the Northern Keep and all the fools within it, they could do what they had speculated on so many times, travel the world, together.

A soft, whisper of a chime drew her attention back to her desk. She secured her door and went back, sitting and pulling from the hidden drawer a crystal half-sphere. Chandra waved her hand over the magical device and then waited. A red mist drifted from the top of the crystal, spiraling and becoming dense. A face, deeply cowled and hooded, formed from the red mist, staring at her with eyes of burning blood. "What is it?" she demanded.

"Your operatives near Mistriver are dead." Xaemus reported.

"Good," the traitor replied. "I'll inform my master." Chandra had been resistant to that word, at first. No creature, man or woman, Human or non-Human, should hold that much power over her. Still, her master had never, not once, forced the issue. Chandra had been the one to first use the word, after so many promises had been made and kept. Unlike House Calonar, unlike even Rashid, nothing her master had ever said had been proven false. No service had ever been demanded, only asked for, in return for generous rewards. Years had passed now, and Chandra had found that she no longer shied away from addressing her master as such, so great had been the rewards and gratitude for her many betrayals. "I'll have another list of targets by tomorrow," she held up the parchment Rashid had given her. "There's been a shift in tactics. The agents will be in the company of veteran House Guard. Will that be a problem?"

The monster of Davenor shook his head. "Once I know the groups' composition and disposition, the rest is simple."

"Contact me tomorrow night for the next list." She waved a hand over the crystal, ending the communication. There was a knock at her door, so Chandra returned the magical device to its hiding place. "Yes?"

Vincent, Chandra's newest partner, entered. "I heard there's new orders."

"Not yet. Tomorrow. We'll be going out in a few days to help bring in refugees." She waved him in.

The much younger man, only last year being inducted into the Service, entered and closed the door. He approached and sat down on the same chair Rashid had used only minutes before. "I'm getting worried," he confessed. The partners had long ago dismissed any formality, despite Chandra's seniority, allowing Vincent to speak his mind when they were alone. "We're losing a lot of people out there. Agents are wandering off-mission, missions are falling apart, objectives are… confusing."

Chandra artfully sighed. She reached under her desk and produced a small bottle of Uldra spirits and a pair of glasses. "I wish I could give you better information," she lied while pouring the drinks and handing one to Vincent.

"You're in the Council meetings," the young spy pointed out. "Do these decisions make any sense to you?"

The traitor laughed bitterly. "Does anything nobles do ever make sense?" she asked, raising her glass. Vincent was the son of shopkeepers in Railling. His family had lost their business, though, due to interference and over-taxation from local nobility, and this had left a resentment in the young man.

The spy, little more than a boy, really, drank and shook his head. "You'd think Rashid…"

"No," Chandra said firmly. "None of that." She poured them both another drink. "He does the best he can with what he's got."

"Morale's taking a real hit," Vincent advised. "He doesn't talk to us, doesn't keep us in the know like he used to."

"He's taking the assassination attempt badly," she excused. "We all are."

"Some more than others," he replied carefully. "Do we have any more data about possible traitors in the Service?"

Chandra shook her head. "Plenty of data. None of it reliable because it all points to each other." This, of course, because the traitor herself was manufacturing most of the supposed evidence. She had turned a few other agents, but not many, and spent the past several years imbedding them across Lanasia to further her master's designs.

Chandra glanced at her young partner. "Funny, how you knew to send Ilse back to the princess at just the right moment," the traitor noted. "Rumor is that you're sweet on her. I'd think you'd take every opportunity for time alone."

Vincent smiled faintly and shrugged. "You're not the only one who likes to keep an eye on things, you know."

She nodded with an approving look, but inwardly, the traitor began reassessing. "What else have you noticed? Aside from Ilse's new dress. You know, the one that's perhaps a little too tight around the backside?"

Vincent actually blushed. He was an excellent agent, very nearly the prodigy Chandra herself had been. Yet, he was still male, and young. She allowed her mouth to continue the conversation, even as her mind continued in its calculations.

"I know that a lot more agents have disappeared than the Council knows," he said. "Whether that's deliberate under-reporting, or Rashid..."

Again, Chandra put a hand up, twisting her face into a careful mask of loyal sternness. "I said none of that." She sighed then, artfully, and poured them another round. "I... probably shouldn't tell you. But I..." the traitor looked at him. "It'd be... nice, to have someone to bounce things off of." She drank, checking that he did so as well. "Besides, if you're sticking your nose into things anyway, it might keep you out of trouble." She breathed deep and structured her lie, so that it held mostly truth. "Rashid is... missing things. He's sending out orders that don't make a lot of sense." She showed Vincent the error-filled parchment the spymaster had delivered earlier.

The young spy looked at the list and spotted the mistakes nearly as quickly as Chandra had. "Deliberate or delinquent?" he asked.

Chandra shook her head. "I won't believe it's a deliberate act," she truthfully lied. "I think he's just getting caught up in his own cleverness."

"What does that mean?"

She poured another round. "We all know there's at least one traitor on the Council, and that at least some of the Service has been corrupted. Rashid keeps sending teams out on these strange, contradictory assignments. He could be trying to smoke out those who've turned."

"That doesn't make much sense. How could that work?"

"Welcome to my personal Underworld," Chandra replied. "I don't understand it either, but, over the years, some of his plans have been... involved. God," the traitor sighed, holding her head. "The whole damned world has gone made. Friends are enemies, enemies are monsters. I just don't know what to do, who to trust."

Vincent finished his drink and stood. "Keep the faith," he advised. "Prince Rogan is on his way home with the Archaeknights. General Killdare is maneuvering to get back as well. All we have to do is hold out. The traitors, whoever they are, can only do so much as long as we stay loyal to each other. Besides," he said with a grin. "We're

House Calonar. We always beat the bad guys in the end." He smiled and walked out, closing the door behind him.

Chandra stared after her young, but annoyingly-perceptive, partner.

Chapter 19

The upper floors of Castle Calonar, in contrast to the purposeful storm below, were deceptively serene. The business of government had moved away, to the rooms and halls below, leaving the royal family in peace. Beyond respecting the core of House Calonar in this difficult time, an unspoken taboo had formed: no one wanted to risk seeing the hero of the Northlands as he decayed. King Cylan was the last of the Heroes of Fate, those legendary champions who had saved Lanasia time and again. The priest Mortimus had died peacefully in seclusion. Sir Talius Ironheart had fallen in battle. Khaine, founder of the Walkers had vanished into the unknown wilderness. The lost Heroes, Samantha and Tienel Uskera had been defeated. None of the Heroes remained, none but Cylan Calonar, and his people were being forced to witness his living decay.

In these horrible times, all of House Calonar seemed to be collapsing. King Cylan himself was poisoned and withering. Queen Nora had suffered some mysterious breakdown. Princess Kyla had been injured in a recent assassination attempt. Prince Rogan was gone yet again on some perilous mission, taking with him Baroness Aebreanna Tressalon and Sir Beraht. Baron Rashid Tressalon was withering into himself, a victim of his own failures in recent months. And now, Princess Karen had… changed. The people who lived and worked within Castle Calonar were increasingly uncomfortable with the deterioration of the Noble House they had sworn to serve.

Mary and Ilse, handmaidens to Princess Kyla, brought their mistress her meals and cleaned her chambers. They also supervised the handful of staff willing to enter those haunting upper chambers. Once, to serve the Royal Family was the highest honor to the castle staff, one struggled for and coveted. Now, only the most devout could stand approaching the rooms of people who had been legends, nearly demigods, but were now fading into mortality.

As she reached the floor reserved for Princess Kyla, Baroness Aebreanna, and Tomas, Mary once again gave silent thanks for the new Uldra inventions. She was pushing a heavy cart laden with meals for all those dwelling in those foreboding rooms. In years past, a team of castle staff were needed to carry the meal trays up the many flights of stairs to the members of House Calonar. Now, however, Mary could do it alone. The cart was perfectly balanced, even with the many plates, bowls, utensils, and other accouterment of dining. The wheels were, in fact, a set of bizarre contraptions, each composed of several, rotating wheels; these spun around each other and extended as needed while Mary pulled the large cart up the stairs, somehow smoothly climbing like some mechanical beast of burden.

Opfern had accompanied Mary up most of the winding stairs. The younger girl, like Mary, had been one of the few who maintained her devotion to her charges. They chatted about unimportant things each day, when they traveled together to the kitchens, retrieved the meals, and returned to the upper floors. Opfern was the only person, besides the Queen, who had regular contact with King Cylan. She never spoke of him, and firmly rejected all inquiries with hard eyes and a disapproving frown. Mary never asked her the status of the Royal Family; the increasingly-haunted look in her friend's eyes, the growing veil of sadness she stoically tried to keep hidden, these were all Mary needed to know that time was running short.

That day, after the meeting of the Advisory Council, Mary and Opfern had, as always, went for the midday meal. When they passed by the Tressalon quarters, both women paused at an unusual sight. Princess Karen, dressed in some new, flowing dress of blue and grey, and wearing a small gold circlet around her blonde hair, was speaking with the Twins, Rasha and Jalad Tressalon. The children of the Baron and Baroness Tressalon, were, in normal times, the pinpoints of nearly all chaos in Castle Calonar. They were irrepressible in their boundless enthusiasm. Both often seemed to nearly vibrate with energy, laughing and running throughout the great castle, exploring and playing and causing the staff no end of exasperation. Since the departure of their mother, though, the Tressalon Twins had gone almost unseen. They spent most of their time in their family's rooms. When they were seen, often the brother and sister were only ever in the company of their father. As Rashid wilted since the assassination attempt on Kyla, the spymaster had seemed to become dependent on his children.

Once, Karen had been a frequent companion of the Twins. The once-introverted princess had difficulty making new friends, and the three children had been raised together. They shared the same tutors, the same bodyguards, and many of the same interests. Despite Karen being a year or so than the two, she remained in their company even as she approached her time of maturing. Now, she was noticeably taller than the twins, and beginning her difficult physical adjustment into adulthood. Rasha and Jalad, however, seemed determined to hold on to their youth for as long as possible.

Mary and Opfern paused at the end of the hallway separating the Tressalon quarters with those of Kyla and Prince Rogan. All castle staff knew to wait at the outskirts when important matters were discussed, and Karen had the same intent visage as had come to dominate her in recent days. Somehow, this had transferred to the Twins, as well. Brother and sister stood still, intent, listening as their older friend spoke seriously with them. At last, Karen glanced at the waiting women. her pearlescent eyes passed over Mary, as though the princess could not bear to look at her too long, and fixed on Opfern. As was becoming increasingly common, Karen's gaze focused on the person and looked beyond. Mary had learned the signs of the new Truthsayer's vision, of her as-yet inexperienced expressions as she saw what the Wind of Fate revealed. Karen looked at Opfern, and an instant of great sadness washed over the princess' young face.

"Lunch," Opfern said hesitantly, having seen the same thing Mary had.

Karen nodded and turned back to the Twins. She whispered one last thing before leaving, continuing on with the innumerable errands that seemed to fill her current days. The Twins came forward.

"We'll take it," Rasha said, her pearlescent eyes shadowed with new worry.

"Are you sure?" Mary asked.

Jalad helped his sister. "Father doesn't want to be disturbed." The Halvan twins, small reflections of their father, spoke sadly, but firmly. They took the food and drink and returned to their quarters, firmly shutting the door.

Mary and Opfern glanced at each other, but the younger shrugged away the concern both felt. The maid never wavered in either her loyalty to House Calonar, or her dismissal of all things she felt were outside of her duty. Mary watched as her friend returned to the staircase and resumed her trip back to the side of her Queen.

"Stop being so damned stubborn!" Ilse's voice echoed down the hall, carried as much by the acoustics of Castle Calonar's architecture as from the priestess' growing frustration.

There was a response muted by the closed doors as Mary resumed her approach. The handmaiden nodded to the group of soldiers standing outside Kyla's quarters. Since the assassination attempt, the assignment had changed. Before, when the Archaeknights were present in the castle, one of their number would stand at this post. A single member of that legendary group was enough to thwart any threat, and their loyalty was unquestionable. When Ward had taken his team to support Prince Rogan's mission, he had left Lukas, the traitorous Archaeknight-in-training. After that monster's failed assassination attempt, the Advisory Council had reached a fast consensus, and the protective force around the noble family was modified. Now, a group stood outside the princess' chambers: two soldiers assigned by Klug Rainer, two of the City Watch assigned by Remm Stonebearer, one of Rashid Tressalon's agents, and one of Esha's adepts. A similar group stood at the Royal Apartments. This mixing of agencies reduced the chance of treachery, but reinforced the growing suspicion plaguing House Calonar's forces.

Even Mary, handmaiden to Kyla and her near-constant companion, was subject to the heightened security. She stopped several paces before the door. One of the guardsmen stepped forward to inspect the cart Mary was pushing. Upon it was lunch, just as it was each time, each day, that the handmaiden made this same trip. Despite the familiarity, still she stopped and was inspected each time she left from and then returned to Kyla's quarters. The guardsman carefully lifted each silver lid and looked under each dish. "How long this time?" Mary asked, nodding towards the door.

Another guardsman laughed slightly. "I think her Highness is trying to get some fresh air."

"What part of 'bed rest' do you not understand!?!" came Ilse's shouted demand.

"Ah," Mary answered as the adept came forward with a small crystal. The meal and cart just checked by the soldier was now mystically inspected. The grey-robed apprentice passed the magical device over the entire cart and all its contents. She also, Mary noticed, subtly passed it over the guardsman, as well. Trust and camaraderie, once the foundations of House Calonar, had become fleeting since rumor of a traitor had spread. Normally, the handmaiden said nothing when she spotted these little acts of mistrust; this time, she acted. "No," Mary whispered, putting a hand on the adept's as her inspection-crystal passed more over the soldier than the meal.

"But-"

The handmaiden held up her hand. "No," she repeated. Mary then raised her voice a bit, looking at each of the bodyguards in turn. "No more of that. No more suspicion, no more accusation. We all serve the same House, the same city. Don't let them divide us." The handmaiden then made to push the food-laden cart forward. With only the briefest pause, the other guardsman nodded and opened the door for her. As Mary passed, she saw from the corner of her eye the other servants of House Calonar looking at each other and sharing a tense, though warming, set of smiles and nods.

"You are impossible!" Ilse snapped over her shoulder, emerging from Kyla's bedchamber. The harried priestess seemed on the verge of an exhausted explosion. Seeing her partner-in-suffering, Ilse approached while shaking her head. Normally, her long hair was kept in a simple Northlands' braid, much as Mary kept her own. As their princess' confinement continued, however, along with her ongoing attempts at escape, Ilse's hair was becoming less a modest style of reserved femininity, and more a tangle of frustrated animosity. "I swear," she said, taking a small batch of nuts from the tray without thinking and sampling them, "the next traitor gets a clean attempt!"

Mary had tried protecting Kyla, of course. As a handmaiden, her life was dedicated to the service and protection of her princess. She had not failed to try, only to succeed. Lukas had tossed her aside like she was nothing. Mary's only success had been in delaying the would-be assassin long enough for Ilse to arrive with her great magic, granted by the Harvest Mother. "You know that's not true," Mary smiled at her friend.

"Ugh!" Ilse replied, as frustrated with herself as with anything. Mary made a point, as she always did, of not looking around the room. She did not look through the open door to Prince Rogan's study, where Kyla had been attacked. She did not look back at the short hall through which she had just passed, where Lukas had forced Mary down and beaten her. Ilse herself had healed her friend's body, removed all the marks, all the blood and every physical sign of suffering. Still, Mary felt the wounds, the sting of slaps and punches. Most importantly, the handmaiden did not look at the spot on the floor, still stained despite hours of intense scrubbing, where Lukas had been mutilated by the magic of Kyla's unborn son. "You're even quieter than usual," Isle noted.

Mary glanced up, away from the places she had not been looking. She put a gentle hand on a box lying amidst the food her friend had been tasting. "I found it," the handmaiden and archivist of House Calonar whispered.

Ilse set down the small cutlet of roasted meat she had been bringing to her mouth. She glanced at the box, only noticing it once made aware of the box's presence. "You're sure?"

Mary took her friend's hand and guided it towards the box. "You tell me."

Ilse breathed in. As a priestess of the Harvest Mother, she was imbued with mystical sensitivity, much more so than Mary or any other person without training and experience. The box was almost a living thing. "It didn't want to be found," Ilse whispered, then tilted her head slightly. "Until now...?"

Mary nodded. "I found it in the Temple archives. It was sitting on a shelf, in plain sight. I must've gone past it a hundred times this winter and spring. I never even noticed it, until this morning."

Ilse looked at her friend. "Are you going to give it to her?"

There was a long, heavy pause. Kyla and the Queen had assigned Mary to explore the archives of the Temple of the Lady of Light. In recent weeks, the archivist and handmaiden had been exploring the past Sisters Superior of that order, Kyla's predecessors. Her mission had been to find exactly what lie in the box. "Should I?" Mary asked.

Ilse was her closest confidant. The two women had arrived in the Northern Keep at nearly the same time. Both were daughters of common fathers, raised to venerate House Calonar. They had both worked in the castle at many of the same tasks until Ilse had been accepted as an acolyte at the Temple of the Harvest Mother. They had been roommates and co-conspirators for years. They had even been appointed as Kyla's handmaidens together. Though, in reality, they acted as the princess' ladies-in-waiting as much as anything else, despite their mutual lack of noble title. "What's wrong?" Ilse asked.

Mary wanted to tell her about the horrid vault under the Sylvai Shrine. She wanted to confess to Ilse all the fears, all the wretched truths learned in that terrible place. Princess Karen's transformation, her imbuement with Truthsight. Queen Nora's diminishment and breakdown. Worst, Mary wanted to tell her best friend of the rancid knowledge that the city would soon die, with nearly everyone in it. No, the young woman realized. That was not the worst of the knowledge Mary was now forced to endure. The worst was the gnawing, gaping doubt for those in whom she had placed her loyalty.

Mary was about to say everything. She was on the very cusp of unleashing all she knew, all she feared, all she suspected. The young woman was at the precipice of a terrible cliff with the ground crumbling under her feet. She so desperately wanted someone, anyone, to share in her fall. She looked into her friend's large, inviting eyes, seeing there the comfort Mary could find, the easing of her own burden but transferring at least a part of it to another. And she stopped.

"I just miss Tomas," Mary half-confessed. "I miss having him… to talk to."

Ilse's wide-open face revealed her disbelief. The priestess was not a woman of deception. Her emotions were as plain on her face as the summer sun was in the sky. She did not press, however. "I need a break," the other handmaiden said. She quickly arranged the meal on the tray and turned to leave. Ilse put a light hand on her friend's arm. "When you're ready."

Mary took her friend into a hug, refusing the tears that seemed to always press from behind her eyes. She paused, and looked at her friend. "I think I've got a handle on things here," she said, speculatively. "You could take a little time to go down and visit with someone."

Ilse blushed slightly and looked away. "I don't know what you're-"

"Come on," Mary interrupted. "The way you've been looking at him? The way you put a little more swing in the hips?" The handmaiden swung her own in great exaggeration of the same motion she had noticed Ilse making whenever Vincent was within sight. "Or the way you 'accidentally' dropped that tray and had to bend over to pick it up?" Mary let one of the silver lids fall to the floor and then, greatly exaggerating, bent over to retrieve it, throwing a wicked look over her shoulder at the now-furiously blushing Ilse.

The priestess mumbled excuses, refusing to meet her friend's eyes. Mary once more hugged Ilse. "He's been looking," she whispered. "He tries to hide it, but every time you walk in the room, his eyes are all over you."

"Really?" Ilse whispered back.

"Why don't you go take him some lunch?" Mary suggested. "Those agents all work so hard, and I know for a fact he's in his office. You could pick up some food for all of them, and maybe give his a little more… attention?" Ilse looked at her friend, biting her lower lip with eagerness flooding into her eyes. She nodded and left, nearly bouncing as she made her way from the Princess' quarters.

Mary breathed deep and walked into her princess' bedchamber. The room was immaculately clean. Ilse was compulsive in that regard, unable to leave a place disorderly. Each chair was purposefully set, each table without dust or debris. The bed was made, with only one corner of blankets folded up as silent evidence of Kyla's most recent rebellion. The windows were open to invite in the warm summer breeze, and the blue and grey curtains tied back in celebration of the day. The doors to the balcony were also open, in defiance of Ilse's demands that they be kept shut. Mary shook her head and went out, knowing exactly to where their belligerent princess had gone.

Kyla was, as best they could tell, in the final months of her pregnancy. So few Halvans were ever born that virtually no one living understood the nature of carrying a baby of that mixed race. The King was Halvan, of course; the great irony of history being that the world's greatest hero was one of that disdained race. Each of his three children had inherited the same mystical affinity and pearlescent eyes. Queen Nora, employing her Truthsight, had revealed that Kyla's son would also be Halvan. As such, Ilse and the other healers assigned to the princess' care were all struggling to predict the progress of Kyla's first pregnancy.

"Lunch!" Mary said with forced positivity.

Her princess was lying on a divan, her pearlescent eyes closed and her chin raised towards the sun. "Is the warden gone?" she asked in a flat voice.

"Ilse was called to the Temple," Mary lied, arranging the cart beside Kyla. Her princess' advancing pregnancy had begun to take serious effect on her small body. Her already-impressive breasts had swollen even further. Her stomach was growing, even more so than for a Human. Kyla was smaller than normal, reflecting the Sylvai lineage of her Halvan race, and so her child was large in comparison. Several attempts had been made to modify the princess' clothes, or even to sew new dresses to accommodate the awkward disproportions of her changing body. In the past week, with the arrival of summer's warm days and nights, Kyla had simply abandoned this effort. "The clerics instructed that you stay covered," Mary reminded her princess.

Kyla, jewel of House Calonar and beloved by the Northlands, stretched languidly, running her hands along her bare stomach and breasts. "His Highness enjoys the sun," she argued. "And so does his mommy."

Mary took a light blanket from within the bedchamber and placed it over her princess. Very nearly before the cover was set, it was snatched off, hurled aside by some unseen hand. Kyla looked up at her handmaiden and smiled. "See?" she said innocently.

Mary picked up the blanket and brought it back to where Kyla reclined. The handmaiden sat beside her princess and place a light hand on her extending stomach. "Your mommy was hurt, remember?" she said softly. "She needs to rest and be kept safe, so we're going to make her, ok?"

The child within sullenly remained still, and Mary placed the blanket once again over Kyla, though she pulled a corner aside to allow the sun to continue glowing down upon her stomach. The handmaiden then pulled the cart closer and held a plate to Kyla.

"How was the council meeting?" the princess asked intently.

Mary carefully explained the new strategy. Kyla listened while eating her meal, but her pearlescent eyes remained fixed on her lady-in-waiting. "Stop," the princess commanded, setting aside her food. Kyla leaned as best she could towards Mary and narrowed her glowing eyes. "What's wrong?" she asked.

The handmaiden stood and busied herself with the meal, shuffling plates needlessly.

"Tell me," Kyla insisted.

Mary breathed deep. "I honestly don't know how much I can... how much I should..." The handmaiden again took a deep, steadying breath. "Highness, your mother... your sister..."

"Karen has the Truthsight," Kyla guessed. "Mother passed it to her."

Mary nodded.

"And they had you accompany them. You saw... whatever is down there."

"Some of it," the handmaiden answered. She walked to the balcony railing and looked out. From high atop Castle Calonar, the city was still beautiful, despite the bustle of war preparations. The forest beyond was even more serene, more breathtaking. Mary knew this sight was a lie, a falsehood disguising the horrible violence occurring out amidst those trees. "Your mother was clear that I wouldn't see everything, and would understand less."

Kyla leaned back, reclining once again as she almost incidentally moved the blanket away from her torso to let the warming sun caress her body. "Aunt Alexia talked to me a few times about the Truthsight," the princess said softly. "She explained how it affected Mother and why I wouldn't inherit it, why it had to pass to Karen." Kyla looked at Mary. "Has she changed?"

Mary turned away from the lying forest. She nodded. "It's not a great change," she said both to herself and her princess. "She's still your little sister." 'I think' were the words the handmaiden did not add. "But now she talks like your mother does... did."

"Where is Mother now?"

"Still resting. Cardinal Tain is watching over your father."

Kyla further threw aside the blanket, waddling herself to the edge of the divan. "Let's go."

Mary moved forward, putting a restraining hand on her princess. "You're supposed to be resting."

"I've been resting for weeks!"

"Days."

"Too long!" Kyla snapped. "We're in a crisis! I'm supposed to be in charge; how can I just lounge around up here while...!?!"

Mary insistently guided her princess back onto the divan. "You're not 'lounging around,' and you damned well know it." Although the handmaiden's voice was as soft and submissive as always, her words, especially her use of profanity, communicated her unflinching resolve. "You almost died." She put a hand on Kyla's stomach. "He almost died. As a mother, your first responsibility is to your child. Ilse says you have to stay off your feet. So, you're staying off your feet, for him."

"Oh, what would she know!?!"

Mary said nothing, only stared at her princess with unflinching eyes. Kyla could only bear that gentle onslaught so long before grumbling, "Fine!" and lying back. Her handmaiden returned the blanket to its proper place, once again arranging it to allow the sun to shine on the sleeping heir of House Calonar. "I just feel so…!" Kyla grumbled, but accepted the glass of water.

"We all need to feel useful," Mary agreed. Her eyes went to the box. "Especially when our loved ones are in danger, and there's something we can do to help."

Kyla followed the gaze. "What's that?" she asked, finally made aware of the box.

Mary hesitated one last time. Then, "Princes, when you gave me the task of searching through your Temple records, do you remember what you told me?"

"Yes. I told you that the power of past Sisters Superior was great, and that we could use the secrets they held."

"You also told me that, if I were to uncover anything dangerous, I should trust me heart as to whether or not I pass the secret on to you."

Kyla nodded. "Since you're not a Sister, you wouldn't be able to use anything you discovered. That's one of the reasons I named you my archivist." She put a warm hand on Mary's. "I'm trusting you with the responsibility to separate what we should know and what we should forget."

"I'm not sure I'm the right person anymore," the handmaiden replied quietly. "Perhaps Medaka. She has the most experience of anyone. She's been guiding me in my research."

"Medaka's a Sister," Kyla reminded. "Anything she found, she could use."

"Your Highness…" Words failed. Mary stood and again looked out on the deceptive tranquility of Wildelves Wood. "I don't know if I trust… myself. How can I know the secrets I uncover are supposed to be uncovered. How do I know I'm not unleashing something… terrible."

"Mary, come here."

The handmaiden obeyed. She sat down beside her princess, who pulled her into a tight embrace. "I don't know what you saw down there. I don't think I'd want to know. My mother chose you because she trusted you. As far as I know, Mother and Aunt Alexia only ever allowed two women to accompany them down there." She rested a cheek against Mary's shoulder. "And now three. I can't think of any greater… I can't image the trust she had in you. If my mother believes in you that much, then so do I. Whatever you think should be done, that's what we'll do."

Mary said nothing for a little while. Her eyes remained on the forest and the horizon, and her thoughts drifted. "Who were the two women?" she asked.

"What?"

The handmaiden leaned into her princess' embrace. "Who were the other women who… went down there?"

"Did you ever meet Raven?" Kyla asked. "Aunt Alexia's partner?"

"Her Walker? The dark-haired Sylva?" Mary shook her head.

"Raven was one. She went everywhere with Aunt Alexia. Protected her, shared everything."

"Did it change her?"

Kyla shrugged slightly. "That happened before I was born. I never knew Raven before. But she was quiet, reserved. She had this… look in her eyes."

"And the other?"

"Samantha," this Kyla said with ice growing into her loving voice.

"The Hero of Fate? The one who…?" None in the Northlands spoke much of Samantha of the Hill People, the Gunrsvein woman who had joined the Heroes of Fate. Everyone knew the legends of that mysterious woman, of course.

Kyla only grunted. An angry kind of sound that spoke more than any words. Samantha was the dark shadow of House Calonar. Stories spoke of a love affair with King Cylan, sometimes before his marriage to Queen Nora, sometimes after. In some tales, Samantha of the Hill People was a seductress, a rival of the beloved mother of the Northlands. In others, she was a pitiable victim, lost to powers beyond her understanding.

"Wait," Mary paused, considering. "If Raven accompanied the Lady Alexia, then Samantha…?"

"Accompanied Mother," Kyla finished grimly. Her handmaiden understood that tone, that tension, and dropped the subject. The implications roiled in her mind, though. Raven the Walker, stoic warrior and companion of the Lady Alexia. Samantha of the Hill People, dark secret of House Calonar. And now Mary.

"I…" the handmaiden and archivist did not make a conscious choice. The words came as though of their own volition. "I think I might have found the secret that your predecessors most wanted to be left forgotten. But… it's the secret you could most use."

"It's that dangerous?" Kyla asked, looking up at her archivist.

"I really don't know, your Highness. I'm not entirely sure how it… what it is."

Kyla put her hand on her friend's shoulder. "Mary, if this secret is as dangerous as you fear, then maybe we should leave it to history."

Mary stood. "No," the archivist said firmly. "It's… I've read most of the diaries of past Sisters Superior. They kept making these references to something I didn't understand. Now I do." She turned and looked full at her princess. "In the past, the Sisters of the Lady of Light had a power that helped their warriors to defend, to protect. It made them stronger, more united." Mary looked out on the city, almost sensing the tension, the recriminations and suspicions that pulled at the seams of the Northern Keep like a worn dress on the verge of tearing. "They were a light of hope and sisterhood in dark times."

Mary moved back to the food tray and put a hand on the box. "Have you ever heard of a Sister Superior named Raenama?" she asked.

Kyla thought a moment. "No, I don't think so."

"Raenama was a Sylva maiden who dedicated herself to the Lady of Light. She lived in Pelsemoria during the Uldra Uprising. In the final years, there was an outbreak of Starfell Plague in the capital."

"I remember from my history lessons," Kyla nodded. "The Sylvai Empress ordered an evacuation of the city. The Uldra learned about it and tried to attack. That led to the Battle of Denisylor Valley."

"The histories of the Uldra Uprising focus on the battles, the movement of armies and the terrible slaughters." Mary smiled ruefully. "They focus on what the men were doing. But they make only brief mention of the plague. Pelsemoria was in chaos. People were getting sick. They didn't understand the disease. Suspicion and paranoia was everywhere. Riots were starting to break out. There was no way for the Empress to save anyone." Again Mary put a hand on the box. "Raenama lived through this. She only had a handful of Sisters with her, and they were all but helpless to bring peace."

The handmaiden and archivist sat on the edge of the divan. "Highness, in all that chaos, Raenama discovered," she paused, considering. "Or... perhaps she was shown..." She shook her head. "In any case, Raenama revealed a power to the other Sisters."

"What was it?"

"A new type of magic," Mary replied. "Or an old one. A Wind of Magic unheard of. Raenama is vague about how she discovered it, something about visitors from the distant west. She implies that Stalline the Wise knew of the Wind, but few others."

"The first adept," Kyla whispered, considering. "What was this Wind?"

"Dreams, your Highness. Raenama had power over dreams. The Wind of Dreams allowed her, and her fellow Sisters, to communicate through dreams, to share those dreams between many people. She helped unite the city, to pacify it, allowing for the evacuation."

"Why hasn't anyone ever heard of this?" Kyla demanded.

Mary retrieved parchment scrolls from a large pocket in her white apron. "This is from the chronicle of Venna, Sister Superior during the reign of Emperor Chlodocar Majestos. She says that, after the collapse of the Sylvai Empire, the Republic took control and abolished all religions except Adamism. The Sisters of the Lady of Light were forced into hiding. Venna tells of a small group of Sisters who refused to hide.

Instead, they tried using the Wind of Dreams to manipulate the new government, to try and take control."

"I remember that chronicle," Kyla nodded. "A group of renegade Sisters broke away and set up a temple in Pelsemoria. As I remember, they were arrested and executed." She looked at Mary. "But there wasn't any mention of the Wind of Dreams."

Mary nodded. "I'm putting together different sources to better understand what was happening. The key to understanding it all was the chronicle of Raenama. She says that, after the Uprising, she fled with a few others to Maka."

"What was she doing there?"

Mary smiled. "Well, among other things, she was having a son named Khaine."

Kyla blinked. "Raenama was the mother of Khaine? The Sylvu Walker who joined with the Heroes of Fate?"

The handmaiden and archivist nodded. "She also says that she taught some of the mysteries of the Wind of Dreams to Khaine though, since he wasn't a Speaker, he could never master it. Raenama learned of the renegade Sisters and secretly returned to Pelsemoria. They had been seduced by the Wind of Dreams into something darker."

Mary looked with serious eyes at her princess. "There's something about the Wind of Dreams. Something... seductive. The few Sisters who remained after the collapse of the Sylvai Empire became split. Half maintained the traditions of loving support, led by Raenama, resisting the seduction of the Wind of Dreams. The other half embraced Venna's more assertive powers. These dark Sisters were drawn deep into the Wind of Dreams, embracing its darkness, its potential for nightmares. They used it to control men, to twist their minds and their hearts into obedience."

The princess' face went deathly pale. "That's impossible! None of our Sisters would ever do such a thing! It goes against everything the Lady of Light stands for!"

"Venna herself confirms much of this, Highness. She speaks of the danger of the Wind of Dreams, of becoming lost within it. But, she believed her renegade Sisters could control the Wind, use it to pacify the Republic and end the persecution of non-Adamic religions. A secret war was fought in the streets of Pelsemoria and in the nightmares of its people. Dreams became battlefields."

Kyla shook her head, the terrible possibility of such power, and its abuse, playing across her beautiful face. "What happened?" she finally asked in a small voice.

"Raenama feared the Adamic Chuch, once it learned what was happening, would hunt down and destroy all the remaining Sisters of the Lady of Light. In an act of desperation, Raenama challenged Venna to some kind of duel within their Dreams. Her diary and Venna's don't go into any detail about their battle. The result, though, was that Venna was left powerless. She surrendered herself to the Church, and died on the pyre. Her followers were also stripped of their powers, but allowed to flee the city."

"And Raenama?"

"Her diary ends there. A few later Sisters Superior mention her and Venna, but there's no mention of what happened to Raenama after Venna's death. They also sometimes speak of the power those women held, but as the centuries passed, these references stopped sounding like history and started sounding like legend. My guess is the secrets ended with them.

"Then the Wind of Dreams was lost?"

"No, Highness. Raenama recorded the basic disciplines of the Wind of Dreams." Mary opened the box and drew from it a small scroll. It was bound by a golden ring upon which was engraved a sitting cat with three four-pointed stars around its head. "The chronicle warns that only a Sister Superior can break this seal." She handed the bound scroll to Kyla.

The current Sister Superior of the Lady of Light held the bound scroll reverently. Kyla's pearlescent eyes were locked on the golden symbol, the holy sigil of her goddess. "Mary," she asked in a hushed voice. "I…"

Mary put a hand over her princess' as they held the bound scroll. "You trust me," she said gently. "I must trust… I trust you."

Kyla looked out at the city. "Too much is happening too fast. My father, my mother, my husband, all… unavailable." She grimaced at her swelling belly. "And his Highness here is making things complicated too."

"Your sister seems to be… asserting herself," Mary offered.

Kyla nodded. "Good. But I want someone who I trust, who I know." She sighed. "Someone who's still herself." She looked up at her friend. "I need you to do something for me."

The barracks of the Calonar House Guard had groups of soldiers in rough formations. Blocks of men in armor were being organized by the bellows of perpetually-angry sergeants. Runners were speeding this way and that, trying to bring order to the chaos unfolding. Supplies were being brought forward and horses saddled. Adepts and agents from Rashid's service milled about as well. Standing in the center of the maelstrom, his voice and his will bringing order, was Colonel Klug Rainer.

The veteran blinked in surprise as Mary approached him. In her hands was a golden cord and a scroll. The handmaiden lifted these, showing them to Colonel Rainer. "What's an aide-de-camp?" she asked.

Chapter 20

Chaos reigned in the northern sections of Wildelves Wood. The village of Willowmoss, a community of both Human and Sylvai, was ablaze. Smoke clouded the air and chocked the frightful cries of the desperate people. Domestic animals ran in all directions, bleating their own terror. Blood adorned every structure, a grisly paint befouling every home and shop. Bodies bled into the small pool before the Adamic chapel. Children wailed over their fallen mothers. Hope was fading against the rising darkness.

A column of refugees was fleeing south. Human and Sylvai marched together, equally scarred with blood and soot. Precious few possessions were clung to by the miserable people. A handful of wagons rolled along with the people bearing the injured and whatever supplies could be saved in their desperate retreat. The people were reduced to little more than hopeless animals.

Near the back of the dredging column, an older woman collapsed. Whether she fell from exhaustion or hopelessness could not be seen, but either or both were likely. Many of the refugees shambled past her, as though not seeing or, more likely, past caring. She lay there until three men spotted the old woman and hurried to help her. She looked up with eyes empty of tears, but, when seeing them, she cried once more. They were Calonar House Guard.

The soldiers were part of a small force, no more than a dozen men, riding north. The warriors stopped upon seeing the refugee column and dismounted. The sun seemed, if only for a moment, to break through, shining off their polished breastplates. The blue and grey surcoats fluttered in a brief southern wind, and the guardsmen moved without need of orders to help the desperate people. Food and water rations were distributed. The weak and elderly were placed upon the soldiers' horses. The old woman who had fallen was gently lifted, carried with reverence to a wagon, which the warriors of House Calonar themselves began pulling.

The commander, a captain by the rank insignia, barked orders. Half of his men remained helping the refugees, the rest spread out through the nearby trees. "Don't try to hide!" the officer called to his men. "Make yourselves known! We're House Calonar, dammit! There are people who need help!"

The soldiers stood tall in their breastplates and helmets. The men sweeping through the trees began making shouted calls to each other and for any other survivors. Poleaxes, the traditional weapons of the Northlands and the symbol of the

Calonar House Guard, were raised, waving in the air to offer hope for any other refugees.

They were answered with screams.

"Form up!" the captain barked to his men. Five of the soldiers remained with the column. The others coalesced into a wedge formation, their poleaxes extended. "Forward!" came the order.

The guardsmen picked up a quick march, covering distance as they advanced back up the road, but conserving their strength for what lie ahead. Within moments, the small detachment had closed upon the source of the screaming. A band of mercenaries had broken off from the pillaging of Willowmoss to descend on a handful of survivors who had been desperately trying to sneak away. Seeing this, the captain of the Calonar soldiers barked, "Duty!"

In reply the soldiers answered with a single, unified "Hooah!"

"Honor!" their commander cried.

"Hooah!" they replied.

"Humility!" came the last, completing the traditional motto of House Calonar.

"Hooah!" the soldiers' answering roar shattered the fear of the assaulted villagers, spearing it instead into the hearts of the mercenaries.

The battle was brief and vicious. The pillaging of Willowmoss abruptly stopped. Vagris' bandits and murderers were courageous when attacking desperate and often unarmed villagers, the sight of a detachment, however small, of the wrathful guardsmen of House Calonar bearing down upon them caused most of the mercenaries to break. The leader of that pack of scum, a brutish Shamashi, tried barking orders at his men in broken Velish, thundering at them to stand and fight. For his courage, the defenders of the Northlands cut him down first. The mercenaries who had been promised theft and rape, an easy campaign of terrorizing helpless victims, could not withstand the organized advance of the Calonar House Guard.

"No prisoners!" the captain barked, thrusting his poleaxe into the back of a mercenary as he tried to turn and flee. "No mercy! Send these bastards straight to Underworld!"

The bandits and thieves broke into individuals and pairs, trying to spread out and away from the disciplined soldiers. The guardsmen dispersed their close formation, breaking into a trot in groups of three and further engaging the enemy. The handful of mercenaries who had not fled at the first sight of the guardsmen were either cut down or forced into retreat in only a quarter-hour.

"Form up!" the captain called. "Let the rest of the scum run home! We're getting these people back to the Keep!"

The soldiers returned to the refugee column. Upon seeing the blood-smeared breastplates and victorious poleaxes raised high, a joyous cheer arose from the exhausted villagers. They kissed and hugged their defenders, offering them praise and blessings. The captain allowed the small celebration for only a few minutes, growling orders to get the column moving again. The large group was only just about to begin their trip to safety when there was a brief commotion from the rear. The captain looked in time to see the two men guarding the back of his formation fall, lifelessly, to the ground. "Down!" he barked, taking a knee and scanning in all directions. "Circle, civilians at the center!"

As quickly as they could, the remaining guardsmen herded the re-terrified villagers. The dirty and disheveled people were forced to the middle of their few wagons, and the soldiers ringed them with their poleaxes pointed out. "Who... what is it?" someone whispered in the suddenly-silent forest.

"Quiet!" the captain snapped. "All senses! Slow. Even. Ready."

One of the soldiers collapsed with a choked gargle, his hand going to the small blade in his throat.

"Umbra!" one of the refugees wailed.

"Steady!" the captain growled.

A thin line of rope dropped from the overhead branches, wrapping itself around another soldier's neck. The screaming man was pulled up so fast his comrades could only grasp at air. The struggling, horrified soldiers reached the dense canopy and his screams suddenly stopped. A moment of stillness passed before the victim's head fell back to the ground.

More screams, more terror filled the refugees. The captain tried calming the crowd, but was having little success. Another rope shot from the nearby shrubs, dragging another screaming soldier away. Three men, ignoring the shouted warnings of their commander, ran after their comrade. Sounds of violence and horror erupted from the trees. Metal clashed on metal. There were screams that echoed all around and then silence. Four heads, one at a time, rolled out of the treeline.

The refugees broke, scattering into the surrounding Wood.

"Enough of this!" the captain roared. Jumping to his feet, tossing aside his poleaxe, the guard commander tore his sword from its sheath and raised it high. "You want me!" he challenged. "I'm right here! Fight, coward!"

Xaemus detached himself from the shadows. The monster of Davenor shot across the road, spinning the dual-bladed sword feared by all who knew of it, and disappearing back into the surrounding trees. All this happened in the space between two heartbeats. The remaining soldiers looked at one another, then at their leader. The captain's body fell one way, his head another.

Eight days and several assassinations later, Xaemus was moving through the shadows as he entered the central pavilion of the mercenary camp, passing without alerting the two Bellonari guards standing watch. Even all the years of intense training the warriors of that Brotherhood underwent were no match for the skills of the monster of Davenor. His brutal training by the Coven of Midnight Sun made him second to none in infiltration. Neither of the two men, both dressed to match the odd conglomeration of mercenaries that had formed Vagris' army, had any indication Xaemus moved to within arm's reach of them. Had the *Xesh'lin* wished, he could have taken the life of either or both men; of course, there would have been neither challenge nor advantage in such an action.

On this morning, many days after the fall of Willomoss, Xaemus was required to speak with Vagris. Rather than navigate the various guards and sycophants who surrounded the warlord, whenever compelled to address the mercenary commander, the monster of Davenor did so by the most direct means possible. Thus, none of the mercenaries, captives, *Xesh'lin* slavers, or Bellonari who had taken up residence in Vagris' expansive encampment noticed as the hunter moved among the various tents towards the warlord's own large pavilion.

Once inside, Xaemus noted without surprise that Vagris was not there. The general of this mercenary army rarely spent much time in his own tent. Despite his many faults, the warlord was a good leader. He took great care to inspect his warriors and give personal instructions to each detachment before they left on another raid. The Bellonar General could also be off indulging in one of his personal grotesque entertainments. Xaemus decided, rather than perusing his target, he would wait.

The hunter's patience was rewarded quickly. After only a few hours, the entrance flaps parted and someone entered. It was not Vagris, Xaemus immediately noted, but a slave. She was *Sy'lva*. She was not a maiden, as the *Xesh'lin* had first surmised, but was rather in the midst of the Change. She had yet to swell into full maturity, but was well underway. Further, the girl had been forced into the Veil. The thin, white fabric covered the top of her head and, most importantly, her eyes to prevent exposure to her enthralling tears. The Veil was held in place with a small silver chain tied under the bridge of her small nose and at the back of her head. No, the hunter realized, not silver, but platinum. She had been forced into one of the costumes Humans so loved to use in the humiliation of a *Sy'lva*: light and silken and doing little to hide her nakedness.

A moment passed before Xaemus realized the truth. This was Komalan, the Speaker's daughter taken by Vagris weeks ago. The warlord had bound her in this humiliating outfit not seen since the fall of the Human Republic. Her growing mane, the living symbol of her life and her feminine grace, had been shorn to almost nothing; all the better, of course, for securing the veil. The righteous authority of her gait had been replaced, crushed already in the bonds of her servitude to an insipid Human.

She still bore the Wyrdmark upon her now close-cropped hair, her dully-glowing eyes, and her weathered flesh. Before coming to this forest, Xaemus had not seen a

Vagris sat down and held out his hand. The Daughter of the Wyld placed a cup in his outstretched hand and filled the cup with wine. "What tasks?" the warlord demanded. "Fak'Har hasn't told me of any other operations."

"Our employer tells you only what you need to know."

"Apparently, I need to know what in Underworld you've been up to," the Bellonar General countered. "Since my operations have been conflicting with yours."

"Indeed." The hunter moved to a large map on the table at which Vagris sat. Xaemus pointed. "I have been tasked with the removal of specific targets in preparation for your assault. Members of Calonar's intelligence service, certain officers within the House Guard. Adepts, when the opportunity is presented. With the raids your forces are conducting, those targets are either grouping with large numbers of soldiers, making my work take longer than projected, or they are retreating to the Keep, which will extend the timeline even more significantly."

Vagris glanced up at his ally. "I thought you were the monster of Davenor," the warlord mocked. "Isn't it true no target can escape you?"

"This is correct. However, the amount of time each target is beginning to require has begun to interfere with Fak'Har's overall timeline. My tasks are meant to expedite yours, when the siege begins."

"In other words, you're starting to look bad to the Shadowed Mage." Vagris stood and handed the empty cup to his *Syl'va* slave. The warlord shook his head. "I won't slow the progress of my operations just to help you preserve your reputation."

"I will be clear," Xaemus said without emotion. "I do not fail in the tasks I undertake. I have specific targets to eliminate at specific intervals. Your military operations are threatening to delay that. Eliminating the forces protecting my targets is becoming unfeasible. Therefore, if you do not slow your raids, I will delay your operations by eliminating your army's leadership."

Vagris narrowed his eyes. "I don't respond well to threats," he stated flatly.

"Nevertheless, you do respond. And, in this case, you will respond obediently."

The Bellonar weighed his options before answering. "Very well, Xeshlin. Since I can't afford to lose too many of my captains, and having you killed would be more trouble than it's worth… for now, I'll limit my raids."

"Good," the hunter replied. Turning to leave, his eyes of burning blood passed over the Daughter of the Wyld and held for a moment. Xaemus paused. "One final matter before I return to my tasks," he said.

"Quickly," Vagris demanded.

"I would purchase your new slave."

The warlord started and turned, glancing first at the hunter and then to the *Syl'va*. The Daughter of the Wyld gave no indication of emotion, offering no hint of an opinion. "Why?" Vagris asked.

"My reasons are irrelevant to you," Xaemus replied. "I desire the slave and have funds enough for a reasonable price."

Vagris narrowed his eyes. "The reasons are not irrelevant, I think. The slave represents an investment of acquisition and training." He glanced over at the *Syl'va* and sniffed. "I'm not about to just hand off all that effort without good reason."

The hunter did not respond at first. "I have an interest," he finally said. "That is all that matters. Your interest would best be served in selling her to me."

"Does this have something to do with her mother being a Speaker?"

At the word, the title of nobility that was all that remained of the lost *Im'peri'a*, Xaemus' eyes of burning blood flickered to the Daughter of the Wyld. She gave no betrayal of emotion. The hunter's grip tightened on his weapon as the memory of the Speaker's fate, her end upon the pyre, returned. With a blade on both ends of the long hilt, his weapon was unique, known and feared throughout *Ar'ae'el* for all the lives that had been lost at either of its deadly ends. Vagris had faced that weapon once before and lived; the likelihood he would have to face such a trial again grew.

"There are slaves aplenty to be found in the Wood," Xaemus said slowly. "Get another. This one will be sought by the Coven to whom you have bound yourself. They will pressure you, first with treasure, then power, then threats of violence, until they have her. I would have her first."

"I'm still waiting for a reason why I should sell this one to you," Vagris countered. The warlord was visibly aware of his lack of a weapon. True he had a dagger on his belt, but in battle with the monster of Davenor, he would certainly prefer a proper sword. "Especially if the Coven of the Puma's Leash would offer so much for her."

The hunter moved his weapon slightly forward. The threat was obvious to both men, although neither betrayed the slightest emotion on their face. "Have you grown so confident in your Bellonari training that you would test yourself against me?" Xaemus asked.

"I'm not just another member of the Brotherhood," Vagris pointed out. "I'm a General."

"You are a General of the Bellonari through deceit and poison," the Hunter reminded. "You did not face Beckett through honorable combat."

"How many have you poisoned?" the warlord asked. "At least one."

"True. King Cylan is falling to the *kay'ay'eil'nas*, brewed and delivered by my hand. I, who infiltrated the Northern Keep, past the soldiers of House Calonar, and even the fabled Archaeknights, to poison the last surviving Hero of Fate. What have you accomplished General? Not even the death of Rogan Eigenhard, as you claimed for so long."

Vagris growled at the *Xesh'lin*'s words. Among the Bellonari Brotherhood, Xaemus knew the warlord still carried the shame of his dual failure, not only for the survival of the traitor, but also for Vagris' false claims of success. "You push too far," he warned. "I have a dozen of my brothers in this camp. Not even you, with your precious sword, could stand against that many Bellonari."

"Perhaps that is so," Xaemus conceded. "But there are a few factors you must consider. You would still have to explain the deaths of so many brothers to the other Generals. Another failure which they would not tolerate. More importantly, you would have to explain your failures to Fak'Har, and the Shadowed Mage would be even less forgiving upon his arrival. Without the Bellonari to protect you, Fak'Har would make a mockery of your flesh." The hunter pointed one tip of his double-bladed weapon at the warlord. "But all of that is assuming you survived your battle with me."

Vagris smiled then. He grinned with vile amusement and spoke a single word. *"Queltuasor."*

Xaemus froze.

The Bellonari General continued to smile but turned and gestured for the *Sy'lva* to bring him another cup of wine. "That's right hunter. The Brotherhood learned her name long ago: the secret you hoped had died with the Coven of Midnight Sun."

Taking the cup his slave brought, Vagris turned back to Xaemus. "The Brotherhood knew someday you'd become a problem. We dedicated a great deal of effort in uncovering that name. All so that, when the time came, one of the Order could take control of your weapon."

Xaemus said nothing. He held his weapon out, extended, in front of Vagris. "Try," he said.

"It's enough for you to know there exists the chance. You cannot have my slave, not at any price. You want her, but not as a slave. I know that now, and that gives me an advantage. The Coven of the Puma's Leash wants her, and that also gives me an advantage. I know the name of your weapon, and that gives me an advantage as well. I'll keep my word and reduce the raids, but only because it suits me. In the meantime, return to your duties, and don't return unless I, or our employer, call."

The hunter lowered his arm. "You believe you have power over me," he said. "And you are fool enough to think you can control the Sorcerous Sisters. You are not the first to believe this. You are correct that I have an interest in your slave." Xaemus closed the distance between himself and Vagris, until there was none separating them. "Understand a simple truth, General. I will return often to check on her welfare. You will not be aware of my presence. Should any harm come to her, by your hand or any other, you will have to test the limits of this control you believe you have, since I will kill you… eventually."

Xaemus turned and departed.

Chapter 21

Once, only hours before, this town had been called Snowholm. Northernmost of the communities loyal to House Calonar, this had been the home of generations of loyal citizens. Long before King Cylan had crowned himself, the people of this land had long since seen him as their true sovereign, not some emperor or council of entitled nobles in the luxurious south. Snowholm's reputation was one of dedication to House Calonar, providing food, raw materials, textiles, and recruits for the Northlands' military. Of all the towns, villages, and farmsteads scattered across King Cylan's domain, Snowholm, so the saying went, was the heart of loyalty.

Little wonder, then, that Fak'Har would choose this place as the first to fall.

"Pull back! Pull back!" The man, a sergeant by the rank insignia on his dented and soiled armor, was trying to organize his soldiers. The town was in flames. This was not like the destruction of other, smaller communities at the hands of Vagris' mercenaries. In those cases, thatch roofs were set ablaze. Crops had been destroyed. People were either killed or rounded up for sale to the *Xesh'lin*. Livestock was slaughtered or taken. Panicked refugees scattered. Little of that was in evidence in the place once called Snowholm.

Everything was burning. Wood, stone, flesh, all of it became little more than fuel. Screams at first filled the air but within minutes were lost amidst the roar of the growing inferno. Farmland was fast becoming a charred hellscape. People had been slain whether they tried to flee or stood to fight. Nothing had been stolen; all was lost in the onslaught. The garrison of Calonar House Guard had stood, and been burnt. A handful of them, under the desperate command of this sergeant, now tried to organize the pitiful, desperate flight into something more like a retreat.

"On me!" the sergeant yelled again, waving his bloody arm. Its partner, holding the man's sword, was gone, consumed by the fire. "Everyone, on me!" He waved his remaining arm in the air, trying to draw the attention of his few remaining guardsmen. None listened.

Even the legendary loyalty and discipline of the Calonar House Guard had broken. Impressively, they had stood for almost a full minute in the face of the advancing Uldra warmachines. They formed their spear wall, interlocking and advancing their poleaxes, barking reassurances to each other. Their defense had been set at the western edge of the town they were sworn to protect. The soldiers had flinched, but not fled. They had grumbled uncertainty at what advanced, but held true. They shouted slogans and mottos to one another, swearing to die to the last man.

And then the Uldra warmachines had let loose their fire.

The great metal beasts, each larger than ten oxen, were called land-ships by their builders. These abominations rolled on spiked wheels of bronze and iron, lumbering over all obstacles, be they walls, trees, or people. A metal head protruded from the top-front of the contraptions, and swiveled like an eagle's. Smoke belched from the rear of the land-ships, a choking, noxious cloud that rained ash for miles around. When these hideous things approached the stoic warriors of House Calonar, their armored prows split and opened, like the fanged maws of some Underworld nightmare. From those cavernous mouths projected a great lead tube, and from these came a flood of fiery destruction, as though a volcano had lowered its mouth and released all its fury.

The entire formation was consumed in seconds. The first three ranks were simply gone, vanishing from existence. Those behind were ignited, their screams overwhelming for a brief moment the roar of the land-ships. These fortunate ones collapsed into ash within a few heartbeats. Those in the rearguard, the reserve meant to defend from irregulars or other flanking forces, shrieked in wave upon wave of heat that melted weapons in their hands. Their armor, breastplates and helmets became smoking liquid that seared into their blistering flesh. Those capable fled. Those incapable fell to the ground, begging for the White Lady's mercy.

This mercy did not come. Instead came Fak'Har's profane warriors. The Uldra land-ships opened from the side, great ramps descending, slamming into the darkened earth. Wordlessly, garbed in armor of black iron, creatures that had once been men marched forth. From a distance, they might appear as knights, but only from a great distance. The unliving knights had barbed spikes upon their plate armor and carried greatswords with serrated edges. Their heads were covered with horned helmets, and their faces were covered with dark masks shaped into all the horrors of the Underworld. They moved in unison, heedless of the burning ground or the begging men. They slaughtered all the living in their path.

The sergeant looked about and saw nothing but destruction. The land-ships had advanced behind the profane warriors into Snowholm. He had fled with the few surviving guardsmen, as their homes burned and their families and friends died screaming. At the southern edge of the immolated town, the sergeant found what remained of his courage. Either that, or some still-rational part of his mind did the basic calculations. Wildelves Wood lay three days travel to the south, and word of the mercenaries hunting amidst those trees must have reached his ears. He was a one-armed man with no weapon, no comrades, and no hope remaining.

The guardsman squared his shoulders and strode to the center of the road. He looked about, but could find no weapon, so he awkwardly pulled a dagger from his fraying belt. A line of seven profane warriors were marching down the street, slowly unyielding in their steady pursuit of survivors. The sergeant stood before them with his small blade and the last tatters of his duty and loyalty. The warriors did not pause, nor gave any indication of his existence, except that the one most in-line with him raised its greatsword.

A small blade, little more than a needle, but coated with a deadly toxin, embedded in the brave man's neck. He fell, painlessly dead before his body hit the ground. From a nearby tree where he had watched, Xaemus offered the only mercy his nearly-dead heart allowed and the only one available. One of the profane warriors turned its helmet in the *Xesh'lin*'s direction, but then turned back as the creatures continued on their way. The monster of Davenor watched as the place once called Snowholm burned. He listened to the fading screams of the people whose only sin was loyalty to a decent man and, perhaps, an overly-ambitious family. The hunter of men and women stood and witnessed as the merciless, mechanical slaughter continued. He would not look away. Xaemus kept his eyes of burning blood focused on the horrors of Fak'Har, the creature to whom the monster of Davenor had sold himself, and considered.

Chandra pushed back a lock of her plain brown hair as she counted the dead. She did not want to be out here. There were so many other, more important things she needed to be doing in preparation of the coming siege. But Rashid had insisted she come out, to take personal leadership of the various teams helping to rescue refugees. He would stay in the castle, ostensibly to supervise and attend any Council meetings. In truth, Chandra knew, the decaying spymaster lacked the energy to leave the castle, let alone the city. The Mindfog had taken root, the traitor knew, and needed to be continued. A few weeks without would probably not be enough to clear his thoughts, but still Chandra needed to get back and continue her ministrations.

"How many were there?" Vincent asked in a whisper, scanning the surrounding trees for possible threats. The heavy mist of the mid-summer morning made vision of little use, and the omnipresent mercenaries made even this brief pause a danger.

"Looks like ten," the traitor replied in an equally-low voice. "Maybe twelve."

Vincent turned and knelt beside his partner. He drew his dagger and used it to pull free a scrap of uniform still clinging to a gnarled bone. "Not much left," he noted.

"The animals wouldn't have left a lot." Chandra stood and smooth the gray wool tunic she was wearing. Casually, making it part of the innocuous movement, she hid the crumpled dispatch. The damning message communicating Prince Rogan's orders needed to be destroyed, especially with Vincent so intent on his examination. The traitorous spy crossed the small clearing in which they stood to another set of remains.

She searched for evidence, just as her junior partner did, but with the intent not of revealing it, but disposing. "We're lucky we found anything at all," she muttered.

Vincent pulled the hood back of his dark green cloak, staring at the scrap of cloth he had pulled free. "They're our guardsmen," he noted. "From Woodwall."

"Probably messengers," Chandra lied. "Or scouts."

Vincent glanced at his partner with unreadable eyes. "Pretty big group for messengers or scouts," he pointed out.

Chandra shrugged, pretending not to be paying attention to him. Her partner's observations were becoming increasingly problematic. She stood and looked about, considering her options. "With all the mercenary attacks, they're probably just being extra careful."

"Why would the western forts be sending scouts this far from Woodwall?"

"Could be any number of reasons," the traitor replied. They were alone. The soldiers with whom they had been traveling this past week were ranged out, searching for refugees. Chandra and her troublesome partner had only a few minutes, at most, for what needed to be done. "We haven't heard from Woodwall since autumn. Can you see any dispatches or other evidence of what they're up to?"

Vincent turned away, kneeling again in the mud for a closer inspection. His eyes were away, his back turned. Chandra moved on silent feet towards him. Her hand drifted to the poisoned needle she kept secured in her sleeve. One puncture, and this problem was resolved.

Vincent dropped a bone he had been looking at. "It might have been the mercenaries," he mused.

"They must have been caught in an ambush and cut down." Chandra kept her voice even and slightly descending, so that, from her target's perspective, she would sound stationary.

"I don't think so," Vincent replied. He held up something small and metallic in his gloved hand to catch the broken sunlight shining through the dense forest canopy.

"Find something?" Chandra asked, only a few steps away. The needle was out and ready.

"Throwing star," her partner answered. "Poisoned."

There was a crash in the brush and Vincent stood suddenly. "Xaemus," he grunted and spun, looking about.

Chandra hid the boiling frustration threatening to betray her and dropped the small needle into the mud. She held up her hands in placation. "It's just our escort," she grimaced. The spy had made little effort to mask her annoyance with being forced to travel with the lumbering guardsmen. Now, her irritation was more genuine. A trio of soldiers came stomping out of the trees, talking to each other in near-shouts. Chandra stepped on the needle, further burying it. Now she would have to replace the tool and its poison, as though she did not already have enough to do if ever she could get back to the Northern Keep. "What is it?" she half-growled at the guardsmen.

More than a dozen mercenaries exploded from the trees behind the three Calonar soldiers. The loyal guardsmen turned and stood, engaging as best they could in the uneven ground. The killers seemed to have been caught as unprepared as had Chandra and her men, as none were wearing armor and one was even only half-shaved. Hastily-drawn weapons were swinging and the trees filled with the sound of steel-on-steel violence.

The largest of the mercenaries, a great beast of a man with coal-black hair and the acrid stink of someone thoroughly-unfamiliar with bathing, spotted Chandra and Vincent. He shouldered aside one of the guardsmen and hefted a spiked mace. The big lug grinned in evil, lustful hunger as he eyed Chandra, disregarding the small, unassuming Vincent.

"Well, hello handsome," Chandra said derisively.

The thick mercenary charged at them, growling, "Surrender, bitch! I'll even let you live after!"

Their attacker swung his spiked mace at Chandra's legs, obviously trying to cripple, rather than kill her. She flipped aside to land next to Vincent. "Fragrant one, isn't he?" her partner observed.

"Give up!" one of the mercenaries shouted. "We've got you outnumbered! This can be easy, or we can put you down and keep the girl screaming for days!"

"Girl?" Chandra sneered, almost negligently flipping her hand in the air and sending a flat-bladed dagger flying. The weapon buried itself in the speaker's throat. The large attacker in front of the two spies barked his outrage and swung again. Chandra and Vincent knelt under the wide swing. She then rolled over top of her partner, launching a pair of knives at the lumbering man.

A mercenary leapt forward and swung his sword at Chandra's head. The spy ducked under and rolled to the side as Vincent charged forward on nimble feet, making lightning-quick slashes with his long daggers. The sword-wielding mercenary died gargling in his own blood.

Chandra spun around Vincent to face another man who had clearly meant to stab her partner in the back. The back-stabber flinched away from the series of kicks and jabs Chandra threw at him, grunting as a guardsman stabbed him in the side.

The swirling melee continued. The mercenaries were herded, corralled into a tight group facing the unbreakable defense of the guardsmen. Attempts to flee or even dodge were countered by a flipping, spinning spy, only to be turned about, confused, and left to face a grim-faced soldier. Attempts to attack were expertly parried by the guardsmen, only to end with another thrown blade in the back. Attempts to charge were neutralized by severed tendons and a blade in the throat.

Finally, the last of the mercenaries roared and charged at Chandra, lifting a battleaxe over his head. She and her partner leapt to either side of the larger man, rolling on the ground in nearly-identical movements and using their blades to open his ponderous belly. The soldiers and spies of House Calonar, breathing heavy but flushed with victory, gathered in the center of the small clearing. Pats and compliments were shared. As seemed inevitable in these trying times, though, their joyful celebration was short-lived.

A pressure built in the air. The edges of Chandra's longer hair stood. They all tasted a growing, metallic tang. Blue energy sparked, snapping at them like a frantic dog, fleeing a larger predator. There was a rush of sudden wind thrusting against them and a flash of blinding light. And then, all was quiet.

A woman suddenly fell from several feet in the air. The guardsmen rushed to her aid without hesitation, one cradling her in his arms while another lifted a waterskin to her lips. She was Human, of average height. She wore the flowing robes common to women in the Endless Sands, though her pale flesh and green eyes spoke of some other heritage. Her clothes were tattered and stained with hard miles, and her breath came in harsh, choking gasps. She blinked uncomprehendingly, her eyes unfocused as she greedily drank. When, at last, some sense returned, she looked at the men and at their heraldry. "Calonar?" she gasped in a near-whimper.

"Yes, ma'am," one of the guardsmen replied. Chandra could not remember his name, having made little effort to learn it. "We're from the Northern Keep."

The woman began sobbing. She clutched at the sleeves of the man cradling her, burying her face in his armored chest. Her shoulders slumped in relief as much as exhaustion. Chandra, walking forward with Vincent, sighed impatiently at the drama of the woman's magical arrival and jerked her head at the junior spy. Her partner took the silent command and approached. He knelt and tried getting the nearly-hysterical woman's attention. "I'm Vincent," he said gently. "I serve Baron Rashid Tressalon. What's your name?"

The robed woman took several deep breaths, seemingly unable to control herself. Vincent leaned in, pushing aside some of the long, sun-bleached hair from her face. "I think it's Naya," he told Chandra.

"That explains the robes," the traitor muttered.

"And the teleport," Vincent added.

Chandra nodded, half to herself. Naya was one of the few adepts in the Service. She had been assigned to the Endless Sands, on the border with the western Uldra tribes. "Any dispatches?"

Vincent gently reached for the messenger bag slung across Naya's shoulder. From this, he pulled a thick roll of parchment scrolls, tied closed with grey ribbon and bond with black wax. This was the method of the Service to mark important documents. As he withdrew the dispatches, Naya suddenly grabbed his wrist, her training and instincts to protect the sensitive intelligence overwhelming her exhaustion. She blinked through weariness and tears, and looked closer. "Vincent?" she said.

The junior spy put a reassuring hand on the woman's. "It's me, Naya," he soothed her. "You're safe."

"No," she gasped, eyes once again going wide. "The others."

A flock of birds, all of different species that would normally never associate, dropped from the sky at alarming speed. Although some of the birds flared their wings at the last second in a desperate attempt to land, most hit the ground with audible force, and many of these did not move again. A falcon that had managed a forced-crash close to Naya and the men blurred in a release of magic. When the effect passed, Chandra blinked in surprise at Sora. The Speaker, a female in her prime, wore a disheveled green dress. Her opalescent eyes carried little of the typical hazel glow, barely a flicker, in fact. Her cedar mane hung limply, many strands even carrying a new, premature grey. Her skin, which should have been the color of warm sand, was blotched and sallow. Like Naya, Sora was gasping at breath and lying near-prone on the moss-covered ground.

One of the guardsmen went to the Speaker, cradling the exhausted Sylva in his lap while his comrade saw to the others. Of the dozen or so birds that shared in Sora's plummet from the sky, only four blurred into their natural forms. The rest were still on the earth. "What in Underworld...?" Vincent muttered.

Sora weakly pushed away the water offered by the guardsman supporting her. "More approach..." she gasped. "From the south." The Speaker tried to stand, but lacked the strength. Her entire small body trembled in a state beyond exhaustion.

Naya also tried to rise, tried calling to magic, but the brief flicker of blue energy within her eyes faded almost as soon as it appeared. Even that effort brought about a greater exhaustion. "Take the messages," she gasped. "Leave us. Run."

"Yeah," one of the guardsmen rumbled. "That's not happening."

Vincent turned to Chandra. "Well?" he asked.

She considered. Every instinct told her to run. They were three soldiers and two spies. The handful of spell-slingers were exhausted and of no use. The dispatches were obviously the important element of the situation. Any reasonable agent would take the asset and go. More importantly, she had to see what was in that bundle before risking the information getting out. Vincent must have seen the decision forming in her mind, because he walked to Chandra, handing the parchment roll over. "Go," he said. "Take the horses and make for the Keep."

She grabbed his shoulder as the junior spy made to return. "You too," she commanded.

Vincent glanced back at her. "They won't leave Naya and the others behind," he replied. "And neither will I." The junior spy glanced at the Naya. "They can't ride. You'd have to support them, which would slow you down."

The guardsmen were gently moving Naya, Sora, and the surviving Speakers together, picking up their spent bodies and placing them together in the questionable shelter of a large tree's enfolding roots. The soldiers' faces were grim, saying louder than any possible words could that their duty was there, protecting the innocent, the helpless. "There's no point in dying here," Chandra offered. "The mission is this dispatch."

"So finish the mission," her partner replied.

The traitor moved away. She glanced back once, seeing the guardsmen readying their weapons and making dark jokes to one another in defiance of their approaching deaths. Vincent said nothing, but stood with them. He did not look at his retreating partner. Chandra continued, finding their horses and taking them all. She would not risk a survivor or, worse, someone with intelligence recovering a mount and getting away. The traitor could return to the Keep now. She had a plausible reason, and the means of fast travel. A little editing of the dispatch she held would even help in her campaign of misinformation.

As Chandra rode away, the sounds of fighting echoed through the trees. The steel-on-steel was accompanied with oaths, curses, challenges, and taunts. These were soon followed with screams. The traitor smiled softly.

Chapter 22

Mary glanced up at the sky through the thick forest canopy. Not for the first time, she had to adjust the awkward helmet Colonel Rainer had insisted she wear. The thick nose and cheek guard was forever grinding against her face. The leather interior had long since acquired a horrid stink. Worst of all, in the heat of midsummer, the helmet seemed to absorb all her sweat, pouring into her eyes each time she shifted her head. The handmaiden and newly-appointed aide-de-camp sighed once more and used the sleeve of her ugly soldier's tunic to wipe away her eyes.

"Leave it," Rainer said, also not for the first time. The colonel had objected initially at Mary's presence on this mission, but grudgingly gave way after reading Kyla's appointment. He had, however, adamantly refused the handmaiden's attempts to wear a proper Northlands dress. Instead, hideously early on the morning of their departure from the Keep, he had taken her to the House Guard barracks. A supply clerk had taken her measurements and provided the same uniform and equipment any undersized guardsman would wear.

"Why are we waiting here?" Mary asked. They were seated on a pair of horses along with a dozen soldiers. Rainer had ordered Lieutenant Aloisa ahead with the rest of the detachment, who were still inspecting the battle site ahead. Even after nearly two months moving through the forest, still Mary could not adjust to the military saddle Rainer insisted she use. As the daughter of a farmer, she had spent little time riding, her husbandry instead limited to plow, milking, and herding animals. What little riding she had done after coming to the Northern Keep had, of course, been oriented towards the proper side-saddle of a decent woman. After weeks of bouncing around on the thick leather contraption, following the twisting route back and forth from village to village, Mary had adopted the unfortunate, yet necessary, habit of sleeping face-down.

Rainer grimaced. "Safety," he grunted. Mary had almost given up on casual conversation with the colonel or any of the guardsmen. At least, she had given up during the day. When the military men were active, as they rode from one community to the next, they were stoic to the point of being made of stone. Their eyes constantly scanned the trees. They rarely spoke, and then only in the briefest words and the lowest voices. They were not tense, not like Mary had been for the first several days. Instead they just seemed… ready.

Aloisa was returning from the small clearing ahead. The lieutenant was an enigma to Mary. Tall and strong and fierce, she seemed almost a man trapped within the wrong body. She was as stoic, as unrelenting, as any of the guardsmen during the day. Whereas Mary struggled with her military saddle and the equipment forced upon her, Aloisa wore the armor, helmet, and sword as though born to them. The Gunrsvein warrior-woman did not walk so much as march, a purposeful stride that seemed to force aside the air and challenge the forest to block her path. She reached Rainer's horse and held up the pieces of a broken poleaxe.

"How many?" Rainer asked.

"Eight confirmed," his second replied. "We're still counting the parts."

The colonel grunted. A wave of anger played across his weather-beaten face. Klug Rainer had been a jovial man for most of his life. In Castle Calonar, Mary and the other servants had heard of the veteran guardsman's habit of making light of every situation. His good-natured jabbing of even Prince Rogan had been the source of much delighted gossip among the people of the Northern Keep. In recent times, though, the burden of command had squashed much of Rainer's joviality. Their mission into the northern forest had not been an easy one. More and more refugees clogged the roads and depleted their supplies, requiring frequent convoys to be sent back and forth from the city. The greater strain, though, had been in the past few weeks, as the number of refugees had dwindled, but the number of bodies had increased. The grey at Rainer's temples and in his short-cut beard seemed to visibly advance with each plundered village, each slaughtered community. New creases appeared on his face with each looted farmstead. He rarely made jokes anymore, and his good nature, when it appeared, was visibly strained.

"We haven't found any more refugees for three days," Mary pointed out gently, struggling with one of her stirrups. "And this is... how many Guard units?"

"Five," Aloisa answered, handing the broken poleaxe to her commander. Seeing Mary's difficulty, the lieutenant walked over and adjusted her foot. The Gunrsvein warrior-woman silently showed Mary how to fix her soldier's boot into the stirrup so that it wouldn't slip out again.

"Thank you," Mary said, and Aloisa shrugged before returning to Rainer's side. The handmaiden was at a loss of how to behave towards the Gunrsvien warrior-woman. Aloisa was very beautiful, in a hard, almost predatory sort of way. Mary often noticed the guardsmen's eyes trailing along their lieutenant's body, but only when they thought Aloisa would not notice. She did nothing to outwardly discourage their visible attraction, the warrior-woman even seemed to enjoy making sport of them. Around their campfires, the Gunrsvein lieutenant joined in the raucous jokes and bawdy tales with her own amorous conquests of innocent farm maids and innkeepers' daughters. And yet, there seemed to Mary to be some invisible line, some unbreakable point of discipline; a number of the younger guardsmen had earned bloody noses or blackened eyes in the first week of their mission, learning the hard way where that line existed. The lieutenant was a soldier, by bearing and ability, and yet she was also a woman, and seemed somehow to exist in both worlds.

"They were hit at night," Aloisa was telling Rainer, "while most of them slept."

The colonel grunted again. "Their sentries?"

"First to die, most likely." The lieutenant gestured to the left and right, indicating where small groups of guardsmen were gathered. "Both died from poison, needles to the back of the necks." She then nodded to the main group in the clearing ahead. "The others died in their blankets. Slit throats and single stabs to the hearts. It probably didn't take more than a minute or two at most."

"Xaemus," Rainer growled.

Mary glanced at him. "How do you know?"

"We don't," he replied. "Not for sure. But this is his style."

"Quick, quiet, and deadly," Aloisa agreed. "And we know he's in the area." She shook her head, the long tail of her tightly-braided blonde hair nearly thrashing in the warrior-woman's anger. "At least, he was."

"Do you know how long ago it happened?" Mary asked.

"Weeks," Aloisa answered. She pulled a scrap of cloth from her belt. It bore the sigil of House Calonar, two crossed diamonds, and was spattered with a crust of something brown. "The blood's long dried," Aloisa said, handing the scrap to her commander. "And the animals have already done their business."

Mary started at the implication, suddenly suspicious of the real reason Rainer had insisted she remain back with him. In the two months of their search of Wildelves Wood, the colonel had taken many actions both subtle and not, obviously trying to protect the princess' aide-de-camp from the worst of what was happening. At each scene of battle, Mary was told to stay back with a protective detail, for her safety. At each burned village, again she was made to wait in the surrounding trees with her detail, for her safety. Whenever they came upon a column of living refugees, Mary was not only allowed, but encouraged to interact with the desperate people, offering whatever comfort she could. Whenever they came upon a column of the dead, however, Rainer made her stay back, for her safety.

"Send them back like the rest?" Aloisa asked. Each time they encountered live guardsmen, the soldiers were taken in, fed, and made to accompany them on their mission if able, or sent to the Keep if not. Mary noticed, however, that each time remains were found that needed to be sent back to the Northern Keep, these harried survivors were the ones tasked with the dubious honor that would take them to a place of safety.

Rainer nodded. "Gather them up," he ordered, "identify them as best you can, and pick out..." he glanced around at the group of guardsmen whose haunted eyes spoke louder than words the horrors they had survived. "Pick out men for an honor guard home."

As their path took them further north, the air became foul. They stopped finding any survivors. The villages, whether Sylvai or Human or both, were all dead. The people were either gone, or their bodies had been consumed by the forest. They pushed on, their hope of finding anyone diminishing with each mile. Despite the cold stone and spent fires, still the air became increasingly noxious.

"What is that?" Mary demanded a week after they found the last group of dead guardsmen. She held a hand to her face, trying to block the thickening air. "It's not more... more dead is it?"

Rainer halted their column. "No," he grimaced, glancing at Aloisa.

The lieutenant nodded. "We need high ground to see for sure."

"Not much of that around here," the colonel noted.

"What about up there?" Mary suggested, pointing at the thick canopy.

"We've got no Sylvai," Aloisa chuckled. "So unless you know a chipmunk..."

"I can climb it," the handmaiden replied. She looked down and plucked a finger against the chainmail shirt Rainer ordered her to keep on during the day. "Not in this, though."

"No," the colonel grunted.

"Sir," Aloisa objected. They stared at each other as Mary looked on, some silent argument playing out between the two career soldiers. Finally, Rainer sighed and nodded. The Gunrsvein warrior-woman then looked back to Mary. "Let me help you."

Mary dismounted and looked around. "That one," Aloisa suggested, pointed to a very tall tree.

"No," the handmaiden objected. "The upper branches are too thin. They'll break." She inspected several candidates. "That one," she said, pointing to a shorter but broader oak tree. The young woman then started struggling out of her chainmail, as always needing Aloisa's help. The Gunrsvein warrior-woman had Mary out of the helmet and armor in under a minute. Mary hesitated, glancing at the tree and then at her military clothes. "It's got to go," she sighed, undoing the heavy leather belt.

"How much?" Aloisa asked with the faintest grin teasing the corner of her mouth and an arched eyebrow somehow pointing towards the nearby soldiers.

Mary grimaced at her. She pulled free the heavy leather belt and tossed it at the warrior-woman, followed by the leather bag typically riding over her shoulder. The handmaiden then sat on the mossy ground and pulled off the thick boots before standing and, after only a moment's hesitation, removed the linen trousers. This she only did when she noticed that the surrounding guardsmen were not looking at her. The handmaiden had feared that her scandalous disrobing would draw the heated attention of so many strong men, but the warriors of House Calonar were, as always, professionals. The soldiers had assumed defensive rings around Mary's tree, facing out. They stood wearily, as though protecting a precious treasure against any possible threat. Even Colonel Rainer had dismounted, passing his horse to one of the teamsters at the supply wagons, and moved about his men, rather than ogling the young woman in a state of undress. Of all the guardsmen, only Aloisa faced Mary.

"Need a hand up?" the Gunrsvein warrior-woman offered.

Mary, keeping the long tunic, turned her back on the older woman and, without pause, scurried up the tree. Summers of her childhood in Snowholm had been spent amidst the trees. A Sylvai village had been nearby and the children of both communities often played together. Though not as naturally dexterous, the Humans learned the art of tree-climbing from their neighbors, and Mary was a natural. Even years later, and lacking the invincibility of childhood, still the handmaiden moved with a natural fluidity amidst the branches of the great oak.

Up she went. Higher and higher into the branches. The tree she had chosen was not the tallest available, but it nonetheless towered over many of its siblings. Mary continued her way up, needing to pause and draw in the strangely-acidic air. During her climb, a part of the young woman's mind noticed the lack of animals. During her childhood climbs, Mary could remember encountering the denizens of the forest from time to time. Every climb seemed to bring her close to squirrels and chipmunks and even the occasional owl among the branches. Looking down, her sharp eyes sometimes spotted hares or deer. Now, however, there was nothing. During her climb, she did not encounter any startled or irascible animals whose into whose home she was intruding. When she paused and looked about the forest floor, she saw only the guardsmen encircling her tree.

As Mary climbed higher, she began to hear a strange sound. Wildelves Wood tended to blunt noise. The trees and their great canopy were often like a blanket lying atop its people, especially in the full bloom of summer. As the handmaiden climbed higher, though, this blanket receded, and the sounds of the world became accessible. But, as Mary made her way up, she did not hear birds or even the wind. Instead, she heard a great, terrible, dark roar. The sound was distant, but constant. She had been to the sea once, long ago. Her father, not long before his death, had taken her on a trip to Ironheartshaven, the great adventure of her young life. She had marveled at the sea, at the great, roaring water that rose up and crashed down upon the rocks, only to pull back, rise up, and crash down again. the sound had been, at first, jarring. It had been like the heartbeat of the world, like a great heard of horses, like the roars of magnificent animals. The song of the sea had been all these things and none of them. When Mary reached the highest possible point on her oak, and looked to the north, she saw the source of that strange roar and gasped. She saw why the air was growing thicker, more noxious with each day. She saw the death of the world.

A tiny fleck, like the first snowflake of winter, landed on her cheek, but Mary only barely noticed. It was not snow, nor even white. It was black, and the horrid nightmare-flake was in the company of a great many brothers. Mary stared, she did not know for how long. She stared and struggled to breathe and silently prayed that she had merely gone insane, that what she beheld was not truth, not reality, but some nightmare of her deluded mind. The horror she beheld, though, refused to become unreal.

"Slow down!" Aloisa cried as Mary scrambled down, far too fast. She skipped finding safe footing. She nearly hopped from one branch to the next. She embraced gravity and the silent hope that it would claim her. Even when she missed a handhold or a step, when she stumbled down only to briefly catch herself, even then, she did not slow. Finally, her luck gave out and the branch upon which she hopped broke and she fell.

The world spun as Mary finished her downward trek much faster than had been her ascent. She hit unyielding branches but kept going. She was bruised and battered, but kept going. She was crying, sobbing at the death of the world, but it kept going. She as in Aloisa's arms, both women on the ground and the warrior growling about something unimportant, but it kept going. Rainer was yelling, demanding to know something, but it kept going. Mary was screaming, and it kept going.

A sharp slap across her face brought the handmaiden back to sense. She was holding her burning cheek and blinking away tears. She was sitting on the moss-covered ground. Aloisa was kneeling in front of her, unyielding and stern-faced, but with the smallest hint of compassion in her wintery eyes. She was holding Mary's shoulders and speaking to her in a calm, steady voice. Rainer was standing above and behind, waiting.

Finally, Mary found strength enough to say something. "The world is on fire."

They moved as quickly as possible. The supply wagons had been immediately abandoned. Supplies had been divided as best as possible to the men large enough to carry the extra burden. Armor, helmets, poleaxes, and spare equipment were all left behind. The guardsmen kept their shortswords, the clothes on their backs, and all the food and water they could carry without burden. Mary did not regather her things, but was hauled onto Aloisa's horse. A large, slow man was put on her mount. The wagon horses were pressed into similar service, the most experienced among the detachment riding bareback. They moved as quickly as possible along the roads leading south, with the flames chasing them the whole way.

The wind became constant. It pushed at them like an angry wall. The heat slowly grew. The air thickened. The dark snow, ashes of a dying world, fell amidst them as though taunting their efforts to escape. They could hear the roar of the forest, the dying wail of Wildelves Wood. They did not stop any more than was absolutely necessary. The horses needed little prodding. The men on foot did not run, but still moved quickly along the flat road. They had even tried continuing on during that first night, but a broken ankle had convinced them the folly of that. The moon and stars had been lost behind the soot-stained clouds, so when the sun fled the Northlands, they were force to stop. None slept. Everyone tried hard not to look north, to see the angry orange and red glow that grew steadily brighter.

The Walkers found them on the third day. There was a distortion, as though the trees gathered together and then parted, though they did not move. A large group of Sylvai warriors, their armor the color of the forest before its death, and their manes tied in firm scalp locks, ran onto the road along which Mary and the guardsmen all fled. The Walkers looked terrible, soot-stained and gasping for breath. Many had fresh, angry burns on their face and hands. Their quivers were mostly empty and several of the warriors were missing their bows and blades. Wounds decorated most of the Walkers, and many where still bleeding. Last to appear was a woman, a young Sylva who was not dressed as a warrior, but instead wore a lose brown dress. Now, her clothes were torn to near-shreds, her great, flowing mane was burnt to almost nothing, and she was bleeding from several angry wounds across her body.

A blast of Umbral fire roared after the Sylvai, and they stumbled away, many rolling along the ground. Several nightmares also came through the mystical opening in pursuit of the Walkers. The monsters stood as men would, upon two legs. In their hands, they each carried horrid weapons of evil, hook-pointed greatswords with serrated edges that dripped gore. The not-men wore plate armor the color of a moonless night with spikes that, like the evil weapons, carried bloody chunks of recent victims. They did not speak, nor make any sound, but continued marching towards the Sylvai.

One of the Walkers rolled to his knee. He was lean, as all the Sylvai warriors were, but carried more muscle, more sheer power, than Mary thought was typical. He had the dark skin more common to the Sylvai of Maka, the mysterious western continent. His arms were bare, exposing the swirling silver tattoos those strange, foreign warriors often possessed. These tribal marks covered most of his flesh, and glowed, as though pulsing with the anger the stoic warrior himself did not express. Instead, this cool Walker brought his bow to bear and loosed his final three arrows in rapid succession. So fast was his draw and release, in fact, that the missiles were all fired before the first found its target. Three of the unliving knights stumbled back with Sylvai arrows now lodged in the visors of their black helmets.

The Sylva rolled to her knees, only a heartbeat behind the mysterious Walker. She grabbed a handful of dirt from the side of the road and flung it at the approaching nightmares, yelling in the language of magic. The flung earth wrapped itself around the not-men and hardened, becoming inflexible stone that trapped their arms. The dark-skinned Walker leapt forward, using his priceless Sylvai bow in melee. He spun the weapon over the head of the first unliving knight, bringing it down behind its legs, then forcing his shoulder into the creature, knocking it to the ground. The Sylva gestured and spoke more words of magic, and the earth formed into rough hands that grabbed at the monster hand held it down. The Walker wheeled just as a second creature broke free of the Sylva's restraint and raised his greatsword. The horrible blade came down and broke the Walker's bow, but the foreign Sylvu did not hesitate; instead, he dodged the attack and twisted, spinning around and behind the unliving knight. The Walker then wrapped the bowstring around the monster's head, slipping the garrote into the gap just below the helmet, and pulled. The unbreakable bowstring sang and glowed, and the unliving knight's head fell free of its torso. The Sylva pointed to the rest of the monsters and snarled in the Sylvai language. In response, the Walker discarded his broken bow and darted forward, catching a blade tossed from one of his comrades. The Sylvai called upon her magic one last time, and the blade caught fire. The Walker drove this into the visor of the unliving knight, and the weapon exploded, destroying the creature's head as well.

"Guardsmen!" Rainer barked, drawing his sword. He was not riding a horse, as he had given that to the soldier who had broken his ankle. On foot, the colonel darted forward. The soldiers at the head formed into three ranks of twenty men and marched forward with blades at the ready, their commander in their center. The nightmares reoriented on this new threat, moving into their own line.

Aloisa moved up with Mary sitting behind her. The lieutenant barked orders to the remaining guardsmen, forming them into smaller squares, ready to relive or reinforce and oriented in all directions.

"Heads and limbs!" the dark-skinned Walker shouted.

"You heard the man!" Rainer thundered. The lines of guardsmen advanced. The three nightmares reached them and swung their hideous greatswords in overhead strikes that seemed as though they could shatter stone. One soldier tried to raise his shortsword as though to deflect the strike of the center not-man, but the horrid greatsword crashed through his upraised blade and cut a terrible wet gash into the screaming man's torso. Rainer, beside the doomed soldier, swung his own blade, cutting into the gap at the shoulder and removing the creature's arm. It oriented on the colonel, kicking the dead man off its greatsword and rising it again. Two guardsmen from the second rank, though, darted ahead, one cutting off the remaining arm and the other removing a leg. When the nightmare fell, Rainer swung his sword at the gap beneath the helmet, removing the creature's head.

The other two were also defeated in rapid order. The guardsmen coordinated their strikes without need of command. They severed limbs and removed heads. The battle, such that it was, ended in moments. Aloisa rode forward and Mary shuddered against her back. Rainer was kicking at one of the helmets, and something like a head rolled out. It might have been Human, once. It was decayed beyond death, though. The waxy, yellowed flesh had withered almost to nothing. The teeth were exposed in a lipless grin, and the nose was nearly gone. There was no hair. Worst of all, the eyes, deeply sunken into the skull, still looked at Rainer, tracking his movements.

"They are not of the living," the Sylva said. She held out a hand, and the dark-skinned Walker was there, helping her to stand. He made as though to pick her up, but she waved him off. The pair moved to the closest of the unliving knights. "Nor are they of the dead." She kicked the head away. "They suffer no pain." She looked at Rainer. "And they can be reassembled. We have seen this happen."

"How do we… finish them?" the colonel asked.

The Walker shook her head. "If such a way exists, we do not know it." He stood immediately behind the Sylva adept, absently tracing a hand along her arm. In response, she leaned back slightly, as though taking both comfort and strength from his solid presence.

Rainer looked to a nearby sergeant. "Scatter them as best you can," he ordered. The colonel then looked to the horizon, where the orange and red glow was now visible, even in the day. "Quickly," he added.

Mary looked at the adept. "Amatria?" she started.

The Sylva, one of Esha's students who had earned the rank of archwizard at last year's Harvest Festival, offered a short bow to Rainer. "I also would offer my gratitude for your timely intervention," she said. The Fire Mage glanced at Mary and smiled slightly. "Hello *yalda'fila*. My surprise at finding you here is not insubstantial."

"Yeah," the handmaiden smiled. "We're pretty surprised ourselves." She glanced at the taller Sylvu standing behind her.

"My *eam'dy*," Amatria said, raising a hand without looking behind and caressing the Walker's chin. "Your people call him Longshot."

Longshot nodded a greeting, though the motion seemed more a response to her touch, her gentle stroking of his jawline.

"Can you get us back to the Keep?" Rainer asked.

Amatria shook her head. "My power is spent. I used what little remained to bring my *eam'dy* and his Walkers here. I fear we are the last of those still alive. If I can rest for a few hours, my abilities should be restored enough for one last translocation."

"I don't think we can wait," Aloisa pointed out with a nod to the glowing horizon.

The colonel gave a look to the approaching fire. "Let's go." He turned to Aloisa. "Any who can't walk get a horse."

Longshot glanced back and spoke in the Sylvai tongue. His words were not harsh, but still carried the urgency of their situation. The Walkers all stood, though some unsteadily. Effort was needed to convince them to ride, but finally reality gave way and they mounted. The column continued south as quickly as possible. Amatria was given a horse, as her still-bleeding leg gave mute evidence of her need. Longshot mounted behind her, and the two pressed together as they rode.

"We haven't found any Speakers," Mary told the Sylva as they continued south. "And less than a hundred Walkers. There's been no word on Sora or the Sylvai in the southern parts of the forest."

"The rest are almost certainly dead by now," the Fire Mage replied with little emotion. "Sora was coordinating the Speakers and Walkers of the southern villages. All contact with those areas has been lost. This great burn spreads across the entire forest, consuming everything. We must assume those not within the safety of the Northern Keep have fallen."

"Or worse," Longshot added grimly.

"Worse?"

"Taken," the Walker said shortly.

Aloisa glanced over her shoulder at Mary. "Taken by the Xeshlin," she said gently. The Gunrsvein warrior-woman looked at Amatria. "I hope none of the Speakers will suffer that."

The Fire Mage shrugged. "We have no ability to influence their Fate," she replied in a tone of forced neutrality. "I have learned that most of the Walkers fell in conflict with the mercenaries or the profanities Fak'Har now inflicts upon us. Sora and the Speakers would likely have added their magic to the battle, but if they became exhausted…"

"Many more have been lost trying to save villagers from the flames," Longshot added.

"Do you know what started that?" Aloisa asked, glancing back towards the inferno.

"Mechanical beasts," Longshot answered. "Uldra perversions of life. Fak'Har arrived with many Uldra technicians from the western clans. They have created machines that belch fire. The profanities ride within them."

"Amatria," Mary said, her heart twisting. "You said they came from the north, and the fire…"

"I do not know the fate of Snowholm," the Firemage answered her unspoken question. Her voice maintained its forced neutrality, but new tears grew within her opalescent eyes.

Longshot put his arm around her and pulled her, if possible, even closer, whispering "*Aebre'kystos*" into her ear. "The Walkers have abandoned the northern reaches of Wildelves Wood," he said to Mary. "From what we have witnessed, little hope can endure of the survival of those communities."

They continued in silence. Mary tried as best she could to contain her emotions, but the shuddering sobs she choked back, the tears she forcefully wiped away, the unwanted memories and fears that surged forward, all of these would not be denied.

Aloisa felt Mary's sorrow, as much as she heard it. The warrior-woman glanced back. "Your family?" she asked.

"I'm from Snowholm," the handmaiden answered. "My mother still..." She could not continue.

Mary had been riding with her lands lightly on Aloisa's waist. The Gunrsvein warrior-woman took one of those hands and put it over her heart, holding tightly. She said nothing to Mary, only let the grief rise and wash over them both.

Chapter 23

The mind-bending blue light passed, and they returned to a city transformed. Amatria had needed hours to recover enough strength to transport them home. She had tried several times, but failed. And so, the column had continued their march, their desperate retreat, from the burning forest. Finally, with the deafening roar and furious blast of the inferno very nearly upon them, Amatria had dragged together enough magic, straining as though she were tearing the continent apart, and triggered the crackling blue light of translocation.

They all, Sylvai and Human, Walker and soldier, and Mary herself, gasped and panted in the suddenly-fresher air. They looked at each other, then to the north. The sun had set, casting its amber glow upon the world. The fire, which had been charging up to them, was now distant, its roar reduced to a distant grumble, and its deadly blaze adding to that blood-soaked twilight. Mary noticed, in the unemotional corner of her mind, that her hair was singed and crisp, at least a few inches having been seared off. She held up a hand and noticed that her skin was reddened, having absorbed much of the inferno's heat. The handmaiden blinked away tears that worked feverishly to clear the charred forest from her eyes, and the sorrowful mourning from her heart.

Aloisa twisted in the saddle, looking back at her. The Gunrsvein warrior-woman looked every bit as spent as Mary felt. Her pale skin was equally reddened. Half her body was smeared in the soot of the dying Wood. The long braid in which she normally kept her blonde hair was loose and singed. Through her arms, still clutched around Aloisa's torso, Mary felt the rapid beat of the barbarian's heart and the deep rise and fall of her breaths, desperately collecting breathable air for the first time in days. They two, warrior and handmaiden, looked at each other, the realization of their survival slow to dawn.

The soldiers and Walkers surrounding them were also stunned to silence. Some heads were bowed in whispered prayers of thanksgiving, others were raised in silent relief. More than a few fell to the ground, exhaustion finally allowed to take hold. They were safe. They were alive. Eventually, one by one, they all looked to the Northern Keep, the beacon of peaceful sanctuary.

The city was girded for war.

The gate was still open and inviting, but a hundred guardsmen stood at the ready in front of it, a wall of advanced poleaxes held level at the unexpected arrivals. The walls bristled with archers, bows ready and arrows in hand. The bastions, the great fortresses spaced evenly along the walls, had new devices, insect-like machines of iron, wood, and rope clung to the tops and sides of these large stone buildings. They were like the crossbows of Alvaro, but so much larger, manned by a dozen soldiers. Smaller cousins of these angry machines, each still needing two men to operate, lined the walls' battlements, and many of these, pulled back like a loaded and ready crossbow, were now pointed at the new arrivals.

"*Zqurpiae,*," Aloisa said softly, her gaze, like Mary's, on the new engines of war. "Old Sylvai design. 'The Scorpion.'"

"And those?" Mary asked dully, nodding to the larger machines nesting on the fortresses.

"Ballistae. An Uldra adaptation of the technology."

Colonel Rainer raised his hand, waving his arm in wide, seeping arcs. "It's us!" he bellowed. "Klug Rainer! We've got survivors! Clerics up!"

At the recognition, the war engines lining the walls were turned away. The guardsmen before them raised their poleaxes and stood aside. The call went back and was answered almost immediately by a team of clerics from the Temple of the Harvest Mother. The priests and priestesses ran forward, already saying prayers to their goddess, summoning her Life Magic, which they applied to those soldiers and Walkers lying on the ground, unable to rise. A second group, Sisters of the Lady of Light in their short skirts and loose blouses, also ran forward with pitchers of clean, cool water. These were greedily lapped up by the survivors. Whole gallons of restorative water were greedily drunk, though somehow the Sisters' pitchers never ran dry.

Mary started when she saw Medaka, the senior-most of her sisterhood, come forward as well. She smiled at her young student and held up her own pitcher. "Welcome home," she said warmly. The handmaiden drank, the water more delicious than any wine Mary could remember drinking, and more refreshing thana a hundred days of peaceful life in a garden-paradise. She drank and drank, until the need for air overrode her need for the comforting coolness of the sanctified water.

Mary handed the pitcher to Aloisa, who took it and drank just as eagerly. The Gunrsvein warrior-woman also held up the pitcher to let its cool water spill over her head, bringing a relieved gasp. She then handed the still-full pitcher back to Medaka. "Have there been any others?" she asked.

The Sister of the Lady of Light nodded. "Remm made it back," she said. "About a week ago, he led a column of refugees along with a hundred Uldra clansmen. They were a little worse for wear, but alive."

"Since then?" Aloisa asked.

Medaka shook her head. "Nothing." She looked out at the smoke-filled horizon and its angry orange and red glow. "We'd nearly given up on you."

"Medaka," Mary said then, her voice near to breaking.

The elder Sister looked up. The young woman, feeling very much like a pain-filled child, looked at her teacher, lips trembling as the unavoidable truth came crashing upon her fraying soul. "Snowholm," she said in a broken whisper. Medaka nodded and set down her pitcher. The Sister held out her arms and Mary dropped from the horse, collapsing into her friend's embrace. She sobbed and shook. She could not speak, could not think. She only cried and mourned the loss of her mother, her childhood friends, the home she had, in the silence of her heart, hoped to show one day to Tomas.

Medaka said nothing. She only held Mary. The priestess stood, cradling her young student and friend against her heart. There was nothing to say, after all. War had come, and taken many. Tragedy, ever the companion of War, was working her will against them all. Aloisa dismounted, handing her reigns to a nearby priest, and joined in the embrace. They stood there, the three women: a warrior, a scholar, and a cleric, holding one another against the evil of those times through which they all suffered. In the twilight of the Northlands and its ruling House, all Mary and her friends could do was suffer and try to help one another go on.

"Where is he!" Colonel Rainer's voice once again cut through everything. The three women all looked up to see the grizzled veteran, red-faced in rage rather than from the inferno, pointing towards the walls. "Where is that little highborn bastard!?!"

A horse of perfect white was trotting through the gate. Upon its back was an impossibly gorgeous nobleman, the curls of his blonde hair dancing in the wind of the approaching forest fire. His elaborate, golden-inlaid armor was as decorative and beautiful as himself and his horse. He had a cloak of crimson velvet attached to his right shoulder, and a rapier rested in a jewel-encrusted scabbard on his left hip. "I hear we have one more band of refugees." His voice, operatic and high, flowed across the gathering of road-weary survivors. When he said the word 'refugees,' his face looked as though the word was noxious in his mouth.

"Who in Underworld is that?" Aloisa nearly growled.

"Baron Hans of House Wurst," Mary answered. Strangely, the appearance of the man who had once thought to seduce her brought a welcome change to the handmaiden. The aching chasm within her chest was filled, if only slightly, with the comforting warmth of amused contempt.

Unlike Mary, who could look at the preening star of House Wurst as a source of comedy, Colonel Rainer looked as though he might skin the arrogant nobleman. The veteran stormed through the group of survivors, soldier and Walker alike making way no matter their weariness. As he approached, Rainer looked up at the self-delighted baron. "Are you forgetting something, major?" he asked, putting particular emphasis on Hans' lesser rank.

The son of a noble family could not, and perhaps did not even try to hide the contemptuous sneer on his full lips. "Forgive me… colonel. Your rank was given to you so recently, and your appearance is so... common, the formalities slipped my mind completely." Hans, if possible, drew himself even taller in the saddle, and raised a salute.

"You were in command of the defensive preparations in my absence, major. Is that correct?" Colonel Rainer said each word deliberately, purposefully.

"Indeed. An honor my family has held for three generations."

"And were my orders, in any way, unclear?"

"Such as they were," Hans said in something only vaguely resembling a murmur. "However, I had hoped that you would defer to my judgement in strategic matters. After all, I have been schooled in the art of war, whereas you... Well, no doubt your time amidst the common soldiery was... informative."

Mary noticed that the few soldiers who had been standing near Hans took several steps back as the colonel walked forward. "So, you took it on yourself to change my orders while I was out trying to rescue survivors? Is that right?"

"I would be quite please to explain the superiority of my-" The baron's words were cut into a startled yelp when Rainer took hold of the nobleman and jerked him from his ornate saddle. Hans fell to the ground and tumbled there, his cloak of flawless crimson tearing and his beautiful armor denting. He awkwardly got to his feet with one hand going for the rapier at his side. Rainer, though, intercepted him with a soot-stained boot to the chest, further denting the weak breastplate and sending the gasping nobleman back to the ground.

"Stay there," Rainer growled. "If you stand without permission, if you say a word, if you draw a blade, your noble lineage ends here."

Hans must have seen something, heard something, within the colonel. He slowly pulled his hand away from the rapier and held it out, staying in the dirt and trying to regain his breath. "Lieutenant Aloisa!" Rainer barked without breaking his stare down at the cringing nobleman.

"Sir!" the Gunrsvien warrior-woman answered.

"You're in command of the walls' preparations!" The colonel pointed to the area in front of the walls. "I want a ditch, at least twenty feet! I want a ring of stakes along the glacis."

Aloisa looked at the walls, running both left and right for hundreds of feet before curving away. She glanced back at the glowing, smoking horizon and its visible approach. "I don't think we have enough time, sir," she pointed out.

Rainer, still holding his eyes on Hans, grimaced. "Concentrate on the ditch, then. Start here. I want twenty feet down, and a hundred long each day, for as long as we've got."

"And how long is that?" Hans finally snapped. Blood was trickling from his nose and he stared fiery hate up at Rainer. "How long do you think you can waste digging a useless ditch?"

"Six days," the answer came.

All eyes turned. Princess Karen stood with a small bodyguard at the gate's edge. She seemed older, in just the few months Mary and the others had been gone. A great sadness hovered behind her pearlescent eyes. Although she stood tall, defiant of the lack of height shared by all the women of House Caloanr, still there seemed a great weight on her narrow shoulders. A golden circlet in her blonde hair gathered the last tatters of sunlight able to break through the thickening black clouds. Her hands were not clasped in front of her waist, as had once been her habit when forced into public address. Instead, she stood with hands upon her only just-widening hips, the bow of her mouth an unflinching line, and her pale skin untouched by cosmetic.

"Your Highness," Rainer said, bowing.

"Colonel," she replied, nodding. The princess and de facto leader of the Northern Keep looked around the assembled soldier and Walkers. "These are the last," she said in a voice of utter neutrality, as though all the emotion of her words had been sapped by the awful weight of foreknowledge. "Bring them inside and see to their needs." She looked back at Rainer. "You have six days to complete your work, then the gates must be sealed."

Rainer bowed again. He looked around the assembled warriors and citizens of the Northlands. "You heard your princess," he nearly roared. "Get to work!" The colonel looked down. "You report to the Auxiliary."

Hans gasped. "I am to command the Auxiliary!?!"

"No," Rainer corrected. "They have a commander, and capable leaders. As a citizen of this city, you'll join them and follow orders."

The nobleman got to his feet, heedless of the colonel's earlier threat. "I am the baron of House Wurst!" he declared. "My family has generations of military training, leadership, and ability!"

"And you are a preening fool," Rainer countered, stepping forward and forcing Hans to take a step back. "You are a disgrace to the name and all that's wrong with inherited titles. You'll help defend this city like everyone else. You'll earn what's been given to you."

"Absolutely not!"

Rainer pointed towards the forest's edge and the encroaching inferno. "Then leave. You either help, or you leave."

He sputtered, indignant.

Karen raised her voice. "The city is, of this moment, under martial law. All citizens, residents, and those who wish shelter within its walls will obey the orders of our military commander. Or they will be subject to his disciplinary actions. Colonel Rainer, and his designated subordinates, speak with the full support and authority of House Calonar."

Rainer narrowed his eyes at Hans. "You work, you fight, or you leave. Now." Without another word, the colonel turned away, giving orders for the preparations of the city's defense and the care of the last survivors.

Aloisa walked up to the open-mouthed Hans. She looked around and spotted a shovel. The lieutenant retrieved the tool and forced it into the hands of the baron of House Wurst. "Start digging," she commanded. When it looked like Hans would refuse, she stared at him through narrow, unfeeling eyes. "I won't give you the choice, boy," she said calmly. "Disobey, and I'll just take you into the trees. You won't come back."

He dug.

As the gathering in front of the city's gate broke apart, everyone seeing to their tasks or being led inside for care, Mary waited. She stood, staring at Karen. The princess gave a few instructions here and there, reinforcing Colonel Rainer's own orders. Finally, she sighed and turned to look at Mary. The youngest member of House Calonar waved away her bodyguards and approached, clearly steeling herself as she stood before Mary.

In the instant the handmaiden made to raise her hand, Karen shook her head. "Not here," she commanded. "More than anything, people need to see House Calonar's authority. They need to trust and believe." Karen turned and walked back through the gates. Mary followed.

The pair entered the city and then turned, going into a nearby storage room built into the walls. Once inside, Karen stopped. The princess sighed again and turned. "No one will see us here-"

Mary slapped the leader of House Calonar. The strike was more than a slap, really. She hit the noble princess so hard that Karen was forced to the ground. "You knew," the handmaiden accused. She stood over the younger girl, barely beginning the journey into womanhood, and stared hatred into the girl's soul. "You knew."

Karen held a hand to her lip, coming away with traces of blood. She sighed again and nodded. "Yes," she admitted, "I knew. The moment I looked at you, in the ziggurat, when I received the Truthsight, I knew. I saw that you would never again see your mother. That you would learn of the death of Snowholm while out, searching for survivors with Colonel Rainer and Lieutenant Aloisa."

"You could have told me."

"Yes," Karen admitted. She remained on the ground, looked up at Mary through her Halven eyes of glowing pearlescence, seeing beyond the now and into all the maybes. "I could have told you. But you would have left. You would have rushed back to Snowholm, to warn your friends and try to save your mother. And you would have been captured. Instead of learning of your home's destruction, you would have witnessed it. You would have seen your mother dying in the flames. And right now, at this very moment, you would have been stripped naked and bent backwards over a Xeshlin altar." The Truthseer paused, still staring at Mary. She waited, watching an event that was never to be through eyes far too young to behold such brutality. "And now, right at this moment," she said with tears attempting to offer a shield against the young Truthseer's eyes and her heart, "a Xeshlin priestess would be walking up to you. Your eyes would be staring at the golden glyphs slashed into her purple loincloth, the only thing she's wearing." Another pause. "She brings up the knife and slowly cuts, this way," Karen pointed a finger high towards Mary chest, then drew a line down, between her breasts, to far below her heart. "You would still be alive right now, as she slowly reaches in, under your ribs, and wraps her fingers around your still-beating heart. Now, she would start to squeeze." Another pause. "Now you would be drawing your final breath as they use your blood, your suffering, and your death to fuel their magic."

Karen closed her eyes, rubbing at them as though trying to force away what her Truthsight revealed. "If I had told you what I saw, you would now be dead. And we still need you here." The princess stood.

"What gives you the right?" Mary demanded.

"Right?" Karen snapped. She took a step forward, standing only a breath from the handmaiden. Though the little princess was far shorter than Mary, the Truthseer seemed as though she towered over the handmaiden. "You think this is a right? Some gift or power or great purpose? Do you think this is some game? If I passed this to you, and I could, you would kill yourself." The princess stomped to the door and pointed outside without looking at a nearby cart of tools. "Do you see that pick there? If I were to pass you the Truthsight, you would scream and scream, and then you would run out and you would thrust your head onto that pick, right into your eye, if only to stop seeing."

Karen turned back to face Mary. "Do you want to know how my father will die? Because I know. Do you want to know what my mother will suffer after the siege? Because I know." She gestured again out the door, this time waving towards the entire city. "Do you want to know how many different ways this city can fall? Because I've seen them, every last one, and all the screaming deaths that go with each possible destiny. In all the different paths, along all the twisting routes Fate has laid before us, there is one, ONE in which this entire world does not burn. I have to condemn hundreds to their deaths, thousands to suffering, all in the hope of guiding us along that one path to salvation."

The Truthseer breathed. She took in calm, clearly trying to gather within her young self the same serenity both her mother and the Lady Alexia, her predecessors, had possessed. "Do you remember the morning we went to the ziggurat?" she asked then.

Mary nodded.

"Do you remember that boy, the page, who tried talking to me before we left?"

Mary nodded.

Karen looked back out the door, towards Castle Calonar resting atop the great hill that overlooked the entire city. "When we got back. Later that same day, I saw him. I looked at him." She turned back to Mary. "He will be the father of my daughter, my only child. I don't love him, and I never will. I'll lie with him only to produce my daughter, the next Truthseer. He'll love me, and I'll use that to seduce him." Tears formed in her pearlescent eyes. The girl's lip quivered, but only slightly. "I don't think I'll ever have love," she confessed, "not like you have. Every time I see someone who knows me in adulthood, they all reveal me, alone. I will be just. I will be merciful. I will be remembered long after my death. And I will be alone." She blinked away the tears and took another deep, sighing breath. "I also know how that boy will die. How he MUST die."

The princess glanced around and spotted a small stack of boxes. She sat upon it. "I meant what I told Colonel Rainer, and what I told you. This city will come under attack, and the people must defend it. We must hold long enough for an escape to become viable, so that certain people get to safety." She looked up at Mary. "I know who I'll choose to live, and who must remain to die."

"Why not send them now?" the handmaiden asked in a whisper.

"You've seen the fire," Karen answered. "But only part of it. Fak'Har's Uldra are burning the entire Wood. We have to wait until the fire is finished. And even then, we need the mercenaries and Fak'Har's creatures focused here, so that those who must survive can escape to safety."

Mary considered all this. She considered the terrible weight of the Truthsight. She considered the decisions Karen was making on behalf of Fate itself. She considered the lives and the deaths and everything in between the princess was orchestrating in some vague hope of escaping a distant cataclysm. "So," the handmaiden finally said, "we're made to suffer for some distant event we'll never see."

Karen actually chuckled lightly. It was not a laugh, but rather a stuttering sigh. "You won't believe me now, but you will later." She looked again at Mary. "The Truthseers, me, my mother, Aunt Alexia, all the women going back beyond the foundation of the Sylvai Empire, we've all been trying to minimize your suffering."

Mary's face must have revealed her disbelief.

"As I said." The princess stood and straightened her dress. She checked her lip, confirming the small bleeding had stopped. "We have work to do. There are only six days left before the siege begins."

The Heroes at Home

II

Wall

Chapter 24

The people of the Northern Keep had informally named the city's gates long ago. The northeastern entrance was often called Merchant's Gate, as that led to the mercantile district as was most commonly used by trade caravans. In the south was Farmer's Gate, so named since most of the communities to the south had been the food source of the Northern Keep for generations. In the west was Uldra Gate, since the mountain clans were most common there, using the entrance closest to Ulheim for the delivery of their stone, precious metals, and manufactured goods. On the morning of the seventh day after Colonel Rainer had led the final survivors home, now they sat outside the eastern gate, called Defiant by the people.

There were no memorials, no statues or carvings or other commemorations at Defiant Gate, and the King himself had tried to discourage the name. Still, every citizen of the Northern Keep knew the tale. On a bright summer day, a hundred knights, leading ten thousand spearmen, stood arrayed before the eastern gate. Duke Cylan had ridden out with only Remm Stonebearer and a small detachment of his House Guard. The Lord of House Calonar had meant to parlay, to meet and talk in the hopes of a peaceful resolution. He made an impassioned plea, a noble statement of his desire for coexistence. He pointed to the Adamic church, an expansion of the tiny chapel that had fallen into disrepair from the negligence of Velaross. Duke Cylan had tried to make peace, but the Inquisitors had wanted only war.

The battle had been sudden and furious. The Holy Inquisitors had attacked without warning, hurling their magic at the Elector Lord of the Northlands. They forgot, or chose not to consider, Duke Cylan's own great mystical power. He repelled the dishonorable ambush. The hundred knights lowered their lances and charged, but met the grim, unyielding defense of the House Guard. The charge ended at the tips of the Northland poleaxes, as did the lives of the hundred knights. The Inquisitors tried ordering their spearmen into an assault, but failed. Duke Cylan had called on them directly, offering sanctuary and new, peaceful lives in his lands, both for them and for their families. The common men threw down their spears and left, most returning in the years that followed. Mary's own ancestor was one of those, a man who returned to Alvaro only to gather his family and return. He was granted a farmstead in Snowholm and lived in peace all the rest of his days. This was the legacy of the Defiant Gate.

"And now it's our turn," Mary whispered to herself. She sat astride a perfectly-groomed horse. Ilse had taken over Kyla's care for the day, everyone knowing that Mary herself was needed elsewhere. Kyla had one of her own gowns altered for this very occasion, clothing her handmaiden and friend in the rich blue and grey of House Calonar. The golden cord that marked Mary as her princess' aide-de-camp, a title she still did not understand, rested on her shoulder, shining in the sunlight.

Mary took a moment to absorb the radiance of the returned summer sun. The clouds had opened yesterday. A great downpour had come as though from nowhere. The miasma that had hung over the city, the choking veil of the forest's death, had been washed away. The city had been cleansed, soot stains vanishing overnight. With the dawn, the clouds had relented and moved west. The sun had broken through and baptized the city in the late summer's warmth. But the sight that was revealed brought a wave of sorrow worse than any fear of the Great Burn.

Wildelves Wood was dead. For as far as anyone could see, the forest was gone. In place of that vibrant, sacred remnant of what the Sylvai called the Eternal Forest was a graveyard of nature. Scorched earth blackened everything. The charred, desecrated skeleton of the Wood looked like the skeletal fingers of a murdered man, pleading to an uncaring sky for a mercy that would not come. Patches of smoke still rose, though only sparingly, like the final breath of a violated mother. There were no animals amidst the carnage, nor birds in the sky. There was nothing left. Nothing but War.

From the high points of the city, the people could see the invaders. Large groups of warriors moved amidst the blackened landscape. They circled the Northern Keep like a flock of carrion-feeders. They did not draw within arrow-shot of the walls, nor make any great preparation for an assault. No, their purpose was containment, of isolating the prey for the kill. Had any thought of escape occurred to the people of the Northern Keep, such an idea would be quickly ended. There could be no escape, for that light cavalry paced about the perimeter of the defenders' vision. These jackals were eager for victims, for any fools who might draw close or try to escape the larger predators.

To the east, along the highway that had, for centuries, offered merchants, explorers, refugees, and adventurers access to the Northern Keep, waited the main army. Human mercenaries made up the bulk of this force, and they were gathered in loose bands that stretched for a mile in both directions. They bore armor and weapons from across Lanasia. Velarossi longswords were as common as Alvaran rapiers. Gwyndd longbows were held ready alongside Pelsemorian crossbows. Pikes and spears, mail and padded vests, helmets and coifs. Nearly the entirety of Lanasia's martial societies were present, ready to ravish the Northern Keep.

At the center of the evil host were a dozen of the horrid warmachines of the corrupted Western Uldra. These did not growl in angry hunger for more destruction, but sat in dead slumber, waiting for their treasonous creators to bring them once again to un-life. Their engines were silent. They did not belch vile, noxious smoke, and their wheels of bronze and iron were still. Their bows were open, displaying the fire-belching cannons that had lain waste to Wildelves Wood, a clear threat of the same fate for the Northern Keep. Their crews and inventors clung to the metal beasts like parasites. These were not the Eastern Uldra so common in the Northlands, the men and women of the mountains of great size, bellowing voices, and good humor. These were as corrupted as their warmachines. Their beards were burnt to almost nothing. They were all soot-stained and garbed in thick hide, though their flesh seemed gray even in areas not stained by their insidious mechanisms. They did not boast or shout or carry-on in the great displays so common to the Eastern Uldra; instead, these beings only glared in hatred, trembling as though eager for another target. Even their size seemed stunted, the corrupted builders only a little taller than the surrounding Humans, but so much more broad than was typical for their race.

Behind these were Xeshlin, dozens of that murderous, traitorous race. Each stood within the shadow of something larger, the burnt husk of a tree, the warmachines of the Western Uldra, and even larger Humans. They acted as though the sun was a pain for them, and every inch of their colorless skin was covered, enfolded within reddish-brown, billowing cloaks. From the sparing folds of their cloaks, Mary could see strange padded armor, dyed to match the cloak. In their hands they held the implements of torturous slavery: whips and chains and clubs. Deep hoods covered their faces, such that Mary could see nothing of their faces, except the eyes of burning blood that looked out in lustful anticipation of the horrors to come.

Far back from the lines of warriors and machines, under the protective cover of a large, thick canvas, were a half-dozen Xeshlin females. This, then, must the Coven of the Puma's Leash, the magical women who dominated the slavers. As frightening, as inhuman as the males were, their tyrannical females were far, far worse. They stood beneath their covering, their shield from the bright summer sun, licking their colorless lips. They each bore the same sigil: green flame erupting from a dark chalice that formed the face of a predatory cat. On the surface, they were as beautiful as their Sylvai cousins, with perfect features and flawless grace. They did not wear armor, but only gowns of what seemed redish-brown silk, a material so sheer they may well have painted their bodies in it, rather than worn the fabric. They had golden chains around their necks, upon which were fixed gemstones of red. In their hands, each of the blood-mystics held scepters that bore blood both recent and old. At their waists were belted the curved knives feared across the world, those used to carve the still-beating hearts from their victims as fuel for their insidious Blood Magic.

In front of the corrupted Western Uldra were the abominations of Fak'Har. They stood in rows of twenty-five. Each seemed like a nightmare statue, blaspheming the tradition of a holy knight. Their plate armor, black enameled and covered with spikes, was still and silent. They held their barbed, serrated greatswords before them, unflinching as though the horrid tools of suffering were weightless. Faces could not be seen behind the slits in their massive helms, and the gaps of the umbral armor showed only darkness beneath. Even the mercenaries avoided these monsters, staying well away and never looking towards them.

At the head of this host, this assembly of greed and evil, waited three men. At their center was Vagris, the infamous traitor of the Republic Legions who had spent much of the past ten years pillaging his way across southern Lanasia. He was the picture of military discipline and pride, his half-plate polished and new. He had a shield at his side that bore no heraldry, and carried a sword sheathed at his hip. His helmet was crested with a horsehair plume that matched the coat of his patient stallion. To his left and right were figures of darkness. On the one side was likely Xaemus. The monster of Davenor was smaller than Vagris, yet carried himself with the undeniable presence of the White Lady Herself. He entire body was covered with varying dark colors, with leather and heavy fabric, so that only a tiny strip of his impossibly-pale flesh was visible near his eyes of burning blood. In his hand, he held the double-bladed sword that had ended lives uncounted. To the other side…

Mary had never seen Fak'Har before. Few had. Stories filled everyone's childhood of the great evils of the world. The Sorceress Vara, who had slaughtered the children of Velaross and stained the basilica's dome red with their innocent blood. Tienel Uskera, called the Greysoul, who would steal the souls of wicked children when they slept at night. There was Kelinva, Dark Empress of the Xeshlin, who visited nightmares upon pious maidens and tempted adolescent boys with horrid corruption. Ravana, the Mad Vaeyen, who sought to devour young heroes just as she had Kyle Calonar. Karnat the Death Mage, who visited the Plague of Walking Death upon the world, still haunted graveyards at night. All of these horrors were known to the world, but none of them matched the terror that was the Shadowed Mage.

Nothing could be seen of Fak'Har. He was robed and cowled. He was a shadow made solid. He carried no staff, nor bore any other of the typical implements of an adept, save for a leather belt with a scroll case hanging from his right hip. His horse was as dark as he, and as still as the abominations he had created. So still these figures were, in fact, that the eye seemed to slip across them, as though the mind refused to acknowledge their realness. The Shadowed Mage sat and waited, facing the defenders of the Northern Keep with all the emotion one has when looking at a beetle, already rolled into a useless ball.

"Let's do this," Colonel Rainer grunted, nudging his horse forward. Their military leader was resplendent. His breastplate caught the sun and amplified it. The sigil of House Calonar, the crossed blue and white diamonds, seemed almost to beat at the center of his chest, defiant as all the forces of the Northern Keep were in the defense of their home. His helmet was not adorned as was Vagris', having no great plume or other decoration. It was the same bascinet helmet used by all the House Guard, but burnished to the same lustrousness as was his breastplate, greaves, and gauntlets. He had no ornamentation, in fact, not even his insignia of rank, nothing to differentiate him from the other guardsmen arrayed on the walls.

"Hold your peace, colonel," Karen said, moving her own horse alongside Rainer. "Let them do most of the talking." Like Mary, the princess was gowned in blue and grey. The sapphire silk of her dress was woven with a pattern of blooming holly, each crimson flower gleaming from tissued gold. Her long hair was perfectly arranged with a Northlands braid, interwoven with pearls matching the string around her neck. A circlet of gold inlaid with sapphires adorned her brow, matching the sapphire pendant formed into the cross-diamond sigil of House Calonar that hung at the base of her necklace.

"I still think you should have waited behind the walls," Rainer grumbled as they rode forward. "Or at least worn armor."

Karen's pearlescent eyes were calm, even more so than had become common in the past weeks. "Don't worry," she said softly. "They won't attack just yet."

Mary rode with them, though she did not know why. Karen had told her to do so earlier, and the handmaiden had shrugged away any questions her mind manufactured as useless. She would understand in time, or not at all.

"Nervous?" Lieutenant Aloisa asked.

Mary glanced at the Gunrsvien warrior-woman. She appeared nearly the same as Rainer. With a polished breastplate over chainmail, a belted sword, and helmet. From a distance, only the tight blonde braid spilling from the back of her helmet made any differentiation between Aloisa and any other guardsman. "I guess I should be," Mary answered. "But…"

Aloisa nodded as their small group halted. "It's the calm before the storm. Don't worry, there's always plenty of time to wet yourself before the fighting starts."

Chandra and Rashid said nothing. The two, both dressed in dark grey and wearing leather vests, had appeared at the gates in preparation for the parlay. They had not been summoned, but Karen seemed unsurprised at their presence, as she always was. Rashid's inclusion did come as something of a surprise to Mary. The spymaster had not been seen in weeks. Rumor swirled of his deterioration, his self-flagellation over the attempted assassination of Princess Kyla. Now, the handmaiden saw the rumors understated the facts. Rashid was withered to a ghost of himself. Dark circles hung around his sunken eyes, which stared emptily out from an expressionless face. His hair had none of its prior lustrousness, and his skin was sallow. His clothes hung from the frame of his body, and he sat near to Chandra, deferring to her in all things.

"Be weary," Esha, the last member of their group, said. The tiny Sylva archmage was almost comical in her wartime apparel. Traditionally, adepts of the Arcane Guild wore no armor of metal, as the restraint and touch of steel could disrupt the employment of their magic. Esha obeyed this tradition, but only to an extent. She still had a leather vest on, the smallest anyone could find or make, and a leather cap over her head. The great archmage and Tower Mistress of the Northern Keep looked very much like a child wearing her father's clothes. The sleeves of her soldier's tunic hung low over her hands, constantly needing to be pushed up. The leather cap was constantly slipping down over her eyes, and her perpetually-singed mane stuck out from every opening.

"You didn't need to wear all that, you know," Mary whispered.

"You may have no great discomfort at the thought of an arrow in your chest," Esha whispered back, once again adjusting her cap and sleeves. "I, however, have seen the effects of Human foolishness and will not be caught unprepared." Her cap slipped forward again.

"So," Vagris said as he pulled his horse to a stop in front of them. "This is what remains of the Northern Keep's defenders." The warlord made no effort to hide his contempt as he looked at the opposing party. "A withered spymaster and his… escort. A pair of noble ladies better suited to the kitchen than the battlefield. A pair of commoners masquerading as officers." His contemptuous eyes went to Esha. "And… that."

The archmage stared hatred with her opalescent eyes. The glare, however, was marred by her cap once again slipping forward.

"Can we just get right to it?" The colonel's voice was steady, as peaceful as the surface of a pond. Mary knew from experience, though, that only the veteran's experience and discipline kept his growing anger in check.

"Oh," Vagris laughed. "Let's 'get to it,' by all means." The warlord drew himself even taller in his saddle. "You're surrounded and outnumbered. You have your walls and whatever other preparations you've made, true." He glanced over his shoulder at the waiting warmachines of the corrupted Western Uldra. "But I've got those. They can get through your walls in a matter of minutes. As is the custom of the Legions, I'll give you the chance for honorable surrender before the ram touches the gate. If you refuse, your lives are forfeit."

Karen nudged her horse forward one step. "Did you have some specific requests, Vagris?" she asked.

The warlord made a show of looking past the young princess. "And where are the adults?" he asked with a sneer. "Your father is all but dead by now, true, but surely your mother is still about? Or at least your sister. Or is she too busy… caring for the men?"

Rainer went to the hilt of his sword, but Karen put a light hand on his. Her gaze never broke from Vagris, looking through the warlord, and past him. "Just because your own mother was an adulteress," she said gently, "doesn't mean all women are."

Vagris hissed and also reached for his sword. "Stop," the word came with resonating power. The warlord froze in place, his muscles locked and his eyes jerking about in confusion.

Fak'Har pushed his own mount forward. The deep hood of his robe regarded Karen. "So," the sound came from the shadows. "Your mother passed you the Truthsight. A desperate gambit."

"No," Karen argued. "Not a gambit, just the Wind of Fate aligning as it must."

"You know, then, what must happen."

"I do. I also know what might happen." The faintest hint of a smile, a curl of her lips betraying the advantage of knowledge, passed over the Truthseer's face. "Do you want to know how you die, Scion of Fate?" she asked calmly. "Do you want to know how much longer you have to live?"

"One of us will die," Fak'Har conceded. "Which of us remains undecided."

"I've decided," Karen argued. "My mother decided. Aunt Alexia decided when she set the Final Host on his path. Your brother was wise enough to stay away from this conflict. You, however…" the princess shrugged.

The Shadowed Mage said nothing for a time, his gaze seemingly locked with Karen's. Finally, after a tense eternity, he turned away. "Give them the demands, let them refuse, and we can begin." He did not wait, but instead continued back to his waiting army.

Vagris jerked forward with a startled gasp. The warlord glanced behind at the withdrawing Fak'Har, a sneer telling his feelings on being commanded by the Shadowed Mage. He straightened, though, and did as instructed. "Our forces are superior to yours," he pointed out. "Killdare and the bulk of your army is on the other side of the Sentinel Mountains. Eigenhard and your Archaeknights are half a continent away. Your non-Human allies are dead or scattered." He stared at Rainer. "We only want House Calonar. You can keep your king for as long as he lasts, and you can even keep that queen of yours, as well. Kyla," he nodded at Karen," and her sister, come with us. Two lives for a city. Surrender the Calonar daughters to us, and my army will leave. Refuse, and I will force my way in and burn the Northern Keep to the ground. I will slaughter every man. Your old women will also be put to the knife. Your boys will be sold to the Xeshlin. Your girls will be given to my men. Every non-Human, Uldra and Sylvai, will be given to the Sorcerous Sisters for sacrifice to their Demon-God. Everything of value will be claimed. Every building will be torn down. Every trace of this city will be erased from the world. Those are my terms."

Rainer looked at Karen, and the princess nodded. The colonel turned back and shook his head. "Legion traitor, you have no standing here. Your warmachines will never breach these walls. Your abominations will be destroyed. Your mercenary scum will be scattered, hunted down, and killed." He looked to the south. "General Killdare is already on his way." He glanced over his shoulder at the Sylvai Walkers, Uldra miners, and city irregulars, all lining the walls. "Our allies are here, and ready." He nodded behind the warlord. "And that breath on your shoulder? That's Prince Rogan, coming for vengeance.

Vagris seemed on the verge of a retort, when Xaemus nudged his horse forward. "Slaughter is not unavoidable," the monster of Davenor said in a voice seemingly indifferent to bloodshed. His eyes of burning blood had been scanning the House Guard standing ready at the open gate, and the defenders, both military and civilian, upon the walls. "The offer is a good one. The Wood has already burned, but not all who lived within or beside the trees were put to sword or flame." The Xeshlin glanced back and hissed something in the horrid tongue of his people, the language sounding more like ice breaking under a sudden heat than true words.

From the rear, the Xeshlin warriors, under the hissing orders of the Dark Coven, came forward. As they moved into the burning light of day, the slavers pulled their heavy cloaks and hoods tighter around their cursed flesh. The males held leashes of barbed leather, to which were connected trains of prisoners. Each was bound by iron, with the manacles securing their wrists to the heavy leather belts at their middles, and their ankles were forced close together, limiting the length of their steps. They were gagged with something resembling a bit for a horse. They had each been shaved of any hair, and the many cuts showed the savagery of the process. They were all nude and barefooted, with innumerable marks upon their flesh speaking to the savagery of their new owners. There was a great variety amongst the prisoners, their eyes hopelessly downcast. Humans walked beside Sylvai and Uldra. Male and female were bound equally, as stripped of dignity as they were of clothing. A great and growing clamor rose from the walls and even Mary gasped.

They were the people of the Northlands. The Uldra, Mary did not recognize, though Remm, holding command at the walls, could be heard swearing with all the rage of a fire-mountain as he called out name after name and swearing vengeance for each mark upon his friends. Others called out the names of friends, family, and loves thought lost in the predation of the mercenaries or the Great Burn. Mary herself saw Vincent amongst the prisoners, as equally cowed as all the others. To her later shame, the handmaiden gave almost no thought to these and all the other people. Her eyes instead went from sorrowful face to sorrowful face, looking, seeking, but not finding. Until that moment, she had hoped, desperately clung to one shred of hope, that her mother still lived. Mary could not find that one face amongst the lien of hopeless prisoners.

At last, Mary glanced at Karen. The Truthseer had been waiting for the look and shook her head, those pearlescent eyes saying clearly that the handmaiden's mother was not among those taken. A brief, but powerful wave of shame rose in Mary's soul. She could not tell as her eyes watered if she was saddened that her mother was dead, or relieved that she had been spared the horrors of Xeshlin enslavement.

"Is this a threat?" Rainer growled. "We all know what you damned Xeshlin do with your captives!"

Xaemus held up a gloved hand, shaking his head. "You misunderstand," his voice answered as though echoing from some open, waiting tomb. "This is an enticement, a supplement to Vagris' generosity."

The colonel narrowed his eyes.

"Stand down your defense," Xaemus offered. "Disband your citizen militia and return your House Guard to its peacetime status. The Northern Keep will be left untouched. The army before you will leave the Northlands. And..." the Xeshlin glanced behind. "These prisoners will be returned to you."

A chorus of hissing erupted from the Sorcerous Sisters. The Dark Coven sneered and growled in the words of their horrid language, their eyes of burning blood nearly taking true flame at the possibility of being denied their orgy of sacrifice. Xaemus said nothing. The monster of Davenor only turned slightly in his saddle and glanced back. His own eyes, the same burning blood as the priestesses, held a greater threat, a more terrifying possibility. Whereas the eyes of the Dark Coven were the writhing flames of an inferno, Xaemus' gaze was that of lava. More destructive and more unyielding. Even the Sorcerous Sisters, the nightmarish predators who ruled the Xeshlin, could not bear the terrible weight of that gaze; they stilled their hissing objections and feel to silence.

Vagris seemed nearly as upset as did the Dark Coven, though his anger was held within his stiff back and frozen face. He did not look to Xaemus, but he also struggled to suppress a wrathful tremor. "The offer is made," he said through gritted teeth. "The prisoners for the princesses. Peace or war?"

Colonel Rainer, commander of the defense of the Northern Keep, said nothing for a long moment. He did not look to Princess Karen for instruction or confirmation of what was in his heart. He did not need to do this. The shouts from the walls had silenced. The stirring of the city's defenders stilled. The resolve of House Calonar, both its noble members and the people sworn, not only to serve it, but for whom that family had sacrificed so much, joined together. Their resolve swelled like a thousand tiny ripples in the sea merging into an unstoppable wave. Hands gripped weapons, faces locked in grim lines, and shoulders squared against the horrors to come.

"This," Rainer held up his arm, his voice growing into a great roar. "This is the Northern Keep. We defied the Inquisition. We defied the Mad Vaeyen. We defied the Greysoul. You're just another in a long list of scum who've learned the same hard lesson. This is House Calonar, and we do not yield!"

The roar was taken up by the companions behind Rainer. The roar swelled and rose to the city's walls, taken up by the defenders there. The roar swelled into the city, taken up by all the people. The roar rose and crashed against the mercenary army.

Chapter 25

"What's your strategy, colonel?" Karen asked.

After the parlay, the city was sealed, both from within and without. Colonel Rainer led their small party back through the gate, and the guardsmen worked the great mechanisms that sealed it. A watch was ordered and preparations made for what must come. Outside the walls, the mercenaries continued their blockading patrols and pulled their main force back in preparation for the battle ahead. The siege had begun.

The leaders of the Northern Keep had moved to the House Guard barracks. There, Colonel Rainer, Princess Karen, Mary, Rashid and Chandra, Esha, Amatria and Longshot, Remm, Cardinal Tain, and Lieutenant Aloisa gathered in a small conference room. This, the princess told them, would be the war council that organized their defense, under the leadership of Colonel Rainer. The Baron Tressalon said nothing, and seemed as withdrawn as always. His second had tried to make excuses for him, but Rainer had put his foot down, and demanded that the two agents participate in the strategy meeting. With Karen's backing of the order, the two spies obeyed.

Rainer was leaning over the center table of the room, upon which was drawn a rough map of the Northern Keep. "A city this size is hard to defend in a siege," the colonel said, waving his hand over the expansive map. "Since we don't know where the enemy might attack, we have only two options: bunch up or spread out."

"Explain," the princess said.

Rainer moved his hand around the city wall, stopping at several points to make a fist. "We reinforce specific bastions, concentrating our forces at key points. That way, wherever the attack comes from, there'll be a response force nearby. Once the attack comes, the rest of our forces move to support." He opened his hand and waved it across the entire city. "The only other real option is to spread ourselves across the entire wall, but that would make response too slow."

Aloisa pointed at the castle. "What about defense-in-depth?" she suggested.

"What's that?" Mary asked.

"We make a token defense of the wall," the lieutenant explained. "We follow the colonel's idea and set up in the strongest fortresses." She gave Rainer and level expression. "Like you said, sir, we don't know exactly where the enemy will attack, and we've seen what those warmachines will do. The walls won't hold." She pointed at a random spot along the wall. "But there's only a few of those things, and they'll likely need all of them at one spot to punch through our defenses. So, we let them."

The Gunrsvien warrior-woman drew a finger from the wall, back into the city. "Whatever breach they make will still be a bottleneck, a choke-point for their forces. Once we know where the enemy will punch through, we deploy the Uldra." She glanced at Remm, "The miners can wait in ambush, hitting them from the sides."

The tattooed Uldra grinned and nodded.

Aloisa then glanced at Amatria and Longshot who, as always, stood pressed together as close as was possible. "We also hold back the Walkers. When the Uldra engage their forces as they come in, the Sylvai can use their missiles to drive them, force them into battle with Remm."

Longshot nodded, his arms enfolding Amatria. Since the parlay, the Sylva had been distracted, her mind struggling to focus just as her eyes were visibly fighting to hold back tears.

Esha stood on her tiptoes to see the map. "I believe my students may also be of service in this strategy," the archmage pointed out, once again pushing her cap out of her eyes. Remm reached down and picked up the tiny Sylva with one massive hand, lifting her so that she could sit at the corner. He also firmly removed her cap. When the great magical practitioner looked like she would give voice to her indignation, Remm only held up one thick finger, as big around as was her delicate-seeming neck. Esha pouted a bit, but then crossed her arms over her small torso. "Like the Walkers," she said somewhat sourly, "we can use our skills to force the invaders into specific locations."

"No, little flower," Aloisa objected. There was an odd degree of respect in the Gunrsvein's voice. Mary noticed that, when she spoke to any official, even Princess Karen, the warrior-woman rarely offered more than the most perfunctory tokens of courtesy. Even Colonel Rainer received her customary rough-and-tumble attitude. She was never overtly discourteous, but rather seemed little interested in treating those of rank any differently than others. Esha, however, received a clear deference from Aloisa. "For a defense-in-depth to work, mobility is the most vital asset. We will need your magic, and that of your students, to ensure our forces can get from place to place."

"I fear I do not understand," Esha admitted.

Rainer leaned over the table. "A defense-in-depth means breaking our forces up. It's done when a smaller force faces a larger one. Rather than fighting straight-on, we break or forces into chunks. When the enemy advances, they'll spread out. We concentrate our assets in specific areas, waiting in ambush and attacking sections of their forces when they can have numerical advantage. When enemy reinforcements come, we pull back and redeploy, letting a different detachment attack in a different area. It's slow work, and costly, but that strategy can defeat a larger force." He looked up at Aloisa. "Though, it's usually used in the open, not when confined to a city."

"Still viable," the lieutenant shrugged. "In fact, it should work even better."

"How so?" Cardinal Tain asked. The old clergyman had arrived at the same time as the others, having been summoned by Princess Karen before the parley had even begun.

"We know the city," Aloisa explained, "they don't. The streets offer plenty of ambush points. We can hide within the buildings and attack when they pass by."

"Unless they burn the city just like the forest," Mary objected softly.

Rainer shook his head. "You heard Vagris. They want plunder."

"It's probably the only thing keeping an army that big together," Aloisa added. "They're working on the promise of sacking the Northern Keep."

"Additionally," Esha said, "such an inferno would be as big a detriment to Fak'Har and Vagris as it would us."

"Quite so," Cardinal Tain mused. "Such a blaze would prevent them from advancing on the castle too quickly."

"And our reinforcements are on the way," Rainer agreed. "Time isn't on their side."

"So, we just give up on the walls?" Chandra demanded. "Those are the strongest fortifications ever made! What's the point of all the work if we're just pulling back? We might as well just open the gates!"

Rashid seemed for a moment to stir himself from his misery. "Maybe we should... There must be a way to..."

Chandra put a comforting hand on the spymaster's arm. "We don't think planning for the worst is the best way to defend this city."

Karen turned to a counter and poured a small glass of wine. The others were not paying attention to the young princess. After all, the youngest Calonar had spent nearly all her life working to blend into the background, to avoid the direct gaze of people. As such, even in these recent months, when she had stepped forward to lead in the incapacity of her parents and her sister, people tended to forget Karen was there until she spoke. Mary was certain that she alone, having spent more time with Karen and her sister than any other, saw the princess mix a small vial of some dark powder into the wine.

Rainer looked at Chandra, his eyes hard. "I won't throw lives away on pride. Fak'Har's warmachines negate the advantage of the walls. If we're going to survive, we have to be flexible."

"We can't just make a single plan," Chandra argued, "especially one based on the assumption of failure."

Karen brought the wine around and handed it to Rashid. As engrossed as she was in arguing with Rainer, Chandra did not notice Rashid drink.

"And if the warmachines were neutralized?" Karen asked as she walked back to her place at Rainer's side.

All eyes went to the princess.

"How?" Aloisa asked.

"The process doesn't really matter," the Truthseer replied. "My sister can neutralize them. The point is, how does that affect our strategy?"

Rainer leaned back, his fists on his hips. "Well..." he mused. "We've been talking like we know the walls will fail. But that's based on those fire-breathers." The colonel looked to his second. "What do you think?"

Aloisa closed her eyes a moment. "What's our goal?" she asked.

"To not die," Esha replied immediately. Remm patted her on the head, which she slapped away in irritation.

"The little flower is quite correct," Aloisa agreed. "The survival of the people is our main goal. The city is second."

Mary spoke up. "Is there any chance we can hold out until Prince Rogan returns? Princess Kyla has been in contact with him for months now. They're getting close."

"Do we know when the prince will get here?" Rainer asked Karen.

The Truthseer took a breath and closed her pearlescent eyes. She then looked from one person to the next, stopping at Aloisa. "Anul 31st," Karen revealed. "We must hold only until then before Rogan arrives with General Killdare. Together, they have more than enough forces to defeat Vagris' mercenaries and Fak'Har's monsters."

"Twenty-three days," Mary breathed, the faintest spark of hope rekindling in her heart for the first time in months." Karen glanced at her and nodded.

Rainer once again leaned over the map. "Alright, that changes things. We know the walls will hold," he glanced at Karen. "Right?"

The princess paused a moment. "The warmachines will be neutralized," she said. "They will not be a factor." She looked at Remm. "Though their operators will still be a problem."

"Not for long," the Uldra said menacingly.

Rainer nodded. "Alright, then they'll have to do it the old-fashioned way." He stared at the map. "There's really only three ways to attack a walled city. Over, under, or through." He looked at Esha. "Over?"

The tiny archmage shook her head. "Siege equipment moves slowly. My students and I will destroy them before they reach the walls. If the *Xesh'lin* witches try to use their power, I will educate them on true magic." Esha's attempts at ferocity or any degree of anger were often comical, though none of her friends and associates would say so. Her tiny, fragile-seeming body simply did not lend itself to ideas of physical violence or even direct confrontation. In that moment, though, Mary started at the Sylva's vicious growl. She exceeded even Remm's hatred for the traitorous Western Uldra when she spoke of the Sorcerous Sisters of the Xeshlin. All the world knew of the animosity the Sylvai held for their traitorous cousins. Rumor, though, whispered of a greater rivalry, a soul-rending blood feud between Sylvai adepts and the Dark Covens.

"So long as the little flower can handle anything larger, we can handle scaling ladders," Aloisa added, also startled at Esha's seething hatred for the Sorcerous Sisters of the Xeshlin. "I'd wager a year's pay that our guardsmen can handle Vagris' mercenaries."

"Through?" Rainer asked.

Esha shook her head. "I've already activated the wall's enchantments. The gates are sealed."

"And defended," Remm added. "Any ramming team that tries to get close will get all kinds of fun dropped on their heads."

"That leaves under." Rainer looked at Amatria.

The Sylva archwizard breathed in, steeling herself against whatever conflict was roiling within her and seeming to draw strength from Longshot. "I am not an Earth Mage," she admitted. "But I still have some familiarity with the local geography." She paused, pinching the bridge of her nose. "I believe too much rock and clay exists within the ground for effective tunneling. Doing so by hand would require more time than the attackers have. Doing so otherwise would require magic."

"We would detect any such attempt," Esha added. "And counter it."

"We still need a contingency for the penetration of the city."

All discussion stopped. Heads turned and mouths opened. Rashid had spoken. Not in broken words or slurring speech. His voice still croaked with ill-use. Dark circles hung over his eyes, but those eyes now held some small, returning portion of the gleam of brilliance. Even as those around him watched, the spymaster stood a little taller. "All these developments are a good thing," Rashid added, running an idle hand through his dark hair. "But we always need a backup."

"Agreed," Rainer said, clearly as startled as everyone else. Everyone, Mary noted, except Karen.

Rashid leaned over the table, examining the map. "You mentioned something about a defense-in-depth?" he asked Aloisa.

The lieutenant nodded. "That was when we thought the walls would fall."

"They still might." The spymaster picked up a quill and began marking areas near the artillery firing positions closes to the castle. "We should plan for a case in which there's a breach. Identify rallying points for our forces so that they can fall back and then mobilize for a counter-attack." Rashid looked up at Rainer. "Do we have an evacuation plan?"

"We're surrounded." The colonel shook his head. "There's no way to get people out as long as the mercenary irregulars are patrolling."

Rashid looked at Karen. An entire conversation seemed to silently pass between the two. "It will only become viable once there's a breach," the princess told him.

The spymaster nodded and looked back at the map. "If a breach happens," he glanced up at Karen again, who nodded, "then all the mercenaries, traitor Uldra, and Fak'Har's creatures will funnel into that one area."

"If they get access into the city," Aloisa added, "even the patrolling mercenaries will likely try to get in."

"Why?" Mary asked.

"Money," Rainer said flatly. "Vagris has promised booty, and it's all in here. If the wall goes down, those mercenaries will want to collect their pay.

Rashid nodded. "Vagris will likely lose control for a while at that point." He looked at Remm. "Can you dedicate some City Watch to an evacuation?"

"Better the auxiliary does it," the Uldra argued.

"Alright." The spymaster looked at Rainer. "So, in the event of a breach, we have the auxiliary lead as many people..." he looked to Karen.

"The castle," she answered, not needing the question spoken.

Rashid nodded. "To the castle, then. Regular forces pull back as well, including the artillery crews, who'll have to sabotage their engines."

"Already taken care of," the colonel said. "The Sylvai engineers have installed a failsafe into each engine. The crew can disable them when they abandon."

"Good," Rashid nodded. "Then the auxiliary and City Watch can protect the people as a rear-guard, holding back anything that tries to grab prisoners during the evacuation."

Remm nodded.

"Hopefully, none of this will be necessary," Aloisa added. "We know Prince Rogan is coming with reinforcements. We only need to hold out for twenty-three days. That's not long for a siege."

Rashid again glanced at Karen, who nodded, her face grim. "Right," the spymaster said. "But let's have this plan ready... just in case."

"That just leaves the disposition of our forces along the walls," Esha pointed out.

"The enemy doesn't have the leadership for too many assault points," Rashid pointed out. "They'll hit in just two, maybe three locations at most."

Rashid dipped a quill in ink and wordlessly handed it to Karen. The Truthseer circled the area at Defiant Gate. "Or just one." The spymaster nodded and looked at Rainer. "We focus on that spot," he said.

The colonel looked from Karen to Rashid and back. "Alright," he said neutrally. He leaned in and nodded to Aloisa, who took up parchment and quill. "An even distribution of guardsmen at these points. Maximize ammunition and supplies in the nearest fortresses. Reinforcing auxiliaries to the close-by buildings, and City Watch at the gate itself. Order artillery to reorient to probable axes of advance on Defiant Gate.

Supply dumps behind each fortress." Colonel Rainer straightened and looked at Cardinal Tain. "Clerics will set up there as well," he said.

The elderly churchman nodded. "We will divide our efforts," he said in a soft voice. "My priests will evacuate the wounded for treatment and offer final rites when necessary. The clerics of the Harvest Mother will act as on-site medics for minor injuries and staff the treatment sites. Medaka will have her Sisters bringing food and water, and will take care of the families of those fighting."

Mary put a hand on the old man's shoulder. "You should coordinate all this from the castle," she suggested.

Tain smiled again and put his hand over hers. "No, my child. My place is here, like every other citizen."

"What about the King?" Rashid asked pointedly. "Who will care for him, keep him alive?"

Cardinal Tain looked at the spymaster. "Queen Nora relieved me after she recovered from her, ah, illness. She is once again tending to the King. She has more than enough strength to see him through until the Prince's return with the Seal of Life."

"I mean no offense, your eminence," Rainer said with a gentle shake of his head. "If the wall fails, if we have to fall back and fight a defense in depth, people will need to hurry to the castle. You..." the veteran gestured helplessly at the cardinal's frail, broken body.

"I," Tain finished with a forgiving smile, "do not move fast in the easiest of times. All the more reason for me not to take up space better used by the young and able bodied." He shook his head. "My mind is made up, my children. I will stay in the city I have served for so many years. Come what may, I will share its Fate."

Colonel Rainer nodded grimly. "So, who's running the clerics at the wall itself, besides Medaka?"

"Your daughter," Aloisa grinned.

Rainer looked as though he would object, that he might charge off and order Ilse away from the dangerous areas, but stopped. "Fine," he grumbled. "No telling that girl anything anyway," The colonel straitened. "Is there anything else?"

Heads shook. Hands were clasped and all of them took a moment to whisper words with Cardinal Tain. Mary said nothing, but she feared as the others did, that the old man, like so many others, would not survive the siege. Rainer and Aloisa left to issue orders. Remm helped Esha down and they, along with Amatria and Longshot, went to mobilize their respective groups. Karen asked Mary for an escort back to the castle. As the two women left, the handmaiden noticed Rashid pull Chandra aside.

"Little bitch must have dosed you," Chandra panted, leaning against the wall of a boarded-up shop. The night was well under way and she had planned a great many activities, all of which had been preempted by Rashid's sudden lucidity. Months of slow dosing, of gradual application of Mindfog, all gone in a moment.

Rashid had taken her aside after the others left. His questions had come quickly and harshly. Chandra had made her excuses, planned and well-worn words meant to dissuade suspicion from her, redirecting it elsewhere. Rashid, though, had seen through her lies almost immediately.

"Where are all the damned agents!?!" he had hissed while leading her back towards the castle. "Where's Vincent? Where's the imbeds who were supposed to be helping organize the City Watch? Where are the people we've been training to infiltrate the mercenary army?"

"You sent them all outside the city," Chandra had replied as they wound through the various back alleys and side streets with which they were both most familiar. "The Council wanted our help in the evacuation, so you ordered everyone out, into the forest."

"Like Underworld I did!" the spymaster had almost snarled. He paused as they had passed through the dark, silent mercantile district. Breathing deeply, he had kept blinking and rubbing his eyes, obviously trying to force away the last of the Mindfog. "I would never do something that stupid! No matter how many I sent out, I'd always keep a few teams in the city!"

"Rashid," Chandra had tried to say as she slowly, subtly applied a powder to her left hand. "I still have the orders. Orders you wrote up. Don't you remember?"

The spymaster had narrowed his eyes. "Yeah," he had said then. "I do rememb-"

Chandra had struck, but not fast enough. Rashid had caught her right wrist, the one holding a dagger stabbing for his middle. At any other time, had the spymaster been at his best, Chandra knew she was no match for him. Fortunately, whatever that damned brat of a princess had slipped him, the effects had not fully dissipated the Mindfog. Her dagger had been a feint; the compound in her left hand was the true attack. The traitor held her hand over Rashid's mouth and nose, suffering his blows to her abdomen until his eyes rolled up and he fell.

Chandra sat beside Rashid as he slept in that alley, collecting her breath and her thoughts. Months of work, gone. Months of planning and preparation, ruined. The siege had begun. Her master had been specific in his requests. Chandra was supposed to be spending the next few nights sabotaging the trebuchets, setting off the failsafe on each engine. Vagris and Fak'Har would be making their preparations for the first assault, and that could come at any time. The traitor looked up, but the moon was already dipping low. She could still complete her work; she had enough time at least for those trebuchets that would likely be used in the coming assaults.

There was a faint vibration coming from the inner pocket of her leather vest. Chandra reached in and withdrew the small communication crystal. It was pulsing black. Her master was trying to contact her. Chandra knew what her benefactor, her co-conspirator and mentor would say. Sabotage the siege equipment. Stay focused on the plan. Forget about Rashid. Just kill him and be done with it. Her master knew of her feelings for him, and had even promised the power to resurrect him should the spymaster need to be killed. Chandra had seen this done before. Her master had the power.

The traitor looked to Rashid and then back to the pulsing communication crystal. She closed her eyes and imagined a map of the Northern Keep. They were in the mercantile district now, closer to the castle than anything else. She would need at least an hour, likely more, to reach the nearest significant trebuchet. She would need all night to sabotage enough to complete her master's request. Chandra opened her eyes and glanced to the west. Her safehouse was near Uldra Gate, at the farthest western end of the city. She had prepared for their escape. She had a hiding place, but it was not ready. There were no supplies yet. She would need to sneak back into the castle, likely needing multiple trips, to gather what they would need when they finally left the Northern Keep behind.

Rashid snored slightly.

Chandra could not hold back the smile from her lips. He did that only when he felt safe. Rashid slept in absolute silence when they were on mission. He only ever snored when they were relatively safe, usually after he made love to her. The traitor picked up her dagger and glanced again at the pulsing communication crystal. She looked out, to the far end of the alley, and spotted an unattended, empty cart. Large enough for a man, she considered. With that, she could smuggle Rashid to the safehouse. She did not have much there, except her supply of Mindfog. Her plan could still work. Her master was more than able enough to see through the destruction of this insipid Noble House. They could still escape to a new life.

The communication crystal was still pulsing, reminding her of her promise to her master. She swore to help bring about the death of House Calonar. In return, she and Rashid would be given all the wealth they could ever need to start a new life. Chandra leaned back again against the wall and closed her eyes. Perhaps Tramaya, she considered. Tramanese merchants often came to the Northern Keep, with their spices, porcelain, and silk. Their homeland was supposed to be beautiful and cultured, to say nothing of far from the madness that was consuming Lanasia. Her master could easily provide her safe passage to the orient. Her, and Rashid. All she had to do…

The traitor again looked in the direction of the trebuchets. Her master had sworn that Rashid could be resurrected, cleansed of any dark memories and all knowledge of the Sylva witch. Chandra's hand closed on her dagger. One quick motion, and it would be done. She looked at Rashid, who continued to gently snore. He used to joke,

Chandra recalled, about where he would die. Back, before the Sylva witch, they had often sat together and talked. He had once told her that he had a vision of his death, that it would be dark and closed in, a place of stone. The traitor looked around. Stone buildings to both sides, and the moon had disappeared behind the distant rooftops. Just one motion, one slice, and she could complete the last tasks her master had asked of her. Then, they could be gone, wealthy and safe and together. All she had to do...

Rashid snored. Chandra looked at him, then down at her hands. One held the dagger, the other, still coated with some of the sleeping powder, held the pulsing communication crystal. She chose, and the crystal shattered against the stone wall. She would need the entire night to get them to the safehouse. She would see Rashid secured and give him a strong enough dose of Mindfog. Then, she would begin planning for how and when to infiltrate back into the castle and get the supplies they would need. The entire city would be focused east, towards Defiant Gate. They should be safe enough in the western districts near Uldra Gate.

As she loaded Rashid into the cart and pulled a tarp over his sleeping form, she was careful to make him as comfortable as possible. A memory intruded as she did so. They had been in the City of All Sins, years ago, when the Service had still been in its infancy. They had been on their way to free that idiot Rogan and his pet Uldra from another dungeon. Chandra had needed to smuggle Rashid into the city, and done so by hiding him in a cart, much like this one. The woman did not fight the smile that bloomed once more on her face, perhaps the first genuine one of its kind in years. The memory of that mission was a good one, the last time she and Rashid had worked together. Just as they would again.

Chapter 26

Opfern arrived pushing a small cart. The maid showed none of the harried activity of most of the rest of the city, instead radiating a mask of calm and certainty. Mary was not fooled, though. Like her, Opfern was dedicated to her service and would never let her own uncertainty affect her mistress.

"How's the Queen?" Mary asked, accepting the cart in the foyer of Kyla's chambers.

"Her Majesty is quite comfortable," Opfern replied automatically, falling back to the same formula she always used when asked these same questions. "She continues in her work keeping the King heathy, now that Cardinal Tain has returned to the church."

Mary paused and put a gentle hand on her younger friend's shoulder. Opfern was a little shorter than she, making the maid's efforts at avoiding eye contact easier. There were no words for a few moments, but Mary could feel the tension in Opfern's body. The slightest tremor, unperceivable to the eye, ran through the maid. She said nothing, would say nothing, even as the well-worn words that had become as much a part of her mask as any expression, cracked. Mary turned her friend and put her arms around the younger maid. "How much longer?" she whispered.

"I don't know," Opfern whispered back. She wrapped her own arms around Mary and relented in her control, however briefly. "He doesn't move, doesn't answer. His eyes barely move. We have to give him broth; it's all he can…" A spasm of grief shook her body. Mary took this into herself.

"She doesn't leave his side," Opfern breathed. "She's pouring all her magic into him, keeping him alive… breathing." The maid shook her head slightly. "I don't think they can… it can't go on much…"

"The Prince is coming," Mary said, willing her words to be true. The handmaiden did not let any of her doubt, her own uncertainty, bleed into Opfern. She held her friend and sent to her all the confidence she, herself, wondered if she really felt. "Just sixteen more days. They have the Healing Sphere and they're coming with General Killdare and the army."

Opfern sniffed and wiped away her tears. "Has… has the Princess heard from…?"

"Just last night," Mary lied, looking at her friend with a warm smile that did not pass any deeper than her face. "They've left Ironheartshaven gathering more forces as they march. We have to keep them all safe for just a little while longer."

Her friend smiled at the thought, the hope that the champion of House Calonar was on his way. The maid turned to the cart and handed to Mary the small tray she had brought. "Right," Opfern said. "You're right. We keep them going, whether they like it or not." This, she said with firmness, even a little mock anger.

Mary took the tray bearing the steaming kettle and cup. Again lying with a smile, the handmaiden set the try onto a nearby table and turned back to her friend. "The most important thing in service to the House..." she began to say.

"Is seeing to their souls as well as their bodies," Opfern finished, mimicking Roland's paternal baritone. The saying was a common one for the head of the castle's staff. He said it often to everyone, and both Mary and Opfern had heard his refrain more times than could be counted. They smiled at one another, warmed at the recollection of so many lessons, so many corrections from the old butler. Opfern squared her shoulders and pulled the small cart bearing the meager meal for the withering King and Queen.

Mary was alone in the foyer. With her friend's departure, she stood in the empty room, briefly able to let go the false confidence that she forced upon all those around her. She breathed and pushed the aching despair, the terrible loneliness, back down into the hollow pit. As was becoming her habit in those small, scattered moments of freedom, Mary looked down at the rings on her finger. She stared at the one, tracing a finger across it. Gold that Esha's magic had turned flawless white, fashioned into the image of the ribbon she had given Tomas. A small diamond at the center. The handmaiden closed her eyes and let her memories drift back.

He had proposed at the banquet ending the Harvest Festival. The night that followed his victory in the tournament was such a joyous one. Food and dancing. Music and good company. They had mingled with the elite of the Northern Keep, dressed in fine clothes their royal patrons had provided. They held each other as they danced, they held each other as they talked. They even, Mary recalled with the faint echo of a wicked grin, let their hands explore just a little when they sat at the royal table. And then, when the night could not have become more wonderous, he had knelt and asked her that one, simple question, and given her the ring.

And then the Death Mage attacked.

And then the sorceress Vara sent her storm.

And then the Prince took him away on another adventure, leaving her here.

"Is the water here?" Medaka asked, sticking her head through the open door from the receiving room.

Mary straightened and forced the tears back down again. "Just arrived," she said in a voice of forced confidence. The handmaiden took up the tray and walked forward. Medaka, dressed as always in a skirt and light blouse of rich purple, stopped her student with a hand on the shoulder. Mary said nothing and did not even look up at the taller woman. Knowing concern flowed from the Sister's heart, and the handmaiden knew from experience that Medaka could draw the deep sorrows from one's soul with barely a glance, so Mary did not look. Instead, she pulled her shoulder away and walked ahead.

They passed through the receiving room and into Kyla's bedroom. The princess was reclining in her bed, wrapped in a light robe of blue silk. This had, in recent weeks, become her habit. None of her dresses fit any more. The growing princeling bulged from her small body, contorting her once-perfect curves. Walking had become awkward, making all other activities, from bathing to having a toilet all the more problematic. Even dressing had become an arduous, time-consuming odyssey, full of foul language. With summer winding down but the days still long and warm, Kyla had finally given up on clothes altogether. Confined as she was to her chambers, and most often to her bed, the princess sullenly refused to cover herself at all. On those few occasions when anyone besides Mary and Ilse were in her company, Kyla's only concession to feminine modesty was the blue robe tied as loosely as possible around her massive stomach and breasts.

Ilse, dressed in her gray cleric's robes, was seated beside the princess, holding a small device in her hand. It was a long wooden handle, with a gold frame extending forward. Within this frame was a small, flat crystal, that cast a warm light over Kyla's body as Ilse ran it along her stomach. In her other hand, the priestess of the Harvest Mother held another lens of glowing crystal to her eye, looking through it as though inspecting something. "Breathe," she commanded.

Kyla made more of an irritated sigh than a true breath. The princess glanced at the door, noting the return of Medaka and Mary. "Are we ready?" she asked.

Mary nodded and took the small tray to the table resting beside the open balcony. She wiped clean the already pristine cup and poured into it a portion of steaming water. Medaka joined the handmaiden, drawing a tiny box from within her lose blouse. It was wooden, but engraved with gold and silver, and had the image of a sitting cat on its lid. Opening this, the Sister of the Lady of Light drew out a very small silver spoon and began depositing the herbs within the box to the steaming cup.

"Do you know the histories, the diaries?" Mary whispered to Medaka.

"I do," the Sister whispered back, focusing on measuring the herbs.

"Then you know the warnings," the handmaiden and scholar pointed out. "This is very dangerous. Dream Magic is corruptive to…"

"Can be corruptive," Medaka corrected. "Some Sisters were corrupted, others resisted the corruption." She stirred the steaming potion. "We must trust Kyla."

"Are we sure this is safe for the prince?" Ilse asked yet again. Having assumed the duty as Kyla's primary physician with the absence of the Queen, the priestess of the Harvest Mother had grown increasingly over-protective of the sleeping future heir of House Calonar. Ilse had become almost tyrannical in her treatment of the princess, dictating meals, rest, and all other aspects of her noble lady's life.

"You know," Kyla mused irritably, "a lady in waiting is supposed to obey, not command."

"Yes, your Highness," Ilse said as she always did, indifferent to her princess' orders.

Mary brought the tea to Kyla's bedside. "Technically, we're not ladies in waiting," she corrected. "We're not even ladies."

"Of course you are," the princess argued absently. "I signed the patents for Ilse's father just yesterday."

All the women blinked. "What?" Ilse asked.

Kyla glanced at her friend, confused. "He didn't tell you?"

"He. Did. Not." Ilse's voice was a calm as always, but its customary warmth was entirely gone.

"Oh dear," the princess mumbled, accepting the tea from Mary and sipping.

"Maybe he was keeping it as a surprise," Mary offered.

"Mmm." Ilse's voice still carried none of summer's happiness. "Highness," the priestess said calmly, "would you please elaborate?"

Kyla sipped again. "Well," she said, blushing to her roots. "In recognition for his leadership in this crisis, and his bravery, my family has granted him knighthood and a hereditary lordship."

"I see."

"We'll have the traditional ceremony once Rogan gets home," the princess continued quickly. "And after Fak'Har is defeated, we'll work out the land grant."

"Mmm." Ilse stood and walked over to the table on which Mary had placed the small tray. On this rested a gold display stand holding a crystal half-sphere. The priestess picked up the magical device and waved a hand over it. There was a brief pause, during which a soft red light gently blinked within the crystal, and then the light became a mist that rose from the surface of the crystal. The mist coalesced into the gruff face of Klug Rainer, commander of the Northern Keep's defense and father to a visibly-irritated Ilse.

Colonel Rainer was looked away, barking commands to some unseen person. "Are you girls ready up there?" he asked absently, then started when he actually looked forward. "Ilse? What's going on? Is everything ok up there?"

"Hello… Father." The priestess' voice could have shattered stone.

"Uh, ok. What's… What happened?"

"I just wanted to talk for a moment before we began."

Rainer looked around. "Now's not the best time, Squirrel." He jerked his head to the side and barked another command. "The mercenaries are forming up. We can hear the Uldra warmachines starting."

"This will just take a minute. Father."

"Uh… ok."

"Was there something you wanted to tell me? Father."

"What in Underworld are you... Wait, is this about that knighthood?" Ilse's eyes narrowed dangerously.

A metallic roar echoed through the magical transmission. Rainer ducked and called for others to do so as well. The red mist distorted for a moment and then corrected, revealing the colonel crouching behind cover. "Look, Squirrel, this really isn't the time! Whatever you girls are doing up there, you've got to get-"

There was another roar of mechanical evil. Through the open door leading to the balcony, Mary could see a flash of hateful fire erupt beyond the city's walls. The handmaiden went to Ilse and firmly pried the crystal half-sphere from her hands. "Colonel, are you ok?" she asked.

"Yeah! I think they're still starting up!" he ducked again as there was another machine-roar. Beyond the balcony, Mary could see another burst of flame, this time joined by another.

Mary put a hand on her friend's. "We have to do it," she said firmly.

Ilse nodded and returned to Kyla's bed. Medaka joined her, sitting on the princess' other side. The purple-clad Sister of the Lady of Light took the now-empty teacup and set it on the nightstand. "Remember," she said to Kyla, "Focus. This isn't like communicating with Rogan; there's no connection of love to follow. You have to center your thoughts on the minds you want to touch." She glanced at Mary. "There will be other things within the Dream," the elder Sister then said. "Darker things. You must avoid these. They will seem like they can help, like they are useful. Shun them, at all costs."

Kyla nodded and took a deep breath. She settled against the pillows and clasped her hands over her heart.

The outer door opened and Karen entered. The youngest Calonar walked in with all the regal bearing of a queen and glanced at Mary. "The attack's begun," she said.

There was another blast of fire from beyond the walls, this followed by several more. Through the magical half-crystal, Rainer cursed and ducked lower behind his cover. "Yeah," Mary agreed. "We noticed."

Karen looked at Kyla. Her older sister nodded and closed her eyes.

"Just a gentle touch," Medaka advised in little more than a whisper. "A suggestion, a quiet hint. Do not use the darkness."

Kyla's breathing grew deep and steady. A soft golden glow emerged from deep within herself. Behind her closed lids, the Sister Superior's eyes flickered.

More baleful eruptions shot out beyond the walls, but very close to it. "Forget the arrows!" Rainer shouted. The terrible roar of metallic evil became constant, a flood of hate. "Keep under cover! Move back from the blast-site!" The colonel was stumbling in a low crouch, and Mary could see flames behind and around the veteran guardsman. "This Druugshit isn't getting any better, girls!" he grunted, diving behind something large and heavy.

Karen walked up to stand beside Mary. "Just a few more moments, colonel."

"Something's wrong," Ilse said.

Mary and Karen turned. Kyla was flinching, her breathing growing short. Her head jerked from one side to another as she mumbled soft sounds of distress. Ilse had taken her princess' hand and was feeling with her other along Kyla's now sweat-beaded brow. The golden aura glowing from Kyla was flickering, and trances of darkness seemed to swirl just beneath its surface. Medaka was holding the golden charm of a sitting cat that hung around her neck, grimacing. "I don't understand," the elder Sister admitted.

"It's Fak'Har," Karen told them. "He knows what Kyla is doing. He's trying to stop her." The youngest Calonar moved to her sister's bed and climbed onto it. She opened Kyla's robe, exposing her swollen stomach. Karen reached out a hand, but paused, almost flinching. The Truthseer glanced her pearlescent eyes at Mary, and the handmaiden saw the briefest flash of near-sorrow on Karen's face. Mary remembered, in that one, brief moment, that even despite her Truthsight, despite her status as a princess of House Calonar, Karen was still a girl, little more than a child.

The Truthseer and princess shook off her hesitation. She put her hand on Kyla's abdomen and leaned in, whispering. Another light joined with the golden aura, this one of pure white. The two auras blended together, intensifying. The darkness eating away just beneath the surface flinched and then writhed. Sparks of mystical power shot from Kyla's body, and all three women gathered around her jumped away. The gold and white auras intensified even more, banishing the darkness. A horrid scream, one of pain and outrage, echoed out from beyond the walls. From the magical half-crystal, Rainer risked glancing up in confusion.

Kyla became calm and peaceful again. The gold and white auras remained, merged together, and a gentle smile appeared on the princess' face. Her mouth moved, as though she were whispering. Her head tilted, just a small bit, and she continued hinting, suggesting, offering.

Outside, beyond the walls, Mary heard the hateful, mechanical roaring stop. She glanced out, past the balcony. The fire had ceased. From the red mist still drifting up from the magical half-crystal, Rainer stood and looked out. "What in Underworld?" he marveled.

"Colonel," Mary said, "What's happening?"

"I think…" the guardsman, a veteran of countless battles and supernatural threats, looked about in open-mouthed confusion. "I think… whatever you girls are doing, it's working."

"What's happening?" Mary asked again.

"The warmachines have stopped. They're still active. There's still smoke coming from them, but the fire stopped. They closed back up again and they're... just sitting there."

Karen walked to Mary's side. "Colonel," she said firmly. "Tell your people to get down."

"What? Why? What's happening?"

"Now, colonel!" the princess snapped.

Rainer relayed the order and took cover. A metallic screech tore through the air, clearly audible even from high atop the castle. Mary rushed to the balcony and could only stare in shock. The handmaiden had heard of fire mountains. Her teachers had spoken of those terrible monsters of the earth, peaks that vomited flame and smoke and death. She had never, though, imagined seeing one. Out, beyond the walls, a cluster of eruptions were pouring liquid flame into the sky.

Karen reached into the sleeve of her blue and grey gown, pulling from it another of the magical communication devices. She waved her hand over the surface of that crystal half-sphere. The red mist formed and coalesced immediately into Esha and Amatria. "Now," the princess commanded, and the image faded.

A great wind, furious and terrifying, exploded around the castle. It bellowed across the Northern Keep, hurling itself from the west and crashing across the city's walls. Just as the horrid eruption of liquid fire was arcing up in preparation for its devastating descent, the wind bellowed into the geysers. The evil, deadly shower was forced back, away from the city and its defenders, falling instead upon the army that had formed up to await their chance to despoil the city and its people. Screams of horror and pain echoed, both from the distant walls, and from the crystal half sphere Mary still held. Through that magical red mist, Rainer stood and stared out. "God's love," the veteran gasped in wide-eyed horror at what he saw.

Karen put away her own communication crystal and moved beside Mary on the balcony. "Colonel, what do you see?" she asked firmly, but also gently.

"It's..." words failed the soldier. The guardsman shook his head and stared. "The warmachines are... gone. They exploded. There's just... metal husks. I don't see any Uldra. The soldiers behind are... most are dead. Some are... are running. There's fire everywhere." Rainer turned away, shaking his head. He took a deep breath and faced Mary and Karen. "It worked, whatever you did. The walls are secure."

Karen nodded. "They won't attack until the fire goes out. You have one week. Let your people rest." She glanced at Mary, her face saying louder than words what the girl trying to be a princess and Truthseer was feeling at what she had unleashed.

Rainer's image dissolved into red mist that descended into the crystal half sphere. Mary returned the device to its holder. She then turned back to Kyla, seeing Ilse and Medaka checking on the princess. "How?" Mary asked.

"Through dreams," Karen replied stoically.

"The corrupted Uldra were... asleep?"

"No. A Dreamwalker can enter a person's mind, even when they're awake. She can whisper into their thoughts, give them hope or fear, confidence or doubt." Karen looked at where her sister still slept. "She can even alter how they see the world around them."

"Illusion?" Mary asked.

"More or less," Karen shrugged. "Kyla changed how the corrupted Uldra saw the controls of those warmachines. She made them destroy themselves."

"And, the darkness?" Ilse pointed out.

"Fak'Har knows about Dream Magic," Karen answered. "He's interfered with Kyla before; he's the reason she hasn't been able to regain contact with Rogan since they left Pelsemoria. When he sensed that she was whispering to his Uldra warsmiths, he tried to stop her." The princess's pearlescent eyes lowered. "My sister needed help, so her son..." Another flash of the briefest sorrow crossed Karen's face. She straightened then. "Kyla shouldn't have to risk this again, not for a while."

A sudden outcry drew all their attention to Kyla. She was curled up and awake. Her face was flushed and her hands went to her stomach. Ilse and Medaka held her, trying to soothe the expectant mother. Mary darted forward and, without thinking, pulled aside Kyla's robe. The handmaiden gasped at the sight of blood.

"Ilse, Medaka," Karen said calmly, "use your magic."

The women, priestesses both, took action. Medaka called upon the Lady of Light to ease Kyla's pain. The princess' face grew easier, her breathing steady. Ilse called upon the Harvest Mother, and the bleeding stopped. Mary put a hand on Kyla's abdomen. She felt the child within, twisting, jerking, clearly in distress. The handmaiden looked at Karen, who could not meet her gaze.

Chapter 27

The siege engines fired nearly as one, sending great blocks of heavy stone hurling through the sky. The missiles, each nearly the size of a small cottage, exploded into the assembling mercenary ranks and the blackened trunks of dead forest. The screams of charred trees mingled with those of broken men. Those near to the impacts but not outright crushed, their bodies reduced to so much pulp, were sent flying. Limbs were torn, torsos crushed, and lives ended. Blood and horror and the terror of another volley filled the air. Lookouts, guardsmen specially trained for their task, called out corrections. Runners relayed these back to the trebuchets at their firing positions deep within the city. The crews made adjustments and reset their massive weapons. The great arms were pulled back and the massive counterweights reset. Teams of laborers and animals moved the ammunition up to be attached in the great slings. Orders were shouted, and the terrible siege engines fired again, once more sending the impossibly-massive stones arching up. Within three shots, five at most, the engines of the Northern Keep were hitting the mercenaries with frightening accuracy.

Nearly a week had passed. Although initially shocked at the explosive end of that first engagement, the defenders and people of the Northern Keep had rejoiced in their victory. The warmachines of the corrupted Western Uldra had been a source of terror to the people. Stories had passed from the survivors of the forest and the Great Burn of the horrifying fire those creations employed. Their sudden, explosive destruction had been so poetic in its correctness that a great number of improvised celebrations had broken out after that first battle. When the threat of further assaults had seemingly passed, many townspeople had even scaled the walls to look out and see the burnt shells of the terrifying warmachines. The people had rejoiced and found new hope, new camaraderie, even as Mary and her friends worked to heal Kyla.

Mary, Ilse, and Medaka had not spent the week in celebration. Their princess, though magically healed, was greatly weakened by the use of Dream Magic. None of the women knew how or why the unborn prince growing within Kyla had been harmed by the effort. Karen had, as became her habit, disappeared. Her orders were relayed through messengers, but the Truthseer kept herself unavailable. In desperation and worry, Mary had even tried consulting Queen Nora, and her more experienced use of Truthsight, but Opfern had been unyielding. No one was allowed to disturb the royal couple, under any circumstances.

So, the ladies in waiting had tended to their princess as best they could. They limited her movement, enforced bedrest, and carefully monitored her food and drink. All of this, of course, being a great source of irritation to the expectant mother herself. In a desperate bid to reduce her number of jailors, Kyla had banished Mary back to her duties alongside Colonel Rainer.

Lieutenant Aloisa had initially resisted Mary's presence on the wall. When the handmaiden had found the Guard leaders after being banished from her princess' bedside, the Gunrsvein woman had looked as though she would refuse and try to send the handmaiden back to the relative safety of Castle Calonar. Rainer, however, had acquiesced to Kyla's order. "Put her back in armor," was all he said, glancing at Mary's Northlands dress.

Aloisa had obeyed, and replaced the equipment Mary had abandoned amidst the Great Burn. The lieutenant had taken Mary aside to a nearby supply dump and rummaged through the spare uniforms and equipment. "Strip," she had grunted at the waiting handmaiden. When Mary had begun to sputter an objection, the Gunrsvein warrior-woman had cut her off. "Do you want to be here or not?"

"Not really," Mary had muttered. "But the Princess ordered-"

"Then shut up and strip. If you're going to be this close you need protection." Aloisa had fished out an undershirt and leggings small enough for Mary. The handmaiden had grudgingly taken off her dress. "That too," the lieutenant grunted, nodding at Mary's ankle-length chemise.

"Absolutely not!"

"Then you're going back to the castle," Aloisa had said flatly. "This is a warzone, not a party. You need to be able to move fast. You do what I say, when I say. Any objection, any failure, and you're gone."

"The colonel-"

"Will listen to me." The warrior-woman had leaned in, an evil grin on her face. "Or do you want to test that?"

Mary had grumbled, looking around. Seeing that they were alone in the small building, she had pulled off the chemise, more than a little uncomfortable. The weather was more than warm enough so that the handmaiden was not chilly, despite the morning's coolness. Each day maintained late summer's radiant heat, and yet the nights and dawns carried the promise of coming autumn.

Aloisa had handed over the underclothes and helped Mary dress. Aloisa then rummaged and pulled out a breastplate. She glanced at the handmaiden, specifically at Mary's chest, and then back at the man-shaped armor. "Nope," she grunted, tossing the metal shirt aside.

"Where did you get yours?" Mary had asked, indicating Aloisa's armor. The lieutenant was, by no means, small-chested, and her polished breastplate reflected this.

There was no specific molding to accommodate Aloisa's breasts, but the armor was noticeably more pronounced at the chest in comparison to the average guardsman's.

"Special made," the warrior-woman had answered. "Women aren't forbidden from the House Guard, but it's pretty uncommon. I offered to pay a smith for my own equipment, but the Colonel forbade it.

"So, all your equipment had to be customed for you?"

"Any good breastplate is customized to the wearer," Aloisa had shrugged, pulling out a chainmail shirt. "Mine's just a little more custom than most. Hold up your arms."

Mary had done so, and the warrior-woman draped the metal shirt over her body. It was a little tight in certain places, but not so much that it greatly limited her movement. Aloisa had her move about, testing that mobility and, satisfied, retrieved one of the smaller bascinet helmets. "I hate those things," the handmaiden muttered.

"Everybody does," Aloisa had answered. "Right up until they get hit in the head." She firmly placed the helmet over Mary's head, doing little to adjust the handmaiden's hair. Finally, the lieutenant retrieved a shortsword and belted it around Mary's waist.

"I don't know how to use this," the handmaiden had objected.

"It's mostly for show," Aloisaa had admitted, settling the weapon in place. "We want to make sure you look as much like the other soldiers as possible.

"Why?"

"So an enemy archer doesn't know you're worth an arrow."

Both Aloisa and Colonel Rainer had grown increasingly surly as the days had passed. Vagris had pulled his army back, into the skeleton that had once been Wildeleves Wood. His outriders still patrolled, still maintained the siege. There were no further assaults, though. No enemy artillery was employed against the city, no infantry formed for attack, no adepts brought their terrible art to bear. Longshot's Walkers, Esha's students, and the Guard lookouts on the walls, all reported the same: the enemy was waiting for something. Even Princess Karen remained silent, only repeating her terrible countdown. Vagris had needed three days for the firestorm to pass and regain control of his forces. But then the renegade Legion commander had not pressed the siege. Instead, they had waited.

"Something went wrong," Rainer had muttered on the morning of the fifth day.

"Well," Mary had replied, looking out at the burnt and twisted ruin of the Uldra warmachines.

They were walking the battlements around Defiant Gate, as they had begun doing each day. Mary continued in her duties to observe and report back to Kyla, the princess one again bed-ridden after her traumatic employment of Dream Magic. Colonel Rainer checked all the siege equipment each day, Mary at his side. He spoke with each unit commander, inspected weaponry, and monitored morale. Ironically, it was the colonel himself who had become increasingly tense.

"No, something else," Rainer had nearly growled. He was looking out from the battlements on that fifth day, staring hatred into the obscuring ruin of the forest. "They had a plan. Vagris would have been ready for the warmachines' failure. Something else happened."

"What?" Mary had asked.

The colonel could only shrug. When the attack had finally come on the morning of the seventh day, Rainer had been almost relieved. Mary was standing with Colonel Rainer and Lieutenant Aloisa at the walls, the warriors watching with almost predatory intensity as the mercenaries had formed into blocks of men, clearly preparing for an assault. The military leaders had waited, watching for something only their trained eyes saw. Finally, when the blocks of men were gathered and moving forward with scaling ladders, Rainer had given the order to fire. The trebuchets launched their deadly barrage again and again. The observers atop the nearest fortresses kept shouting down corrections, and the siege engines made their corrections.

"Maintain fire at points seven, eight, twelve, and fourteen," Rainer ordered to a runner. He turned to Aloisa. "Let's keep them bunched up until they get in range of the wall engines."

The lieutenant nodded and send runners with preparatory orders to the large, crossbow-seeming weapons set along the walls. "Have we spotted any enemy engines?" she called up to the nearest observer.

"Only infantry so far!" the guardsman called down from the top of the tower. "No Uldra, Xeshlin, or those bastard monsters!"

Rainer grunted at the news. "He's testing us."

"What?" Mary asked.

"Vagris," the colonel explained. "He's sending in the least useful of his troops. He's learning what kind of defenses we've got in place."

"So, this is just…?"

"A probe," Aloisa finished. "If they actually break through, great. But Fak'Har and Vagris really only want to watch and see what we do."

"Why would those men agree?" Mary asked. "Why would they throw their lives away?"

"Not much choice," Rainer answered. "They were picked for the opening assault. It's a garbage job, but someone has to do it. If they tried to refuse, they'd be executed."

"Plus," Aloisa added, "if they do manage to break in, they'd be the first to start looting."

"Carrot and stick," Rainer agreed. He turned to a nearby sergeant. "What's the status of the ballistae?"

"Batteries five through seven ready to fire. One through four and eight through eleven don't have a good angle, so they're holding."

"What about twelve?" Aloisa asked.

"Malfunction," Rainer grunted. "They're trying to repair, but they might be out of action for a while."

Esha, once again wrapped in ill-fitting armor, was clambering up the steps to join them. "Glad you're here, little flower," Aloisa said warmly.

The tiny archmage smiled. "I found a natural pause in my other responsibilities," she said happily. "I thought, with all the activity here, I might find some use."

"Your students?"

"They have already dispersed along this section of the wall. They are sheltering within the fortresses and stand ready to assist however you need."

"How many of those explosive javelins did your people make?" Rainer asked.

"They are not precisely javelins, colonel," the Sylva objected primly, holding up a tiny finger. "My design consists of an integrated shaft composed of four-"

"Esha!" Rainer snapped.

"My students completed enough for each of your applicable ballistae to fire two," the archmage said softly. She looked saddened at the rebuke, her chin dropping slightly and her opalescent eyes going wide as she looked up at the brutish colonel.

Aloisa cleared her throat roughly, her own gaze becoming hard and frosty. "I'm sorry, Esha," Rainer sighed as though from a memorized formula. "I shouldn't have snapped at you."

Esha continued starting at the aging veteran with wide eyes, an artful tear forming, but not falling.

"And...?" Aloisa prompted.

The colonel shot his lieutenant an irritated look. "And... You should always know how grateful I am for all your help." Rainer's words were clearly rehearsed.

Esha brightened. "Why, thank you colonel," she said happily.

"Now," Rainer said through gritted teeth, "would you please make sure the ballistae crew know how to load and fire your... devices."

"Most certainly, colonel!" The archmage very nearly skipped to the nearest fortress, casually adjusting once more the overly-long sleeves of her soldiers' tunic.

The colonel sighed heavily again and shook his head. "Have each battery load standard shot first," he told the runners. "Esha's... devices," this he said with another irritated glance at the grinning Aloisa, "get loaded second. After that first shot, the special... whatever... are to be kept in reserve. Only fire them at a triple-horn."

Seeing the runners dispatched, Rainer turned fully to Aloisa. "What's the status of the guardsmen?"

She jerked her head down to the area behind the walls, where units of soldiers wearing breastplates, helmets, and carrying Northland poleaxes waited. "I've got the companies spread out in this area to man the walls, plus the remaining regulars positioned for reinforcement at specific breaches. The auxiliary are evacuating all civilians from the surrounding district. Remm has the Watch and the Uldra at the gate, in case of an assault there."

Rainer nodded. "Alright," he grunted and turned to face the unfolding battle. "Let's get this started."

The blocks of mercenaries were being herded. After the first several deadly volleys from the trebuchets, Colonel Rainer ordered them to shift their fire to the enemy's flanks. The massive boulders began landing on either side of each mercenary unit. This caused the invaders to bunch together, desperate to avoid the missiles as they approached the walls.

Rainer watched, waiting. Mary's entire body tensed, desperate for something to happen. She looked from the colonel to Aloisa and back, but neither officer moved nor spoke. They were waiting, obviously, but Mary's untrained eyes could not see for what. The mercenaries crept closer and closer, holding ladders between their lines and shields above and to the front and sides.

"Let's give those shieldmen something to worry about," Rainer said at last.

Aloisa nodded and turned to the nearby bugler. "Single blast," she ordered.

The guardsman raised a Druug horn to his lips and blew a single, long note. Human archers stood and positioned at the small arrow slits. They knocked, drew, and released, sending a rain of thin missiles out. The mercenaries shouted warnings to each other and raised their shields, fending off the arrows. The vast majority of the shots did nothing but bounce harmlessly off metal shields or lodge into those of wood and hide. A very few enemy soldiers screamed and fell, arrows taking them in the arm or the leg. Despite the rarity of damage, the archers continued firing.

"That's right," Rainer murmured. "Keep your heads down. Little more."

The mercenaries, appearing like turtles as they crept closer to the walls, continued their approach.

"They're not shooting back," Aloisa noted.

"Probably saving it for the real assault," Rainer mused.

The mercenaries drew closer. They crawled ahead, their shields held high and their ladders ready. Shouted orders bounced from one block of men to the next. The war-turtles adjusted, spreading out to approach a wider section of the wall. Shouts came down from both directions that the archers were tiring, their shots becoming less accurate. The furthest-advanced of the mercenaries passed the burn hulks that had been the Uldra warmachines and paused. Before them was the glacis, the wide ditch Aloisa had seen finished only a day before the arrival of the invading army. Within that dry moat was an array of sharpened stakes, all pointing out at the mercenaries as though the city had grown fangs, and dared the invaders to approach any closer.

"Alright," Rainer finally said to Aloisa, his eyes on the mercenary units and an evil grin on his face. "Hit them."

The Gunrsvein warrior-woman grinned darkly, a sinister light in her eyes of winter ice. "Double blast," she told the bugler.

The guardsman again raised his Druug horn to his lips, but this time he sounded two long notes. In response, the archers ducked back down, swinging and rubbing their arms. The mercenaries, only just beginning to try and navigate the glacis and its sharpened spikes, looked up in near-panic, just as the scorpions and ballistae let loose. Large bolts shot from the walls with horrific power and shocking accuracy. The ballistae missiles lanced through shields, whether metal or hide, with indifference, skewering several men and scattering the enemy formations. The scorpions, smaller siblings to the large ballistae, sent their own vengeance into the mercenaries. Men once under the cover of their compatriots' shields were assaulted by dozens of bolts, any one enough to carve out a man's heart. The mercenaries wavered, shouted commands trying to pull back within their protective formations.

"Reset the trebuchets," Rainer ordered.

The runners leapt to their duty. Within minutes, the falling stones no longer landed to the left and right, they crashed directly atop the wavering enemy. The mercenaries, already at the edge of their morale, broke. A great cheer went up from the defenders along the walls, accompanied by taunts and jeering of the defeated invaders. As word spread of the mercenaries' retreat, the cheerful outcries spread through the soldiers waiting behind the walls, and from there into the city.

"Do we use the special shot?" Aloisa asked. "Really send them running?"

Rainer considered, watching the disintegration of the enemy formations. "No," he decided. "We've only got two shots. Save them."

"Is it over?" Mary asked.

The colonel nodded. "For today, probably. Vagris will need to restore order before he can launch another assault." He turned to Aloisa. "Set lookouts and rotate the men. Make sure the artillery is checked and let the archers have a nice, long rest."

Mary found herself at the Sylvai restaurant. She had not intended to go there, yet her feet brought her to this meaningful place. After Lieutenant Aloisa had departed to implement Rainer's orders, the colonel had politely, but firmly, suggested that Mary return to the castle until the next assault. The handmaiden, having no other purpose at the walls, complied. She sent a brief report via the magical communications device, including her intent on returning. Kyla's shouted voice came from behind the image of Ilse's face, though, forbidding Mary from coming back before midday.

The plaza in which the Sylvai restaurant operated was one of those without a trebuchet. The cobblestone area was clear, absent any sign of the siege except for the lack of customers at the normally-busy restaurant. In fact, only one diner sat at the outdoor tables, who greeted Mary's arrival with a grin and a raised glass. "Great minds think alike, it seems," Aloisa noted.

Mary stared, blinking. The warrior-woman had not only arrived ahead of her, but had also managed to take off her armor, instead wearing the blue and grey uniform of the House Guard.

"If you plan to leave your mouth open," the Gunrsvien warrior-woman said, "you should at least put some food in it."

The handmaiden approached. "How did you beat me here?"

"If your current pace is indication, quite easily." In sullen obedience, Mary's pace had been unhurried. She had passed by the soldiers and workers as they made preparations for the next assault, whenever it would come. She had passed by the homes and shops, most closed or dedicated to the support of the city's defense. She had barely acknowledged the occasional friendly greeting from this citizen or that. Her mind had drifted from one thought to the next, seemingly determined to avoid a few critical facts. "Are you joining me or not?" Aloisa asked.

Mary shrugged slightly, trying to sit but fumbling. The sword she had been wearing was still belted at her waist, forgotten. Once the assault had been broken and the handmaiden directed to leave, no one had retrieved her wartime equipment and Mary herself had been so lost in her mind's efforts to dodge unpleasant realities that she had simply walked away, still garbed for battle.

"You must really enjoy the touch of steel," Aloisa noted, standing. "Why are you still wearing the mail?"

Mary looked down and realized that she was, indeed, still dressed in the chainmail shirt. A glance up revealed that she still wore the helmet, as well. "I didn't know how to take it off," the handmaiden shrugged.

"Fair enough." Aloisa stood and crossed to Mary. The lieutenant took the helmet and placed it on one of the empty chairs at the table she was using. "Lift your arms."

Mary complied and Aloisa pulled the chainmail shirt from her shoulders. The blessed touch of fresh air was a joy. Her skin pimpled against the layer of sweat that had accumulated across her entire torso. She could not help but cradle her breasts for a moment, suddenly free of the restrictive metal embrace.

Aloisa unbuckled the sword from Mary's waist. "Wonderous, isn't it?" she noted with a smile, returning to her seat. The lieutenant balled up the chainmail and placed it with the helmet. "Nothing quite like that feeling when you take the armor off." The warrior-woman sat and picked up her glass. "Keep the shirt and trousers," she advised. "Wear them the next time you come to the walls. I'll keep your armor. Just come find me first and we'll get you dressed again."

"Thank you."

The Gunrsvein shrugged. "Are you going to eat?"

Mary sat absently, still demanding that her thoughts remained as long as possible on the sensation of freedom. Aloisa looked at her across the rim of her glass, saying nothing. The handmaiden glanced around. "Are they even open?"

Aloisa nodded. "*Fu'iel*," she called, waving.

Mary glanced over her shoulder and saw the proprietor, a portly Sylvu, speaking with a sergeant from the City Watch. "You speak Sylvai?" the handmaiden asked as the restauranteur nodded and waved.

"Yes. After I was purchased from my family and brought here, I made a point of learning all the languages of the Northern Keep."

Mary glanced back at Aloisa. "Purchased?" she started. "You're a slave?"

"No longer. Colonel Rainer was the one who purchased me. When we arrived, he tried to explain that I was no longer his property, that slaves were forbidden here." Aloisa shook her head. "A foolish idea."

"You... you liked being a slave?"

"We are all slaves," the Gunrsvein replied. "We are all bound by those powers beyond our control or understanding. We cannot control who our parents will be, nor our killers. We can do nothing about the weather or the seasons." She shrugged again. "We are all bound by our dooms."

"Doom?"

"Our... how do you say it? Our destiny. The story of our lives was written long ago by uncaring gods. We merely act out that story."

"You almost sound like an Uldra," Mary noted.

"The Uldra know much. Not as much as the Gunrsvein, of course, but much."

The Sylvu restauranteur arrived. "Our offerings are minimal," he apologized. "We can offer a simple lunch only."

"*Ey'hi'rava'enim'neth'gal*," Mary said.

The restauranteur bowed and left. Aloisa looked in surprise at Mary, who matched her typical shrug. "I don't speak all the languages of the Northern Keep," she said in answer to the unspoken question. "But I know a little Sylvai." She accepted the glass of wine the restauranteur brought her with a smile. "Why were you sold into slavery?" she asked while sipping. "If that's not impolite."

Aloisa snorted into her own glass. "I still do not understand this idea of 'impolite.'"

"Your people... don't believe in manners?"

"We have excellent manners. But if you offend a Gunrsvein, you will know. There is none of this..." she waved a hand across the city, "confusion of meaning. But to answer, my father sold me to ease the burden of the family."

"I don't understand."

Aloisa leaned back in her chair. "Winters are hard in my homeland, and summers short. There is little open land to farm. We must raid for most of what we need. I was too small to help with the raiding, so I was little more than a burden to my family."

"Too small?" Mary pointedly looked at the warrior-woman's large body. Although she lacked the greater muscle of many professional soldiers, Aloisa was equally as tall, and she had no delicacy or frailty, filling out her Guard uniform.

"For my people, I am small. My father took a woman from Nebel in a raid. At first, my mother was just a slave, but soon they married and she gave him several children. Most of my brothers and sisters favored our father. I favored our mother. I was the smallest, the weakest. My father knew I would have trouble taking a husband, and I would not be a great help in raiding. Our family had no farmland. I was of little use. He took me back to Nebel and sold me to the warrior who had led the town's defense, who had killed many of my people."

"Colonel Rainer?"

"Not a colonel at the time, but yes."

"I'm surprised he agreed to buy you," Mary admitted. "House Calonar is very strict on its views of slavery."

Aloisa shrugged again. "The people of Nebel understand the Gunrsvein, as well as any outsiders can. There has been much contact. Much trading and fighting and fornication. My people often sell unwanted children there. The slaves are not called slaves, but are kept as servants and often marry into families. Rainer's wife taught me your language and your childish ways. I ate and learned with his children, and was treated the same as them. When Rainer came to the Northern Keep, I came with the family as well. When his son joined the House Guard, I did also."

"You don't want to go home?"

The warrior-woman again gestured across the city. "This is now my home. My doom brought me here, so here I stay until my doom takes me elsewhere. I admit that I do miss some things from my home, though."

"Like what?"

"Your forest was nice, before the Great Burn, but it was too flat. In my home, the rivers run through great valleys, with mighty waterfalls that catch the light of the sun in a beautiful mist. We have many hot springs, instead of these..." Aloisa made a face, "these indoor bath-places of yours." Her icy blue eyes grew distant. "And the winters are hard in my home, so we must come together. Our halls are loud and joyous. We take our comfort with each other, and celebrate our community."

The Sylvu restauranteur came with a tray of food. As he warned, the meal was simple: a thick stew of mostly vegetables. The smell suggested the perfect seasoning for which his family was famous, but it held none of the intricate complexity Mary had come to expect from the best dining in the Northern Keep. They both thanked the restauranteur, who set their table and left. Aloisa watched him leave, her eyes taking in his soft body. "Also, the men in my homeland are considerably more worthy. The males here are so… delicate."

"You like brutish men?" Mary asked, somewhat sarcastically.

Aloisa looked at her, her face level but for the slightest curve at the corner of her lips. "I take pleasure in more delicate things," the warrior-woman admitted. "I prefer them, in fact." She sampled the stew. "But I will need a man at some point, of course, to father my children."

"Is that all you want a husband for?" Mary asked. "To sire your children? What about love, companionship?"

"As I said," Aloisa replied, tongue teasing at her spoon, savoring the taste of her meal. "I prefer more delicate things. Men in this place seem of little use besides physical labor and seeding."

"So, any prospects for your… seeding?"

Aloisa shrugged indifferently. "Not many. I must consider who would provide me the best children. The strongest, most cunning, most intelligent." The lieutenant looked at Mary, her head tilting in consideration. "Your man might be useful in this."

Mary choked for a moment on a vegetable. "What?"

"Well, he is not the largest, but he is fast. He won the tournament last year, and that suggests great potential. He seems intelligent enough, for a man. Most importantly, you have already broken him, so he would be obedient."

"I didn't break Tomas!" the handmaiden said indignantly.

"Did I not see him wearing the clothes your wished?" Aloisa asked in confusion.

"Well…"

"And the other changes in his appearance. The hair, being clean-shaven. Were those not your wishes?"

"I mean…"

"And he made an offering to you of a perfectly-adequate treasure." The warrior-woman pointed with her spoon at the ring on Mary's finger.

"I… he's… Wait, adequate?" Mary nearly sputtered at the implied insult to her betrothal ring, clutching it to her heart.

"I did not mean to insult the offering," the Gunrsvein insisted. "The opposite, in fact. Gossip says there is some great enchantment on the ring." She looked up at Mary. "Is your man a user of magic?"

"No, the enchantment was done by Esha."

"Ah. If the little flower put her mark on the ring, then it is all the more valuable. Your man shows great wisdom in his offering to you. If I may ask, what enchantment did the little flower place upon the ring?"

Mary's eyes drifted to the ring. She traced a light, caressing touch along its surface of flawless white gold, formed into a replica of the ribbon she had given to him as a token for the joust. "It turned white when I put it on," she nearly whispered. Her thoughts drifted back, to the banquet following Tomas' great victory in the tournament. The food, the dancing, most mostly importantly, the great culmination, when he had dropped to one knee and asked her to be his wife.

"It…" Aloisa was staring at her with a skeptical look on her face. "It… turns white?"

Mary snatched up the spoon and stirred her stew in irritation. "It's symbolic," she insisted.

"As you wish," the Gunrsvein woman shrugged. "If we do decide to use him for seeding, make sure your man presents some treasure to me that is a little more… appropriate for me."

The handmaiden shook her head. "I can't believe you're so casual about… seeding."

"We would wait until he seeded you first, of course," Aloisa conceded. "That would be only proper. But after, I would happily offer any reasonable compensation. Money, goods, or services." She looked up at Mary again, the same suggestive curve dancing upon her lips. "If you prefer, you could even participate in the seeding."

Mary blushed all the way to her soul. She stammered, uncertain of what exactly the Gunrsvein was suggesting, but also almost fearful she knew exactly. "Can we not talk about… seeding?" she finally asked. "I'm trying to eat, after all."

"As you wish," Aloisa shrugged, continuing her meal. "Shall we instead talk about whatever you do not wish to talk about?"

"What do you mean?" Mary asked, not wanting to understand.

"For many weeks, you have carried yourself as one does who knows many unwanted things. I assume this comes from the Doomsayer."

"Doomsayer?"

"Karen. She reveals destinies, does she not? Many in the Guard whisper of her new sight."

"They shouldn't gossip about House Calonar."

"Do you wish to speak of her prophecies?"

Mary said nothing, instead picking at her stew. Aloisa did not press her, but neither did she offer a change of subject. Instead, the lieutenant just sat and ate and waited. After their meal was nearly done, Mary at last said, "Did you know that I'm a baroness?"

"I assumed you had some title or other," Aloisa answered. "You serve a noblewoman, after all."

The handmaiden shook her head. "I was just a servant. It's not even my title. Kyla… the princess showed me a copy of the patens of nobility. It was written by her and has been agreed to by Velaross, Alvaro, and Ironheartshaven. Tomas has been granted his own Noble House, and named the hereditary Lord of Pelsemoria." She picked at the last of her stew. "I'm now the Lady of House Fidelis, Baroness of Pelsemoria. Or, I will be, once we marry. If we marry."

"Is that a high rank? Baroness?"

Mary shrugged. "It's lower than a duke or king, but more than a knight."

"That is good, then. You have status and wealth and land."

"I don't know how much wealth and land. Pelsemoria is a ruin. Tomas' job... my job will be to lead the rebuilding."

Aloisa leaned back, taking up her wine glass and staring at Mary. "And yet, you do not seem happy with your title. You even speak of not marrying your man. Did the Doomsayer reveal something?"

Mary was about to answer, but paused. She started several times, but her voice made no sound.

"Knowledge is a difficult thing," Aloisa observed. "Childhood is easy. We are told how things are, and we accept this. Then we go into the world, and learn that life is not so easy, so simple. I came to this place and met many wise people. Few of them ever seemed happy."

"She's never said anything about my marriage," Mary whispered. "About my future."

"But others, yes? The Doomsayer has revealed what will befall others?"

The handmaiden nodded. "Many others."

"So you suffer your good fortune because you know of so much hardship others will suffer." Aloisa shook her head. "You Adamics," she chuckled. "So set upon your miseries."

"What does that mean?"

"Today, we won a great victory." The lieutenant nodded across the plaza at a couple. A guardsman was holding the hands of a shopkeeper's daughter. They stared into each other's eyes and whispered things that brought a flush of excitement to them both. "Look there," Aloisa instructed. "Tonight, they will take pleasure in each other. Tomorrow, that boy will be back on the wall. Perhaps the enemy will attack, perhaps not. Perhaps the boy will die in the next assault, perhaps he will live to return to her bed. They know none of this. They care for none of this. All they know is the joy they will have tonight.

"Tomorrow your man may return with Rogan. He may not. Tomorrow, there may be blood and death, or there may not. The Doomsayer has revealed much to you, and that is your burden. But the darkest tomorrow remains that: tomorrow."

Aloisa stood and put several coins on the table. She retrieved Mary's helmet and chainmail shirt. Before she left, the woman put a hand on the handmaiden's shoulder. "Do not ignore your burdens, but do not let them bury you. Find what joys life will offer, for as long as they are offered."

Chapter 28

Xaemus hated what had become of the forest. Not for the
irreparable damage done to the Wyld; like all his cursed race, the *Xesh'lin* hunter had
never felt the touch of the living world within his withered soul. Nor was the loss of
life especially significant to the monster of Davenor; he had drawn the blood of every
race in his unending search for the Dark Empress. Xaemus did not even especially
care for the displacement, murder, and enslavement of the people once living within
the now-dead forest. They all hated him, after all; was it not natural for him to hate
them?

No, these were not the reasons Xaemus felt so ill-at-ease within the scorched land
surrounding the Northern Keep. The noxious cloud of ash hanging over their
encampment meant little to him; his face was forever covered anyway, filtering out
the worst of the toxic air. The mercenaries had taken to wrapping their mouths and
noses, and the wet breath of many said this did not protect them. The blackened soot
that clung to all the tents, all the equipment and men, and profaned every hand and
face, meant little to the monster of Davenor; as a *Xesh'lin*, he had to stay covered in
any case to protect from the burning sun, and to conceal the scars of his shameful
defeat. The vengeful mud clung to his boots as wrathfully as it clutched to all the
invaders who had destroyed this place; but this, also, was of little note as Xaemus was
accustomed to all manner of inhospitable terrain. His centuries-long quest had taken
him to every corner of this cursed world.

Xaemus hated what had become of the forest for one, simple reason: it now
reminded him of home.

Walking amongst the blackened husks of dead trees was like walking amongst the
ironwood forest surrounding Mount Godsfire. Centuries of eruptions, of succeeding
blankets of ash, had hardened the trees until they were as forged metal. The *Xesh'lin*
had learned to harvest this resource, even as the males were leading slaves in the
harvesting of Wildelves Wood. The enthralled males labored alongside those in more
physical chains through each night, not with axe and saw, but with the magical devices
crafted by the Sorcerous Sisters. As he approached the mercenary camp, Xaemus was
uncomfortably reminded of such work camps at home; *Xesh'lin* overseers supervising
Human laborers, using the tools provided by the Dark Covens to fell the ironwood,
only for the black rods to then be hauled away. The sight of such forced labor, the

sound of cracking whips and screaming flesh, the smell of hate and decay, all colluded to pull Xaemus' thoughts back to his abandoned birthland.

The feeling was even worse once he arrived in the mercenary camp. Humans abounded here, as they abounded in Davenor. Slaves were everywhere in the Blighted Lands. They were currency, pets, toys, and tools to be used and then discarded. Their eyes never left the ground, never dared make contact with those of burning blood, for fear of attracting the attention of their owners. Here, the mercenaries, though not slaves in the most technical manner, had adopted the same caution. No man, regardless of size, skill, or experience, dared look full into the gaze of a *Xesh'lin*, especially the monster of Davenor. They had witnessed too much of the Dark Coven's work.

Another blood-rite was being performed, as Xaemus approached the heart of the mercenary camp. Vagris had encouraged the *Xesh'lin* to build their altar beside his own pavilion. The Sorcerous Sisters were a source of power, after all, and the Bellonar General was drawn to such things. Even now, Vagris was standing outside his large tent, a cup of steaming tea in his hand as he watched the Dark Coven performing its most sacred, most profane, ritual.

And she stood beside him.

She was a slave. Of this, there could be no doubt. As had become the custom of the Humans during the millennia-long reign of their Republic, Vagris had dressed her in little, more a decoration of Sylva flesh than any protection from the soot and ash. Her bare feet, so delicate and meant for fine slippers, sank into the clinging mud. Her sculpted legs did not press or pull at the sucking ground as did those of most others, including Xaemus himself; she stood passive and uncaring as only the most noble soul could. Her torso, though covered with that pitiful gauze likely meant to excite the lusts of Vagris and his scum, barely took in breath. Her body had continued its change in the weeks since Xaemus had last seen her, swelling more fully into maturity, into readiness. His nose, and the most primitive parts of his body, caught her scent on the pitiful breeze; her body was nearly ready for its first reproductive cycle and was reaching out, calling to surrounding males, though she, herself, made no effort at seduction. A small, decorative chain of silver and steel was clasped at her graceful neck, her shapely waist, and her supple wrists. She held the tray bearing Vagris' tea kettle as though it had no weight, unyielding even in her servitude. The Veil still covered her eyes, locked in place around the upper-half of her emotionless face, protecting her owner and his men from the enthralling power of her tears. She was perfect.

Xaemus knew what was happening to him, to his body and mind. Whenever he breathed in her air, he was intoxicated. His heart sped, as though it would lunge from his chest to throw itself at her divine feet. His eyes of burning blood narrowed and could not be pulled free from their worship of her, the near-readiness of her body.

His arms and legs tensed, ready to obey her slightest command. His pride ached to prove himself worthy of her, to defeat all others so that she might choose him. His mouth dried, desperate for the water only she could provide. Though she wore the chain, he was the slave.

The conscious part of his mind, the weakening center of his rational self, tried arguing against biology. This was a remnant of his species' primitive past, it insisted. Once, long ago in brutal antiquity, the *Sy'lvai* were targets, prey because of their small size. Females needed to choose only the strongest, those mates most capable of protecting her during the long pregnancy and her children during their even-longer infancy. In the distant past, once a male had proven himself worthy of her, a female would enthrall him with her tears, binding him forever to her protection and her service. This was the most complete slavery, the most unbreakable bond, the most absolute devotion, one for which males yearned.

Even the *Xesh'lin*, cursed offshoot of the *Sy'lva'i*, felt the call of the tears. Males competed with each other, performed acts of creative brutality in the desperate hope of being chosen by one of the Sorcerous Sisters. Wealth was nothing. Victories were nothing. Conquest and acclaim and achievement were nothing. A male's only hope for any real status in Davenor was to be chosen. And, for centuries, Xaemus had shunned this practice.

Another male of his cursed race was approaching. Three of them, in fact. So, Xaemus thought, this is the moment of their attempt. They were carrying the cutting rods fabricated by the Dark Coven, likely trying to remain unnoticed. The Sorcerous Sisters have reached the point of deception, of waiting until Vagris is wholly distracted by the ritual to take her. Xaemus had been correct in the priestesses' near-obsession with possessing a Daughter of the Wyld. They would not be able to resist the lure of controlling her, of attempting one of their conversions, to unlock the power contained within her soul.

The first would-be abductor died silently. His head made no sound when it left the body, and neither portion of useless meat made sound when they reached the ground. The second must have sensed the White Lady's approach, but his throat opened before he could do more than make a partial turn. The final male who thought himself worthy enough to lay hands on her did not even reach an arm's length of the Daughter of the Wyld. Xaemus did not kill him, though; far better he serve as messenger.

"Tell them," the monster of Davenor hissed into the whimpering male's ear. "Tell your mother and her sisters of your failure. And before they take your manhood, your tongue, your kidneys, and then your heart, tell them one more truth." Xaemus turned the enthralled male, the weak, pathetic, unworthy creature who had dared threaten the Daughter of the Wyld. Xaemus' eyes of burning blood blazed into this pitiable thing's soul. "Tell them, she is protected."

The enthralled male was sent stumbling away, whimpering as the beaten dog he was. Xaemus knew he would retreat to his mother's tent. He knew, just as that failed abductor must know, the destiny awaiting him for his failure and, worse, his embarrassment of his owning priestess. But, he was enthralled. He could not help but return to his mistress. This was the destiny of all enthralled males, to be tools, at best to be pets, used and discarded by the females who dominated them.

The Dark Coven of Midnight Sun had thought to enthrall Xaemus, and died for their hubris. Other *Xesh'lin* females had tried and similarly failed. As word had spread of the monster of Davenor, a great many Sorcerous Sisters had tried to enthrall him, to entice him into their servitude, and failed. When he had left the Blighted Lands on his quest, any number of power-hungry females had sought him, and been shunned. Xaemus kept his flesh, his soul, his dedicated love, for the one in all the world worthy of it: Kelinva, his Dark Empress.

But now, he wavered.

She was aware of his presence. Xaemus was certain of it. She always knew when he was there. The Dark Coven of Midnight Sun had taught him to call the shadows, to merge into the darkness that accompanied all light. Centuries of practice, of learning the skills of every warrior-cult, granted the monster of Davenor his ability at remaining unobserved. And yet, she was aware. She made no movement, nor acknowledgement. She did not betray her knowledge of him; her glory was such that she would not even grant him her distain. He was not yet worthy of it.

Vagris must have sensed something, as well. He did not know of Xaemus' presence, but he felt the shift in his slave. The Bellonar glanced behind and down at her, looking upon her with an arched eyebrow. Even his dull Human senses could detect her readiness. Perhaps, Xaemus considered, this was why he so insistently kept her in his personal service. Like all his Brotherhood, Vagris bent towards challenges, constantly testing himself. Perhaps he sought to prove his mastery over his biology, to shun her even as his body must yearn for her. Xaemus wished to kill the male for his impudence.

Vagris glanced around and Xaemus allowed himself to be seen. The Bellonar snorted in derision and turned back to the Dark Coven's spectacle. "Finally finished with your reconnaissance?" he asked.

"Obviously," the monster of Davenor replied. He moved to stand near her, making the movement seem as though he were standing beside Vagris. She made no response to him, teasing him with her control, her quite dignity and reserve.

"The traitorous Uldra have not abandoned you?" Xaemus observed, nodding towards the separated tents of the warsmiths. The corrupted barbarians of the west were tinkering with some new devices, objects of brass and copper and ironwood.

Vagris glanced at the few remaining traitorous Uldra. "Of course not," the warlord snorted. "As long as Fak'Har pays their price, they stay."

"They've lost their precious machines," Xaemus pointed out. "Years of corrupting themselves to relearn some of their mockery of magic, and now their precious inventions are gone." He glanced his eyes of burning blood at Vagris. "What was their new price?"

The warlord nodded at the ritual before them. "Blood Magic. The priestesses are infusing their new tools with power."

Xaemus nodded. The corrupted barbarians had been traveling with Vagris' army all summer, far too long to remain untouched by the seduction of the Sorcerous Sisters. The monster of Davenor had seen some of the traitorous Uldra even join in the priestesses' rituals, contributing their hulking bodies to the various perversions. No wonder that, even with the destruction of their beloved warmachines and deaths of so many of their comrades, the twisted barbarians had chosen to stay and receive more dark secrets from Fak'Har and his allies. In the time of the *Im'peri'a*, females had enthralled both Human and Uldra males, but such perversions had eventually grown distasteful. Even the Sorcerous Sisters shunned the practice, despite their own exploration of corruption. Curious, then that the Coven of Puma's Leash had chosen to enthrall many of these twisted barbarians.

Before them, the next victim was brought forward. The Dark Coven had built one of their altars to *Ethroi'sa'kai*. Where they had found basalt stone Xaemus did not know, nor did he care. As always, the altar had been formed roughly, with hard edges. It was curved, so that the victim could be placed upon it with her back arched upwards. Horns of ivory were attached at each corner. These, Xaemus knew, would be from an elephas of the Blighted Lands. By custom, when a Dark Coven would dispatch some of their members on foreign adventure, they first sent their enthralled males to the southern savannahs to slaughter one of the great beasts. Like every other element of life with the Sorcerous Sisters, this was a test. The elephas would kill many, crushing the hunter-males or worse, crippling them. These unworthy ones would be left to die, exposed to the sun or torn apart by scavengers or savage Humans. Xaemus' eyes of burning blood scanned the nearby males. There, in the place of honor nearest the Sorcerous Sisters, a Xeshlin male stood, nude but for his ceremonial red loincloth and decorated with the marks of victory. The male who had made the killing blow was anointed with the tattoo over his heart, the personal mark of the Coven's leader, and given the honor of tending to the High Priestess' needs. As the latest victim was pulled screaming onto the altar, the anointed male held the knife ready. Had he not freed himself from servitude to his own Dark Coven, Xaemus himself would likely have been in that position at some time.

"What did you find?" Vagris asked, sipping at his tea.

Xaemus said nothing at first. He watched as the victim was forced onto the altar. Her arms and legs were held fast with cold iron, each chain connected to one of the ivory horns. Two of the lesser priestesses, their red sashes as yet unadorned with the glyphs of achievement, came forward and cut away the offering's dress. "Nothing. There is no sign of reinforcement to the south." Xaemus did not know why he lied. His duty to the Shadowed Mage was to report when Eigenhard and Killdare arrived in the Northlands. His obligation was to report the armies' advanced scouts, even now ranging into the desolated forest. Despite this, he lied.

"General Killdare is certainly taking his time," Vagris mused. He held out his cup and she refilled it without needing to look. "I expected his advanced scouts by now. Frostfront must be a bigger complication than we planned for."

Xaemus said nothing, instead trying to focus his thoughts and attention to the mockery of religion unfolding before them. The Human girl was most likely a maiden, for such pure blood would be needed for the work required. "She's from Snowholm," the monster of Davenor noted.

"Yes," the Bellonar confirmed. "From the prisoners we took before Fak'Har started burning the forest."

The girl's voice had gone ragged from screaming. Her wide eyes darted about, as though in search of some rescue. They all did that, Xaemus recalled. Each time he had been forced to watch the rite, he had seen the victim looking around for some chance at hope. None ever came. Instead, the High Priestess and her sisterhood stepped forward. Each of them wore only the red sashes; there was no sense ruining perfectly good clothes time and again, after all. Those light, flimsy decorations were, Xaemus knew, white when first awarded to a Sorceress Sister upon completion of her novitiate. The first act of that nascent priestess was to sacrifice her defeated rivals, their blood staining the new sash red. The Sorceress Sisters all had numerous glyphs of gold, bronze, and silver decorating their sashes, showing the many achievements. The Coven of Puma's Leash was influential, Xaemus realized, with so many decorated priestesses. Odd that such powerful females would leave Davenor; typically, errands requiring travel outside the Blighted Lands were left to less dominant groups. "I will replace my supplies and go east," Xaemus said then.

"Eigenhard will likely come from there," Vagris agreed. "We'll need as much advanced warning as possible."

The High Priestess stood before the altar and held out her hand. Her anointed male came forward and offered her the knife. Each Dark Coven had a different style in their implements, Xaemus knew. This one had no serrated edges or hooks or barbs. Odd, as most priestesses preferred inflicting as much suffering and damage as possible. This one was just a simple, curved knife, resembling a puma's claw. The victim saw it, though, and found the strength to renew her screaming. One of the other Sorcerous Sisters knelt at the head of the altar. This one must be most in favor at the moment, Xaemus mused. That younger-seeming priestess leaned forward and locked her eyes of burning blood with those of the victim. She opened her mouth and breathed in the girl's terror, taking in the power to enhance her vitality. "You will continue your assaults?" Xaemus asked.

"Just as soon as the priestesses here are finished building my siege engines," Vagris confirmed. "And empowering those new Uldra devices. After our recent setbacks, I'm making a more coordinated, multi-axis attack."

"Fak'Har's accomplice within the city has failed?"

"Not that he'll admit, of course," the warlord grunted. "But those damned trebuchets were supposed to be incapacitated. We were supposed to be free to attack days ago. Instead, nothing but silence."

"The traitor has ceased communication?"

"Not a whisper. So, Fak'Har has… instructed me," this, Vagris said with almost a sneer, "to completely redesign our strategy. I've had the infantry launching a few probes, more to drain the Keep's resources than anything else. Once the Sisters are done and the Uldra have dug their tunnels, the real attack can begin."

The monster of Davenor looked passed the altar, where the High Priestess was drawing the knife down the victim's chest. When the maiden started coughing spurts of blood, the younger Sorcerous Sister kneeling over her face began licking at the terrified girl's mouth, reveling at the power released. Xaemus saw great piles of the harvested wood, blackened and ready. Several of the new engines were mid-construction already. "Ladders," Xaemus noted. He glanced once more at the corrupted Uldra. "And digging tools." The traitorous barbarians were building cylinders of brass and bronze. Each was covered with knobs and dials, and glowed from within with an umbral red.

"And a few rams," Vagris added. "The sisterhood has promised me they can enchant the rams to penetrate the walls."

The monster of Davenor looked back to the altar. "So many gifts will take a great deal of power," he pointed out. The High Priestess had given the knife back to her anointed male and was reaching one delicate hand into the girl's chest. She would be gentle, Xaemus knew. Her fingers would just barely slide along the victim's still-beating heart. An experienced priestess could prolong the suffering, leeching a great deal of magic from the sacrifice.

"We have plenty of slaves," Vagris pointed out. The cages near to the priestesses' tents were filled with Humans and *Sy'lva'i* and, surprisingly, even a few Eastern Uldra. They pressed together, turned away from the altar and the girl's gruesome death, holding one another and trying to shield the young and the small from the horrible truth of how most of them would end.

Xaemus once again looked past the altar where the High Priestess was leaning closer to the victim. She would be squeezing now, gripping the heart tighter and tighter until it burst in her hand. The monster of Davenor looked past this, feeling little need to witness the barbarity yet again. Instead, his eyes of burning blood went to the men tied to stakes facing the machines under construction. "The imbuing sacrifice?" he asked.

Vagris nodded. "The High Priestess says that her rams will need the souls of loyal men." He waved his teacup at the sacrifices tied to the stakes. "Those were Calonar guardsmen taken not far from the city."

The girl was dead. The High Priestess was raising her heart, chanting her dedication to *Ethroi'sa'kai*. Xaemus glanced away, knowing this was his only safe moment. All eyes, willing or not, would be locked upon the conclusion of the rite. The High Priestess would tear a chunk of the heart with her teeth, smearing the blood upon her hateful face and colorless body. She would then call forward her anointed male and feed him the piece of the heart from her own mouth. The heart would then be passed from one Sorcerous Sister to the next, each eating a piece and gifting it to her chosen male. Once the heart was fully devoured, they would celebrate the death with wanton carnality. Others would be allowed to join, if they so desired. Xaemus had seen enough of these mercenaries to know that some of the killers would join enthusiastically.

A thought occurred, and the monster of Davenor looked about the gathering. The men assembled to witness were the worst of Vagris' scum. The true killers: murderers, rapists, torturers, many of these creatures Xaemus himself had helped escape Ubelheim last year. Most of them had been bound for execution. These dark souls should have been uncontrollable; at best, Vagris should only have been able to unleash them. And yet, they were obedient, dedicated to a cause, rather than the immediate gratification of their vile hungers. As Xaemus looked around, he began to finally understand. Males such as these existed in Davenor, after all. Such monsters were drawn to the Dark Covens, to the freedom to explore their destructive desires. The beasts in the form of men stared in almost ecstatic rapture at the High Priestess as she pushed her anointed male on top of the altar and mounted him. She gestured to one of the nearby killers to join, which he did with great enthusiasm.

Xaemus glanced again at Vagris. His eyes were cold, detached, calculating. He observed how uncontrollable beasts were, essentially, domesticated. How the loyalty of monsters was enforced. The Sorceress Sisters were enthralling these men, these horrid killers. They were allowing the indulgence of the most forbidden joys. All that remained was controlling the Dark Coven, and that calculation Xaemus could see playing out behind Vagris' eyes.

Xaemus let his eyes of burning blood turn away. She was unmoved. Xaemus saw that the horrid Red Thirst that was seeping through them all washed past her like an ineffectual breeze. She did not shift, did not stir in the slightest. The power of the Sorcerous Sisters had no grip upon her. She was above their hunger, their weakness. Like the night sky, she drifted above them all, as beautiful as she was untouchable. "I have need of your slave," the monster of Davenor said tightly.

Vagris only waved his hand dismissively.

Xaemus stepped towards her. He did not approach too close. He had not earned the privilege. She did not move. "You will come with me." He had meant the words to be a command, an insistence. Somehow, though, as they left his lips, it had lost its power, instead sounding as a question, an almost desperate plea.

Still, she would say nothing to him, would not grant her the song of her voice. Instead, her opalescent eyes still downcast, she turned towards him, expectantly.

Xaemus walked away from the disgusting spectacle unfolding. They would take one hour, he knew. Regardless of the participant's stamina or desire, the Sorcerous Sisters would indulge their hunger for one hour exactly. If their males could not endure, they would be cast aside for others, forever shammed and shunned. Xaemus cared little of this. Instead, he walked into Vagris' pavilion. He paused at the entrance, turning and holding aside the flap for her.

She walked through without acknowledging him. She moved to a table and set down the tray and kettle. She said nothing, only waited in perfect indifference.

"I would speak with you again," he said. Once more his voice betrayed him, sounding less than a command than a request.

She said nothing. She only waited.

"I would spare you from the rite," he tried again, but got no response. "I do not want you to suffer more than you already have. I want you to be safe. I…" His words failed.

At last, she blessed him with her voice. "You are under the haze," she observed, her honey words caressing his ears as much as they did his heart. "You feel my *shey'iel'enim'or* and the pull of the blood rite. Your mind is not your own."

Xaemus wanted to argue, wanted to denounce the hateful religion of his people, but he knew the truth of her words. Her scent was powerful now, placing the haze upon all nearby males. In normal times, she would have already chosen a mate, and the two would isolate until the change was finished. That, combined with the inebriating power of the Dark Coven weighed heavily on the monster of Davenor. "What do I do?" he asked, he almost begged.

At last, at long last, after an eternity of punishment, she relented. She raised her chin and let the hazel glow of her opalescent eyes fall fully upon him. His body took a step forward of its own volition, heedless of his weakening objections. She held up a hand, and his body stopped. He was not enthralled, but his body was fully under her power. If she would but command it, he would devastate the camp, slaughter all those in her way, carving a path to her freedom.

But she did not command. "You must choose," was what she said. "What do you want?"

"You," was his choked reply.

She shook her head. "Beyond this moment. What do you want? Answer."

Commanded, he had to obey. "To serve," he said.

"To serve whom?"

"One who is worthy."

"Is that why you seek the Dark Empress?"

He nodded. "My Coven was unworthy. They only wanted a tool, a weapon for their petty schemes. They conspired and plotted, they maneuvered for minor power and status. There was nothing grand in their actions, nothing... I want a mistress of worth."

"And how will you know if she is of worth?"

He paused. Such a question had never before entered Xaemus' mind. From the moment he chose rebellion, to free himself from the Dark Coven of Midnight Sun, he had been fixated on finding the Dark Empress, believing she alone was worthy of his servitude. "I... don't know."

"Go," she commanded. "Find out."

Commanded, he had to obey.

The camp was quiet. The night was advancing. The rite had finished, the hour passed. The mercenaries who had not participated were almost certainly in the shelters of their tents. Those who had not were even further afield, desperate to be away from the perversion of the Sorcerous Sisters. Those who had tried to participate lay scattered about the altar. All were either nude, or else their clothes were in shreds. Some still struggled to catch their breath, some did not breathe at all. The offering still lay on the altar, as motionless as some of the celebrants. It would be taken away and burned before the next sacrifice. The captives were also silent in their pens, few slept, but none dared move against the possibility of being chosen next. The few guards were on the outskirts of the camp, pointedly staying away. The Dark Coven were all gone, retreating to their quarters to be bathed for the next rite. They would have another hour of rest and restoration.

Xacmus stood amidst this carnage, this carnality, with an empty soul. The horrid umbral magic had passed. The Coven's acolytes would be at work, harnessing the summoned power into devices and containers for later use. The *Xesh'lin* had been separated from the Winds of Magic long ago. The Last Empress had punished them for their betrayals, forcing the Dark Covens to form and discover this new, horrific source of mystical power. The Umbra were willing teachers, and the Sorcerous Sisters eager students. Even in his childhood, during his training by the Coven of Midnight Sun, Xaemus had felt nothing but distain for their rites. But, he now worried, would the Dark Empress be any different?

Kelinva had been the founder of the first Dark Covens. She had created their rites, been the first to employ the power of suffering, horror, and death. She had enthroned herself in Davenor, leading her people in the conquest of that continent and transforming it into the Blighted Lands. As the Dark Empress, she had converted Xaemus' people to the worship of *Ethroi'sa'kai*. She had subjugated not only the Humans native to Davenor, but the males of her own race. Kelinva was what the Sorcerous Sisters aspired to be.

The barest whisper of a sound drew Xaemus' attention. He moved into the shadows, slipping towards its source. He was near the stakes upon which the intended victims to empower the siege equipment were tied. They were all silent but one. A male Human, young, though not a child, was grunting, trying to maintain his silence against his many wounds. He was being untied by a *Xesh'lin* male.

The *Xesh'lin* was the average of any of their race. His eyes of burning blood darted about in worry. His lean body shook with fear, but also with determination. He was dressed as any of those in service to the Dark Coven would be, but did not bear the marks of the recent rite. There was no blood upon his lips, nor was he as desiccated as the other unclaimed males. Moreover, he lacked the added muscle of an enthralled male. He could be unattached, Xaemus mused, as yet unproven and so available to any of the Sorcerous Sisters. Too little time had passed for any rejuvenation, though. Those who had survived the rite, who had proven their worth in pleasuring the priestesses, would be, even now, undergoing a mystical rejuvenation so that they might be of service in the next rite. Xaemus was curious, so he waited and watched.

The *Xesh'lin* finished untying the Human. They both collapsed under the young man's weight. Having been tied for so long on the stake, the Human would not be able to move his arms and legs for a while. The *Xesh'lin* hissed for him to try, to overcome his injuries. He whispered urgent pleas for hurry, for their extreme danger. The Human tried. He defied the cuts and gashes; he pulled at his limbs, demanding his body obey. There was little result.

The *Xesh'lin* finally pulled the Human onto his shoulder, trying to leverage his much-lesser weight. The pair began an awkward, hissing stumble away from the stakes and towards the dubious safety of the camp's perimeter.

"You are going the wrong way," Xaemus observed, emerging from the shadows.

The pair spun, the Human dropping to the ground and the *Xesh'lin* raising his hands. He bore no weapon, but instead had his hands outstretched, twisting into the gestures that would harness the Winds of Magic. Although Xaemus was blind to the Winds, as were all his cursed race, still he recognized the forms employed by the Sylvai and the Humans. "How are you doing that?" he asked, curiously. None who bore the Mark of Kelinva could summon the Winds, and most especially not a male.

The *Xesh'lin* spotted him, and his eyes of burning blood widened in fear. His gaze went then to Xaemus' double-bladed weapon, and then back to his covered face. "Xaemus!" he gasped.

"And you are Xathias," the monster of Davenor deduced. "The one born of magic. The one whose Coven somehow restored his connection to the Winds." Xaemus tiled his head. "I heard your priestesses killed you."

"Clearly not," Xathias sneered. The younger *Xesh'lin* was making an obvious attempt at bravado, at laughing in the face of his terror.

"Indeed. So you have traded servitude to your Coven for servitude to House Calonar."

"Where else could I find training?"

Xaemus nodded. "Logical." He glanced at the Human, who was still trying to force his body into obedience. He then looked at the other bodies still tied to the stakes. "Are you a saboteur, or a rescuer?"

"Why should I answer?"

"I could kill you and question the Human," Xaemus suggested. "Even if you survive my attack, you would need magic to do so, and that would stir the entire camp."

Xathias narrowed his eyes of burning blood. "Yet, you have not stirred your allies."

"I am curious. Satisfy my curiosity, and perhaps you can survive this night."

"I was sent to infiltrate this camp. To sabotage the siege engines during construction."

"Again, logical" Xaemus conceded. "You would have an easier time than any other, knowing the ways of the Dark Coven." He nodded to the Human crouching beside Xathias. "Why rescue that one, though? You could have finished your work and be gone. Why risk discovery for that one, rather than any other?"

Xathias glanced down at his Human and then looked back to the monster of Davenor. "A debt exists between us."

"A debt? Ah, that is how you escaped your Coven." Xaemus nodded approvingly. "Agents of House Calonar extracted you." He looked at the Human. "And this one was part of that operation."

"I will balance the debt," Xathias declared, once again raising his hands. "By any means required."

Xathias said nothing. He did not move. He stood, considering. "Loyalty," he mused. "Even to the point of self-sacrifice." The monster of Davenor glanced back, towards the dark pavilion of Vagris and to the sheltered quarters of the Dark Coven beyond. "Such a thing is almost unheard of among our people."

"Your people," Xathias snapped.

"You foreswear your race?"

"Do you not?"

Xaemus again considered. "Like you, I escaped my Coven. But I still had… hope for our future."

"With Kelinva," Xathias snorted. "You think the Dark Empress is any different? Any better?"

Once more, Xaemus was silent. The two *Xesh'lin* stared at one another, neither eager to begin a conflict. The monster of Davenor turned then, and pointed with his double-bladed weapon in a direction different from that Xathias and his Human had been traveling. "That way," he advised. "The traitorous Uldra are digging tunnels. One team happened upon a smuggler's route into the city. They withdrew to consider its best use, so there will be only a few guards. Go two miles. You will find a great stone in the shape of a crouching male. The tunnel will take you into the city." He turned away.

"Why?" Xathias asked.

Xaemus paused. He glanced back, uncertainty for the first time entering his eyes of burning blood.

Chapter 29

Mary started when Kyla jerked to wakefulness. The princess gasped for breath and her pearlescent eyes darted about. Her handmaiden was there, at her bedside. She put a cloth cooled with water at Kyla's brow, not only to wipe away the sweat, but to offer comfort. "It's alright," Mary whispered. "We're here. You're safe."

Kyla's breathing steadied. She leaned into Mary, who wrapped her arms around her princess. The handmaiden rocked gently, reassuringly, much as one would a child. Both women put a hand to Kyla's distended stomach. The unborn prince was thrashing about himself, sensing his mother's distress, or perhaps objecting to yet another exertion. "It's alright," Kyla whispered to him. "It's over."

Ilse rushed into the bedchamber. The young priestess saw what was happening and rushed to Kyla's bedside, sitting on the opposite side as did Mary, also putting her arms around the princess. "Again?" she asked, her eyes directed to the handmaiden.

"She insisted," Mary replied.

"That's three nights in a row," Ilse pointed out.

"And three interceptions," Mary agreed. "Let's call Esha."

"I said we should do that from the start."

"I know, I know."

"Um," Kyla interrupted irritably. "Do I get to say something?"

"No," both Ilse and Mary said in unison.

"You insisted on doing this," the priestess accused.

"Despite what we all thought," the handmaiden added.

"So now, we're taking charge."

"Like we should have in the first place."

Once Kyla was eased back to comfort, and the unborn prince was able to drift back to sleep, Mary and Ilse stood. "I'll call Esha," the handmaiden said, going to the small table on which rested the mystical communication device."

"We should bring Medaka in as well," Ilse suggested, moving to the outer rooms. She paused at the door. "I think we should talk to my father, as well."

"Why?"

"We've lost another method of communication with the outside world," the priestess sighed. "My father will want to know."

Mary sent the messages out, calling for an impromptu strategy meeting. When she finished, the handmaiden started when she returned to Kyla's bedchamber. The princess was, once again, defying orders and moving to get up. "Highness!" the handmaiden barked.

"I'm not lying in bed for a Council meeting!" Kyla insisted. With an exasperated sigh, the noble jewel of House Calonar had to resort to rolling to the edge of her bed. Even had Medaka and Ilse not ordered her to bed rest for the remainder of her pregnancy, Kyla would likely have been forced there anyway. Her frame was so small, thanks in large part to her Halvan bloodline, that carrying the child of a full Human was much more burdensome than was typical for a gravid woman.

Mary rushed to her princess' side, almost catching her before she rolled off the bed. "Highness," the handmaiden said again. "You know-"

Kyla waved her to silence. The argument had become stale, both women knew. The princess had been made very weak after the bleeding from her assault on the Uldra warmachines. Already threatened by the assassination attempt, the unborn prince had been still for nearly a day. Ilse and Medaka had worked frantically, employing not only their medical skills, but their magical ones, as well. At last, with the next dawn, the little prince had once again moved, and Kyla herself had stabilized.

Since then, Mary and Ilse had become even more tyrannical over their noble charge. Every movement of the princess was curtailed, limited to only the most vital. Kyla took her meals in bed. They half-carried her to the bathing tub. They kept her wrapped in blankets. Any objections were harshly overridden, regardless of Kyla's rank. And the princess had grown increasingly frustrated.

Mary set her princess at the edge of the bed, and pulled several pillows for her to lean against. "If you insist-"

"I do," Kyla snapped. "I'm still the regent. I lead House Calonar until my husband returns or my father is healed."

"Your sister-"

"Is barely twelve. The Church and the law may call her an adult, but I don't. She shouldn't have to bear all his herself."

Mary sighed and retrieved the rolling chair. Esha and Remm had arrived with it the day after Kyla's bleeding. The mismatched pair had presented it as an alternative to any walking the princess might be forced to do. It was a grand thing, with large wheels that gently rolled not only in circles, but yielded up and down to the slightest imbalance, keeping the passenger level. Mary rolled this to her princess' side and locked the wheels.

Kyla looked at this with evil in her pearlescent eyes, then directed the hateful gaze up at her handmaiden. "Must we?" she demanded.

"Highness," Mary said with the patient tone one would use with any child. "If you insist on attending this meeting, and won't let us have it in here, where it would make sense…" she nodded to the rolling chair.

"Get me a robe," Kyla sighed. The princess had steadfastly refused all her attendants' efforts to dress her. She nearly hissed any time one of them brought forward even a shift, complaining of its scratching against her stomach and breasts. Kyla's skin had become exceptionally sensitive, reacting even to the gentlest breeze. Often preferring nudity in even normal times, the princess had become almost fanatical in her avoidance of any material rubbing against her body.

Mary went to a wardrobe and retrieved the one garment her princess conceded to, and even then, only for as brief a time as was absolutely necessary. The silk robe of flawless blue was so soft it seemed as though the late summer sky had woven itself into fabric. Mary draped this over Kyla's small shoulders and helped her into the sleeves. On any other woman, the robe would be voluminous; on the gravid princess, it just barely covered her. Kyla had ordered the sleeves hemmed until they just barely covered her elbows. It could not be closed completely, so Mary had improvised a second belt; one tied just beneath her expanding breasts, the other beneath her swollen stomach. This gathered the front of the robe away from Kyla's legs, leaving them exposed from the knee, but flowed out behind her in a great train. The princess' chest was only barely covered, as little of her sensitive skin as possible in contact with the silk that she insisted grated on her like wool. Her stomach bulged out, totally uncovered, but Kyla insisted her little prince preferred that.

Mary retrieved a brush and did her best to tame her princess' unruly mass of blonde hair. This finally accomplished, she leaned in and leveraged Kyla into the rolling chair. Setting her legs onto the raised rest so that her feet were extended slightly forward, Mary then organized the blue robe as best she could to maintain as much of her princess' unwanted modesty as was possible. This done, the handmaiden unlocked the wheels using the bizarre levers Remm had shown her, and pushed the increasingly-heavy jewel of House Calonar out to the sitting room.

Medaka was already there. God alone knew how the elder Sister of the Lady of Light traveled so quickly; her Temple was far from the castle, and yet she was always quick to arrive upon any summons. Further, despite the late hour, Medaka was as well-made as always. Her hair was flawless and the faint cosmetics she wore, so subtle you could only barely notice them, masterfully applied. Her purple skirt was without wrinkle and the red cord marking her as an elder Sister was perfectly arranged. She stood at the window, chatting with Ilse as Mary and Kyla entered. "Is everything alright?" Medaka asked, her voice as gentle, yet as firm, as always. Her words were not directed at Kyla.

"No change," Mary shrugged.

Esha walked in then, her blue robes even more rumpled than usual and her burn-singed hair an almost artful arrangement of unkemptness. The tiny Syla did not look as though she had been sleeping, for her opalescent eyes were as wide as ever in her waking hours, and she did not carry the sullen lack of focus as was so common in the woken sleeper. Instead, the tiny archmage was flushed as though disturbed from a great exertion, almost certainly yet another of her bizarre experiments.

With Esha also came Lieutenant Aloisa. The Gunrsvein woman towered over her tiny Sylva companion. Although she was not wearing her armor, still her frame was thick and powerful, made to seem even more so when in such close comparison to the diminutive Esha. Like the archmage, Aloisa's hair was a disordered mess, her normally tight braid absent and revealing just how voluminous her hair really was, spilling over her strong shoulders and down her powerful back. Even her blue and grey uniform was disheveled, seeming as though it had been hurriedly thrown on. Like Esha, her unadorned face did not seem as though the warrior-woman had not been disturbed from sleep, but from great exertion.

"What were you two doing?" Kyla asked.

Aloisa seemed about to reply, but Esha swatted the much taller woman in her hard stomach. "Oh, nothing," the tiny archmage said cheerfully. "Just a little side project. Something to indulge my curiosity."

The lieutenant glanced curiously down with the barest hint of a grin, but shrugged and said nothing.

"Let's take this into the dining room," Kyla instructed. The princess then threw an arch look up at Mary. "If I can't go to the council chambers, I can at least hold a meeting somewhere looking a little official."

"As your Highness commands," Mary said without inflection. She wheeled her princess into the dining room, pulling away the chair resting at the head and placing Kyla there. The handmaiden lowered the footrest and locked the wheels once her princess was in place, and moved to the chair beside her.

The others came in as well, and took seats. Ilse and Medaka sat on Kyla's other side and Esha took the last of the places. Aloisa grabbed the chair Mary had moved and pulled it behind Esha, where she loomed over the diminutive Sylva.

A knock on the door announced Rainer's arrival. With the colonel came Remm. The massive Uldra loomed over the guardsman, much as Aloisa had loomed over Esha. Unlike the women, however, the men did not seem as though they had been disturbed from some great exertion. Ironically, the men, however, were even more disheveled. Rainer had dark circles under his sunken eyes, and he clearly had not groomed his beard in days. Remm was as unruly as ever, his thick leather tunic stained with food and glowing embers, frayed and torn and in desperate need of replacement. His hair was a wild nest of tangles and knots. Only the extensive tattoos covering half is face and body seemed organized, the twisting curves somehow seeming elegant against the indifferent ugliness of the Uldra.

The men entered the dining room and stood. Remm crossed his massive arms over his equally-expansive chest and said nothing, only waiting. Rainer folded his arms behind his back and nodded to Kyla. "Princess," he said respectfully. The colonel glanced at Ilse and smiled softly. "Squirrel," he said fondly to his daughter.

"What's the story with that nickname?" Mary asked, looking at her friend, but Ilse threw a hostile look back.

"Did you not tell her ladyship about that time when you were eight?" Rainer asked.

"Ladyship?" Ilse started.

Rainer looked in surprise at Mary. "Did the baroness not tell her friend about the promotions?" He shook his head in mock sadness. "So many secrets these days."

"Stop causing problems, father," Ilse snapped. "You're not one to talk about keeping secrets, anyway." Word had spread of the heated conversation, although there had been only one voice heard, between father and daughter. Rainer had failed to inform Ilse about his knighthood, as he had failed to inform most everyone, especially the soldiers under his command. Ilse had ensured that word spread, and that everyone properly address her father as "Sir Klug," despite his objections.

The colonel raised his hands in surrender. "I believe the message said we needed to talk about something important," he pointed out, almost desperate to change the subject.

"Has anyone seen Rashid or Chandra?" Kyla asked.

Heads shook. "Chandra was at the walls yesterday," Aloisa offered. "I am unsure what she was doing. We did not speak."

"Was Rashid with her?" the princess asked.

Aloisa shook her head. "I have not seen the spymaster since that last strategy meeting."

"Nor me," Rainer added. He glanced around. "I just assumed he was still in his rooms. That he was back…" Everyone knew of Rashid's withering in recent months. The spymaster had been seen little outside his quarters and, even then, he was a shadow of himself. Castle gossip insisted that he was lost to self-recrimination for his failures leading to the assassination attempt on Kyla.

"I hoped he was coming out of it," Kyla grumbled, shaking her head. She glanced at Mary. "You said he seemed to be getting better."

"At that last meeting, he was very active," the handmaiden insisted. "He almost seemed like himself towards the end."

"Well," Kyla sighed, absently rubbing her stomach, "check on him. I'd really like my spymaster's advice right now." The princess straightened and glanced at Medaka. "I tried to Dreamwalk again."

The elder Sister narrowed her eyes. "I warned you against that," she pointed out with a glanced exchanged with Mary.

"We need to know where Rogan is," Kyla argued. "And General Killdare."

"And she wanted to see her husband again," Mary added, holding Medaka's eyes. Kyla threw her friend a hostile look.

Esha spoke up. "My understanding of the Winds of Dreams suffers from many limitations," the archmage said. "But all magic requires effort, exertion, putting stress upon both the body and the mind. I was given to understand that, after the incident in which you neutralized Fak'Har's warmachines, you were placed on even stricter bedrest to protect the child."

"She was," Ilse said irritably.

"I've Dreamwalked to Rogan before," Kyla pointed out defensively. "It's never any real exertion."

Mary cleared her throat meaningfully.

"As long as we don't do any of that," the princess added in annoyance. "Dreamwalking is as natural, as effortless as breathing, really."

"Although," Medaka interjected, a shadow passing over her face, "any form of magic has risks. Isn't that right? Risks particular to each Wind?"

"Indeed," Esha nodded. "Each of the Winds of Magic carry their own challenges, their own-"

"Dangers," Mary almost whispered.

"The Wind of Dreams is no different," Medaka continued. "It can provide great power, but there is a... temptation."

"For what?" Aloisa asked.

"For the dream to become a nightmare."

"I'm only trying to communicate with Rogan," Kyla insisted.

"But," Esha argued, "you do so against the magical barriers emplaced by Fak'Har."

"And to do so," Medaka added, "you must draw on the more harsh elements of the Wind of Dreams."

Esha glanced at Medaka. "You said the Shadowed Mage interfered when the princess attacked the Uldra?"

Medaka nodded.

"Then we must assume the Shadowed Mage has at least some faculty with Dream Magic," the archmage concluded. "Certainly much more so than I, and perhaps at least equal to the princess' current ability."

"Is he still blocking your communications?" Rainer asked.

Esha nodded. "My voice has been limited to the Northern Keep since the siege began, and was being curtailed during the Great Burn. None of my students can even translocate or communicate within the city, so great is Fak'Har's interference."

"I thought the walls were supposed to protect our spell-slingers," Remm pointed out.

"The enchantment I constructed does offer protection," the archmage nearly sulked. "Were those defenses not in place, I suspect many of our adepts would be incapacitated by the Shadowed Mage, perhaps worse."

"That's why I risked Dreamwalking again," Kyla insisted. "We need to contact the outside. We need to know where help is."

"But it didn't work," Mary added. "The princess tried for the last three nights. All blocked." Her eyes again went to Medaka. "And each time, she's tried drawing deeper from the Wind of Dreams."

Esha nodded, her mouth twisting into a tiny grimace of thought. "We must assume that Fak'Har has manipulated his magical blockade so as to disrupt the lost Winds, as well as the doctrinal ones. The Shadowed Mage is at least as knowledgeable of Dream, Shadow, and the others. He will have prepared for them."

"Princess," Rainer said. "When was the last time you spoke with Prince Rogan?"

"More than a month ago. They had just left Pelesemoria."

"Not since?"

Kyla shook her head. "I've been able to see him, but not... talk." She hesitated, her brow furrowed in thought. "It's hard to explain. Dreamwalking isn't like being in the waking world. There are no solid points of reference except for people, other dreamers."

"The Wind of Dreams is the least substantial," Medaka explained. "Of all the Winds of Magic, it's the least anchored to this world."

Kyla nodded. "I can't really tell where someone is or what they're doing when they're awake. But, if they're asleep, I can see through their memories, their dreams. I haven't been able to pull Rogan in to my dream again so that we can..." the princess glanced guiltily at Mary. "So we can talk."

"Uh huh."

"But," Kyla hurriedly continued, "I have been able to see his dreams. Before the siege began, they had already arrived in Ironheartshaven."

"Impressive," Rainer mumbled. "Only a few weeks' travel time from Pelesemoria to Ironheartshaven."

"They have the Archaeknights with them," Aloisa reminded her commander. "One of them can manipulate the wind."

"He had his team and the Archaeknights," Kyla confirmed. "He'd been in contact with General Killdare, and they were coordinating their plans to reach the Keep."

"Makes sense," Rainer agreed. "The Prince will gather forces from in an around Ironheartshaven. He'll be able to build a force at least equal to the General's, but they'll need to arrive at the same time."

"Why?" Ilse asked her father.

"Like the Princess said," the colonel shrugged. "Coordination. If either the Prince or General Killdare arrive too soon, they'll have to face Vagris alone. That's risky considering what kind of assets he has. But, if their two forces arrive at the same time, they'll outnumber the enemy." The veteran guardsman tuned back to Kyla. "Highness," he said gently. "It would be... advantageous if we could coordinate with them as well."

"I know," Kyla agreed. "That's why I was trying to make contact." She shook her head. "I just can't break through. I can't even see outside the city anymore."

"Given time," Esha mused, "no doubt your proficiency with Dream Magic would improve. I would assume, as with any discipline, practice would enhance the abilities of even a Dream Mage."

"But we don't have time," Mary argued. "And the Princess can't risk practicing now, can't risk the... dangers." She meaningfully looked at Kyla's exposed stomach.

"Indeed," the Sylva agreed. "Though the Princess' condition would offer one advantage."

"What advantage?" Ilse asked.

"Supplemental power," Esha shrugged. "We have already seen compelling evidence that the prince-to-be possesses formidable arcane potential. He has already brought it to bear while still within his mother's womb.

"My God," Mary gasped and all eyes turned to her. She looked at Kyla. "Lukas. When he tried to kill you, when you were incapacitated, your son called on the Fael."

Ilse nodded. "And when you attacked the rouge Uldra. Karen whispered something to the baby; I think he helped you, gave you the strength to break through Fak'Har's interference."

"And he paid the price," Medaka reminded.

They were all silent for a time. Esha sighed and leaned forward. Aloisa had needed to stack a number of books on the archmage's chair to allow Esah to sit high enough, and these shifted a bit with the brilliant Sylva's movement "Princess," the archmage said in her tiny, soft voice, concern radiating from her large, opalescent eyes. "The point should be well-considered. Within your unborn child, you have a great arcane potential. I suspect that your son could help you break through Fak'Har's interference again. However, as I stated before, employing any of the Winds of Magic comes at a cost."

"And the Wind of Dreams has its own dangers," Medaka added.

"Indeed," the archmage continued. "We adepts are drained by employing the Winds. Great stress is placed on our bodies, consummate with the feat we are attempting. The Shadowed Mage is one of, perhaps the most powerful wielder of magic to ever live. Like Cyras Darkholm, Fak'Har has mastered most, perhaps all, of the Winds of Magic. No one adept could possibly stand against him." She glanced at Medaka. "If there are no other Dream Mages...?"

Medaka shook her head. "Not in Lanasia."

Esha sighed and nodded, the stack of books on which she sat once again shifting under her slight frame. "Then there is no one else to aid you. There is only your unborn child. You have the ability, even now, to overcome Fak'Har's interference, even as you did before, and bring your Dream Magic to bear. But to do so would require putting an incredible stress on both you and your son. Even a grown adept would suffer under such a strain. An unborn child would not be able to endure such hardship."

"We think the princess is in the final weeks of her pregnancy," Ilse offered. "Perhaps the final days. Of course, no one really knows, since so few Halvan children are ever born. He should be far less vulnerable now than in earlier times." The priestess looked at Kyla. "But there is still great risk. Trauma, injury, overexertion by the mother, all these things can harm the child."

Kyla leaned back. "So, no more Dreamwalking."

Nods came from nearly everyone.

The door opened again, this time without a knock or other announcement. Karen entered, looking the same as she always did since gaining the Truthsight. She was well-groomed and unruffled, the hour of the night as unimportant as would be the hour of the day. The youngest Calonar stopped at the doorway and looked at them each in turn, breathing deep and nodding. "Friends are about to return," she said, her young voice level and without emotion. "I need the City Watch," this she said to Remm, who nodded without hesitation. "You three also need to be there," she pointed in turn to Rainer, Aloisa, and Ilse. "I've already sent others ahead."

Without another word, the nascent Truthseer turned and left. The assembled people glanced back at Kyla, who shrugged. "You heard her," the princess said. Everyone stood, going about their tasks. The princess put a hand on Mary's. "You go too," she ordered.

"Highness-" the handmaiden started to object, but Kyla shook her head.

"I want to know what's happening. Medaka can stay here while you're gone. Go and report back to me."

Chapter 30

The mercantile district was silent. The new Uldra gaslamps still burned, casting their soft golden light across the empty streets. The cheery beacons always stayed lit through the night, their minders only extinguishing them at dawn. The most adventurous of nocturnal customers would have long since sought out their beds when the city was at peace. Now shops were closed, some even boarded up. The quarters in the floors above were still as Karen led them through the clean streets.

They arrived at their apparent destination with hours to go before morning. Distant Ulheim lacked even a hint of pre-dawn light. The building to which Karen led them was one of those boarded up and seemingly abandoned. The princess and Truthseer nodded at Remm, who removed the obstructing boards nailed across the door. The ancient Uldra showed neither strain nor hesitation as he cleared the obstruction and opened the door, leading his small team of watchmen inside. They quickly searched, both the empty shop itself and the equally-vacant quarters above before Remm returned to the door and nodded to those waiting outside.

Karen led the rest inside. The shelves were bare. Mary could not recall having ever entered this place, nor did its stand out in her memory. Ilse ran a finger along one of the bare counters which stood nearest to the door and came away with a layer of dust. Rainer glanced behind the same counter his daughter was inspecting and found only empty cupboards. Aloisa sniffed the air, wrinkling her nose at its staleness. The place had been abandoned long before the siege began.

Without pause, Karen walked to the rear storeroom. The princess gestured for Remm and his watchmen to follow, with Mary and the others trailing behind. This storage space was far larger than the shop. Large boxes were stacked along the walls and in the rear, leaving only the center of the room empty. Remm's watchmen moved with experience into this room, searching along the obstructed walls, but careful not to disturb the unknown boxes. The Uldra himself, the white of half his body nearly glowing in the dim light, stood in the empty center, gesturing for Karen and the others to wait at the door.

The watchmen finished their initial clearance of the room and looked to Remm for instruction. The elder Uldra pointed at one of the boxes, near the back but sitting alone. "That one," he said. His watchmen went to the single crate. Two approached while the others formed a weary perimeter. One man pulled a metal rod from his belt, different from the wooden clubs the Northern Keep's City Watch normally carried.

Using this, the watchman worked at the box, freeing one side and pulling against the thick iron nails holding the lid in place. With a reluctant creek, the wood came free. The watchman stepped away as his partner grabbed the lid and lifted, allowing the first man to look inside.

When the watchman jerked his head at Remm, the Uldra approached. "Huh," was all he said before glancing at Karen.

"They're meant for use once the infiltrators arrived," the Truthseer explained.

"What is it?" Rainer asked.

Remm reached in and pulled out a spiked maul.

"It's Uldra-sized," Mary noted.

Remm glanced at her and nodded, hefting the massive weapon in his hands.

"How many?" Aloisa asked, her eyes moving around the many boxes in the room.

Remm glanced again into the crate before him. "A dozen or so," he answered.

"Do all the boxes...?" Rainer asked, his eyes also scanning the many boxes.

"Yes," Karen replied.

"Like Anninihus' dead things and their weapons," Aloisa observed to her colonel.

Ilse gasped at the memory, shuddering in recollection and pressing into her father. Rainer put his arm around his daughter. Her friend had not spoken of that fight. The only details had come from Tomas. They had spoken the night of that encounter, while Mary had tended to his wounds. The Death Mage had been smuggling bodies into the Northern Keep, along with terrible weapons of pain and suffering. Tomas and Prince Rogan had discovered the cache and Anninihus had activated his abominations. The creatures had nearly killed them all until Esha's timely magical intervention. Ilse had been there, had also faced the horror of the Death Mage's creations.

"That was an early attempt," Karen said as her pearlescent eyes scanned the room. "Anninhus was commanding the first creatures Fak'Har had created, while he was still perfecting the process to make his unliving knights." The Truthseer was, Mary quickly realized, not looking at the various boxes, but at the various people. She paused at one of the watchmen, staring at him for a moment while the man blinked in discomfort. The princess then pointed at one of the boxes near to him. "Move that one aside," she commanded.

The watchman did so. A few of his comrades moved to help, but stood back in surprise when they realized the box in question was empty. It was pulled aside with little difficulty, revealing a trap door. Remm stepped forward. "Where's it go?" he asked.

"Outside the city," Karen explained. "It used to lead to a small clearing in the forest, but the Great Burn collapsed the far end. The rogue Uldra discovered the tunnel a few days ago and have been working to clear and reinforce it."

"They're going to use it to infiltrate the city," Rainer said grimly.

"Not anymore," Aloisa added.

"Is that why we're here?" Mary asked dubiously. "To stop the rogue Uldra?"

"No," Karen said. "Some friends are coming back. They were directed to the tunnel. Here they come now." She glanced at Remm. "Open the door; they're wounded and exhausted."

Again obeying without hesitation, Remm moved to the trapdoor and pulled it open, the rusted hinges squealing a futile protest against the great Uldra's strength. All was quiet for a moment then, until a trembling hand was raised into view and a gasping voice said, "A little help would be most appreciated, if you would not mind."

Remm reached down, taking the offered hand, and pulled.

"Vincent!" Ilse gasped and ran forward. Mary saw that it was, indeed, the young spy. He was nude, his emaciated body covered in still-bleeding wounds. His face was a patch of discolored abuse and his breath bubbled red. The priestess took him into her arms and held him close, her tears starting to wash away his injuries.

"Ilse?" the young spy weakly said. "Is it... are you real?"

She nodded. She kissed his face and held him close. The spy began to cry. "They showed me..." he gasped. "They looked like you while they... They sounded like you... They tried to make me think it was you... I didn't believe..."

Mary glanced at Rainer. The colonel stood with one eyebrow raised as he watched his daughter and the young man in her arms. He had an unreadable look in his eyes, but the handmaiden thought she saw the barest hint of a nod.

Remm had reached into the tunnel gain and came up with a Xeshlin. Mary needed a moment to realize it was Xathias, so odd he looked. The recently-promoted archwizard was nearly as nude as Vincent. He wore only a scarlet loincloth, torn and stained from their escape. His once-long, free-flowing hair of colorless white had been shorn close, and his face no longer bore a thin beard. Instead, the renegade Xeshlin was unshaven and rough, silently telling of their hard trek. His eyes of burning blood were weary and drooped in relief. Like his companion, Xathias' body was a patchwork of small cuts and bruises, though his were miniscule compared to Vincent's grievous injuries. "Welcome home," Remm said.

The Xeshlin nodded and stood straight. He glanced at Karen. "The camp was where your directed me," he reported. "I did as you instructed; the siege engines those witches are constructing will fail."

The princess nodded.

Xathias glanced back to the tunnel. "My covert identity should be intact," he offered. "Though I will need some explanation for my sudden disappearance. I might be able to reinfiltrate the Coven."

Karen shook her head. "You've accomplished what you needed to. If you return, the Sorcerous Sisters will identify you. They'll complete the ritual that-"

"I am familiar with the procedure," Xathias interrupted with a raised hand. "I know what befalls those of my gender who demonstrate facility with the Winds of Magic."

"We could always use another spell-slinger on the walls, anyway," Remm offered. "Once you're rested."

The renegade Xeshlin straightened his shoulders. "I need little," he said firmly. "A good meal and some appropriate clothes will restore me as much as is needed." He turned his eyes of burning blood to Rainer. "I will report to my teacher, and be with you tomorrow."

"The next assault?" the colonel deduced.

Xathias nodded. "The equipment is nearly complete. With the dawn, Vagris will make his next attempt."

Rainer glanced at Aloisa. "Then we need to make sure everything's ready."

The Gunrsvein lieutenant nodded and left. Rainer started following, but paused at the door, glancing back at his daughter. Ilse had lain Vincent onto the floor. The priestess was whispering to her goddess, calling upon the Life Magic of the Harvest Mother. She held her hands just over Vincent's brutalized body, a soft light glowing between them as Ilse passed along, focusing as needed upon those areas of greatest injury.

Mary walked over to Rainer. "She'll need some time," the handmaiden said gently. "We'll take him back to the castle with us. I'll ask Medaka to help, to heal his mind and heart while Ilse takes care of his body."

The colonel stared at his daughter. "Somehow," he said with the faintest hint of a smile, peaking around the very edge of his lips. "Somehow, I think she's got both covered."

Ilse glanced up at her father. The two shared an unspoken look. Her father finally let the smile that had teased his face come fully to the surface. He looked down at his daughter and nodded.

Ilse needed almost an hour to heal Vincent enough for the trip back to the castle. Remm used the time to send a pair of his watchmen to retrieve a carriage. They could only find a wagon, but the Uldra shrugged in acceptance. Once Ilse declared Vincent well enough for the trip, the men picked him up under the priestess' firm command and gently placed him in the transport.

Rainer gave his daughter a brief kiss. "Take care of him," he said.

"I will, father," she whispered.

Remm then lifted Ilse and put her on the wagon beside Vincent. Without preamble, he ordered the rest of his men to see them safely back to the castle. This done, the Uldra turned back to Karen. "What about that?" he asked, nodding towards the tunnel.

"We need to seal it," Rainer declared.

"No," Karen countered. She looked at Remm. "The rogue Uldra are digging tunnels under the city's walls."

"Sapping," the Watch commander grunted. "Like the Sylvai at Uldron."

"What?" Mary asked.

"The Siege of Uldron," Rainer mused. He glanced at Remm. "That battle was twelve thousand years ago. No records of it survive."

"Thirteen," Remm corrected.

"How do you know what happened? Even the Sylvai don't have any surviving records of that war."

"They're lying," the Uldra grunted. "Shiny-eyed sissies kept records of everything. They just want the rest of the world to forget." His eyes, both the black one and the blue, grew distant for a moment, haunted by an ancient grudge, an undying and unanswered injury. "But a few of us remember."

"What's sapping," Mary asked again, trying to break the awkward silence.

"I thought it was just a theory," Rainer offered. "I've read about it in a few doctrines, and General Killdare and I talked about it once. When you assault a city's walls, you normally only have two choices, over or through." The colonel nodded to the distant walls. "The enemy tried over last time; they wanted to use scaling ladders. Next, they'll try rams to breach the gate."

"And the walls themselves," Karen said, her pearlescent eyes looking at and through Rainer. "The Dark Coven has been working to build and enchant several rams so that they might breach the walls."

"But that won't work either," the colonel added. "Even without Esha's protective spells, a casemate wall is specifically designed to counter breaching. That would mean they could only defeat the wall with sheer numbers." He looked at Remm. "Unless they sap." The veteran led Mary to one of the counters and drew into the thick dust coating it. "Instead of attacking the wall itself, you go under it," he explained, drawing a rough image of a wall. "You dig a series of tunnels that lead under the wall, into the ground the wall is sitting on. Then you fill the tunnel with wood and oil and light it on fire. The tunnel collapses and takes a section of the wall with it." The guardsman glanced at Remm. "It's been tried a few times, but never successfully."

"It's been done," the bifurcated Uldra insisted. He nodded towards the distant enemy. "Castle Kordenel. An Uldra clan sapped the walls." He looked meaningfully at Rainer. "They were from the west," he said. "The traitors will know how to do it."

"Then we have a problem."

"No, we don't." Remm squared himself. "I'll get all the clansmen in the city together. Most of them were miners; they know tunnels and digging, and we needed to take care of the traitors anyway." He glanced at Karen. "This is the time to do it?"

The Truthseer nodded.

"Then that's it," Remm declared. "I'll take my people into that tunnel and we'll deal with the traitors." He glanced at Rainer. "You handle the fight above, and we'll handle the one below."

The warriors nodded and clasped hands. The Uldra paused as he turned, his mismatched eyes of blue and black turning to the cheery gaslamps he, himself, had designed and his people had installed. The commander of the City Watched looked back at Rainer. "You might want to turn these off," the Uldra suggested. "Things are about to get a little loud."

Colonel Rainer also looked at the gaslamp and nodded.

Remm departed and Rainer followed, bowing to Karen before he left. The princess walked outside the shop and stood in the street, looking at the wagon as it made its slow way back to the castle. Mary walked up beside the girl. In the light of the Uldra gaslamps, they could see Ilse sitting beside Vincent. She was holding his hand, talking softly to him. Even from the growing distance, Mary could almost feel the love radiating off the two, made all the stronger from their sudden and unexpected reunion.

"I could have let him die," Karen whispered.

"What?" Mary asked, startled.

"Vincent's return wasn't Fated," the Truthseer explained. "His capture was. His torture by the Dark Coven was. Nothing could change that. But he could have died in that camp. His suffering would have been done. Now, he'll live an entire life with the pain in his body, and the pain in his soul. He'll remember the sight of Ilse torturing him, of evil women taking her form and her voice, of laughing at his abuse. He'll never really recover.

"When I sent Xathias out to sabotage the Xeshlin siege engines, I could have told him to leave the prisoners in place. He would have resented the order, but obeyed. Vincent would have died with the dawn, along with the other captives. He could have been at peace."

Mary glanced at Karen, seeing once more that this was not a Truthseer holding power of Fate and the lives of all mortals, but a little girl struggling to find a way through lives filled with suffering. "So, why did you free him?"

The young princess sighed and rubbed her eyes, as though she could wipe away the suffering she had witnessed when looking at Vincent. "He'll be useful later," the Truthseer revealed. "He and Ilse both. They'll be strong allies for Rogan in the years to come. And…" She looked at Vincent and Ilse, who were holding hands and staring into each other's eyes.

Mary looked as well and, for just a moment, thought she saw as Karen did. She saw the suffering, the pain and hardship. But she also saw something else, something more. "And, this way they have more time together," the handmaiden finished.

Chapter 31

A strange mist poured out from the desiccated remains of Wildelves Wood. From amidst the blackened trunks, the skeletal fingers still reaching to an uncaring sky for mercy from the Great Burn, a thick cloud of black and grey rolled towards the Northern Keep. The morning sun, still climbing from Ulheim's peaks, cast an ominous glow on the mist, unable to penetrate the evil that slid towards them. All the warmth of the late summer was lost to that encroaching cloud. It moved like a thing alive, like some wretched miscarriage reaching out, hungering for the living.

"Is that natural?" Rainer asked.

Esha, garbed once again in her oversized protective gear, stood on a crate Aloisa had brought up. Still the tiny archmage had to stand on her tiptoes to see over the battlements. "This has been summoned," the Sylva said grimly. She began whispering, her voice so soft that Mary could not make out the words, even if she could decipher the complex language of magic. The handmaiden was standing beside Esha, having arrived only moment before, and stared at the oncoming mist with the same dread as most of the city's defenders.

Esha paused in her whispering magic, closing her opalescent eyes tightly in concentration. Then, she gasped and would have fallen from the box if not for Mary and Aloisa, who caught the tiny archmage. "Fak'Har is aiding them!" the Sylva hissed.

"What?" Rainer snapped, looking back out to the encroaching mist.

"The Shadowed Mage has lent his own power to the Dark Coven's!" Esha clambered back onto the crate and leaned out to see the mist. "He is using it to hide their approach!"

A runner arrived and saluted. "Sir! Bastion Seven reports!"

"Calm down!" Aloisa snapped. "And stop saluting the Colonel!"

The runner flinched and blushed. "Sorry ma'am!"

"And lower your damn voice!"

"What's your report?" Rainer asked.

"The... cloud has stopped. It's staying out of arrow range."

The colonel looked out himself. "Yeah," he nodded. "It is stopping. Out of ballistae range, too."

"But not the trebuchets," Aloisa pointed out.

Rainer nodded and glanced at Esha. "Can you dispel that mist?"

The archmage looked out at the mist again, twisting her mouth in concentration. "With Amatria and Xathias, yes. Give the word, and we can unleash a concentrated effort that will overwhelm Fak'Har and his *Xesh'lin*..." Her tiny body nearly shook with barely-restrained anger.

"You're adorable when you want to say a bad word, you know," Aloisa teased.

Esha put her tiny fists on her equally-small hips and faced the Gunrsvein woman who towered over her.

"Let's get Amatria and Xathias up here," Rainer said to the runner, who nodded and left.

"What do we do in the mean time?" Mary asked.

Rainer nodded and called for more runners. "Have all engines in range orient for maximum coverage of that mist. They're to spread out their shots as much as possible. All scorpions and archers to hold fire until Esha's magic works. They're to fire normal shot until a triple-blast, then load the special shot."

"The trebuchets won't hit much of anything," Aloisa pointed out as the runners departed.

Rainer shook his head. "They don't have to hit anything. I just want whatever is creeping up on us to know we can range them. I want them nervous before they get to us." The colonel moved to the edge of the battlement and called down. "All irregulars to the gate. Guard reinforcements stage in front of assigned bastions!"

"How do you think Remm's doing?" Mary asked of no one in particular.

"The Uldra will do their job," Rainer insisted, rejoining them. "There's nothing we can do about it anyway." He paused and glanced at Esha. "Can we?"

The tiny archmage shook her head. "Once I was informed of the rogue Uldra's strategy, I tasked a number of my students to try and locate them, but they are shielded. I believe the Dark Coven is protecting them from our divinations and interceptions. This is, no doubt, why I did not sense their attempt at circumventing my wards on the walls already. I fear we must trust to Remm's strategic instincts, betrayed temper, and tunneling experience."

Aloisa looked down at the ground before the walls. "I do not envy them having to wage war like that," she mused. "Trapped under the ground, fighting in darkness against their own kin."

"We have our own worries," Rainer pointed out.

"What are they waiting for?" Mary asked, again looking at the mist. It was pulsing, almost thrashing, but held its distance from the city.

"Could be anything," Aloisa answered.

"I think they're trying to coordinate," Rainer countered. "The princess said the rogue Uldra were going to try to sap the walls. If they can open holes in our defenses, Vagris won't have to throw his men away on another assault."

Mary looked down at the imposing stone construction on which they stood and the glacis with its wooden stakes before it. "If there's a chance the wall could come down…"

"If this wall fails," Aloisa laughed, "we are all quite screwed regardless."

Rainer grunted. "We win or lose the fight for this city here."

Suddenly, the ground seemed to give voice to a bizarre, hollow roar. Then another, and another. The thick stone vibrated beneath Mary's feet, and the mist before them recoiled. The vibration gave way to jerking, as though the world herself was under some violent attack. The earth beneath them shook back and forth. Loose stones and shingles feel from rooftops. Crates and stacks of equipment were overturned. Esha fell from her box, caught in mid-fall by Aloisa just as Mary herself was caught by Rainer when her footing failed. An unfortunate few were not saved, however, tumbling over to fall back into the city. "Groundquake!" someone shouted, and the call was taken up by others.

What came next made a mockery of the groundquake. There was a dull roar, as though a horrid Vaeyen had been awoken from its ages-long slumber, then another and another. The charred, skeletal trunks surrounding the Northern Keep, all that remained of the once-lush Wildelves Wood, swayed. Many toppled or even shattered. Within the city, buildings shed stone and tile, and the weaker ones collapsed outright. The whole world heaved and screamed in the agonized throes of vengeful kinslaying. Even from so far above, with the ground attempting to shield them all from the hateful fury of the Uldra, the sounds of their wrath echoed out. Cracks appeared in the fields before the city walls, and these writhed. The glacis Aloisa had dug before the walls collapsed into darkness, opening a massive chasm before the wall. The world's spasming increased, and there was one final detonation. The ground sank and heaved, showering both defender and invader with earth and stone.

And then all was still.

Esha, cradled against Aloisa's breastplate, blinked her opalescent eyes. "I believe Remm has engaged the rogue Uldra," she noted.

Aloisa glanced over the battlement. "Is this a good thing, or a bad thing? she asked.

"The walls're still standing," Rainer pointed out, getting to his feet and helping Mary do the same. "We're still here. I'd call that a good thing." He glanced over the battlement. "Your glacis is… a little deeper now."

"Will that help us?" Mary asked, also looking over the edge of the wall. The low trench was, indeed, deeper. In fact, the stake-lined depression had been replaced with a large crevasse, its bottom lost in shadows.

"It'll sure as Underworld make Vagris' job harder," Rainer shrugged as he walked to the other side of the battlement. "What's happening down there?" he called.

A few shouted replies came up. Many were wounded, but most only lightly. The clerics of the Harvest Mother were already deploying, bringing that merciful goddess' healing magic to bear. Mary looked out onto the Northern Keep and sighed in relief. Here and there, a few of the buildings had succumbed to the Uldra's vengeance, but not many. The city was intact and, for the moment, safe.

"Colonel!" Aloisa called out, nodding beyond the battlements.

Rainer and Mary moved to look. The field separating the Northern Keep from the dead forest was broken. What had been a flat, gentle plain was now a jagged riot of cracks, sinkholes, cliffs, and exposed stone. The blackened husks of the Uldra warmachines had been torn to pieces, with only scattered bits of iron, copper, and bronze remaining. The broken field was now a monument to the devastation of Fak'Har's invasion. The cloud of debris had replaced the obscuring mist, but was clearing. Shapes had appeared within that ominous cloud. At first only the most vague silhouettes, but quickly taking form. They were men, or something in the shape of men. Mary shuddered when her mind finally identified them.

Fak'Har's blasphemous creations were marching out from the mist. They were even worse than Mary's recollection. Standing taller than a man, their plate armor was still as black as a moonless night, with horrid spikes decorated with the bones and flesh of their victims. They did not carry their greatswords, though. Instead, the unliving creatures were pulling at large wooden constructions.

"Damn!" Rainer swore. He rushed back to the edge of the battlement. "Battering rams!"

"But how?" Mary demanded, glancing again at the fissure that had opened and the nearly-impassible broken field.

"That's how," the colonel replied grimly, staring hatred out into the skeletal forest.

The handmaiden looked, and trembled. The mist and debris cloud had continued to clear. Behind the advancing horrors, a large canopy was once again held up by mercenaries. Beneath this protective cover, safe from the late-summer sun, was the Coven of the Puma. The Xeshlin priestesses were chanting and waving their arms in unison, gesturing towards the broken field. In response, the earth began to smooth, to level itself into lanes for the advancing battering rams.

"Damn!" Rainer swore. "They'll clear a path or bridge." The veteran shook his head. "Damned spell-slingers." He turned and roared down. "Gate, and wall sections five and seven!"

Below, the call was echoed and soldiers moved. Further reinforcements were moved to those areas. Mary stared out at the approaching threats. They looked like bizarre houses built of blackened wood. Each rolled upon many wheels. They had arched roofs covered in shields like improvised shingles. The frame was open, revealing a single, great log within each, connected to the houses by chains as though they rested in some evil cradle. The front of those single, massive logs had been capped with spiked iron. The engines were pulled by Fak'Har's unliving monsters, who made no sound, not even a grunt against the great mass of the engines.

"Ballistae ready!" Aloisa shouted. She looked at the colonel. "Special shot?"

"No!" Mary called out. Rainer looked at her. "Last night! Karen said they would fail!"

"If the Dark Coven built those engines," Esha warned, "they will have some counter to my wards on the gate and walls!"

"We can't let them reach us!" Aloisa insisted.

Rainer stared at Mary. "Faith," was all the handmaiden said.

The veteran guardsman looked at her for a moment. "Load special shot!" the colonel barked. "Take aim but do not fire!" He squared himself. "Let's see what happens."

The rams continued their way forward, moving inch by inch through the lanes opened by the Coven of Puma's Leash.

Rainer leaned back. "Longshot!" he called down the line.

The lead Walker, crouching like all the archers and awaiting command, stood and looked over.

Rainer jerked at thumb at the approaching engines. "See what happens!"

Longshot nodded. The Walker tuned and raised his bow. He sighed a target and selected an arrow. In one, fluid motion, he knocked, drew, and released. The missile lanced out with flawless aim. It reached out and would have struck one of the unliving knights directly in the small opening at the visor, but broke. Some feint red light slid along the monster, intensifying for only the instant of the arrow's impact, before fading again.

Longshot glanced at Rainer. The colonel grimaced nodded. "Hold all," he commanded, and the Walker returned to his waiting crouch.

Esha was once again standing tip-toe on her box, trying to see over the battlement. "Fascinating," she breathed. "Some kind of barrier, but flexible, able to move, to respond to the subject's mobility."

Aloisa glanced down with a smile. "You could sound a little less enthusiastic, little flower."

After an interminable approach, the rams finally reached the fissure. Far behind, the Xeshlin priestesses again deployed their stolen magic, and the stone on either side of the yawning crack reached out, clasping to one another and forming bridges for the advancing rams. The defenders above were silent, stoic, waiting for the revelation of Fate. The engines stopped just short, one in front of Defiant Gate, and the others on either side, at sections of the wall between the bastions. The unliving knights moved along the great logs and took up handles that stuck out at even points. As one, the monsters pulled back, far back. Mary held her breath, clinging desperately to her belief in Karen's Truthsight.

The rams were released and launched forward. The sliding, insidious red light manifested again, collecting at the front of the great logs, dancing along the spiked iron heads. Swinging upon their great chains, the logs rushed ahead, unstoppable. And then, they were stopped. In the instant the red light of the rams contacted the gate and the walls, a matching light of blue gathered at the impact points. When these two touched, the results were explosive.

Mary was thrown back again by the explosions. As one, all three of the rams detonated, sending out a mighty shockwave. Directly behind, a shower of wood and chain and iron and unliving knight were hurled away from the Northern Keep, back into the enemy. Mary blinked and shook her head, both sight and hearing clouded by the thunderous death of the Dark Coven's battering rams. Looking about, the handmaiden saw almost everyone else equally stunned by the spectacular failure of this latest assault.

Esha, however, immediately twisted free of Aloisa's protective arms and climbed back onto her crate. The tiny archmage excitedly leaned forward as far as she could. "Ooo!" she said in near joy. "Spontaneous interaction of equal and opposite waveform energies!" the Sylva squealed happily. "Particle excitement to the point of mutual annihilation!" In her glee at this newest experience with combustion, Esha clambered up the stone, suddenly sliding forward. The Sylva would have fallen over the wall had Aloisa not been there to catch her. "Energetic manifestation, amplification, and detonation!" she called back, seemingly oblivious to her peril.

Aloisa pulled Esha back, and the tiny archmage slid a hand along the interior of the battlement. she pulled her viewing spectacles from within her oversized armor and used them to study the stone. "Hmm," she said in fierce concentration. "Mutual dissipation of stored energy."

"Esha!" Rainer said urgently.

"Hmm, what?" The tiny archmage was clearly immersed in her most recent obsession.

"Esha," the colonel tried again. "What in Underworld just happened?"

"Oh, yes, excellent. The competing energies of my wards and the Coven's enchantment interacted at a sub-solid level initiating-"

"Esha, for the love of God!"

The archmage paused, blinking. "Ah… rams touched wards. Boom."

"Thank you." Rainer moved to look out from the battlement.

"There is an unfortunate consequence of this good fortune, however," Esha warned.

"And what is that, little flower?" Aloisa asked.

"The sudden application of two inverted, competitive energies at such a minute point of contact-"

Rainer was thumping his head against the unyielding stone of the battlement. Esha looked to Aloisa, who could only shrug.

"Ah, the power of my protective wards, which I embedded into the wall, is now expended."

Mary knelt beside Esha. "You mean, we're no longer protected?"

The archmage shook her head. "Oh no. No, no, no, no. Well…" she thought for a moment. "Essentially, yes. We still have the protection of the stone itself. But any mystical protection is, for the time being, gone."

"Will it… recharge?" Aloisa asked.

"Eventually, yes. Even if the wall were to be destroyed, the stones themselves would carry my wards. They will replenish their protective energies over time."

"How long," Rainer asked. He held up a hand. "Short answer, please."

"Weeks. Perhaps months." Amatria and Xathias arrived, climbing up the stone steps to join them on the battlements. "In the meantime," Esha continued, "my students will act in place of the wards, countering any employment of magic."

"Alright," Rainer said. "They'll be massing for another assault. Vagris'll have to, now." A runner arrived with a parchment. This, the guardsman handed to his commander with a salute.

"Why?" Mary asked.

"After two failed assaults," Rainer absently replied while reading the parchment, "he'll have to strike now. His mercenaries'll start deserting without some kind of victory." He paused, grimacing. "Well, this is strange."

"What now?" Aloisa asked.

"I ordered the gaslamp system disabled during the siege." He glanced up at his second. "With Remm gone, we needed to consult the plans." The colonel handed over the parchment. "They're missing."

"Missing as in misplaced?" Aloisa asked, scanning the report.

"Missing as in stolen." Rainer shook his head. "Just one more thing, I guess. Have the Watch investigate when they're able." The colonel glanced at Esha. "How long until you three can get rid of the last of that fog?"

"We need only a few minutes to prepare," the archmage replied confidently.

"Alright." Rainer looked back onto the field. "Do it. Let's see if we can scare them off before the attack."

"You think that's likely?" Mary asked.

Rainer only glanced at her.

The air around them was filled with the sounds of fighting, screaming, yelling, and dying. The mercenaries had run forward carrying more assault ladders. They were, however, limited in their avenues of advance. The broken field was impassible for any large group, so the attackers had to follow the lanes opened by the Xeshlin priestesses.

Because of this, the Northern Keeps' defenders were able to orient their missiles onto these few passages, and their deadly storm became viciously accurate. Scores of mercenaries fell against the combined fire of the archers, the scorpions, and the ballistae. Dozens fell, but hundreds reached the wall. The ladders came up at many points, but the mercenaries were not the first up. Instead, the assault was led by Fak'Har's unliving knights. The armor of these creatures repelled the missiles from Longshot's archers and the scorpions. Only the massive bolts from the ballistae could penetrate the metal and magic protecting the monsters, and these were too few, took too long to reload to fell more than a handful of the horrid abominations.

"Breach!" the call came from further down the wall. Mary looked and saw an entire squad of guardsmen confronting one of the unliving knights. Reinforcements rushed to that spot, but in the crush of the narrow battlement, they could not defeat the creature. Longshot sprinted to that point. He dropped to his knees and slid beneath the great swings of the monster's greatsword, dropping his bow. The dark-skinned Walker instead drew a pair of Sylvai blades and slashed. Spinning in circles with his arms outstretched, Longshot sliced at every gap in the unliving knight's armor. He separated each section of limb, feet from thighs, thighs from legs, wrists from forearms, forearms from arms, arms and legs from torso. Finally, with two great swipes, the Sylvu warrior separated the monster's head. All these pieces, he kicked from the battlement.

With the defeat of the unliving knight, the guardsmen pushed back at the invading mercenaries. They thrust and slashed with their poleaxes until the fighting drew too tight. Then they dropped their traditional Northland weapons and drew their swords. The engagement was brutal, bloody, and merciless. Blue and grey was splashed with red. Screaming invaders were killed or thrown bodily from the wall. Some few managed to escape the rage of the defending guardsmen, tumbling down to the streets below. The irregulars met these doomed fools, the citizens of the city who had taken up arms for their beloved home. Those men who did not die at the hands of the Calonar House Guard, instead fell to the fury of the people.

Rainer had firmly put Mary in the nearest bastion, absolutely forbidding her to leave the relative protection of its guards. From there, she watched, pale-faced and emotionally numb, as the second assault unfolded. She watched the scorpion crews continue with their engines, firing shot after shot into the crowds of mercenaries pushing to reach a ladder. She watched as Longshot's archers send a deadly rain sleeting down on the attackers. She bore witness to dozens, perhaps hundreds of deaths. A sudden bang to the side opposite where the battle was unfolding made Mary start. A scaling ladder had struck on that currently undefended portion of the wall.

"Amatria!" Mary called.

Her childhood friend, who had been assisting the aim of the scorpions looked over. The archwizard noted the ladder and moved forward. "Step back," she commanded, raising her staff. Mystical words came spilling from between her lips, and she wove the complex gestures with her free hand vital to the summoning and control of the Winds of Magic. One of Fak'Har's unliving knights raised its helmeted head over the battlement, and a gauntleted fist reached up to take hold and hoist the monster up. "I think not," Amatria said firmly. She pointed with her staff, and a spark of blue light appeared. It pulsed for a moment, then arced to the very tip of the creature's helmet. The unliving knight stiffened, jerking. It made no sound, but rancid smoke poured out from its visor. When Amatria ended her attack, the monster fell back, locked in one position like an ornamental suit of armor. It tumbled down, knocking several screaming mercenaries from the ladder. Amatria narrowed her eyes and spoke another word, pointing at the ladder itself. The wood exploded in flame, collapsing under its own weight and that of the dying men holding it. The threat defeated, Amatria nodded at Mary and returned to her work, aiding the scorpion crewmen.

The defenders were staying ahead of the latest assault. Reinforcements continued arriving from all directions. Fresh arrows were continually brought up for Longshot's archers. Ammunition came for the scorpions and ballistae. The trebuchets behind them continued to drop their great stones amidst the approaching army, responding quickly to the corrections sent from the observers in the bastions. Each ladder that came up was met with buckets of pitch, stones, and a concentration of missiles. When an unliving knight managed to breach the battlement, it was met with a surge of guardsmen, supported by magic from Esha's students or the archmage herself. The tide of the battle seemed to be favoring the defenders of the Northern Keep.

The success of Colonel Rainer and his warriors, however, was not coming without cost. Piles of mercenary dead lay at the base of the wall and in the streets below. But, among the distained fallen, there also lay the blue and grey form of a guardsman. Screaming wounded were pulled from the battlements, to the tender care of the clerics. Ilse had reluctantly left Vincent's side, and then only with the young man's unyielding insistence. Now, the young priestess moved constantly alongside her fellow clerics of the Harvest Mother. Everywhere, the glow of Life Magic brought what aid it could to the injured. Far too often, though, these men and women had to call instead for a Sister of the Lady of Light. Medaka led these priestesses, who gave comfort to the dying, easing their fear and offering them peace in their final, pain-filled moments. Kyla had ordered that all her attendants help with the battle, overriding their arguments to remain at her side. Mary saw her friends helping however they could, while she did little more than bear witness to the slaughter.

The handmaiden peaked around one of the ballistae as its crew worked to reload. "Amatria," she called again. Her Sylva friend joined her and looked to where Mary indicated. A large knot of the unliving knights had gathered at the gate. Together, they carried one of the spike iron caps that had been upon the tips of the Dark Coven's battering rams. "What are they doing?" Mary asked.

"Some small charge may remain within that iron," Amatria mused. "Even if none does, their strength alone may be sufficient, with the Mistress' wards no longer active."

"We've got to stop them!" Mary insisted.

"Indeed." Amatria reached into her robes and pulled out a small communication crystal. She activated it and called to Xathias. In a few moments, the rouge Xeshlin appeared. Amatria explained the situation, and the two archwizards formed a plan. The Sylva closed the communication and returned the arcane device to her robes. She then ordered the crew to pull their engine back. She began chanting and forming the necessary gestures. Mary looked out and, in the bastion opposite theirs from the gate, she saw Xathias matching his fellow archwizard. The two drew upon the Winds of Magic, but in different ways. Amatria's spell drew upon water; as though from the air itself, tiny globes manifested and gathered, joining with one another as they danced around the Sylva. Across, in the opposite bastion, Mary noticed Xathias gathering fire in the same way that Amatria gathered water. The two did not signal one another, did not communicate in any way that Mary could tell, yet still unleased their magic at the same instant. Amatria send a thunderous tide against the unliving knights that were now beating against the gate. The small, rushing water struck at the monster's legs, causing most to fall and the rest to stumble back. At the same time, Xathias' fire struck from above, heating the black armor such that it glowed. Amatria's water hissed into steam, seeping into every opening, every exposed point of the creatures, even as Xathias' fire melted the armor. A handful of mercenaries had joined with the unliving knights, but these retreated, screaming at the onset of the magical attack. When at last the combined assault ended, there was nothing left of the unliving knights but cooling, steaming, useless lumps of twisted metal.

"Look out!" Screams came from the city behind them. In answer to the continuous assault by the city's trebuchets, an assault of smaller rocks came flying out of the dead forest. With cries and curses, the defenders of the Northern Keep took what cover they could, within buildings, behind walls, or under upraised shields. Bodies were crushed, scorpions destroyed, and buildings reduced to rubble. New screams of pain and despair echoed out. Mary looked and saw uniformed guardsmen, armed irregulars, and the City Watch, all lying alongside crushed clerics. Their trebuchets were firing into open terrain; sometimes they hit but most often they did not. Every one of the enemy's missiles, though, landed within the confines of their city, and each caused death and damage.

"I thought Xathias disabled their engines!" Mary exclaimed, taking cover.

"He sabotaged the battering rams alone," Amatria snapped. "Clearly the Shadowed Mage ordered the construction of catapults!"

Outside, the hail of stones continued. They fell without precision, landing as often within the city as they did against the walls. The assault on the battlements abruptly ended as a series of falling stones came down onto the combatants, killing friend and foe alike. The mercenaries halted their climb up the ladders, pulling away from the walls. The unliving knights stood as though lacking orders, and these few atop the walls were soon crushed by the newest attack.

Rainer tumbled into the bastion, followed immediately by Aloisa. In her arms, the great Gunrsvien woman was cradling Esha. The three were harried and bloody. Aloisa's helmet was gone, and the tight braid in which she kept her hair was a loose mess. Rainer was clutching his left arm, blood falling from his limp fingers. Esha's oversized armor was torn, as though it was nothing more than loose cloth. Aloisa looked down at her in concern. "Are you alright, little flower?" she asked.

Esha nodded, her opalescent eyes pinched in pain and worry. She looked up at Aloisa and smiled. "I told you my armor helped."

"What do we do, Colonel?" Mary asked, wincing as a large stone struck their bastion.

The veteran guardsman looked to Esha. "Can you stop this?" he asked.

"We can," the archmage confirmed. "But doing so will block our trebuchets as well."

"Do it!" Rainer barked.

Esha went to Amatria, and the two joined hands, chanting in the language of magic. Rainer turned to Aloisa. "Get runners to our engines. Cease fire and hold!"

The lieutenant nodded.

The mystical chant rose and intensified. Esha and Amatria raised their hands, their voices matching the ascent. Finally, they brought their arms down and released their spell. Mary, who had no affinity for the Winds of Magic, nonetheless could feel the power of the archmage and her students. The handmaiden felt as though a sudden blast of warm air thrust against her and out, past the bastion. The thunderous crashes continued, but only overhead. There was calm silence in the city itself. Mary risked a look outside the bastion. A wall of shimmering light shone over the walls. The rocks Fak'Har's engines were hurling hit this and broke apart, as though striking an immovable mountain.

Aloisa shouted to runners, relaying orders for the conservation of ammunition.

Rainer also leapt to the battlement's edge and called down. "Fire brigade! Search and rescue! All auxiliaries mobilize! Get the wounded to the castle! Leave the dead!"

The impacts of rock overhead stopped. Mary looked up, but saw that the magical barrier was still in place. She glanced out of one of the ballistae's firing points, and saw that the mercenaries and the unliving knights had pulled back, far out of range of the Keep's archers. "What happens now?" she asked.

There was a terrible impact against the wall itself. The entire bastion shook with the impact, and everyone inside threw themselves to the floor, covering their heads. "That," Rainer said sourly.

Fak'Har's catapults had adjusted their aim. Now, instead of raining death into the city, they hurled their stones against the walls. "How long can we take this?" Mary asked, wincing against another impact.

"This is good Northlands granite," the colonel replied, picking himself up. "Designed by Uldra stonemasters. It'll take them weeks to break through just the first wall."

"Indeed," Amatria noted. "One must wonder at the strategy. Fak'Har must know that time is not an asset for him. The Prince is returning with reinforcements. He does not have the option for a lengthy siege."

Rainer shook his head. "This is just a distraction," he declared. "Vagris is playing out the Siege of Castle Kordenel: assaults to assess enemy weak points, demoralize with catapults, then mass for a combined attack." The colonel turned to Aloisa. "Get the guardsmen reset; stage in the bastions, ready to defend against the next assault." She saluted and left.

"When will the next attack come?" Mary asked.

Rainer squinted his eyes. "Let's force the issue." He looked at Esha. "Can your people block the stones?"

The archmage nodded.

"Do it."

Esha's students gathered in the bastions along the western section of the walls, under the leadership of Amatria, Xathias, and the archmage herself. On Colonel Rainer's order, the adepts spread out along the battlements. Mystical words joined together into a great, echoing chorus. The stone continued, but so did the song. At last, the adepts paused and waited. A stone hurled through the air but then exploded yards from the walls. Another stone then detonated, and another, and another. Each time a stone flew out from the dead forest, it was destroyed.

There was another long pause in the violence. The defenders waited. They could see movement amongst the blackened trunks, but nothing came. Midday came, and with it, food and drink. Medaka led her Sisters of the Lady of Light along the battlements, giving whatever comfort, support, and reassurances were needed by the guardsmen and Esha's adepts. The lack of enemy response to the deployment of the city's adepts was becoming unnerving.

Longshot had maintained his vigil atop the battlements. His opalescent, Sylvu eyes scanned the distance without pause. His Walkers also maintained their watch, but in rotation. Their leader refused to be relived, though, grimly surveying the battlefield. Rainer and Mary approached him. "Anything," the colonel asked.

"They are preparing," Longshot replied calmly. "For what, I cannot see."

"Do you think they'll attack again," Mary asked. "Or will they wait for tomorrow."

"They will come," Longshot replied, turning towards Mary. The handmaiden happened to be facing in the right direction, only by the purest luck seeing the attack coming. She threw herself forward, knocking Longshot down only a fraction of a heartbeat before an arrow would have speared his head.

"Down!" they both shouted together.

The sky filled, darkening even the late summer sun. Arrows filled the air, arching and striking against stone and flesh. Several adepts, their grey and blue robes turning red, were struck and fell screaming. Guardsmen leapt onto the unprotected wizards and mages, their armor deflecting what might have killed the vital adepts. The soldiers grabbed their charges and bodily pulled them into cover, against the battlement walls, into the bastions, or down to the cover of the streets below.

The hail of arrows continued, and Rainer half-dragged Mary back into the nearest bastion. Longshot tumbled in behind them. "They certainly are enthusiastic," the Walker noted.

"How long can they keep this up?" Rainer demanded.

"That depends entirely upon how much ammunition they have," Longshot replied. "At the very least, their archers will tire. Vagris will have to begin rotating them. The intensity will soon diminish."

Esha and Aloisa came up the interior stairs. "My students cannot continue their protection whilst these archers maintain their fire," the archmage announced. "Even if the rate decreases, the threat is too high!"

"Then," Longshot said calmly, "we must encourage them to stop." The Walker called down the line to the nearest of his comrades in Sylvai, and the called continued. The Sylvu warriors, keeping low and tight against the battlement walls, spread out. Rainer kept Mary within the bastion, but both went to the door to see what was happening.

Longshot went down the line of his Walkers, giving instructions to each in Sylvai. He then deployed those archers from the guardsmen, setting them between the Walkers. Finally, he went to the center, directly above Defiant Gate. "Alright, my people," Longshot said in Gunnic. "Stand ready. Humans, you are suppression, fire as quickly as you can. Worry not for your targets, only give them worry for you. Walkers, you must spot the enemy and loose."

The archers, both Human and Sylvai, waited. The hail of enemy arrows continued, but soon slowed. The missiles continued to fall, but instead of a constant, demoralizing assault, the attack became sporadic, unpredictable.

"NOW!" Longshot called.

As one, all the archers stood with bows raised and arrows knocked. The guardsmen begin loosing arrows as fast as they could, sending a sheet of their anger back at the enemy. The Walkers were more precise. They stood and looked. Each spotted a target and let fly a single arrow. The mercenary archers screamed, those who did not die immediately from a Sylvai arrow in the eye or the throat. They withdrew a bit, seeking shelter within the dead trucks of Wildelves Wood.

"Let us show them the flaw in their reasoning!" Longshot called out.

Another hail of Sylvai arrows flew from the walls, dancing in amongst the blackened trunks. Another score of enemy archers screamed and died. The rest withdrew further, desperately sending arrows back to fall far short of the walls.

"Now that is just pathetic," Longshot grimaced. "One last time, my people!" The Walkers let fly one more barrage of arrows, and the mercenary archers were sent screaming into flight.

A great cheer arose from the walls, joined by those struggling in the streets behind them. News of the victory spread, and the whole of the Northern Keep gave voice to their relief, their joy at surviving another battle. The defenders upon the walls, Walkers, guardsmen, and adepts, embraced each other and celebrated. Amatria ran to Longshot and hurled herself into his arms, melting into one another as the setting sun shone upon the victorious Northern Keep.

Chapter 32

The sun completed its daily trip without seeing another assault from Vagris' army. The mercenary dead were left where they fell in the broken fields before the Northern Keep's insurmountable defenses. Every living thing capable had long since fled the Great Burning, leaving no carrion feeders to feast upon the corpses now strewn before Defiant Gate. Even the insects had retreated against the hateful advance of Vagris and the Uldra warmachines, leaving nothing, not even the Wood itself, to tend to the gruesome canvas on display.

Gentle dusk came and spread her starry curtain over the battlefield. A peaceful cool hinting at the approach of autumn replaced late summer's heat, offering relief to the warriors and adepts exhausted by the day's struggle. Colonel Rainer ordered rest and restoration. The Sisters of the Lady of Light brought food and drink. The clerics of the Harvest Mother tended to those wounded who had remained at their posts. The Adamic priests gave final comfort to the fallen. Of these all, Cardinal Tain's clergy had the most work.

"Do we have the White Lady's count?" Rainer wearily asked as he removed his helmet.

"The Adamics are still working," Aloisa replied. The imposing Gunrsvien woman was still in her armor, instead helping Esha as the tiny archmage struggled out of her own protective equipment.

Cardinal Tain sat wearily on one of the few surviving chairs. "I will have the final count by morning," he said, the weight of his sworn duty pressing down on his already-weary shoulders. "But the number will be high."

They had left the walls. A building near Defiant Gate had taken a direct hit from Vagris' catapults, punching a great hole in the ceiling and knocking down half the walls. The upper floor had partially collapsed, but the front shop was still more or less intact, but for the exposed roof. Without a coordinating word, the war council had assembled in this place to discuss their status.

The brief trip had been morbid. The joyous victory of the setting sun had been short-lived. The reality, the cost of the Northern Keep's triumph was quick to assert itself. The streets were filled with the dead and dying. Clerics of the Harvest Mother hurried about, trying their best to save those who could be saved, while Adamic priests knelt over those who could not. The Sisters of the Lady of Light were already tending to the newly widowed and orphaned. It seemed to Mary that every wall, every bench, every face was blood-smeared after the day's horrid struggle. The soldiers who had been relieved from the wall sat in small groups, their heads bowed and their eyes lowered. The auxiliaries worked like grim shadows to clear rubble as they continued their increasingly-hopeless search for survivors. There were no more cheerful cries of victory and determined celebration. The cost was simply too high. Even the chestnut trees in a nearby plaza seemed subdued, drooping against the siege.

"Longshot?" Rainer asked, pulling up a wobbly chair and wearily setting himself down upon it.

The dark-skinned Walker, his opalescent eyes as weary as any Human's, grimaced as he removed his leather gloves. "Forty-three of my people are wounded and will be unavailable for the next assault," he reported. Longshot leaned his bow against one section of destroyed wall and began working at his arm guard. "Twelve Walkers have already passed beyond the Veil. Another eight will likely make the journey before dawn."

"How many does that leave you?" Aloisa grunted, pulling free Esha's ruined leather vest.

"Eleven, including myself."

Amatria and Xathias arrived then. "We have set the students to rest," the Sylva reported, moving beside Longshot and enfolding herself in his arms.

"One wizard and four mages are remaining at their posts," the rouge Xeshlin added. "They will rotate through the night." The archwizard, finding no seat, leaned against a countertop, breathing deep the cool night air. Autumn was approaching, this much was certain. Summer was diminishing with each day, and the evenings carried the growing promise of the next season.

Esha nodded, running her small hands over her tiny body and relishing being free of her armor. "I fear your warsuit is too damaged for use, little flower," Aloisa said, looking at the great tear in one side of the vest. "You will need another."

The archmage shrugged. "The armorers will have more important duties."

"Any word from the castle?" Rainer asked.

Mary reached under her own mail shirt and retrieved the small communication crystal. She pulled it free and inspected the half-sphere. "No," she told the colonel.

"But you reported in?"

The handmaiden and aide-de-camp nodded. "I spoke to the Princess about an hour ago. Ilse and Medaka are already back, organizing the wounded." Mary looked at Rainer. "They're running out of space, though."

The colonel nodded, rubbing his eyes. "Any recommendations?" he asked.

"Princess Karen has been doing something she calls triage. The critically wounded are being sent to the Temple of the Harvest Mother. Those who cannot be saved go to the Adamic Church, and those with only minor injuries and the lost children are being sent to the Temple of the Lady of Light."

"Who goes to the castle itself?" Aloisa asked, moving to the ruined doorframe.

"Princess Karen is choosing certain people. She goes among the refugees. She picks out small groups, families mostly, and sends them up to the castle. Everyone else is sent to one of the temples."

"Any word from Rashid or his spies?" Rainer asked, his tone communicating his lack of hope in the question.

"Do I qualify?" a voice replied. They all turned and started at the sight of Vincent, clothed once more in the black and grey of House Calonar's intelligence service. He stood wearily, his face still lacking much of its color, but resolute.

"Does my daughter know you're here?" Rainer asked.

"She was busy," the young spy replied lightly. He entered the ruined shop and leaned against the same counter as Xathias. The two nodded at each other, but said nothing. "I didn't want to disturb her while she's trying to help people."

"She's gonna have your hide when she finds out," the colonel objected with a shake of his head. "Mine too, probably."

"I have to be here, sir," Vincent said firmly. "I can stand and help, which is more than what a lot of people can do right now."

The two men shared a steady look. Finally, Rainer nodded. "Alright. But you get to explain it to her."

A pair of Sisters of the Lady of Light brought in small bundles. "From the Sylvai restaurant," one said, handing out the packages. Mary took hers and opened it, finding a small assortment of vegetables and bread, some cheese and meat.

The second Sister set down a small cask, opened it, and then handed small wooden cups to each of them. This done, the two priestesses left, continuing their duty to bring comfort to the defenders.

"Are there any other spies still active?" Aloisa asked through a large bite of meat.

Vincent shook his head. "I haven't seen any. The forest operation took a heavy toll on our people. The rest, trainees mostly, were acting as runners between the artillery teams. At least four were killed in the bombardment."

"And the rest?" Rainer asked while taking the cup Mary had poured for him.

"Missing." Vincent opened his package and began eating a carrot.

"Where's Rashid and Chandra?" Aloisa asked.

"Missing," the spy said grimly. "No one's seen either of them since after the first assault. Apparently, Rashid sent a message for the Twins to stay in the Royal Apartments."

"Why?" Mary asked, handing him a cup.

"I don't know. That little maid of the Queen's won't let me in to talk to them."

"Opfern," the handmaiden smiled. "She's a little territorial about the King and Queen."

"That's one word for it," the young spy said sourly. "I can only hope Rashid's working on something, some plan."

The colonel shook his head. "We can't go looking for individuals right now. After this is all over, then we can start searching." He drained his cup. "We need to plan for the next assault. The question is, what will Vagris throw at us?"

Aloisa lifted Esha onto a counter, letting the tiny archmage sit cross-legged while eating her meal. "We have neutralized his catapults," she pointed out.

"And his archers," Longshot added. The Walker was gingerly sampling from his own meal package, using the barest tips of his fingers to selected a morsel and bring it to Amatria's lips. In return, the Sylva archwizard took items from her meal and fed them to Longshot. "To say nothing of Princess Kyla's neutralization of the Uldra warmachines," she noted.

"Has there been any word about Remm or his people?" Rainer asked.

Heads shook. Since the terrible groundquake, there had been no sign of Remm Stonebearer or the Uldra he had taken to confront their traitorous kin. The City Watch had switched to subordinate commanders in their leader's absence. "We saw no rogue Uldra amongst the mercenaries during their assaults," Esha pointed out. "This, combined with the fact we are not, currently, awash in barbarians, strongly points towards the success of Remm's vengeance."

"But did he pay the price for that victory?" Mary asked gently.

They were all silent a moment. No one wished to point out that they were observing a moment of silence. Remm and his Uldra were amongst the most fierce, resilient of all people. They had gone into those tunnels willingly, even eagerly, intent on avenging the betrayal of their kin. One look into the broken fields spoke of the ferocity of that engagement, that retribution. There seemed little hope of anyone, even Remm Stonebearer, surviving the cataclysm. So, they said nothing for a few moments, honoring their friend and his people.

"So," Rainer stood and arched his back. "Vagris has tried the warmachines, catapults, archers, and sapping tunnels."

"And two failed assaults with his infantry," Aloisa added.

"Right. He knows we've countered these; he won't want to keep wasting resources on something that hasn't worked. So, what does that leave?"

"Magic," Mary said softly. All eyes turned to her. "Vagris may be leading the army and organizing the attacks, but Fak'Har is still out there, isn't he? Him and the Xeshlin priestesses. Wouldn't that be a resource Vagris would want to use?"

"The Shadowed Mage may or may not be employed," Xathias said then. "But if our enemies are to bring their arcane assets to bear, I think they will first use the Dark Coven."

"Why?" Rainer asked.

"The pattern," the rogue Xeshin replied. "Vagris first sent a mercenary assault, and only then brought to bear his ranged weapons. He uses his most expendable assets first. Between the Sorceress Sisters and the Shadowed Mage, the *Xesh'lin* will be the more expandable."

"Infantry, archers, and artillery I can fight against," Rainer mused. "But magic women…" He looked at Esha.

The tiny archmage glanced up from her meal, a smear of cheese on her small cheek. "*Xesh'lin* priestesses have no magic in and of themselves," she said through a mouthful. "They steal it from other living beings. They use Blood Magic, Umbral rites, parasitic rituals that harvest natural arcane energies. So, if they do personally join in the next assault, how much power and of what kind depend entirely upon what they are able to scavenge beforehand."

"They have a great many prisoners," Xathias said quietly.

Vincent nodded, a dark shadow passing over his pale face. "I saw Humans and Sylvai," he reported. "Some Uldra too. Hundreds of people. They… harvested many of them to build those rams and catapults. But they still have more."

"There will be a…" Xathias twisted his face into a snarl of hatred and contempt, "celebration." The rouge Xeshlin sniffed at the night's air, grimacing. "I had hoped the scent was only in my imagination, my memories. But I can sense them." He closed his eyes of burning blood, hanging his head in shame. "Even this far away, the Coven's pull is strong. They will bring the worst of Vagris' mercenaries into the… celebration. They will spend the night sacrificing and indulging all the appetites of the males. They will enslave a large group of mercenaries."

"*Xesh'lin* females would enthrall the males of other races?," Amatria said, the disgust in her voice clear. Her fingers absently tracing along Longshot's chin. She glanced up at him. "Shave," she commanded. "Soon."

In response, the Walker took her hand and kissed the tips of her fingers.

"I did not say enthrall," Xathias corrected. "I said enslave. The Sorceress Sisters will lead the mercenaries in an orgy of carnality, of violence and narcotics and copulation. They still have the tears, and have learned to produce them at will, rather than only during a fertility cycle. Mixed with their Blood Magic, the Sorcerous Sisters will use their corrupted tears on a large group of the worst of Vagris' killers. By the end of this evening, the males will be without fear or mercy. They will be freed from any morality." The archwizard glanced meaningfully at Rainer. "I have noted that certain kinds of Human males are especially vulnerable to a Dark Coven's seductions.

"They will take the day to rest, to recover from the exertions of the rituals. When the sun sets on the morrow, the *Xesh'lin* will emerge with their new warrior-slaves. The Coven will direct the next assault."

Rainer leaned back in his wobbly chair. "So, on the next assault, the mercenaries won't break."

"Fanatics," Aloisa spat. "Always more trouble than they are worth."

"But in the short term," the colonel argued, "exactly what Vagris would want." He looked at Xathias again. "Will the priestesses attack directly?"

The rouge Xeshlin shrugged. "They may. The celebration is a double-edge sword. The Sorceress Sisters can amass great power. I have seen even small rites, with only a dozen or so celebrants, still grant a Dark Coven considerable energy. But in doing so, the females themselves suffer a..." The archwizard tiled his head, searching for a word. "I suppose, an intoxication is the best way to describe the effect.

"When a Dark Coven performs the rite, they absorb a great deal of power, the essence of their victim's lives. The Sorceress Sisters lose their inhibitions, what little remains of their own morality. They can empower their enslaved males, but they become somewhat enslaved themselves."

"To what?" Aloisa asked.

"Blood-madness. To the drawing of blood and the inflicting of suffering."

"So, they'll be just as uncontrollable as the mercenaries?" Rainer asked.

"No. They will be in control of themselves. They will be capable of harnessing and unleashing their stolen magic. They will, however, be almost desperate to do so in the pursuit of pain."

Chapter 33

Xaemus tried to ignore the celebration, but failed. The monster of Davenor had not witnessed the Crimson Delight since leaving his blighted homeland. He had wandered across the world, seeking any sign, any witness, any possible lead on the location of his Dark Empress. He had purposely avoided his own people, leaving any area once word arrived of *Xesh'lin* slave raids. Most amongst his race believed either that Xaemus hated his own kind, or feared them, fleeing against the wrath of the Covens.

In truth, the Sorceress Sisters were the reason for his self-imposed exile, but not in the manner the *Xesh'lin* commonly believed. Xaemus cared little about the bounty placed upon his head. Similar rewards existed in most cities. Occasionally, some fool would attempt to collect, but these encounters always resulted the same, with one less fool in a world full of them. Legend had spread in recent centuries of Xaemus' quest in search of the Dark Empress. The irony of this was lost on no one, least of all the monster of Davenor. Kelinva had founded the Dark Coven; she had empowered the Sorceress Sisters, teaching them the Umbral blood rites. What unfolded, even now amongst Vagris' mercenary army, was the direct result of the Dark Empress' design. For reasons Xaemus himself did not fully understand, he sought to restore the Midnight Queen of the Sorceress Sisters.

He had known what effects would unfold. Xaemus had been a slave of the Coven of Midnight Sun. He had seen them perform the Crimson Delight. The monster of Davenor, perhaps better than any living male, understood what was to come. Still he dallied. The days belonged to Vagris and his captains. The mercenaries fought and suffered and died, as Humans were wont to do. But the nights... the nights belonged to the Sorceress Sisters.

Cries of passion and suffering filled the night air. Xaemus stumbled through the street, trying to shut out the sound. This was the culmination of the Crimson Delight. The Dark Coven of the Puma's Leash had spent weeks leading Vagris' worst killers through all manner of debauchery. Pleasures of flesh, of food and drink, of narcotics, were all explored, each night bringing some new, corruptive pleasure for the Humans. On this final night, a cloud of debaucherous evil danced upon the wind. Grunts and squeals, screams and moans, were the only sounds left amongst the dead trees of Wildelves Wood.

The warlord himself was absent, of course. Vagris was not a fool. He and his fellow Bellonari had ordered the majority of their force into a different camp, outside the Sorcerous Sisters' sphere of influence. The professional, experienced soldiers, the true mercenaries, were kept out of the Crimson Delight, protected from its mind-altering effects. The plan had been made for tomorrow night's assault, and then Vagris had taken away those over whom he wished to maintain control. The rest he fed to the hunger of the Sorcerous Sisters.

As he hurried through Vagris' encampment, Xaemus tried not to see into the open tents. This was a part of the Coven's corruption. Indulgences were on display, inviting. Even the shelter of modesty was stripped from the victims of the Crimson Delight. The remaining slaves had been dispersed amongst the most brutal of Vagris' killers, supposedly gifts for loyal service. Male and female, Human and Sylvai, all the captured prisoners were, in truth, only fuel for the Umbral ceremony. The monster of Davenor tried not to look, to be reminded of those rituals to which he had been forced to participate, but he failed. No group was smaller than four. Most of these involved several mercenaries taking their dark pleasure with a slave. Even as the Humans ravaged their prisoners and each other, blades drew blood from every exposed piece of flesh. This was lapped up by the corrupted warriors, even as the narcotics provided by the Dark Coven were liberally sampled. The horrid pleasure only increased as Xaemus drew towards the center of the encampment.

The altar was still in place. The Humans believed the final sacrifice had been the previous night. Xaemus knew better, of course. They were all the final sacrifice, the crescendo of the Crimson Delight. Though their bodies would live on, their souls would be forever broken, corrupted beyond recovery so that, when they died, the Umbra would be waiting to eternally feast upon them. The denizens of Underworld were patient; they did not demand immediate death, preferring instead that these corrupted Humans would live on and spread their corruption. The monster of Davenor did not want to look, did not want to see and be reminded of his forsaken past, yet his eyes of burning blood still wandered to the center of the celebration.

The Sorceress Sisters themselves were arrayed on and around the altar. The insidious priestesses had arranged themselves and their offerings in concentric rings. Status amongst the Dark Coven was reinforced by the appointment of placement; the High Priestess would have named who would be allowed at which ring. With them, they had victims specially selected from amongst the slaves. Mothers and sons, fathers and daughters, brothers and sisters. In a horrid twist of Fate, the *Xesh'lin* had even located a set of twins, adolescent boys, who were chained upon the horned altar itself. These were the special prize for the High Priestess herself. She would lead them through the worst possible acts, violating the most primal taboos. She would take her pleasure with them, even as the other Sorceress Sisters took theirs with the other familial slaves. Even now, the grotesque, seductive power of the Dark Coven rushed out to consume Vagris' killers.

He had tried to warn Vagris. Even as the sun began its final descent that day, the monster of Davenor, once again acting for reasons he did not fully understand, had tried to convince the Bellonar General of the folly about to unfold.

"Why allow this?" Xaemus asked, "You have mercenaries aplenty, and they've already built your siege equipment. Why sacrifice a portion of your forces only to empower them further?"

"None of my Bellonari participate in this ceremony," the general replied as he packed the last of his equipment. Most of his personal articles had already been removed from his pavilion, leaving the two warriors alone in an empty tent. "My brothers have moved outside the camp to avoid its corruption and taken those soldiers I can control with them."

"And yet, you leave enough for the Sorcerous Sisters to use in their ritual."

"I'm curious," Vagris admitted. He finished belting on his breastplate. "I've seen most forms of magic in the world, but the Blood Magic of the Xeshlin remains something of a mystery. I, like most, always assumed this was some deliberate effort on your race's part, trying to maintain secrecy."

"No," Xaemus confirmed. "The Dark Covens would like nothing more than to share their devotionals with the world. This was Kelinva's First Commandment: to convert all to the worship of *Ethro'sa'kai* and the Umbra." The monster of Davenor, glanced out the open flap. Slaves worked under the lash of enthralled males, preparing the altar and the rings for the night's ritual. "The men you leave behind are damned, you realize."

"Once the siege is over, their purpose and usefulness is over anyway," Vagris shrugged.

"Where is the Shadowed Mage?"

The general nodded towards a tent opposite from his own, on the other side of the altar and its rings. "He said something about his own preparations."

Xaemus looked as well into the imminent maelstrom of wrenched corruption. "If you stay and watch," he warned, "you will be drawn in. You will be made to participate."

"I'm well aware of the danger," the Bellonari General replied. "Thus, our evacuation." He pulled on his helmet and belted on his sword. "I've taken reasonable precautions to protect my best assets. If the priestesses can provide a powerful, expendable weapon," he shrugged once more.

"You are a fool, Vagris," Xaemus growled. "You think to sample the Crimson Delight without being corrupted by it. Even if you do not personally indulge, you are casting victims into the Coven's furnace. The Umbra will still have a claim upon your soul." He stopped then. The monster of Davenor ran his eyes of burning blood around Vagris' tent, a horrid suspicion dawning upon him. "Is she one of the slaves?" he asked in a voice that could shatter stone. "Have you given her to the Sorcerous Sisters?"

Vagris glanced at him. The slightest pause held between them, somehow forcing away even the insidious pull of the Crimson Delight. Even now, hours before the ritual would begin, still there was a building of horrid power. Finally, the Bellonar shook his head. "No. I had her removed to a tent at the far edge of the camp. She's under guard by my brothers. Though, not for your sake, or hers. I need a reliable servant, and, as I understand, most of the females will be used up tonight."

Xaemus turned to leave. "No," he corrected. "Not some. Not most. All. The Sorceress Sisters do not tolerate competitors."

The Bellonari guarding her tent stood rigid when Xaemus appeared. The monster of Davenor said nothing, only stared at them with his eyes of burning blood. The two Humans glanced at each other, and stood aside. Xaemus then entered the tent.

It was much smaller than Vagris' pavilion, matching the design of those used by the mercenaries. There were no wooden bunks, though, but rather a single cot lying at the tent's rear wall. A tray of uneaten food sat on the ground, as did a pitcher of water, still full. A single lamp burned in the center of the tent, sitting upon a small wooden table. This was the only light within, a pinprick of shelter against the howls of rancid joy roaring out from the mercenary camp.

She was there. She was kneeling at the table, her head bowed and her eyes closed. Her hands were folded in her lap. She was, as always, wearing the ridiculous outfit forced upon her by Vagris, some absurd attempt at humiliation and sensuality. She wore it as an Empress would wear the most regal of gowns, though. Her shoulders were not bent like a slave's, instead firm and level. Her face was not twisted in fear or lost to the Crimson Delight; she was calm, collected, coldly-indifferent to the horrors unfolding outside. She did not tremble, either from fear or from desire; the power of the Dark Coven was lost upon her. She was beyond them, above them, serene as only a glacier of flawless ice could be.

The Veil was still chained to the top half of her face. Once again, Xaemus had to fight the urge to tear that blasphemous thing free, to restore to her the power that was her birthright. Even in the dim light, he could see the faint glistening of Tears at the corner of her perfect eyes. They would still be potent, he knew, still capable of enthralling at the slightest contact. Ten thousand generations called out from the past, demanding that he submit to her, to take on the Tears and become hers. But there was more, as well.

Xaemus was *Xesh'lin*, one of the cursed race. His skin and hair had no color. He was burned by the light of day. He had no magic, no connection of any kind to the Winds. His wounds did not heal. His eyes of burning blood forever looked out on a world that despised him. He was bound, by oath and by history to the Dark Empress. Worst of all, even with his rebellion from the Dark Coven of Midnight Sun, he was still vulnerable to the seduction of the Sorceress Sisters. Even there, standing at the open flap of her tent, he felt the siren call of the Crimson Delight. Some wretched part of him wanted nothing more than to go, to submit himself to the Sorceress Sisters, to obtain the satiation that only the ruling females of his race could offer.

But, with that near-compulsion, there was another feeling. The closer he drew to her, the less he felt the pull of the Crimson Delight. He had, nights before, felt the pull of her biology. Her change was complete, and her scent, combined with the seductive power of the Sorceress Sisters, had nearly overpowered him. But now, all was serene. The cool safety of winter drifted from her, pushing away the angry heat of summer. Here was shelter from the hateful storm. Here, Xaemus found peace from not only the Dark Coven, but from his past.

Always before, she had waited, passively, until he spoke. She would not even look at him unless he commanded it, denying Xaemus the pleasure of submission to her authority. Always before, she had maintained the stillness of her servitude, her unfeeling indifference to what Fate had forced her to endure. But now, at last, she commanded him.

"Kneel," she said without looking up.

Xaemus set down his weapon, the double-sided blade that had spilled more blood than entire armies. He knelt, arranging the folds of his black robes and ensuring that his face remained covered. He would not offend her eyes with the sight of what lay beneath his cowl and mask.

"Why do you come here?" she asked without infliction, her voice empty of curiosity. "Why do you return, time and again, thinking I do not know you are there? Why do you stare at me?"

"I…" Xaemus had every intention of answering, but could not find the words.

She opened her opalescent eyes, warming his soul with their hazel glow. She kept them fixed upon the small lamp, however. "Do you think I am Kelinva reborn?"

"What?" The question was so sudden, so unexpected, that Xaemus was nearly stunned to silence.

She stared into the flame. "Your quest is well known. You seek the Dark Empress. I was taught many things before my life was taken. Many secrets were shared. Centuries ago, Kelinva learned of reincarnation from the Shadowed Mage. Each time she is killed, her soul is reborn within the body of a blood relation. My mothers traced their ancestry to the Empire, through the noble houses in service to the Empress."

Xaemus said nothing, utterly unsurprised at the revelation of her descent from the only truly-noble blood left in this wretched world.

"Kelinva was also of noble birth, in service to the Empress. The specifics of her bloodline were erased from all records. No one living knows into what body the Dark Empress can be reborn, which family, which bloodline, carries the curse of her reincarnation." Finally, in a wave of comforting, emotionless cool, she looked up, locking her opalescent eyes into his of burning blood. "Do you believe that I am Kelinva reborn?"

"I do not know," Xaemus answered.

"But you suspect?"

"I do. I sensed something within you. You have the nobility of the lost Empire. You do not move through the world, instead, it yields before you, as it should."

She was silent for a time. A part of Xaemus' mind was vaguely aware of the debauchery outside, but this was only a small part. Nearly all his focus was upon her. She stared into the small flame, her noble face unreadable. Finally, she held a hand to her chest. "A great emptiness lies here," she said. "I am cold, even in the summer. I do not feel the sun's warmth. I can feel the Winds of Magic, though I do not call upon them. I do not hate, nor love, nor care at all."

She once more looked up at him. "Kelinva was many things, but none of them cold. She was a creature of passions, of hunger for desires fulfilled. I do not believe I am your Dark Empress." She kept looking at him, staring her opalescent ice into his very soul. "And you do not care," she observed.

"I do not. You are noble, born of a bloodline flowing from the mists of both our races' beginnings. You are solid and unyielding, the Wind of Earth made flesh. You are perceptive and supportive, the Wind of Air given form. You are power and grace, the Wind of Fire made manifest. You are wise and irresistible, the Wind of Water. You are to become a matriarch, the embodiment of the Wind of Life. You are inflexible and beautiful, the Wind of Death. And you are the mistress of all things, the Winds of Time and Fate. You are the entire world, all of creation."

"And yet, I am a slave," she pointed out.

"You are a slave for only as long as you choose to be," he argued. His words shifted, then, to Sylvai, the oldest known dialect. "Command me," he said in those sacred words. "Say you wish to leave, and it shall be so. Say you wish this army destroyed, and it shall be so. Say anything you desire, and it shall be so." He bowed, prostrating himself before her. "This, I swear, now and forever."

She was silent again. "You offer the Oath of Binding?" she asked in ancient Sylvai.

"I do."

"You would submit yourself to my Tears, forever lost to my command?"

"I do."

"No." This, she said in the grunting Velish of Humans.

She denied him. He had made the sacred oath, and she denied him. He had offered her all that he was, had ever been, and could ever be, and she denied him. "Why?" he whispered, staring into her eyes.

"I am a slave, and I would not enslave another. I have no will. I have no desire. My life ended with the destruction of my village. I have no name, no purpose."

"Then let me help you find it anew." He gestured beyond the tent. "I have searched the world for centuries, and found nothing worth the odyssey. Let me walk beside you on your search. If you find no meaning here, find it elsewhere. Let me take you away from this place, from the Coven of the Puma's Leash and all those like them, who would use you, corrupt you. Let me be your protector and companion."

She stared at him. She remained kneeling and staring. The small lamp burned between them, casting them both in an equal glow that was as much shadow as it was light. She considered for an age as the Dark Coven led the fools outside into the darkest violations. Finally, she nodded, the faintest hint of a motion. "If I agree to this, I ask one thing in return first."

"Name it, and it shall be so."

"I will take the Emptying."

"No!" Xaemus gasped. "You cannot!" He gestured at her. "Your Change is complete! You have a matron's body, ready to grow new life! You are…"

"Already empty," she finished. "I was born to be a Matriarch, but that life is dead. If I am, in fact, Kelinva reborn, but as yet unrealized, then I will end her line here. For centuries, my mothers before me have enthralled their males, ensuring their own protection, but I will not bind another to my will."

"The Emptying will sap your greatest strength," he argued, waving a hand at her womb. "You will be unable to create life!"

"Yes. I will sacrifice my access to the Wind of Life to strengthen all others. I will make myself unusable to Kelinva and to her Dark Covens."

Xaemus shook his head, such a sacrifice unthinkable to any descended from the Eternal Forest, lifespring of the world.

"You took the oath," she pointed out. "You said whatever I wish, it will be so."

"The oath is unbinding without the Tears," he argued.

She shook her head. "The oath will be all the more binding. There will be no compulsion, no irresistible biology mandating the oath, forcing your obedience. If you keep you word, it will only be because you choose to do so."

Xaemus opened his mouth, as though to speak, but once again could find no words. "What do you need?" he asked in resignation.

"Only a witness."

She stood then, and motioned for him to do so as well. Xaemus was *Xesh'lin*, and so had no access to the Winds of Magic. Despite this, he could still feel her gathering of power. The ground on which they stood twisted, rocks and lumps of earth rolling in circles around her bare feet. A breeze pushed against the tent flaps. The flame of the small lamp grew taller and reached for her. The water that had been resting in its pitcher slid up and around, rolling in a wave around her body. The sounds outside quieted, as though the couple slid away from the world, held tight in a small universe of their own.

Words floated from between the tiny bow of her mouth. Xaemus did not understand the words, for they were in the language of magic. He did not understand, but he could feel. She spoke forbidden words, sounds of sacrifice, of power, of sorrow beyond imagining. She gave sound to a terrible song, one of transcendent misery. Even the withered tatters of Xaemus' soul recoiled from the words she spoke, that all *Sy'lva* matriarchs knew. Legend alone held tales of honored mothers, revered females who sacrificed their greatest gift in times of terrible crisis. These matriarchs were all nameless, unknown to Time and Fate, their destinies sacrificed.

Xaemus watched as she was changed. Her cedar mane, shorn to almost nothing, darkened and grew, until it was as black as a raven's wing and flowing as the midnight sea. Indeed, instead of a gentle cascade, a flowing river of color, her mane stiffened as though it became a thing of living night, containing therein what could be tiny reflections of muted light, or all the starry heavens. Her flesh of warm sand cooled, the color draining, flowing away, retreating from the onset of a winter unending. She became the cold itself, a living avatar of frost, of fresh, untouched snow. The veil, the hateful prison scores of brutal Humans had inflicted upon generations of *Sy'lva'i*, flared, burned, and vanished in a halo of magic. Her eyes of hazel opalescence, once pools of innocence forced to reflect the horrors of her life, stilled. Those perfect orbs hardened as the color retreated, giving way to a dark power. She closed her eyes as this change completed and, when she opened them once again, the opulence within had been replaced by radiant rubies. The night sky contained within her mane seemed to leak outward, to seep into those gemstone eyes. The pale flesh surrounding those orbs of terrible power were stained a sooty black that matched her raven mane. She floated for an immeasurable time, staring at him. Her expression was unreadable, and yet her aura, even to one as dull and unworthy as Xaemus, was nearly divine. Here was one who would look upon the world, and the world should look away. The monster of Davenor prostrated himself again, reverent to this one finally worthy of his loyalty. He knelt before her but did not bow, did not flinch or look away, instead keeping his cursed eyes of burning blood fixed on hers of radiant ruby.

Then, the spell was finished and she gently returned to the ground. The earth and the air and the flame and the water all returned to their places. "It is done," Xaemus said. He stood and held his fingers up, only a breath away from the shadow stains around her ruby eyes. "You no longer have the Tears," he declared.

"No," she replied in a voice that spoke with the chorus of all the Winds but one. "From this day, I am Dy'lnnd, 'she of the Ebon Tears.'"

Chapter 34

Runners were sent out and the informal war council met once again at the ruined shop near the city walls. Midday had passed and, with it, the heat of the day. The sun was well into its descent by the day Mary and Ilse arrived, casting long shadows over the weary city. Days had passed since the last assault; Colonel Rainer had used that time to rest the Northern Keep's defenders, yet still faces were long as the two young women made their way towards the small ruined shop.

"It can't last much longer, can it?" Ilse asked, also noticing the sagging shoulders and drawn faces of the nearby warriors.

Mary grimaced. "They've already endured so much," she pointed out. "But there's no real end in sight."

The two women passed through the broken doorway. Within Rainer was speaking with Longshot and Amatria. The dark-skinned Walker showed little of the growing desperation so plainly written upon the Human faces. His stance was relaxed, almost casual, and his leather armor, though showing repairs since their desperate retreat from the Great Burn, was untouched with any more recent damage. Amatria was similarly composed. Her hair and cosmetics were perfect and her blue robes without wrinkle or blemish. The two Sylvai stood near to one another, as was their habit, and whenever their attention wandered, their hands unconsciously sought each other out.

Rainer glanced at Mary and Ilse, nodding his greeting. "How're things at the castle?" he asked.

"The same," Mary replied. She moved to one of the intact counters and removed her helmet, letting her long hair flow freely. Aloisa had not been present to help her into her warrior's garb, but another soldier had taken on the duty.

"The King and Queen are still in isolation?" the colonel asked.

Ilse nodded. She crossed the room and gave her father a hug. "Opfern isn't even bringing solid food up for them anymore," she nearly whispered. "Only broth." She looked up into Rainer's eyes. "I don't think he has much more..."

Their small group was silent. Cylan Calonar had been the defender of the Northlands for longer than any of them had been alive. His magic, his warrior's skill, and his diplomacy had maintained peace in their homeland through countless trials. Even the Xeshlin Invasion had barely touched the Northlands, thanks in large part to the presence of the Lord of House Calonar. He was the last survivor of the Heroes of Fate, the last of that legendary group who had fought the worst horrors to ever exist. And now, he was dying in what was perhaps their darkest hour.

"And the Queen?" Amatria asked gently.

Ilse wiped away tears. "Very nearly as drained. She is pouring every ounce of her magic into the King, just to keep him breathing. She is sacrificing herself, just to buy time."

Longshot leaned against the counter, this small motion possessing all the lithe dexterity of his race and his warrior's path. "Have we any updates on the approach of General Killdare or Prince Rogan?"

Mary nodded, finding a stool and sitting upon it. "Whatever interference Fak'Har has in place weakened recently," she told them. "It's still there, but Kyla was able to see through whatever he's doing. She spotted the Prince while he was dreaming. He's only a week or so away. He's coordinating with General Killdare, maneuvering their forces into the forest."

Rainer glanced at Longshot. "Make sure word of that spreads through the Walkers," he instructed. "I'll do the same among the guardsmen and City Watch. We've got to give them something to hope for."

Mary glanced beyond the broken walls of the ruined shop. "We saw some of the soldiers on our way here," she noted. "They look…"

"On the edge," Rainer finished. "Most sieges aren't won or lost on the battlefield. They're won or lost here," he tapped a gloved finger against his temple. "If we can hold out long enough, repel enough of their assaults, Vagris won't be able to keep his mercenaries here. They'll desert."

"There will be no desertions," Xathias argued. The rough Xeshlin arrived wearing heavy robes, protecting his cursed flesh from the heat of the descending sun. "The Crimson Delight is complete. The Dark Coven has now enslaved the minds of the mercenaries."

"What does that mean, exactly?" Rainer asked.

"I have seen them do this before. The Crimson Delight is their primary means of maintaining their rule over the *Xesh'lin* and the slave Humans of Davenor. They have spent these past nights leading the mercenaries in a great bacchanal. They began a fertility cycle amongst all the Sorceress Sisters, mixing their tears with various narcotics." The Watermage glanced at Amatria and Longshot. "The females of my kind do not content themselves with only enthralling their mates, and especially not a single male. Nor would they perform the mutual enthrallment, as I understand many *Sy'lva'i* still do here in Lanasia."

Amatria took Longshot's hand, but said nothing.

"So, it's stronger than Sylvai enthrallment?" Ilse asked.

Xathias nodded. "And more insidious. The enthralled males have had all decency stripped from them, but also all fear, all doubt." The rouge Xeshlin nodded his deeply-cowled head beyond the walls. "For those males, nothing in this world exists except the command of their mistress. If the Sorceress Sisters will it, the mercenaries will hurl themselves bodily upon our walls, climbing up with only their fingernails if necessary."

Rainer leaned back against a section of broken wall. "So," he mused. "The next assault will be the final one."

Amatria glanced at Mary. "You said that Princess Kyla was able to locate her husband because Fak'Har's interference as weakened?"

The handmaiden nodded.

"Curious."

"Care to share?" Rainer asked.

The archwizard narrowed her eyes in thought, absently running a hand along Longshot's arm. "He has dedicated himself to disrupting all our communication and divinations beyond the forest. That he has relented, even if only slightly, speaks of some alternate priority."

"Which is?"

Amatria glanced at Xathias, who shrugged. "We would need to consult with *Parden* Esha."

"Where is Esha?" Ilse asked.

"Aloisa went to get her," Rainer answered.

"But, that was hours ago," Mary pointed out slyly.

"I'm aware."

"Regardless of what the Shadowed Mage is planning," Xathias interjected, "we can anticipate the next assault."

"Go on."

The rouge Xeshlin made a half-glance towards the afternoon sun. "The mercenaries are now under the dominion of the Crimson Delight. They are fearless, true, but also useless without their mistress' presence."

"That can happen," Amatria pointed out. "In an imperfect or forced enthrallment, the male can become dependent on the female's presence. In her absence, he becomes increasingly unfocused, suffering mental and physical degeneration until their reunion." She glanced meaningfully at Rainer. "Rashid…" she pointed out.

"So, the mercenaries need the Dark Coven," Rainer mused.

"And not only to avoid the withering effect," Xathias added. "The Sorceress Sisters will need to give them every command in response to any change in the situation."

"What happens if we kill the Dark Coven?" Mary asked.

Xathias looked at her. "Whenever a Sorceress Sister dies, all her enthralled males are killed immediately. Without her presence, her control, they become little more than animals. Wild, uncontrollable. They attack anything that moves until they are spent. The withering takes them eventually, but his requires days. In the meantime, they kill everything in proximity, feeding on flesh and blood."

Mary shuddered, then looked at Rainer. "If this happened before the next assault..." she suggested.

Rainer nodded and glanced at Longshot. "Could your people do it?"

The Walker nodded, his arms enfolding Amatria. "What they have done is a perversion of our most sacred tradition. The enthrallment is meant to bind two people in mutual love and devotion. Their degeneracy calls out for vengeance. If these witches show themselves, my brothers and I will see them dead."

"This will not be so easy," Xathias warned. "The Crimson Delight empowers them. The Dark Coven will be at its most formidable now. Each Sorceress Sister will have the power of an archwizard, perhaps more. If they appear at the next assault, they will not cower in the reserves. They will be as enervated as the males, as eager for blood and suffering. They will employ their foul magic."

"Can your people deal with them?" Rainer asked.

Amatria and Xathias glanced at each other. "Perhaps," the rouge Xeshlin answered. "The cost will be great. There will not be many; the Covens keep their numbers small. But those few will have significant power. If we must engage directly..." He shook his cowled head. "Those of us who survive will be of little use to you for the remainder of the siege."

"Does that mean the Dark Coven will be equally spent?" Mary asked.

"I suppose so," Amatria acknowledged.

"What're you thinking?" Rainer asked.

"The next assault will have the Xeshlin priestesses at the head. They'll be blood-maddened, just like the men. Amatria, Xathias, and all the Keep's adepts will fight them. No matter who wins, both sides will be drained. We won't have our magic, but neither will Vagris. If the next assault fails, he'll have nothing left. That just leaves the maddened warriors."

"Berserkers," Aloisa said suddenly. "There are ways of handling berserkers."

All heads turned. The Gunrsvein lieutenant had arrived with Esha. The warrior-woman was dressed in her uniform, though this was rumpled. Her great length of blonde hair was only barely restrained in her customary braid, this looking as though in great need of repair. She stood as solid as ever, as immovable as stone, but there was also a great softening in her eyes, as though the hard, Northlands ice that once rested in her skull had melted into twin pools of crystal water.

Beside her, Esha was the same as ever, perhaps even more so, as the great archmage had reverted to her pre-war self. The Sylva no longer burdened herself with armor, instead returning to her customary blue robes. These were rumpled and singed as they had always been, the collar, sleeves, and hem fraying from detonations, immolations, and innumerable distractions. Her burn-shortened hair was its usual unkempt mess but her skin carried a new flush and her opalescent eyes glowed more brightly than ever before. Mary noticed a small detail, a new knot on Esha's Guild braid, one entwined with a few threads of golden hair.

Rainer must have seen all that Mary did, but he said nothing. A raised eyebrow was his only comment at the state of his lieutenant. "And how do we fight... what did you call them?"

"Berserkers," the lieutenant supplied. She and Esha entered the ruined shop. The Gunrsvein woman picked up Esha and placed her on a counter, leaning against it herself. The archmage crossed her legs and smiled brightly, scooting nearer to the rigid warrior-woman nearby. "This happens amongst my people," Aloisa continued, apparently trying to ignore Esha as she played with her long blonde braid. "Men, especially, seem vulnerable. Battle-madness descends, and they hurl themselves at the enemy. If there are no enemy to be found, they seek out bloodshed wherever it can be found."

"Do they always die once overcome with this battle-madness?" Amatria asked. As though without thought, the archwizard was mirroring Esha, idly running her fingers through Longshot's tightly-bound hair.

"No," Aloisa answered. "Once they've spilled enough blood, they usually come out of the madness. If not, they're killed."

"How do you fight against them?" Rainer asked.

"Tactics," the Gunrsvein warrior declared. "They cannot think, so you must. Attack them at range, wear them down with missiles. Slow their approach. Force them to tire, climbing over obstacles. Once they reach your lines, use spears. Treat them like you would a rabid animal. Put them down at distance."

"Well," Mary shrugged, nodding beyond the walls. "The ground is plenty rough already."

Rainer nodded, his eyes lost in thought. "Between the cave-ins, the destroyed warmachines, and all the trebuchet impacts, there's no direct line of advance anymore."

"And the trebuchets can keep scattering them on the next charge," Aloisa added, irritably slapping away Esha's hand. In response, the mischievous archmage began playfully poking at her much-larger companion.

Rainer glanced at Longshot. "Can your people lead the Guard archers? Help them pinpoint their shots?"

Longshot considered, leaning into Amatria as the Sylva continued trailing light fingers through his hair. "Yes, but we cannot achieve both tasks. Either we engage the Xeshlin seductresses, or the Human berserkers. Trying to do both would lessen our utility to the point of negligence."

"I honestly don't know which will be the bigger threat," Rainer admitted. He looked to Xathias. "What do you think?"

"The Sorceress Sisters are the greater threat, by far," the rough Xeshlin replied without hesitation.

"We'll handle them," Esha confidently declared. The tiny archmage glanced at Rainer. "If you can protect my students and me from physical harm, then we'll take care of those *Xesh'lin* witches."

"That's it then." Rainer straightened, both his back and his shoulders. "Everyone pass word about what Princess Kyla has learned. We only need to hold off for another week or so. This next assault may decide the entire war." He nodded to Esha. "Our adepts will engage the Xeshlin priestesses. Longshot's Walkers will lead the city's archers again; they'll wear down the berserkers as they make their way towards the walls." The colonel looked to Aloisa. "The scorpions and ballistae will use the last of their ammunition. Don't wait for orders, just break up any big groups for Longshot to hit. Triple-horn for the last of the special shot. I'll have the spotters direct the trebuchets onto Fak'Har's monsters. The Guard will engage any breach points along the walls."

Colonel Rainer looked around. "Any other suggestions?"

"Colonel," Mary spoke up.

He looked at her. "What about Fak'Har himself?" the handmaiden asked. "We know he's doing something, preparing for something, otherwise Kyla wouldn't have been able to see past his interference. What do we do about him?"

Rainer nodded and glance around, but saw only looks of uncertainty. "There's not much we can do about the Shadowed Mage. I've never heard of him engaging in personal combat." Nods from all the others confirmed this well-known fact. "He's always stayed in the background, manipulating, like Cyras Darkholm. We can only hope that he sticks to his habits. If Fak'Har does appear… we'll just have to adapt."

Chapter 35

"They're forming up!" Aloisa barked. She was standing at the battlements just over Defiant Gate, looking out on the ruined field stretching out before the Northern Keep.

Mary glanced out from one of the ballistae's firing points. At the edge of the broken field, amidst the charred, dead trees, figures were visible among the shadows. The moon had risen full, even as the sun had set behind gathering clouds. A threatening autumn wind had gathered and even now blew in from the north, promising another hard winter. No orders had been needed; the defenders had deployed themselves along the walls even as the day's light retreated from the horrors to come.

Women emerged then from the blackened forest. Mary needed a moment before her mind realized the truth. Not women, grotesque mockeries of women. They were nude but for flowing loincloths stained red as though from the blood of a thousand screaming victims. Jagged runes, twisted mockeries of Sylvai glyphs, slashed themselves in gold down the loincloths, collecting the bright moonlight. Their flesh and flowing manes were without color, made more so by the gathering night. Their eyes of burning blood seethed and glowed with harvested power, matching the stains decorating their bodies from the unholy celebration that hand empowered them. In their hands, the monstrous Xeshlin females held barbed whips and serrated blades. They were crowned with obsidian, and had matching chains around their necks and hips, these glittering with embedded rubies. They hissed and licked their lips, as though relishing the thought of a bloody feast to come.

Amidst these horrors were beings that had once been men. They still wore some of the armor, though only in bits and pieces. Men from across Lanasia gathered as near as possible to the Xeshlin females, snapping at each other to be closer and reaching out fearfully for some passing glance, some indifferent touch, from the females who had enslaved their souls. The men's bodies were a riot of torn clothing, ruined armor, and recently-scarred flesh. Dark blood was stained on them, on their fingers and their mouths. Their hair was unkept and their eyes were devoid of thought.

Not all the mercenaries had been corrupted by the Xeshlin priestesses. The berserkers made up the center, the great mass facing the Northern Keep. But on the flanks, and in reserve, the city's defenders could see more sell-swords, gathered in smaller groups. These kept well away from the Xeshlin and their bestial former comrades.

"Vagris is smarter than I gave him credit," Rainer admitted. The colonel was standing at the door to the bastion into which he had firmly placed Mary. He was looking out on the gathering enemy, the same as all the other defenders.

"What do you mean?" Mary asked.

"He didn't let the Xeshlin enslave all his mercenaries." The veteran nodded to the other groups of seemingly-rational warriors. "He kept a large part preserved, still answerable to him. He'll throw away the berserkers to breach the walls, then still have a viable force to sack the city." The colonel shouted down to a runner. "New orders to trebuchets and spotters!" he bellowed. Open sheaf! Spread volleys! Continuous fire on my command!"

"What's happening?" Mary asked as the runners darted away with the artillery's new instructions.

"Vagris is holding some of his assets back," the colonel answered. "He's betting the Xeshlin and their berserkers will breach the walls. He won't deploy the bulk of his force if he doesn't have to. We need to discourage the mercenaries from getting involved and keep those berserkers scattered for Longshot." He nodded to the broken field. "Once I give the command, our artillery will open up with everything they've got. They'll cover as much of the area as possible. Maybe they hit something, maybe not, but the enemy will see how impossible it will be to approach the city."

One of the Xeshlin females, this one having the greatest number of blasphemous glyphs on her flowing loincloth and an obsidian tiara trimmed with gold, raised a long-nailed hand in the air. The berserkers tensed in readiness, as did their blood-streaked mistresses. The nearly-taloned hand came down, and the battle-maddened men charged.

"Triple blast!" Rainer roared. Before his voice even faded, it was matched with three terrible blasts from his bugler. As one, the trebuchets positioned within the city flung their great missiles up and away. The ballistae and scorpions also let fly. The broken field became a killing one. Stones and javelins and bolts filled the air, to the accompaniment of the screaming dead. The berserkers did not cry out in pain, even as their bodies were crushed or impaled or riddled with barbed metal; their voices only carried despair at being denied fresh blood and failing their mistresses.

"Longshot!" Rainer called out. "Archers on your command!"

Much further down the battlements, the dark-skinned Walker nodded. He glanced around one of the stone covers and waited. The berserkers drew closer, as uncaring of the missiles as they were of their dead and dying comrades. The Xeshlin Sorceress Sisters came forward as well. Each female floated along the ground, her bare feet sliding inches above the broken field. They hissed growled commands at their enslaved males, demanding blood and suffering. Several scorpions took aim at these monstrous females, but their bolts struck some red-tinged force, some nearly-invisible shield that enveloped each of the Xeshlin priestesses. A ballistae also took aim and let fly, but its great javelin shattered against the red shield of the Dark Coven.

Rainer saw this, even as Mary did. He glanced back, into the same bastion. "Esha!" he called out. "They're coming!"

The tiny archmage stood and nodded. Aloisa, who had been standing at the opposite door as Rainer, approached the Sylva. The two women said nothing. The Gunrsvein dropped to a knee, though she still loomed over the diminutive Esha. They looked into each other's eyes, sharing an entire conversation in the one look. The archmage reached up and lay a tiny hand on Aloisa's cheek. Then, Esha squared herself and marched forward, needing not to bend over to remain within the protection of the battlements' wall. The archmage reached into her blue robes and retrieved a communications crystal. She activated it and said, "Stand ready, students. Your final examination is upon us."

The howling berserkers continued their mad charge across the broken field. Their groups were quickly broken up by the uneven ground and the unceasing barrage from the city's artillery. In twos and threes at most, but mostly alone, the blood-mad warriors howled as they sprinted towards the walls.

"They don't have ladders!" Mary exclaimed.

"I doubt they thought of that," Aloisa replied, moving to join Rainer. "They'll try to climb the stone barehanded or with their weapons."

As though in response, the Xeshlin priestesses waved their arms in great circles. The air shimmered around their slight bodies, as though some insidious power was gathering into them. The Dark Coven pointed ahead, to where their enslaved males were charging, and the ground ripped and heaved. Earth and stone piled atop itself, forming great ramps. The mystical constructions began directly in front of the charging, shrieking berserkers, and continued rising, gathering more material into themselves. The world itself seemed to be reached out with chthonic fingers, lunging towards the walls of the Northern Keep.

Esha reached the crate that had been emplaced beside Longshot. She clambered up, needing only minimal assistance from a nearby guardsman, and looked out onto the broken field and its approaching digits, upon which clung berserker mercenaries like ticks upon a desiccated hound. "Hmm," the tiny archmage said, as though looking at nothing more consequential than some new type of plant. She reached once again for her communications crystal, and into she said, "Xathias, stasis. Amatria, disruption."

The chthonic fingers, having very near reached the walls, stopped suddenly. The earth and stone writhed in place, like a thousand, thousand eels trapped in a barrel and desperate to escape. The berserkers holding on to the rams howled in frustration. Many leapt from their mystical siege ramps, only to fall to the distant ground. Those who survived their descent continued to clutch at the ground, dragging their broken and useless bodies closer to their intended victims.

Mary saw Amatria, in a bastion further down from her own, gesturing and chanting the words of magic. Behind her were a group of blue-robed students and grey-robed apprentices, all matching the Sylva archwizard's motions exactly. On the broken field, in response to Amatria's magic, the chthonic ramps shuddered and shattered, those pieces still held in Xathias' magic. This, at last, relented, and the chunks of destroyed earth and stone fell to the ground, burying the grasping berserkers.

"Now!" Longshot barked. The Walkers and the archers all stood. They knocked arrows, took aim, and loosed.

Those amongst the berserkers who had not been killed, either from the fall or the sudden destruction of their ramps, were quickly felled by a new volley of arrows. This was joined with more great stones from the trebuchets, more bolts from the scorpions, and more javelins from the ballistae.

On the broken field, the Xeshlin priestesses hissed their frustration and waved their hands. The shimmering red that protected them extended, shielding their enslaved males as they picked themselves up and resumed their charge. Amatria and Xathias led a magical onslaught upon the red-trimmed shield, but to no avail. Arrows and stones and bolts and javelins shattered against it, while the berserker mercenaries continued their charge.

"This is my task," Esha declared.

"Hold!" Longshot called out, and the Walkers and archers ducked back behind the battlements.

The tiny archmage stood on her tiptoes and held up her staff. She spoke the words of magic, gesturing at its very tip. A pulsing light appeared upon the staff, collecting at its peak and rotating through every color known and unknown. Esha continued her chanting and gestured from her staff to the broken field. The prismatic light leapt joyfully from its perch and landed gently upon the red-rimmed shield. Esha narrowed her eyes and made tiny gestures with her fingers. The light pulsed and changed in response, altering its form and the array of its many colors. The berserkers continued their mindless charge and the red-rimmed shield continued with them. Suddenly, the prismatic light seemed to wiggle into the shield, sliding not past it, but instead arching within it, spreading in further and further tributaries until the shield was fully enveloped in Esha's prismatic spell. The tiny archmage made a little, self-satisfied smile, and snapped her finger. The shield exploded into nothingness.

"Again!" Longshot ordered, and the Walkers and archers stood and let fly, joined by the other artillery.

More missiles filled the air and the berserker mercenaries were cut down. Their blood and bodies littered the broken field, and the Xeshlin priestesses hissed their frustration. The Dark Coven halted their floating advance and once again gathered their insidious power. They each doubled over as though in pain from such a magical tension, and then straightened, flinging their arms wide. Horrid blades of impossible darkness, each radiating an umbral red power, lanced out from the sorceresses. These speared into the stone with little effect. Many, though, found openings in the battlements. Mary watched in horror as an archer was caught in the chest by one of the evil blades and hurled back into the street below. She looked out and screamed. The archer was writing on the ground; the Xeshlin spell melted into his flesh, becoming a wretched mass of dark tentacles that slowly devoured his body. Other men, Human and Sylvai, had been caught by the magical attacks and lie screaming and writing in the horror and agony of their violent, pain-filled deaths.

Another volley of the insidious missiles flew and more defenders were caught, impaled and sent screaming to the ground. Esha leapt from her crate and rushed to the edge of the battlement. She spoke the words of magic and gestured at the victims of the Xeshlin's wretched spells. A great, white light enfolded each of the victims. Their screams were suddenly cut off and the light faded. The writing darkness was gone, as were most of the bodies of the victims. Esha glanced back and a sneer. "Well, that will be quite enough of that," she said primly.

The tiny archmage went back to her crate and clambered up, disregarding shouts to stay down. She raised her staff, speaking the words of magic again, and swung her arm out in a great arc. When the next barrage came from the Xeshlin priestesses, the dark missiles exploded in golden light. Esha reached for her communication crystal. "Xathias, Amatria. Counter now!"

Another barrage from the Xeshlin was again intercepted by Esha. When this happened, though, arcs of blue lightning erupted from the bastions on either side of Defiant Gate. These caught the sorceresses on either end of their line by surprise. The females had time only for a startled yelp before they were destroyed by the blue lightning. The magical attack then arched from the first targets to the next on either side of the Xeshlin line. These priestesses had time to re-erect their shields, intercepting the strikes from Xathias and Amatria. The high priestess at the center snarled and hurled a crackling whip of purple and black at the far bastion in which Xathias stood. The rogue Xeshlin broke off his own attack and erected a hasty shield with the help of his nearby students, only just barely intercepting the mystical whip.

Esha again spoke words of magic and joined in the battle of spells. Rays of pure white lanced from the tip of her staff, cutting down one of the Xeshlin priestesses. The high priestess hissed and gestured at Esah, sending out another barrage of dark blades. The archmage, though, called upon a great wind that turned the blade aside, casting them spinning away. Amatria threw another bolt of blue lightning, keeping the priestesses to the right occupied with nothing more than protecting themselves.

Xathias also led a distracting assault. He and his students bombarded the Xeshlin line with stones ripped up from the broken field and cast once again at the Dark Coven. Those priestesses on the left were forced to shield themselves are their comrades from this assault, unable to make any offensive moves. This left only the High Priestess herself to face Esha.

Both magical women tore open reality to gather mystical weapons. Driving ice, bursts of flame, unseen horrors, and onslaughts of boiling water were cast one against the other. The broken field writhed beneath them all as though the world was made angry at such a violation of nature. Esha launched attack, defense, and counter-attack, all with a calm, almost casual air. The high priestess, though, began sweating, gritting her teeth and straining to draw upon more energy. At last, having expended a great burst of magic to send a flood of vile green tentacles grasping at Esha, the high priestess collapsed, exhausted.

The high priestess picked herself up from the ground, even as Esha manifested spinning disks of green and gold light, using them to destroyed the tentacles. The Xeshlin sorceress looked about and snarled in the hateful speech of her people, pointing at the three remaining members of her Dark Coven. The male Xeshlin at her side leapt forward. They drew hook-bladed knives from their belts and murdered their compatriots near the other Xeshlin sorceresses. They then grabbed the females themselves and dragged them screaming nearer to the high priestess. She gestured, and her enslaved males butchered the other sorceresses. The high priestess then made a pulling gestured, and evil red mist rose from the sacrificed Xeshlin females. This mist collected around the high priestess' outstretched arms, restoring her vitality until she once again floated above the broken field.

A green light gathered from all around, rising from the earth and the city and even the sky. This power collected into gently-rotating whirlpool around Xathias, who had emerged from his bastion. The high priestess saw this and oriented on the rogue Xeshlin with a snarl of hatred.

But then, another light of red gathered around Amatria, who had also emerged from her own bastion, opposite Xathias. The Sylva archwizard faced the high priestess with grim resolution as she harnessed her own magic. In return, the Xeshlin sorceress again hissed and glanced from one archwizard to the other.

Rather than launching an attack, both Amatria and Xathias pointed at Esha, standing stop the battlement above Defiant Gate. The swirling lights of green and red floated out, merging into the tiny archmage's outstretched arms. This magic united within her small torso, sharing their colors with one another and reaching back to join with the archwizards on either side. Together, the three powerful adepts merged their magic, united themselves, giving and receiving with equal measure, each amplified by the presence of the other. As one, the three pointed at the High Priestess, alone now but for her few enslaved males, standing above the broken field. The swirling light of many colors reached out from all three, creating a great bubble around the High Priestess and her slaves. The Xeshlin tried striking out, tried employing her stolen magic, but her wrath could find no purchase against the gentle glow summoned by the three comrades.

The swirling light of many colors enveloping the high priestess and her slaves intensified. It collapsed in, onto the bodies to the Xeshiln. They screamed and thrashed about, but to no avail. The light of many colors captured them and lifted them high. The light intensified, brightening until it shattered the night. Then, the light was gone, and with it the Xeshlin.

"Well," came a voice of infinite evil drifting out from the darkness. "I think that should just about do it."

A figure came walking out from amongst the dead trees. It was robed and cowled, much as the Xeshlin were in the burning light of day. The figure did not seem so much to move as to flow from one shadow to the next. The darkness seemed to reach for it, to blend into the creature approaching them, only to retreat once the figure had passed by. It passed through the broken field, giving not the slightest glance towards the dead and dying, the bleeding and broken. It flowed up along one of the larger uprisings of earth and stone, to stand exposed to the defenders of the Northern Keep.

"Fak'Har!" Mary gasped.

"Triple horn!" Rainer thundered. "Fire everything!"

The scorpions and ballistae let fly. Word was passed back to the trebuchets, which once more cast their great stones aloft. Esha's explosive ammunition detonated in the Shadowed Mage's very face. Bolts and arrows and javelins and stones all struck. They all failed. The bolts shattered upon nothing well before reaching the shadowed target. The javelins passed harmlessly through. The great stones changed their trajectories, falling far from the calm form of the Shadowed Mage. Longshot and his archers all stood and loosed their arrows as fast as they possibly could. The arrows stopped midair; the hung for a moment and then fell to the ground. On and on the missiles came, but nothing could harm the Shadowed Mage, who soon began chuckling at the impotence of the Northern Keep.

"*Yall'een!*" Longshot swore, leaping atop the battlements and letting fly arrow after arrow at the Shadowed Mage.

Fak'Har did not flinch. Instead, with a casualness of motion reserved for idle days of summer, pulled back the hood of his impossibly-black robe. His face was a twisted mockery of Cyras Darkholm's. His grey hair was pulled back in a tight knot and he had innumerable scars decorating his flesh. His eyes, not the merry blue of the Trickster Mage, were like the calm sea moments before a horrific storm. The Shadowed Mage glanced at Longshot, and he smiled again. Fak'Har pointed a finger towards the defiant Walker. The arrows that had been halting midair slowly turned, orienting at their originators. The Shadowed Mage made an idle toss of his hand, and the arrows shot out, with greater, impossible speed than they could ever have had if launched from a bow. Cries of pain and death echoed from the walls as the Walkers and archers died. Longshot cursed and flung himself back behind the battlement.

The assault of bolts and javelins and stones continued. Fak'Har glanced to his left and right, and then to above Defiant Gate, where Esha stood trembling. The Shadowed Mage grinned and gestured to the left. A thousand bolts of lightning tore open the sky and the bastion in which Xathias and his students had been sheltering exploded. Screaming bodies fell along with massive construction stones. The entire structure collapsed in on itself, taking the guardsmen within as well as Xathias and his students.

The Shadowed Mage then pointed to the right, at the bastion in which Amatria was sheltering with her students and Mary. "Out!" the handmaiden screamed, diving from the stone structure. The bastion exploded, just as had the first, killing those within or sending them falling. Mary was dazed for a moment, but found herself still atop the battlement, being dragged away by Aloisa. The Gunrsvein warrior-woman was bleeding from a gash atop her head, but still moved with all the unwavering resolution she ever had. She rested Mary against the battlement wall, beside where Rainer had placed Ilse, having pulled his daughter out ahead of Mary. The handmaiden saw Longshot, sprinting towards the ruined bastion, screaming Amatria's name. "What do we do!?!" Mary demanded.

Esha looked down at them, and then out at the Shadowed Mage. Fak'Har was standing calmly, as though waiting. The tiny archmage sighed and dropped her staff. She then spoke words, calmly, but clearly, in the language of magic.

From the broken field, Fak'Har laughed. "It's been a long time since anyone's given me the Challenge. I accept." The Shadowed Mage drew a circle in the mud and stepped within.

Esha reached into one of the many pouches resting along her belt and used fine white sand to draw a circle atop of the bastion's stones. She also stepped within.

Both adepts raised their arms and began chanting, calling to the Winds of magic. Rainer glanced at Aloisa. "Tell everyone left to open fire," he commanded.

Ilse held up a trembling hand. "No!" she exclaimed. "You can't!"

"Now's the time," her father insisted. "While he's distracted!"

"You can't!" Ilse repeated. "As soon as they drew those circles, they became connected. It's a duel, one of the oldest traditions from the Sylvai Empire! If you interfere, you'll disrupt the magic between them! You'll kill Esha!"

"Damn!" The colonel nodded to Aloisa. "Make preparations. If this goes south, be ready to pull back."

Aloisa nodded and moved down to the street below. Rainer looked at the two injured young women. "It think it's time you make your reports to the Princess," he declared.

"I'm not leaving you here, father!" Ilse said flatly.

"And I'm not leaving without her," Mary added.

Rainer shook his head, grumbling.

Esha was sweating. Streams of tension and effort poured down her face, staining her blue robes. The air around her shimmered as though some great heat had wrapped itself around the archmage. Her lips never stopped moving, nor did her hands; both continuously calling upon the Winds of Magic. Fak'Har seemed to be doing little better, though, Mary noticed. The Shadowed Mage was hunched over and visibly trembling at the effort of dueling Esha.

The shimmering then stopped. Mary had only a moment of relief before the duel resumed, but in a much more ostentatious way. "Down!" Rainer barked, pushing Mary and Ilse to the stone floor and covering them with his armored body.

Fire and ice, wind and rain, solid sound and weapons of aether flew about. For every attack of shadow or green flame Esha suffered against, the archmage retaliated with golden light and red hail. Mary risked a glance over the battlement wall and saw the ground open beneath Fak'Har's feet. The Shadowed Mage was briefly enveloped by the angry fire at the world's center, but, when the flames returned to their home, what lay within Fak'Har's protective circle, including the Shadowed Mage himself, survived. With a sneer, he ripped three of the dead trees behind him out of the ground. With a word and a gesture, he imbued them with orange light and hurled the terrible missiles at Esha. The archmage did not flinch, but sent a trio of crackling balls flying out, impacting and destroying the magical attack.

"Back off the walls!" Rainer ordered. He gestured to the surviving guardsmen and Walkers before nearly picking up Mary and Ilse and half-dragging them down the nearby stairs to the relative safety of the street below. Aloisa was moving soldiers and civilians back, away from the walls, and had a carriage waiting. "You two are leaving!" the Gunrsvein woman commanded

"But-"

"No buts!" Rainer thundered, to the accompaniment of another horrible detonation atop the walls. "Even if she wins the fight, this whole damned area is going to be flattened!"

Aloisa and Rainer practically dragged Mary and Ilse onto the waiting carriage, but they all paused when there was a sudden quiet from above. They each looked up and saw the archmage, still standing atop the battlements, but panting and withering. From beyond, down within the broken field, they heard Fak'Har's terrible voice.

"Enough of this!" the Shadowed Mage roared. Then came words. Terrible words. Impossible words. Words that ate into one's soul.

Ilse screamed and held her head. "The Umbral Language! The words of Underworld!"

Cracks appeared in the great city wall. These cracks were filled with an evil, pulsing light of red and purple, of black and green. The light pulled at the stone of the wall and the surrounding buildings, tearing free chunks of stone. This caused more cracks to appear, and the great stone wall of the Northern Keep began to groan.

"Back," Rainer said very calmly. "Back, back, back!" The colonel looked around. "Everyone get BACK!"

The flames of Underworld itself spurted out from the cracks in the wall. These became gouts that slithered up the stone. The fire leapt into the sky, swirling into a maelstrom above Esha's upraised head. More and more flames, more and more heat, more and more evil erupted from the weakening walls to gather above Esha. The Umbral storm raged and grew, then collapsed to a pin-point of evil. All was quiet, then, and still.

An explosion like nothing heard before erupted, roaring across the city and into the dead forest beyond. The flames of Fak'Har's final spell erupted out, destroying everything they touched. Those men and women still atop the wall were consumed, a pitiful few leaping in desperation. The wall itself became a thousand, thousand chunks, hurled in every direction to rain down on the city and the mercenaries gathering outside. The world descended into screams and horror and despair and suffering, then dissolved into white.

Mary regained some part of her senses. She blinked and looked around, trying to sit up. The carriage was destroyed, splintered wood and a mutilated horse being all that remained. Ilse lay near her, unmoving. Garbled sounds drew her eyes around, where guardsmen were scrambling to rouse survivors. Mary blinked and looked to the eternal wall that had, for generations, protected the Northern Keep.

Mary sat up, only dimly aware of the blood covering some part of her face. She blinked again and looked to her side. Aloisa was there, her own face and hair a tangled mess of blood. The Gunrsvein warrior, unflappable, stoic in the extreme, stared with open eyes and open mouth at what was in front of them.

Defiant Gate was gone. Not destroyed, not broken, gone. A great hole existed where that monument to the Northlands' stubborn survival once rested. The walls to either side had collapsed. Here and there, broken pieces of bodies stuck out, unmoving.

"Esha!" Aloisa screamed.

The tiny archmage, Tower Mistress of the Northern Keep's Arcane Guild, teacher and mentor to generations of Northland adepts, loyal advisor to House Calonar, was gone.

Rough hands were on them, pulling them up. Rainer and a handful of guardsmen were lifting Mary, Ilse, and Aloisa. The colonel had slapped Mary across the face and was screaming something at her, but the handmaiden could not force her mind to comprehend what was happening, nor was she really sure she wanted to. Rainer looked back, and Mary followed his gaze. Beyond the rubble that had been Defiant Gate and the city's wall, Fak'Har stood amidst the broken field, a vast avenue of smooth earth now stretching from the exposed city, to the waiting mercenaries. The Shadowed Mage was smiling still and holding his hands out, as though presenting a gift. From all around the Dark Scion, the mercenary army charged.

Rainer turned and roared, "RETREAT!!!"

The Heroes at Home

III
Castle

Chapter 36

Mary stared in confusion at what her eyes beheld. A massive portion of the wall was gone. Defiant Gate, that symbol of their home's resilience, the people's unwavering survival against all aggressors, had simply ceased to exist. The bastions on either side were rubble. Stone still fell, tumbling to the ground like so many errant stones cast down a riverbank by some idle child. The buildings nearest Defiant Gate, shops, storage, and homes, had been reduced to shrapnel. This had been propelled out and away, into the city, where a devastating field of crumbling ruins now stood, markers of a proud city looking now standing like a forgotten graveyard. Bodies and parts of bodies were scattered amidst the few survivors of the walls' defense, a poisoned rain forever cursing the Northern Keep.

Colonel Rainer, failed commander of the city's defense, was grabbing her, lifting her, and bellowing orders. Mary heard his words, but could not comprehend. He was gesturing to the handful of guardsmen and reservists still standing, still capable of standing, and to those only barely moving. These, Rainer was trying to organize. They checked the nearest intact bodies, most finding nothing but meat. On the rare occasion that a survivor was uncovered, this person was picked up and carried away. Supplies were left. Arms and armor were left. Tattered banners and uniforms were left. The dead were left. Only the living were extracted from the ruins of Defiant Gate.

The reality pressing in was anathema to Mary's mind. The young woman kept blinking, as she looked around, trying to force the world back into reason. She had lived her young life in Snowholm, a peaceful town at the norther edge of House Calonar's domain. Her father had served that noble family, as so many fathers and mothers had. They, and the Northern Keep itself, were spoken of, not in hushed veneration, like most Adamics used when speaking of Velaross, the Holy City. No, their noble rulers and capital were spoken of in with the warmest, proudest honor. House Calonar had stood for millennia, fighting for the common people even during the rule of the Sylvai Empire. Cylan Calonar himself had waged war for the people of the Northlands, defending them as one of the fabled Heroes of Fate against the Xeshlin, the Nenic Twins, and the Greysoul. The Northern Keep had been a refuge since the fall of the Republic, a bastion of peace and security as the continent descended into civil war. The great city of the Northlands could not ever, would not ever, fall.

But, like a mighty warrior fighting his last battle, the Northern Keep had suffered a mortal wound, and now lay dying. Mary turned her eyes and not only beheld, but truly comprehended, the sight with which she was confronted. The walls were breached. Defiant Gate had been destroyed. Many, perhaps most of the city's best defenders lay under mounds of jagged rock. Beyond lay the broken field, where so much of Vagris' army had been turned away. But now, the warlord himself, a traitor of the Republic Legions, stood with his mercenaries. They were also stunned by Fak'Har's evil magic. They were collecting themselves and looking at the exposed city. They were pointing and starting to move.

"We need to get out of here," Mary said calmly.

"Oh, really?" Rainer snapped sarcastically. Mary looked, and the veteran guardsman was helping load another moaning soldier into the back of a wagon. Ilse and Aloisa were already aboard, the Gunrsvein warrior-woman's head being cradled in the priestess' lap. The lieutenant was barely moving, and hardly breathing. Ilse was using her goddess' magic to try and restore her friend, but the worry on her face spoke louder than words. The work, such as it was, finished, and Rainer called on the small team of men standing in place of a horse. "Let's go!"

"Wait!" a voice called with desperate urgency. Mary turned, wiping some errant blood from her eyes without considering whether it was hers. Longshot was rushing to them. The dark-skinned Walker moved across the rubble-strewn area with all the grace of his people, all the fluidity of his warrior-kin, and all the urgency of a man in love. In his arms, he carried Amatria, who clung to him as though he were the last sane thing in a world gone mad.

"Hold!" Rainer barked, and ran to the approaching Walker. He took Longshot's burden into his own arms, letting the Sylvu warrior leap down from the ruined building across which he had been sprinting. Together, they returned, even as Vagris' mercenaries made their way across the broken field.

Rainer handed Amatria up to the waiting guardsmen in the wagon. She was only barely moving. Her left leg looked as though it had been crushed multiple times. The bloody mess of fabric and flesh ended only an inch or two below the knee, and the remaining stump was impossibly twisted. Her blue robes were torn to the point of uselessness. Her bared torso was a canvas of wet gashes and tortured bruises. Her right breast was gone, looking as though it had been torn away. One of her ribs visibly poked out from the skin. Mary could see the twisting organs inside her nearly-open stomach. Neither of her arms functioned, though the left seemed as though it might someday respond once again to the archwizard's commands. The hair on one side of her head was only just a mangle of torn, bloody whisps. Her nose and cheeks were caved in, and she was missing several teeth. Somehow, the Sylva was conscious, and her opalescent eyes were fixed upon Longshot.

The Walker was in little better shape than any of the surviving guardsmen. His armor was gone, either destroyed or cast off to allow of unimpeded movement. His green and brown tunic and hose were torn and bloody. His scalp lock was missing and for the first time, Mary saw that his great many was even longer than Amatria's, falling freely across his strong shoulders to spill down his back. He stood without the slightest regard for his many wounds, most of these still fresh and wet. Instead, his back was straight and his opalescent eyes unwavering. His weapons were gone, just like his leather armor, with only an empty scabbard still riding on his hip. He glanced back at the gaping hole where Defiant Gate once stood.

Rainer and Mary both followed his opalescent gaze. Vagris' mercenaries had reached the ruined wall and were pouring into the city.

"We need time," Rainer noted.

Longshot glanced down and retrieved a nearby shortbow, its fallen guardsman-owner no longer having need. "You shall have it," the Walker said with grim finality, slinging the nearly-full quiver onto his back.

"NO!" Amatria commanded and demanded, somehow reaching up in desperate disregard for her grievous wounds.

Longshot turned back and smiled. He quickly moved to the side of the cart, where Amatria was trying to rise but being held down by Ilse. The Walker took his lady's hand in his. He placed the gentlest possible kiss upon her fingers, then held her palm against the beating of his heart. They said nothing, only staring at one another for only a brief moment, the world vanishing into their shared, opalescent gaze. An eternity together was spent in that second, before Longshot pulled away, his face never losing the smile of loving devotion as he looked upon the Sylva to whom he had enthralled himself.

"No," Amatria said again, desperately trying to rise, to maintain her sight of the Sylvu to whom she had enthralled herself. "No." Her hand remained outstretched, as though it was still held by his.

Rainer took Mary's shoulder. "Move out!" he barked. The surviving guardsmen strained and got the cart moving. Within seconds, they were in a rolling trot, heading as fast as they could towards the dubious safety of Castle Calonar.

Mary glanced back as the colonel led her away.

Longshot had turned away. He fired one, then two, then three arrows at the onrushing mercenaries. Three men were dead before the first had time to fall. The warrior, the last surviving student of Khaine, founder of the Walkers, spun under and around a thrown spear and sent his own missile flying, killing the attacker. A pair of mercenaries charged, screaming at the Sylvu, but Longshot leapt over them. He pulled another arrow from his scavenged quiver and buried it into one man's neck, only to pull it free, turn, knock, and fire it into the second's eye. The dark-skinned Walker, champion of his people, retrieved this arrow and fired it into yet another of the mercenaries. More invaders came, and more died. Longshot did not relent as he made Vagris' army pay for every life lost upon Defiant Gate.

A small group thought to bypass Longshot. The Walker was dancing as much as moving amongst the uneven mounds that had once been the district nearest to Defiant Gate. A half dozen men, leering with the easy target retreating under Rainer's leadership, swung wide to avoid death at the hands of the champion Walker. These fools died as easy as their brethren, though. Arrows retrieved from bodies were sent flying with barely a glance. Longshot seemed to know every movement, perhaps ever thought, of the mercenaries. The small group that had wanted to circle around and pounce upon the retreating wounded fell as one group, arrows erupting from their throats and eyes.

Mary kept looking back as they retreated. The streets became clear soon after leaving the area. Once free of the rubble that had been Defiant Gate and the surrounding neighborhood, their pace increased. She joined with Colonel Rainer, grabbing hold of the cart and pulling. She looked back and tried to see the last defense of the Northern Keep's walls. Longshot leapt and spun. He vaulted and rolled. He fired arrows into attackers near and far. He retrieved arrows from bodies as he danced past. He deflected sword strikes with his bow and drove fist and elbow and knee into faces, joints, crotches, and stomachs. When grabbed, he spun and twisted and killed. When cornered, he leapt and rolled and killed. When attacked, he defended and countered and killed. A dozen mercenaries lay dead around him. Then a score. Longshot did not stop, did not even pause. He gained for his Amatria and the others the time they needed to retreat.

Mary lost sight of the small battle as they continued their desperate retreat. Sounds of violence continued and spread. The very last she saw of Longshot, last disciple of Khaine, was of the Walker using the broken pieces of his scavenged shortbow to mercilessly beat a whimpering mercenary.

They mercenaries caught them just outside the city center. "There!" came a shout from behind. Mary glanced back and saw a group of more than twenty men, charging at them from one of the main boulevards. The four guardsmen pulling the cart full of wounded stopped and spread out, drawing swords or grabbing whatever improvised weapons on which they could lay their hands. Colonel Rainer stood in the center as the haggard defenders formed a line and braced, grim-faced yet unwavering.

The mercenaries hurled themselves forward, their eyes alight with murder, plunder, and all the joys to be had with fresh captives. They were less than a hundred yards, though, when a new surprise took them. From the allies and side streets, from left and right and behind, over a hundred of the City Watch fell upon the invaders.

The blue-capped policemen and fire brigade of the Northern Keep, while not as trained or as unbreakably disciplined as the House Guard, were nonetheless committed to the defense of their home. The Watch hurled themselves onto the mercenaries, swinging shortswords and their patrol batons. Screams filled the air. The enemy were cut down or beaten. The Watch was merciless, relentless, vicious in their counter-attack. Within moments, the mercenaries, those few who survived, were sent bloodied and scurrying back to the safety of their fellows.

One of the Watch, a silver disk on his blue cap marking him as a patrol leader, stepped up to Colonel Rainer and saluted. "We thought you wouldn't mind if we stepped in, sir," he said.

Rainer smiled and sheathed his scavenged shortsword. "Not at all. What's our status?"

Several of the watchmen relieved the Guard at the wagon, beginning to pull the wounded further into the city center. "Vagris sent detachments south and north once they were inside the walls. They're opening more of the gates, letting in the rest of his force that was out maintaining the siege. Right now, there's a fighting retreat all over the city. The Guard..." he looked to Rainer with deep sorrow. "What's left of the Guard, that is, is retreating to their barracks in the southern district."

"Who's in command?" Aloisa asked wearily, rising to a seated position with Ilse's help.

"Nobody," the watchman shrugged. "At least, not that we've heard."

"What about the Watch?" Rainer asked.

"We're fully deployed. Anyone near Defiant Gate started pulling the wounded back; they're heading to the castle. The rest of us, mostly those of us on other gates or assisting the trebuchets, have re-formed into our neighborhood detachments. We're hitting and running, keeping Vagris' mercenaries confused."

"How long can you keep doing that?" Mary asked gently.

The watchman grinned at her. "This is our city, our neighborhoods, our streets. We know them. Most of us were raised here. We can keep them running in circles for days."

"We don't need days," Aloisa pointed out. "We need one week. Just until the Prince and General Killdare get here."

"We'll get the time," the watchman swore. "They may have broken the walls, but this city still has some fight in her."

Rainer nodded, thinking. "That's good, but it's only a delay. Send runners to any neighborhood detachment they can find. Have every large group send a representative to me. We need to coordinate."

There was a thunderous explosion, far to the west. Another quickly followed, then another and another. A line of smaller explosions continued, seeming to spread out and away from Defiant Gate, sending new walls of smoke into the already blighted sky. "What in Underworld?" Rainer growled.

Mary stared, her mind working. They had paused just outside the city center, and the handmaiden was leaning against one of the Uldra gaslamps. She looked up at the cheerily-burning light, understanding forcing its way forward. "Oh God," she gasped. "Run!" she then screamed.

The guardsmen and watchmen looked at her in confusion, even as Mary darted forward and grabbed the cart herself. She strained to get the heavy vehicle moving. "The lamps!" she yelled. "They've ignited the lamps!"

Rainer looked back in open-mouthed shock, then leaped to the cart himself. "Pull!" he thundered.

Everyone capable threw themselves at the cart full of wounded. They forced the heavy thing back into motion, dragging it further into the relative safety of the city center. This location, though ringed by the gaslamps, had none within it. The great marble fountain remained, still pouring water.

More explosions clawed at the Northern Keep. Blue and green flames shot up and spread outward. The Uldra had installed their system throughout the city, in every neighborhood and along every major street. All of them were interconnected, so all of them were exposed to Vagris' simple, ruthless tactic. From the city center, Mary and the other survivors of Defiant Gate watched as the Northern Keep died.

The inferno followed the Uldra gaslamp system. A cascade of explosions turned into a horrifying symphony. The smaller detonations continued and were joined by others. The thunder of a thousand, thousand summer storms arrived all at once. Shockwaves hit them from all directions. Every pane of glass shattered. Stone and wood were crushed. Buildings were knocked aside. Carts and benches and merchant stands simply vanished, atomized. The firestorm followed, consuming everything left standing. Mary stood and watched the Northern Keep's death throes, unblinking and unthinking.

The heat reached them and was terrible. Mary could feel her flesh cooking. Her hair smoked as she shielded her face against the invisible, baleful avalanche. "Into the water!" someone shouted. Mary turned but, before she dove into the fountain, she glanced back at the cart of wounded. Ilse was dragging a guardsman into the water. Aloisa was tossing Amatria into the life-saving water, heedless of her own injuries. Rainer was standing in the cart, grimacing against his reddening skin as he handed the wounded out to others, leading a chain gang that moved their helpless comrades into the water. Mary joined in, helping as she could, and looked around for more to whom she could give aid once the cart was empty. Someone grabbed her, though, and bodily threw the handmaiden into the fountain.

The water was a blessed relief. Her flesh felt as though it was on fire, like the city itself. Mary closed her eyes and let herself float in the cool water. Last summer, she and Tomas had swum in the now-ruined gardens. She had passed to him the letter left by the Lady Alexia. He had shown her the note, instructing them both to enjoy their time together. Mary smiled, even as she let herself sink, at the memory of that day. She had removed her clothing artfully, strategically, letting Tomas see as much as he wished through those side-long glances he thought were so subtle. They had held their hands as they swam through the serene waters of the gardens. They had held each other, their exposed, purified bodies pressed close. She had encouraged him, sometimes needing to actually take his hand and move it to those places she wished to be touched. He had blushed, adding to the warmth of his hardening body, and the pleasure she felt at his touch.

Where was he now, Mary wondered as she sank deeper. No doubt her Tomas was riding alongside Prince Rogan. They were coming to her rescue, to save them from Vagris and Fak'Har. The day was young, but he was an early riser. He would be up and moving, demanding that they move faster. Perhaps he was already astride Urge, his great chestnut warhorse. Somehow, Mary knew that, even at that very moment, her Tomas was riding, pushing as hard and as fast as he could. He was on his way, with Prince Rogan, the Archaeknights, and General Killdare's army. She only had to…

Mary opened her eyes and forced herself to the surface of the fountain. The wounded, guardsmen, and watchmen were all around. The handmaiden helped some of those too weak to swim, moving them to the edge of the fountain where they could rest against the marble wall. Ilse, Aloisa, Rainer, and the others still capable also gave aid to the wounded. Mary looked to the colonel. "Fire brigade?" she asked.

The veteran shook his head. "Hopeless," he grunted.

"There has to be something!" the handmaiden insisted.

Rainer looked out on the burning city. He had sworn to defend the Northern Keep, Mary knew. His failure was unavoidable, undeniable. The colonel did not weep for his city or his people. He only stared at the flames, at the pyre his leadership had built. For weeks, Klug Rainer had been decisive in his every action, his every decision, his every movement. Now, Mary could only see a broken old man. His shoulders were slumped. The inferno dancing upon the broken remains of his home also caressed his weathered face. His scavenged shortsword was gone, with only an empty scabbard flapping uselessly against his leg. Rainer's hands were limp at his sides, lacking even the strength to form a fist in defiance of what the veteran saw. "It's over," Mary heard him whisper.

She stood, moving as best she could in the waist-deep water. The handmaiden moved to Rainer's side and put a hand on his arm. Mary turned him, forced his gaze away from the burning city, and to the frightened, demoralized, and wounded people in the fountain. "They are alive," she pointed out. "You duty doesn't end until they're safe."

Uncertainty clouded Rainer's face. He was about to speak, but Mary raised a hand. "Your daughter is still alive," she added. "If you want her to see another dawn, then you aren't allowed to give up."

Rainer looked to Ilse. Her priestess' robes were soot-stained and soaked. Her long hair was matted to her face, a face that was set in determination as she continued employing her training and her goddess-given magic to ease the suffering of the people around her. Ilse glanced at her father and smiled, not the bright smile of her joyful childhood, but the confident smile only a loving daughter can share with a good father.

Rainer saw this, and squared his shoulders. His hands tightened into fists, and his face locked, once more, in stoic determination. "Right," he said in a voice of command that forced back the flames, the heat, and the sullen despair that was the worst threat of all. The colonel looked about. "Every able body, strip and tie up your shirts! We don't have buckets, so we're improvising!" He glanced at the watchman. "Form your people up! We're making a bucket line!"

"To where!" The watchman demanded. "With what!?!"

Rainer grimly pointed to Castle Calonar in the north, rising untouched above the burning city. "If we have to," the colonel declared, "we'll move inch by inch, but we're getting to that castle!" Colonel Rainer, veteran of the House Guard and a hundred campaigns in the service of his Noble House, then returned to the bellow that had, for decades, been his best tool of leadership. "Now move your asses, you sorry sons of bitches!" he thundered.

Every able body amongst them obeyed. Those still wearing armor cast it aside. They stripped their shirts and tied the garments into bags. Every man stripped to the waist and added his clothing to the effort. Soon, they spread out into a double line, passing improvised bags full of water forward and empty bags back. The fountain, though no longer spraying, was still full. Under Colonel Rainer's leadership, the survivors spread themselves out from that blessed sanctuary, and took the water with them. They began pouring that life-saving fluid onto the burning street to the north, making a path to the sanctuary towering above them all.

Rainer barely glanced when he saw Mary join in the work. Beside her was Aloisa, also helping to move water forward. Every able hand and every useable piece of clothing contributed to the effort. Ilse remained with the wounded, keeping them alive and as comforted as possible, but she stripped free her robe, working in the thin shift beneath without qualm. Mary felt a momentary flash of shame at how quickly her friend had cast aside her modesty for the sake of others, and did the same. Aloisa noticed this and grinned, doing likewise.

Their progress was slow, but steady. The fire was a stubborn opponent, and their improvised bags leaked terribly. The advantage of this, however, was that each of them remained soaked in protective water as they battled the fire. The flames only reluctantly gave way, but were forced into a grudging retreat. The survivors gained ground, a foot at a time, as the morning gave way to midday. The smoke burned their eyes and their lungs, but they continued. They limbs ached and burned, but they continued. Floating embers, time and again, found their vulnerable skin, but the survivors continued. Each block north they moved was a titanic victory, and on they continued.

"This isn't working anymore!" Mary yelled over the roar of the flames. Their line had grown too long. They were now single file, passing the improvised sacks forward to continue the effort. But, by the time the bags would reach the front, all the water therein was gone, either escaped from holes or simply boiled away. The handmaiden shook the tied-up shirt, damp but otherwise empty, to emphasize the problem.

Rainer grunted. "There has to be a way!" he insisted.

From behind, there was a sudden chorus of surprise. Mary, Rainer, and Aloisa glanced back, and saw all the remaining water in the fountain suddenly rise up as though it were a living thing. Moving like some great ocean serpent of legend, the water rose and swayed, seeming as though it were looking about, before hurling itself to the left and right. A massive tide rushed against the burning buildings, forcing away the flames and the smoke, crashing again and again to beat back the inferno and form a safe channel for the survivors.

As one, they looked ahead. Vincent and a dozen grey-robed adepts had arrived on horseback. The student-mages were waving their arms and chanting in the language of magic. With them came a large group, perhaps a hundred or more, of the castle staff led by Roland. They had poleaxes and swords, carried litters and led extra horses. Mary saw this, and nearly collapsed in relief.

"It's about damned time!" Rainer barked.

Vincent rode forward, his young face showing relief nearly equal to that as Mary felt. "Sorry, sir," the spy said. "But we had a little..." his words failed. The young man's eyes had drifted past the colonel, to the fountain behind. He saw there Ilse, still with the wounded. Vincent stared at the priestess, the afternoon sun bright upon her singed hair and burnt shoulders. The spy charged his horse forward, uncaring of any other. He flung himself from the saddle and took Ilse into his arms. He kissed her and held her. He whispered her name as though it were the sweetest of magical incantations. Ilse, for her part, held him even tighter, tears flowing and kisses falling.

Aloisa handed Mary a large shirt, sniffing loudly. The handmaiden took the offered garment and, pulling it on, glanced at Rainer. The colonel's face betrayed conflicting emotions as he saw his daughter, still undressed for the effort to save their lives, was held in the arms of a man who clearly loved her. The father said nothing, but only nodded.

Chapter 37

Even with the newly-arrived help, the survivors needed most of the day to reach the base of the escarpment upon which Castle Calonar rested. Vincent, the grey-robed adepts, and the castle staff who had left behind the safety of their fortress-home all lent their aid, but still the trip was an arduous one. The inferno that had been the Northern Keep held the mercenaries back for most of the day. The flames that had threatened to consume Mary and her friends was equally dangerous to the invaders, and so they saw few signs of the enemy as they made their way north. Still, there were many wounded, most unable even to walk. The litters Vincent brought were insufficient and even the horses were too few. Again, Colonel Rainer ordered the improvising of nearby material, burnt wood and torn clothing offering the minimal requirements for improvised slings and litters. They had to leave behind nearly all weapons, all armor. Only Rainer himself and a handful of battle-capable guardsmen remained armed. All the others, including Mary, worked to carry or support those in need.

They had to stop and rest often. Smoke had formed a seemingly-permeant cloud over the dying city. The sun was nearly lost and the world had gone dark as night. Only the omnipresent glow of the inferno raging through most of the Northern Keep gave any illumination. Breathing was a chore, even for those without serious injury. Burdened with the wounded made every step a labor, every drawn breath a ragged gasp. Ilse had overseen the tearing of much of their clothing, including her priestess' robes. These, she soaked with whatever water the grey-robed apprentices could summon, and then ordered everyone to cover their mouths and noses. The wet cloth helped against the oppressive smoke, but only a little.

Mary felt as though she had somehow slipped into Underworld. The scene pressing in all around was exactly how the handmaiden had envisioned the infernal realm. Great, oppressive darkness clung to everything. Their weary, exhausted faces were illuminated only by the inferno's shifting red and orange glow. The heat was a living thing, searing flesh and scarring the soul. Every moving shadow held some threat of violation and violence. Worst of all, the only possible salvation lay in a shining fortress far overhead, often obscured by the hateful, choking darkness. Still, she and the others forced themselves onward, one step at a time.

At some point, the sun must have set during their slow trek. Aloisa was the first to spot the torches, and she pointed them out to Mary. The handmaiden looked, and saw pinpoints of light moving about the shattered ruins of her home. "Mercenaries?" she asked wearily.

The Gunrsvein warrior-woman, a comparatively-small guardsman braced against her powerful shoulder, nodded grimly. "They need light for the looting."

Mary cleared her throat of some smoke, spitting out a great wad of something dark. "How far?" the handmaiden asked.

Aloisa shrugged. "Can't say. Too much smoke. Not far."

"They'll be busy a while," Rainer grunted, shifting the weight of the wounded man he supported. "Vagris won't be able to organize them until the fire is out and the looting is done."

"Will they attack the castle?" Mary asked.

Neither warrior answered, but their faces, even concealed with wet cloth and soot, spoke clearly the answer. As they drew closer to the escarpment, the wandering torches grew in number and proximity. Sounds of fighting, sporadic and vicious, filled the air, as did the screams of women and children. Murder, theft, and rape added their own horror to the burning world. They found bodies in the street. Those homes not yet destroyed by the inferno were open and looted. Husbands and fathers lay with improvised weapons. Sons and brothers were similarly butchered. Few women or infants were to be seen though. "Slaves," Mary muttered darkly.

"The Xeshlin are dead," Aloisa reminded her, catching the handmaiden's thought. "But there'll be others."

"Nothing we can do," Rainer added. "We save who we can."

The mercenaries reached the gatehouse protecting the base of the escarpment before the survivors did. The sounds of conflict had been intensifying as they drew clearer. Moreover, they no longer heard the screams of victims and the laughs of celebrating mercenaries, but rather the bright steel-on-steel of professional conflict. Colonel Rainer halted their group, setting down the wounded and calling forward every able-bodied warrior. Mary stayed at the head of their group, with Aloisa and Ilse remaining as well. Vincent, however, moved forward, despite Ilse's brief protest.

The warriors disappeared into the smoke and darkness. Mary was tense, trying to breathe and to see through the pall of death and destruction. The sounds of fighting intensified, and she could hear Colonel Rainer's roaring commands. There was more steel striking against steel, more screams. Then, there was quiet. A few garbled shouts went back and forth before Vincent returned, wiping fresh blood from his shortsword. With him came not only Rainer and his warriors, but a large group of guardsmen, still wearing their armor and wielding their poleaxes.

"Grab the wounded," Colonel Rainer commanded. "Get them moving up the switchbacks."

Ilse ran forward and embraced Vincent. They held each other only a moment before she broke away and, with a brief hug for her father, returned to her oversight of the survivors. The fresh guardsmen assumed the burden of carrying the litters and the walking-wounded. Mary went forward with Aloisa, letting the large Gunrsvein woman lean on her shoulder as they went. The smoke cleared and they saw the guardhouse. The Oolaug River tributary that formed the castle's moat was littered with debris and dead. Its waters ran nearly black, only barely reflecting the red and orange of the inferno. The stone bridge crossing the moat was intact, though scarred with fire and violence. At their approach, the pair of iron portcullises were raised, allowing the wounded to pass through. Bodies were littered on either side of the near guardhouse, nearly all of them Vagris' mercenaries. The air seem clearer here, at the base of the escarpment upon which Castle Calonar stood. Mary could breathe for the first time in hours.

"What's your status?" Rainer was asking the sergeant of the guard.

"A handful of attacks," the guardsman replied. His helmet and chainmail were blood-spattered, but intact. Similarly, his poleaxe showed signs of fighting, but still gleamed in the feint light. Mary's heart rose at the sight of a uniformed, equipped, and battle-ready guardsman, especially one surrounded by so many of his fellows. "Probes, I think," the sergeant was continuing. "Small groups, for now."

"That'll change," Aloisa pointed out as she and Mary approached the two men. "Are there any other points of resistance?"

The sergeant shook his head. "We don't know. All contact within the city is lost. We can't see more than a few hundred yards from down here, and I'm told the visibility isn't much better from up there." He jabbed a finger up towards the castle. "There're rumors of surviving Guard units assembling at the barracks. Townspeople are either fleeing there, coming here, or heading towards the west gate."

"Why the west gate?" Mary asked.

"Vagris has called in all his forces," the sergeant replied. "There's nobody outside the walls anymore. People are hoping to get out and reach Woodwall."

"How many refugees have passed through here?" Rainer asked.

"Not many," the sergeant replied. "And none in the past few hours." The guardsman sergeant glanced about, leaning in so that the passing survivors would not hear. "Sir, orders have come from Princess Karen." The sergeant glanced at Mary and Aloisa.

"Go ahead," Rainer said. "At this point, we all need to know everything."

"Sir, the Princess had commanded that I'm to have the apprentice-mages destroy the bridge. She said I would know when to do it. I've been waiting, trying to give as much time for refugees as I can. Then that Vincent kid took the mages and went after you. He said the Princess sent him on a specific mission."

"You can do it now," Mary said softly. "You can destroy the bridge."

All eyes went to her. The handmaiden shrugged. "We'll be the last."

Aloisa nodded. "By now," the Gunrsvein woman said, "anyone who could make it here, has. Anyone who can't…"

"Let's do it," Rainer agreed. "Sergeant, let's get this last group through, then lower the portcullis on both sides. The grey-robes can blow the bridge and we'll all get up to the castle."

The wounded were moved across the moat as quickly as possible. A handful of the guardsmen went with them up the switchback road winding up to the castle. Most remained to seal off the moat. Aloisa, being wounded herself, could have gone with them, but the Gunrsvein warrior-woman insisted on remaining to supervise the grey-robed mages. They needed a great deal of time, being only apprentices. Mary watched with Colonel Rainer as the adepts-in-training took barrels of some sticky, viscous gel from several barrels and applied it across much of the bridge. To this shimmering layer of slime they added a dark powder.

"Couldn't they just use magic?" Mary asked as the grey-robes continued their world.

"Full wizards could," Rainer answered. "But these kids don't have the power or the knowledge. They have to do it the hard way."

"Colonel!" a lookout called from the city-side guardhouse.

Rainer and Mary looked to where the guardsman was pointing. A large group of mercenaries were forming up down the street. They were the typical assortment of killers, with weapons and armor from across Lanasia. All were pointing at the guardhouse and the bridge.

"Damn," Rainer muttered.

"What do we do?" Mary asked.

He glanced down at her, then at the road where Ilse and Vincent were supervising the last of the wounded as they began the climb up to Castle Calonar. The old soldier, veteran of so many campaigns, then called down to Aloisa. "How long?" he asked.

"Ten minutes!" she called back.

"Damn," the colonel grunted again. He narrowed his eyes at the mercenaries, who were getting into assault lines and clearly making ready to attack. Rainer nodded and looked down at Mary. "You've got one more job to do," he said.

"Colonel?"

"You're Princess Kyla's aide-de-camp, right?"

"I suppose. Though, no one's ever told me what that means."

"It means you bear witness," the old veteran said grimly. "You report back, and you make plans to keep these people alive." He turned and marched over to where the remaining guardsmen were checking their gear. "You," Rainer said, pointing at the youngest soldier. "Give me your gear."

"Sir?" the confused young guardsman blinked.

"You heard me," Rainer growled. "Hand over your gear and then help get the wounded up to the castle."

"Sir I-" The guardsman's protests were cut off by a hard look from the Colonel.

"What's your name, son?"

"Simon, sir," the guardsman replied.

"Simon." Rainer nodded towards his daughter and the wounded survivors. "That's your duty. Get those people up to the castle. Understood?"

The guardsman nodded and saluted once more. The young man then reluctantly stripped off is mail shirt and helmet.

Ilse walked up with Vincent. "Father?"

Rainer looked at his daughter. "Do your job," he said gently. "See to the wounded." He pulled the mail shirt over his head and shoulders, setting it in place. He then took Ilse in his arms and held her tight for a moment. "We're so proud of you Squirrel. Me, your mom, your brother. I'm so proud of my little girl, there are days I think I might just burst."

"Daddy," Ilse tried to say again, tears flowing from her eyes.

Rainer held her at arm's length, looking down at his daughter with a wide, proud smile. "I'll say hi to your mom and your brother for you." He then turned to Vincent.

"Sir," the young spy said. "I'll do it. I can-"

Rainer held up his hand, ending any objection. He then held that hand out, taking Vincent's in his. "You've got a job," the father said with a nod to his daughter. "Do it well. Live every moment for each other." The colonel took Simon's helmet and placed it on his head, then took up the young guardsman's poleaxe, another of the kind of weapon he had carried for so many years in service to House Calonar. He grinned as he looked down at Ilse. "How do I look?" he asked with a grin.

Ilse could say nothing, only stare at her father through veiled eyes. Her breathing was heavy again, though not from the smoke. She stared up her father as though burning the image into her mind, clinging to Vincent and trying to force back a tide of emotion that would destroy her.

Rainer turned and stepped away. He paused at Mary's side. "Help them," he said simply, and the handmaiden nodded. Aloisa had returned from the bridge, looking at her commander with curiosity. "Sir," she began to say. "What...?"

"You have command, lieutenant," Rainer said with finality.

"Sir-"

"One week. You hold out for one week. These people will survive. You aren't relieved until General Killdare and the Prince get home."

Rainer made to move past his lieutenant, but the large Gunrsvein woman stopped him with a hand on his shoulder. "Sir," she said.

"No," he replied with finality. "This is my job. You do yours."

She stood for a moment, her hand on his shoulder. Then, Aloisa briefly took Rainer into a rough embrace. "Thank you, sir," she whispered, "for everything."

Rainer smiled again, softly, and nodded to the Gunrsvien girl he had brought to the Northern Keep, taken into his family, and treated as one of his own. "Find happiness," he told her. "You deserve it."

Colonel Klug Rainer then marched forward. The remaining guardsmen formed up around him. Simon, the young soldier left behind, closed the near-side portcullis and broke the control lever. He then moved up the switchbacks, joining with the wounded who had paused in their trip up to the castle.

Beyond the gatehouse, the mercenaries were lighting more torches and bringing up incendiaries, no doubt to try and burn the defenders blocking their way. Rainer did not allow them the chance, though. He ordered the portcullis open and led his guardsmen out at a march. They quickly formed into a triple-line. The first line had its poleaxes extended, and Colonel Rainer led them from the center. The middle line held their weapons above the heads of the men to their front. The final line held their poleaxes high. The mercenaries abandoned their fire and re-formed into lines to meet the guardsmen. The first rank of invaders died screaming. Then the second. They tried to move around, to climb over the rubble to either side and flank the impenetrable wall of Northland poleaxes, but were met with the guardsmen's third rank. These flankers were cut down even as more of their compatriots fell to Colonel Rainer.

The mercenaries screamed as they died. They screamed in frustration as the grey-robes made ready to destroy the bridge, the only feasible way onto the switchback road leading to Castle Calonar. They screamed in agony as Northland poleaxes were stabbed into their torsos or slashed, separating limbs. They screamed for reinforcements to be brought up and screamed for a withdrawal. Those in the back died trying to advance. Those in the front died trying to retreat. Colonel Klug Rainer led an assault into the very teeth of the assembling enemy without pause.

More and more of the mercenaries were drawn to the battle. Like carrion eaters, they circled and gathered their courage to attack. Like buzzing insects, they flittered about, looking for an opportunity to feast. Like parasites, they tried to weaken, to latch onto some vulnerable spot, but found none. Dozens, then scores, and then hundreds of the invaders came, only to fall against the guardsmen of House Calonar.

Colonel Klug Rainer did not advance. He did not press the attack, despite his advantage of training, discipline, and commitment. He held his soldiers at the gatehouse and the bridge. He formed successive rings, encircling the only access to the bridge across the moat. The mercenaries tried to attack, and fell. More and more came, but they all died. This victory, this time desperately needed, was not without cost. First one, then two guardsmen died. A third, then a forth fell to a lucky strike or a cowardly arrow or just the press of numbers. Colonel Rainer held the line, but he lost his men. More and more soldiers in blue and grey lay amidst the rubble. The ring defending the gatehouse and the bridge contracted, until only a handful remained.

Ilse clung to Vincent, her breathing shallow and rapid. She could not be pulled away, could not even be made to look away. Both the young spy and Mary together tried to force her back, to spare her the sight of her father's final stand. At last, Aloisa arrived with the grey-robes. "It's time," she said in a hollow voice.

Ilse and Vincent remained silent, staring. Mary took a breath and said, "Do it."

Chapter 38

Roland escorted them up the switchback road. The trip took most of the rest of the day, burdened as they were by the wounded. They had no carts, no horses. They only had supportive arms and the improvised litters made from their tattered clothing. The climb was wearing, though more from the sights that greeted them than from the burden of so many who had suffered in the ill-fated defense of the city.

The Northern Keep was a burning ruin. As Mary and the other survivors, escorted by the castle staff who had come to their aid, climbed the switchback road, they rose above much of the smoke that clung to their home. The afternoon sun only grudgingly broke through the death-pall, and what it illuminated nearly destroyed what hope they still clung to. Some few budlings, scattered here and there, stood. Most were little more than rubble, a broken wall here, a hollowed frame there. The city's road system was still visible, but only because those paths were the only rubble-free lanes. Patches of fire still bloomed like the final gasps of a dying man, burning for a moment only to fade away.

Few of the great constructions of House Calonar remained. The Adamic Church was an empty shell, its sacred pool a blackened mire. The barracks of the House Guard was little more than a desecrated gravestone, already populated. The Temple of the Lady of Light still stood, but its pristine white columns were now charred bones, protruding from a dead city. The home of the Harvest Mother's clergy was similarly broken, half its walls were collapsed and those within now beyond saving. The great memorial at the center of the city, the fountain in which Mary and the other survivors had sheltered, was even now being stripped of its precious metals. The handmaiden felt nothing as the thought dawned upon her, the golden words of peace and acceptance, declaring the Northern Keep a sanctuary for all, were being torn apart.

Vagris' mercenaries were like ants feasting on a corpse. There was no cohesion, no military coordination among the invaders. They were scavengers, parasites scrambling about in their grisly feast. Mary did not know what treasures would remain after the city's fiery death. The mercenaries, though, seemed determined to uncover every one. Some of the evil men were visible through the funeral pall, loading their spoils onto horses. As they climbed higher, seeing more of their dead city, Mary noticed a great many of the mercenaries leaving, riding their horses out of the now-open gates.

"Will Vagris have any left to attack us?" Mary asked, almost to herself.

"Some will remain," Roland told her. The chief butler was supporting a young guardsman as they climbed, ignoring completely his aging body and old wounds. "There will be some who don't care about theft. They'll only want more killing and… other things." His greyed, wrinkled face was set in stone, but his weathered eyes spoke of having witnessed old atrocities.

The sun had slipped behind Ulheim by the time they reached the castle. The shadows of those great mountains, dark fingers grasping at the ruins of the Northern Keep, added to the gloom of the dead city. A cold breeze had arrived with the sun's departure, blowing away not only the last traces of summer's heat, but also pushing at the chocking miasma hanging over the city. In years past, Mary had yearned for that first autumn breeze. It normally carried the taste of home and hearth, of holidays and community. Last year, the arrival of autumn had celebrated her love with Tomas, the culmination of a long, vibrant romance. This time, however, that wind carried nothing but death.

The castle's courtyard was in chaos. The air itself sang a dirge of hopeless, aimless preparation. Rows of bodies, some breathing, most not, were laid out along one wall. Only a handful of Harvest Mother acolytes remained, lacking any supervision from seasoned clergy. No Adamic priests or Sisters of the Lady of Light were visible, no one to offer comfort against the coming night. The only guardsmen in uniform were young trainees or retired veterans, those who had been unable to join in the defense at the walls. Castle staff scurried about, trying to offer what help they could, but clearly not knowing what to do.

Roderick sprinted forward to help Roland. The stablehand took the wounded guardsman, and guided him to a nearby blanket. "What's our status?" Roland asked, unable to hide the relief his old body felt.

"The same," Roderick answered. He helped the wounded guardsman to the ground and rolled one end of the blanket to support the man's head. The stablehand then turned back. "There aren't any more refugees coming in, not since you left."

"There won't be," Mary said without feeling.

"The bridge has been destroyed," Roland confirmed. The old butler turned to a pair of downy-cheeked boys wearing the uniforms of House Guard. "Close the gate!" he ordered.

With a heavy, thunderous bang, once of finality, like the closing of a tomb's door, the great iron gates of Castle Calonar closed. There followed a moment of silence. All work in the courtyard ceased and all eyes turned to the gate. No one in living memory could recall the castle's gates being closed. Many, in fact, had thought them to be decorative, incapable of closing. Even when the Northern Keep had come under attack from the Inquisition, from Xeshlin raiders, even from the Greysoul himself, never had that gate closed.

More castle staff came forward and took charge of the wounded. They moved the moaning, weak survivors to what blankets remained, but without organization. This lasted only a few heartbeats before Ilse stepped forward. "Who's in charge of this?" she asked a grey-robed acolyte.

"No one," the girl replied. "We're just..." she shrugged.

"Alright," Ilse breathed. She turned to a group of too-young guardsmen. "You three," she said firmly. "Go into the castle proper and scrounge whatever wood you can. We need poles about the length of a man's body." The priestess then looked at a small group of Harvest Mother acolytes. "And you," she said, "start cutting cloth into squares, one yard at each side. We need more litters. You four," Ilse pointed to a gathering of castle maids. "Any excess clothing needs to be cut into bandages. Strips about four finger-lengths thick and the length of your arm. Then put them in boiling water until needed."

Many eyes went questioningly to Roland. The chief butler raised an eyebrow. "You heard her," he said clearly. "Get to work."

Ilse rapidly organized those of able body in the courtyard. She triaged the wounded, having those who could be saved moved together and organized according to need. She assigned acolytes to specific groups with specific tasks. Supplies were inventoried and distributed. Castle staff were dispatched to improvise what was needed. All of this Ilse did rapidly, but with grim determination, only incidentally accepting the cleric's robe one of the acolytes brought her.

Lieutenant Aloisa stood as steadily as her injuries allowed. Looking about, she called to Roderick. "Who's senior ranking among the Guard?"

The stablehand glanced at a few of the old veterans. "One of them, I suppose."

"No officers?"

"Just you, ma'am."

Aloisa sighed and nodded. She then moved to the veterans and began speaking with them.

"What about the royal family?" Mary quietly asked Roland.

The head butler grimaced. He glanced about then nodded to a quiet corner near the empty stables. "It won't be long," Roland told Mary quietly when she joined him. "Opfern tells me the King is barely breathing. The Queen is pouring all her magic into him, but accomplishing little. She's killing herself trying to keep him alive. The Twins are with her." Roland looked intently at Mary. "You know about their... abilities?"

Mary nodded. The great secret of House Calonar was the peculiar magic of the Tressalon twins. "They can't really control it though, can they?"

"The Queen is desperate," Roland answered. "Opfern says that she's trying to guide them through some means of using their magic to keep the King alive."

"Is it working?"

Roland could only shrug.

"And the princesses?"

"Kyla is almost ready. The child will come any day. I've assigned a few acolytes to care for her."

"What about Medaka?"

Roland nodded out, past the castle's walls. "She went out yesterday. She said she needed something from the Temple."

Mary's face paled. "She went out before the breach?"

The head butler nodded. "The lookout said they saw something strange happening at the Temple, after the mercenaries got in. Lights, explosions, strange magical... things. I suppose the Sisters put up some kind of fight." He glanced at Mary. "You saw the Temple?"

She nodded. "What about Cardinal Tain?"

Roland shook his head. "The last anyone knew, he was still at the Church. He and his priests were determined to keep the doors open."

A shouted commotion caught their attention. Across the courtyard, Aloisa was yelling at someone huddled against the wall. The cringing figure was wearing the tatters of a white cloak and had folded himself into a tight ball. Aloisa was pointing out towards the city and snarling accusations of cowardice. Finally, the lieutenant drew her leg back and started kicking the cringing figure.

A pair of veteran guardsmen moved forward and grabbed Aloisa, pulling her back. The cringing figure uncurled enough for Mary to blink. In the same moment, she was both shocked and completely unsurprised. "When did he arrive?" the handmaiden asked.

"He was the first one in," Roland answered. "We saw Defiant Gate explode and the reserves start to mobilize for defense. He came running through the castle gate less than an hour later."

Mary looked at Margrave Hans Wurst without feeling. The cringing nobleman, filthy and pathetic, had soiled himself under Aloisa's assault. He wiped blood and mucus from his nose and looked at Mary. He seemed as though he might say something, might try to invoke the relationship between them that had only ever existed in his mind. The handmaiden turned, putting her back to the coward and deserter, and started walking towards the castle's large doors. Roland fell in beside her.

"And Karen?" Mary asked.

"She's been busy at something," the head butler replied. "We're not really sure, but she's been moving about for days."

The great double doors stood open, and a similar chaos was inside. Mary climbed the steps, but paused when she saw Karen walking out. The two women shared a brief look, but neither spoke. Mary was well aware by now of the princess' Truthsight; there seemed little left to say.

"Where's Vincent?" Karen asked.

Mary nodded towards where Ilse was giving commands. Vincent stood at her side, looking as though he would never leave. During their climb up the switchback road, the pair had been inseparable. They had not spoken to each other. Vincent had offered no platitudes after the death of her father. He had not tried to lessen her grief. He had only held her close. Ilse, even now, leaned towards the young spy. Her voice and face radiated calm authority, even as her body seemed to reach for Vincent in search of support.

"Get him," Karen commanded.

"He needs to be with Ilse," Mary countered. Her voice was flat and immovable.

"Bring her as well," the princess replied. "We also need Aloisa." Karen turned to Roland. "Inventory our remaining supplies," she commanded. "We need enough for five days. The rest needs to be packed and made ready to move."

"Highness," the head butler stepped forward. He glanced about and lowered his voice so that only the three of them could hear. "Are we abandoning the castle?"

"Not quite yet," the Truthseer replied. "But soon."

Their small group, all that was left of the war council, met in an antechamber off the castle's main hall. This room, Mary realized, had been used by representatives of House Calonar to meet with minor functionaries and envoys from other nations. It was sparsely decorated, with only a single table and three chairs. The blue and grey carpet was rolled up and set against one of the walls. The windows were closed to retain as much of the day's warmth as possible, while also keeping out the smoke of the dead city beyond. Mary's eyes kept going to the House Calonar coat of arms hanging over the dark fireplace. The silver and white diamonds no longer gleamed as they once had, the handmaiden realized. The soot of the Northern Keep's death had penetrated even here.

"You need to go to Rashid's apartments," Karen was telling Vincent. "Make sure you're not seen. When you're there, you'll find Chandra leaving. Follow her, see what she's doing, then report back."

"I can't leave," Vincent said with finality. He and Ilse sat on two of the chairs, as close as possible to one another. He held the priestess' hand gently, but firmly, and their shoulders were touching.

"You must," Karen replied, staring at him. "You need to find out where she's being going."

"Why?" the young spy demanded.

"So she can know," Mary said softly. They all glanced at the handmaiden, who was standing at the window, looking out. The ruins beneath them still sputtered the occasional flame, and smoke still drifted into the uncaring sky. Beyond the Northern Keep's corpse, the charred, ruined forest lay dark and quiet, bereft of life. Nothing seemed to lay beyond the charred bones of Wildelves Wood. The world had fallen into night.

"What?" Vincent asked.

"That's how her Truthsight works," Mary explained without looking away from the gathering darkness. "She can only know something if someone else will learn it. She needs you to go find out whatever Chandra has been doing so that she can know it by looking at you. If you never go, you will never learn the information, and Karen can't know it by seeing your Fate."

They all glanced at Karen, who shrugged.

"Seems an awkward way of doing things," Aloisa muttered.

"I didn't make the rules," Karen said, somewhat sullenly.

Vincent glanced at Ilse. She forced a smile and nodded. "I've got work to do here, anyway," she said.

"Yes, you do," Karen agreed. "You need to organize the wounded and the castle staff. Anyone who can't contribute to the final defense needs to be ready to go once Vincent returns."

"Go where?" Ilse asked.

"And what final defense?" Aloisa demanded.

Karen sighed and rubbed her eyes. "There will be one, last attack," she told them. "Fak'Har will need time to recover from Defiant Gate. Once he does, he'll personally lead his monsters against the castle."

"What about Vagris and his mercenaries?" Aloisa asked.

"Once they finish looting the city, most of the mercenaries will desert. Vagris will also try to escape, once he gets word of Rogan's arrival." Karen looked Aloisa squarely in the eyes. "You've already been named commander of the defense," the Truthseer pointed out. "This is your final responsibility within that duty. You need to organize what forces remain. You need to buy enough time for as many people as possible to escape and for Rogan's team to arrive."

"How long do I need to hold?" the lieutenant asked.

Karen rubbed her temples and shook her head slightly. "It's unclear," she confessed. "There are a lot of decisions between here and there. A lot of people have to make a lot of choices. How long our relief takes depends on all of those choices."

"But they will get to us?" Ilse asked in a small voice.

Karen nodded. "At least some of Rogan's team and the Archaknights will reach us. How many and when..." the princess shrugged.

"How long?" Aloisa asked.

"Five days. Fak'Har will regain his strength and attack in five days."

"Well," the lieutenant mused, "that should be plenty of time. After all, he's got to get across the river and climb the escarpment."

"He'll arrive at the castle walls in five days," Karen insisted. "He'll use his creatures and his magic to reach us."

"Great," Aloisa muttered. She stood. "Alright, I'll get to work. We'll hold until the Prince arrives." The lieutenant marched out of the room.

Karen turned back to Vincent and Ilse. "Once you get back from learning what Chandra knows, you and Ilse will start leading the evacuation."

"If we need to defend the castle-" Vincent started to object, but Karen held up a hand.

"You and Ilse must lead the survivors to safety. You'll both be needed later, along with others I'll be sending with you. Take them west, to Woodwall. Once this is all done, we'll meet you there."

The couple nodded and stood, leaving Karen and Mary alone in the room. The handmaiden said nothing, only continued to stare out the window. "Aren't you going to ask?" the princess sighed.

"No," Mary replied. "There doesn't seem much point. You already said Prince Rogan's team is on their way. You said they'll reach us. At least, some of them, anyway."

"I can't see Tomas' destiny," Karen admitted. "He's Fatetouched: able to change the Wind of Fate. I don't know if he'll be one of those who reach us."

"Is that why Cyras Darkholm chose him?" Mary asked softly. "Why the Trickster Mage sent him here?"

"Not just the Trickster," the princess noted. "My mother, Aunt Alexia, and even Fak'Har. Everyone with some access to the Wind of Fate knew these events were before us. We all knew this war was coming, as well as what lay after. We all also knew that Tomas was Fatetouched and would have an important role in what was to come. Cyras and Fak'Har were likely trying to manipulate him into accomplishing their own goals."

"And you?" Mary asked. "What did the women of House Calonar want from him?"

"To meet you," the Truthseer admitted. "We wanted him to have some joy in his life, before all this had to happen." Karen sat wearily. "Tomas was Fated to come here. At least, certain people here were Fated to meet him, to get close to him. I think there's more to his destiny than I know, but I'm not experienced enough with the

Truthsight to figure it all out." The princess looked again at Mary, who continued looking out, past all the death, into the east. "Are you sure you don't want to ask?"

The handmaiden shook her head. "What comfort would knowing bring me?" she replied. "We'll either see each other, or we won't. I'd rather have the-"

"You'll see him again," Karen interrupted, almost with realizing. The words sprang from her lips of their own volition, as sometimes happened to the inexperienced Truthseer. "You will be reunited. That, at least, is Fated."

Mary said nothing. She continued looking out, to the east, as though searching for some hint of the next dawn. "So, what am I doing for the next five days?" she asked.

"Choosing."

The handmaiden turned back, facing the Truthseer.

"I need you to choose," Karen said softly. "There are a few people who will be important later. I'll make sure they leave with Ilse and Vincent. But there are others who can survive." The Truthseer again rubbed at her temples. "All their Fates are intertwined. None of them will be especially important, but they'll still have impacts on the world. It's like seeing tiny stones thrown into a river. They'll make small ripples, small changes, but nothing I can make sense of." Karen looked up at Mary, once more seeming like the young girl she really was. "I don't know how to separate out who lives and escapes the castle. I need help choosing."

"You need me to choose who lives and who dies." It was not a question.

The princess nodded. "Just like I've been doing since we came out of the ziggurat."

Chapter 39

Xaemus entered Vagris' pavilion, moving through the shadows to avoid notice. Within, the warlord himself was standing at the large table dominating the center of the tent, surrounded by the only four Bellonari who had survived the destruction of Defiant Gate and the inferno that had engulfed the Northern Keep. The Humans were visibly exhausted and filthy. Most, all except Vagris, were soot-stained, having only just escaped the great blaze that consumed Calonar's city. Three of the deadly warriors had wounds. Their armor was battle-scarred, and their eyes dropped as they struggled to focus on their commander's words.

"How many were lost?" Vagris asked.

"Almost half," one of the Bellonari replied. "All the ones enslaved by the Xeshlin are dead, and that was nearly a third of our force. Of the remainder, they charged into the city. Scouts opened the other gates within a few hours, letting the outriders in as well. When Fak'Har set fire to those gas lines…" the Bellonar, a Human from Tramaya, shrugged.

"What about the survivors?" Vagris growled.

"Once the blaze passed," another of the Bellonari, this one a Human from the Gwyndd Islands, said, shaking his head in disgust, "those jackals lost all discipline. Most are still in there, looting anything worth the taking."

"A few are indulging other appetites," the last, a Velarossi, added. "Whatever civilians survived the fire are being hunted down. The men and children are being butchered, the women are being made sport of."

Vagris waved the audible disgust in his subordinate's voice. "They've served their purpose," he declared. "They got us in. How many do we still command?"

"None," the Tramayan snorted. "Or nearly none. Some have already taken their plunder and fled south. Most of the rest are still scrounging the ruins."

"They'll flee just as soon as they have enough," the Gwyndd added. "Or once we try to reimpose discipline."

The Velarossi pointed to the map of the Northern Keep spread out on the table before them. "That castle's visible from anywhere in the city," he declared. "And so's that damned escarpment it's sitting on. The second we try to force the mercenaries to assault it, they'll break."

"Do we have anything left?" Vagris demanded. "Any viable force?"

"Just Fak'Har," the Velarossi replied. "Him and those things he created."

"Where is our employer now?" the Tramanese asked.

"Resting," Vagris grunted. "The duel exhausted him."

"And his creatures?"

"The Shadowed Mage has them at work on that ramp of his."

"How long to finish it?" the Tramanese asked.

"Normally, I'd say two or three months. Those creatures work nonstop, though. They need no rest, no food or water, and no overseers to force them onward. They'll have it ready in days, a week, at most."

"And Fak'Har will order the assault the moment it's ready," Vagris grimaced.

The Gwyndd leaned in. "If we're to leave," he said, "now's the time."

"The Brotherhood has little more to gain here," the Velarossi agreed. "We've broken the Northern Keep and scattered Calonar's forces. Even with only a handful of soldiers, that castle can withstand any siege."

"And we know Eigenhard is on his way," The Gwynnd added. "He'll have gathered his forces by now. Even if we were still at full strength, he and Killdare would outnumber us, and their soldiers would be far better trained and far more disciplined, than this rabble you've put together."

"And yet," Vagris argued. "There remains the point. Eigenhard is on his way. We're all sworn to kill the traitor."

"At the cost of our lives?" the Tramanese asked. "We have no viable means of engaging Eigenhard's forces. Any attempt to do so would only be suicide, a waste of our lives."

"There's the threat of the Shadowed Mage," the Velarossi pointed out. "Fak'Har has made his desires plain. He wants the Calonar girls. This entire adventure was predicated on our capturing or killing them. If we abandon this campaign before securing those women, the Shadowed Mage will almost certainly retaliate."

Vagris held up his hand for silence. "Are we all agreed that we should leave?"

Nods from each responded to his question.

"And are we also agreed that the Shadowed Mage is too dangerous, too unpredictable, to risk angering." Again a round of nods.

"Then I propose the following. We let the mercenaries continue their pillaging, using their disorganization as our excuse for inaction. We allow Fak'Har's creatures their time to build that ramp of his."

"The mercenaries will see it's construction," the Tramanese pointed out. "They'll know when it's ready."

Vagris nodded. "And they'll scatter when they think the order to assault the castle is imminent. That will cause confusion."

"And opportunity," the Velarossi added. "Cover."

Vagris nodded again. "We wait and we seemingly obey. When the time comes, Fak'Har has already said that he'll lead the assault himself. That will be our window."

The warlord glanced at the Gwynnd. "In the meantime, we'll need fresh horses and supplies ready at a moment's notice."

"Easier from inside the city," the warrior noted. "Further from Fak'Har's tent and notice. We can move ourselves in, acting like we're trying to restore order among the mercenaries, and stage near the northeastern gate. When the time comes, we all head there, get our supplies, and leave."

Vagris straightened. He brought his fist to his heart. "Blood, strength, and honor," he said.

The other Bellonari mirrored his gesture and his words. They all filed out, leaving their commander alone, staring at the map. Xaemus waited until the sounds of their movement faded, then stepped from the shadows, opposite from Vagris. "Where is she?" he asked.

The Bellonar General glanced up, annoyed. "And have you abandoned your duty to the Shadowed Mage?"

"As you intend to?"

Vagris snorted. "You have no more loyalty to that madman than I. Have you even made a single reconnaissance to the south or east since last I saw you."

"I have journeyed much these past days," the monster of Davenor replied. "I have seen much. What I have witnessed convinces me that my time here is at an end."

Vagris reached for a nearby decanter and poured himself a small glass of wine. "Then, we at last find ourselves in agreement on something."

"Where is she," Xaemus asked again. "I will not repeat myself again."

"The slave?" Vagris snorted. "I haven't seen her since you did whatever magical nonsense that was with her." He waved a hand. "An infertile Sylva is as useful as a lame horse. Take her, for all the good she is now. She's probably still in that tent."

Xaemus moved rapidly through the nearly-deserted camp. He did not bother slipping through the shadows, though there were those aplenty in the dirgeful night. Some few wounded mercenaries had made it back to their camp, only to find no assistance waiting. A few tents, scattered here and there, contained the moaning dying. Wounds gaped open, leaking crimson life onto the charred ground. The stench of infection forced itself into the mouth and nostrils, even through the heavy cloth Xaemus forever kept wrapped around his face. Any animal capable of carrying a man was long since taken and gone. The slave pens were empty, but for the rotting flesh of the victims of the Sorcerous Sisters. Even Fak'Har's blasphemous creatures were gone, now in the city constructing the Shadowed Mage's newest abomination.

Her tent was open and unguarded. Xaemus rushed in, and was himself surprised at his relief. She remained, kneeling at her small table, waiting as she always seemed to be. Even without the consideration of Vagris or the security of his warriors, still she wore the insulting garb of a slave. Still she was barefoot, her graceful limbs exposed to the jagged, desecrated earth. Her body was still on display, the ludicrous outfit forced upon her enhancing her wonderous body, rather than offering her the dignity of modesty.

As always, she was aware of him, when she should not have been. She looked up at him, her ruby eyes unwavering and unexpecting as they drifted past the great raven mane that flowed without restraint down the perfect marble column of her neck and around the graceful curves of her shoulders and breasts. There was no question in her gaze, for there never was. She did not press him for information or action. As ever, She of the Ebon Tears only waited.

"Our time of departure has come," the monster of Davenor declared.

"My owner?" Her voice, when she blessed him with it, was the song of winter: perfectly cool and yet possessing indefinable power.

"Your owner no longer. You are free, as you have been all your days, and must be for all those that remain. I swear it."

"His soldiers?"

"Dead or deserted. He is alone, but for a handful of his Bellonari. Even now, they plot their escape, as well."

"The Coven of the Puma's Leash?"

"Dead. A few of their lowest, unenthralled males may yet live, but they are scattered."

"And the Shadowed Mage?"

"No threat to you." Xaemus felt as though he were swelling, growing in strength and determination. The monster of Davenor fell away as he knelt before She of the Ebon Tears. "I swear to you that no threat will ever again besiege you. No shadow shall ever again befall you. No power shall ever again stand against you. I bind myself to you, for all my days, if you will accept me. I swear myself to your service and your defense, if you will accept me. I will be yours, in this world and the next, if you will accept me."

She of the Ebon Tears stood, looking down at him. She placed a light, blessed touch on his chin, raising him so that his gaze of burning blood met hers of radiant ruby. "I have no tears to enthrall you," she reminded him. "There can be nothing between us, except a promise."

"My promise shall be more binding than any tear, any oath, any spell or curse. I am yours, if you will be mine."

"Bare yourself to me," she commanded.

Xaemus hesitated. For years, since his encounter with the mad Uldra, Beraht, he had kept his flesh hidden. Since time immemorial, the *Sy'lva'i*, and their hated *Xesh'lin* cousins, had flaunted their physical beauty. They bore their faces and bodies, knowing how envious the lesser races were for the perfection they had been granted by the *Sa'kai*. But Xaemus was a thing scarred, deformed. He was the monster of Davenor, twisted into a hideous grotesque by the mad Uldra and his axe. He kept that shame forever hidden, safely concealed. Even to She of the Ebon Tears, he had only ever revealed a portion of his disfigurement, and then, only from the safety of deep shadow.

"Bare yourself to me," she again commanded.

With trembling hands, Xaemus obeyed. He pulled back the dark hood and removed the cloak. He slowly let drop the heavy cloth covering his hideous face, and opened his shirt. All of this, all the defenses he had against the gaze of those who might see his monstrousness, he let fall to the ground. He remained kneeling, his head bowed in shame, unable to see what must be revulsion in the radiant ruby eyes of She of the Ebon Tears.

Once again, she blessed him with a light touch. The very tips of her fingers took his chin and raised his face. Her strength should have been as nothing, and yet, her touch was as irresistible as the winter storm. He looked up, and saw into her face... compassion. She looked at him, not with revulsion, not with scornful mockery. She looked into his eyes of burning blood with tenderness. Her gaze of radiant ruby did not move to his scars, his malformed chest or his twisted face. Those eyes, like the dawn of a new day after a horrific night, only open to him, welcoming him. She did not see the twisted body of the monster of Davenor. She saw only Xaemus.

"For all my trials, I welcome your aid," she said in the ancient *Sy'lva'i* tongue, furthering the ritual as old as the *Sy'lva'i* themselves. "For all my threats, I welcome your protection. For all my nights, I welcome your touch." She bent down then, and forever locked his eyes with hers. "You are mine, and I am yours." They both closed their eyes and parted their lips. She took his face in her hands and brought her face to his. The last words, the completion of the ages-old ceremony, she breathed into his soul. "May it be now, and forevermore."

Chapter 40

Xaemus, companion to She of the Ebon Tears, left her in the tent. He had wanted for them both to leave, to vanish into the night together. She had objected, and reminded him of her state of undress and their need of transportation. Xaemus could slide between the shadows, but she had no such ability. She would need clothing fit for travel, and a horse upon which to ride. As was now his sworn duty, he left to acquire for her the things she needed and desired.

The mercenary camp was far too deserted. There would be few supplies, if any. Thus, Xaemus had to enter the ruins of the Northern Keep in search of what they needed. This offered few opportunities, but he knew there would be some. Vagris' mercenaries were scattered throughout the dying city, seeking anything of value. There would be horses here, and clothing. In fact, the mercenaries' actions would be advantageous to Xaemus. He would not have to ransack house after ruined house in search of supplies. The sell-swords would have done all that work for him. He had only to find some of Vagris' men.

He moved quickly, forgoing his usual emphasis on stealth. Time was short, shorter even than Vagris or Fak'Har knew. Xaemus' eyes of burning blood went to the great ramp under construction. Only hours had passed, and already the evil thing rose above the broken rooftops. Fak'Har's creatures had begun at the city center, using the ruins of the old fountain that had once stood there for their first construction materials. Layer after layer of earth and stone and wood and even decaying flesh were heaped, one upon another. The black-armored creatures did not move quickly, but did their work instead with an unrelenting purpose. Even in the few moments Xaemus spent watching, he could see the ramp rising higher and higher. Days only would be needed before Fak'Har would assault the castle.

That is, if he had the chance.

Fak'Har had given Xaemus a great many duties in the months of his employ to the Shadowed Mage. He had performed many detestable actions, from freeing prisoners meant for Ubelheim to assassinating leaders of House Calonar's military. He had cut off communication by slaughtering messengers and mages. He had done all this in the expectation that Fak'Har would reveal to Xaemus the location of Kelinva, his Dark Empress. The last of his assignments had been reconnaissance. He was supposed to be ranging far to the south and the east, giving warning once the rallied forces of House Calonar approached. Xaemus was supposed to give the alarm when Eigenhard and Killdare were within striking distance.

What neither Fak'Har nor Vagris knew was that Xaemus had found another purpose for his hated life. He was no longer sworn to the service of the Dark Empress. He no longer cared for discovering Kelinva's newest incarnation or bending himself to her. Instead, he was now the companion to She of the Ebon Tears. After two centuries of searching, at last he had found one worthy of his devotion. He had no use for the Shadowed Mage's information, and so no longer performed those duties demanded for that payment. Instead, he had spent the past days watching, protecting, and waiting. Fak'Har's behavior at Defiant Gate had been the catalyst. The fool had invoked the dread language of Underworld and brought down a curse upon himself. He would infect all those around him until he was inevitably dragged into the waiting maws of the Umbra.

In fact, that curse was already manifesting.

Vagris had thought it was Fak'Har who had ignited the gas lines. Xaemus had been there. He had seen the Umbral shadows reaching out, breaking the lines across the city. He had seen the sparks of insidious magic. The burning of the Northern Keep had not been Fak'Har's intent, it had been his curse. What was more, Xaemus had long since spotted the advanced scouts and messengers moving back and forth from the south and the east. Eigenhard would not arrive alone, nor would Killdare. Instead, Fak'Har's curse insured that both their forces, either one of which more than enough to destroy Vagris' survivors, arrived together. They would be upon Fak'Har and Vagris within days. Had Xaemus still desired the location of the Dark Empress, he would have told his former employer. Instead, he remained silent, and made ready an escape for She of the Ebon Tears.

Together, they would leave this place. Where they would go, Xaemus did not know and was uncertain as to whether he cared. He would be at her side, wherever she journeyed. That was enough for him. Even now, moving rapidly amidst the ruins of the Northern Keep, he felt the serenity of purpose. She had expressed her command, her desire to be away from this place. He would see that fulfilled.

Xaemus found the three mercenaries outside what had likely been a shop. The Human males were laughing and toying with a Sylva. She was aging, though not yet elderly, still holding much of the beauty of her youth. Her matronly body spoke of at least one child in her long life, though likely that was long ago. Now, her dress was in tatters, burnt and nearly useless. How the Sylva had survived the city's burning, Xaemus did not know, but her great mane was burnt short, now barely falling to her shoulders, and her flesh was reddened.

The mercenaries had encircled her, forcing the Sylva to a corner of her destroyed shop. Her opalescent eyes shed tears, though her face seemed resigned. Enough of her body was exposed that, even had the Humans not been otherwise inclined towards dishonoring her, their weak minds would be enflamed now. They dropped their weapons as their approached her, leering and almost trembling in anticipation of the attack. One was even already opening his clothes in his eagerness to feel the press of her flesh.

The first died silently. The second, the creature who was opening his clothes, followed almost immediately after. The third whirled, his hand going to a weapon that was lying behind Xaemus' left foot. Panicked eyes went to the Xeshlin's weapon, and then back to the warrior himself. Realization must have had dawned upon his primitive mind, because the doomed fool turned as though to flee. He managed a single step before his own head was sent tumbling to join his fellows.

"Will you take me to your priestesses?" The Sylva's question carried a note of resignation. Xaemus had heard that same tone before, in the voices of his hated race's many victims. Some tried to fight, others to flee. But inevitably, there came a moment when those captured by the *Xesh'lin* realized that they must be given to the Sorcerous Sisters, that they were doomed to a horrid, torturous death.

Xaemus turned his eyes of burning blood to the Sylva. "Not since I slaughtered my Coven have I doomed any to the knife of the Sorcerous Sisters," he answered. "Nor will I ever. You are free."

The Sylva looked at him in confusion. "You are the monster of Davenor, are you not?" she demanded.

Xaemus glanced around the ruins of her shop. There were still some tattered bolts of cloth, some boxes and mirrors and other indicators of her trade. "You are a seamstress, are you not?" he asked.

"Once."

"As I was the monster of Davenor, once."

The Sylva looked at him in curiosity. "Then, what are you now?"

"I am the companion of She of the Ebon Tears. She would not want you enslaved or otherwise dishonored." Xaemus nodded beyond the ruins of her shop. The mercenaries had tied up five horses. Three of these were loaded down with the spoils of their plundering. "I have need of only two of those," he told the Sylva. "The other three, and what they carry, are yours. Do with them as you will. I have seen other survivors escaping to the west."

Without another word, Xaemus moved out of the ruined shop, to the waiting horses. He untied two and mounted one, preparing to leave. He heard the Sylva's voice, from the charred doorway. "Thank you," she said.

Xaemus did not know what to say in response. In his two centuries, he had never heard those words spoken to him. In all his travels, all his actions, no one, not the

Coven that had made him, not any of his victims, and certainly not any of his employers, had ever before spoken those words to him. He half-turned in the saddle, glancing back at the Sylva seamstress. She stared at him through her opalescent eyes, the same kind of eyes that had only ever looked at Xaemus in hatred and fear. The companion of She of the Ebon Tears could only offer an awkward nod before leaving.

Xaemus returned to the mercenary camp. On his way out of the ruined city, he had come upon another small group of mercenaries. Like their compatriots, they had been looting, but unlike the others, these Humans, showing more foresight that most Humans seemed capable of, had also ransacked a restaurant for food and supplies. The bodies of the family, Sylvai by the looks of them, lay scattered over tables and on the burnt ground. The mercenaries had barely bothered cleaning their victims' blood from their weapons before looting the restaurant, not only of silver or other valuables, but also of the foodstuffs contained therein.

Xaemus said nothing to the Humans as he killed them. He was not avenging the Sylvai family, these restauranteurs who had only died in the protection of their home and their business. In truth, Xaemus cared little for the portly Sylvu and his children. They were dead, and thus no longer of any concern. However, the supplies the mercenaries were stealing would be of great use to Xaemus and She of the Ebon Tears. He did not think she would mind his killing of these murderers, and most certainly not in the pursuit of resources they would need. Therefore, their deaths were quick and almost unworthy of note.

The companion of She of the Ebon Tears tied up the two horses, one with a riding saddle, one burdened with supplies, at the edge of the encampment. His weary eyes of burning blood were everywhere as he approached her tent. This was the time of greatest uncertainty, of vulnerability. Should any of the mercenaries come back, or realize what he was doing, should anyone warn the Shadowed Mage, all could be lost.

Xaemus reached her tent, and stopped, a great, familiar darkness returning to his soul.

Fak'Har stood outside her tent, looking directly at Xaemus.

They stood thus, for several moments. Neither spoke. Neither moved.

Finally, the Shadowed Mage grinned at Xaemus. "I have one last task for you," he said in the hissing tongue of the Xeshlin.

"And if I refuse?" the companion of She of the Ebon tears replied in *Sy'lva'i*.

Fak'Har held up his hand. A lock of her raven hair was caught between his fingers, trying to escape in the gentle breeze.

"Where is she?" Xaemus asked, his voice as cold and undeniable as Death Herself.

"Don't bother," Fak'Har replied, waving the hand holding her hair. "I've already sent her away. You really shouldn't have left her alone here, you know."

Xaemus raised *Queltuasor*, the poisoned double-blades forged at the command of the Dark Empress herself that had struck fear across the world for more than two centuries. The companion of She of the Ebon Tears lowered himself into a combat stance and commanded his body to readiness. "I will not ask again," he declared.

"And you'll never find her if you try anything foolish," the Shadowed Mage declared. Fak'Har summoned a stool out of the darkness and sat upon it, seemingly unconcerned at the barely-contained violence only a few feet from his exposed throat. "Don't worry, I only need one last little favor, and then you and she can go off and do... whatever it is you think you'll do. If you succeed, I'll release her to you, unharmed. Otherwise, as I said, you will never find her."

Xaemus forced his body to uncoil, forced the quiet calm that preceded his doing terrible violence on another living creature back into the far corner of his mind. "Speak," he said.

Fak'Har glanced over his shoulder. Castle Calonar rose above the dead city. Even in the night's moonless darkness, the castle was visible atop its great escarpment, as was the ramp rising to meet it. "My assault will be a little uncontrollable," the Shadowed Mage admitted. "There's no telling what will happen once my creations breach those walls." He snorted and rolled his hateful eyes. "Quite literally, in fact. The Prophecy is utterly silent about what will happen once my attack begins. You will infiltrate Castle Calonar and bring me the younger of his daughters."

Xaemus narrowed his eyes of burning blood. "I thought your interest lay with Kyla."

Fak'Har shrugged. "Things change. I've already taken care of her pregnancy. Better to start fresh with some other woman with a great magical lineage. The younger Calonar daughter though, has inherited the Truthsight. She's as yet unskilled in its use, but still a formidable obstacle. I'll need to control her as we move into the Inversion."

"You want me to kidnap a girl-child and bring her here," Xaemus stated.

"Not here." Fak'Har nodded to the south-east. "Take her to Citta Muore in the Rainer Mountains."

"The Velaross Duchies are a war zone," Xaemus pointed out. "Between the Gwyndd and Xeshlin invasions, to say nothing of the idiot dukes themselves, that will not be an easy trip."

"But that is where you will go," the Shadowed Mage replied with a grin. "You will take the younger daughter of Calonar to Citta Muore. I'll meet you there after my business here is concluded. We'll swap girls there."

"And if you do not survive your business here?"

"I will. No matter the resolution of the castle, I'll survive and go to the Velaross Duchies. Regardless, though, my servants have your Dy'lnnd with them. They will be at Citta Muore in two months."

Xaemus narrowed his eyes of burning blood.

"And if you show up without the Calonar daughter," Fak'Har advised with a raised finger, the one from which her lock of hair still dangled, "they'll destroy her body and soul. You only get your Dy'lnnd back if you arrive with Karen Calonar."

The Xeshlin stood rigid for a moment. Then, he nodded the briefest of nods. "So be it."

Chapter 41

"How long?" Kyla asked wearily.

"Another few days," Mary answered.

Both women were on the princess' balcony, ostensibly for fresh air. In reality, Kyla had insisted on seeing the ramp for herself. Mary had arrived that morning, almost desperate for some relief from the onerous duty Karen had forced upon her.

"How many have you gotten out?" Kyla asked, her pearlescent eyes locked on the hideous construction inching its way towards them.

"Two hundred," her handmaiden replied, also with eyes locked on Fak'Har's newest attack. Castle Calonar rested on a great escarpment, a tall hill with steep slopes on all sides. For centuries, the fortress had seemed impregnable, unassailable by any enemy. The Shadowed Mage was now proving that belief utterly false. "Ilse and Vincent are organizing more groups."

"That's good," Kyla nodded. She stared as the monstrous creatures, the blasphemous knights of the Shadowed Mage's creation, continued their work. For days, the black-armored things crawled across the ramp like insects, like horrific beetles, pushing rock and wood and chunks of things best left unidentified. More and more of the ruined city was stripped for materials and carried or dragged to the ramp. It now rose higher than any remaining structure in the Northern Keep, save for Castle Calonar. "When do the evacuations continue?"

"I've already picked the next seven groups," Mary said in a hollow voice. Her eyes went from the horrid construction out beyond the walls. Her gaze did not even pause at the great hole where Defiant Gate had once proudly stood. Instead, she once more sent her eyes and her hopes out, beyond her castle-prison, the ruined city, and even the immolated forest. Somewhere, to the east, Tomas was on his way. With him came Prince Rogan, Baroness Aebreanna, Sir Beraht, the Archaeknights, and the great army of General Killdare. "They'll be ready to go as soon as Ilse and Vincent finish organizing their supplies."

"Two hundred and seventy survivors," Kyla noted. "And more tomorrow." The princess glanced at her handmaiden. "And we know they'll be safe?"

Mary nodded. "You sister said so. All the mercenaries are here in the city, or fleeing south. The survivors will reach Woodwall in a few weeks." She looked to Kyla. "We can still get you and your family out, your Highness."

Kyla, beloved first daughter of the King and Queen and jewel of House Calonar, grimaced, putting a hand to her massively-swollen stomach. "His Highness here is not up for travel," she said in mock irritation. "For good or bad, this is where I'll deliver."

Mary put her own hand on Kyla's, both of them holding on to the future heir of House Calonar. "Any day now?" she asked.

Kyla nodded. "Any day. Medaka..." The princess' eyes misted. There had been no word of the Sister since she had left and disappeared into the inferno that had consumed the Northern Keep. A chance remained that Medaka had escaped the ruins, along with some others. From the castle, lookouts had spotted a great many people fleeing the city and its invaders, heading west. However, few believed Medaka would abandon them in such a way, least of all Kyla and Mary. "Before she went out, Medaka said the labor pains would begin soon."

Mary glanced back at the two Harvest Mother acolytes, both collapsed on cots in the princess' rooms, exhaustion having finally overwhelmed them. "We really should have Ilse up here," the handmaiden said, not for the first time.

"She has more important things to do besides hovering over me," Kyla replied firmly. "And so do you, you know."

"The choices are made for the day," Mary shrugged. "My job is done, for now. Besides," she smiled at her princess. "A handmaiden's duty is at her lady's side."

Kyla rolled her pearlescent eyes. "You really have to stop calling yourself that," she reprimanded. "You're not a handmaiden any more. You and Tomas both received his patents of nobility. You're Mary, the Baroness of Pelsemoria and my lady-in-waiting."

Mary shrugged away the titles, looking once more at the great ramp reaching towards them, visibly growing like some horrid finger, pointing its way to their doom. "Maybe," she whispered.

"Karen told me last night that she saw you and Tomas reuniting."

Mary nodded. "She told me."

"You don't believe her?"

"No, I believe her. The Truthsight has never been wrong. But it has been... misleading."

"She's still new to it," Kyla objected, rising to her little sister's defense.

"I know. Tomas and I... we'll be together. But when, where," the handmaiden shrugged.

Kyla held her friend's hand even tighter against her swollen stomach. Her son seemed to reach out as well, offering comfort, even from the womb. "Have faith," she whispered, glancing back at Fak'Har's ramp. "It's all we have left."

A knock started the acolytes to wakefulness. One went to the apartment door and admitted Vincent, who came out to the balcony. "We're dispatching the next group," the young spy reported. "Another will be leaving within the hour."

Kyla nodded. "Good. Still no signs of trouble?"

Vincent shook his head. "The passage is clear. I walked its length again last night. And the area around its exit is on the outer edge of the gardens. The mercenaries are all avoiding that area."

"Nothing to steal," Mary sniffed.

Vincent shook his head. "I think it's more than that," he argued. "When they first began sacking the city, our lookouts spotted several groups heading towards the Sylvai Shrine. There were… disturbances. Lights, sounds, strange winds. A few men were seen running away, and the mercenaries have been avoiding the gardens ever since." He nodded out, towards the empty fields that had once, seemingly a lifetime ago, been the lush city gardens. "Even the fire didn't reach into the gardens."

"The Uldra gaslamps weren't installed there," Kyla pointed out.

"Maybe," Mary mused, her narrowed eyes going to the gardens and her memory to the structure resting beneath them.

"What is it?" Kyla asked.

"Secrets," Mary answered. "Secrets and mysteries."

"You sound like my mother."

"The Queen is wise," Mary said piously, and Kyla punched her in the shoulder.

"Speaking of," the handmaiden continued, looking back to Vincent. "Were you able to convince them?"

The young spy shook his head. "Opfern still isn't letting anyone in. I was about to force the issue, but the Queen herself came out. She still refuses to move the King. He's…" Vincent's eyes went to Kyla as his words failed.

"He's too weak to survive the trip," Kyla finished sadly. "I saw him last night. He can't be moved, and we're not leaving without him."

"At least, we could move your sister," Vincent suggested. "We should ensure the safety of someone in the House."

"Good luck with that," Mary snorted.

Kyla nodded ruefully. "Whatever comes, House Calonar makes its stand here."

They were quiet for a time, watching the nightmare monsters continue at their work, raising the ramp closer and closer. Aloisa had the handful or archers left to her fire a few shots that morning, probing, but to no avail. The range was fine, but none among the boys or aging veterans left to defend the castle had the skill or strength to properly engage Fak'Har's creatures. Arrows went wide or struck the heavy, black-enameled armor and fell away, useless. So, the Gunrsvein lieutenant had ordered them to save their remaining ammunition for the final assault.

"Any clue where Chandra went?" Mary asked.

Vincent shook his head. "I scouted the area where the passage exited, but couldn't find any sign of her. She might have spotted me. I thought about a further reconnaissance, but Princess Karen was clear that I needed to return with news about the tunnel. I wanted to go out again, but Ilse said no."

"Any sign of Rashid?"

Vincent shook his head. "With all the activity in that tunnel now, Chandra's got no way back into the castle so, whatever she's up to, she's stuck out there."

Kyla pursed her lips. "All this time," she mused, "we thought Rashid was suffering from the separation, from being away from Aebreanna too long. We though his trouble came from their forced enthrallment. That's why she hasn't left the city very often." The princess glanced back at Vincent. "Could we have been wrong? Rashid had problems whenever he spent too much time away from Aebreanna, but never this bad, even for long separations. Could it have been Chandra doing something to him?"

"There's just no way of knowing, princess," Vincent admitted. "I don't know much about Sylvai enthrallment, and Aebreanna was always resistant to talking about what happened after the Greysoul kidnapped her. She was especially silent about the enthrallment with Rashid. Without more data, I just can't answer that."

They were quiet again.

"Oh," Vincent chuckled, glancing at Mary. "I caught your boyfriend again."

Mary made an exasperated groan. "How many times is this?" she asked.

"Five. The noble Baron of House Wurst has tried five times to sneak out with the women and children. For this latest attempt, he actually put on a dress."

Kyla snickered, but Mary only rolled her eyes once more.

We could just execute him for desertion," Vincent half-heartedly suggested.

"He isn't worth the time or the effort," Mary nearly spat. "Just forget about him."

"Do you have any idea where the tunnel came from?" Kyla asked, changing the subject again. "Who built it or how?"

Vincent chuckled. "Actually, that's one mystery I was able to solve." He reached into his tunic and pulled out a scrap of parchment. "I found a couple of arcane marks inscribed on either end of the tunnel. One of them was at the entrance, here in the castle, and the other was at the exit, at the edge of the gardens." He handed the parchment to Kyla.

The princess looked at it in open-mouthed shock. Mary leaned over to see. One of the marks was a bizarre confusion of lines, turning back in on itself like some impossible knot. "Who's mark is that?" she asked.

"The Trickster Mage," Vincent answered.

The other, even Mary, as uneducated as she was in magic, could identify. Every adept in the world of a certain power adopted some mystical sigil, some sign that was their personal identification within the Winds of Magic. This one, every citizen of the

Northlands knew within their very souls. Two birds, one light, the other dark, flying in tandem around the crossed-diamonds of House Calonar. "Lady Alexia," Mary breathed.

Vincent nodded. "And that stonework is pretty worn," he said. "It looks like the tunnel was part of the original construction. Remm could have told us exactly, but I'm guessing that, when Castle Calonar was being built, Cyras Darkholm and the Lady Alexia joined their power to build a hidden passage very nearly to the edge of the city."

Kyla held the parchment against her heart, closing her pearlescent eyes and whispering a prayer to her aunt, the matriarch of her Noble House. "She knew," Mary said aloud. "Years, centuries ago, she knew this all would happen."

"And gave us a means of escape," Vincent agreed.

Kyla smiled, beaming a renewed hope, not only for her House or her people, but for life itself. Then, her smiled suddenly vanished and her brow furrowed. She squinted and curled, her face grimacing into an ugly knot. "Platypus!" she said in a hoarse, choking growl.

"Platypus?" Vincent repeated.

"Ohhh, flabbergasted," the jewel of House Calonar said then.

"What?" the spy stared in confusion.

Mary held her princess, straining to support her greatly-increased weight. "Breathe, Highness!" she said uselessly. "It will pass!"

"What in Underworld is happening?" Vincent demanded.

"It's a contraction, idiot!" Kyla snarled at him and his entire gender.

"It's time!?!"

The two acolytes darted out onto the balcony. "It's time!?!" they both repeated.

"IT'S NOT TIME YOU-" Kyla's outburst cut shot as she suddenly took a deep breath, able at last to uncurl.

"It's not time," Mary repeated in a calmer, yet still annoyed, voice. "Medaka warned us that there would be contractions before labor truly began."

"So, what do we do?" Vincent asked.

"Oh, I'll tell you what to do!" Kyla snapped. The princess then stopped and, with wide eyes, looked down. "Dammit! I pissed myself!"

"It's alright, Highness," Mary said soothingly. "We'll get you into a nice bath."

An amused snicker drew every feminine eye to Vincent. The young spy, instantly recognizing his folly, took a half-step back. Kyla's gaze began to burn, to seethe with pearlescent power as a nimbus of mystical energy began steaming off the raging jewel of House Calonar.

"Highness," Mary said carefully. "Remember, no magic."

Kyla took several deep breaths, struggling to restrain the mystical onslaught onto this offending male for fear of the damage it could do to her unborn son. At last, the shining aura dimming back into her skin, the princess just told Vincent, "Run."

He did.

Chapter 42

Mary met with the other leaders left in Castle Calonar in their small antechamber. "This is the last of the groups," she said, handing over a list of names to Vincent.

"We still have time," Ilse insisted, ever at Vincent's side.

In response, Mary looked at Karen, seated once again at the small table. The Truthseer shook her head. "That will be the last possible group out," the young princess told them. "You have all the names. We'll need to seal the tunnel before the assault begins."

"The ramp isn't finished yet," Vincent pointed out.

"It will be," Aloisa countered. "Tomorrow morning. Midday, at the latest."

"Dawn," Karen replied quietly. "They'll have the ramp finished at dawn. The assault will come at midday."

"Wait." Ilse was looking at Mary's final list. "There are only eight names on this. The groups have all been of ten or twelve."

"You two will be in that last group," Karen said.

"What?"

"No!"

The princess held up a small hand. "You both have important choices ahead of you. Our people will survive this, and another conflict lies ahead. The people will need someone to lead them to the safety of Woodwall. I must remain. Aloisa needs to command the defense." Mary noticed that Karen could not bring herself to look at the Guard lieutenant.

The Gunrsvein woman nodded. "I could never run from a fight anyway," she added.

"And I doubt anyone could convince Mary to leave," Karen pointed out with a smile at the handmaiden.

"Your sister's contractions are continuing," Mary reported. "Her water could break at any moment. I'm staying."

Karen nodded and looked back to Vincent and Ilse. "That only leaves you two. To be blunt, we don't need a spy right now. And all the wounded who can be saved are among the refugees. You're our only remaining cleric. Your duty is to them."

"My duty is to House Calonar," Ilse objected. "As was my father's and my brother's!"

Mary crossed the room and took her dearest friend into her arms. "They did their duty," she whispered. "And now you do yours, as we all do." The handmaiden stood back, holding on to Ilse's hands. "My place is at Kyla's side. Opfern is staying with the King and Queen, helping the Twins. Aloisa is leading our last defense. Your duty is to lead the people to safety."

Ilse looked as though she would object. She wanted to speak, to find the words to argue. She could only close her eyes though, and whisper, "You shouldn't have to be alone when…"

Mary smiled through her tears. "Go. Both of you."

Vincent nodded in agreement. His objections were no less stern than Ilse's, but he remained silent. Aloisa stood and crossed to them, taking the young spy's hand before exiting the small room. Vincent and Ilse stood for a moment, holding Mary's hands. At last, they also left to organize the final group in their flight from Castle Calonar.

Mary remained for a time with Karen. She went to the counter running along the far wall and poured two glasses of wine. She set one before the young princess and sat down as well, sipping at the delicious red drink. "So," the handmaiden said, "this is it."

Karen nodded.

"You said there's another conflict ahead," Mary pointed out.

"There's always another conflict," the princess replied. "Stalline, the First Mage, defeated and imprisoned Ramalech, but there was another conflict. The Sylvai defeated and conquered the Khepri and then the Uldra, but there was another conflict. My father and the Heroes of Fate defeated Kelinva's invasion, but there was another conflict. Tomorrow, Rogan and Tomas arrive. They'll get to the castle and end this war."

"But there will be another conflict," Mary added.

Karen nodded. "The moves are already being made. The traitor on the council is still out there, plotting what comes next."

"I thought Chandra was the traitor."

"She was serving another," the Truthseer revealed.

"Who?"

Karen told her.

Mary leaned back in her chair, shaking her head. "What was all this for?" the young woman asked. "Why all this suffering and death?"

The Truthseer sighed and closed her eyes, rubbing at her temples. "Ten years ago," she paused. "No, it's twelve now, I think. Twelve years ago, Tienel Uskera wanted to gather the Seals of Stalline. My family fought and defeated him. In that fight, the Emperor was killed, along with nearly all the Elector Lords. Pelsemoria was destroyed and the Republic collapsed. Aebreanna was kidnapped and tortured by the Greysoul, causing her to accidentally enthrall Rashid and conceive the Twins. All that suffering and death, just to beat him."

Karen looked at Mary. "Tienel was Fated to gather the Seals. That was the first step in the final conflict of the Prophecy. But, whether the Greysoul was successful or not was flexible. If he had opened a portal to another world, he would have escaped the conflict, but a horde of Umbra would have escaped Underworld. The Republic would have still collapsed, war would have still erupted, and the Northern Keep would have still come under siege. By stopping the Greysoul, my family spared hundreds, maybe thousands, from suffering at the hands of the Umbra."

"Then, what did all this," Mary gestured out the windows. "What did this save?"

"Most of our army was away when the attack came," the Truthseer answered. "Many of our people will survive, far more than if we had openly fought a war with Fak'Har. The forest would still have burned. Our city would still have died. But now, Rogan will have General Killdare and an army for what's to come. He'll have Vincent and Ilse. He'll have Woodwall. All to face what comes next."

"What does come next?"

Karen looked out the windows. "The Inversion, the Return of the Dark Empress, and the Rise of the Demon-God. If we had stood and fought, Rogan would have been alone, without support. Now…"

"Now, he has a chance," Mary finished.

Karen nodded. "Or, at least a better one when the battle comes. He'll have resources, allies, support."

"Will he have Tomas?" the young woman asked suddenly.

Karen rubbed her temples. "I'm not sure," she admitted. "Vincent and Ilse don't interact with Tomas again. His path lies away from the Northlands, either to the south or to the west. I think Rogan will have the choice to go with him, or stay here. But, I'm just not sure."

Mary said nothing. She sipped at her wine and considered the implications of what Karen had told her. Finally, she stood. "I should get back to Kyla."

Karen nodded. "She'll need you tomorrow." The young princess then sighed again.

"Where will you be?"

The Truthseer smiled sadly and stood herself. "Oh, I have one more part to play in this. We have a visitor coming. I'll need to greet him." With that, Princess Karen left.

Mary waited a moment, then walked out of the anteroom. She went, not to Kyla's apartments, but first towards the castle's chapel. Roderick the stablehand intercepted her on the way. "Can I have a moment?" he asked.

Mary stopped and sighed. "You're leaving, Roderick," she said flatly.

"I should be here to-"

Mary gestured for silence. "I've had this conversation already, many times, and I'm tired of it. Karen herself put your name on the lists. You go with the last group. You'll help Vincent and Ilse get the refugees to Woodwall, and that's final."

"Let him stay!" a pitiable voice demanded. Unsurprised, Mary threw a contemptuous look at Baron Hans. "If he wants to die here, let him! Give me his place!" The pretty nobleman was dressed in a torn dress, his armor and sword long abandoned.

Mary stared at this man who had thought himself so grand, who had spoken of her as a prize, as some toy to be seduced and, no doubt, then abandoned. "There's another war coming," the handmaiden said softly, though with steel in her voice. She glanced at Roderick. "You'll be needed at Woodwall to help Prince Rogan fight it." Mary looked around the castle. "This battle is already over, already decided. We need you for the fight ahead." She then turned and passed with barely a glance at the cringing, sobbing champion of House Wurst. "You," she sneered, "nobody needs for anything."

As she moved towards the chapel, Mary spotted more people, more names she recognized from having put on the lists. She avoided these as best she could, and preemptory dismissed all those too persistent to understand her avoidance. She was tired, so very tired. Tired of choosing who would live and who would remain. She was tired of bearing witness to death and destruction, to suffering and the loss of hope. She wanted to be free of all this, all the burdens and unsought responsibilities that had so tarnished her soul.

She paused only a moment when she saw Karen. The princess was standing with someone, a boy who seemed vaguely familiar to Mary. The pair were near to the last group of refugees, assembling for their departure. Karen had taken him aside, and the two were speaking, very quietly, with an intent look about them. The boy, downy-cheeked and awkward, was almost pleading with the princess. Karen, in response, whispered something to him, standing tall and assertive in her blue and grey Northlands dress. Where once Karen had been painfully shy in speaking to anyone, but most especially to anyone of the opposite sex, now the princess and Truthseer stared unblinking into the boy's tearing eyes.

The memory came, then, to Mary. A scene much like this, even in the same place. Karen and the boy, standing to the side of the great double-doors that provided entrance to the castle's main hall. He had tried to talk to her and she had wilted from the attention. That had been the day, Mary recalled, in which Queen Nora had taken her daughter and Mary down, into the ziggurat hidden beneath the Northern Keep. That had been the day in which Karen had been cursed with the Truthsight.

This, then, was the page. Karen had prophesized that he would become the man she could never love. The one who would love her and father her daughter.

The page blushed and nodded, his eyes downcast. Karen gently put her lips to his cheek, bringing a flush to the boy's face. She gently, but firmly, pushed him away then, to join with the last group that would escape Castle Calonar. The princess turned away and moved towards the grand staircase, glancing to Mary as she passed. The two women shared a moment, and Karen sadly nodded.

Mary at last entered the empty chapel. She stood at the doors, letting her memory slip into the warm comfort of the past. Her dress had been of the purest white that day, she recalled. Sewn by Valaera, it had delicate lace around the long sleeves and collar. The brilliant Sylva seamstress had embroidered blue patterns along the neckline to match the blue satin band around her waist. Her veil, more lace provided by Kyla, had been held in place by a crown of fruiting holly. Her great train had been held by Kyla and Baroness Aebreanna, the two noblewomen seeming perfectly comfortable acting in service to a common girl.

Mary walked up the short aisle, even as she had that day, nearly a year ago. Karen and Rasha Tressalon had walked ahead of her, scattering flower pedals, and Jalad, Rashid's son, had followed behind, carrying the golden bands on a velvet cushion. As she walked, Mary let her eyes go to the altar and to where he had stood. Her Tomas had been perfect, stoic and strong in his blue and grey uniform, tailored perfectly to enhance his body, made hard by months of training with Prince Rogan. He had looked at her; she had felt his eyes locked upon her, as she made her way to stand with him before the altar.

She now stood where she had all those months ago. The King had held her hand as she walked, and then went to the front pew to sit with his wife and daughters. Mary held up her hand, even as she had then, as the crimson ribbon had tied their hands together. She looked down at the ring on her finger, the band of white gold fashioned into the ribbon that, even now, Tomas carried as he came to her rescue.

"Mary," he had said, filling her entire soul with love for him. "My heart has called to you for all my life. You give me hope and joy, and I will love you always. My life is yours, along with all I own. I pledge myself to you, and only to you, now and forever."

Tears flowed from Mary's eyes. For the first time since he had gone to support Prince Rogan in his dangerous mission, tears came not from Mary's loneliness or fear, but from her loving memory of him to whom she had pledged herself. "Tomas," she had said and whispered again now. "I have dreamed of you without knowing you. I have missed you before meeting you. I promise myself to you, body and soul, that I might hold you and love you always. I pledge myself, now and forever, to you."

And then they had kissed. Mary put light fingers to her lips, recalling the feeling of her Tomas, pressing in, holding her. They had kissed to the cheers of their friends and the joy of their hearts. "I love you," she whispered once more.

Chapter 43

Dawn came, as it must. Kyla had insisted on being taken to the castle's main hall. Mary had pleaded, cajoled, and even threatened, but the princess was resolute. "We're not safe anywhere," she had pointed out. "Where I sit won't matter much."

Sullenly, Mary had taken her princess down to the main hall. The trip was exhausting for the two women. Kyla was almost unable to bear her own weight and that of her son, leaving Mary to all but carry them down the flights of stairs. By the time they reached the main hall, both were drenched in sweat and trembling with exhaustion.

Aloisa saw their arrival and ran over. "This is very stupid," she pointed out.

"Tell her," Mary grunted as they lowered Kyla onto a bench.

"My House is under attack," the princess panted. "And I won't hide in some closet."

"You could deliver any time," her handmaiden insisted.

"My water hasn't even broken yet. There's plenty of time."

Aloisa stood, grim-faced. "I can't spare anyone to protect you, princess," the Gunrsvein woman said.

Kyla waved away the thought. "Deploy our people however you need to. Mary and I'll be fine."

Aloisa jerked her head at Mary, who made sure Kyla was a secure as possible before crossing the room. "Are you sure about this?" the Gunrsvein woman asked.

"No," Mary admitted. "But there was no talking her out of it."

The warrior-woman sighed. "Fine. Is the evacuation finished?"

Mary nodded. "The only ones left are you and your people. The princess and I will be here, apparently. The King and Queen are upstairs in the Royal apartments, with Opfern and the Tressalon Twins."

"And me," Roland added, limping forward. Both women turned and started. The old butler was dressed in a shining breastplate and had a sword belted at his waist.

"With respect," Aloisa began, but Roland shook his head.

"I'm too damned old to be running through some tunnel," he stated firmly. "I've served this family all my life. If this is its last battle, then this is where I'm standing."

Aloisa looked as though she might object, but Mary put a hand on her arm. "Actually," the handmaiden interjected, "we do need someone to look after the people upstairs. The Queen will want to be kept updated on the fight and, if the worst comes…"

Roland nodded. "You're just trying to keep me out of the fight. But, it's a good point." He glanced at Aloisa. "I'll handle things upstairs. You take care of things down here."

They clasped hands and Roland began the climb up to the Royal Apartments. Aloisa pulled a borrowed helmet over her head and settled it. "Well," she sighed. "I guess it's time to get things started."

Mary nodded, but looked around and saw only fear. Young boys and old men, all dressed for war in borrowed or improvised equipment. Hands shook and eyes that had beheld far too much suffering for so few years struggled to hold back tears. Many faces turned to one another in search of hope, or at least some scrap of purpose, but found none. These were the names Mary had chosen, the lives she had condemned to a hopeless defense. These were her victims.

"I chose you," Mary said then, surprising all, but most of all herself. Heads turned to her and she cleared her throat. "Princess Karen has the Truthsight. Word has spread of this, and it's true. The gift was passed from Queen Nora to the princess. We've all come here through the Wind of Fate. We were meant to be here, together, in this moment. The Truthseer of House Calonar chose me to choose you." She looked around and walked in a circle, holding each defender in her eyes, if only for a moment. "I picked your names for this. You, before all others, are meant to be here. The Princess tells me that Fak'Har will be defeated. We need only hold. Prince Rogan and General Killdare will be here at any moment. We need only hold. Today sees the downfall of the Shadowed Mage and his unholy creatures. We need only hold."

Mary stood in the center of the main hall. "Your families. Your friends, your wives and daughters and injured comrades are, even now, escaping to Woodwall. But they need time. Esha died protecting Defiant Gate, but her students are still here, fighting with us." The handmaiden nodded to the great staircase.

All eyes turned. Autumn had come and brought a renewal to all mystical Sylvai. The tattered, cedar whisps of Amatria's hair had been restored, regrown into an auburn mane that flowed defiantly in the midday breeze. Her hazel eyes, bruised and weakened, had opened that morning with amber resurgence in their opalescent glow. The horrid mockery of flesh that should have been the color of warm sand instead of the panorama of bruise and gore, had greeted the new day healed, a radiant dark gold to match the new season. Amatria stood, braced with an improvised crutch yet the worst of her injuries restored, among her remaining, grey-robed students.

"Amatria and her mages have sealed the tunnel and could have tried escaping as well, but hey honor their teacher's memory and her courage."

Mary pointed to the handful of archers. "Longshot and the Walkers held the enemy back for weeks. They survived the Great Burn and could have fled the Northlands, but they stood with us."

She pointed to Aloisa. "Colonel Klug Rainer survived Defiant Gate and reached the castle, helping me and many others survive as well. He could have hidden, lived a few more days, but he stood at the guardhouse and gave us the time we needed to reach safety."

Mary looked at them all once more. "Now it's our time. House Calonar has fought many battles. Many before us have fallen carrying the blue and grey into glory. We have battled the Inquisition, the Xeshlin, the Greysoul. All have thrown themselves against the blue and grey we now wear." She gestured down at herself. That morning, she had risen and, instead of a traditional Northlands dress, Mary had put on the grey pants and blue tunic she had worn while standing on the wall with Colonel Rainer.

"Many of us will not see the next dawn. But our names will carry on. We have all learned the names of those who stood with the Heroes of Fate at Velaross and the Battle of the Bloody Fields. We remember those who stood with the King at the Battle of Defiant Gate. We remember those who fought with Prince Rogan against the Greysoul. These names are calling to us now. They want to know, will we earn our place among them? Are we deserving of the blue and grey? Are we House Calonar?"

The remaining defenders, boys, old men, wounded, and tired, raised their arms and roared.

Fak'Har's creatures hurled themselves at the walls. Ladder after ladder sprung up from the wide ramp, slamming into the ancient stonework of Castle Calonar. A handful of mercenaries, blood-soaked and frenzied at the thought of more slaughter, were the first to hurl themselves over the battlements. They were also the first to die. The defenders, old men and boys, fought with the merciless tenacity of seasoned men defending their families. Screaming invaders were met with poleaxes, swords, spears, and bare hands.

Three men, wrapped in Velarossi chainmail, reached the battlements and lunged themselves at a pair of boys. The invaders must have been expecting immediate flight, for when the boys, both proudly wearing the blue and grey of House Calonar, stood their ground and leveled their spears, the murderers paused. The two boys did not hesitate, though, but rather advanced, jamming their weapons into the chests of two of the invaders. The third, wide-eyed and suddenly aware of his own mortality, turned to flee, but was met with a thrown javelin that buried itself into the killer's back.

Four more of Vagris' most vile murderers leapt over the battlements and rolled down, into the courtyard. They landed with surprising dexterity, coming to their feet, weapons drawn and eyes burning for victims. Rather than targets, though, they met a wall of grey-haired veterans. These old men advanced on the killers, their faces showing neither fear nor mercy. Upraised shields and blades were forced aside from mighty sweeps of Northland poleaxes. Men whose arms had not born the burden of battle for countless years returned to the training of their youth. Perfect sequences of swipe-parry-thrust-riposte were executed with the finesse only experience and determination could provide. The killers were, themselves, cut down in seconds.

Screams drew Mary's attention back to the walls. From the doors to the great hall, she saw a clutch of five guardsmen, all wounded but still holding their weapons high, cut down by a pair of Fak'Har's unholy knights. The black-armored creatures let the blows of the poleaxes fall where they would, ignoring what should have been mortal wounds struck through the gaps in the spiked plate. Instead of falling or even acknowledging the attacks, the two monsters raised their greatswords and struck, cutting four of the wounded guardsmen down with massive swings of the serrated blades. The last stumbled back, losing his poleaxe as the unholy knights advanced on him.

Then, a half-dozen grey veterans were there. Two of the men each bodily grabbed the wretched monsters, leveraging their own strength against Fak'Har's abominations. They forced the creatures to the ground, while their two fellows grabbed the greatswords and drove those down, splitting the evil knights in half. The rest picked up their own blades and began chopping, cutting away section after section of the unholy plate armor and whatever might lie within.

The last of Vagris' mercenaries saw that Death that awaited him and looked about for some leverage, some means of gaining advantage. He laid his eyes on Amatria, propped onto her crutch, and the small band of grey-robed mages surrounding her. The killer grinned and advanced, holding his sword high and almost trembling in anticipation. Amatria, her group sheltering in the empty stables, saw his approach and sneered. She barked a command to her mages and pointed at the mercenary. As one, the grey-robes made a series of gestures, chanting in unison. A crackling blue flame appeared between each of their hands, building in heat and intensity. At Amatria's command, the mages hurled their fire at the mercenary, surrounding the screaming man in an impossible fire that consumed him in seconds. The fire did not die, though, but instead branched out into small orbs. These, the mages directed with words and gestures and Amatria's guidance, impacting, again and again, Fak'Har's unholy knights. Each of the black-armored creatures hit by a fiery orb was hurled up and away, to fall silently from the walls and the escarpment.

Aloisa led from the battlements. At the breach-point where the ladders were raised, she surged forward with a handpicked team of guardsmen and veterans. This formed the core of the castle's defense. Aloisa and her group stood firm against even Fak'Har's abominations. The Gunrsvein warrior-woman did not test her strength directly against the unholy knights, but rather fought smarter, quicker, and trusting in her fellows. When a greatsword came down in an unstoppable arc, Aloisa would dodge. When a monster tried to swing a great slash, she and her team danced back, only to advance again. They did not used their sheathed swords, but rather raised axes, tools for battling lumber, rather than for war. These, however, made for better weapons against the black-armored creatures. When a greatsword came down, Aloisa or one of her team would swing at the joints of the wielding arms. When they danced back to avoid a slash, they then darted back in and chopped off feet, thighs, and legs. Black-armored pieces fell like a constant rain from the battlements. Despite this, Aloisa and her team were forced back, step by step.

"Archers!" the Gunrsvein called. "Visors!"

The handful of archers they still had emerged from the shelter of the great hall. They formed successive lines along the staircase leading down to the courtyard. Together, they raised their bows and let fly a storm of arrows. These missiles struck the growing tide of unliving horrors at the walls, most missed. A few, though, struck true. Arrows filled the narrow visors of the monsters. Unfeeling though they were, still the creatures needed sight, needed to spot their victims before they could strike. The unholy knights stumbled as more and more arrows flew, and more and more of the creatures lost their sight. They began swinging wildly, striking their brothers as often as the defenders. This Aloisa could not withstand, and ordered her team back, away from the maddened attacks.

"Amatria!" Aloisa called as she dropped from the battlements. "Hit them!"

Amatria looked and snapped orders in the arcane language. Her mages concentrated and redirected their blazing orbs. The spheres of blue fire ceased their dance and instead swirled around the blinded monsters atop the battlements. Again and again, the mystical weapons lunged in, knocking down one of the unliving knights. These would stand, only to be struck down again. Many were forced back to the wall's edge, and sent tumbling over the side.

A great cheer went up as the last of the unholy monsters was sent flying off the wall. But his was cut short with a single word, spoken with all the vile hatred possible from a single mortal being. "Enough!" he roared. There followed a shocked silence, and then horrid veins of purple and red light began splitting the stonework of the castle's walls. The pulsing light spread, growing, and Aloisa ordered her people back.

There was an explosion. Shattered stone flew in all directions. Dozens were felled by the deadly shower. Screams filled the air and those still able desperately grabbed at the wounded, pulling them back. Mary looked at where that section of the wall had once been. The sight was clear of the devastated city beyond. The smoke had mostly cleared, but still there clung to the ruins of the Northern Keep. The ramp they had all watched being built rested just beyond the gaping hole in their primary defense. An entire horde of the unliving knights waited atop it. At their center, his face twisted into frustration, was Fak'Har.

The Shadowed Mage pointed at the defenders of Castle Calonar. "Kill them all," he commanded, and his abominations obeyed.

The fighting renewed with a ferocity that mocked the first assault. Steel on steel became a constant, unwavering song, accompanied by the growing screams of the dead and dying. The wounded were cut down where they lay, begging for an impossible mercy. Aloisa and her team formed at the base of the stairs leading up to the central hall. They became unmovable, unwavering, a flexing yet unrelenting defense from which the archers continued their unceasing volleys. Amatria and her mages retreated back, behind the relative safety of Aloisa's perimeter. Her adepts continued launching their mystical attacks with increasing desperation. The strength of their magic was visibly fading, though, withering against the unending tide of evil unleashed by Fak'Har.

"As you said, monster," Kyla said from behind Mary. "Enough." The princess, barely able to stand, moved forward to the very center of the open doorway. She shook off Mary's insistent pull, staring her indignant hatred at the man who had murdered so many of her people.

"And what little trick do you have for me, princess?" Fak'Har mocked. "Will you finally bring that wonderful Calonar magic to bear?"

"The baby!" Mary hissed, but Kyla waved her to silence.

"No, monster," the jewel of House Calonar declared. "Not my family's magic. Mine."

Kyla closed her pearlescent eyes and raised her hands. "For our loved ones," she said in a voice that echoed out, beyond the castle. She brought her hands to her heart and a golden nimbus radiated out from her soul. "For our community." The Sister Superior of the Lady of Light was lifted, floating into the air as her golden nimbus intensified, as her Dreams manifested in the physical world. "For each other!" She opened her eyes of blazing, golden pearlescence and held out her hands to the defenders before her. "May the Lady of Light grant us Her protection! As we help each other, so shall the Goddess-Pure help us! So may it be!"

The golden nimbus poured out. Kyla's Dream of healing, of strength and will, infused them all. Gentle fingers of divine blessing poured forth, enveloping the defenders of Castle Calonar. Their eyes glowed with renewed purpose. The wounded stood, their bodies restored. Broken weapons were reformed. Empty quivers were replenished. Blades and bows, axes and poleaxes, shined with a holy light that made a mockery of the sun.

Fak'Har and his unholy creations were forced back, shielding their eyes from the purity of Kyla's devotion, both to her goddess and to her people. They all, ally and enemy, felt her unbreakable, undeniable love, her Dream made manifest through the

Lady of Light. The invaders withered, weakening against such selfless compassion. The defenders were rejuvenated. As one, Aloisa and all those who had followed her into battle stood tall and stared ahead. They lifted their weapons and charged.

The unliving creatures had been wounded by the presence of Kyla's Dream Magic, but not destroyed. They fought back. Fak'Har snarled orders to them in some hideous corruption of the arcane language. Amatria, still crippled but standing as though her grievous injuries were nothing more than the most minor of aches, led her mages in an assault on the Shadowed Mage himself. He deflected their magic, but was kept occupied, unable to lend his own support to the surging battle in the courtyard. Fire was met with black water. A wall of furious wind was just barely deflected by a wall of manifested shadow. Beams of light met shields of darkness. Amatria led her students through attack after attack, unable to penetrate Fak'Har's mystical defenses. Despite the ferocity of the magical battle, Amatria could not force the Shadowed Mage away.

Aloisa's defenders forced the unliving knights back, one step at a time, from the castle's great hall. They battled with a ferocity impossible to common soldiers. Two grey veterans, suddenly feeling the strength of their youth returned, leapt upon one of the black-armored creatures. They wrestled it to the ground, ignoring their own wounds and instead roaring their fury as they ripped the thing apart. Three boys darted under the great swings of the blasphemous greatswords, rolling under and between the armored legs of the nightmare creatures. They drew kitchen knives from their belts and cut, stabbed, and sawed at the vulnerable backs of the monsters' legs. Archers found the skillful aim they had been lacking, and now every one of their inexhaustible arrows found its mark. Still the creatures attacked, surging forward as they could.

The battle quickly devolved into a stalemate. Neither Amatria nor Fak'Har could find purchase against the other. Neither Aloisa nor the unliving knights could gain ground. Kyla's blessing gave them all unending strength, but the defenders could use this only to avoid being overwhelmed. Fak'Har's insidious creations were tireless and merciless, but they did not have the numbers to overwhelm the castle's defenders.

"Fak'Har!" Kyla called out from the great doorway. "It's me you want! Stop this madness!"

The battle paused. Amatria held back her grey-robed mages. Aloisa pulled back her defenders. The unliving knights paused and stepped back, their greatswords held ready. All the fighters eyed one another as the unofficial truce began, and every living heart waited for the outcome.

"Call off your creatures!" Kyla demanded. "You've destroyed our city, ruined our castle! Our people are scattered! What more could you possibly want!?!"

The Shadowed Mage grinned as he looked to the jewel of House Calonar. "You cannot image the things I want, princess," he sneered. "You cannot image what I've sacrificed, what I've done, all in the name of trying to limit suffering!"

"Limit suffering!?!" Kyla cast her arms about. "Look around you! All you've done is CAUSE suffering!"

"What is this compared to the world!?!" Fak'Har demanded. "The Demon-God is coming! His return if Fated; it WILL happen! And what then? Your precious city would burn anyway! Your beloved people, your cursed House, all dead! All I have ever wanted is to limit the suffering that must, inevitably come!"

Kyla stared at the Shadowed Mage. Then, she said, "What is your goal here, Fak'Har? What do you hope to achieve? Vagris and his mercenaries are gone, run off or dead. Most of your creatures are also destroyed. My father…" the princess forced control back into her voice. "Your poison is nearly finished. What else do you want? Me? My child?"

The Shadowed Mage laughed. "No, princess, not any more. The Prophecy says your idiot husband will sire the One Who Comes upon a noblewoman from a powerful magical heritage. My brother and I both thought that was you." He sneered. "But it doesn't have to be. There are other candidates. More pliable, more worthy. Once you're gone, that fool Eigenhard will inevitably take his comfort with one of them."

Kyla put a hand to her stomach. "My son?"

Fak'Har smiled again. "You asked what I want, princess? I want you dead. Or, at least, I want that mongrel in your belly dead." He cocked his head to one side. "How about that for a negotiation, princess? I'll call off my creatures, end my attack on your people. All you have to do is let me cut that parasite out of your gut."

A new aura grew out of Kyla. The golden Dream turned dark, nightmarish. Arcs of pure magical energy manifested around the Sister Superior of the Lady of Light. Mary was forced back as Kyla's power snapped off her body, contacting nearby wood and stone and shattering chunks of it. The nightmare of wind gathered the jewel of House Calonar, lifting her as her eyes blazed with sapphire pearlescence. Her face twisted into rage. Her great, flowing blonde hair came alive, sharing in the power her body was producing. It swirled about as though some serpentine creature with a will of its own, seeking a victim, a source of the rage radiating from Kyla.

More bolts of nightmares made real leapt out in lances and arcs. Aloisa and the defenders flinched away, trying to maintain their perimeter, but fearful of their princess' magic. Several of Fak'Har's unliving knights were struck and exploded into flickering sparks that quickly died. More of Kyla's nightmare shot out, impacting with a dome of Shadow Magic Fak'Har raised to defend himself. Through this, the jewel of House Calonar snarled her rage.

"Highness!" Mary called out. "This is what he wants! The baby!"

Kyla's eyes widened. The nightmarish aura pulsed and vanished, and she fell to the ground. Mary rushed to her side, supporting her princess as she gasped and held her stomach. Her handmaiden looked down and gasped. A bright red stain had appeared on Kyla's dress, at the meeting of her legs. Kyla held her friend and looked down herself. "No," she sobbed. "What have I done?"

"Be still, princess," Mary said. "It'll be alright."

"No," Fak'Har mocked. Stood tall, having been forced to a knee against Kyla's power. He grinned at the princess and Mary. "It won't be alright. One more push should just about do it." The Shadowed Mage raised a hand and called to it all the nearby shadows. But then, he paused.

A horn, at first gentle, quiet, like the first blush of dawn, drifted across the air. It repeated, stronger, closer, more urgent and challenging. From the south, the horn grew in power and clarity, calling out to the defenders of Castle Calonar.

"Killdare!" an aged veteran atop the battlements called out. Mary looked, and saw the old man pointed urgently to the south. "General Killdare is here! He's in the city!"

All was quiet for a moment. Then, another horn, this from the east.

"Rogan!" Kyla gasped.

Another defender, this a boy standing atop a different section of the battlements called out. "The Prince! Prince Rogan! The Prince is here!"

Fak'Har's eyes widened. He looked to the south, then to the east. He turned back, his unliving knights awaiting his command. The Shadowed Mage looked to Kyla. The jewel of House Calonar, gasping, bleeding, but undefeated, grinned. "Time's up, Fak'Har!"

Ruins

Chapter 44

Alexia had once called Wildelves Wood the last remnant of the Eternal Forest, that primordial homeland of her people. It had been a lush evergreen sanctuary, both a nurturing mother and protective father for the people who had made their homes amidst the ancient trees. The forest had been like a curtain, an obscuring veil laying atop the Northlands. What occurred within the branches of the Wood was for the Sylvai alone to know, they, and their protectors in House Calonar.

Now, it was a charred wasteland. The earth was an evil crust, broken under each step. Their passage had stirred a noxious grave-cloud, a funerary remembrance that slithered into the mouth and nose, and down the back of the throat. Where once there had been gentle, rolling hills adorned with mossy glades and sparkling streams, now there was only a flat graveyard. Blackened stumps, stripped of branch and leave, poked up from the desecrated earth like unmarked gravestones.

Even the mercenary camp they had passed through was lifeless. Weather-beaten, abandoned tents had been scattered about. Bodies of Human, Uldra, Sylvai, and Xeshlin had been half-heartedly stacked, stripped of anything of value. Lone figures lay, here and there, abandoned to die from illness and wounds. Now, those corpses were bloating in the autumn sun, adding their own miasma to the dirge of Wildeleves Wood.

Finally laying eyes upon the Northern Keep, though, was what nearly broke them. Smoke rose from the dead city to join the grey sky. Defiant Gate was gone, leaving behind a gaping wound in the mighty walls that should have defended Mary and all the others. The great stones on either side of where Defiant Gate should have been were already crumbling, collapsing one building-piece at a time. Beyond lay the Northern Keep, exposed. Buildings were crushed and burnt. The streets were littered with corpses, Human and animal. None of the great constructions remained. The Temples to the Harvest Mother or the Lady of Light were desecrated ruins. The spire of the Adamic Church was broken and fallen. The barracks of the House Guard was half-collapsed, and looked to lose the remaining pieces.

"Are we too late?" Aebreanna asked quietly. The Sylva had risen that morning renewed by the changing of the seasons. Her great mane had darkened to amber, just as her flesh had darkened to golden tan. Tomas had looked to her in hope, but she had only shaken her head. The Wyrdmark had once more failed to restore her face.

In the center of the city rose a new monument to evil. Layers of building material lay one atop the other. Stone, wood, and darker things Tomas' mind refused to identify, rose up from the center of the city, where the squire knew the fountain should rest. It reached up, an impossible extension of Underworld itself, to clutch at the great escarpment upon which Castle Calonar should have stood protected. Instead, the castle's outer wall had been crushed, an impossible hole punched through the heavy stone, and dark creatures were swarming inside.

"What in God's name is that?" Tomas demanded.

"Breaching ramp," Beraht growled.

"What do we do, Rogan?" the squire whispered.

The knight, anointed heir to House Calonar and protector of the Northlands, gathered Stick's reins. The irascible black warhorse was pawing at the dead earth, snorting his rage and quivering in anticipation of vengeance. Rogan glanced over at Earl Konrad. "Take command," he told the leader of the Ironheartshaven forces. "If we did this right, Killdare should be approaching from the south. Coordinate with him. Sweep the city, building by building. Look for survivors, and find any of Vagris' mercenaries."

"Prisoners?" the large Northlander asked. He was a man of few words, as Tomas had learned in their weeks-long march from Ironheartshaven. Though not the most senior of the noblemen who had joined them in this campaign, he was a natural leader: practical, intelligent, creative, and with an unshakable loyalty to his men.

Rogan shook his head. "Not this time." He glanced back at the ruined city. "It doesn't look like we'll have the resources for prisoners. Kill anyone with weapons. If they throw down their arms and surrender... it's your choice." The knight then looked to Ward. "We're going ahead," he declared. "Keep your people close, there's no telling what tricks Fak'Har has left."

The Archaeknight leader nodded.

Rogan led his small group, his own team with the Archaeknights, forward. "We stop for nothing," the knight growled as they rode. "Anything that gets in our way is moved. We've GOT to reach the castle." With that, Stick leapt forward.

They charged through the broken field without pause. Deriel's horse hit an unseen hole, though, and stumbled. The Sylvu Archaeknight leapt from his saddle, employing the power gifted to him by the King to take flight. Rogan glanced back and, seeing this, motioned for the young warrior to continue along with them. They galloped through the strange, mostly-smooth path stretching in front of the hole that had been Defiant Gate, but were forced to a pause because of all the debris blocking the road.

"Recon," Ward called to Deriel. The young Sylvu flew up and forward. The Archaeknight leader glanced at Gendo and Kara. "Clear it."

Kara closed her blue eyes and focused, pointing at the obstructing stone. She raised her hands and the stones, large and small, lifted themselves from the ground. Gendo, the Tramanese Archaeknight, concentrated, and a wave of force spilled out, knocking the rubble from their path.

Deriel swooped back to them. "After about a hundred yards, it becomes clear," he reported. "I think the Uldra gaslamps exploded. It's created channels across the city."

"Lead us," Rogan commanded.

The young Sylvu gestured towards the castle. "Do we go to the switchback road?" he called down. "Or to the base of that thing? It leads directly-"

"I can see where it leads," Rogan interrupted. He nodded his head at the massive ramp. "Take us to that. If it gave Fak'Har an easy entrance, it'll do the same for us!"

Within a few minutes, it was clear their current pace was unsustainable. Stick and Urge had the endurance to gallop all the way to the castle, but none of the other horses could. Aebreana's Mayva was too small to keep up with the great warhorses. Ironically, Beraht's Sus was large enough, but lacked the endless stamina of Stick and Urge. Even the horses ridden by the Archaeknights were having trouble keeping up with the two well-bred, trained, and experienced warhorses.

"We need a moment to consider," Aebreanna declared, calling them all to a stop.

"No time!" Rogan snapped, making as though to keep going."

"If you try to maintain this pace, you and your squire will arrive alone!"

"And we'll be too saddle-sore to be much good," Tomas added. "We need to be smart about this."

"Fine!" the knight snapped. "We'll make a canter." He nudged Stick forward, but at a more constant pace the other horses could maintain.

Their approach, though steady and reasonably quick, seemed intolerably slow to Tomas. He kept glancing up at the ramp, seeing the horrid black forms that had to be Fak'Har's unliving knights, crawling up the hideous construct, pouring into the castle's courtyard. Less than an hour had passed since they had passed through what had been Defiant Gate, an impossibly-long time for a battle.

"Rogan," Tomas said to his knight.

"I know, kid," Rogan growled. The prince of the Northlands was refusing to look up. He made a visible effort to keep his eyes down, on the path ahead. They were so close now. After months of travel, endless hundreds of miles across Lanasia and back. After facing the Sorceress Vara and the Triumvirate of Frostfront. After defeating Vagris' mercenary ambushes. After traveling to Uldron and surviving the Druug helter. After the flight from Dayvic and the infiltration of Tordenia. After passing through Dagon'ay and Otherworld. Even after facing and defeating the Shadowed Mage himself, now they were within sight of Castle Calonar and their loved ones.

They drew closer. The sounds of battle drifted down from the castle. Steel on steel, oath and scream, magic and archery. All of these taunted Tomas and his friends, invisible signals that the fight above was becoming increasingly desperate. Shapes flew from the castle battlements to crash far below. They saw screaming mercenaries sent flying over the edge, to disappear into the ruins of the Northern Keep. They also saw the dark forms of Fak'Har's monsters plummet silently to the ground. Still they went on.

Something caught Tomas' attention. It was like the ghost of a memory of movement at the corner of his vision. He tried to shake away the distraction, but could not. Whatever it was nagging at his senses was persistent. Finally, the squire spared a glance away from the ramp, drawing tantalizingly near. He looked down one of the avenues blow clear by the detonation of the Uldra gaslamps. With a snarled oath, Tomas reigned in Urge. "Rogan!" he hissed.

His knight also reigned in and looked to where his squire indicated.

Not even a hundred yards down the street, the rubble-strewn path littered with burnt bodies, crushed homes and shops, and overturned carts, was Vagris. The traitorous commander was exiting a building still relatively intact alongside four other warriors. They were all garbed in chainmail and traveler's cloaks. They were loading supplies into a small wagon, and saddling their waiting horses.

Rogan's eyes burned with an undeniable lust for revenge. His hand went to Talon, belted as ever on his hip. "Rogan," Tomas said softly, but urgently. When the knight looked to his squire, the young man glanced meaningfully at the ramp, and the besieged castle. Rogan snarled, torn between two impossible choices. Finally, he looked to his apprentice. "Take command," the knight growled. "Get to the castle! Stop Fak'Har!"

Tomas put a hand on his knight's shoulder. "Rogan, what about-"

"He's not getting away with this!" Rogan snapped, pushing away his squire's hand. The prince of the Northlands looked to Ward. "Give me two," he said, drawing Talon.

"Gendo," the Archaeknight leader ordered. "Rei."

The two, husband and wife, moved their horses up beside Rogan. The three readied weapons and then charged. Tomas watched for a moment, then shook his head clear. "Let's move!" he commanded.

As they rode, another flicker of something forced Tomas' attention away from the path ahead. They were only a few blocks away from the base of the ramp. The buildings here seemed to have survived the worst of the Gaslamp firestorm, but then been stripped. Fak'Har had used the buildings themselves as construction material, breaking down stone and wood, harvesting every available piece. The ruins around the center of the Northern Keep were no longer soot-stained, no longer battle-scarred. Instead, they seemed as though in the midst of deconstruction.

Thomas was ignoring everything as they rode, everything but the base of the ramp. Still, some flicker of movement, some indescribable disruption, waved at him. In the months since their departure from Tordenia, the young man had grown increasingly trusting of his sensitivity to the Winds of Magic. He was still untested, unsure of how his power worked, but he had begun to trust when that power was trying to alert him of something.

The young man pulled Urge to a stop and looked around. He did so less with his eyes than with his entire being. Rogan's advice of employing all his senses, beyond sight, came to mind. Tomas listened, he felt the shifting of the breeze, he smelled the destruction. More than that, though, he reached out, into the Winds of Magic.

Aebreanna pulled her Mayva up beside her young friend. "Describe it," she suggested.

"Something... illusive," the nascent sorcerer replied. "Like it's trying to hide. Like it doesn't want to be noticed. A rodent, burrowing into the ground." Tomas almost closed his eyes and reached further out. The Winds blew this way and that, as was their habit. The gentle randomness was as it always was. He could even feel the use of magic above, where adepts were waging a battle with Fak'Har. But there was something else... nearby.

"There." His eyes snapped fully open, and his finger was already pointing to a wall in mid-deconstruction. Something or someone had pulled a piece of the Winds, tucking them over themselves like a blanket folded over itself.

Aebreanna looked, her opalescent eye far more acute than Tomas' Human one. She spied and cursed. "Chandra!"

Beraht had come forward as well, an almost null-spot within the Winds of Magic. "What's she doing out here?" he demanded.

The spy, having clearly realized she had been spotted, bolted from her hiding place. Instead of running to them, however, to those who should be her friends and allies, Chandra ran away. "What's going on?" Tomas demanded.

Aebreanna narrowed her opalescent eye and handed the reins of her Mayva up to Beraht. "I shall find out," she said menacingly.

"Aebreanna!" Tomas objected, pointing up the ramp.

The lithe Sylva pulled her bag free from her shoulder and handed it to Tomas. "Get the Seal of Life to the King," she commanded. "All else is secondary. I have suspicions, and will see them satisfied." With that, Aebreanna leapt from Mayva's saddle, vaulting up to a portion of wall and nearly gliding away.

Tomas was about to object, to demand Aebreanna return, but Beraht put a hand on his small friend's shoulder. "Forget it, kid," the great Uldra advised. "Females are hard enough to herd. That one is impossible."

The squire grimaced and turned back to the ramp. "Alright," he growled. "Let's ride."

The base of the ramp was only minimally guarded. Three of Fak'Har's unliving knights stood in a rough half-circle. The first was obliterated by Beraht as he galloped past, one swing of his great Uldra waraxe enough to send pieces of the black armored creature flying in all directions. The other two turned to attack, but were intercepted by the Archaeknights. Sarah rolled off her horse and tumbled along the ground, tying up one knight's legs and sending him to the ground. There, Khwezi leapt upon the creature's back and, laying his hands on the black-enameled armor, caused it to turn red, steaming, and melting into a heap of unusable slag. The last unliving knight faced Asaya and Ward. The Halvan woman drawing a great gale that forced the monster stumbling backwards, to the waiting leader of the Archaeknights. Ward grabbed the abomination and brutally ripped off his head and limbs.

"Alright," Tomas noted. "Time to climb." He looked up the steep ramp and grimaced. When Urge put a hoof upon the haphazard construction, the wood and stone and flesh gave way. "This will take a minute or two."

Beraht dismounted and joined his small friend. He also grimaced and nodded. "You're right, kid," he said. "I'll buy you some time." The great Uldra looked to Deriel. "Get me up there!" he barked.

The young Sylvu meaningfully looked Beraht up and down. "There's no way." He glanced at Asaya and Kara. "Unless…"

The two men glanced at each other and nodded. "Stand ready," Asaya advised.

Deriel walked to Beraht and all others backed far away. "Yeah, no problem," Tomas muttered. "Everybody just go and do whatever."

Kara sheathed her heavy daggers and gestured. Deriel and Beraht slowly lifted off the ground by her invisible, mystical power. The young Sylvu moved behind the great Uldra and grabbed him, nodding to his teammates. Asaya then joined her own power to the effort. A horrific wind appeared from nowhere, twisting around Deriel and Beraht in a twisting funnel. The two males lifted up, higher and higher, raised by Asaya and guided by Kara. They were hurled up in to the grey sky, arching under Deriel's control to the Castle. Tomas looked up and saw the two fly over the battlements. Even from so far down, Tomas heard Beraht roaring a challenge, a taunting, distracting bellow at Fak'Har.

"Alright," the squire said. "He's giving us a chance. Let's ride!" He once again nudged Urge forward, but once more the ramp gave way under his warhorse's weight. "Damn!" Tomas swore. He grimaced and shook his head, looking at Ward. "We'll have to climb it."

The Archaeknight leader nodded and dismounted, his team doing the same.

Tomas slid from Urge's back, but the chestnut stallion moved to block him. "It's got to be this way," the squire argued, but his mount refused. Tomas reached up and patted his warhorse on the neck. "I don't like it either," he confessed. The squire glanced back and saw a small group of mercenaries trying to approach. "Think you can handle that?" he asked.

Urge glanced over and snorted in contempt. Tomas slapped his warhorse on the flank and the chestnut stallion reared, charging into the new targets.

There was a crash and a surge within the Winds of Magic. Tomas looked up.

"How many times must I kill you, Uldra!?!" Fak'Har's exasperated voice came crashing down the ramp as Tomas and the Archaeknights charged up. There was another flash and surge, and Beraht was sent roaring through the sky. Like some great stone tossed by a siege engine, the son of Uldron arced up and away, crashing into the upper floors of the castle's main hall.

"C'mon, c'mon!" Tomas demanded. The Archaeknights needed little encouragement, following him as best the unstable ramp would allow. Their climb was difficult and frustrating. Without the Archaeknights, Tomas feared it would have been nearly impossible. Time and again, he or one of the other mystically-enhanced warriors would slip, losing their footing, and need to be caught by someone. Time and again, Ward had to employ his great strength, and Sara her great dexterity, and the other Archaeknights their own gifts, to maintain the ascent.

Above, they could hear shouting. The sounds of true battle seemed to have faded, but the voices were all the more urgent. Tomas gritted his teeth and continued to climb. At last, they reached the top of the ramp and, without a moment's hesitation, leapt across the small gap, thundering through the broken wall and into the courtyard.

Everywhere was madness. Guardsmen, dead and alive, were scattered across the area. The stables had collapsed, the walls were cracked, the double doors leading to the great hall stood open and useless. Pieces of Fak'Har's unliving knights lay strewn about, but dozens more were intact and advancing on the survivors. The Shadowed Mage himself stood in the very center of the courtyard, raising his arms and calling upon the Winds of Magic. He was facing away from Tomas, looking up to the grand stairs that led to the open double doors and the main hall beyond. Standing on those stairs were more guardsmen. Behind them, Kyla was lying on the ground, groaning and bleeding and very pregnant. Queen Nora stood at the doors, with a guardsman standing behind her holding some bundle of rags.

Mary was there. She knelt, sword in hand, beside her princess. Her long flowing hair was disheveled, and her perfect face was lined with worry. She was not wearing her Northlands dress, having replaced it with trousers and a military-style shirt and tunic. Patches of sunlight were breaking through the grey sky, and a single golden beam shined upon her. In response, echoing that life-affirming ray, a circle of gold shined from her finger. It was the ring of white gold, the stylized metal ribbon she had accepted when she accepted him.

"Words cannot express," Fak'Har was yelling, "How tired I am of all of you!"

Tomas looked, and the Shadowed Mage was leveling his hands at the stairs. At the few survivors... and at his Mary.

When before Tomas had summoned the Winds of Magic, there had been a terrible pressure in his mind. He had felt as though his entire body was being squeezed in some terrible vice. This time, however, there was nothing uncomfortable or uncertain in his soul.

Instinctively, Tomas called out, through the Veil. A chorus of voices, some centuries dead, others only recently having made the journey, responded. Together, as one, they all reached for the Winds of Magic. Earth mages, air mages, fire mages, water mages, life mages, all joined with Tomas, adding his own Death Magic to their mighty arsenal. The chorus did not try to shape their Winds, did not force then into some distortion, but rather harnessed their raw, untamed nature. A kaleidoscope of arcane power erupted from Tomas, blazing out and impacting the Shadowed Mage. Fak'Har screamed in soul-deep agony as he was hurled across the courtyard, impacting with bone-crushing force against the far wall. Somehow, impossibly, the Shadowed Mage picked himself up, standing and snarling hatred at Tomas.

The young man, lord of House Fidelis, liege protector of Pelsemoria, son of Alessandros, squire to Rogan Eigenhard, heir to Alexia, and betrothed to Mary, drew Steelheart, legendary sword of House Calonar. The blade of heroes leapt from its scabbard and shined in the glorious light of the Northlands sun. He roared his challenge to the enemy of his friends, leveled the blade with which he had been entrusted, and charged.

Chapter 45

Xaemus paused after exiting the hidden tunnel to orient himself. Surprisingly, House Calonar had discovered the passage, requiring that he slip amidst the shadows for his own trip through. To the best of his knowledge, the tunnel had remained unused, likely since its completion centuries ago. In his first voyage through this forgotten portal, when he had been tasked with poisoning Cylan Calonar himself, he had seen no signs of use. Indeed, the air was stagnant, undisturbed dust covered every surface, and the stone floor showed no signs of wear. To Xaemus' eyes of burning blood, the tunnel seemed to have been constructed, then abandoned without use.

The state of unuse was especially curious, considering how he first located it. When Fak'Har had tasked him with brewing and delivering the *kay'ay'eil'nas*, Xaemus had, of course, needed some means of ingress. The switchback road was immediately unusable. Each level had powerful detection wards and a dissuasive number of soldiers. Similarly, employing an adept to open a mystical portal would not work, as Esha had established layered defenses to deny any infiltration. Simply climbing the escarpment would not work either; there existed too few shadows to slip into, and hours of climbing in full view of the city would have been disadvantageous. Xaemus' considered strategies had become increasingly exotic as he prowled the city until random chance had intervened.

Xaemus had been on the western outskirts of the city, very near the wall and its gate on that side, when he had spotted a matriarch. The Sylva had emerged from an uprising of rock, one of the innumerable small hills that dotted the western side of the Northern Keep. Xaemus had not recognized the Sylva, but he saw immediately the mark of authority in her. She stood tall, with the grace and bearing reserved only to the greatest, most experienced of matriarchs. He had seen the elder Sorcerous Sisters affect this bearing, though few projected such calm certainty. The Xeshlin had crouched, hidden amidst the shadows, and watched as she emerged from a door so well hidden he doubted if ever he would have seen it otherwise. The matriarch had stood there, dressed in the blue and grey of House Calonar, and looked about. Likely, his memory had altered the event, or possibly he had even imagined, but Xaemus thought the noble Sylva had spotted him, had looked directly at where he hid. She had smiled then, a kind, gentle smile utterly alien to the Sorcerous Sisters who had created him, before turning and reentering the hidden door.

More curious than expectant, Xaemus had investigated, and found the tunnel. This time, the city was in ruin, with few buildings still standing. The outcropping of rock was still there, though bereft of its grassy and tree-covered mantle. The hidden door, also was still there, now stood open. Groups of refugees had been emerging from the secret passage at regular intervals through the night, requiring Xaemus to wait. He needed a few hours to time out the groups, so that he could traverse the tunnel without worry of interruption. True, he could easily slaughter any of the frightened groups he saw, but she would not want him doing that, even in the pursuit of her liberation. The groups stopped with the morning sun, yet he hesitated still. He had only one chance to infiltrate Castle Calonar, one chance to secure his objective and be away; he could not squander that chance.

The Coven of Midnight Sun had taught him patience and resilience. This was how Mother Xelesa had described what she termed his training. She had taken him from his litter, somehow, for some reason, differentiating him from the other young boys. She was not his biological mother, of course, none of his litter knew she who birthed him. This was irrelevant to Xeshlin boys; mother was a title, a rank given to the one who owned him. One by one, his litter-mates would be selected to become servants, to live lives of silent obedience. Some, they were told, would be trained as spies or merchants or craftsmen, depending on the whim of his mother. Any who reached the Age of Choice without being selected would be either given to the Arena, or else offered to the Demon-God. There had been times, quiet, secret times, when Xaemus had wished one of those preferable fates had befallen him, rather than Mother Xelesa.

Xaemus did not like dark places. This was ironic, since he spent so much of his time among them. He was comfortable in the night, as all his cursed race were, so as to be free of the burning sun. The night had stars and moon to shine upon them. But the truly dark places, like the hidden tunnel, forced unwanted memories upon Xaemus. She had not spoken a word to him, only pointed and had her enthralled males place him in chains. They had half-dragged him into a room with only a single torch in its center. The infant Xaemus had been chained to the stone floor, able only to reach a few feet in any direction. Mother Xelesa had brought in a plate, upon which was a single piece of moldy bread.

"You can eat this," she told him in a voice he later learned she believed was loving. "Or you can wait. The bread will attract larger things, larger meals." Her eyes of burning blood, adorned with dark cosmetics, slid to the heavy shadows along the walls. "These, if you can catch them, will provide an even greater meal, if you are patient." The infant Xaemus had not understood, except that she had wanted him to wait. The moldy bread had been placed in front of him, within his reach, and Mother Xelesa had left. When she did, and the heavy iron door had closed and locked, the single torch had gone out.

The tunnel, when Xaemus had first entered it, had reminded him of that room, that first test among a very great many. The stones were similarly fashioned, bearing no tool marks, no rough edges. They radiated power, matriarchal magic mixed with Uldra stink. The great difference lay in the light. Whenever Mother Xelesa gave him some new task in that room, her departure took the light with it. When Xaemus entered the tunnel, the door had quietly closed behind him, but then the light arrived. Soft, heatless orbs, floating just above head-level, emerged from the darkness at even intervals, so that no single stone was left in the dark. These remained illuminated for as long as Xaemus had needed to make his passage, extinguishing as silently as they had been birthed once he reached the far end.

A solid stone wall had waited at the end of the hidden tunnel. This, too, brought back an unwanted memory to Xaemus. Older, but still before his weapons training had begun, Mother Xelesa had once again put him in the room. "Free yourself from the chains," she commanded in that same, seemingly-loving voice. Her instructions were nearly always such: simple words, simple declarations, and simple expectations. She had never once given him advice or instruction. The young Xaemus was given only a task. He either succeeded and was rewarded, or failed, and was given to Mother Xelesa's acolytes for a day.

When he had first journeyed through the seemingly-abandoned tunnel, Xaemus had reached the wall at its end and paused. He probed the stone with one gloved hand, looking for a latch or some other mechanism. Then, the detested memory came again. He had probed at the locks on Mother Xelesa's chains, even as he probed the wall. The young Xaemus had pulled at the chains, straining with all his undeveloped strength. He had twisted at the manacles, trying to wiggle his way to freedom. He had done everything his untrained mind could conceive, but all for naught. Mother Xelesa had stared at him with her darkened eyes of burning blood. Eventually, she grimaced, but only slightly, and turned to leave.

"Mother," the young Xaemus had said. That had been the first time he had ever dared speak to her. Males were not allowed to voice their thoughts, except to slaves. They could answer questions when asked, they could offer opinions, again only when asked, and they could declare their joy at whatever the females inflicted upon them. They could not, however, speak without leave. "Mother," the young Xaemus had said. He had turned, as much as the chains would allow, and fell to his knees before her. He had bowed his head to her, lowering himself until he could press his lips to her bare feet. "Please release me."

A light finger had touched his chin and raised the young Xaemus to look fully into Mother Xelesa's eyes of burning blood. That had been the first time she looked at him with something other than curious indifference. That had been the first time she smiled at him, though Xaemus could learn to fear that smile and the hunger that lay behind it. "Always find the simplest path forward, my Xaemus," she had nearly purred. That had also been when she gave him his name.

Xaemus had forced the memory away as he had stood at the stone wall. He then simply pushed and the wall slowly swung away.

Castle Calonar's layout was simple, Xaemus recalled. When he had infiltrated to deliver the *kay'ay'eil'nas* to Cylan Calonar, he had frequently needed to move amidst the shadows. Staff and functionaries had been everywhere. This time, the place was nearly empty. Xaemus was able to move rapidly up the stairs, reasoning that he would begin his search at the upper levels and work his way down. This plan, as so often could happen, lasted only until his first encounter.

Having emerged from the secret tunnel, he slid towards the nearby staircase, but paused at the approach of voices. Xaemus slid into the shadows and waited. A small group arrived, and Xaemus could only blink his eyes of burning blood in surprise. His target had delivered herself.

"I must once again object, your Majesty," a large, elderly Human male was saying. He had the baring of miliary training, though marred with a heavy limp. He was talking to Queen Nora Calonar.

"We have no choice," the Lady of House Calonar replied. "We have to be there."

"My Queen," the old man started to object.

"It has to be this way," Princess Karen Calonar insisted. His target was older than Xaemus remembered from the last time he had seen her. Humans always aged faster than the *Xesh'lin* recalled. When last he had passed her by, the girl-child had been just that, undeveloped in both body and mind. Xaemus recalled thinking she was deeply introverted, seemingly to wither into her clothes when forced to interact with any group. This Human, however, was much changed. She stood tall, much as a matriarch would, and leveled a steady gaze through those half-breed eyes of which House Calonar seemed so proud. She spoke with the voice of authority and certainty, despite addressing someone far older and, no doubt, far more experienced. "My parents have to be in the courtyard for the final confrontation."

The elderly man sighed and nodded as the two females continued down the hall. Behind him, some warrior from the House Guard passed carrying something. Xaemus needed a moment before he realized the bundle in the male's arms was Cylan Calonar himself. The last survivor of the Heroes of Fate was in the final stages of the *kay'ay'eil'nas*. He was emaciated, very nearly nothing but a skeleton wrapped in yellowed skin. Only a few whisps of hair remained, and his sunken eyes stared blankly. His breathing was shallow and coarse, and the guardsman carrying his king moved as though the once-great warrior and adept weighed nothing at all.

With the small group came the Tressalon Twins. Male and female, the children appeared, initially, much as did Karen Calonar. "Are we sure it's safe down here?" The boy's voice cracked and wavered as though trying to decide which register to use, and downy fur had spurted from his cheek and chin.

"Father's message told us to wait upstairs." The girl matched her brother in his transition, clearly having begun her own journey into maturity.

At the mention of their father, Karen Calonar paused and sighed. "Things have... changed," she said. Most of her group seemed unaware of the knowing tone in her voice. Only her mother, Queen Nora Calonar, glanced back. Xaemus, too, understood the weight of those words. Mother Xelesa had spoken in a similar way when speaking of certain events. Whenever she spoke of the Dark Empress, of their fealty to Kelinva, she had used a similar voice, one pregnant with sorrow and some undeniable obligation.

"Have you seen the future again?" the Tressalon girl asked.

Karen Calonar smiled, though sadly. "Sort of." She glanced at her peer, the two being of similar ages and heights, but paused. Xaemus had heard whispers of the Truthseers of House Calonar, as most people had. Legend and rumor had been confused, though, of which matriarch possessed the Truthsight. Every empress of the Sylvai Im'peri'a had benefited from a Truthseer, females who possessed a connection to the Wind of Fate. Legend stated that this ability had passed from mother to daughter, even as the Crystal Dias had along the royal line. After the collapse of the Im'peri'a, rumor abounded that the descendants of those Truthseers had blended with House Calonar, that one of the matriarchs of that family retained the Truthsight. None seemed to know with certainty, though, if it was the lady Palsilyagathalexia, Nora, or one of her daughters. Clearly, Xaemus mused, the Truthsight rested with the youngest of the Calonar females.

Karen Calonar looked at the Tressalon girl, staring for a hard moment. The princess then glanced around, her half-breed eyes pausing when they fell upon the shadow in which Xaemus hid. "Simon," the young female commanded to the guardsman carrying the desiccated king, "go on ahead."

The Queen again glanced back. Karen looked to Nora and nodded, a silent exchange passing between mother and daughter. "Come," the Lady of House Calonar said, motioning for the guardsman carrying her husband to follow.

Karen Calonar gestured to the Tressalon twins. "We'll stay here a moment," the princess declared. She then turned to the old, limping warrior. "You have to decide," she said with great sadness. "You either stay with us, or go with them."

The old Human glanced from the young princess to the queen and back. "Can you explain?" he asked gently.

Karen Calonar shook her head.

"I swore to your father that I would keep you safe," the old warrior said. "You and your sister." He smiled then, "At least, until I can finally see you safely married off."

Karen Calonar tried to smile, tried to force some warmth into her face and eyes. Those half-breed orbs, though, were too filled with tears. She watched as her mother and the guardsman carrying her desiccated father continued down, waiting until they were well away before turning back to the shadow in which Xaemus hid. "You can come out now."

Something about her voice, her tone and her certainty, was undeniable to Xaemus. Mother Xelesa had spoken to him in that voice. She had commanded him, when training him in weapons, in poison, in infiltration and the manipulation of the Wind of Shadow. At all times, Mother Xelesa had spoken to him in that exact tone, whether in commanding him to violence or in satisfying her hungers.

Xaemus emerged from the shadows. He was not sure why he did so, except that he must. No matter Mother Xelesa's bloody body, her opened throat or dead acolytes, still Xaemus could not help but obey that voice. He shook off the compulsion and declared in Gunnic, "You will come with me, willingly or otherwise." He leveled Queltuasor, the noxious twin-bladed sword, at the Tressalon Twins. "I have no business with you. Run and hide, or stay and die."

"There's no need for that," Karen Calonar said, again in that tone that echoed from Xaemus' past.

"I have a need," the Xeshlin insisted, even as Queltuasor lowered slightly.

The Truthseer of House Calonar nodded. "I know. She's been taken, and you think you need me to get her back."

Xaemus did not show his surprise. He had never before interacted with a Truthseer, but his discipline was nearly absolute. "Yes," he confirmed. "I will take you, and trade you for her."

"I'll be damned to Underworld first!" the old Human barked. He ripped the broadsword sheathed at his hip and limped in front of the youngest daughter of House Calonar.

"You need not die here," Xaemus offered, though he was uncertain as to why. Always before, when any obstacle presented itself, the monster of Davenor removed that obstacle in the simplest, most expedient way possible. This time, however, he paused; she would not want him to kill without reason. "You cannot stop me, and gain nothing in the attempt."

"I gain honor," the old warrior declared. As best he could with his heavy limp, he positioned himself to face the monster of Davenor, his blade in a low guard. "I am sworn to the defense of these children."

"So be it."

Xaemus tried to kill the man quickly, cleanly. He spun his double-bladed weapon, intending to knock the sword from the old warrior's hands. This failed though, when the warrior called upon some unknown reservoir of speed and skill. He did not meet Queltuasor, but rather rolled his blade under it, slashing a surprising counter that cut a strip of fabric from the Xeshlin's sleeve. Xaemus danced back and looked to his shirt in surprise.

"I won't fall so easily," the old man pointed out.

"No," Xaemus nearly sighed. "But you will fall." He darted in and spun Queltuasor, the first blade knocked the old warrior's sword to the side before the second blade slashed at his throat. Again, surprisingly, the loyal male was able to move aside, so that Xaemus' attack missed his flesh by the barest of breaths.

Xaemus was surprised, and this moment of hesitation did not pass without being exploited. The old warrior lunged forward, launching a surprisingly-rapid sequence of strikes, counters, and feints. He used his greater strength and mass to force Xaemus back, relying on pure defense and dexterity to remain free of the man's broadsword. These small victories, however, came with a great price.

The old man limped back, away from Xaemus and shielding the children with his own body. Several small cuts marred his arms and legs. Wet red was spreading out from these points. The loyal warrior blinked and shook his head, his breathing labored. "My weapon has tasted your blood," Xaemus noted with a degree of sadness he did not understand. "The poison is already in your heart. You will be dead in moments."

"Then," the old warrior panted. "These are important moments." He charged again. The great man swung his broadsword at Xaemus' head, then rolled his shoulder and brought the blade back and up. He struck again and again, each attack carrying less force. At last, the loyal warrior stumbled, almost dropping his weapon. Xaemus caught the man before he could fall, and gently lowered him to the floor. The warrior's grip on his sword was weak, but it did not fail, the Northlands blade remaining in his hand. "You fought well," Xaemus offered.

"I…" he struggled to say. "I… serve… my House."

Xaemus nodded. "I envy you, that loyalty. I swear, I will not harm the children. Though I will take Karen Calonar, I will not allow harm to befall her." He was unsure if the old warrior heard his oath. The eyes stared at him, but there was nothing behind them. The breathing had stopped, the old warrior's duty at last finished. Xaemus closed his eyes and finished lowering him to the floor, ensuring that the loyal man's weapon remained at his side.

He stood, then, and faced Karen Calonar. "You will come with me," he commanded.

The male Tressalon twin looked at his sister. "We need help," he said urgently.

"But who?" she asked in reply.

They stared at each other a moment, then, in unison, they said, "Uncle Beraht!"

The wall behind Xaemus exploded. The Xeshlin crouched and stumbled as wood and stone filled the air. Something huge had crashed into the castle. He shielded his covered face as he was pelted with debris. Glancing back, Xaemus saw a shape arise in the cloud, massive, more of an ambulatory mountain than any living thing. The shape took a step, then another, and finally forced away the cloud of dust and debris.

It was an Uldra. Heavy scalemail covered a massive torso. Metal bracers were wrapped around arms the size of tree trunks. Greeves that could have protected a stone column rode on its legs, and steel-shod boots stomped on the carpeted floor. The Uldra's head was concealed, though, for a massive vase was lodged around it. The foul-smelling barbarian grasped about with its right hand, and there was another disturbance in the cloud of dust and debris. An Uldra waraxe leapt into the barbarian's hand, as though of its own will. The lumbering thing used the blunt end of the weapon, smashing it against his own face.

The Uldra shook its head to clear its vision. It had a beard of midnight black, though unlike most of its odious race, the facial hair was not braided or adorned with precious metals. It wore no helmet, having lost it in the impact, but instead wore a strange purple-embroidered ribbon around his head.

"Uncle Beraht!" the Tressalon twins again cried out in unison.

The Uldra blinked and looked at them. "Kids?" it said, obviously trying to twist its blunted mind into understanding. The barbarian then looked to Karen Calonar. "Axe-blunter?" The mountain-creature growled at Xaemus, spinning his waraxe in the air. "I don't know who you are, you piece of Druugshit, but I-"

Xaemus had turned to face him, exposing Queltuasor, his signature, double-bladed weapon. "You!" he hissed.

"Xaemus!" The Uldra called Beraht grinned evilly. Dark joy filled his sunken eyes and a line of anticipatory drool rolled from the corner of his mouth. "Run along, kids," the barbarian laughed. "Me and the Xeshlin have business!"

"Business," Xaemus echoed. "Yes." With his free hand, he tore away the cloth covering his face. He tugged at the robe covering his torso, exposing the truth beneath. Xaemus gestured to his deformed face, the twisted mockery of a smile his lips had become, at the grotesque chasm that had been carved into his chest and stomach. "Yes," he said again, "there is a debt between us."

Beraht hefted his waraxe. "I've got your payment right here!"

The two warriors, the shared hatred of their races undeniable, lunged at each other. Beraht heaved his waraxe, shattering the floor where Xaemus had been standing only a moment before. The Xeshlin twisted and slashed with his weapon, but the blades sparked off the back of Beraht's scalemail. The Uldra roared and swung his weapon again, forcing Xaemus to jump back, flipping in midair. The barbarian did not hesitate to press his advantage, barreling forward and swinging his waraxe in repeating, figure-eight loops. Xaemus tried catching and deflecting the swings, but Beraht's infinite strength was too great to overcome or even redirect. The Xeshlin was forced to keep flipping back, down the hall and further away from the children.

When Beraht raised his waraxe again, Xaemus dropped and spun on one foot, lashing the other leg out. Rather than dodging, though, the Uldra slammed his immovable leg onto the floor. The Xeshlin's strike failed, his leg bouncing off unyielding muscle. The barbarian raised his other steel-shod foot and tried to bring it crashing down upon Xaemus' misshapen chest, but the Xeshlin rolled away. He came to his feet and launched himself forward, making twin, rapid thrusts at Beraht's hideous face. The Uldra was forced to step back using his waraxe to deflect the attacks. The barbarian then lowered his shoulder and thrust forward, knocking Xaemus away.

The Xeshlin spun his double-bladed weapon in a great circle, spinning Queltuasor around and over his back as he danced out of the Uldra's reach, buying himself a moment's pause to reassess. He faced the grinning maniac before him and sneered his contempt. Xaemus began spinning his weapon again in broad loops as he advanced. Without warning, he pivoted as though presenting his back to the barbarian and suddenly slashed downward. He caught the waraxe and forced it away, bringing the other blade around to slash Beraht across the face.

The Uldra roared his pain and fury as blood poured from the fresh gash. Somehow, he grabbed the hilt of Xaemus' weapon and bodily threw the Xeshlin back down the hall. Beraht shook his head, flinging his blood away from his eyes and snarled. Xaemus knew, from years ago, that Queltuasor's poison would not kill the Uldra, nor even significantly slow him. Somehow, through some impossible magic of his misbegotten race, the barbarian suffered none of his weapon's deadly properties. Typically, when faced with such a dangerous opponent, Xaemus would just inflict a passing blow, some meaningless cut, then delay and allow his weapon's poison to do its deadly work. This time, however, he knew he would have to defeat the Uldra the hard way.

Xaemus skipped back, creating more separation. He spun his weapon up, so that its length pointed towards Beraht, along his arm. When the Uldra charged, the Xeshlin dropped one of the blades down towards his own leg, spinning the entire weapon so that the second blade would make a vertical slash. This was meant to be a feint, a decoy, drawing the barbarian's attention, but it did not work. Instead, Beraht blocked the second blade with his waraxe and grabbed again the hilt of Xaemus' weapon before the Xeshlin could bring the first blade up in his true attack. The Uldra physically picked up his enemy and hurled him against a wall.

Hatred alone kept Xaemus moving. He bounced off the wall and ducked under the swing of Beraht's waraxe, spitting blood as he moved. The Xeshlin leapt and extended a leg as though he were kicking the wall, using the force generated to rebound off and launch himself at the Uldra. Xaemus struck with both ends Queltuasor, rapid strikes to the sides, to the top and bottom, twisting to thrust only to spin around slash again. Somehow, the damned barbarian was able to match his speed, blocking, countering, ignoring cuts to the hands, arms, and legs. Every part of the Uldra's malformed body not wrapped in steel was bleeding, yet still he kept fighting.

"STOP!" The shouted command echoed down the corridor. Both combatants paused. They stood, gasping and staring hatred at each other. Beraht was covered in his own blood. Xaemus breathed wet pain.

"This is over," Karen Calonar proclaimed. The female, little more than an infant, stepped between the two hated warriors. She glanced at Beraht and commanded, "Put it down." To Xaemus' great surprise, the Uldra obeyed, lowering his waraxe. Karen Calonar then looked at him. "Put it down," she repeated. And, for some reason, Queltuasor obeyed.

"Do you really think Fak'Har will honor his deal?" Karen Calonar asked him.

Xaemus blinked. He did not mean to speak, did not register even that he was speaking, until he spoke, "No."

"No," the Truthseer of House Calonar echoed. She stepped towards Xaemus, waving away Beraht's growled warning. "You will stand before the Dark Empress," Karen Calonar predicted. "She will command you, and you will have to make a choice. What that choice will be," the Truthseer shrugged.

"What about-"

"Dy'lnnd has been taken south, just as Fak'Har said. But he has no control over her. He handed her over to one of the Sorcerous Sisters."

"They died at your walls," Xaemus objected.

"No, one didn't fight. One remained behind. She was warned by Fak'Har that the rest of her coven would be killed. Besides, she wasn't part of the Coven of the Puma's Leash. She was an infiltrator."

"For whom?" the Xeshlin grumbled.

"The Coven of Mount Godsfire. They think Dy'lnnd might be the Dark Empress, so she's being taken to their new High Priestess."

"Where?"

"You already know. Fak'Har already told you."

Xaemus stared down at the young Truthseer. "If I arrive without you," he said. "If I arrive alone-"

"You won't be alone," Karen Calonar promised. "You'll have help." She glanced behind at Beraht. The Uldra stared at her and snorted in derision. "The Xeshlin also have Medaka," she told him.

Beraht started. He stared at Karen Calonar, his entire body trembling in fury. His dim eyes went from the Truthseer to Xaemus. The *Xesh'lin* looked back at him, warring impulses of vengeance and his overwhelming loyalty to She of the Ebon Tears.

"They don't know what she really is," she told the Uldra. "Only that she's important to you and that you'll be important to the Dark Empress. Both of you. If you fight together," Karen Calonar told them both, "you will free Medaka and Dy'lnnd. If you oppose each other, both women will die on a Xeshlin altar. Choose."

Xaemus and Beraht stared hatred at each other. Ten thousand generations screamed at them through the Veil to obey the vendetta, to answer blood for blood. The Uldra victims of the Dark Empress' Soul Magic cried out for vengeance. The Sy'lva'i warriors crushed at the base of Uldron's walls demanded payment for their sacrifice. The slave-warriors butchered for entertainment, the merchants hunted for sport, the soldiers calling out from blood-soaked battlefields and the sailors grasping up from watery graves. All of them demanded the obedience to vendetta. Most powerful of all, an encounter now decades past stood between two younger, less-experienced warriors, and the scars both still carried.

The warriors stared hatred at each other, and chose.

Chapter 46

Chandra ran through the ruins of the city, fighting the urge to swear. Word was spreading that Prince Rogan and General Killdare were approaching, far sooner than they should have been able. That idiot Fak'Har was not supposed to break through the walls for days yet, let alone by obliterating a massive portion of the city's defenders. He was supposed to be trapped in a grinding, house-by-house assault within the walls. Instead, the colossal fool had ignited the Uldra gaslamp system. Instead of Chandra slipping out and making her way through crowded, terrified streets, here she was running through a burned-out husk of a city.

Too many things had gone wrong. Chandra's master had assured her that she would survive, that witch Aebreanna would be dead, along with her mongrel children, and Rashid would be freed of her spell. Chandra had dreamed for ages, since long before her master had recruited her, of the day she and Rashid would ride forever away from the Northlands. They would laugh together, and he would finally see her value. His mind would no longer be enslaved to that Sylva whore. He would... they would both... be free.

And since when did anyone else know about the passage? Chandra fumed at the memory of its discovery. She had conducted what was supposed to be her last reconnaissance, and realized that idiot Vincent was following her through the tunnel. She had only just barely avoided him! Thank Fate that he did not continue the search, or she may have had to kill him, attracting far too much attention. Worse, rather than using the tunnel to escape himself, or even taking that insipid priestess with whom he was so infatuated, the staggering moron told everyone of the passage's existence. An entire flood of refugees filled it, making her and Rashid's escape all the more problematic.

With so much movement, of Vagris' mercenaries and the castle's refugees, Chandra and Rashid had not even been able to make their escape from the city. They would never make any real distance, especially with Killdare's army out there somewhere, without horses, so Chandra had gone out in search of some. Instead, she had found Rogan and the witch.

Now she was running for her life. Aebreanna would pursue her. She had to. The witch had spent years thwarting Chandra's every action, every ambition. She would come after her now. But the spy had time. She could get back to the safehouse, back to Rashid. The western districts were least-touched by the gaslamp explosion. Most of the buildings were still in good condition. She weaved her way amidst the burnt, but standing, alleys. Chandra would have liked to move faster, to go straight to her safehouse, but she had to be careful.

With the sun dipping behind the ruins to the east, Chandra at last reached the innocuous-seeming house. She had been gone too long. Too many hours had passed. The spy had intended to go out only to secure horses and supplies, but had been delayed. She was unsure if Rogan's self-righteous squire had spotted her, but he had Aebreanna with him, and the chance of discovery was just too great. Chandra looked around, carefully assessing the area. She had not given Rashid another dose of Mindfog for hours, almost half a day. Far too long.

There was nothing. The neighborhood was looted and deserted. The castle refugees had seemed to leave, the last of them gathering under the leadership of that fool Vincent and his insipid priestess hours ago. They were all gone now, through the western gate, likely heading for Woodwall. The abandoned neighborhood was as quiet as a tomb.

Chandra entered the safehouse and closed the door behind her. The furniture was overturned or destroyed. The mercenaries had long since looted the area, even forcing their way into the safehouse, but had failed to find the trapdoor leading to the hidden basement. She went to the hidden door and worked the mechanism to unlock it. This was the final safeguard, of course. This was a place to put prisoners from which they could not escape. A shame, really, that she had been forced to use it on Rashid, but he would understand, eventually.

Chandra climbed down the staircase and turned, only to duck the swipe of a knife. Lightning-fast jabs, strikes, and sweeps came. The spy blocked as best she could in the dim light, trusting to instinct and training. The knife came in and she grabbed the hand wielding it, twisting the wrist and stripping the weapon away. In the same motion, she grabbed the arm and pulled, leveraging her weight to throw her attacker to the ground.

Rashid rolled on the stone floor and came back to his feet. He turned to face Chandra with murder in his eyes. "Mindfog!?!" he growled, throwing a small bottle to her feet. "How long?" He darted forward and threw another sequence of jabs at her stomach and face. "How long, damn you!"

"Rashid!" Chandra panted, blocking his strikes and trying to put distance between them. This was all but impossible, though, in the tiny basement. It was only a single room, barely large enough for two people to stand beside one another with their arms outstretched and not overlap their fingers. "Please! I can explain! You can be free of her!"

Rashid's eyes became nearly wild. He grabbed Chandra' left arm and spun her, twisting the limb into a painful, joint-burning lock. "How long, traitor!?!"

"I just wanted to help you!" Chandra insisted. When Rashid applied more pressure, she stepped into the direction of his lock, bringing her arm close to her body and twisting. She slipped through his grasp and faced him, driving her knee into his groin.

Rashid doubled and fell. Chandra's eyes widened. "I'm sorry!" she gasped. "Please, let me explain!"

"Explain?" he grunted, slowly regaining his feet. The spymaster was moving as though against a tide. He was struggling, Chandra realized, still under the effects of the Mindfog. "You can explain this?"

"You're under her spell," she reminded him. "She enthralled you, enslaved you! She poisoned your mind with her tears!"

"And you helped me by poisoning me with Mindfog?" Rashid's eyes, though still unfocused, were getting visibly clearer. "By locking me in this cell? What have you done, damn you!?!"

"They deserved it!" Chandra insisted. "This whole House! They forced us to serve them, to keep them in power! Without us, they would have fallen years ago!"

Rashid paused, staring at her. "What did you do?" he whispered. His eyes darted to the ladder leading up and out. "What have you done!?!"

The spymaster leapt for the stairs, but Chandra intercepted him. "No!" she screamed. "Just let me explain!" They fell back and Rashid screamed, stiffening. Chandra looked, and pulled the knife she had still been holding out of his back. Blood covered her hands and stained the front of her shirt. She dropped the knife and looked to Rashid.

He had rolled slightly, looking at her. His breath was weak, and fading. His eyes were wide, but going dark. "Traitor," he whispered and collapsed.

Chandra knelt there. "I'm sorry," she whispered. "I didn't mean... We couldn't... I don't..." Her hands shook. The blood that painted them fell in heavy droplets to the stone floor. She reached out, feeling at his neck. There was no pulse. She drew that hand along his lips, leaving a red smear. He was free, she realized. After a decade or more of horrid slavery, he was free of Aebreanna. She closed his eyes and adjusted him so that he lay as though sleeping. She had freed him. Chandra reached down and pulled free his gold ring, the only adornment he wore. She kissed his hand when she did so, and placed the ring on her own finger.

The sun was beginning to set when she exited the safehouse. Chandra carefully closed the door, doing so with as little noise as possible. She did not want to disturb Rashid. He had earned his rest, after all. The spy breathed deep, trying to let the tension in her body relax away. She had done a good thing, after all. No man could possibly want to remain enslaved to a Sylvai witch. Far better to be free. Rashid was a true man: strong, intelligent, protective, devoted. If he had control over his mind, he would have found a way to free himself from her. But, Sylvai tears were just too powerful. He would have wanted to be… He would have taken any destiny, rather than remain a slave. If he could have, he even would have thanked her.

After all, Chandra recalled, they had spent many years together, before the witch. He had helped her escape that slave caravan, and together they had killed the Xeshlin who had bought her. They had traveled Lanasia together, learning the spy's trade. They had even founded the agency together, and made House Calonar what it was. All of that while sharing so much time together.

She brought the golden ring to her lips, then held it to the door. He would rest well, now that he was free. A soft smile of contentment slid onto Chandra's face, until she turned around.

Aebreanna was standing across the street, staring at her.

Chandra froze. A thousand excuses, a thousand half-truths, a thousand impossible lies all came flooding into her mind. Her mouth formed beautiful lies that would convince Aebreanna of their enduring friendship, even as Chandra's many untruths had done so many times through the years.

But Aebreanna was changed. Chandra saw that immediately. Beyond the evil Wyrdmark and its obvious effects on the witch's body, the Sylva had returned a different being. Her arrogance was still there, of course, Chandra doubted any force in all the worlds could destroy the witch's arrogance. She still stood arrogantly tall, despite her tiny body. She still looked down her nose at the world, though now only through one eye. Her long mane, that ugly, animal flood of fur now spilled over half her face. Her clothes had changed, as well. Aebreanna had typically worn leather, dyed in soft, natural colors. Now, her vest was black and studded with silver. Her many Sylvai blades were gone as well, so that now only a single dagger was belted at her waist. More than anything, though, was the feeling of the witch. Aebreanna had been, although an arrogant bitch, still a creature of passion. The monster standing before Chandra now was cold.

Her one, glowing eye was not on Chandra's face, it was on the hand upon which rested Rashid's last gift to her. It still bore his blood, as did her hand, a necessary sacrifice to free him. Aebreanna looked up, her face still an emotionless mask. "Does he live?" she asked in a voice as devoid of feeling as a glacier is devoid of summer.

For some reason, some impossible, foolhardy reason, Chandra spoke the truth to this woman for the first time. "He's free."

Emotion, at last, shown on Aebreanna's face. Chandra had seen such feeling before, but only in the darkest of souls. Hunger was there, a terrible need. Some vile persona seemed to flow into Aebreanna, and the Sylva did nothing to fight it off. She slid a hand to her belt, where rode the single dagger. "Do you know what this is?" she asked in a voice full of the promise of something terrible.

"No," Chandra admitted.

"It is the Darkshard. It is a cursed thing, crafted of Soul and Shadow." She drew the blade. "It is your destiny."

They circled each other like predatory cats. Chandra drew her own blade, the very same knife that had liberated Rashid. Aebreanna saw the blood upon its blade, and her eye narrowed. She did not sprint, did not make sudden, rough motions. Instead, when the two women engaged, they did so as dancers. This was there way, the guiding principal of their every interaction: a flowing tide that spun one around the other.

Aebreanna had come to the Northern Keep as an enemy agent, Chandra recalled as they circled one another now, in the burnt western district. She had been in service to the Greysoul. Despite this, Rashid had brought her to the Northern Keep, her and that pet Uldra of hers. The spy glanced about, seeking some means of advantage, or escape, but saw none. Aebreanna kept her eye locked. Even in that first meeting, when Rashid declared her to be a guest, under observation, Chandra had hated the woman.

They moved towards each other. Chandra tried stabbing low, aiming for the witch's kidney, but Aebreanna grabbed the wrist. She was still holding the Darkshard back, for some reason, keeping it away from Chandra even as they pitied their strength against one another. This was her habit, the spy knew. The witch never committed everything to a single attack, a single strategy. Even her seduction of Rashid had been careful, calculating, employing a variety of means, from dangerous enemy to innocent victim.

Chandra grabbed her blade with her free hand and forced the knife forward, into Aebreanna's body. The witch twisted at the last second, so that the strike dug into her thigh, rather than piercing her kidney. This was probably the Sylva's greatest advantage, Chandra knew, her flexibility in both body and mind. Of course Rashid had slept with her. Why would he not? Her body was appealing, at least as much as an undeveloped Sylva's could be. Chandra had even been tempted to join them in their dalliance, thinking it to be only that. But Aebreanna had adjusted, twisting Rashid's mind away from casual sensuality and into total slavery.

Aebreanna pulled the knife from her thigh, still using only one hand, and spun, pulling Chandra over and around her shoulder to flip into the charred dust of the street. The spy regained her feet and turned, just as the witch made broad attacks from the left and right. Something was still holding her back, though. Her blows from the right were hard and angry, a match for the snarl curling the side of her mouth. But those from the left, from the hand holding the Darkshard, were as impassive as that hidden side of her face. Chandra grabbed Aebreanna's outstretched hand, mirroring the same throw the witch herself had just used, and slipped the Sylva over her shoulder.

Like Chandra, Aebreanna was not deterred. Immediately coming back to her feet and turned to face the woman who dared compete for the man she had enslaved. They made a series of light strikes at each other, probing, testing. Aebreanna stabbed the Darkshard towards Chandra's face, but still without great power. The spy deflected this strike and countered, slashing a light red line across the witch's abdomen, just below her leather vest. Aebreanna seemed not to notice the injury, but instead dropped the Darkshard low and jabbed it towards Chandra's own middle. The spy grabbed that incoming wrist as she had done in countless battles before, and struck just above with the handle of her knife. This strike should have dislodged the Darkshard, should have sent it flying from Aebreanna's grip, but it failed. Something kept that evil blade in her hand.

Aebreanna struck with her open left hand, beating on Chandra's back and shoulder before grabbing her off-arm and twisting it up into a horridly painful lock. The witch then began kicking, driving her knee up into Chandra's chest and abdomen, forcing the air from her lungs. Desperately, the spy dropped her knife and grabbed the back of Aebreanna's outstretched knee with both hands, driving her shoulder into the witch and forcing her away.

Chandra stumbled back, frantically trying to regain her air. Aebreanna paused herself, as though waiting. The witch was patient, after all. She had not pushed her seduction of Rashid, had not ever forced the issue. She had allowed him to pursue her, allowed him to assume the assertive role. She had allowed him to make every overt action, drawing him in.

Chandra did not wait until she had fully regained her breath, but instead shot forward before Aebreanna could be ready. She raised a fist and struck at the witch's face, but the Sylva caught the blow with her left hand, blocking the attack, only to jab that hand forward, into Chandra's eye. The spy made a wild, blind swing with her other arm, only to have that blocked, before moving forward to grab Aebreanna. She was stronger than the Sylva, after all. She should be able to leverage that and force the witch to the ground. They grappled for only a moment before Aebreanna spun and, with only one arm, flipped Chandra head over foot, rolling over top of the witch and spilling to the ground again.

Chandra felt strangely comfortable in this moment. Rashid had done something similar to her, after all, a decade ago. He had returned from the mission to rescue Aebreanna from the Greysoul enslaved. He could not pull himself more than ten paces from her. His eyes had been forever locked on her body. He had become a prisoner of the tears, of his lust for her. Chandra had tried to intervene on the morning of their wedding, to somehow force him free of the spell. He had rejected her though, laughing at her concern and entering the Sylvai shrine where she would seal her enchantment upon him. Chandra had not entered, but instead had fallen to her knees in the dirt outside.

Now, Chandra looked up at the woman who had beaten her, who had enslaved the man she... "He was only with you because of the tears," she said.

"Perhaps." Aebreanna looked down on her just as she had for all these years. "And yet, he was still mine."

Chandra screamed at her enemy and lunged forward. Aebreanna said nothing, did nothing. A strange sadness washed over her face, and her right arm seemed to flinch, without her intention. Chandra stopped and looked down at the Darkshard, impaling her heart. She looked up, into the terrible darkness, the awakening evil, within Aebreanna's glowing eye.

The Sylva leaned in and whispered in her ear, "Just as your soul is now mine."

Chapter 47

"Vagris!" Rogan's voice was like an avalanche, and unstoppable tide thundering against a shattering cliff. He leveled Talon, his trusted longsword, at his most hated enemy, and charged. Stick, never in need of encouragement, snorted his eagerness, his hideous hunger, to finally be let loose to inflict suffering on those most deserving of it. Rogan did not try to guide, steer, or otherwise control his warhorse. The knight just let go. He dropped the reigns and trusted to Stick, his oldest, most reliable, most constant of companions. Together, in this moment, there were of one mind.

Vagris saw his approaching death and cursed. "Stop him!" the warlord snapped at the four Bellonari escorting him. The warriors, men from across Lanasia and trained in the same deadly skills Rogan had learned, spread out in a tight line of leveled weapons across the ruined street.

"Take them!" Rogan snapped.

Rei leapt from her horse and flipped in the air. Mid-flight, she gestured at the Bellonari. Umbral portals appeared and horrific nightmares surged out. Things unnamed with tentacles, clawed limbs, serpentine bodies, screaming mouths with endless rows of fangs. Their scaled flesh shifted from one hideous color to the next. Their too-many eyes narrowed like some feline predators, only to then spiral like the twisted mirror of one's own madness. Even for the Bellonari, trained, disciplined, and unbreakable, these were impossible to face. They screamed and back away.

Gendo also left his saddle, rolling to the ground and coming up on one knee. He raised the great spear with its curved blade, and brought the weapon's blunt end down. The earth recoiled from the strike, a wave of stone and rubble rolling down the broken street. The Bellonari, already backing away from Rei's illusions, were violently thrown from their feet and dashed upon the ground.

Rogan and Stick, only a half-step behind Gendo's mystical attack, thundered past the Bellonari. Vagris ran around the waiting cart, putting it between him and his enemy, but Stick leapt across the obstruction, clearing it with room to spare. Seeing this, the warlord ran towards a nearby building, most of it still standing, but risked a glance behind his shoulder. In a move unrehearsed, unpracticed, and capable only through the near-manic hatred they felt, Stick charged the traitor and, at the last moment, lowered his head and dug his forelegs into the lose earth. Rogan was thrown from the saddle, hurling himself at Vagris. The two men collided and were forced through the window in front of which the Bellonar General had been standing.

Both Rogan and Vagris crashed through the glass. In almost identical movements, they both rolled across the wooden floor of the nearly-intact shop and came back to their feet, facing each other with swords in hand. There were no words, for none were needed. Here was Vagris, the man who had betrayed Rogan and tried to murder him, the man who had orchestrated and led the destruction of the Northern Keep and the slaughter of its people... Rogan's people. Here was Rogan, the traitor of the Brotherhood, the only failure in Vagris' career and the source of his shame. No words were needed between these men. Their hate was beyond speech, beyond thought.

They came together in a crash of steel. Strike, thrust, parry, dodge, block. They were men equally trained by the Brotherhood. Vagris ripped his sword from its scabbard and held it low, Rogan mirroring the motion with Talon. The knight's gaze was torn down, though. "Zhu Shasho," he snarled at the man who could have been his brother.

Vagris raised the Tramanese blade. "My prize, for killing Silverhorn." The traitor held his sword in a low guard and Rogan darted in, words lost, thought lost. Even their hatred, somehow, was lost. The knight was passed hatred, past rage. This was the man who had murdered his mentor. Vagris had not killed Silverhorn, had not defeated him; the traitor had poisoned Rogan's teacher and stolen his sword.

Rogan held Talon held above his shoulder, swinging the longsword in a hard chop. Vagris brought his own weapon up the block, but rolled his shoulder. Rogan instantly sensed the building counter and stepped back, just as Vagris' blade struck the open air that had, only an instant before, had been occupied by Rogan's torso. The knight did not hesitate, but raised and twisted Talon for yet another attack, this one probing his enemy's defense. Vagris blocked the flicking cut, but immediately countered, striking against Rogan's shoulder. The knight twisted, bringing his hands up and Talon's point low, deflecting the warlord's cut, only to immediately swing his blade in a dancing loop, slashing against his enemy's chest. Vagris blocked the latest attack and both warriors raised their blades, but with light steps they back away, circling, assessing.

Rogan could not fight the snarling hatred crawling across his face. Each strike was a reminder of that night. The ring of steel and they were back on that rooftop. The impact of a sword, and they were arguing about the assignment. "She's a child!" Rogan had hissed.

"She's a target!" Vagris had insisted. "She's our mission!"

"They want us to rape a child!" Rogan spit as though choking on the words. "What in Underworld has happened to the Brotherhood that this is acceptable! Where's the honor in this? Where's the decency?"

Vagris had stopped and put a finger in Rogan's chest. "Your masters both thought they could fight with honor," he had pointed out. "Look what happened to them."

Rogan roared in fury and raised Talon. Vagris began raising his own blade, but the knight shifted the angle of his attack, instead sweeping from the side. The warlord was able to adjust his block and counter, forcing Rogan a step back.

The knight had seen more examples of his former-brother's contempt for decency on the ride in. They had passed the Sylvai restaurant Kyla so loved, and passed the bodies of the family who ran it. The place had been ransacked, and the father still had the kitchen knife in his hand, unspotted with blood.

Vagris narrowed his eyes. The warlord leaned back slightly and slowly brought his weapon into a low guard. He feinted upwards, drawing Talon up, but then looped his blade down and under Rogan's sword, rolled his shoulder until his weapon was level, and lunched in.

Rogan saw the attack coming, but could do nothing to defend. It was a perfect strike, flawlessly executed, a model for the manuals. Vagris was everything a Bellonar was supposed to be in these modern times, skilled, strategic, ruthless. Rogan had undergone the same training as his enemy, but lacked the merciless precision. However, the prince of the Northlands had also received training from a lunatic Uldra.

Rogan dropped Talon and stepped into Vagris' strike. He twisted and grabbed the warlord's arm, yanking him off-balance and stepping back, pulling Vagris down and away, tumbling to the ground. The warlord lost his sword and had to tuck his shoulder, rolling as best he could back to his feet.

Vagris came back into a light stance, almost bouncing on the tips of his toes. The warlord was smaller and lighter than Rogan, even in chainmail. The knight did not dance or hop, he only stood, chin slightly down, glaring his hatred for the man before him. Neither glanced at the blades that had slid across the floor. Neither looked away from the killer before him.

They each moved forward. Rogan kicked a light, probing foot and Vagris' shin, but the warlord only hoped back and darted his own tentative punch. Rogan jerked his head back and continued to circle. Vagris advanced, flicking more probing fists. He lightly kicked at Rogan's shins and hip. The knight did not respond. He was no match for skill and precision, so he would not try. Vagris danced in once more, his body declaring to Rogan his intent for a meaningful strike. Rogan ducked under the jab and struck at his enemy's middle, working his way up Vagris' body with punch after punch, finishing with a hard forward jab across the warlord's face. The knight tried to follow up with another blow to the face, but Vagris ducked this and countered with a quick double-jab, knocking Rogan back. The knight stumbled and let himself fall to the ground, rolling away to gain precious seconds and come back to his feet, his arms raised and ready.

Vagris came forward, punching Rogan in the face. The knight exaggerated his response, ducking low. When the warlord came in for another attack, Rogan jabbed his elbow out, catching Vagris at the bridge of his nose, before grabbing his enemy by the back of the head and driving his fist into the warlord's jaw. The Bellonar General stumbled, trying to clear his vision, but Rogan was on him, driving another hateful punch to the side of the man's face and forcing Vagris to the ground. This time, it was the warlord who rolled, who had to buy time in a directed tumble that brought him back to his feet. Rogan came in, but Vagris spun, crouching low and pivoting on one foot, the other lashing out to take the knights' legs out from under him. Rogan hit the floor but was back to his knees, but not before Vagris was standing over him, grinning through a mouthful of blood. Rogan tried to punch, to jam his fist into his enemy's crotch, but the warlord caught this, snarling "You dirty fighting-!!!"

Rogan answered by suddenly surging up, ducking his head in and then lashing it up, so that the back of his skull impacted Vagris' chin. The warlord stumbled back, and the knight grabbed his shoulders and slammed the front of his skull into the man's nose. Both stumbled back. Rogan fell against a counter, a hard, wooden surface that held him up. The world was a blur, red and spinning. He breathed and coughed and spit out a gob of blood he had no use for.

The knight turned and leaned against the counter. Vagris was on the opposite end of the same wooden support. The two men, panting and bleeding, stared at each other. Wearily, they stepped out, facing one another. Rogan moved as though to punch, but suddenly found himself lacking the strength. Vagris deflected his outstretched arm, using the momentum to push Rogan down. He then grabbed the back of the knight's head and forced it down against his upraised knee.

Rogan snarled through spit and tears, grabbing Vagris and shoving him back. The warlord could not regain his footing as Rogan pushed at him, throwing punch after punch into his middle. Finally, Vagris was slammed against the back wall and Rogan immediately launch a quick double-strike onto the man's face. The warlord was able to make a desperate block of yet another punch, once again grabbing the back of Rogan's head. The knight twisted this time, however, using his hands as a push and block of the upcoming knee. So, Vagris grabbed Rogan about the neck, pulling him down into a chokehold. In response, the knight balled his fist and drove that into the warlord's groin. When Vagris doubled over in pain, Rogan, using the advantage of being beneath his enemy, bodily picked the warlord up and dove forward, driving them both into the unyielding wooden floor.

The men lay there for only the briefest moment. They began grabbing at each other, snarling and cursing and spitting blood at each other. They tried grabbing, they choking, they tried doing anything they could to find purchase. Vagris savagely bit Rogan's outstretched hand. The knight ground his knee into the warlord's groin. Rogan punched Vagris. Vagris kicked Rogan. The warlord tried kicking his enemy away, but Rogan twisted the foot away and leapt atop the Bellonar, grabbing his shoulders and slamming him into the ground again and again and again. He then jammed his thumb into Vagris' eye, the warlord screaming as a fountain of blood and pus and gore erupted from his face.

Rogan knelt overtop of his most hated enemy, his greatest betrayer, the man who embodied everything the Bellonari had become, in defiance of what Silverhorn, the knight's great mentor, had believed. Rogan punched the face that had taken control of the Brotherhood. He punched the face that had betrayed and tried to murder him. He punched the face that had led a mercenary army in burning Wildelves Wood. He punched the face that destroyed the villages of the Northlands, sacked his home, and threatened his family. He kept punching long after the screaming stopped, long after the moving stopped. He kept punching until there was nothing but flat, cold meat under his fists.

Rogan Eigenhard, prince of the Northlands and champion of House Calonar, stepped out of the ruined shop. One of his eyes was swollen shut. His nose was broken. He was missing a few teeth. His body screamed its need for rest and healing. In one hand, he held Talon, a gift from the King and from Remm Stonebearer, before Rogan had left to rescue Aebreanna. In the other hand, the knight held Zhu Shasho, the blade of his mentor. He blinked his one good eye and looked around,

The other Bellonari were dead. Rei and Gendo were finishing them and moving towards him. Gendo's eyes were wide and Rei's hand was covering her open mouth. They said nothing as they stared at their prince. Stick walked up, having chased off the Bellonari horses. The black warhorse nudged Rogan's shoulder, and the knight patted his oldest friend on the head. Stick nudged Rogan again, half-turning him towards the castle. The knight blinked again and looked up at his home. He then grabbed Stick's reigns and said, "Let's ride."

Chapter 48

"Time's up, Fak'Har!" Kyla's taunt echoed off the castle's cracking walls.

The Shadowed Mage grinned at the princess, and Mary felt a renewed terror rising in her soul. "Really?" Fak'Har sneered. "Your man-toy will still need an hour to reach us. More than enough time to finish my business."

"No more, Fak'Har," the princess insisted. "No more death, no more suffering." Kyla motioned about the broken courtyard, filled with the dead and dying. "What more could you possibly want? My city is destroyed! Thousands are dead! Families broken forever! You've destroyed Wildelves Wood and massacred the Sylvai! The Uldra are at war with one another! What more is there to gain here!?!"

"The Inversion is upon us, princess," the Shadow Mage replied with surprising sincerity. "I would catalyze it, hasten its passage." Fak'Har's tone shifted then, Mary thought. The barest hint of uncertainty, of dark reflection, perhaps even of regret, passed over him. "The suffering has only begun, Kyla," he said. "House Calonar had to die, it was Fated. The Inversion will make all this," the Shadowed Mage waved his hand to encompass the castle, the city, and the forest, "it will make this all seem as nothing. And even then, the Dark Empress will return, and bring with her the Demon-God." He pointed at Kyla's stomach. "Would you really bring a child into this world, only to watch it suffer over the next five years?"

"There is always hope, Fak'Har," Kyla insisted, a hand going to her unborn son. "There is always a chance. Each generation has Fatetouched, people who can thwart the Prophecy, change things for the better."

"Or the worse," the Shadowed Mage countered. "You never knew your brother," Fak'Har reminded. "He died before you were born. Kyle Calonar was supposed to be the Heir of Calonar. He was supposed to lead the fight against Kelinva and her Demon-God, and sire the One Who Comes. But a Fatetouched intervened, just as she did at Velaross to save your father. Kyle Calonar was the last possible chance to thwart the rise of Ramelech, but he was killed. And so, we got your precious Prince Rogan."

Fak'Har glanced at Mary, his insidious grin slipping further from his lips. "And now we have another of these damned Fatetouched," he said. "Another foolish child, stumbling around the world, causing chaos." The Shadowed Mage shook his head. "Enough of this foolishness. All I've ever wanted was to minimize the suffering of the Prophecy, to make the end of things as painless as possible. But you, you and your cursed family and my fool of a brother all think you can stop what's to come." Fak'Har sneered up at the Calonar sigil, engraved in the stone above the large double doors leading into the main hall. "Heroes," he spat. "All you've done is draw out what could have been simple, quick, and painless. No more." The Shadowed Mage raised a hand, calling to it the inky darkness from all around. "Now, you die, little princess, and the Heir of Calonar will find someone more pliant to grow his seed."

Mary stepped in front of her princess. Kyla tried grabbing for her, but the handmaiden was as stone, immovable, unflinching. She drew the sword Colonel Rainer had given her and raised it, her ignorance of fighting irrelevant in the face of her duty.

"Oh, please," Fak'Har snorted. He flicked a hand and Mary was sent flying, crashing against the wall beside the hall's doors.

The air was knocked from her and Rainer's sword slipped from her untrained hand. Kyla was there, beside her, as the world swam back into focus. The princess was saying something to her, tears streaming from her face. She held up one of her small hands, and a glowing light appeared. "No," Mary gasped, grabbing her hand and pushing it away. "No magic."

The handmaiden sat up, ignoring the burning protest coming from her ribs. She coughed, and quickly wiped away the small fleck of red that dripped from her chin. Mary looked about and saw Rainer's sword. She grabbed the hilt and once more lifted the weapon, standing in front of her princess. "You won't hurt her," Mary swore.

From the steps, Aloisa barked a command and the remaining defenders roared their accompaniment to Mary's defiance. The soldiers formed a wall, overlapping what equipment they had, whether it was dented shields or blunted poleaxes. Behind that unflinching line, Amatria and her grey-robed mages reached out and called to their hands crackling blue energy.

"We are House Calonar!" Aloisa roared, and the other defenders shouted their agreement.

"And today," Fak'Har answered, "House Calonar dies." He once again called the shadows to his hand and, with an almost negligent flick of the wrist, the Shadowed Mage send tendrils of evil lancing forward. The defenders of House Calonar stood firm. They caught the insidious attack on their weapons, their shields, their armor. Amatria and her mages raised prismatic shields that tried to block the Shadowed Mage's attack. They held, growling and roaring and snarling their defiance against Fak'Har's evil, but they could not hold. The tendrils of purplish black writhed, twisting through Amatria's magical shields. They penetrated the shields and the upraised poleaxes. They burrowed through armor, reaching hungrily for the soft flesh beneath. Aloisa and the few defenders screamed a painful chorus as Fak'Har's magic touched their flesh and began burning deeper.

Mary jumped forward, reaching out with Rainer's sword. She slashed at the hideous tendril spearing into Aloisa's chest. The weapon of purplish-black flinched, releasing the Gunrsvein woman, and reared back. She collapsed to the stone steps, gasping and coughing blood. Fak'Har's tendril loomed over Mary, swaying like a serpent ready to strike. It twisted and shot down at the handmaiden, who held her ground.

"NO!" A golden light, edged with blue lightning, appeared around Mary and the surviving defenders. The light not only stopped Fak'Har's attack, it dissolved the evil tendrils entirely. Mary glanced back and saw her princess floating once more. The invisible wind of magic once more buoyed her up, causing her long hair to dance about her head and her robe to billow about her gravid body. Kyla's eyes shone with the power of her magical legacy, and her entire body glowed with a radiant aura of gold and blue. Like a divine mist, her nightmarish Dream drifted out, caressing the unliving knights and sending them stumbling back, jerking as though suffering some impossible malaise. Kyla's nightmare even reached out to Fak'Har, but slid against the dome of shadowy evil he erected.

"No!" Mary screamed. "Kyla, STOP!"

The princess did not stop, though. Her golden Dream infused the people who stood, ready to die in defense of her family. It comforted them, easing their pain and once more closing their wounds. Like a mother's blanket, the shining Dream surrounded each of them, offering solace against the darkness. The unliving knights were forced away, stumbling against each other and their own legs. The horrid creatures were corralled against the gate, as far from the survivors and the great hall as was possible. The nightmarish Dream gathered itself together, building in intensity, solidifying into images of dragons and Druug and faceless warriors. These phantoms advanced on the unliving knights, ready to destroy them forever.

And then, Kyla screamed, and the Dream vanished.

Mary looked once more at her princess, and gasped. Kyla had collapsed to the ground. Her handmaiden rushed to her friend's side. Kyla's water had broken, and with it came far too much blood. Mary looked to the princess' flushed face, and both women shared a look of mutual fear, mutual horror. "Not for me," Mary whispered. "Not for us."

Kyla screamed again, contorting.

Fak'Har let his protective dome fade. He breathed what was almost a sigh of regret, then shook his head and advanced once more.

"No!" a woman's voice demanded. Mary looked, as all eyes did. Queen Nora stood at the center of the great double doors leading to the castle's main hall. The Lady of House Calonar seemed to have aged decades since last Mary had seen her. Her hair, once shining blonde with only subtle streaks of old age was now entirely silver. Her beautiful face, once a rival for her daughter's in its enchanting glory, was now deeply creased, the skin hanging off protruding bones. Her sunken eyes were still their glorious blue, but beset with heavy, dark rings. She stood tall, despite the withering of her body, and her gaze was level and steady upon the Shadowed Mage. "No more, Fak'Har," the Queen of the Northlands commanded.

"Your Majesty," the Shadowed Mage sneered with a mocking bow. He made a show of looking behind and beyond the Lady of House Calonar. "And what's this?" Fak'Har said in derisive surprise. "The great King of the Northlands has graced us with his presence.

Mary and all those in the courtyard looked, and despaired. Simon, the young guardsman Colonel Rainer had ordered away from the guardhouse, was carrying some frail husk of yellowed flesh and protruding bones. It was not a body; it could not be a body. Mary's mind recoiled from the though, the possibility of anything living being so withered. Her rational thoughts, though, rebelled against the handmaiden's will and identified the limp doll hanging from Simon's arms.

"Behold!" Fak'Har laughed. "Behold the champion of the people! Behold the King of the Northlands! Behold the greatest adept to ever wield staff or spell! Behold the Black Duke of the Northern Keep! Behold the last of the Heroes of Fate! Behold, Cylan Calonar!"

The greatest hero to ever live feebly turned his head. Blind eyes looked out on his broken home. A mouth, barely capable of drawing breath, was open and drooling. Clawlike hands, which once bested Vaeyen, Xeshlin, warlords, and Umbra, hung impotently, barely twitching.

"Oh, to see the great leader brought low," Fak'Har continued to mock. He glanced at Queen Nora. "Worry not, Lady of Calonar. I'll end his suffering." The Shadowed Mage moved forward again, but stopped. A look of confusion marred his evil face. He glanced about, then looked up.

"FAK'HAR!!!" came a roar that would sunder the mountains themselves. All faces turned up, and hope was restored. From out of the setting sun came an Uldra. "Round two, bent-wand!" Beraht thundered as he came flying out of the sky, bolts of holy power arcing from his mighty waraxe. Fak'Har cursed and dodged, just as the great warrior impacted the ground. There was an explosion of dust and stone. Debris was sent flying in all direction. Everyone in the courtyard stared as the cloud settled. Beraht stood in the center of the small crater his arrival had created. The great Uldra warrior looked about, raising his weapon. He spotted the Shadowed Mage and roared, leaping once more.

Fak'Har desperately restored his dome of protective Shadow. Beraht impacted it with a great clap of thunder. The magical defense was shattered and Fak'Har was forced once more the tumble out of the way as Beraht's holy weapon created yet another small crater. The Uldra swung his waraxe in might arcs, seeking the head of the Shadowed Mage.

Fak'Har snapped an order to his unliving knights, and the monsters responded. They swarmed towards Beraht, their greatswords upraised and their pace, for once, urgent. The Uldra turned and swung his great waraxe. One of the creatures was caught by the holy weapon and exploded into a shower of armor pieces and the dust contained within. Beraht swung again and again, destroying more of Fak'Har's blasphemous creations. One of the creatures reared up and tried to bring its greatsword down, but Beraht caught the weapon with his free hand and, with a jerk, broke the unholy blade. He then stabbed the shattered blade into the creature's visor and kicked it away.

Fak'Har barked words in some hateful mockery of the language of magic, and bands of midnight black wrapped themselves around Beraht's wrists and ankles. The Shadowed Mage stood and raised his hand up, causing the Uldra to rise into the air. "How many times must I kill, you, Uldra!?!" Fak'Har demanded. He swept his arm up in a large loop, and there was a great explosion. Beraht was sent flying back into the air, arcing overhead and crashing into the castle.

The Shadowed Mage gasped for air, seemingly on the verge of exhaustion. He shook his head, though more, it appeared, from exasperation than anything else. Fak'Har turned back to Queen Nora and the handful of survivors gathered around her. He walked towards them, moving into the center of the courtyard. "Words," he snarled, "cannot express how tired I am of all of you!" The Shadowed Mage raised his hand again and called to them his horrid power.

"Now, you-" An earth-shattering flood of pure magical force avalanched through the courtyard. Fak'Har was caught in the center of that catastrophic tide. He disappeared for a moment, swallowed into its power and thrust across the courtyard to impact the fall wall.

The setting sun broke through the grey sky. Beams of light spilled down onto Castle Calonar. Mary was warmed by one of these beams. She, and all those present, living and unliving, looked. Mary's eyes filled, her heart leapt, feeling as though it would burst from her chest. Rainer's sword slipped from her grip. Her hands clasped together and the ring he gave her felt as though it would ignite in loving flame.

Standing, framed in the glory of the setting sun, and raising high the legendary sword of House Calonar, was Tomas. The ribbon of Mary's mothers was tied about his scabbard, its tails flapping like a battle standard. His breastplate gleamed and his long hair danced in the rising wind. With him were the Archaeknights, the great defenders of the Northlands, standing at attention and awaiting his command. "Fak'Har!" her champion and husband-to-be thundered. Tomas leveled Steelheart at the fool who had threatened her, and charged.

Chapter 49

Somewhere behind him, Tomas heard Ward order the
Archaeknights to destroy Fak'Har's unliving knights. This was good, some rational
part of his mind mused. This left the Shadowed Mage for him. The Archaeknights
spread out through the courtyard. Sarah leapt into the air, faster and nimbler by far
than any other. Her red hair lashed about, even as her arms and legs and her long-
handled blade did. She literally danced upon the shoulders of the unliving knights,
throwing them off-balance, stumbling into the attacks of her teammates. Asaya let fly
her whistle, and a mystical gale knocked a dozen of the monsters from their feet,
allowing the blonde Halvan woman to dart amongst them, slashing with her twin
rapiers. Kara grabbed one of the black-armored abominations with her magic, lifting
it and slamming it back to the ground again and again, shattering the monster. Teka
Ironhands moved around the edge of the courtyard, running to the side of Kyla and
Mary and bringing her Life Magic to bear on the bleeding, pregnant princess. Deriel
attacked from above, his power of flight keeping the young Sylvu well out of reach
and allowing him attacks of opportunity as his teammates presented them. Ilaywin's
magical arrows found every gap in the unliving knights' armor, detonating with a flash
and destroying the monsters from within. Ward led his team into the midst of
Fak'Har's creations, and destroyed them.

The Shadowed Mage faced Tomas with a sneer of contempt. He flung a spell at
the charging squire, but Tomas flicked Steelheart and dispersed the magic. Fak'Har's
eyes widened in understanding, clearly identifying the legendary sword of House
Calonar. Tomas reached the Shadowed Mage and Steelheart came down in a deadly
arc. Fak'Har vanished and reappeared several feet away. The squire turned and
charged again, swinging his sword in an effort to end the monster once and for all,
but the adept vanished once more.

Fak'Har reappeared in front of Tomas. The Shadowed Mage laughed and clapped
his hands. In flashes of magic, more Fak'Hars appeared. A dozen, then a score, of
mirror-replicas of the Shadowed Mage surrounded Tomas. The young warrior laid
about with his legendary sword. Tomas swung Steelheart, and each phantom was
dispersed upon contact with the venerable blade. The squire spun his blade and
dispersed more of the illusory Fak'Hars. More appeared, though, and advanced on
Tomas with daggers of shadow. He glanced about, the rational part of his mind
making a swift calculation. He grimaced and sheathed Steelheart, opening his

thoughts. The nascent sorcerer did not just open himself to the Winds of Magic, but to the Veil itself, closing his eyes and whispering. He called out for help, and Alexia responded.

Tomas opened his eyes with an opalescent glow. He and Alexia glanced about the courtyard and they smiled. Together, they clapped his hands, sending out a wave of magic that dispersed all illusions. Fak'Har, the real one, stumbled back with a snarl. Tomas and Alexia thrust their hands then to the ground and thick, thorny vines erupted from the flagstones. These living weapons reached out and slashed at the Shadowed Mage. They drew streams of blood and screams of pain. Fak'Har growled in the mockery of the language of magic and lashed out with blades of purplish-black. Tomas and Alexia twisted their hands and arms in a complex pattern, chanting in the language of magic and summoning a tiny whirlwind. They let this mystical construct free, spinning it out at the Shadowed Mage. Fak'Har again snarled a spell and dispersed the newest attack. He then called a pilar of midnight fire and sent it charging towards Tomas and Alexia. They spun aside and gathered many nearby stones, flinging them at the Shadowed Mage.

"We have no time for this!" Alexia whispered in their mind. "Cylan's life fades by the second!"

"Can we beat him?" Tomas asked. Fak'Har reached out with another spell and sent several greatswords dropped by defeated monsters flying at them.

"Not in time!" Alexia answered, leading them through the creation of a magical shield that repelled the deadly missiles.

"Then what do we do?" They conjured elementals of air and earth, which attacked Fak'Har. The Shadowed Mage repelled their combined assault and dissipated the mystical creatures.

"The Archaeknights," Alexia advised. "They can occupy him while we heal Cylan."

Tomas glanced around the courtyard. Ward was picking up one of the unliving knights and hurling it off the escarpment while Drystan teleported across the area, gathering the wounded near Teka. Khwezi, the Davenorian, was combining his mastery of fire with Fikri's control over water. The pair were effectively neutralizing many of Fak'Har's monsters, but were unable to decisively defeat them.

"They're occupied," Tomas pointed out, dodging them aside as the Shadowed mage sent a hail of armor pieces at them.

"You can solve that particular problem," Alexia said. "Use your affinity with the Wind of Death. Attune your sight to the creatures."

Tomas did as his friend instructed, letting her take charge of the fight against the Shadowed Mage. While Alexia sent elemental bolts at Fak'Har, the squire opened himself up to the Wind of Death. The White Lady was everywhere, nearly overwhelming Tomas. So many had fallen, and were soon to fall, that the squire could not differentiate one object within the Wind of Death from any other.

"Focus," Alexia whispered.

Tomas did, concentrating on one of the unliving knights. He saw it then, the solution. Fak'Har had mixed together several of the Winds in creating his blasphemous nightmares. The point, the central purpose, of that process had been to suppress the Winds of Thought and Death. Tomas had no facility with the Wind of Thought, having only briefly experienced its weakest form among the Khepri, but the Wind of Death was his to command. While Alexia defended them from several of Fak'Har's tendrils of evil Shadow, Tomas called to the White Lady. He pointed to the unliving knights, to these perversions of the natural order. There was a lock of Shadow on each of the monsters, a shell that prevented the Wind of Death from touching them. Tomas concentrated and directed the White Lady away from the despairing wounded, denying them for a moment Death's release. With his magic, the squire reached into each of the unliving knights, and offered the White Lady a means of access.

"No!" Fak'Har shouted, sensing what Tomas was doing. The Shadowed Mage tried desperately to disrupt the squire's spell, to counter or even misdirect what the nascent death mage was attempting. Alexia, though, denied him. She forced him to respond only to her magical attacks.

Tomas did not feel as though he were attacking Fak'Har's monsters. His magic, the Wind of Death, was not an evil one, nor something meant to inflict suffering. In fact, the White Lady and Her death mages were harbingers of peace. Tomas realized that now. The monsters battling the Archaeknights were only more victims of Fak'Har's evil. They suffered from within their black-enameled prisons. They called out for help, for the freedom of the Veil, for an end to their pain and horror. Tomas offered them this. He reached out, through the Wind of Death, and guided the people trapped within those horrid, violent shells into the waiting arms of the White Lady.

Across the courtyard, the unliving knights collapsed. The pieces of their spiked, hideous armor simply fell apart. Their serrated, barbed greatswords fell to the ground. Their helmets clanged uselessly to the flagstones. Dust was all that rested within the armor, and this was caught in a liberating breeze that carried the victims within out, across the Veil. Tomas heard their joyful cries, their relived expressions of gratitude to him as the White Lady guided them home.

"Archaeknights!" Alexia called out. She pointed at Fak'Har.

Without need of further command, Ward and his team launched themselves at the Shadowed Mage. Ilaywin fired arrow after mystical arrow, forcing Fak'Har back. Khwezi, Fikri, and Asaya added their elements to the barrage. Kara hurled stones and broken weapons and bits of armor at him. Sarah and Ward advanced on either side of the Shadowed Mage, preparing to hurl themselves at him.

"Now," Alexia whispered, "while they have him occupied. Use the Seal."

Tomas nodded and ran towards the stairs leading up to the double doors and House Calonar. He reached into Aebreanna's bag, still draped over his shoulder, and retrieved the Healing Sphere.

"NO YOU DON'T!!!" Fak'Har lashed out with a wave of shadowy evil. The Archaeknights were sent hurtling from him. He reached out with his magic and grabbed a heavy dagger, calling it to his hand. The Shadowed Mage reached back, preparing to throw the blade at Tomas, but paused. He glanced aside, at Kyla and Mary, and grinned. He threw the knife with a snarl of Shadow Magic, speeding it and granting the weapon greater lethality.

With a wet, heavy impact, the dagger impaled Mary's chest.

Tomas' love, his intended wife, the very beating of his heart, looked down in surprise. She then looked at her champion, seemed as though she would say something, and fell.

"Mary!" Kyla screamed, and crawled to her handmaiden's side.

Tomas stared in shock, frozen. Then, his very soul twitching in fury, he spun and tore from Alexia her magic. Thorned branches erupted from the flagstones at Fak'Har's feet, wrapping around the Shadowed Mage. They tore into his flesh and raised him up, crucifying him in midair. Tomas tightened his grip, and the branches and vines twisted deeper, bringing an agonized scream from Fak'Har'

"Choose!" the Shadowed Mage managed to yell. "Use have the Seal of Life, boy!" He looked at Tomas, then to the two groups at the entrance to the castle's main hall. "It will only work for one! You can only heal one!" He then screamed again as the thorns it deeper.

Tomas looked to Mary, cradled in Kyla's arms and bleeding her life away. The squire looked to King Cylan Calonar, faded to almost nothing. He could sense the White Lady's question. She would claim one, but had paused, awaiting Tomas' choice. Alexia was silent; the young man could feel his friend's loving concern, but also her impotence. He was the Fatetouched, the one who walked outside the Wind of Fate. The choice was his.

"God forgive me," Tomas whispered. He looked up and screamed, "Your Majesty!" throwing the Healing Sphere up to House Calonar.

A guardsman who had been carrying the King but set him down, caught the Seal of Life and handed it to Queen Nora. The Queen of the Northlands took the Healing Sphere and held it to her husband's chest, invoking its quintessential magic. "HEAL!" she demanded. The soft white light of the Seal of Life shifted to gold. It's brilliant luminescence filled the courtyard, spilling out, further and further. The Healing Sphere became blinding, shattering the growing shadows of dusk.

"NO!" Fak'Har screamed, his defeat more painful than the thorns chewing upon his flesh. "YOU DON'T KNOW WHAT YOU'VE DONE!"

The light faded then, and all was quiet. Every breath was held, and the entire world awaited what must come next. There was a crack of distant thunder, a rumbling of an approaching storm as all faces turned to the entrance to the castle's main hall. Standing tall, his robes partially askew to reveal a toned, powerful chest, was Cylan Calonar. Full, strong, restored to his vigor. The last of the Heroes of Fate stepped forward. His Halvan eyes blazed with his magic.

"You killed my people," the King of the Northlands accused. He floated up, lifted by his power. "You burned my forest and my city," the Lord of House Calonar's voice was steady, even, and yet filled with the ultimate possible authority. "You hurt my friends, my family, MY DAUGHTER!" The sky went dark, as black as the deepest night, but for flashes of lightning and the thunderous aura of the last of the Heroes of Fate.

King Cylan Calonar waved absently at Alexia's natural prison, and the vines and branches fell away, dropping Fak'Har to the ground. In their place, lightning blazed out. These were not the instant flashes to be seen in a common storm, though. These were celestial arcs that blazed into life and remained. The crackling, deafening shackles wrapped themselves around the Shadowed Mage's arms, legs, torso, and neck. Fak'Har may have been screaming, for his mouth was wide and his tongue bulged, but nothing could be heard, nothing but the pronouncement of the Northlands king.

"You will suffer."

The lightning tore at Fak'Har. It cut away his robes and his flesh. His hair caught fire, and the flames were joined by ones erupting from his eyes, his nostrils, his ears, and his mouth. Piece by piece, the Shadowed Mage's body was torn asunder, only chunks of well-cooked meat falling to the ground.

All was, once again, silent. The sky cleared, revealing evening had come. The peaceful stars shared a quiet sky with the blushing moon. The sun had finished its retreat behind the mountains of Ulheim. The King was standing with his wife, momentarily weakened, but restored. The Archaeknights were picking themselves up and shaking off the release of their master's power. Luwina and the surviving defenders were looking at each other, shocked at their continued life. The Healing Sphere, depleted for a time, sat on the ground, only a feint hint of its white light spilling into the courtyard. Kyla sobbed and cried, straining through her contractions, and the ongoing bleeding from her womb. At the open, double doors leading from the castle's main hall, Karen, the Tressalon Twins, and Beraht were walking out, looking about in confusion, all but Karen. At the breach in the castle's wall, Rogan and Aebreanna, accompanied by the Archaeknights Genma and Rei, arrived, trying to understand what they were seeing.

There was a gargled gasp. One of the guardsmen, a woman, Tomas absently realized as her helmet fell away and a long braid spilled out, was lurching away from the other soldiers. She grasped at her head and screamed as her body was enveloped in Shadow. The darkness consumed her, but then faded and was gone, taking the female guardsman with it.

Off to the side, almost forgotten amidst the cataclysmic events just witnessed, Tomas cradled his love. Mary was gasping her last, staring up at the man to whom she had sworn herself, and who had sworn himself to her. He held her hand to his face, the hand that bore the simple band of white gold, fashioned into the image of a ribbon. Tears flowed from his eyes as they looked at one another. Neither spoke. Mary's breathing slowed, eased, then stopped. Tomas still held her hand to his face, still looked into eyes that could no longer see. He still held her close, and made no move to ever let her go. On her finger, the ring that had bound their souls gently changed, the white returning to yellow.

Chapter 50

Tomas worked through the night. He kept his body busy, his muscles straining, his eyes and ears distracted. Little was left in the gardens, that made his work take all the longer, requiring all the more attention and effort. He spent hours gathering wood, useable wood. His search of the wasteland that had been the gardens proved fruitless, so he expanded into the neighboring streets. When the Uldra gaslamps ignited, they took most the city with them, but the western districts were still relatively intact. This offered the resources he needed.

No one came to bother him. Most likely, they were busy with their own griefs. Rogan had gone to Kyla's side and, with Teka Ironhands and Queen Nora, they had gone into the castle. Tomas had seen the look in the eyes of the Arcaheknight healer, though, and knew what must come. Aebreanna had taken her children somewhere, and the cries of despair from the Twins spoke of Rashid's fate. Beraht too had left, saying something of the Temple of the Lady of Light. No one thought to ask about Princess Karen.

Even when the elements of Killdare's army reached Tomas, they left him alone. Likely, word had already spread. Prince Rogan's squire had become known, after all. First he had been champion of last year's Harvest Festival, then he had joined in the fight against Anninihus the death mage. Rumor had run fast of Tomas being the one who finally ended that fiend. Gossip had a way of traveling faster than the wind; the final events of the siege must have reached the army by now.

Now and then, as Tomas worked, he heard sounds of violence. Remnants of Vagris' mercenaries were being dug out of their holes. Killdare's forces had been ordered to move carefully, securing the city and clearing it, one ruined building at a time. Torches moving amidst the darkness spoke of the effort. Tomas did not care; he had a more important duty.

The horizon was blushing with the first hints of rosy dawn by the time Tomas was ready. He had gathered more than enough wood, often resorting to broken furniture and collapsed building material. By good fortune, he had found a cart, and this made transporting the fuel easier, more efficient. Unfortunately, constructing the pyre had required little actual thought, allowing his mind free reign to drift though memories, both pleasant and not.

Everything was gone now, Tomas' mind pointed out as he stacked the wood. He had seen the remains of the Sylvai restaurant, where they had their first real date. He had also seen what remained of the restauranteur and his family. As he had carried her down the ramp, the moon had illuminated what remained of the Guard barracks and parade field. Bodies littered the field where he had fought in her honor, won the tournament for her glory. He had seen the southern district, where the temples of the Lady of Light and the Harvest Mother once sat. There were only ruins there, now, broken and already crumbling. Some part of Tomas' mind wondered if the sick children they had visited survived. He had passed the fountain in the city center with her in his arms, near to where she had performed that beautiful dance, supposedly for the entire city, but really, for him. The fountain was nearly empty, splashed with blood and worse. And, of course, there was the blasted, wasted gardens.

The sun was just peaking over the eastern horizon, seeing a dead city. Tomas knelt over the small campfire he had built, finishing with the last of the kindling. He forgot how many times he had seen this done, and done it himself, back in Pelsemoria. Hardly a week went by after the night of Kyla's Madness without somebody needing its final rites. The young man had grown quite adept at building funeral pyres. Fitting, somehow, that he should have this one last pyre to build, before he leaves.

Tomas did not need his eyes or his ears to know Karen approached. She moved through the Winds of Magic without touching most, yet shined within the Wind of Fate. She was like a beacon, a burning lighthouse within the currents of destiny. Much had changed since Tomas had left the Northern Keep with his friends. The world itself had seemed to shift. This paled, though, compared to the change in little Princess Karen.

"Are you still even her?" Tomas asked dully.

"I'm not really sure," the little girl said. Not really a little girl, Tomas admitted to himself. Even without the strange alteration in her, she had begun her change to womanhood. Karen was still early in that difficult time, but already showed signs of growing into the same maturity enjoyed by all the women of House Calonar. "I can barely remember who I was before the Truthsight."

Her voice was the greatest of changes, Tomas decided as he positioned the kindling around the base of the pyre and within its many layers. This supposed girl spoke with a woman's voice, with an empress' voice, really. Certainty, authority, and more regret than any young person should possess. "I was expecting Cyras," Tomas admitted.

"He wouldn't come," Karen told him. "He's afraid of you, the same as Fak'Har."

Tomas snorted in contempt for why anyone would be afraid of him.

"You're Fatetouched," the new Truthseer of House Calonar reminded him. "All your choices lie outside the Wind of Fate. Unpredictable, uncontrollable. Both of them tried to manipulate you into this series of events, to control how you'd react."

"You're leaving a few people out," Tomas noted, but Karen said nothing. He finished with the pyre and turned back to his love. "Cyras Darkholm, Fak'Har, Alexia,

Queen Nora." He paused. "You. All of you have been manipulating people, manipulating events, to try and affect what's to come."

"Yes," Karen admitted. Then she grimaced. "Though, I don't think I'm very good at it."

"I'm sure you'll get better with practice," Tomas said, lifting Mary and placing her on the pyre. He adjusted her carefully, ensuring the dignity and poise she deserved to have in traversing the Veil. He stood for a while, looking at her face. The rising sun cast a warm glow upon her. Tomas adjusted the few errant strands as they danced about in the gentle breeze. "How's Rogan?"

"Mourning," Karen answered. "Kyla lost the baby. What comes next will be very hard for him."

"When will they move her?"

"General Killdare is preparing a large convoy. It'll depart for Woodwall in about a week. We're all going." She glanced about. "There's not much point in trying to stay after all this."

"The Death of Calonar," Tomas said, quoting what little he knew from the Prophecy.

"But not the death of the people," Karen countered. "We survived, because of you, and Mary, and Rainer and Esha and all the others."

"Sacrifices for the grand plan."

"The alternative is worse."

"The Return of the Dark Empress," Tomas said without caring much. "The Rise of the Demon-God."

"But first, the Inversion."

Tomas turned and picked up the torch he had set within the campfire. "Your problem," he said flatly. The young man turned back to the pyre and ignited it, ensuring the fire was well-born before backing away.

"You still have one last part to play in all this," Karen said.

Tomas snorted again, locking his eyes upon his love as she began her journey through the Veil. "The Final Host," he muttered. "That's what Cyras called me."

"Yes. The Inversion has begun. But before Rogan and the others can respond, one of the Scions has to die. Either Cyras Darkholm or Fak'Har; the Trickster, or the Shadow."

"So, we're not even pretending that your father killed Fak'Har?"

"I already told them he survived, just as he survived Tordenia. He can reincarnate in another body. He jumped into Aloisa, stole her body."

"Which you knew would happen."

"I knew it could happen," Karen replied. "Whenever a Fatetouched acts within an event, Truthsight becomes blurry. I knew you would have a choice, to either heal Mary or my father. If you healed Mary, Fak'Har wouldn't have needed another body.

He'd have just left. The Truthsight has limitations, especially with the Fatetouched. I don't even know which one you'll kill."

The flames grew higher, brighter. The smoke drifted up, carrying her to God. "Simple choice," Tomas noted.

"Cyras wanted it that way." Karen stood beside him. "He wanted you fixated on his brother, rather than on him."

"I don't even know where either of them have gone."

"I can tell you. I've seen people who will encounter both of them in the future. I know where you can go, or at least, where you can start looking."

Tomas said nothing for a little while, but just stood, staring at the pyre and his departing love. "I don't think she'd want me to seek vengeance," he mused.

"Probably not."

"I should want it, though." He thought about that. Alexia had gone back, beyond the Veil, leaving him to his mourning, but Tomas knew what she would say. "I should be furious, with Fak'Har. So why aren't I?"

"You'll find your rage again," Karen promised. "Rogan was the same way when Anninihus killed his first love. He felt very calm, until he didn't."

"If I don't seek one or both of them out...?"

"The Wind of Fate will shift. It will bring one or both of them to you. One of the Scions will die. The choice of which has been left to you."

"Does it really matter which of them I go after?"

"It does, but I'm not sure how or why, not yet. Truthsight doesn't reveal everything. There are gaps around a Fatetouched, including the consequences of their actions."

"Did you know what would happen to her?"

Karen did not answer at first. She glanced nervously at Tomas, whose eyes remained on the pyre. There was no emotion in his voice, no accusation, no condemnation or forgiveness. The young man himself did not know how he would react to the answer. "Yes," the Truthseer answered truthfully. "From the moment I looked at her with the Truthsight, I knew this was a possibility. I knew if you healed my father, then she'd see you one last time, and that Fak'Har would kill her." The little princess breathed deep, tears falling from her young eyes. "I knew Esha would die on the wall. I knew the forest would burn. I knew hundreds would be taken by the Xeshlin. I saw it all: every death, every tortured scream." Her haunted eyes turned to Castle Calonar. "I saw my nephew, born in blood, crying once, and then dying." Her breathing was labored, gasping. "I saw Kyla and Rogan, holding each other in sorrow. I saw Beraht, standing in the ruins of the Temple of the Lady of Light, holding the purple headband Medaka gave him. I saw Chandra murder Rashid, and Aebreanna..." Her young, as yet unfinished body shook with the horrors she had already beheld, and those lying ahead. "And I had to let it happen."

"Why?"

"So that there'd be survivors. Vincent and Ilse are already heading to Woodwall, and the Western Forts themselves survived. House Calonar's army survived. Rogan will have a chance now, when the time comes for him to fight the Demon-God."

"Sacrifice hundreds, to save thousands."

Karen shook her head, fighting to maintain her composure, and failing. "Sacrificing thousands, to save an entire world."

They were quiet again, each facing their own grief, the individual burdens thrust upon them by the Wind of Fate. Tomas looked around. "We had lunch here," he said.

Karen wiped away tears and nodded. "And you swam in the creek over there."

Tomas looked and saw where she was pointing. "Yes," he agreed. "Alexia had left a note. She told me to enjoy the times while we had them." Tears began to come forth, not in a great flood, but just a few. "And we did."

He half turned. "I once asked your father, if he could be free, what would he do."

Karen nodded again. "Take his family and ride away."

"If I were free, I would've never come here. I left Pelsemoria to save my people, but my burden brought me here. I met a beautiful woman here, and earned her love. If you could be free, princess, what would you do?"

The Truthseer thought a moment, but shook her head. "I don't remember." She glanced towards the Sylvai Shrine. "I think Karen Calonar died in the ziggurat. I barely remember her, being her. She wanted... she wanted friends, happiness. She wanted to be an aunt who was fun to be with, to see her sister's children grow. She wanted to see Rogan crowned king." The Truthseer took a deep, shuddering breath. "But Karen Calonar is gone. I won't ever be the fun aunt. My niece... Rogan's child will be the One Who Comes. He won't ever be a king, and I won't ever have friends, not really."

Tomas put a hand on her shoulder. "You've got one, at least."

"A Truthseer touched by a Fatetouched," Karen said through a force smile. "God knows what kind of havoc you're causing in the Wind of Fate right now."

Tomas smiled. He let more tears fall as he looked to the horizon. "Yeah. I'm good at that." He sighed, breathing in the fresh, cool breeze blowing in from the north. "I'm very good at that."

To Be Continued

Tomas' Journey
Concludes in:

The Southern Invasions
Book 5 of the Master of Fate

ABOUT THE AUTHOR

William Price Jr has published numerous short stories and poems, still searching for truth amidst his many made up stories. After retiring from his military service and teaching, he lives in New Hampshire.

www.ingramcontent.com/pod-product-compliance
Lightning Source LLC
Chambersburg PA
CBHW011343010726
47493CB00011B/2931